JEN WILLIAMS started writing about pirates and dragons as a young girl and hasn't ever stopped. Her short stories have featured in numerous anthologies and her debut novel, *The Copper Promise*, was published in 2014 to huge acclaim. Jen was nominated in the Best Newcomer category at the 2015 British Fantasy Awards and her following two novels, *The Iron Ghost* and *The Silver Tide* were both shortlisted for the British Fantasy Awards Novel of the Year. All novels in the Copper Cat Trilogy, *The Copper Promise*, *The Iron Ghost*, and *The Silver Tide*, are available from Headline in the UK. *The Bitter Twins* is the second epic novel in The Winnowing Flame Trilogy. Jen lives in London with her partner and their cat.

Praise for *The Ninth Rain*:

'There is so much to praise about *The Ninth Rain*: the world-building is top-notch, the plot is gripping and the characters just get better and better. A sublime read'   *SFX*

'Absolutely phenomenal fantasy – a definite must-read'
                                                                    Adrian Tchaikovsky

'Williams portrays her characters as flawed but humane, propels the plot with expert pace, and excels at eldritch world-building'
                                                                    Guardian

'*The Ninth Rain* is a fast-paced and vibrant fantasy romp through a new world, full of pe⟨...⟩ne with and enemies you'd happily ⟨...⟩w

'A cracking story that grips you ⟨...⟩ let go'   ⟨...⟩ox

Praise for Jen Williams' Copper Cat Trilogy:

'A fast-paced and original new voice in heroic fantasy'
Adrian Tchaikovsky

'A fresh take on classic tropes. . . 21st century fantasy at its best'
SFX

'Williams has thrown out the rulebook and injected a fun tone into epic fantasy without lightening or watering down the excitement and adventure. . . Highly recommended'
Independent

'A highly inventive, vibrant high fantasy with a cast you can care about. . . There is never a dull moment'
British Fantasy Society

'Expect dead gods, mad magic, piracy on the high seas, peculiar turns and pure fantasy fun'
Starburst

'Absolutely stuffed with ghoulish action. There is never a dull page'
SciFiNow

'An enthralling adventure'
Sci-Fi Bulletin

'*The Copper Promise* is dark, often bloody, frequently frightening, but there's also bucket loads of camaraderie, sarcasm, and an unashamed love of fantasy and the fantastic'
Den Patrick

By Jen Williams and available from Headline

The Copper Cat Trilogy
The Copper Promise
The Iron Ghost
The Silver Tide

Sorrow's Isle (digital short story)

The Winnowing Flame Trilogy
The Ninth Rain
The Bitter Twins

THE BITTER TWINS

JEN WILLIAMS

HEADLINE

First published in Great Britain in 2018 by
HEADLINE PUBLISHING GROUP

1

Cataloguing in Publication Data is available from the British Library

ISBN 978 1 4722 3520 6

Typeset in Sabon LTD Std by Palimpsest Book Production Ltd, Falkirk, Stirlingshire

Printed and bound in Great Britain by Clays Ltd, St Ives plc

Headline's policy is to use papers that are natural, renewable and recyclable products and made
from wood grown in well-managed forests and other controlled sources. The logging and
manufacturing processes are expected to conform to the environmental regulations of the
country of origin.

HEADLINE PUBLISHING GROUP
An Hachette UK Company
Carmelite House
50 Victoria Embankment
London EC4Y 0DZ

www.headline.co.uk
www.hachette.co.uk

For Dad,
with Love.

1

'What to do with all the flesh, and all the bone? That was the question no one had considered, of course.

'Human beings are not, after all, simple bags of blood. At the end of all the fighting, the battlefields of the Carrion Wars were heaped with bodies – actual hills of bodies, corpses so numerous that they dammed rivers and caused floods. The crows and the ravens and the other scavenging birds turned the sky black. It was quite a sight. I made many drawings, many paintings.

'Obviously, once we had taken what we needed, we left them there – it was not Ebora's problem, what became of those bloodless bodies, and the plains people were, quite understandably, reluctant to come and collect them, so the human corpses stayed right where they were and rotted into the ground. The animals had their feed, and the bones were left to litter the battlefields like grains of rice cast onto the floor. Sometimes, when it is quiet here in my rooms, I listen and I think I can hear the ghosts calling me, crying out in their hundreds, their thousands. I want to get up and sketch them, but I sit with the charcoal in my hand and do nothing. There is *no imagining their multitudes, and no way to capture it on canvas.*

'I did not fight in the Carrion Wars, but I was there to witness the horror. Arnia curls her lip at me and says nothing, but it is clear enough what she thinks of that. I think it is important someone is here to witness these things, or at least, I used to think so. Perhaps if I hadn't been there to witness the slaughter and carry those heavy images in my head, I would have made different decisions and we wouldn't be where we are now, with the burdens we now carry.

'I still hear the ghosts sometimes, and they call me unto death, where I belong.'

The words of Micanal the Clearsighted, taken directly from what I must assume is his most personal journal. Quite the gloomy sod, but I cannot deny there is real poetry in his writing – which is not surprising, given that he was Ebora's most celebrated artist: a genius in a nation of masters. And whatever I might think about his tendency towards melodrama, there are clues here – to the reality of the Carrion Wars and the devastation the crimson flux wrought on the Eboran people – that are without doubt, a staggering gift to my own studies.

Extract from the private journals
of Lady Vincenza 'Vintage' de Grazon

'What have I done?'

Hestillion clung to the silver pod, hugging it to her chest as though it were the only solid thing in existence. There was a yawning sensation in the pit of her stomach.

'What is wrong, Hestillion Eskt, born in the year of the green bird?'

Hestillion looked up. She was kneeling on the floor of a

room unlike anything she'd seen before. The walls were a soft, fleshy grey, punctured here and there with odd fibrous growths, small lights hanging at the end of each. The ceiling above her was a shifting mass of black liquid: the same black liquid that had reached down for them from the corpse moon. She could still feel the strange prickly sensation it had left against her skin – it had been obscenely hot, like the hand of a person wracked with fever. With a jolt, she remembered where she was.

'I am *inside* the corpse moon.'

The queen moved into sight, then, moving languidly on legs of the shifting black liquid. Her face, a white mask resting on a bed of the stuff, seemed to grow more certain as she looked at Hestillion: the features a little stronger, a little more distinct. She smiled, an uncanny stretching of her lips.

'The corpse moon? That is what you call it?'

Hestillion took a breath. 'No, not truly. It's what the humans called it. They never saw it alive, after all. Not the ones that are around now, anyway.'

The queen tipped her head to one side. 'We like it. The *corpse moon*.'

There was a hum, and the room shook faintly, a soft vibration that travelled up through Hestillion's slippers and into her bones. Seeing her look of surprise, the queen stepped over to her – the movement strange and elongated – and, leaning down, pressed a narrow finger to the floor. Immediately, the soft grey material grew translucent, bleeding outwards like grease on thin paper until, to Hestillion's horror, she could see the landscape speeding away below them. She gave a little cry, almost falling backwards.

'We travel up and away now, you see,' said the queen. 'We are worn and broken and old, but we can do that.'

Hestillion swallowed hard. They were so high in the sky she could barely fathom it. Her beloved Ebora was there below, recognisable from its marble and its wide streets, but as she watched, a white shape moved in front of the impromptu window. A cloud. They were above the clouds. *This must be what it is to fly with the war-beasts*, she thought, and she gripped the pod a little tighter. It was cold.

'This makes you uncomfortable.' It wasn't a question as such, and when Hestillion looked back up at the queen she saw that the creature was peering at her in genuine curiosity. More alarmingly, the ceiling above her was moving, and long glistening appendages began to ooze out of the black liquid: seven of them, like long multiple-jointed fingers. As she watched, pale orbs began to push through at the end of each, rolling wetly to clear themselves of the black mucus.

Hestillion scrambled to her feet and drew herself up to her full height. She very deliberately did not look at the eyes in the ceiling.

'What is this? Why have you brought me here?' Before she could stop it, another question leapt on the tail of the last. 'What *are* you?'

'You are interesting to us, Hestillion Eskt, born in the year of the green bird. And you helped us. We shall help you.' The patch of translucence suddenly grew, racing away beneath Hestillion's feet; it was as if she stood on thin air, a terrible drop yawning away below. Her stomach tried to climb out of her throat, and summoning every bit of willpower she had, Hestillion made herself look directly at the queen's face.

'Stop it. This is not . . . helping me.'

The queen shrugged, and once again the floor was a solid thing. The eyes in the ceiling retreated too, oozing back into the shifting wetness.

When she trusted herself to speak again, Hestillion kept her voice low. 'You do not owe me anything, Queen of the Jure'lia.'

'Queen . . . of the . . . worm people. What interesting words you have. It is to be savoured. Besides which, we owe you very

4

much. You spoke to us, sought us out and roused us from the chill death of the roots. If you had not done that, we would have slept forever, trapped, and might not even have woken when your stinking tree-god crawled back to life. You interest us, very much, and we would not leave you behind. We have said this.'

Hestillion blinked. This was the first example of emotion she had seen from the Jure'lia queen, aside from mild amusement or curiosity. It was easier, and better, to focus on that than the wave of guilt the creature's words had prompted. Carefully, she placed the war-beast pod on the floor, letting it lean against her legs. She could not quite bear to be out of contact with it, but her arms were beginning to shake – a war-beast pod was not light.

'I am not a prisoner here, then?' Hestillion lifted her chin, aware that even standing as tall as she was the queen towered a good three feet over her. 'I could leave?'

'Leave? You are welcome to leave, yes.' The queen gestured at the floor again, and this time, to Hestillion's horror, it began to grow not only see-through, but soft. Her foot sank down into it, followed by the other, and there was a terrible sensation of something easing away beneath her.

'Stop! Stop it, that's not what I meant!'

The floor grew solid again, and the queen smiled her cold smile. After a moment, she lifted her long arms to the ceiling and fibrous black tendrils came down to meet her. Rising from the floor, she sank into the pool of black liquid as though she were sinking into a bath, and then she was gone. Belatedly, Hestillion realised that there were no doors in the room, and no visible way out.

'Leave, and go where?' she said to the war-beast pod. Kneeling, she wrapped her arms around it and closed her eyes. 'Back to the people I've helped to destroy? I would be better off falling through this floor, in that case.'

5

Something was poking into her chest. She reached within her dress and pulled out a rectangular card about as long as her hand. It had been folded so many times it was slashed with creases, but she remembered the picture on the front of the tarla card well enough: green shapes like twisted fingers against a dark background. The Roots. Aldasair had given it to her years ago, and she had kept it, although she couldn't have said why, and when they had prepared to pour the growth fluid on Ygseril's roots, she had tucked it inside her gown. For luck, she supposed. Feeling a fresh surge of disgust at her own stupidity, she slid it back where she had found it and put her arms around the war-beast pod again. It remained cold under her touch, and she wondered why she had brought it.

2

The ice was thinning.

Peering over the side of the well, Eri could see the smudged shape of his own head and shoulders looking back at him: a dark mirror. He wasn't sure how he knew the ice was thinner, aside from a blurred memory of a hundred winters asking the same question; he had done this before, after all, over and over again. It was possible to think of that as being caught between mirrors. A hundred, a thousand images of himself, the same over and over, caught in this dark mirror forever. Stepping neatly away from that thought, he pressed his hands to the big rock he had lifted onto the lip of the well, and gave it a quick shove. It plummeted down and there was a satisfying crack, followed by a *sploosh*.

'Good.'

He would have water from the well again. Through the winter he had taken water from the great steel buckets he had brought indoors just before the cold months truly took their grip on Ebora, and occasionally from handfuls of snow, but mostly he had stayed inside, safe within the walls of Lonefell. But water from the well would be fresher, and not taste of metal. It was one of the things he looked forward to spring for, after all. Mother would be pleased to hear of this sign of the warmer months – she would be glad to get back to the gardens.

The bucket was stiff with frost, but the rope he had kept indoors to save it from the wet rot. In moments he had a bucketful of water as clear as the sky, and before he poured it into the basin he took a mouthful straight from it, grinning as the shock of the cold travelled through his teeth.

'*Brrr.*'

Basin in arms, Eri walked back through the frosted gardens. It was too soon yet for shoots, but he could imagine them there, waiting under the ground like tiny green promises. Back inside Lonefell, he took the basin straight through to the kitchens and added more wood to the fire, waiting for the stove to warm. From there he went down the cold stone steps to the larder, grabbing a candle as he went. The larder was a vast place, and the yellow warmth of the candle did not quite light its furthest corners; if anything, it only served to deepen the shadows on the empty shelves.

'Empty shelves.'

Eri stood and looked at them, a cold worm of worry waking up to twist inside his chest. He had perhaps two shelves of food left down here, if that. Jars of pickled vegetables he had made himself with the last of the vinegar, dried and salted meat from the rabbits he had managed to trap last summer, a pair of ancient cheeses wrapped in thick cloth. He was afraid to open those in case they were completely lost. Time was running out, if there was any left at all.

Eri snatched a packet of the dried meat off the shelf and left, heading up to the kitchens, humming tunelessly to himself, murmuring the occasional word as the fog of forgetfulness lifted.

'On the fifth day we shall dance, my love . . . and on the sixth you shall sing to me . . .'

He put a small amount of the water on to boil, and put some strips of the old rabbit meat in to soften. A handful of dried herbs and some salt went in next. It would be a warm dinner, at least.

Leaving that to cook – for want of a better word – Eri wandered down the corridor away from the kitchen, walking without thinking to his mother's rooms. The walls here were covered in bright paintings: of the lands beyond the Tarah-hut Mountains, of the war-beasts in their battle glory, of old Eboran heroes, their armour shining impossibly bright. His mother and father had made the inside of Lonefell bright with paintings and stories, and every room was stuffed with bookcases, each heaving with books. When they took their son into seclusion, they had not wanted him to be bored.

His mother's room was bright with early morning sunshine – he had already been in here to draw her curtains – and she was a still shape within the bed. The sheets were crisp, and embroidered with a great forest, animals peeping out from between the trunks and branches.

There was a chair by her bed, so Eri sat on it, remembering as he did so that when they had first come to Lonefell, this had been his favourite chair, even though his legs hadn't quite reached the ground at the time. Now the upholstery was thin, and here and there little puffs of white stuffing were showing through like the thinning hair on an old man's head.

'It's cold, but the ice is melting.' He looked across the bed at the far side of the room as he spoke. His mother was a series of soft curves that he didn't quite focus on. 'Not long now and the garden will be blooming again. Although . . . well, I hope the vegetables do better than they did last year, Mother. I don't know what it is – maybe it's just that the soil is tired. Everything around here seems tired.' Eri stopped, and after a moment he pulled the corner of the blanket back, and with only a small amount of difficulty slid his hand into his mother's. He still didn't quite look at her. 'When we came here, I thought it was all a great adventure. That we were pilgrims of a sort, I suppose, striking out on our own to find our way. You and Father made it seem like that, I think – all of Father's stories, all the books he brought. He was so excited to read them with me, I remember. And our garden. We were going to grow so many things in it. Exotic foods as well as everything else, and of course I had a whole suite to myself, full of toys. You must have employed every artisan in Ebora, to bring that many toys with you.' He cleared his throat, and squeezed his mother's cold fingers.

'I'm sorry. Now, I realise it must have been terribly sad for you both. Leaving everything behind to come all the way out here. I found some letters . . .' Eri paused, shivering violently. His stomach growled and when he pulled his jacket closer around his chest, his fingers brushed against ribs that were too prominent. 'It's not that I'm snooping, Mother, it's just that I've read every book twice, three times, some of them, and Father didn't mind.' He bit his lip, then continued. 'I found letters from your mother, and from Father's parents. They weren't happy about what you'd done, by the sounds of it. Letters full of pleading, and threats. I didn't realise you had told them they couldn't see me, but then I suppose I never thought about it.'

A fly had got into the room. It buzzed once past Eri's ear, making him shiver again, and then threw itself repeatedly against the far window until he stood up and chased it out with a roll of old parchment. That done, he stood by the glass and looked up at a clear sky. Nothing up there today, at least.

'I think I'm seeing things.' He looked back at his mother, then just as quickly looked away again. 'Things in the sky. But that can't be. Ebora is dead – it died a long time ago, probably when those letters from my grandparents stopped coming.

10

Right? I just need to eat more food, that's all, and that will be easier soon, it will be easier . . .' Eri raised a trembling hand to his forehead and pushed away the hair that had fallen into his eyes.

'Oh, speaking of which . . .'

He straightened his mother's blankets, bending down to brush a dry kiss against her waxy skull, and then hurried back to the kitchens. His meagre broth had congealed into something that would at least be more flavourful than water, and he quickly slopped it into a bowl. That done, he carried the bowl, spoon sticking out of it, down another long corridor to his father's study. In here, the books were watchful, too quiet, and the maps on the wall all looked like lies, so he picked his father up and took him back out to the gardens. There was a series of low stone benches facing the frozen pond, and here he sat and slowly ate the hot gruel, his father set upon the ground next to him.

'You can feel it's warmer, can't you?' The taste of meat, salty on his tongue, had cheered him up somewhat. 'I didn't tell Mother, but the larder is nearly empty. This thaw couldn't come quickly enough.' He paused to yank a piece of particularly tough meat from between his teeth. 'Ugh. The rabbits will be back in a few weeks, and if we get some really fine weather, I can range further. I know what you'll say, but the Wild is still a good distance from Lonefell and there's a chance of some deer to the east, I'm sure of it. A whole deer would keep . . . would keep me . . . us . . .'

A shadow cast them into darkness. Eri looked up, his heart in his throat, and there it was *again*. He jumped up so violently his boot hit the bucket of bones, causing a dry clacking noise he automatically ignored. Above them a dragon soared, slow and magnificent in the golden light of the morning. She was low enough for Eri to see the wide pearly scales of her stomach, each as big as his hand, and the fine white feathers of her wings.

'It can't be real. Such things don't exist anymore. I mean, they just don't. Father?' Eri looked down, directly into the bucket of bones – something he very rarely did – and the bare yellow reality of his situation was as cold and as shocking as the well water. He gasped, wrenching his eyes away, and looked back up to the dragon. She was turning to the west, banking slowly like an eagle, and it looked as though there was someone riding her. After a moment, the dragon opened her jaws and a bright jet of violet flame leapt forth, like some sort of fantastical flower. It dissipated, and Eri realised he could hear something, something even more extraordinary; the sound of laughter in the wind. It had been decades since he had heard laughter – it was difficult, for a moment, even to remember what it was.

Eri stood and watched the dragon until she was a tiny dot on the horizon, his broth quite forgotten and cold. His father did not venture an opinion.

3

My dearest Marin,

By Sarn's broken old bones, I hope this letter finds you safe. I have sent it on to the last address I had for you, and I hope that you are still there – the university at Reidn has good, strong walls, and there are lots of people there. If you can, stay there, Marin. Don't do anything stupid (not that you would, darling, but your aunt worries so).

I've sent a letter home to the vine forest too, but I am on the road and have no way to receive replies. There is a certain amount of safety in remoteness, so the House may not have seen any horrors, but I cannot help thinking of the Behemoth ruins hidden within the forest. They were ancient and little more than shards and broken pieces, and everything I've seen suggests that only the remains from recent Rains have been brought back to life, yet . . . Of course I worry.

I travel now with an Eboran woman called Nanthema. I will have mentioned her to you, I think. We're making our way to Ebora, travelling often at night and avoiding the main roads, although I'm not sure that will help. We

13

must be alert at all times, and it is exhausting; if we are not cowering from the distant sight of the Behemoths lurching through our skies, we are hiding from wolves, or Wild-touched creatures. I am hoping to find help in Ebora, or at least more knowledge of what exactly we face. I have much to tell you, Marin darling, but too much to fit in this letter. I will tell you when I next see your dear, handsome face.

An interesting note about this letter. We have stopped in a town called Nōrg, a northern settlement clinging to the Min hills (hills my arse, these things are more or less mountains, my sore feet can attest to that) and they have the most remarkable birds here, huge things that I think must be mildly Wild-touched. They use these birds to send messages, which is, hopefully, how your letter will reach you. However, the woman I spoke to who tends these birds told me that just recently the birds have not been returning. Killed by Behemoth creatures, I asked her? She thought not – it's possible, she thinks, that the birds have been using the corpse moon to navigate by, and now that it is gone, they are getting lost. Isn't that remarkable, Marin? There are always new wonders, it seems.

Extract from the private letters
of Master Marin de Grazon

When the attack came, Esther was ankle deep in muddy sand with her little brother. The day was a blowy one, punctuated with squalls of rain all the colder for coming in off the sea, and they both had their hoods strapped down tightly. Corin's was bright blue and sewn with little fish shapes: a present from their grandfather. He had got it for his nameday only the week before, and was still insisting on wearing it at all times, even at dinner. Inside the great shell they were protected from the worst of the weather, but it was still cold and damp.

14

'It smells,' pointed out Corin.

'Mmm, lovely fishy smell. Smells just like your socks.' They moved deeper inside, Esther leading the way as Corin stifled his giggles. The smooth, pinkish walls were stained with salt and even a few barnacles, but Esther could see what they were after, just ahead. White mounds with black spots, each about the size of her foot, clung to the shell wall. She took out her knife in readiness.

'Here we go, Corin. Do you want to do the first one?'

Up close, the sacs of razor crab eggs were more translucent than white, with bulbous grey shadows inside, covered all over in a thick, shivering jelly. Corin frowned deeply; they did not look much like the tasty morsels of brown flesh their father served up for dinner in the evening, and she could see him wondering already if this was worth all the effort.

'Look, I'll show you.' Esther untucked the oilskin sack from her belt and positioned it under the nearest cluster, then took her knife from its sheath. This, she knew, was Corin's real fascination, so she let the murky light play along the blade for a moment. 'You take the knife, and then, holding the cluster at the bottom, you see, you just slide it up under, next to the skin of the shell. You have to get it all in one go, otherwise it all falls apart into blobby bits.'

In a practised movement, she slipped the blade underneath and the egg sac fell – with a slightly unpleasant *splish*, she had to admit – neatly into the awaiting bag.

'Oh.' Corin's expression was hidden within his hood. 'What's that?'

'What's what?'

It was a hum at first, and then a high-pitched whine that seemed to thrum through the walls of the great shell. Without really knowing why, Esther leaned her hand against the shell wall and felt it vibrating, so deep it made the ends of her fingers go numb.

15

'The noise! What is it?' There was an edge of panic in Corin's voice, so Esther sheathed her knife and, leaving the bag where it was, took hold of his hand.

'Probably just a big ship coming in,' she said, although she knew already that couldn't be right. No ship could make such a racket. 'Let's go and have a look, shall we?'

They walked quickly to the lip of the shell, following its gently spiralling walls with the sand sucking at their boots. Esther's first thought was that an unexpected storm had rolled in; true, the sea was the same steely band it had been earlier, no tossing waves out there, but Coldreef was in shadow. The wooden palisade that circled the settlement was a series of dark jagged sticks, and the cramped houses, with their mismatched walls of driftwood and razor shell, looked too small, dwindled somehow. And then she looked up.

'In Tomas's name.' Esther snatched Corin up from the sand and held him to her like she hadn't done since he was four. 'Corin, we must get inside.'

There was a monster hanging in the sky. To Esther, who had lived in Coldreef all her life, it looked a little like the fat sea beetles she sometimes found dead down by the shore, except it was huge, as big as a thousand Wild-touched razor crabs. It had a bulbous, segmented body, an oily greenish black in colour, with cracks and lines running all across the thing. Here and there were puckering holes that seemed to be expelling a thick black ooze, and odd skittering creatures. Even as she watched, these were falling down towards Coldreef like seeds falling from a tree, many-jointed legs spread wide.

'What is it, Essie? What is it?'

She had been running awkwardly towards the palisade gate, her only thought to get back to their father, but now the monster was descending – if it kept going, it would simply crush Coldreef under it. She stopped, and heaved Corin into

16

a more comfortable position. It never occurred to her to put him down.

'I don't know. I don't – Corin, maybe we should hide for a bit. Back in the shells, and just wait, wait until it's gone.'

'But Papa!'

Esther winced. Corin hadn't called their father that since he was very small. There was a sudden rumble from the monster and it shifted abruptly to one side. The movement did not look controlled, and even to her eye, it looked as though it were struggling to stay upright somehow. Parts of its segmented hide were missing, she realised, and others looked like they were sitting at the wrong angle. There was another noise now too, a high-pitched shrieking –

'Essie! Look!'

The people of Coldreef had realised what was hanging above them. Some were already trying to leave, running out the gates in a blind panic, while others were standing, looking up at the monster as though trying to figure out what it was. Esther saw some arming themselves, and then others falling down as if in a fit. First one, then two, then five or six; something was attacking them, something Esther couldn't see. She hadn't thought it possible for her to feel any more afraid, but a cold surge of terror was filling her throat.

'Back to the shells, come on! Papa will be fine. He'll meet us there. Come on!'

Suddenly, everything was lit with an eerie purple light, like a lightning bolt had hit the settlement. Crying out wordlessly, Esther looked up to see a new shape in the sky – just as impossible as the monster, and in many ways, just as frightening. A dragon flew low overhead, mists of violet flame clinging around its jaws, before it roared forth another fireball. The dragon glittered in the subdued light, making Esther think of the shards of mother-of-pearl she would sometimes find on the shoreline, and there was a young woman riding on its back.

Of her Esther could make out very little, save for a flash of black hair and an odd dark smudge on her forehead. In her arms, Corin began to kick violently.

'Monsters! Monsters!'

'*Shhhh.*' She squeezed him tight. There were more flying shapes coming now, a menagerie of creatures straight out of her childhood stories. For no reason she could think of, her eyes filled up with tears. 'I think these monsters are here to help us.'

Tor saw the holes in the side of the thing, and even though he hadn't seen a living Behemoth so close in well over three hundred years, it was obvious that these were broken places, pieces of the creature that had yet to be repaired. He glanced over to Noon, but she was already gone, Vostok a rapidly dwindling shape as the dragon dived down towards their enemy. Instead, Tor leaned low over Kirune's shoulder and shouted into the great cat's ear.

'That big hole. Let's make it bigger.'

The war-beast growled, a deep rumbling that Tor felt reverberate up through his legs, and then the cat folded his huge leathery wings and they were falling, the Behemoth suddenly looming impossibly large ahead of them. Beyond its bulbous greasy shape Tor could see the bleak little settlement, grim-looking shacks of driftwood and shell now bleeding panicked people. The smell of salt and seaweed was strong in his nose, and for a second he felt a strange welling of euphoria – they would *save* these people – and then they crashed into the side of the Behemoth, Kirune skidding across its surface before digging his claws into the greenish material.

'We need to work on your landings.'

'Like you would do better,' growled Kirune. The war-beast folded his wings away awkwardly – they still looked ungainly to Tor's eye, grey and leathery like a bat's, with short black horns poking out at the joints – and leapt towards the ragged hole. Up close it was possible to see the oddly fleshy interior of the Behemoth; grey, almost translucent pads, white nodules and clusters of yellowish lights. Kirune immediately began to claw viciously at the edges of the hole, peeling back the greenish moon-metal and exposing more of the pale padding. Tor glanced up to see Vostok passing over, her violet fire filling the overcast day with an eerie glow. Her flames licked over the surface of the Behemoth, and Tor saw things moving there, creatures like huge six-legged spiders with pulsating sacs nestled at their centres. Three or four of them seemed to crumple under the dragon-fire, but after a moment Tor saw that they were not dead, they were merely crouching to protect the delicate egg sacs that birthed the burrowers. Noon added her own dragon-fuelled winnowfire to the blast and finally two of them fell away from the surface of the Behemoth, smoking and blistered, but more were seeping out all around them.

'There are burrowers on the ground!' The shout came from above. Tor looked up to see Bern on the war-beast Sharrik flying overhead. The big human had a shining axe in either hand, trusting his harness to keep him in place, while the griffin Sharrik, who had grown to be the largest of all the war-beasts, beat his wings with such violence Tor could feel the wind from them pushing his hair back. Looking over his shoulder, Tor could just make out the ground and the people panicking there, but an answering shout came from Vostok.

'No! We must concentrate on wounding the Behemoth! Leave the humans.'

'You make your holes.' Sharrik's voice was a rumbling boom. 'We have lives to save.'

Immediately Tor felt Kirune's shoulders bunch, and the great cat lifted his head. Eyes like yellow lamps narrowed at the retreating form of the griffin. He gave one last slash at the hole and he was leaping into the air again, wings unfolding with a crack like the wind filling the sails of a ship, and they were diving again, racing to reach the ground before Sharrik. From behind them Tor heard Vostok's roar of outrage.

'No! We must work together!'

Tor leaned forward, gripping the thick fur on the back of Kirune's neck. His eyes were watering at the speed of their descent. 'Kirune! When Vostok gives you an order—'

'I will not be told what to do by a snake!'

Tor hissed between his teeth, but as they neared the settlement it was clear that the situation on the ground was very bad indeed. The packed dirt was seething with a tide of burrowers, and men and women and children were falling as he watched, while others were climbing up onto their roofs to get away. The 'mothers', the strange spider-like creatures, stalked among the chaos, white sacs pulsing as they gave birth to more of the scuttling carnivorous beetles.

Kirune hit the ground hard enough to throw up a cloud of dirt and dust, with Sharrik landing a moment later. The griffin's wings were blue and black, bright against the teeming chaos. Bern gave him a cheery wave, just before Sharrik's great blunt head darted out and snapped the legs off a passing mother-spider. Tor sincerely hoped the big man hadn't heard the growl he had received in response from Kirune.

'Where is Aldasair?'

Bern pointed to the houses behind Tor with the butt of his axe. Aldasair's war-beast was a huge black wolf with grey eagle's wings, her eyes a deep warm amber. She was standing on the roof of a shack, peering down at the chaos below with obvious alarm. Aldasair, Tor's cousin, was sitting very upright on her back, his face utterly drained of colour.

'We'll do what we can.' Tor drew his sword. All around them the people who had initially fallen to the ravenous burrowers were rising again. Their insides consumed and the black sticky residue oozing from their empty eye sockets, they began to converge on the war-beasts with welcoming smiles. 'Drones. Kill them, and as many of the burrowers as you can manage.'

Kirune roared, a sound that seemed to roll around the stricken settlement like thunder, and then he was pounding across the teeming space, his huge paws crushing burrowers into paste. Next to them, Sharrik was a massive, bulky shape, ebony beak slashing and tearing like a blade. Drones fell, their hollow bodies exposed to the bleak daylight, and for the first time Tor heard the screaming from all around them; the howls of pain of those being eaten alive, the wailing of those forced to watch. Grimacing, he forced himself to turn away from it. There was no time to focus on the horror of what was happening.

A spider-mother stalked close by them, and Tor tugged on Kirune's thick grey fur. 'Quickly! Kill this thing!' But Kirune had brought down a pair of drones and his muzzle was buried deeply in their sticky guts, jaws tearing and rending. 'Kirune! Listen to me!'

It was too late. The spider-mother closed its long arms around a fleeing woman, pouring its gift of scuttling burrowers directly over her, and then the great black wolf was there. She caught the mother between her jaws and ripped it away from the woman, shaking it back and forth like a dog with a rabbit, before throwing it away in disgust. On her back, Aldasair wore an identical expression of dismay.

'Good work, Jessen.' He stroked her between the ears soothingly. 'You are doing very well.'

Just then the day filled with green and purple light, turning the shadows crisp and black. Tor looked up to see Vostok wreathed in her own flames, a jet of green fire travelling from Noon's outstretched arms. He followed the direction of her winnowfire and felt his stomach turn over – there was a rupture in the side of the Behemoth, but not one they had

21

made. Part of the creature was opening up, metal skin peeling back as something pale and shining pushed its way through from inside.

'It's a maggot!' bellowed Noon. She was waving at them frantically. 'We have to stop it getting out!'

Tor curled his hands around the harness, preparing to order Kirune back into the air, when he spotted a group of people by the wall of a house. The mother had already been turned into a drone, her eyes nothing more than gaping black holes, but she had three small children with her. They were clinging to their mother, not understanding what she had become, or why she was holding them down, pressing them to the ground so that the burrowers could do their work. Their pitiful cries, more confused than frightened, squeezed at his heart. Gripping his sword firmly, he unstrapped himself from Kirune, and jumped down.

'Go and help Vostok.' He pointed at the underbelly of the Behemoth, where already the maggot could be seen more clearly. 'Stop that thing from getting down here.'

Kirune turned his baleful yellow gaze on Tor and snarled, before leaping away into a thick crowd of the drones. Tor opened his mouth to protest, but there was no time. Instead he ran to the small house, kicking burrowers out of his way as he went. One of the children was already lost, kicking and screaming in the dirt as the beetles inside him ate away everything that made him human – Tor stepped over him, ignoring the painful contraction of horror in his chest – and ran the mother through, bringing his sword up to part her chest into two gaping pieces. With so little left inside her, it was horrifyingly easy. Next to her, the two surviving children screamed, scrambling away from him.

'Wait! I'm on your side!' The door of the hut clattered open and a stout woman grabbed the children by their necks, dragging them over the threshold with impressive strength. The look she turned on Tor was a cold slap; horror, fear and rage twisted into a rigid mask.

'Murderer!' she screamed, before slamming the door shut again.

'Shit.'

'War-beasts! War-beasts, to me!' It was Vostok again. Her violet fire and Noon's winnowflames had blistered the maggot, but it was still wriggling its way out of the Behemoth's port side. Jessen and Aldasair were there, but the wolf was circling with her wings spread, clearly uncertain how to help, while Sharrik was on the far side of the village square, nearly over-whelmed with drones – men and women and children now under the control of the Jure'lia were clinging to his wings and his shaggy hindquarters. One stocky man with a white beard was hanging around the griffin's thick neck. Bern, on the war-beast's back, was busily fighting them off, his bright axes – the Bitter Twins, Tor remembered, that was what he called them – streaked with black fluid.

'Kirune?'

Tor's war-beast had his head down, nose deep in a pile of dismembered drones. Tor yelled again, with no response from Kirune save for a lazy flick of his black and grey stripped tail, so he ran over, glancing uneasily at the Behemoth above them. Judging from the fat width of its body, the maggot was nearly halfway out.

'Kirune! We have to get back up there. Are you even listening to me?' Reaching the beast's side he clapped a hand on his shoulder, and abruptly found himself on his back in the dirt, Kirune's heavy paw pressing on his chest. The cat's blocky head hung just above him, enormous yellow fangs bared.

'I am busy!' There was black ooze smeared across Kirune's short, thick whiskers. His breath was hot and fetid, stinking powerfully of dead things. 'Do not order me about!'

Tor felt his own rage sweep him from head to toe, and with

more strength than he thought he possessed, he shoved Kirune's paw from his chest and scrambled to his feet. Slamming his sword back in its scabbard, he squared up to the cat, who hissed at him.

'Oh, hissing, is it? The great war-beast Kirune, legend of Ebora, hissing at his master because I have demanded he stop playing with his toys!' Tor kicked at the remains of the drones. 'Great Kirune, the whining kitten.'

Kirune growled low in his throat, crouching with his wings folded tight to his body. Tor knew he meant to leap at him, and if he did, that he would likely break every bone in his body, famed Eboran strength or not, but at that moment it was impossible to back down. He was thinking of the scarred portion of his face, and how if the tree-god Ygseril hadn't chosen to birth these war-beasts, there might have been sap enough to heal him – to heal all the Eborans still clinging to life despite the crimson flux. Kirune's tail lashed back and forth over the dirt, his eyes wide and dangerous.

'Tor! Blood and fire, look out down there!'

It was Noon, her voice shrill with horror. Tor looked up in time to see the maggot squirming fully from the side of the Behemoth, and then it was falling, some obscene dropping plummeting towards them even as Vostok blasted it with her flames. Tor threw himself past Kirune just as the maggot landed, crashing in the midst of the square and then rolling over several shacks, shattering them into shards of wood and shell. Up close, the thing was a creamy grey, shining here and there with a sickly pearlescent gleam. The front part, which Tor, for want of any better ideas, decided must be its head, was a darker grey than the rest of it, with a handful of glistening nubs at its top and a dark, pulsating maw beneath that. It rolled once more, and Tor got a brief glimpse of a set of tiny, stubby legs underneath, and then it was busily munching away on the houses it had crushed. Wood, shell, glass, hay

24

and dirt – all was sucked up and consumed, faster than Tor would have thought possible. A few men from the settlement, armed with what looked like steel harpoons and a couple of rusty swords, ran forward and began hacking at its slippery flesh, but a fresh swarm of spider-mothers appeared, overwhelming the men and dragging them, screaming, towards the mouth of the maggot.

Tor jumped up onto Kirune's back and for a wonder the great cat turned from the corpses, leaping across the square with teeth bared. They made it in time to knock one spidermother aside, and Tor reached down and tore the man free with his bare hands, only to see another disappear into the monster's mouth out of the corner of his eye. Then Bern was next to him. The human's bare arms and neck were covered in scratches and bites, and with a lurch of guilt Tor remembered that the last time he had seen him the man had been close to being overwhelmed by drones.

'Where is Sharrik?'

Bern nodded upwards even as he grappled with the next spider mother, his axes flying. Sharrik was above them, his huge shape casting a dark shadow over them all, while Vostok circled overhead.

'Get away!' Vostok was bellowing. 'We must burn it as best we can!'

As if hearing the order itself, the maggot suddenly pulsed, throwing them all back. Its rear end thrashed back and forth, and then with another violent pulse, a thick green liquid began to gush from what, for want of any better ideas, Tor was forced to think of as its arse. The green fluid flowed across the square towards the remains of the small buildings, surging over the rubble and the remaining people, trapping humans and drones alike.

'The varnish.' Tor squeezed the hilt of the Ninth Rain, at a loss. 'How can we stop this? How?'

25

The maggot pulsed again, and more of the stuff surged from its back end, threatening to flood the square and trap Tor and Bern where they stood.

'Bern! Quickly, to us!'

Bern didn't need to be told twice. He climbed onto Kirune behind Tor, and with a cough of protest, the war-beast leapt up into the air, leathery wings beating furiously. It was not easy – as strong as Kirune was, Bern was a heavy man – but they made it out before the varnish reached them, joining Vostok and Sharrik in the air.

'Move, now, out of my way.' Vostok's voice was tight with command, her long serpentine neck already stretching out to funnel her flames directly onto the maggot. Noon had both her hands raised, each fist gloved in her emerald witch-fire – the life energy she drew from the dragon to fuel it produced an especially bright flame.

'Wait!' Tor scanned the ground desperately. How was it possible to miss a giant wolf? 'Where is Jessen? Where are Jessen and Aldasair?'

For a few moments no one spoke. Tor had time to wonder what he would do if his cousin had been killed; to lose both his sister Hestillion and Aldasair, so close to each other, would be too much, and then Bern thumped him on the shoulder and pointed. Jessen was on the far side of the square. Aldasair was still on the wolf's back, and he was pulling children up onto the saddle with him – three or four of them clung to him desperately, while Jessen dangled one small child from her jaws, teeth delicately holding on to the boy's collar.

'There is no time for that,' hissed Vostok. 'Jessen, drop them and clear the area!'

The wolf looked up at them, and even from that distance it was possible to see the defiance in her amber eyes. Aldasair, now fairly swamped with children, wore an identical expression.

26

'Foolish cubs! They will soon move when everything is aflame.' Vostok opened her jaws and Tor could see the violet flames banked there, stirring into life.

'Stop it!' He caught Noon's eyes, and was glad to see that Vostok's rage was not reflected there. 'Noon, we have to think about this . . .'

Above them, the Behemoth was still bleeding its spider-mothers down onto the settlement, while below, the varnish was spreading its green fingers between each broken house. Tor hoped that some of the humans down there had had time to flee, that perhaps they had given them that much at least, but he could see darker shapes trapped in the varnish, and bodies strewn everywhere.

'We have to move it,' said Bern in his ear. He turned then in the saddle, and shouted over to Vostok. 'Pick it up, take it beyond the palisade. Burn it there, on the beach.'

The dragon hissed between her teeth, obviously outraged that her orders were being ignored again, but then Noon leaned down and spoke into her horned ear.

'Very well. All of us together may be able to shift it. Quickly now.'

It was not easy. Bern climbed over to Sharrik in a manoeuvre which Tor was half-convinced would see the man plummet to his death, and then together the three war-beasts descended. Vostok and Sharrik went to the maggot's head, while Kirune grasped at its tail. It was slippery and the big cat struggled to get a purchase on it. Kirune muttered in the back of his throat about how it smelled bad, but eventually sank his long claws into the maggot's hide, and the whole thing rose uncertainly into the air.

The reaction from the Behemoth was immediate. More spider-mothers began to fall on them from above, and Tor found himself working hard to keep them away from Kirune, the blade of the Ninth Rain slashing back and forth like a scythe. Despite their best efforts, they could not lift the maggot very far off the ground, and they left a long line of destruction in their wake as they dragged it beyond the confines of the settlement. There was a grim moment as the belly of the creature caught on the wooden palisade, but then with a sickening tearing they came free again and Tor was glad to see a steaming pile of grey innards on the sand behind them. Once they were clear, Vostok gave a cry and they dropped the maggot, Kirune growling with relief.

'Get clear, all of you, get clear!' Vostok lowered her head again, and this time Noon stood in her saddle, a halo of green fire already burning around her. 'Noon, concentrate your witch-fire on its wound.'

Both dragon and fell-witch released their flames. The blast was so bright Tor had to shield his eyes, but still he looked, watching as the maggot's skin bulged and blistered. The place where they had torn it seethed and boiled, and then its insides were pouring out, splashing onto the beach in a hot torrent. The maggot itself visibly seemed to shrivel, something inside it irreparably broken. The twin fires ceased, leaving a thick pall of evil-smelling yellow smoke, and one very dead giant maggot.

'We did it.' Tor found himself grinning, and he pressed his fingers to Kirune's fur, expecting to share with him a feeling of triumph – but the big cat dipped his head, breaking the contact.

'I think we've annoyed it enough. Look!' Tor turned to see where Bern was pointing. The Behemoth, now flying more crookedly than ever, was turning away from the coast and surging away, gradually picking up speed. There were more holes in it than Tor remembered, and several darkened patches from Noon's and Vostok's fire. That had to be good. That had to be worth it.

'We chased it off,' he said aloud, but no one answered. The

settlement, he realised, was little more than a mixture of shattered houses and green varnish. The bits of it that were still standing were merrily on fire, while a handful of survivors stood down by the shoreline, their arms around each other. Jessen and Aldasair were down there, releasing their passengers to the stunned-looking crowd. Tor realised he could hear a child crying.

'That's got to be worth something, hasn't it?'

4

'Vostok is angry.'

It hardly needed to be said. The dragon had stalked off some hours ago, disappearing into the patch of Wild-wood at the edge of the bleak clearing, but Noon could still feel her rage near her heart, like a banked fire, and she thought the others should know it as clearly as she did. They were resting on their journey back from the distant settlement, and all of them – man and war-beast alike – were avoiding her eyes.

Tor sighed from the other side of their campfire. 'We are not what we should be yet. Of course we're not.' Kirune lay some distance behind him, a dark-grey shape with his head turned away from the humans. He snorted at Tor's words, which Tor ignored. 'With the best will in the world, Noon, she can't expect us to be. So our first skirmish with the Jure'lia didn't cover us in glory. Are we any of us surprised?'

'Glory? Most of the people there died.' Noon bit her lip. It was hard to separate her own anger from the dragon's. 'Their settlement is a ruin. We fucked up. We fucked up, and people died.'

Tor's face on the far side of the fire was bathed in orange

light, turning the purple scars on the left side of his face grey. His expression was grim.

'This is war,' he said. 'You can expect to see much more of it.'

'The glory days of Ebora are long behind us.' This was Aldasair, his soft voice seeming to float over them in the growing dark. Next to him, the giant wolf Jessen was little more than a mound of darkness, her orange eyes hanging like lamps in the gloom. 'Our armies, with their shining armour and singing swords are rust and dusty bones. We are like . . . an echo of something that came before.'

Next to him, Bern looked concerned, and Noon thought he had good reason to be. Aldasair had been nearly silent since the fight, and now he sounded ghostly and lost. Bern pulled the kettle from the fire and filled a tin cup, which he passed to the Eboran.

'It's been a long day. Here, drink something hot.' He cleared his throat. 'The Finneral know those people, a little. We've traded with them, sailing our ships up into that chilly little bay. They have these enormous crabs, you see, and the meat is so fatty and rich it can keep you going for days and days, and they weave this material from the seaweed, sea-leather they call it, tough as your arse it is. We take them our metal and our whale skins and there's a fine old trade, although I imagine . . .' He coughed into his hand. 'I imagine there will be less of all that, for a time.' Beyond the ring of their fire light, the griffin Sharrik had stretched out on the stubbly grass, his thickly furred stomach exposed to the air. The silence was broken by his snoring.

'War is one thing. I know it's going to get much worse.' Noon reached out for Vostok and felt her growing closer, an angry white presence. 'But we are . . . we are all wrong. We need to try harder.'

'And you're an expert on it now, are you?' Tor took the

kettle and filled his own cup. 'A witch from the plains who has spent most of her life imprisoned in the Winnowry wants to tell *me* about how Eboran war-beasts should fight?'

His tone was light, attempting to make a joke of it, but she felt the steel underneath the words. Here she was, stamping all over his birthright after all, and straightaway she felt her own anger growing.

'I know more about being a weapon than you ever will.'

'And you would do well to listen to her, son of Ebora.' Vostok emerged from the trees, moving quietly despite her size. As always, Noon felt her heart lift at the sight of the dragon; even in the night gloom she was extraordinary, her shining scales picking up the orange glow of the fire and igniting a thousand tiny suns. 'Our problems are numerous and complex, and we have little enough time to deal with them.'

Tor looked away from the dragon. Noon knew he would avoid contradicting her directly – he was still half in awe of the first war-beast to be born in hundreds of years, and more than once she had caught him gazing at Vostok with something like longing.

'We destroyed the maggot, killed dozens of drones, and drove off the Behemoth.' He took a sip from his tin cup, and grimaced. 'By the roots, what is this swill, Bern? Anyway,' he shook his head, 'I am calling it a victory, either way. There are people on that coast who are alive now because of us, and not trapped in varnish or stumbling around with their insides missing.'

'You drove off a Behemoth that was already weakened.' Vostok came over to the fire and pressed her long head briefly against Noon's shoulder. 'Lying for centuries in ruins has left them broken – they haven't had their usual period of recovery, and we are presented with a unique opportunity. Of course, we're also in the unique situation of fighting with possibly the worst war-beasts Ebora has ever seen.'

At that, Kirune was suddenly upright, hissing through his bared fangs. Even Sharrik raised his head from the ground, feathers bristling.

'Listen to me. We must fight as *one*. We must move and attack as one unit. Without unity, we are chaos.' Vostok snorted, and Noon laid her hand against the scales on her neck. They were warm. 'It is because you do not have your root-memories, any of you. Our souls should have returned to Ygseril's roots when we last died, but instead we were exiled, lost. We became ghosts, parasite things haunting the wrecks of our old enemy, and now even those souls are lost, dissipated finally into nothing, and in the end it was only I who survived to find Ebora again, carried safe within Noon. Do you even understand what it is you have lost? With your root-memories you would remember all our battles, all our victories, and we would know each other as we should. You would feel Ygseril's roots binding us together, one to another.' Noon could feel the edges of sorrow clouding Vostok's anger, but none of that was apparent in her voice. 'So we must learn to work together without the bonds that would normally tie us. In short, you must learn to take orders.'

'And you must be the one to give them, snake?' Kirune was pacing now, huge paws kicking up dust. 'Because you breathe fire, you must be in charge of us?'

'Now, then, Kirune,' Tor was holding out one hand towards the giant cat, his face alarmed. 'That isn't going to help—'

'I command you because I am your only link to the glory that was!' Vostok thundered. Violet flames danced in the back of her throat. 'Your names were stolen, chosen at random from an old scroll, because we do not know what your names truly were. *True war-beasts you are not.*' The dragon lowered her head, and Noon wondered if this was where all this madness would end: a ridiculous fight in the middle of nowhere, all of them cooked in dragon-flame. 'Kirune, you refuse to bond with your warrior and take vicious pleasure in contradiction. Through your selfishness you lead us to doom. Sharrik, you are brave but you do not think. Your strength can be used for so much more. Jessen, you are timid, possibly the worst and most unforgivable trait in a war-beast. And your warrior is no warrior at all.'

Despite the warmth of Vostok's anger, Noon winced, although Aldasair seemed barely to have noticed. He sat with his head down, his fingers laced around the tin cup.

'And Tormalin the Oathless.' Tor jumped as if struck. 'You are vain, distracted, arrogant and convinced that you are the only true warrior here. If you do not learn to work with Kirune somehow, you will be worse than useless – you will be a liability.'

'I trained for decades while you were haunting Esiah Godwort's wreck, you misbegotten relic . . .'

'Hey,' Noon sat up, 'the war-beasts *died* at the end of the Eighth Rain, Tor, torn out of their bodies when your tree-god trapped the Jure'lia queen. It's not like they chose to be para-site spirits. Who would?' The memory of Vostok's sorrow and confusion at what they had become was still very fresh.

Vostok ignored them both. 'The Behemoth was our target. We needed to work together to drive it off, long before it ever managed to birth a maggot, and yet where were you all?'

'We saved the humans.' Jessen's voice was soft, but for the first time Noon thought she detected genuine anger there. 'We helped the children to flee.'

'*Children*,' Vostok sneered. 'It is war you must be concerned with, not a handful of lives. If we let all the Behemoths flee as we did today, Sarn's children will soon be no one's problem.'

'Vostok.' Noon pressed her lips together. She felt the dragon's need to fight keenly, and it made thinking of anything else difficult. Absently, she pressed her fingers to her shirt; under-neath it, the silver scar on her chest felt too smooth. 'Do you

34

really think we could have killed that thing today? With just four war-beasts?'

Vostok turned her head away, looking back out into the trees as though she had heard something, but Noon knew she was just avoiding the question. That alone made her feel cold inside.

'Has it ever been done before?' asked Bern, his honest face unusually serious. 'Any other battles in your history where the odds were so . . . uh, unfavourable?'

'No,' said Vostok shortly. 'There were always hundreds of us, before.'

'It doesn't matter,' said Sharrik. He rose from the thin grass and stretched out his wings – they were huge, and the darkest blue in the firelight. 'We are mighty! We shall fight!'

'You must *learn* to fight,' said Vostok, but some of the anger in her voice had softened. She settled onto the ground, tucking her legs neatly under herself. 'Unity, or we are lost. We must find a way to be one again.'

'Well.' Tormalin sat back. He met Noon's eyes briefly, and gave her half a smile. 'Perhaps we'll get lucky and find a new brace of war-beasts freshly hatched when we get back to the palace. Stranger things have happened.'

5

This must be the strangest journey I have ever undertaken.

Nanthema and I make our slow way to Ebora, travelling when we feel it's safe, taking turns to sleep. I keep looking at the sky, searching for the corpse moon there like a tongue searching the hole where a tooth was once rooted – I know it's gone, but part of me can't believe it. Since we watched the waterlogged Behemoth remains rise from the sea we haven't seen any Jure'lia as close. A few sightings in the distance, enormous bloated tumours hovering impossibly still over the tops of trees, or, more ominously, above tiny settlements. I feel I can barely describe here what it is like to see these monsters of our history risen again.

It is strange too to be travelling with Nanthema. I find myself almost frightened watching her, as though a part of my past had just forced its way into my present. She is as lovely as she ever was, her eyelashes when she sleeps downy and thick on her cheek, her long, confident stride when she walks. She touches my hand and kisses my cheek, as though we have never been apart, yet I know I must look greatly changed to her, and although she is frightened, like me, she looks around always with curiosity and wonder. It is the thing I always loved most about her.

I am glad she lives. I am very glad not to be making this journey alone.

Extract from the private journals
of Lady Vincenza 'Vintage' de Grazon

'I'm telling you, Vin, there's someone there.'

Vintage paused, squinting into the distance. All she could see on the road was a confusion of broken stones and the debris of years of isolation. There were fewer buildings in this remote corner of Ebora, but there was still a wide tracery of roads, dotted here and there with statuary that once, she suspected, would have been spectacular.

'Your eyes are better than mine, darling. Who is it?'

Nanthema frowned in answer. They had been travelling for weeks, and they were both tired, dusty and hungry, living off what food they could find in the wilds of Ebora, and the occasional rabbit Vintage surprised with her crossbow. There had been no sign of human life for much of that time, with most people hiding within their settlements, waiting to see if the Jure'lia would come for them. Most people, Vintage had cheerfully pointed out, were not stupid enough to be travelling anywhere, but then, they weren't most people.

'Let's get closer and see.'

Although the ice had thawed in the last few days, it was still frigidly cold and Vintage unhooked her crossbow from her belt with numb fingers. To either side of them dark pine trees rose like an ominous curtain, and she began to wonder if people would have turned to banditry yet – that was what humans did, in times of war.

'It's a boy,' said Nanthema.

'A child? By the vines, what is a child doing . . .?' A moment later she saw him, and on the heels of that, realised what he was. 'Nan, that's an Eboran child.'

Nanthema just nodded.

He was sitting on a broken rock, with what looked like a bow made of black wood slung over one narrow shoulder. To Vintage's eyes he looked to be no more than twelve or thirteen years old, but in Eboran terms that meant he could be anywhere near as old as two hundred years. His hair was an ashy blond, long and unkempt enough to curl at his neck, and although his face was finely boned and delicate, he was also much too thin. The furred jacket he wore hung on him loosely, leaving a great gaping hole at the neck, and he was slumped on the rock as though he did not even have the energy to lift his head. He was sitting, Vintage realised, on a broken statue. Judging from the snarling head that lay at his feet, it had once been a dragon. A war-beast, of course.

'An Eboran child,' murmured Vintage. 'I had thought . . . I had assumed . . .'

Nanthema glanced at her, her lips thinned with displeasure. 'When Ygseril's life-giving sap was gone, very few were born. Those that were, were born sickly and ill.' She touched a finger to the frame of her eyeglasses. 'When we found out that human blood could heal us, mothers and fathers couldn't feed their babes enough of it. Of course, we couldn't know that consuming human blood would lead to the crimson flux. . .' She shook her head. 'I can't remember when I last saw an Eboran child.'

'Come on, let's go and see who this poor creature is, and what he's doing out here in the arse-end of nowhere.'

The boy looked up as they approached, and his hands clutched weakly at the bow on his shoulder. There was a quiver of arrows by his feet – Vintage thought they looked ancient – and a steel bucket with a cloth over the top. His eyes were deeply shadowed, and now that they were closer, Vintage could see lines around them, making him look strangely ancient. She wondered how she could have ever mistaken him for a human child – it was a stark reminder of the inherent strangeness of Eborans, with their red eyes and unnatural strength. Travelling with Tor, and now Nanthema, she had started to get a little too used to them. With a little grunt, the boy pushed himself off of the broken rock and faced them.

'Darling, it's a cold day for sitting around on old stones.' Vintage smiled at the boy. 'My grandmother used to say you'd get piles from sitting on cold rocks. I'm sure you're much too young to suffer with such things, but it doesn't hurt to be careful.'

'Piles?' His voice was deeper than she was expecting. 'Piles of what?'

'Well, indeed. There's a question.' They stopped in front of him. The maroon of his eyes was too bright for the gloomy day, more akin to rubies than old wine. 'Are you quite all right?' When he seemed unable to answer, Vintage gestured to Nanthema. 'This is my friend Nanthema. As you can probably tell, she's not a stranger to your lands, but I have never been here before. My name is Lady Vincenza de Grazon, but you can call me Vintage.'

The boy raised his eyebrows at her name, apparently impressed.

'I'm Eri,' he said. 'Eri of . . . I can't remember. Of Lonefell, I suppose.'

'That is your home?' asked Nanthema.

'I suppose that it is.'

'And are there others there?' asked Vintage. She glanced around, wondering if perhaps there could be more Eborans nearby. 'Relatives, perhaps?'

The question seemed to distress the boy. Looking away from them, he turned to the dark woods on the other side of the broken road, and then picked up his quiver of arrows. 'There are small deer in these woods, or at least, there used to be. It's difficult to remember, but I'm sure that I saw them once. But lately I've heard wolves howling a lot, at night, when it's dark, and sometimes in the day too.' His throat moved as he swallowed heavily. 'Do you think that maybe the wolves ate all the deer already?' He paused, and when he spoke again his voice was strangely resonant. 'I need meat.'

'That could well be the case,' said Vintage. 'Are you on your own, Eri?'

Curiously, the boy looked down at the covered bucket, and again he seemed to struggle with the question. 'Food is the problem,' he said. 'I can't really go on pretending it isn't. One jar left in the pantry, the ground too cold for seeds.' He looked back up at them, swaying on his feet slightly. 'Is there food where you are going? Where *are* you going?'

'We're going to the centre of Ebora, Eri, to the palace. Hopefully, there will be people there, or at least, I'm sure they will have left something behind we can eat.' Vintage put on her best smile. 'It's worth a look, don't you think? Would you like to come with us?'

'I'm not supposed to go there,' the boy said. 'I know that much. We were never to go there again.'

'Who told you that? What has happened at the palace?' Nanthema looked sharply at the boy, but he just shrugged.

'I don't know, I've never been. And I can't remember why now, not really . . .' After a moment, he reached down and picked up the bucket by the handle. Inside it, something clacked dryly together. 'I will come and have a look, that's all. I can always come back, can't I?'

Later, when they had stopped to make camp and the boy was asleep by the fire, Vintage found herself staring at his face. It was too gaunt, the skin oddly thin, and somehow she thought it wasn't entirely to do with his hunger. As if sensing her thoughts, Nanthema nodded at the boy and poked at the fire with a stick.

'Born after Ygseril died. Sickly, no root-nourishment there. He looks older than he should, don't you think?'

'Do you have any idea how difficult it is to tell how old an Eboran is, my darling?' Vintage kept her voice lower than Nanthema's although the boy was obviously deeply asleep; his odd growling snores were evidence of that. 'To me, he looks like a boy who has been ill for a long time.'

'He has, in a way.'

Silence fell. They had made their fire near a ring of standing stones. Each was elaborately carved with twisting strands of ivy, although from the corner of Vintage's eye the leaping shadows seemed to turn them into leering faces.

'We should have asked him to take us to his house. I should like to know how many other Eborans are out here, and why they've chosen to be so far from the palace.' Nanthema pursed her lips. 'Before I left, people were moving inwards. Trying to keep close to one another. Being out here, so far from the palace, makes no sense. Shall we see what is in his bucket?'

Vintage shrugged, uneasy. 'It's probably the food he collected earlier today,' although in truth she didn't really believe that. It hadn't sounded like food, not as they'd walked along the road and listened to the contents rattling against the metal. 'Leave him be, Nan. We'll get him to the palace with us, find him some food to fatten him up a little, and perhaps there will be someone there to look after him. The poor lad looks like he could use some looking after.'

Nanthema looked uncertain. She pulled a roll of greased paper from her pack, and peeled it back to reveal a length of dried sausage; she gnawed on the end of it.

'How does it feel, to see a child of your people again, after all this time? It could be seen as a hopeful thing. You were trapped inside that Behemoth for over twenty years.'

'Time hasn't really passed for me, Vin.'

'You know what I mean.'

Nanthema looked up from the meat, and then broke into a wide smile. 'I feel curious, Vin, like I usually do. Hopefully there will be people left at the palace, and then the boy can be someone else's problem. Here, do you want a bite of this?'

Vintage thought of the lad looking at the bucket, of him saying, 'I need meat'.

'Thank you darling, but I'm fine.'

6

The cell – as Hestillion had come to think of it – was almost cosy, in a terrible way. It was never cold, nor too warm, and the dim glow from the bulbous nodules in the walls dimmed for several hours each day, so that it was almost possible for her to recall the normal cycle of days and nights. A few hours after the queen had left her the first time, the wall had split open like a pair of eyelids peeling apart and a squat, formless creature had oozed through, carrying an armful of fleshy brown things like larvae. Hestillion had scooped up the war-beast pod and scrambled hurriedly towards the far wall, but the creature had placed the things on the floor between them, and then made stilted, encouraging gestures at her, as though she were a wary wild animal and it were trying to make friends. When Hestillion had not moved, the thing had shuffled forward on its squat legs and, picking up one of the brownish pods, had peeled the top open. Inside it was a grainy-looking white muck, which it then scooped out with its approximation of a hand, and lifted to where its mouth would have been if it had any features at all. The mime was clear enough. The homunculus carefully placed the open pod down on the floor and then oozed its way back out of the wall.

It had taken Hestillion hours to work up the courage to pick up the pod herself, but in the end her cramping stomach was too insistent, and to her surprise the grainy muck tasted rather like especially bland porridge. She had eaten it, and was not sick, and opened another of the pods. It had contained water with a faintly mineral taste.

Now, the shuffling homunculus – she had no way to tell if it was the same one, or a series of them – dropped off the food parcels every day, and she ate and drank without fear. Yet she was frightened, angry in a way she had never been in her life, and heartily sick of porridge.

The light nodules had brightened again in their approximation of morning when the latest homunculus slipped through the puckered wall opening. Hestillion was crouched on the slightly spongy floor, her arms around the war-beast pod. She thought it had begun to grow warm, and sometimes when she was very still, she thought she could sense the creature inside trying to reach out to her. But then she would remember how she had thought she was talking to the great god Ygseril while she dream-walked, when in actuality she had been simpering and grovelling to their enemy, tricked into finally releasing the Jure'lia queen from her prison within the tree-god's roots. That thought was still too much to bear.

'You. Creature. Can you speak?'

The homunculus stiffened as it placed the food packages on the floor. The things that came each day were identical, as far as she could tell, constructed from the pliable black material that seemed to be at the very heart of what the Jure'lia were; they had no discernible head, just a thick torso, short stumpy legs, and long flexible arms. The digits that split the ends of those arms changed and twisted into whatever happened to be needed at the time.

'I know you can hear me.' Hestillion stood up, reluctantly leaving the faint warmth of the war-beast pod behind. 'I want

44

something other than this gruel. I want real food. If you are keeping me here, you must give me something real. Wine, bread, meat . . .' The thought of bread, freshly baked and full of its own warmth, was like a physical blow, and for a second she was unable to speak. 'Where is your queen? Bring her to me!'

The creature was shuffling rapidly back to the wall, clearly meaning to leave her, and without knowing she was going to do it, Hestillion leapt across the chamber towards it. The wall flexed open in its unpleasant way but she had hold of the thing's stringy arm and she yanked it away from its escape hatch.

'Speak to me! I *know* you can hear me, I know it!'

Under her fingers the creature's arm was tough and stringy, but as she squeezed it the cords of its muscles seemed to turn back to goo, and then it was free of her and slipping back out the hole. Roaring with frustration, Hestillion threw herself after it, and her head and torso slipped wetly through the opening. She had a glimpse of a curving narrow space filled with shadows, the homunculus skittering out of sight around a corner, and then the wall was moving against her, closing around her like a tightening ring of flesh.

'I know you can hear me!'

Bracing her feet against the floor of her cell she pushed forward, trying to wriggle out into the corridor beyond, but the wall actively thrust her back; it was like being spat out with tremendous force. She hit the floor and was back on her feet immediately, but the hole had already closed – the surface was smooth and unyielding again.

For a handful of erratic heartbeats Hestillion stood and glared at the wall, trembling all over, and then she shrieked, a terrible broken noise that left her throat raw and stinging.

'You can! You can hear me! You can!'

Unsteady on her feet, she walked back to the war-beast pod.

It looked small and grey, an incongruous artefact from hundreds of years ago, in the belly of an alien monster. But inside it, she knew, there was a link to Ebora and everything she had abandoned.

Kneeling next to it, she placed her hands on the surface and forced herself to look at it properly. It was not grey truly, but a deep burnished silver, and it was longer than it was wide, although the shape of it was irregular, covered all over with soft bulges. There were no creases in that skin, no wrinkles. Nothing to get her fingernails under.

'I know you can hear me too,' she said softly. 'And I'm sorry if you're not ready, but I need you here now, little one.'

Gritting her teeth, Hestillion bent her fingers into claws and sank them into the skin of the pod. There was a great deal of resistance, and at the first few tries her fingernails just skidded off the surface, but she brought the pod around to brace it between her legs, and using her own weight, managed to lever off a chunk of the pod. It came away in thick, fibrous wads, filling the cell with the clean, sharp scent of trees and leaves. Choking back a sob – how that scent took her back to her earliest childhood – she worked all the faster, peeling away handfuls of the stuff, regardless of how it broke her nails and made them bleed. The skin of the pod was thicker than she had expected, so thick that she began to wonder if there was nothing inside at all, but she pushed away that sickening thought with a grunt and kept digging, faster and faster now. The joint of the smallest finger on her left hand popped and a sharp dart of pain travelled up to her elbow. Hestillion hissed with annoyance and kept going. There had been a change in the texture of the stuff; it was more brittle, crumbling to bits as she removed it, and then she was down to a layer like thick lace.

It was then that something moved under her hands.

Hestillion yelped, unable to stop herself. Purple scales, tiny and interlocked, shifted under her grasp. She had an odd thought – that the pod would be full of snakes, that they would slither out and eat her – and then she was tearing more pieces aside with her bloody hands. The thing inside was shifting weakly, not quite able to pull itself free, and gradually Hestillion became aware that she was murmuring to it, saying quiet soothing things as if it were a baby.

'There you are, there you are, not much longer. Hold on, hold on, my sweet.'

She slipped her arms fully into the pod, encircling the creature, feeling the fluids of its birth surge out over her chest, soaking her already tattered gown. The thing shifted against her sluggishly, slippery scaled skin oddly feverish, and then she heaved. The pod itself split into several large pieces, and she fell back against the floor with the creature cradled to her chest.

For several breaths she was too exhausted to do anything but lie there, soaked in the tree-scented fluid with the weight of her new charge heavy on her torso and her hands throbbing steadily. When eventually she gathered the strength to lift her head, she found herself looking into a great pearly eye. The war-beast was no bigger than a large dog, and it was a dragon, its long serpentine head cocked to one side so that it could look at her better. Its scales were a deep purple, shading to magenta at its throat and belly, while small, dark horns, so purple they were almost blue, sprouted from behind its ears. The creature's wings were small and wet, stuck firmly to its back still. Shaking with a combination of awe and exhaustion, Hestillion touched a hand to its jaw.

'I can taste your blood.'

Its voice was male, but light. He sounded very young. Hestillion nodded uncertainly.

'You can hear me.'

'I can.' The dragon blinked at her owlishly. Although she

had at first thought his eyes were entirely white, she saw now that they were silver at the centre, and oddly reflective.

'Can you see me?'

The small dragon snorted, and with a stirring of his limbs, slipped off her and onto the floor. He seemed to have difficulty standing, his head oddly oversized in comparison to the rest of him. He looked, she realised, very much like a baby.

'I see you. I taste you too. I am hungry.'

'Yes.' Hestillion stood up slowly, unable to take her eyes from the small dragon. War-beasts, she knew well, were born from their pods fully grown – or at least, large enough that it made little difference. This creature, with its undersized pod, had not spent long enough on the branch, and there was a chance it would simply die, too weak to live. But at least now it would have a chance; the first war-beasts in so long should have that much, if nothing else. 'What is your name, my lord?'

The dragon took a few steps forward. He was trying to look at his own feet as he did so, and nearly fell over. His tail was short and stubby, with only the tip touching the floor.

'I don't know. Is there food?'

This was new as well. When they died, the souls of war-beasts returned to Ygseril's roots, eventually to be reborn in his branches centuries later. They would remember who they were, their old forms, and keep all their old memories. It was one of the reasons they were such a formidable force; the war-beasts were Eboran history given flesh. She thought of all the war-beasts dying at the end of the Eighth Rain, when Ygseril had died. She thought of their souls seeking out roots that were dry and dead, and a shiver worked its way violently down her back.

'What do you remember, bright one? Anything you can tell me, anything at all.' He wobbled his head around to look at her. 'And then there will be food.'

He made a huffing noise, and shook himself all over.

'Warmth, sunlight. A rustling noise. Falling.' One of his wings flexed experimentally, black feathers all stuck together. 'I am sorry.'

'Do not be sorry, lord. Here, this is food.' She went over to the gruel pods and began to peel one open, but as the small dragon teetered over to her, he stumbled and fell, legs kicking as he lay on his side. Hestillion scooped him up and took him back to the pod, ignoring the tight feeling of despair that was seeping through her chest. *I have someone to talk to*, she told herself. *I am not alone here.*

'Here, look. Here.' She settled him on her lap as best she could – he was, at least, too big to sit there comfortably – and directed his snout to the open pod. He began to eat, jaws working furiously so that gobbets of the gruel slopped down her robe. When he had finished the first one, she opened the second pod and he thrust his snout inside it eagerly.

'You will need a name, lord.' He did not respond save for a series of wet chomping noises. 'And I suppose I will have to give it to you.' The weight of him on her was as oddly comforting as it was uncomfortable. 'I cannot know what your name was in your past lives, and I am uncertain as to whether I should give you another's name. That would seem . . . unlucky.' She cleared her throat. 'I never thought I should hold a war-beast in my arms. I never thought I would leave Ebora again, but here I am. When I was very, very small, there was a flower that grew in Ebora. It was my favourite, when I was a child – a big purple flower with great velvety petals. It was called cellaphalious. Such a delicate bloom, and hard to grow in any great quantity. Many of our gardeners dedicated decades of their lives to cultivating it, and then in late spring, when all the new plants opened their buds, we would hold a day of celebration. The Festival of Celaphon – a welcoming to the new flowers.' Distantly, Hestillion realised she was crying. Tears were making their way down her grimy face in a warm flood, but it did not matter. 'Celaphon. How is that for a name? Do you like it?'

The young dragon snorted into the pod. 'Celaphon. Celaphon.'

'That's it.' She smiled through her tears. 'You say it perfectly, Celaphon.'

She had just opened the third pod, not thinking what she would do for her own sustenance, when the wall peeled back to reveal the Jure'lia queen. She stepped over the threshold, an intent expression on her face, and the hole healed behind her. Hestillion gathered Celaphon to her chest and stood up, trying to ignore how heavy he was.

'What is this, Lady Hestillion Eskt? What have you done?'

'You knew I had him,' she said. 'You knew, and said nothing.'

'We thought the thing was dead.' The queen's tone was mild, but Hestillion was not fooled. 'A living war-beast, here, among us. Such changes we have seen. Dangerous changes.'

The teeming black ceiling above became suddenly more lively, and underneath her slippered feet, Hestillion could feel the floor growing warm, as though the Behemoth was turning its attention towards her.

'If you want to kill him, you'll have to kill me,' she said. 'This is all I have left. Don't make the mistake of thinking I won't die for it.'

It was a gamble. She still had no real idea why the queen had kept her alive, or why she had taken her into the corpse moon at all – it could not truly be that she felt grateful, after all.

'You are all so concerned with living and dying.'

'And you're not?'

The queen seemed to take a slow breath then, and Hestillion wondered if she had lungs at all, or if it was some pretence meant to disarm her.

'We suppose not. We are concerned with birth, with change,

with movement. With consumption.' Whether it was a contrivance or not, the queen had her head bowed slightly, as though she were truly considering her answers. 'The individual is nothing, when the whole changes and moves on. Still, you have given us a lot to think about, Hestillion Eskt. You told us that this had never happened before – that never in the history between our *peoples* had we spoken with each other, and that is true. A line of communication has been opened. Change has happened. Perhaps that is meaningful after all.'

The newly named Celaphon wriggled in Hestillion's arms. She wished the queen would stop using her family name; she had only revealed that because she thought she was talking to her god.

'I don't care what is meaningful for you or not. I am keeping Celaphon. You cannot have him.'

'A name already? You people and your names.' The queen came further into the cell, her glittering eyes fixed on the young war-beast, and Hestillion regretted telling her Celaphon's name, too. 'But if you do not care what is meaningful to us, Lady Hestillion, why did you come here?'

'I did not come here! You took me.'

Silence fell in the chamber. Celaphon turned in Hestillion's arms, resting his heavy head on her shoulder.

'Did we, Hestillion Eskt? You did not resist. We felt your need to escape.' When Hestillion did not answer, the queen turned back to the wall, which opened at her touch. 'Interesting. There will be more food, for our old enemy. Why not? It is a runt, and will die soon of its own accord.'

With that she slid from the room, leaving Hestillion and the new war-beast in an uneasy silence.

51

7

Ezion,

Forgive this very brief note, but as I'm sure you can imagine it is dangerous to linger too long anywhere, and in this tiny village we have an opportunity to sleep under a roof. I intended to make the most of that.

I hope with all my heart that you are all safe. How are Carla and the children? How is Bernhart? If you have any sense you will be lying low. Invest in foods that last a long time, don't go travelling unless you absolutely must. Don't forget about the staff either, Ezion – they have worked with our family for generations. They are our family. I want you to imagine my face as I am telling you this, and know that if I hear otherwise there will be trouble. (I'm sure you hate this, being given advice by your big sister, but you know I'm right. I think you've always known that).

It will surprise you to hear that I am travelling with the Eboran woman Nanthema. Remember her? I suspect you do. We are heading to Ebora, hoping we'll find some answers there. I will write to you again as soon as I know more. Please kiss Carla and the babies for me, and tell them Aunty Vintage loves them.

Extract from the private letters
of Lord Ezion de Grazon

Noon leaned forward in the harness, hearing the creak of the leather as it stretched to support her, and pressed her hands to the scales on the back of Vostok's neck. Below them, the outskirts of Ebora lay under a fine covering of glittering frost: overgrown fields like a frozen sea, the occasional ruin sitting at the end of an abandoned road. The days were growing warmer as they edged towards spring, but at this hour of the morning winter's teeth still had some bite. It had been agreed that they should take turns patrolling Ebora; every day, they would watch the borders and see what they could see. Since the skirmish at the coast they had heard nothing further of Jure'lia activity, but they had to assume that their enemy was still active. Under Noon's fingers, Vostok's blood surged hot beneath her pearly scales and ivory feathers. Noon grinned to herself. She was chilled to the bone, they were hopelessly outnumbered and everyone was in grave danger, but she was flying a fucking *dragon*.

'How it has all changed,' said Vostok. 'I remember when—'

'Vostok, if you're about to tell me how you remember when all this was a field of golden wheat, or a landing platform for war-beasts made of pink marble, or some bloody thing, please don't.'

'It was an orchard, actually.' Vostok rumbled in the back of her throat, sounding aggrieved. 'Memories are important, child. As well you know.'

Noon bit her lip. 'Yeah. I know. Sorry.'

Memories were a sore subject. The other war-beasts of the Ninth Rain, who had been born from their own silver pods over the course of the long winter, did not remember Ebora in all its old glory. They did not remember anything at all of their past lives – not even their own names, let alone what it was to fight the worm people, to defend Ebora, or to fly in formation with their brothers and sisters.

'We will find a way around it,' she said, trying to sound surer than she felt. 'Tormalin is working hard to make a connection with Kirune, and Aldasair, well, they are both doing everything they can—'

'They all must work harder. They must learn to *listen*. I cannot hold off a Jure'lia invasion on my own.' Vostok brought her great wings down abruptly once then twice in quick succession, causing them to surge higher in the sky. Noon moved her hands back to the reinforced strap on the front of the harness and squinted against the freezing wind.

'What is it?'

'We are not alone in the sky. Something else is flying here. Look, towards the mountains.'

Noon blinked stinging water from her eyes, and peered at where Vostok was steering them. She spotted it almost at once – a small black shape against the grey, edges blurred from the speed of its own wings. Her stomach dropped at the same moment her chest tightened with excitement.

'It's the fucking Winnowry. What are they doing here?' Noon pressed her lips together. It was extraordinary really, but it had been some time since she had spared the Winnowry, and its miserable cells full of fell-witches, a single thought.

Below her, Vostok chuckled. 'You cannot guess?'

'If they think they are taking me back to that shit hole . . .' Noon laughed. She was riding a *fucking dragon*. 'Shall we go and show them what your fire can do, Vostok?'

In answer, the landscape below became a blur as they shot towards the black spot in the distance. Noon leaned low over Vostok's back, keeping the shape in sight as they flew. As they

54

drew closer, she saw that it was indeed one of the Winnowry's giant bats, very like the one she had escaped on herself. There was a woman sitting astride it, wearing a blue and grey cloak, as well as a thick fur-lined hat against the cold. Another fell-witch, and an agent of the Winnowry. She did not retreat as they closed in, although Noon saw her tense in the saddle, her mouth opening to murmur some command to her understandably skittish bat. No bat born in the last few hundred years had seen a living, breathing war-beast. Vostok came close, then held herself hanging in the air, lazily beating her wings so that the wind ruffled the bat's fur.

'Oi! Lost, are we?'

The woman smiled. She was young, not much older than Noon, and her skin was a warm brown. Curls of glossy black hair peeked out from under her hat. She looked like she had a face that smiled often, and there was a confidence in the tilt of her chin that felt out of place in someone about to be roasted by a dragon. The hat and the hair partially obscured the bat-wing tattoo on her forehead.

'Fell-Noon, I presume?'

'That was never my name.' Noon placed her bare fingers against Vostok's neck and sought out the dragon's life energy to generate her witch-fire. She took just a touch, and it filled her chest with warmth in moments. 'And I'm never going back. They must know that by now.'

The woman tipped her head to one side; a non-committal gesture. 'I am not here to bring you home, believe it or not.'

'*This* is Noon's home,' said Vostok. 'Not some human prison.'

For the first time, the woman looked unsettled. 'It can speak?'

'Of course she can fucking speak.' Noon pursed her lips. The winnowfire she nursed within her was itching to be released. 'What do you want?'

'I am Agent Maritza. I'm here because the Winnowry are curious. All sorts of stories are coming out of Ebora, spreading

55

down across the plains.' She eyed Vostok uneasily. 'Looks like they're true.'

'True? How much evidence do you need?' Noon gestured to the empty sky above them. Not long ago, the corpse moon had hung there, unmoving for centuries. When the Jure'lia returned, the old Behemoths had awoken, including the corpse moon – becoming something alive and vital once more. Agent Maritza gave her a rueful nod.

'Fair enough. The worm people have been seen in the skies again, and they've left some of their muck hanging about the place too.'

Noon settled back in the harness, considering. The last thing she wanted to do was have a cosy chat with a Winnowry agent, but the bad winter had closed most of the newly open routes to Ebora. In truth, they desperately needed the information. She could tell from the careful stillness below that Vostok agreed with her.

'Been up to their old tricks, have they?'

Agent Maritza nodded briskly, suddenly businesslike. 'In a few places, yes. They've eaten their fill, puked up that green stuff of theirs, and even left a few drones bumbling about the place.' The woman's mouth turned down at the corners, and Noon couldn't help frowning in sympathy. 'But it has not been as devastating as you might think. It's been patchy, almost. They attack, and then disappear, as if they're confused or unsure. The Behemoths themselves . . .' She paused. 'How much do you know, of what happened?'

'More than we care to tell you,' rumbled Vostok.

The woman blinked, and then continued. 'The old crashed Behemoths scattered throughout Sarn repaired themselves, dragging their shattered bits together. You would not think it possible for them to fly again, but they've managed it.'

Reluctantly, Noon thought of the Behemoth wreck in Esiah Godwort's compound. The man's obsession with studying the

56

ruined thing had outdone even Vintage's passion for Jure'lia artefacts. Although Noon had blown half of it to pieces with her winnowfire, she wouldn't be surprised to hear that it was also floating around the sky somewhere. She remembered the shrivelled corpse of Tyron Godwort, Esiah's son, who had been trapped in the heart of the monstrous structure. The boy had died for his curiosity too.

'They are weak still,' said Vostok, her tone musing. 'Usually they would hide, and have centuries to build and repair their creatures. Now they must limp as best they can.'

Noon placed a hand on the dragon's neck again. *Be cautious. We shouldn't share too much.* Vostok's assent was a warmth in her blood.

'How many war-beasts have been birthed?' Agent Maritza smiled. 'Is that even the right term? And how many pods did the tree-god shed? What condition are they in?' A gust of chilly wind tugged at her hat, and she pulled it firmly back over her forehead. Her bat showed no signs of tiring.

'What makes you think I would tell you? The Winnowry can go fuck themselves. Tell them that from me.'

Agent Maritza snorted. 'You honestly think the Winnowry care about one little runaway witch? The whole of Sarn has more important things to think about now. Besides which, from what I've heard, they've written you off as a dangerous lunatic anyway.'

Immediately, Noon felt Vostok's anger rise to meet her own, and they both moved as one. Noon lifted her hands to shoot a thin jet of winnowfire directly at the agent just as Vostok ducked her head. The green flames burst into a sheet of fire a foot away from the woman, who was yanking hurriedly on the reins of her bat to bring them out of range. Noon leaned back in the harness, savouring the way her stomach seemed to press into her chest as Vostok propelled them up above the hapless agent and her mount. Vostok brought her head low and roared, a stream of violet flame shooting from between her jaws. For a moment, Noon thought the dragon had had enough of Agent Maritza and had decided to blast her and her mount from the sky, but when the heat haze had cleared from her eyes, the agent was still there, although she was struggling to control a very startled and slightly singed bat. The giant bats of the Winnowry may well be trained to deal with winnowfire calmly, but a dragon was another matter entirely.

Vostok roared again, still hanging over the pair with her jaws wide, her violet fire an ominous light in the back of her throat. Agent Maritza, one arm wrapped several times around the reins, raised her free hand and a glove of green fire appeared around it. Noon laughed, delighted.

'Oh, do you really want to see what we can do together, Agent Maritza?' Vostok almost seemed to thrum with power beneath her. The dragon wanted a fight, and so, Noon realised, did she. 'The flames make a very pretty combination. I promise it's worth seeing, just before we melt the eyes out of your face.'

The bat was still struggling to get away, and after a moment the winnowfire coating the agent's hand winked out of existence, and she took up the reins with both hands.

'If you think you're safe out here in the middle of nowhere, you're wrong.' The agent tried to inject a jeering note into her voice, but her face was moist with sweat, and it didn't quite ring true. 'When Sarn falls, so will Ebora.'

The bat arched up into the air and turned, heading back towards the mountain as swiftly as it could go. For a second, it felt like the most natural thing in the world to pursue her, to blast her from the sky with a combination of green and violet fire – they were of one mind, in that place where to Noon things seemed to make sense again. But then she thought of Vintage's voice, no doubt telling her that it was foolish to murder someone simply over an insult. Simply because you *wanted* to.

The woman and her bat were a dot now, a smudge against the grey of the Bloodless Mountains, while all around them the day was filling with brighter, if not especially warmer, sunshine. Noon rubbed her fingers together; they were like sticks of ice, although she hadn't felt cold at all – not while Vostok's anger warmed her.

'Come on, then,' she said, taking up the harness strap again. 'I expect Tor will want to know about this.'

8

Tor stood in the courtyard with his arms crossed, and watched the big man attempt to wrestle the griffin to the floor.

Or at least, that's what it looked like he was doing. Bern the Younger actually had a long thin length of rope in his hands, and was trying to take measurements, but Sharrik was having none of it. He had pressed his body flat to the flag-stones, like a cat that did not want to be picked up, and he kept unfurling his enormous wings, none too gently pushing Bern away.

'By the stones, Sharrik, will you not keep still? It would hardly take a moment if you would stop fidgeting about.'

'I do not want that harness.' The griffin's voice was a low gravelly rumble. 'I want armour, with jewels on, and gems. Like in the paintings.'

'Yes, well.' Bern the Younger stepped back, looking the war-beast down from head to thrashing tail, seeking out a breach in his defences. 'We don't have any of those at the moment, so we're having to make do, my friend. Your last harness did not survive the fight at Coldreef, and I'm sure it's because it was poorly fitted.'

'It is the finest leather we have,' put in Tor. 'I have made sure of that. One day we may find armour befitting your majesty.'

Sharrik turned one huge red-ringed eye on him, as if he sensed mockery of some sort. Seeing the griffin distracted, Bern stepped in under his wing and hurriedly began to stretch the rope around his great muscled shoulder. Not for the first time, Tor wondered at the man's ease with the creature; Sharrik was huge, even bigger than Vostok, their dragon war-beast, and stocky with it. The griffin's thickly muscled legs, those of a great cat, were shaggy with fur, and his thick neck ringed with blue, white and grey feathers. His long wings – the wings of an eagle, like Vostok and Jessen – were a pale blue, with long black flight feathers at the tips. As usual when he saw Sharrik, Tor found it difficult to look away from his great curving black beak. It looked sharper and more lethal than his own beloved sword, the Ninth Rain. Bern clearly felt no such unease around Sharrik, but then, he and the griffin had grown close, in the way that war-beasts and their companions did, over time. Or were supposed to, anyway.

'Vostok said that is what we are due,' said Sharrik, although his tone was less certain than it had been. 'Jewels and such. We are to be celebrated, feasted.'

'There we go, nearly done.' Bern straightened up and Sharrik lifted his wings menacingly. Tor wasn't sure if the man was foolish or brave, but then again, he was so tall and broad across the shoulders, if any human had a chance of wrestling a griffin into submission, it was probably Bern the Younger. He had come with his people to help rebuild Ebora, and had been present in the Hall of Roots when Ygseril had birthed the silver war-beast pods. Since then, most of his people had returned to Finneral, but he had remained, continuing to clear away much of the devastation wrought by centuries of disuse, and lending a strong hand where it was needed. He had since witnessed the birth of each war-beast, side by side with Aldasair.

'Now, if you'd stopped behaving like such a baby about it, this would have all been done an age ago.'

Tor turned away as Bern continued to coax the griffin into having his measurements taken. They were in the biggest court-yard in the palace, a place that had once sported several small circular gardens and a large pond in the centre. The gardens, all gone to seed or full of dead plants, had been cleared away to make more room, while they had refilled the pond with fresh water. Bern had built a big wooden shelter alongside one wall, and widened the biggest entrance to accommodate the beasts as best they could. The truth was, they were too big to be comfortable in many parts of the palace, and this courtyard was the largest free space they had. The far wall, which had once been covered with a beautiful and ancient mosaic – teeming fish of red and yellow – was now marred with deep scratches, violent enough to have scattered hundreds of the delicate tiles from their beds and exposed the grey clay beneath. He frowned at it.

'Here, look, Vostok is coming back. See how fine the harness looks, Sharrik!'

Tor turned at Bern's words and looked up to see the wide stretch of the dragon's bulk casting them into shadow, her taloned feet outstretched to land. She did so lightly, the violence of her wings briefly buffeting the courtyard with wind, and then Noon was climbing down from her back.

'My lady Vostok. How was the new harness?' Bern approached the dragon respectfully, one hand tugging thought-fully on his neat yellow beard. 'It wasn't uncomfortable in flight? No chafing? You weren't restricted in any way?'

'It was adequate.'

Bern turned back to the griffin, triumphant. 'See? Adequate! Will you stop fidgeting now?'

'We found a Winnowry agent on the foothills, would you believe it?' Noon's cheeks were flushed with the cold, and her eyes were bright. Her black hair was in disarray, half covering the old bat-wing tattoo on her forehead, although Tor had to admit he could not remember an occasion when her hair had been tidy. She was wearing soft, comfortable travelling leathers, with a heavy hood around her neck that she had clearly made no use of. Self-consciously he raised a hand to the scarred side of his face, then forced himself to pluck tidily at his own collar instead. After a moment, he realised what she had said.

'One of those lunatics, here? Are they still trying to take you back to that prison?' He cleared his throat. 'Are you hurt?'

Noon snorted. 'Did Kirune smack you about the head again? There was only one of them, and she didn't try anything.' Behind her, Vostok was greeting Sharrik, their heads together in conference. Bern was scribbling something in a tiny, much-folded notebook he'd retrieved from his belt. 'And if she had, Vostok and I would have blown her out of the sky.' She paused, seeming to see him properly for the first time. Her voice softened. 'Are *you* all right?'

For a moment, he did want to talk to her properly, take her aside, somewhere warm where they could be alone. He remembered how close they had become before, when he had dream-walked into her sleeping thoughts; when she had held him inside the Behemoth wreckage. And later, in the cave . . . Ebora, with its problems and snows and, above all, its war-beasts, seemed to have leached that closeness away from them. Instead, he smiled and said lightly, 'You think everything falls apart when you two leave the palace? I am fine.'

'Hmm. Well. According to this agent, the worm people have been quiet. A few attacks, but nothing like a full-scale invasion. Vostok says that they must be weak, still repairing their old hulks.'

Tor frowned, and folded his arms again. It was bitter in the courtyard, despite the thickly padded robe he had rescued from his family's suite. It was a deep maroon, with a curling pattern of sea monsters embroidered at the cuffs in pale green silk. Thinking of the old family suite made him think of Hestillion – all her things had still been there, of course, her clothes and her hair brushes, the endless pairs of delicate silk slippers. He had moved them all to their parents' old chamber, not looking too closely at any of it.

'Where's Aldasair?' Noon was attempting to flatten her hair and having very little luck.

'In the Hatchery.'

'Still watching?'

'Still watching.'

Now it was Noon's turn to frown. 'There has been no change there, then?'

Tor shrugged. 'Will you come and see? I know Aldasair will be glad to see you.'

They left the courtyard, walking through the empty corridors of the palace, Tor following a route he barely had to think about. He had run away more than fifty years ago – looking to escape the horror of the crimson flux, Ebora's decline, and too many memories to count – and in the end he hadn't managed to forget any of it, despite his very best efforts. On their way they passed another of the interior gardens and saw a group of plains people and Finneral folk, working busily on a series of tanning racks. Tor raised a hand to them, while Noon kept facing straight ahead. She only spoke once they were out of sight.

'They're still here, then?'

'Noon.' Ahead of them the corridor was in shadows, but just in front he could see a set of muddy boot prints – more evidence that Ebora wasn't as dead as it had once been. 'We need them here. You know that.'

'Hmm.'

In truth, the humans who'd stayed behind after the Jure'lia returned had been vital to their survival. The food situation in Ebora had been precarious for some time, and only the fact that there had been so few Eborans still alive had saved them from a slow wasting away. They had existed for decades on the stores packed away by previous generations, and on the passing business of traders willing to sell meats, wines, and any fresh food they had. However, now they had war-beasts to feed, and no infrastructure in place to do so. Bern had spoken to the humans who had elected to stay, and just before the heaviest snows came down, the plains and Finneral peoples had banded together and travelled back through the foothills of the Tarah-hut Mountains, returning with a herd of the small goat-like animals called the fleeten, and after an expedition to the west, a number of great shaggy-coated bovine beasts Tor had never seen before. Bern had told him they were called sods-hair cows by his people, and they were good for milk, meat and a very tough leather. It was, Tor reflected, a development his sister would not have been pleased about. Once, their people had almost seemed to exist in a different world, one of near endless life and beauty. Now, the very people they had slaughtered were ensuring their survival.

Despite all the help from the plains folk, Noon had not been happy to see them stay. Originally from the plains herself, she had her own unhappy history with her people, and it seemed she wasn't especially popular with them, either. The old woman who had recognised her as the young girl who had killed so many of her people had left, at least, returning across the mountains despite the winter weather.

They reached the tall doors of the Hatchery. There were a pair of guards at the door, both Finneral women, and they nodded them through. The long room beyond was bathed in chilly light from the windows on both sides, and a series of silk nests – now supplemented with furs and hides – held their cold, grey charges. Aldasair stood by one such nest, his hands held soberly behind his back, while next to him sat the huge black wolf, her long muzzle pointed demurely at the floor, her back straight, so that she almost seemed to mirror his posture. She looked up as they entered, her amber eyes turning towards them, but Aldasair only moved when she nudged him. He turned to them, startled.

'Cousin?'

'How's it going, Al?'

Aldasair gestured to the silvery pod in front of them. It was small, no bigger than a large man crouching down, and its surface was smooth and unblemished.

'It's growing warm to the touch, this one. Jessen thinks it won't be much longer.'

Tor glanced back to the giant wolf. Of all the war-beasts they had birthed, Jessen was the least communicative, speaking rarely and then usually only to Aldasair, but she lowered her head and spoke, her voice soft.

'I can feel the presence in there, growing stronger. He prepares his strength.'

'And . . . will he be . . . like you?'

Jessen turned away, not answering. Aldasair was looking at the pod again, an expression of anguish on his fine-featured face.

'It's so small,' he said. 'In comparison, I mean.'

'Vostok didn't think that one would live,' said Noon. She was watching Jessen closely, as though reluctant to contradict her words. 'But who knows?' She cleared her throat. An uncomfortable silence grew between them then, and Tor knew they were all thinking of the inert grey pods in the other nests; thinking of them, and deliberately not looking at them. Of the fourteen silvery pods they had left – one had been stolen by his sister, of course – only four had hatched successfully so far. It was a terrible number – even if every one of the fourteen had produced a healthy, fully-grown war-beast they would still have struggled to stand against the worm people. With four . . .

'Have you seen Kirune?' He tried to keep his tone light, but he couldn't quite avoid seeing the look that passed between Noon and Aldasair. It was, to his surprise, Jessen who answered him.

'Kirune has gone out to the Nest,' she said. As she spoke, her bushy black tail made one decisive sweep across the floor. 'To see what he can find, he says.'

'Again?' Tor bit down on the anger in his voice, and plastered a tight smile on his face instead. 'I suppose we should go and get him. Noon, would you mind giving me a lift?'

9

'I do not like this.'

Noon could feel Vostok's discomfort radiating up through her scales; it was in the set of her shoulders, the tight movements of her wings. Behind Noon, Tor leaned forward, and she felt the brush of his warm breath against her cheek despite the frigid air.

'I'm sorry, Vostok, I truly am. Perhaps you could have a word with Kirune, convince him not to go off on his own like this. Then I wouldn't have to impose on you.'

'It is not just that, as you well know, son of Ebora.' Below them, the western outskirts of the city were still and unmoving, with no signs of wildlife or people. 'I do not like to go to the Nest. I cannot see the good in it. Besides which,' she added, a hint of acid in her tone, 'as his companion, *having a word* is your job. I am no diplomat.'

Feeling Tor stiffen in his seat behind her, Noon spoke into the brief chilly silence. 'Kirune is trying to find a way to remember, Vostok. I don't think we can blame him for that. And if he's going to find that anywhere . . .'

The dragon growled low in her throat, but in the strange current of feeling that moved between them Noon could feel her sorrow, as much as she tried to hide it.

'There is nothing there but grief.'

They flew on. The buildings became less and less opulent, then simply fewer in number, until they were flying over stretches of nothing very much. Out here, the snows were deeper, although Noon caught sight of bright patches of moisture here and there – spring was making its presence felt, however slight, and the snow wouldn't be here much longer. A grey shape in the distance began to resolve itself into a low range of mountains – a smaller reflection of the looming Bloodless Mountains to the south-west. They flew on and on, over lands wild and untamed, punctuated here and there with the smaller towns and settlements of Ebora. They passed over them so swiftly that Noon barely had a moment to take them in, but the sight of them reminded her how little she, or any human, truly knew of Ebora. When she had thought of the place at all, she had thought of their dead tree-god, the fabled city and the palace, and the strange, unknowable people who had lived there. It had never occurred to her that of course not all Eborans would live in the city, that there would be men and women whose lives likely resembled those of any normal human.

Vostok flew on, and soon it became apparent that they were heading towards one peak in particular: a solid mound of rock with a rounded bluff. From this vantage point it was a patchwork of grey, white, and a deep, dark green, and then as it grew closer, it was possible to see that something was clinging to its sheer sides. Bands of blue and cream began to resolve into several floors of a huge, complex building, circling the mountain like some sort of unlikely geometric fungus. As well as the rings of low buildings crouched on its craggy face, Noon could see a wide tower directly in front of them, built from shining blue rock. From this distance, it looked extraordinary: the largest single building Noon had ever seen, bigger even than the Winnowry, bigger than Ygseril's palace. It was difficult

69

to see where it began and where it ended, given the snowy slopes disguising its edges.

However, as they flew closer, the cruel light of the wintery sun revealed the truth: it was a ruin. The cream and blue marble was cracked, even shattered in places, and nature had crept spindly fingers into each rupture and sprouted there, so that plants and vines had spread over the walls like an infection. The tower, with its blunt top and wide-silled windows, where once war-beasts had come and gone like pigeons in a coop, was dark and fractured, soot at each window like a howling toothless mouth. This was the ruin that was the Nest.

'You can almost see what it was,' said Noon, not quite able to stop herself. 'I can imagine them all, here. Fire and blood, I *can* almost see it.'

'The last taste of my memories,' said Vostok. 'Do not concern yourself with it.'

Abruptly the dragon dropped down through the air, swooping over the foothills that led to the magnificent ruin, and then up, gliding in the frigid air. Below them in the crusted snow Noon could see fresh tracks – the wide pad of a giant cat – and then they were there, in the midst of the enormous war-beast castle. Ahead of them was a tall outer wall, partially covered in snow and a creeping vine of greenish-blue. Noon turned and looked behind them; there was a narrow track carved into the side of the mountain, although it had been partially hidden with landslides and the virulent advances of nature. In the wall ahead there was a series of small archways, meant for the Eborans who had braved the treacherous path, and next to that, a larger entrance for the war-beasts: a wide, reinforced gate gilded with gold that was burnished and dark now. They flew over the wall, and the interior was a web of circular courtyards and raised platforms. A place for war-beasts to rest and to spend time together, to feed and to sleep away from the chaos of central Ebora. When they had lived.

Tor leaned out again and pointed. 'Here. There he is.'

Kirune was a dark-grey shape moving across one of the circular raised gardens inside the complex, his wings folded tightly to his back. The thick grass around him was frosted white, although Noon could see green patches where the heat from his body had thawed the cold away. Without a word, Vostok brought herself in to land gently, alighting on the grass a few feet away from Kirune. The big cat looked up, startled.

'What do you want?'

Vostok snorted as Tor and Noon detached themselves from her harness and climbed down.

'You should have heard me coming, war-beast. Are your senses so dull?'

To Noon's surprise, Kirune didn't hiss. Instead, he turned back to the grass.

'I have been exploring,' he growled. 'If I look at this place enough, it will come back to me. Something has to be familiar. I have been down under these floating things, and there is a door that leads into the mountain.' He paused, flexing his shoulders. 'But the entrance is covered over with ice.'

Noon looked at Vostok in surprise. They had visited once before, not long after Vostok had been birthed from her own silver pod, but once she had seen the devastation there, the dragon had not wanted to explore further that day. 'Something underneath the Nest?'

'There were halls. Tunnels. It was a place to be warm in the winter.'

'We should go and look,' said Tor. He walked over to Kirune and briefly placed his hand on his fur, but the big cat shrugged him off. 'There might be something in there that could help them remember.'

For once, it was Vostok who hissed through her teeth. 'Does no one listen to me? Without their root-memories, Kirune, Sharrik and Jessen have no connection to our joint past. They

71

were severed from Ygseril, and all that past knowledge is lost forever. This is not some human thing, where you forget where you have put something and later recall where it is.'

Kirune had crouched lower and lower at the dragon's words, his tail swishing threateningly back and forth.

'Who are you to say what we are capable of?' He bared his fangs, huge and curved and faintly yellow. 'You just want to be the leader! That's why you won't let us try.'

'Vostok, what harm could it do?' said Noon quietly. 'Let him see his past.'

'What harm?' Vostok turned her violet eyes on Noon. 'What harm, to make me look at the graveyard of my kin?' Noon opened her mouth to respond, not sure what she could possibly say to that, but Vostok was already turning away. 'Let's go, then. If the old doors are covered in ice, then you will need Noon and me to open them for you, ungrateful cub.'

They made their way down carefully and slowly. Noon and Tor had to climb back onto Vostok's back, as the distance between each of the platforms was larger than any human could jump without serious injury. As they moved, Kirune nimbly jumping along behind, Noon found herself gazing around at the strange interior of the Nest. To her, it was a little like being at the bottom of a pond filled with lily pads. All around them were platforms and gardens supported on graceful curving struts that rose from the ground like the stems of unlikely flowers. Some of the platforms held towering pavilions, now mostly broken or leaning precariously. She saw one that had once held an elaborate fountain shaped like a series of waterfalls, but one of its walls had collapsed and she could see a bright-green splash of algae coating its sculpted rocks.

'This place is extraordinary,' Noon kept her voice low, pitched for Tor, who sat closely behind her. 'Did you ever come here? Before, I mean?'

'Once or twice.' She could hear the frown in his voice. 'As

a special treat, on particular days. Mostly this was a place for the war-beasts alone, and only their bonded warriors would visit regularly. As you can probably tell, it's not exactly easy to get to unless you can fly.' He sighed, and his tone softened. 'It was their sanctuary. It always seemed magical to me, because of them. And then afterwards . . . afterwards, this was a sad place to come. A monument to an enormous loss we could barely comprehend.'

They jumped down from the final platform and landed on a lush lawn, or what had been a lawn once. Now it was a bare scrubland, dusted here and there with tall grasses, partly hidden under the remains of the snow. There were other things here, discarded weapons barely recognisable through the layer of rust, and Noon recognised the bones of a horse, ancient and yellow-brown. Ahead of them, the wall of the mountain rose. It was covered in a thick green moss, bright and oddly beautiful. Noon wondered how much life-energy was contained in the virulent covering, and her fingers itched.

'Eventually, when so many of us were sick and dying, we stopped coming up here at all. We saw lights sometimes, and figured that humans had made it this far, looking for what they could loot,' said Tor. He shifted in the harness slightly, his hand resting on Noon's hip, and then he snatched it away as though he'd touched something hot. 'They weren't brave enough to come to the palace, couldn't face their monsters.' He snorted. 'But the Nest was isolated, and they knew very well that its inhabitants were all dead.'

There was a door in the green wall of the mountain. It was huge, and at the top it was possible to see that it was made of black iron, etched here and there with intertwined serpents. Beneath that a thick slope of ice covered the bottom.

'Soot and bones and ruin,' said Vostok. 'There is nothing here for war-beasts, just evidence of human greed and unpleasantness.'

'I'm sorry, Vostok.' Noon pushed her hair back from her face. The Eborans might have murdered thousands of humans for their blood, but the war-beasts hadn't.

'It is hardly your fault, bright weapon.'

The door rose in front of them. Tor and Noon unstrapped themselves from the harness and stepped down onto grass stiff with frost.

'It looks like they tried to burn the tower,' said Tor. 'Which is especially idiotic. The thing's made of marble. It's not so easy to destroy what Eborans build.'

'Yet time has done the rest,' said Vostok. The dragon peered closely at the ice on the door, and snorted again. 'Noon, this will require your witch-fire after all. I am likely to blast the door to pieces.'

Noon smiled and walked over to the mountain wall. After a moment, she placed both hands on a small patch of the wall that was free of ice, sinking her fingers onto the soft, springy surface of the moss. She reached out and let the life-energy flow into her. It *felt* green, teeming with life, thousands and thousands of tiny plants, all clustered together so close they were practically one. Something about that thought gave her a tight feeling in her chest, and her smile faltered, but a slight cough from Vostok brought her out of her reverie.

'You could not use my energy?' asked the dragon.

Noon stepped back. The wall in front of her now sported a pair of large brown handprints.

'I wanted to see what it felt like.' Without bothering to explain further, Noon conjured up a pair of green fireballs and tossed them gently at the thick band of ice. With a hiss and a series of cracks, part of the ice melted away, and after a moment, Noon produced another two, which she deployed at the thickest remaining sections. Water ran over her boots.

'I think that'll do,' she said, standing back. She caught Tor's eye and saw the half-smile he gave her. There was a time, she knew, when her control over the winnowfire had been erratic, to say the least. Now, with the help of Vostok's control and her own growing confidence, the witch-fire was a tool rather than a curse.

Vostok moved to the door. It was slightly ajar, although wedged in place with debris and rust. Carefully, she hooked her claws around it and pulled, and with a terrible screech that made them all wince, the door came open. Inside they could just make out the beginning of a dusty floor, mosaicked with an elaborate pattern of flowers and twisting vines, but it was gradually lost in shadows, and beyond that was a wall of darkness.

'There were lamps once, that were always burning,' said Vostok. Some of her anger seemed to have ebbed away, to be replaced with a quiet sadness. 'A few Eborans lived nearby, in their own quarters, and they would come and do things like that for us.'

'The Order of the Feather,' said Tor. 'I remember them.' He stepped over the threshold. Just in the door was a wall sconce at human height, and there was an old torch stuck inside it. Tor retrieved the torch and held it out to Noon. 'Would you do the honours?'

A glove of green flame popped into existence around her hand, and she gripped the end of the torch for a few moments until the papery twigs began to crackle and the flame turned orange. Together, with Tor holding the torch, they made their way down the central walkway. It was enormous, with a ceiling that stretched off into the distance. To either side of them, walls that had been carved out of the rock rose smoothly. Noon thought they had probably been covered with a type of plaster, and then they had been painted over. A huge, interconnected mural revealed itself as they worked their way down. Images of Ebora at its pinnacle loomed to either side, with depictions of tall Eboran men and women. Some of the Eborans

75

wore exquisite robes, relaxing in gardens while they took part in creative pursuits. With their lavish, almost unending lives and their strange, ethereal beauty, she could almost understand why they thought of themselves as godlike when compared with their simple human neighbours. Noon saw some figures writing, their heads bowed gracefully over reams of parchment, while other men and women embroidered vast tapestries or played musical instruments. Some of the Eborans wore armour, and these Noon paused to look at more closely. There was armour of grey and silver, black and gold, even armour of stranger colours, like red and blue and green. Seeing her stop, Tor brought the torch closer.

'They would enamel the metal,' he said. Kirune appeared at his elbow. The big cat's yellow eyes glowed a ghostly green in the dim light. 'A vaguely ridiculous practice, but it was fashionable to have the showiest armour, particularly during a Rain – it showed that you were so confident in your abilities as a warrior that you weren't worried if your armour attracted attention to you personally. It's amazing we weren't all wiped out by our own stupidity much earlier, really.'

'There are war-beasts too,' said Kirune quietly. They were huge figures on the murals, stalking across fields and forests like giants. Noon thought many of them had to have been exaggerated for emphasis. She saw enormous griffins, dragons, giant wolves with thick ruffs of fur around their necks, foxes with wings like kestrels, and other less identifiable creatures, things like giant birds with halos of fire around their heads, and one thing that looked like a hulking wild boar, its tusks capped with gold. The war-beasts were also engaged in pastimes, most of which were difficult for Noon to make out. In some scenes they appeared to be playing games that involved chasing or flying, and in others they scooped great furrows of earth out of the ground into obscure patterns. In other paintings, the ones where the Eborans wore armour, the war-beasts were clearly attaining glory on the battlefield. They also wore pieces of armour, much of it shining with jewels and brightly coloured enamel. Curiously, the Jure'lia were not depicted in any detail – there were just anonymous grey shapes where the age-old enemy stood.

'Our artists often didn't like to paint the worm people,' said Tor, as if guessing her question. 'It was considered unlucky, and many said it spoiled the beauty of their work.' He turned slightly to Kirune, who was still staring at the walls. 'Any of this look familiar to you, Kirune?'

In answer, the big cat growled low in his throat.

'Let's keep moving down,' said Noon. 'See what else we can find.'

The passageway ate deep into the mountain. Around them, great pillars appeared, revealed like sentries by the flickering torchlight. Eventually, they came to a huge circular central cavern. The ceiling here was a vaulted dome covered in gold – it glinted and shone in the torchlight – and a number of passageways led off like the spokes in a wheel. In the centre, there was a circular arena, with rows of huge steps leading down to a sandy floor.

'A meeting place,' said Vostok. She was looking at the steps as though she were seeing the war-beasts who had once reclined there. 'The passageways lead to nooks in the rock, places where we could go and sleep, to be alone. They were deep enough for it to be silent in the nooks, even when a great discussion was going on in the hall. Sometimes,' she tipped her head slightly to one side, 'there would be singing contests. Or we would recite poetry.'

Noon moved closer to the edge of the arena, peering down. She tried to imagine Vostok in the centre of the sand, singing to an adoring audience. With some difficulty she suppressed a smile.

'None of this means anything to me,' rumbled Kirune. Noon's amusement faded. 'I want it to become clearer. But it's not. It's just not.'

Vostok sighed noisily. 'Of course it's not. Your memories never returned to Ygseril's roots. You grew in his branches without them.'

Kirune circled around, his paws padding against the stone with barely any noise, despite his weight. His tail was swishing back and forth again, and Noon could see Tor frowning slightly.

'Are there any other places we can look at?' she said, placing a hand on Vostok's shoulder. 'We may as well see all of it, now we're here.'

'There was another place,' said the dragon. 'We kept our most favoured artworks there, the items we gave special honour. Our hoard.'

'Come on, then. Let's see it.'

Vostok led them down another passageway. This one did not have a softly curved ceiling like the others, but rather the walls met overhead in a square archway. The paintings here had become much simplified too – there was only a long, unbroken landscape on the walls, a series of soft, rolling hills in ochre and brown, and overhead, a single golden river led them along the path. Noon found herself glancing up at it again and again; the torchlight seemed to travel on ahead in its waters, glittering and chasing itself. Eventually, they came to another set of huge iron doors, only these were standing open.

'They came in here too! An outrage.'

Noon grimaced. There were bodies on the floor just in the doorway, ancient skeletons now but it was clear there had been a fight. Swords, rusted and brown, lay next to outstretched finger bones, and one skull had been cracked open with an axe that was still embedded in it. Inside, statues had been pushed over to shatter into marble pieces on the floor. Tapestries had been slashed, left to hang in ragged pieces like rotting skin, and paintings had been torn down from the walls, their delicate frames shattered.

78

'The humans must have had a disagreement over who got to steal what,' said Tor softly. 'That makes me feel a little better, at least.' In the centre of the room was a circle of looming figures, each a wooden model of a war-beast. They were simply carved, each facing out towards them, their faces blank.

'What were those for?' asked Noon.

'We would keep our finest armours displayed there,' said Vostok. 'Works of art, every one.'

'Whoever survived the fight must have made a fortune,' said Tor, looking around the room.

It was a sad sight. There were alcoves in the walls, spaces where, clearly, beautiful objects had once been stored, all empty now, and a stale old smell permeated everything. The taste of it tickled the back of Noon's throat, and she swallowed hard.

'Kirune, does any of this seem familiar?'

The big cat lifted his head, then looked away. Noon pressed her lips into a thin line.

'It was still a good idea to come here,' she said. 'It's still important to Eboran history, isn't it? Even if it's all empty now.'

Vostok stalked along the far wall, where a deep alcove stretched the length of the room. 'There was a great piece of Eboran history stored here once, but it is also gone. How swiftly we were disregarded.' The dragon lowered her head, and the arrow of sorrow she felt seemed to pierce Noon's own chest. She rubbed her dusty hands on her shirt and went to the dragon. The long alcove was dusty, and above and below it were many wall sconces for lamps. Once, someone had wanted this area bathed in light. There were rounded indentations in the stone, as though lozenge-shaped objects had been stored there in the past.

'Tell me about it,' she said. 'What was here?'

'It was a record, or at least the beginning of one,' said Vostok. 'A record, still in progress at the Eighth Rain, of all the war-beasts that have ever lived and died. Their names, their forms, their accomplishments. We never knew which souls would return or when, and so often the forms were different.' Vostok paused, and when she spoke again it was hesitantly, as though she were revealing some sort of weakness. 'In the Sixth Rain I was born again as a griffin, my feathers like amber and gold. That would have been captured, in the record, along with my accomplishments, my deeds, my associates. An Eboran man instigated the project, drawing together all the histories and accounts into a central work, and he had sworn to dedicate his life to it. Now it is gone.'

'You mean, a book?' Kirune came padding over. He had been prowling the room in circles, sniffing the broken statutory and muttering quietly to himself. 'What's so important about a book?'

Vostok hissed, and Noon blinked in alarm at the sudden surge of anger she felt from the dragon. Hastily, she reached out to her. *Calm, brave one. Calm.*

'Ignorant cub,' hissed Vostok. 'It was not a book, but . . . a unique creation. And it is lost.'

'Well,' said Noon, keeping her tone reasonable, 'couldn't he have come and taken it away, this man? Perhaps he meant to continue to work on it, when you were all gone. You said it was still in progress.'

'I remember this.' Tor approached, holding the torch closer to the alcove. 'I mean, I never saw it, but I heard about it. Micanal the Clearsighted's great project.' He turned to Noon. 'He was, many Eborans thought, our greatest artist. A genius. And we don't know what happened to him. He upped and left, with a group of dedicated followers – he was probably sleeping with most of them – and went in search of some mythical island in the Barren Sea. The idiot never came back.'

'Would he have taken this thing with him?'

Tor shrugged. 'I've no idea. Maybe he came here and put it

somewhere safe before these idiots tried to destroy the place. I suppose we'll never know, now.'

'Fire and blood. A thing like that would have been really useful.'

Behind her, Vostok hissed. 'It would not have helped them! Nothing can help them, save for listening to me.'

Kirune growled, a low, deep rumble in the back of his throat, and Noon felt her own anger flare up.

'Shut up, both of you!' She saw Tor give her a startled look, and ignored it. 'Vostok, of course this might have helped! We would have had names, dates, pictures. Even if they didn't remember, it would have given them something to start . . . to start building themselves with. Knowing your history is important.' She took a deep breath, remembering that her own history was something she'd rather forget. 'Perhaps we should go. I've seen enough ruined things for one day.'

10

'We would speak with you, Hestillion Eskt.'

Hestillion looked up from the gruel-pod, feeling her cheeks flush with shame. She had been so intent on eating that she had the stuff all over her fingers and her face, and there were dark, stiff patches on her gown where she had cleaned her hands at previous meal times. Next to her, Celaphon was equally intent, his snout buried deep in his own food pod. Hestillion had not seen the queen herself for some time; the only contact she had with anything that could be said to be living were the strange half-formed homunculi that brought her the pods, and she had long since ceased to be ashamed to eat in front of them. The queen, though, was something different. Scrambling to her feet, Hestillion lifted her chin.

'Remembered I am your prisoner, have you?'

The queen cocked her head, as though she didn't quite understand the question.

'We do not forget you, Lady Hestillion. We make sure of it. You are supplied with food here? There is a place for your waste?'

Hestillion felt her cheeks burn again, and furiously ignored it.

'What do you want?'

The queen came further into the room, moving with her strange liquid grace. To Hestillion's eyes, she looked different – the stringy matter of her limbs was more defined, and the black fluid that formed her body was less wet-looking, even lighter in colour, a sort of dark grey-green. Celaphon removed his snout from the pod with a wet smack and stared up at her.

'Your dragon creature. He does not grow.'

Hestillion stepped in front of him, putting herself between the queen and the war-beast. 'He lives.'

The queen blinked, eyelids as white and as hard as shells over glossy black eyes. 'We remember them, you must realise, back through the centuries. Waves and waves of enemies, with scale and tooth, feather and fire, pressing us back, always back. It is possible to see glory in a pestilence, and although all must be consumed, there was respect. That,' she nodded to Celaphon, who had sat back on his haunches to regard her with wide, pearly eyes, 'is an afterthought. An act of desperation by a dying creature.'

'If we are so unimportant, let us go.'

The queen turned away from her at that. 'Come with us. We want to show you something.'

The wall peeled apart and she stepped outside. Instead of shrinking shut as it usually did, the hole remained open.

'You will follow, Lady Hestillion?'

Hestillion glanced down at Celaphon. The dragon was looking with longing at the remaining gruel pods.

'Stay close to me,' she said in a low voice. 'Do not leave my side.'

Hestillion went to the hole, and climbed out somewhat awkwardly. Celaphon tried to follow, but the height of the gap was taller than him. He flapped his poorly formed wings once or twice before Hestillion reached back through and picked him up. He might not be growing, she reflected, but he certainly felt heavier. She put him back down by her feet.

The space beyond her cell was a narrow corridor, the walls curving softly so that when she looked up, she could see only shadows. Now that she looked closely, she could see thin dark lines in the walls, glistening slightly. More of the ubiquitous black fluid.

'We could pull you through the walls, but we imagine you would not find that comfortable.' The Jure'lia queen gestured and the curved surface in front of them split down the middle, peeling back to reveal another, identical corridor. The wall on the far side of that opened too, and then another. The queen began to walk briskly down this impromptu passageway and Hestillion followed with Celaphon scurrying at her ankles. She had the impression of being inside something with many flattened layers, like an onion or a fruit of some sort.

'When I spoke to you before, when you were in the roots –' Hestillion paused, gathering her thoughts – 'you would refer to yourself as *I*, sometimes. Now it is only *we*.'

The queen seemed to stiffen, her shoulders curving in slightly as though Hestillion had dealt her some sort of blow. 'We had been separated for a long time,' she said eventually. 'It is not natural for us to be alone, for so long. It was like decaying, and sometimes . . . it was hard to remember our connections. What we will show you here will help you understand.' Her shoulders shifted, and her tone changed. 'When we come to a new place, we must burrow beneath the land.'

Hestillion looked at the back of the queen's head.

'A new place? What does that mean?'

'We burrow deep, under the skin. Find warmth and darkness, and there we deposit that which will come next.' Ahead of them, more doors tore into being. Hestillion looked around as best she could, trying to get some sense of where she was, but it all looked very similar; fleshy grey walls, bunches of softly

84

glowing nodules. The queen frowned. 'Your undernourished creature. You brought it here inside something, didn't you? What name do you have for that?'

'We called them pods. They are fruits that fall from Ygseril.'

'We secrete that which will come next.'

Hestillion pressed her lips into a thin line. 'Eggs. You're talking about laying eggs.'

'Yes.' The queen looked pleased and they continued walking. Ahead of them the opening was smaller than it had been, and a dim blue light leaked and flickered around its edges. 'When the eggs have been laid, we enter the changing time. We become new shapes – not travelling shapes, but harvesting shapes. We become the tool to change this new place into what the eggs need.'

Hestillion thought of moths and butterflies, emerging from cocoons.

'Why are you telling me this?'

The queen carried on as if she hadn't spoken. 'Our forms change, but we must always remember what we are. That way, we are one. Here, look.'

The opening revealed not a corridor, but a round chamber. Towering at its heart was a tall blue crystal, shining with an inner light.

'I don't like it,' said Celaphon at their feet.

Hestillion nodded slowly, unable to take her eyes away from it. The light the crystal cast was clear and beautiful, the blue of a summer's bird, but it made her deeply uneasy all the same.

'What is it?'

'It is a piece of our memory,' said the queen, as though that explained everything. 'Come and see truly.'

Hestillion followed the Jure'lia queen into the room cautiously, too aware that the walls could close up behind her again. Up close the crystal winked and sang with light, and then abruptly she was looking at something beyond its surface.

A landscape was caught inside it, like a painting behind glass. Hestillion's breath caught in her throat.

'How . . . how is that possible?'

The landscape was a dark green sea pierced with paler green rocks, a sickly yellow sky arching overhead. The ocean tossed and hissed with steam. Hestillion had never seen anything like it.

'A memory of a place we knew, where our eggs hatched successfully. We carry them with us. Do you remember, Hestillion, born in the year of the green bird, when we asked you what held you together?'

Hestillion looked down at the little dragon. Despite his misgivings he was edging towards the crystal's surface, so she pushed him back gently with her foot.

'I remember. I thought you were Ygseril at the time.'

The queen either didn't notice or ignored the sour note in her voice. 'This is what we meant. A memory, a moment of time held in place, at the heart of each Behemoth. So many worlds, Lady Hestillion, we hold in our hearts. It weaves us together, as one.'

'That is . . . remarkable. But why bring me here? Why show me this?'

The queen turned to her then, her tall body curving slightly to bring her face closer to Hestillion's. Up close, it was possible to see that the rigid white mask wasn't completely flawless. Hestillion could see flecks of dirt on it, even a small crack in its shining surface near her left eye.

'Because, for the first time, our cycle is being . . . interrupted. We have been on this world for thousands of years. Each time we emerge to change the world to suit our eggs, we are pushed back. By you. By that.' She pointed one claw-like finger at Celaphon, who cringed against the floor. 'So long, so long in our harvesting forms. Again and again we retreat, recover. Again and again we emerge. And then, this last conflict, to lie cold and inert for so long, without even the chance to recover.'

'Then why don't you leave? This is a bad place for you. So go.'

The queen ignored her question. 'You said this time, it is new. That this . . . communication between us has never happened before. This is why we tell you, because we hope it is true. It's not in our nature, but perhaps it is time to try something else.'

'Peace?' Hestillion glanced down at Celaphon, who had curled himself around her feet.

'Here, come and see. We would be interested to know what you think.'

Hestillion waited for the Jure'lia queen to move, but instead the ground beneath their feet slowly began to drop. It was just the space immediately around them – the flickering crystal with its frozen memory stayed where it was – and strings of the Jure'lia substance stretched long around them as they were lowered into a cavernous room below. To Hestillion, it looked as big as the Hall of Roots in the Eboran palace, but there were no windows. The light came from rings of the glowing nodules that circled the walls – larger than those Hestillion had seen elsewhere – and a series of large raised circular pools, filled with a white liquid that seemed to give off light like a shifting, curling mist. There were unmoving shapes in the pools, but Hestillion could make out no details.

'What is this place?'

'You would call it . . . an experiment.'

Their platform settled softly onto the floor and was immediately absorbed into it. Celaphon stepped away from the space where it had been, whining softly. The queen began to walk towards one of the pools, and after a moment, Hestillion followed.

'You are not like the rest of your people,' said the queen.

87

'Perhaps it follows that this world is not like the others. So, for the first time, we are trying to grow something new.'

They crested the edge of the pool and she pointed down into it, but for the moment, Hestillion refused to look. Instead, she kept her eyes on the queen's mask-like face.

'We nearly killed you last time, didn't we? It was almost the end of all of it, us or you – one of us would perish. Except that's not how it worked out. You were trapped, and we were poisoned.'

'We did not poison you. Your diseases are your own affair,' pointed out the queen, mildly enough. 'Will you look?'

Grimacing, Hestillion turned to the pool. The initial shape of the thing resting in it was that of an enormous man, at least nine foot tall, as far as Hestillion could guess. It lay on its back in the pool, the cloudy white water half submerging it. Like the water, it was white as chalk, and its features were soft and unfinished; Hestillion could make out grey shadows where its eyes were, and a thin greyish slash where a mouth would be, but no nose. Its chest was bulky and wide, and its arms were thick. There was no hair on it anywhere that Hestillion could see, and there were . . . holes. Ragged openings in its chest, its stomach, along its thick arms, and inside it was possible to see that it was hollow and filled with the sticky greenish black substance that was everywhere on the corpse moon. Just like a drone, thought Hestillion. There were strands of pale muscle across these openings, as if it were still knitting itself together. The figure also appeared to be lying on something just below it, but the water was too bright to make it out.

'Well that's . . . disgusting.' Hestillion glanced around. 'There are more of them?'

'Many more.' The queen was gazing down at the figure with narrowed eyes, as if she wasn't sure what it was either. 'We have learned from you, do you see? We are not things that learn, not usually. We birth, we eat, our eggs hatch, we travel and we begin again. But perhaps these shapes are the key.' She turned to Hestillion. 'What do you think?'

'What do I think?' Hestillion took a deep breath, and drew herself up to her full height. She tried not to think about her dirty hair or her stained robes. 'I think that I am a guest and an ambassador here, and it is time you started to treat me as one. You wish to consult me? Then I require rooms, a proper bed, a place to clean myself. Better food than the swill you have been forcing on me. Celaphon and I must be housed in a way that befits our status – as a lady of Ebora and her war-beast.'

The Jure'lia queen went very still. She raised her hand, with its long, tapering fingers, and closed them slowly around Hestillion's neck – they were so long they wrapped easily around themselves.

'We could summon something to eat you,' she said, her voice low. 'Eat all your insides and connect you to us forever.'

'But then I would be just another part of your *hive*, and you wouldn't be able to ask me questions.' The queen's skin – for want of a better word – was warm, just like normal skin. 'What reason is there for me to cooperate with you? I will not spend the rest of my life in a squalid, windowless cell.'

There was a long moment of silence. Hestillion strained her ears for any sort of noise at all, but she could only hear her own breathing, and the fearful panting of Celaphon. They must be very deep in the belly of the corpse moon.

'Windows. Very well.' The Jure'lia queen released her grip on Hestillion's neck. 'You shall be our first guest, Lady Hestillion Eskt, born in the year of the green bird. And everything you know, we shall come to know.'

11

We passed through a section of Wild territory yesterday. We could have attempted to go around it, I suppose, but it would have added days to our journey, and with Sarn, we are always likely to have to cross the Wild at some point – particularly if you want to get anywhere in a hurry. It was in the heart of a stretch of marshland not far from the western borders of Greenslick, and we happened to cross it in the midst of a bad patch of weather. The clouds grew low and dark, and the mists rose up all around us so that we stumbled into the Wild before we truly knew where we were.

Together we had been following narrow tracks of solid land, built and maintained by the people of a small village not far from the marshes, which we passed through the day before. Apparently, they had built special fish enclo-sures within the marsh and consequently needed these paths to get back and forth safely. I had given them coin for a map of the paths, which was parted with very reluc-tantly. From the look the chap gave me, I suspect many are starting to feel that this will be the end of Sarn, and soon coin will be useless.

Passing through the normal marsh into the Wild was not a pleasant experience, to say the least. I'm sure that if my dear Tor were here with us he would have been outraged at the cost to his clothes. The stench! The waters were brown and black and soupy, while enormous reeds grew in clumps so huge we almost became lost in them. Once or twice I got my boot wedged in the sucking mud, and we both became very itchy and sick. Several times I saw something huge moving in the mud, and I walked with my crossbow out for some distance. Eventually, when we had emerged from another great thicket of weeds, we spotted one Wild-touched monstrosity disappearing back into the stinking waters – I don't know what it was truly, but it put me in mind of a vast mole, pink-skinned and blind, with a mouth full of long, yellow teeth.

We have seen no parasite spirits, which strikes me as strange – though something of a relief.

Extract from the private journals of Lady Vincenza
'Vintage' de Grazon

'Extraordinary. Simply extraordinary.'

Vintage had taken her notebook from her pack out of sheer habit, but she only gripped it with one hand, unable to drag her eyes from the sights around her. They stood in front of the gates to the Eboran palace. There were the sweeping gardens, the ornate buildings themselves, glittering with gold and glass, and then above it all, the spreading branches of Ygseril. And there were leaves on them, silver leaves against brown bark.

'He lives.' Nanthema was next to her, one hand pressed lightly to her mouth.

Vintage realised she was swaying slightly. She took hold of the woman's elbow, steadying her. 'Eri, my dear, did you know? Did you know your god was alive?'

91

The boy shook his head. He looked perplexed by their reactions, and he held his bucket tightly in both hands. 'I was never supposed to come here,' was all he said.

There were people on the grass beyond the gate. They stood with tents or around cooking fires, and many of them were performing chores – fetching water, tanning leather, cleaning tools. They looked, to Vintage's eye, ridiculously relaxed. Did they not realise where they were, or what stood behind them?

'Nanthema, I feel like . . . I feel like we might have missed something significant. I also feel like I may throw up.'

They walked slowly up to the gates, which were standing open, and stepped through. No one moved to stop them, and only a few people looked around with any interest. One of these was a huge blond man with a neat beard and a pair of formidable axes on his belt. He had his sleeves rolled up and Vintage could just see a thick band of ink poking out from under his shirt. Wiping his hands on a cloth, he came over to them.

'By the stones, you look like you've had a long journey, if you don't mind me saying.' He was smiling at them warmly, but there was a stillness about his eyes that suggested he was as perplexed about their appearance as they were about the newly living Ebora. 'I'm Bern Finnkeeper and I'm . . . I'm helping out around here, for want of a better way of putting it.' He glanced from Nanthema to Eri and back again. 'I – where have you come from? I thought we knew of all the living Eborans—'

'I'm Lady Vincenza de Grazon, but you can call me Vintage, dear.' Vintage stepped neatly in front of the others, offering her hand. The big man called Bern enclosed it in his meaty fist with remarkable gentleness. 'My associate is Nanthema. She, as you can probably tell, is a child of Ebora, and what with everything happening in Sarn, she thought it best to come home, and, to tell you the truth, I have always wanted to see

Ebora and who could possibly pass up the opportunity? This is Eri, his story is a little more complicated, but I'm sure we'll get it all out eventually but mostly, I suppose, what I would really like to know –' she took a sharp breath – 'is why, by the bones of Sarn, is that bloody great tree alive when it's been dead for centuries?'

'Vintage. Vintage!' The big man took her hand and squeezed it again, looking suddenly very pleased. 'I know your name, of course I do. Listen, Lady de Grazon, there is an awful lot—'

At that moment they were swallowed by shadow. Vintage looked up to see something huge barrelling towards them from above. Her hand dropped to her crossbow automatically, and then the big man Bern was gone; instead, he was rolling across the grass with something enormous, something of fur and feather and brightly shining claws.

'No.' Nanthema's words were softer than a whisper, but Vintage heard them as clear as thunder. 'It can't be.'

The rolling chaos resolved itself into a giant monster. It clambered to its feet, a creature with the body of a great muscled cat, half hidden within ruffled eagle's wings. Its head was also that of an eagle, its throat ringed with blue and white feathers. Vintage looked for Bern, fully expecting to see him gathering his guts from a steaming pile on the floor, but he was pulling himself to his feet and laughing, gamely thumping the enormous creature on the flank.

'You got me that time, Sharrik. You sneaky bastard.'

'Fuck me.' Vintage blinked. Her voice felt like it was coming from very far away. Her voice was the beach and she was the tide, edging further and further out. 'Fuck *me*.'

'I'm sorry about that,' said Bern, brushing himself down. The creature shook itself all over. It was a griffin, Vintage thought, although its cat-like paws suggested that it was a sub-set of the species, as, rightly, it should have the talons and front legs of a bird, although who was to say what a true griffin was anyway? She would have to consult, consult all the books and notes available and . . . Vintage blinked rapidly. *Get a grip.*

'Sharrik has made a game of surprising me,' said Bern. He threw an affectionate glance over his shoulder to the beast, who was now gathering an audience of children. They were tugging on his fur and looking up at him with bright eyes – just as though he were the farmer's prize horse. 'I'm sure he thinks it's very funny, but . . . I'm sorry. This must be a lot for you to take in.'

Vintage realised he was looking at the two Eborans. Nanthema was standing with one hand pressed to her mouth, tears streaming silently down her face, while Eri hid behind her, his face very pale. Vintage took a deep breath, trying to get her heart under control, and she grabbed hold of the big man's forearm. It was as solid as a tree trunk.

'Strong drink, my good man. Do you have any?'

It was late when they got back to the palace. Kirune slunk off immediately, not giving any indication of where he was going, and Vostok declared that she was going to the outer hills for, as she put it, 'a bit of peace and quiet'. Tor and Noon were left alone in the courtyard.

'Well.' Tor rubbed his neck, which was cramping with the sort of deep ache that likely meant a headache later. The scars on his face felt tight and sore – a sure sign that he'd been flying for a length of time. 'I'm not sure whether to call that successful or not.'

'Kirune and Vostok went somewhere together without killing each other, that seems like progress.' Noon smiled faintly as they stepped through the doors into the palace corridor. 'Are you all right?'

'Hmm? Oh, aches and pains, you know. The usual.'

Silence fell between them then. The corridors were lit softly here – they couldn't afford to waste too much oil, after all – and in the dim light Noon's face looked flushed. It occurred to him that it was very rare for them to be alone together these days. There was always someone wanting something, or a war-beast that needed attention. Or the dragon. There was always the dragon.

'You're moving much better, lately,' said Noon. She gestured to his arm. 'Are you . . . getting used to them? The scars?'

Tor shrugged. 'No choice really.' Seeing her look away, he cleared his throat. He knew that she still felt responsible, even though he no longer blamed her – if she hadn't destroyed the parasite spirits in Esiah Godwort's compound, they all would have died there. 'It eases, although the cold makes everything stiff.'

'I'm sorry, there has been so little time lately. With Vostok and the others, and everything else.'

Tor held his breath, half fearful that naming the dragon would summon her.

'You should not feel . . .' He stopped. Now he found he couldn't meet her eyes. 'That's to say, it makes no sense for you to be beholden to me. You don't owe me, and . . .' He sighed, looking back at her face. Her eyes were very dark. 'I cannot demand it of you.'

She grinned then, suddenly, and much to his own annoyance, he felt his heart beat a little faster.

'I never really said, but it was never a chore. Not at all. I never would have thought I would be gladly giving up my blood to an Eboran monster,' she grinned a little wider. 'But I actually grew to like it. You know. A little.'

He could see that she was blushing, and he grinned back at her.

'In that case, I have a very passable bottle of Reidn wine in my rooms?'

Tor considered taking her hand but then thought better of

it. Even so, they walked with more haste than was normal through the winding corridors, and as they caught each other's eye at the door, they laughed together a bit. Inside his suite, a few lamps had been lit and there was half a bottle of wine on the table alongside a half-eaten meal – he couldn't remember leaving that, but then he'd never been particularly fastidious – and the place looked cosy.

'Noon.' He turned towards her and hesitantly put his hand on her waist. She turned her face up to his, quite serious now, and he remembered gently biting her wrist in the cave, when they had faced down the wolves and everything was so cold. All the teachings of the House of the Long Night seemed to have fled him for the moment. 'Noon, I wanted to tell you—'

The dry cough from the other side of the room made them jump apart as though they'd been pinched. Tor spun around, ready to ask what business anyone had to be lurking in his rooms, when he saw a familiar figure in the shadows. He closed his mouth with an audible snap.

Vintage brushed herself down, deliberately not looking at them, but there was no missing the smirk on her face. 'My darlings, am I interrupting something?'

'Vintage!' Noon leapt across the room and almost barrelled the older woman over with the force of her embrace. 'You came back! I mean, you came here! Why did you come here? Do you know . . .? Have you seen . . .?'

'What Noon means, Lady Vincenza, is that there's an awful lot to tell you.' Tormalin crossed the room in a few strides and took Vintage's hand and squeezed it, before pressing his lips to it briefly. He grinned at her. 'You are not going to believe some of the nonsense we've been through.'

'Oh, I'm not?' She swatted at his arm, but she was grinning too, and her eyes were shining a little too brightly. 'I've been through some fair old shit myself, you know.' She reached up suddenly and, putting her arm around his neck, pulled him down into a fierce hug. 'Tormalin, I am so glad to see you well. And, frankly, alive and walking about. When I left you both . . .'

'I was missing half my face, yes. Thankfully, I don't remember much about it, and Noon has helped me to regain some of my strength.' Noon shot him a look for that, and he cleared his throat. 'But why did you leave us? Injured, half dead, and in the house of a man mad with grief. Plus, I must tell you, Esiah's wine cellar was not what it could be.'

Vintage sighed. 'Let's sit down, shall we? We've a lot to talk about, and my arse is still sore from all the walking.'

'I cannot believe that I have lived to see such a thing. I just cannot.'

Once everything had been told as well as it could be, Vintage had demanded to see all the war-beasts, so they had walked together to the Hatchery, where Aldasair still waited with Jessen to see if the smaller pods were close to hatching. Vostok was there too, having returned from her own jaunt around the hills, and was now tolerating Vintage's close examination of her wings, her feathers, her scales and horns. She seemed to have very little fear of the dragon, although she did keep pausing to bow to her.

'You, my lady, are more beautiful than I could ever have imagined. The paintings and statues do not do you justice.' Vostok dipped her head at this flattery, looking pleased. 'And you say you have never been this form before?'

'Not quite so, no,' said the dragon. 'A griffin, a great bird, and a dark dragon with wings like a bat, once.'

'Extraordinary. Just extraordinary.' Vintage paused in her examination to wipe at her eyes. 'Oh, you must forgive me. I just never thought . . . All these years learning about you, you see. All these years looking at dusty old sketches and images carved in the sides of old temples, and here you are. If only,

97

my darling, we did not have to meet under such unfortunate circumstances.'

'You say you were inside the Behemoth when it started to wake up?' Tor was standing with his arms crossed by one of the unhatched pods. Noon had seen him look for Kirune instinctively when they'd entered the hall, then just as instinctively pretend that he was doing no such thing.

'Yes.' Vintage straightened up, although she didn't quite turn away from Vostok. 'I have to tell you, my dear, I very nearly shit a brick. Everything started humming with energy, and parts of it started moving. It was repairing itself, would you believe that?' She shook her head slightly. 'To think, that all that time they were simply dormant. Nanthema and I barely got out of there before the whole thing sealed us away forever.'

'And your companions? When will we meet them?'

'Bern has gone to fetch them,' said Aldasair softly. 'Nanthema, and the boy, Eri.'

'You will let me draw you, I hope?' Vintage looked from Vostok to Jessen. 'I am not a great draughtsperson – not nearly as good as my distant cousin Rolda, anyway – but I will make a brave stab at it. I could easily make it my life's work, drawing you.'

'Vintage, we probably don't have time for that.' Noon crossed her arms over her chest, then realised she was mirroring Tor, so she put her hands in her pockets instead. 'The worm people could attack at any moment. We need to figure out what we're going to do next. We have four war-beasts, when normally there would be at least a hundred, and only Vostok remembers how to fight.'

'Of course, my darling. But just think, all of us together again, I'm sure we can figure it out.'

There was a soft exclamation at the other end of the hall. Bern had appeared with the Eboran woman and the child. The boy was the one who had cried out, but the woman Nanthema had her hands pressed to her face, her eyes streaming with tears.

'Nan, come and see them!' Vintage was beaming.

The woman called Nanthema came slowly down the hall, walking softly as though, if she moved too swiftly, the war-beasts might shimmer and break apart, revealed to be pieces of a dream after all. Her hair was long and dark, like Tor's, and it was loose over her shoulders. A pair of eyeglasses were hooked into the top of her shirt, and they winked in the lamplight. The boy was slight and sickly looking, his red eyes almost lost in shadows, and curiously he carried in his hands a heavy and awkward-looking bucket.

As they approached, Jessen suddenly stood, her big bushy tail straight as a brush.

'Another one comes!' she said, her normally quiet voice shockingly loud in the Hatchery. Noon frowned, wondering what the big wolf could mean, and then she spotted the war-beast pod rocking back and forth in its silk nest. It was one of the smallest, one that she had privately decided would bear them no beasts, but it was moving violently, and even the surface of it was beginning to split as the creature inside tried desperately to get out. Eri and Nanthema were just passing it; the woman stepped back, clearly alarmed, but the boy neatly put his bucket down on the marble floor – it had a cloth over it, Noon noticed for the first time – and went to the pod. Later, Noon would think about that moment often; Eri had gone as if summoned. As if his destiny was reaching out to him.

'I am here to witness a hatching!' Vintage was ecstatic, almost elbowing Tor out of the way to see as they all gathered around, but the boy Eri was there first. Without hesitating, he knelt on the floor and began to pull away chunks of the silvery pod material, the thin muscles in his arms bunching with the effort of it. The clear fluid ran over his hands and soaked his ragged shirt; the sharp green smell of apples filled the room.

'The boy,' said Tor. He met Noon's eyes, and she saw him shrug slightly. 'Should we . . .? I mean, shouldn't someone else?'

'Who else?' said Vostok, who was looming behind them. 'He is a son of Ebora too, Tormalin the Oathless.'

Tor grimaced at that, but Noon saw that it was too late anyway; already there was a sizeable hole in the pod, and a taloned foot was reaching out of it, grasping for whoever might be outside. Eri took a hold of it immediately, and Noon felt her stomach turn over. It was so small, this new beast. Would it even live?

With his free hand Eri pulled at more of the casing, but it was already falling apart. The creature inside it wriggled and stretched, a confusion, for the moment, of wet fur and limbs. One wing popped out as if on a spring, and it flapped back and forth wildly.

'Hello, friend,' said Eri. His voice was shaking. 'I'm here to help you.'

The war-beast slithered out of the remains of its pod onto Eri's lap, and once again Noon wondered at how small it was. No bigger than a large dog, it had a long, foxy face, rather like Jessen's but narrower, with oversized pointed ears, and it was covered in fur that was somewhere between the colour of ash and gold. With another tremor of shock, Noon realised it wasn't far off the colour of the boy's hair. The beast had feet like an eagle, and there were patches of copper-coloured scales on its forelegs and rump, while its wings were leathery and brown.

'Unusual,' murmured Vostok. 'I have not seen such a form for many Rains.'

'Incredible,' said Vintage. She had clasped her hands in front of her chest, and there were tears freely running down her face, although she was grinning as merrily as Noon had ever seen. 'What is she? A type of griffin? Another subset of the winged wolf?'

The war-beast coughed, and flapped its wings once, almost knocking Eri over, but the boy held on to the creature fiercely. They were both now liberally covered with sticky pieces of the pod material.

'Greetings, newest sibling,' said Jessen. 'We've been waiting to meet you for a while now.'

The small war-beast turned to look at her, blinking eyes that were like big blue marbles, but it did not speak.

'Here, let's get you cleaned up.' Aldasair touched the boy's shoulder hesitantly. 'I'm sure we can find some new clothes for you, Eri. You look like you've been living in those for years.'

For a moment the boy looked blank, as though remembering something he'd rather forget, and then he hugged the beast all the tighter.

'He'll come with me, though. We'll stay together now.'

'Of course,' said Vostok. 'That is your purpose.'

'Our new war-beast guest is small enough to stay in a room with you,' said Aldasair. He did not see how Tor winced at that statement. 'Come, I'll show you where you can sleep, Eri.'

The boy got up then, reluctantly putting the new beast down on the marble floor, but immediately the creature pressed itself to his legs so closely that when they made to leave the hall behind Aldasair, Eri almost tripped over the beast several times. He paused and retrieved his bucket as he went.

'So, five war-beasts now,' said Noon into the silence that filled the Hatchery at their departure. 'That's got to make our odds better, hasn't it?'

'Or, we've got four war-beasts and one more mouth to feed, and we're having enough trouble feeding everyone in this palace as it is,' said Tor. He saw the look Noon shot him and he raised his hands apologetically. 'He's barely big enough to carry our bags, Noon.'

'But he'll grow, right?' Noon turned to Vostok and Vintage,

who were wearing oddly similar expressions of consideration. 'You've all grown a little since you were birthed from the pods, it's just that he'll have more catching up to do.'

Vostok rumbled in the back of her throat before answering. 'Yes,' she said, although she sounded far from certain. 'Food, exercise, stimulation. They should all help our newest sibling.'

'Good, fine. Tor, we will just have to find more food. We all will.'

12

This section of the gardens had once been glorious. Aldasair remembered lawns lush with colour; flowers of blue, red, purple, and miniature trees with blossom of pink and yellow. They were the summer gardens, so it was to be expected that they didn't look their best when winter had barely left them, but neglect had done far more damage than an inappropriate season. Still, the grass was thriving now that the frosts were largely gone, and Eri and the new war-beast did not seem to care for the lack of flowers. They tore across the lawns, chasing each other and rolling in the dirt – Aldasair had found clothes for the boy, which were now well on the way to being ruined, but it was difficult to feel sad about that. The room from which he had looted the items had been much sadder, after all.

'Run faster, little brother!' called Sharrik. He stood with Aldasair and Bern, his blue feathers almost luminous in the sunlight. 'He is nearly catching you!'

'How do you know he's a he?' asked Bern.

'The scent. Although it makes little difference to us.'

The new war-beast had yet to speak. Instead, he seemed to communicate through a series of bashful head butts, all of which were directed towards the boy. As they watched, the

103

new beast jumped into the air and almost took off, beating his bat-like wings once, twice. He hovered up there for a moment, and then Eri jumped up and caught him. They barrelled to the ground together. The boy's laughter was like birdsong on the air, light but brittle.

'Where is Jessen?' The two were running off out of sight, and without stopping to discuss it, they moved to follow them, Bern pausing to pick up the bucket. Vostok had indicated that they should keep an eye on the newborn for now, just in case he should suddenly become ill or weak.

'She has gone to hunt,' said Aldasair, feeling a slight constriction in his chest as he did so. Jessen did not enjoy hunting, and she was aware that was a failing in herself, but they needed more food – there was no way around it.

'Hunting!' Sharrik immediately began to bristle, the feathers standing along his great muscled neck. 'Why am I not hunting? I shall hunt!'

'If you are going, at least let me remove that harness. You'll be better off without the weight.' Bern made to reach for him, but Sharrik whipped his head out of reach and with a few beats of his enormous wings, rose into the air.

'I shall bring back an entire herd!' he declared, before launching up and away. The wind from his wings battered them for a moment, and then he was gone.

'By the stones, I don't think he listens to a word I say.'

'He's like you.' Aldasair smiled, and then added, 'He wants to help, I mean. He's eager to be of assistance.'

'You mean he's eager to show off,' said Bern, but he was smiling faintly too. 'Well, if he can find game around here, he'll be lucky. We've all been out and looked, further and further every day – Tor and Noon are flying south now, over the mountains, but the further they go, the more energy they use up, and I'm not sure that does us any good. Even Noon's giant bat has been bringing back the odd rabbit, although I've not seen her for a while.' He sighed, and then lifted the bucket. 'And what is this about, exactly? It barely feels like there's anything in it at all.'

Aldasair lowered his voice. 'Eri will not go anywhere without it. An emotional attachment of some sort, something from his home he cannot let go of.' For a time they stood and watched as Eri and the war-beast attempted to climb a small tree. 'The human woman Vintage found him sitting by the road, and it's clear he hasn't been eating properly for some time. He may have experienced some sort of trauma and he won't speak of his family. I think he may have been alone for a long time. That can do strange things to a person.'

Bern looked at him, his eyes nearly as green as the fresh grass. Aldasair found that he was holding his breath, uncertain what he wanted Bern to say next, but then the big man turned away. 'Time heals,' he said eventually. 'That's what my father always says, anyway. Time, and the company of people who . . . care for you.'

'Your people have nearly all left. Did you not wish to go with them?'

Bern smiled again. 'And leave Sharrik? I know it's not your custom for humans to bond with war-beasts, but I'm afraid that ship has already sailed.' The big man cleared his throat. 'The great oaf has become quite dear to me.'

'There's nothing that says the war-beasts have to stay here.' Aldasair clasped his hands behind his back, carefully not looking at anything. 'Our old rules, the way things used to be – all of that is dust, Bern. You and Sharrik could go wherever you wanted. Finneral must also be in need of protection.'

Bern put the bucket down. 'Why are you saying this, Aldasair?'

'I don't know, truthfully.' He thought of Jessen, hunting somewhere far away. He could feel her, like a knot of tension in his chest, and knew that she was not enjoying herself. 'I don't know why I say anything, half the time. Part of me thinks it was easier when I didn't have anyone to talk to, when the corridors of the palace were silent and we were quietly slipping into death, I . . .' He pressed his fingers to his forehead. 'You should ignore me.'

'Never.' Bern gripped his shoulder briefly. 'You – and the boy – have been through a great deal, and Vostok is right, the war-beasts need to work as a unit. If I leave, that could damage what we have built.' He looked away, and Aldasair noticed that his cheeks were faintly pink. 'And what we have built means a great deal to me.'

'Hoy!' Eri was calling and waving to them. His wan face, still so gaunt, was flushed with colour. 'We've found something.'

He and the war-beast approached, the boy cradling something in his hands. From what Aldasair could see, it was a brightly painted object about the length of Eri's hand.

'We were digging together, and he found it. Isn't it fine?' The war-beast sat at his feet, long foxy nose pointed in the air.

Bern took it carefully from the boy's outstretched palm and showed it to Aldasair.

'By the stones, Aldasair, I think I know what this is. Imagine finding one of these out here, and so intact too.'

It was a clay figurine of a war-beast. Before Ygseril had been awakened and the Jure'lia queen had escaped, he and Bern had taken the last of the figures from the Hill of Souls and buried them quietly in the hills. When he had been a child, it had been a tradition to make such figures in honour of the war-beasts who had passed, and then when the Hill of Souls got too full, they would bury them in the ground so that their spirits might return to Ygseril. To find one out here that was still intact was certainly extraordinary.

'It must be hundreds of years old, yet it looks like it was only buried yesterday.'

The figure was of a winged cat, a little like Kirune, but with great twisting horns bursting from its forehead. The whole thing was painted a bright yellow.

'I know who it is, too.' Aldasair reached out and took the object lightly from Bern's big hands. 'Her name was Helcate, a very distinguished warrior indeed.'

'Helcate,' said Eri. 'Helcate. I think I remember . . . There were stories, my father tells me them sometimes. Helcate. I'm sure I remember her.'

'Helcate.'

The voice came from the ground, and they all looked down to see the small war-beast looking up at them. His voice had been soft, and broken with disuse, but there was no mistaking what he had said.

'Do you remember her?' Bern crouched, bringing himself to the same level as the war-beast. '*Are* you her, small one?'

'Helcate,' repeated the war-beast.

'I think he is just repeating Eri,' said Aldasair, but his lips felt numb. 'He is remembering how to speak, that's all.'

'Either way, I think that should be his name.' Eri put his hand on the war-beast's head and scratched him behind the ears fondly. 'Helcate, my friend.'

'How far is it?'

Nanthema glanced up. They were beyond the realms of the palace, walking down a wide street in the eastern sector of the city. It was growing late, and the dying sun was sending pools of golden light and black shadow stretching across the road.

'It's not far,' she said, and then she stopped. Vintage paused with her. 'I'm not certain this is a good idea.'

'I know it must be painful, and strange, Nan, but how can you stay here and not go and see?' Vintage adjusted her pack strap. The windows of the great houses all around them looked too dark. 'How were they when you last saw them?'

'Old,' said Nanthema, the corners of her mouth turning down. 'Very old. And – Look, they told me to go, Vin. They didn't want me to stay here, watching everyone die. Watching *them* die.'

'I know.' Vintage reached out and very briefly brushed Nanthema's cheek. 'That's what parents do, I suppose. Try to spare their children the pain they have to suffer. But I'll be there with you, Nan. Whatever it is, we can get through it together.'

Nanthema nodded, her long hair sweeping forward to hide her face for the moment.

'All right.'

They resumed walking. There were, Vintage noticed, fresh tracks on the road, evidence that Ebora was not quite as dead as it had once been. A wind rushed down across the ruined houses, bringing scents of newly blossoming flowers, rain and rot.

'Besides, twenty-odd years is not so long in Eboran years, is it? Your parents can't have aged so much while you were trapped inside the Behemoth crystal.'

'They weren't in the palace, Vintage, and I doubt they would deliberately miss the return of Ygseril and the war-beasts. It wouldn't be wise to get my hopes up.'

Vintage nodded, feeling her cheeks grow hot. Always she was supposed to be the wise one, the clever one, yet when she was with Nanthema, it was as though she became her teenage self again, enthusiastic and full of ideas and opinions – not necessarily clever or wise ones.

'Here. The house was just beyond the corner.'

They did not see it immediately, as several sizeable trees had grown up at the intersection of the road, the spaces between them filled with newly budding shrubs and bushes. When they pushed through and spotted the dwelling, Vintage felt a shiver of apprehension move through her. It was a typical Eboran building, flat roofed and single-storeyed, sprawling and somehow organic-looking, but it was mostly hidden under a rust-coloured creeper, which had covered the pale walls and dangled like chimes from the gables. The windows were dark-smeared holes, somehow hungry and strange.

'See?' Nanthema was attempting to sound cheerful, but it came out strangled. 'It doesn't do to be too optimistic. My mother was hardly fastidious but I doubt even she would put up with such a mess.'

They made their way towards it, stepping over rotten strands of creeper and dirt made slippery from melting ice. The scent of rot grew stronger, and Vintage was reminded of Esiah Godwort's mansion. They had found only sadness there, and abruptly she regretted encouraging Nanthema to seek out her parents. *I'm so set on finding the truth that I forget that a comforting lie is sometimes the better path.*

'Nan . . .'

'No, look, we're here now. It would be even worse to walk right up to the threshold and then turn away. I'd be thinking about it forever.'

There was a pair of double doors under an ornate gable, carved once with images of Ygseril. The pale-green paint had flaked away and there were fat deposits of yellow moss clinging here and there like limpets. Nanthema tugged at the handle and the door stuck for a moment before springing open with a gust of foul-smelling dust. Immediately inside it was dark – Vintage could only make out a handful of chairs on a dirt-streaked floor – but moving beyond the receiving room they came to a chamber with windows all down one side in the Eboran style, and the last sour orange sunlight filled the room well enough to see the horrors inside it.

'Nan, come on, let's go.' Vintage reached out for the woman's arm, but she stepped neatly away. 'You don't need to see this.'

'Oh, but I do.' The strangled good cheer was back in

Nanthema's voice. Vintage winced. 'I had to come back here, didn't I? So it's time to see what was waiting for me all along.'

This was, Vintage guessed, a living room of some sort – there was a dining table, several of the braziers Eborans often used for cooking light meals nearby, and the walls were lined with paintings and tapestries – but at some point someone had brought in a makeshift bed and crammed it next to the long table. Perhaps the view from this window was their favourite, she thought, feeling her throat grow tight. Perhaps they'd wanted to be able to see it while they died.

There was a twisted form lying on its front on the floor, its face turned towards the window. The body was not quite completely skeletal. Its long, white hair was still attached in patches to its scalp, and the nightgown it wore was yellowed and stained but largely intact. There was a very large black stain surrounding the body, scuffed and smeared, even disturbed here and there by the trails of insects as they made their way back and forth, but it was possible to see what it was. Impossible not to see.

'She bled out,' said Nanthema faintly. She was standing very still and straight, her arms at her sides. 'My mother got the crimson flux eventually, it seems, although she appears to have been very old when it happened at least. She loved the western garden, you see. My father was the gardener, spent decades crafting it, and he planted all of her favourite flowers out there.' She smiled, and her face was beautiful and terrible in the dying light. 'His garden, the eastern one, was full of medicinal plants, because his true love was science. But he spent more time in the western one, because it was his present to her. So mother came here at the end so that she could look at it, and eventually, I suppose, she could not stop coughing up blood. Vomiting it by the end, I imagine. She has crawled from her bed – do you think she lost her mind at the end? Did she try to get outside, thinking that could save her?'

'Nan, please. Don't.'

'It's interesting, though, don't you think? It's interesting what you can tell from this little scene. I wonder if my father was still alive at this point, or if he died before her.' She turned towards the dining table. There were dishes piled up there, the contents turned black and furry. 'This.' She reached out and poked at a big yellow bowl. 'My father would make tenzin stew and serve it in this bowl – always just this bowl. I think he was still alive and making it for her when she died. Have you ever had tenzin stew, Vin? It's from Jarlsbad, that's where you can get the best tenzin stew, but my father's was quite good too.'

'Nanthema, please. Let's go back outside and get some air. We've seen enough.'

'Yes.' Nanthema turned towards her. The Eboran woman's eyes were dry, although she did not focus on Vintage as she spoke. 'Let's go and look at the garden, because . . . Let's go outside.'

She strode over to the nearest window, and with some difficulty, thanks to the dirt and filth crusted to it, slid it aside. Immediately the room filled with the ripe scent of rotting vegetation.

'Nan . . .'

'Come on. We may as well finish this.'

Outside, the garden was a confusion of long grass and thick clumps of bushes that had burst out of their neat rows. There were a number of fruit trees, the sort Vintage had seen all over the palace gardens; these had grown so wild and so close together that their interlinked branches seemed to form their own ceiling.

'I wish you could have seen this place at its best, Vin,' said Nanthema quietly. 'It really was something.'

'I wish that too.' Vintage swallowed. 'Did they have friends who could have checked up on them? You can't have been all alone out here.'

'It was the end.' Nanthema sounded too calm, her voice

oddly slow, as though she were speaking from a dream. 'We kept to ourselves. Dying is a private thing. Look, here he is. Of course he would be here.'

At first Vintage could not make out what she was talking about at all, and then she saw it. A slumped shape at the base of one of the miniature apple trees. The man had died on his knees, and his body had bent almost double, his head nearly brushing the ground. Insects moved busily across his shining skull, and one of his hands lay face up on the layers of dead leaves. For a moment Vintage could not understand how he was still upright, until she spotted a thick, rust-coloured object between his midriff and the ground. It was a sword, buried in his guts.

'What . . .?'

'Mother died, and Father couldn't live with it.' Nanthema tipped her head to one side, as though she were looking at an especially interesting species of flower. 'I would imagine he was out of the room when she died, and came back to see her sprawled there in a pool of her own blood. He would not want to die looking on her like that, so he went out into her favourite place. He could remember her better there.'

'Nanthema, please.' This time Vintage took hold of the woman's arm and held it until she met her eyes. 'Let's go now. If there's anything here you feel you need, then I can come back for it myself, alone. You've had a terrible shock.'

'A shock?' Nanthema grinned. 'Oh no, it's not shocking. I knew this was what I'd find, I . . . when I left them I knew it would come to this but I didn't think it would smell so much, do you see? That it would be quite so squalid.' She laughed, an odd, choked noise. 'No, you're right. Let's go.'

They were some distance away, halfway back to the palace with the spreading branches of Ygseril in view, when Nanthema suddenly stumbled in the road, falling to her knees, much as her father had. The tall Eboran woman began to shake violently, and Vintage knelt next to her, holding her tight until it stopped.

13

As far as Hestillion was concerned, the windows were both a blessing and curse.

They stretched the length of her new quarters within the corpse moon – not glass, of course, but a permanent translucence to the strange material that made up the Behemoth walls. Through it she could see the changing moods of the sky, the rushing clouds, and Sarn, cold and distant, and that had lifted her heart significantly – it was only when windows were taken away, she realised, that you truly understood what they had always given you. However, it also meant that she was horribly aware of every movement the Behemoth made. The clouds would abruptly rush by, or the ground would fly up towards them, and Hestillion would have to grab on to something to steady her roiling stomach.

Celaphon, at least, did not seem especially concerned by all the queasy movement, but then Celaphon did not seem concerned by anything at all.

'My dear one, do you not feel like eating today?'

The small dragon was lying at the foot of her makeshift bed, his snout tucked neatly under his arm, but at the sound of her voice he raised his head slowly, blinking his odd, blind-looking eyes at her. The latest gruel pods sat next to him, each carefully opened by Hestillion for him to eat from, but he hadn't touched any of them.

'I am tired,' he said, in his ghostly little voice. 'Tired of . . . the food.'

'And I cannot blame you for that, but if you do not eat, dear one, you will not grow up big and strong.'

Celaphon lowered his head again, as though it were too heavy to hold up for very long.

'I do not want to make you sad. But my stomach does not want it.'

Hestillion strode across the room to the far corner. The queen had been good on her word, and had provided her with a new suite. It was still as far from her rooms at the palace as could reasonably be imagined, but there was evidence that some effort had been made on her behalf; a tall nook in the wall for storage, several soft mounds to sit on, even a mirror of sorts – it appeared to be made of a reflective liquid, that would sometimes shiver and ripple while Hestillion looked at it. She often wondered who was looking out. In the centre of the main room was a raised platform covered with the soft grey padding that lined the walls, and on this was a mismatched collection of furs and blankets; it was surprisingly comfortable, although the suspicion that she rested on the pliant flesh of a monster did not make for restful sleep. Celaphon would often curl at the bottom of the makeshift bed, his fevered scales keeping her feet warm.

In the far corner there was a round hole in the floor, and in it was more of the slippery black fluid that was so much a part of the Jure'lia. Hestillion knelt next to it.

'You, in there. I want to speak to you.'

Immediately, the surface of the pool began to boil and jerk, and out of it rose one of the little homunculus creatures that had been bringing her the gruel pods. The shifting oily expanse of its flesh contracted, revealing a hole in what Hestillion guessed was its head.

114

'Yes.' Its voice was an oily whisper.

'I want food. Real food, not this endless muck you keep bringing me. Celaphon needs meat, and fruit, and lots of it. I have asked for this before.'

'We have brought you this before.'

Hestillion pushed her dirty hair out of her eyes, trying to keep her temper.

'Yes, and he ate that! That is how food works. You need to bring more of it, do you understand?'

There was a pause.

'We will bring more pods.'

'No! You will bring meat, and fruit, and you will *keep* bringing it. Do you understand?' The creature stood, its mouth opening and closing uncertainly. 'Where is the queen? Fetch her for me. She must know that she is starving us, and if we are starved, we cannot help her.'

The homunculus was quiet for a time. When it spoke again, there was an odd tone to its voice, as though it were really two voices speaking at once. 'The queen says: there will be more soon. We have no wish for you to starve. More very soon. Look out the window.'

With that, the small creature sank back into the pool and vanished. Hestillion watched it for a while, rubbing her hands on her grimy robe, and then she stalked back across the room. Celaphon raised his head wearily, and she reached down and scooped him up into her arms before sitting on the foot of the bed. He was not as heavy as he had been, and that worried her.

'Dear one, we will have some food for you soon.' The dragon raised his eyes to meet hers, and she forced herself to smile. 'As much food as your stomach can handle. And then how would you feel about trying your wings out again?'

Celaphon's head dipped to rest against her breastbone.

'I will make you sad.'

'No, no, you do not make me sad.' Hestillion squeezed him

115

to her, ignoring all the ways his bony limbs poked into her. 'I only wish for you to be what you are destined to be, Celaphon. It will take time, and patience. That's all.'

'I want to fly. Like in the stories you told me.'

'And you will, Celaphon, you will. You shall be the mightiest war-beast there ever was.'

Ahead of them, the long window was full of orange and pink cloud; a sunset was filling the sky with its fiery light.

'And you will breathe fire too, eventually. Dragons were always the most powerful war-beasts, and you, dear one—'

The view in front of them suddenly lurched downwards, the clouds torn into feathery pieces to either side. Hestillion gasped, and clutched Celaphon closer, but all she could feel physically was a hum that moved through the entire ship, so low it was a sensation rather than a noise. Below them, now that the clouds had been cleared to either side, she could see the landscape of Sarn – somewhere to the east, if she was right, a rich place of green grass and fruit trees – and there was a neat little town crouched in the heart of rows and rows of orchards. Hestillion could see slate roofs and patches of smoke from chimneys, and narrow streets, some cobbled but most simply packed dirt. Cautiously she stood up, and carrying Celaphon with her, walked over to the window.

'What is happening?' asked the small dragon. He shifted in her arms, wanting to get a better view of the window.

'It looks like we might be about to get our dinner.' Hestillion forced a smile on her face. 'Won't that be nice?'

There were people running in the streets, their faces turned up to the monster above them like tiny moons. Lamps were lit, and points of light burst into life everywhere. Gates were flung open, and the humans living in the small town began to flee. And then, from the outer limit of her vision, other shapes began to appear: terrible, spider-like things with many legs, that floated down towards the town like malignant seeds. Soon, they would birth burrowers, which would start converting the people in the town into drones, while the maggots would start to busily eat everything they could before covering the remains in varnish. Hestillion grimaced and began to turn away from the sight, but Celaphon wriggled in her arms.

'I want to see! Don't you want to watch, Lady Hestillion?'

I should watch, she thought, pressing her lips into a thin line. *I should see the harvest of what I have sown.*

Reluctantly, she turned back to the window just in time to see other, even stranger shapes falling down towards the town. For a second she was struck with a new horror – was the queen somehow throwing human victims down from the Behemoth? – and then she realised what she was seeing; the queen had released her 'experiments' from the vats.

They looked like huge, pale humans, as white as paper and naked, although there was little human detail to them that Hestillion could see. They were big, heavily muscled things with no hair, and they each had a pair of bony wings sprouting from their backs. She could see the skin stretched between each bone, and how the wind filled and buoyed them like sails, and then they were too far away, flying down towards the houses with arms outstretched.

'New horrors,' she muttered to herself, feeling cold despite Celaphon's body curled against her. 'And we thought they were bad enough as it was.'

In the end she watched all of it. The town itself was broken into pieces; it went from a neat confection of grey stone and brown slate to a shattered confusion of rubble, people's belongings strewn here and there like innards leaking from a corpse. Most of the people, she thought, managed to get away, although there were still plenty of human figures staggering around when the maggots descended; these final drones were consumed along with any other organic material. The fruit trees vanished very quickly indeed – watching it was almost fascinating, if you could detach yourself from what it was. The two maggots that had been birthed from the belly of the corpse moon grew fat, and then began to excrete their green 'varnish'. Eventually, however, Hestillion began to feel a jarring shudder in the hum that moved throughout the Behemoth, and the big ship began to descend, somewhat unsteadily, before landing hard enough to nearly knock her off her feet. She went to the long window then, and had a glimpse of one of the queen's experiments; the creature was on its knees, its big wings hanging to either side of it, useless or forgotten. And then the window clouded over and she could see nothing.

'What is happening out there?'

'I cannot see,' piped up Celaphon. She had put him down on the bed, where he lay on his side, panting as though he had been for a run.

'Do you understand what you saw?' Hestillion looked closely at the small creature. His pearly eyes were half shut now. 'Do you know what the outside world is? Can you remember that much?'

The dragon made a strange fluting noise. 'I know bits. I know that this is strange. That outside is . . . normal.'

'And your old name? Your previous forms? Do you remember Ygseril?'

'The sound . . . of wind in the branches. That's all.'

Hestillion was just sighing over this when the corpse moon shuddered violently again. The window flickered back into life and they were rising up over the mess of the town. Almost immediately afterwards the passage to the room slid open, and the queen appeared. She looked, as far as Hestillion could tell from her mask-like face, agitated, and she carried a number of sacks in each long hand. A few of them were soaked through with blood, leaving a crimson smear across the floor as she approached.

'Here,' she said. 'Meat.' She dropped the bloodied sacks on

the ground. On the bed, Celaphon sat up, his snout twitching. 'These also are for you.' She passed the others sacks to Hestillion; inside were a number of dresses and robes, and a pair of dun-coloured leggings. Hestillion held them up critically. They were obviously not of Eboran standard, but they were clean and in good repair, which was more than could be said for her current dress.

'Thank you.' She put the sacks aside, resolving to go through them properly later, and picked up one of those containing the meat. As she did so, Celaphon wriggled off the bed, and limping slightly on his poorly formed legs, came to join her. 'What was that place you attacked?'

'A human town.'

'Yes, but which town? Where is it? Somewhere to the east, is it not?'

The queen tipped her head to one side. 'It is a human place. It hardly matters what it has been named.'

'And this is . . . this is not human meat?'

'It is from the animals they keep. We assumed that human flesh would be offensive to you, although we do not understand why. It is all the same.'

'Human blood is . . . Never mind.' Hestillion pulled a chunk of meat from the bag. It was a deep, dark red, and marbled through with thin lines of white fat. Looking at it made her own stomach cramp with hunger, and the smell of blood awoke memories she hadn't contemplated for some time, but she passed it down to Celaphon who clamped his jaws around it gladly. The sound of his happy chewing filled the room.

'It is still very small,' said the queen in a considering tone. 'We remember the war-beasts of old. Are you sure that is what it is?'

Hestillion ignored this.

'I saw your new toys flying out there,' she said. 'What happened to them? What were they there to do?'

119

The queen raised her chin. For the first time Hestillion wondered why she had brought the sacks herself when it would have been easier to send a homunculus to do the job.

'They collected your meat and your niceties.' The queen gestured to the sacks again. 'They went inside the humans' houses and dwellings. We saw, through them, what was to be taken. And they carried it back. Some killed humans too – humans that tried to defend their meat and niceties.'

'They carried it all back?'

The queen paused. She took a few steps further into the room. Her shoulders, Hestillion noted, were draped with a flowing piece of the black fluid, almost as though it were a cloak, and her flesh seemed paler still than when she had seen it last. A dark green, like the leaves of those trees that lived through the winter.

'It's not finished,' said the queen eventually. 'They weaken too easily. Something about the wings . . .' She turned and looked at Celaphon then, who was taking no notice of either of them. 'It is curious, making new things. You creatures are all interior framework. It is most vexing.'

'Your new toys could not fly back up by themselves.'

'We collected them instead, and what they were will go back into the pools to be broken down and moulded anew. We have to be careful now, Hestillion Dream-walker, born in the year of the green bird, as we are not completely healed, and the process is a slow one.'

'There was no white dragon,' Hestillion pointed out. 'And no other war-beasts came to the town's defence. Have you been attacked elsewhere? I know you have other ships.'

The queen looked at her for a long while then, as though considering her answer, but in the end she turned back to the door.

'There is food in the sacks for you also, Hestillion Eskt. We hope it meets with the standards of an ambassador.'

120

14

'Your wings! Keep them tense, Helcate. Use the muscles in your shoulders, direct all of your energy there. Faster now, faster.'

The small war-beast was trying his best, but it was clear to Vintage that he was tired, and he only managed a short flight of around ten feet before he landed back in the wet grass. Vostok snorted her impatience, but Eri looked pleased, his gaunt face bright with pleasure.

'He has been flying all morning,' said Vintage, in a carefully musing tone. 'His enthusiasm certainly never wavers, but I suspect he could do with a brief rest.'

The dragon turned her violet gaze on Vintage. It was still unnerving to be so close to her, but at the same time, there was such a reality to Vostok that Vintage found herself getting used to her presence all the same. Her scent – sap and apples – and the sheer weight of her; it was impossible to look away, sometimes. And yet, despite all the awe and near-religious terror Vintage felt, she was surprised to find something else – that Vostok could be difficult.

'We have no time to rest. The Jure'lia will not be nursing their wounds forever. Eventually, they will turn their eye back to Ebora, and we must be ready. Even the smallest of us.'

'He is growing, though, look.' Vintage nodded to where the small war-beast was trampling the grass with Eri. In the last few days Tor and Noon had brought back a large amount of fresh meat, and Sharrik had done the same, returning with a series of unfortunate deer clasped in his enormous beak. Much of this fresh food had gone directly to the newest war-beast, who had eaten heartily. Some of the human foraging teams had brought baskets of a tuber they had discovered growing out in the grounds now that the dirt wasn't so hard. Vostok had snorted at these, but Bern had boiled them up with herbs and all the war-beasts had eaten them, along with the still-bloody meat. Helcate's head nearly reached Eri's shoulder, which was remarkable progress, and as if in response to his friend, Eri too looked healthier. He had not lost the oddly aged look around his eyes, but his skinny limbs were firmer, his cheeks a little fuller. 'You must be pleased about that?'

'Pleased?' If it were possible for a dragon to look perplexed, Vostok was doing a fine job of it. 'All of this is wrong. A runt war-beast? I am aware this happens to animals and humans, Lady de Grazon, but we have no experience of such things.'

'You mean *you* don't.'

'I beg your pardon?'

Vintage cleared her throat. She tried not to think about how impossible this conversation would have seemed a week ago.

'You are being forced into a role you're unfamiliar with, my lady. You've never had to teach anyone before, or watch someone grow. You were all born knowing your purpose and yourselves. There was never any reason to teach anyone anything, when the knowledge was already there, nestled neatly in your beautiful heads. There was just war, and glory. Now, there is teaching.' Vintage smiled faintly. 'You find yourself a teacher, and you do not like it.'

The dragon was quiet for a moment. Helcate and Eri were laughing together over something, the covered bucket quite forgotten under a tree. Looking at it, Vintage felt a twist of unease in her gut.

'Noon respects you greatly,' said Vostok, after some time. 'She thinks you very clever, for a human. Just because we are bonded, do not think that I must also respect your opinion, Lady de Grazon. You know nothing of war, or of what we are.'

Vintage half nodded, half bowed at that. 'Of course, my lady. But I do find that people are people, wherever I go, and it seems to me that war-beasts are very like people.'

Vostok snorted at that, and when she did not reply, Vintage sensed that the dragon had deemed her unworthy of a response.

'I would love to see the Nest,' she said into the chilly silence. 'Noon gave me some idea of what it was like. It sounds extraordinary.'

'Hmph. There is little point. Much of what was there is lost or has been stolen by humans. Empty spaces, broken things.'

'I have spent much of the last few years looking at empty spaces and broken things, my lady, and I doubt anything I have seen would be as spectacular as the Nest. Noon mentioned a particular missing artefact, something you were especially aggrieved to find gone?'

Eri and Helcate came wandering over together. The war-beast had his wings folded neatly along his back, and his head held high. Despite Eri's best efforts, he had yet to say anything other than his own name.

'You may rest,' Vostok told them graciously. 'But be ready to fly again once you have your wind back.' The dragon turned back to Vintage as Eri began to rummage in his pack for their lunch – cold meat pressed between slices of a tough flat bread Bern had introduced them to. 'The missing item was a special piece by the artist Micanal the Clearsighted.'

123

'I have heard of him, of course. I've even been lucky enough to see some of his works. A painting at the house of a friend of mine, a sculpture in Jarlsbad.'

'This was something else.' Vostok's voice had taken on a distant, wistful tone. 'He was making it just for us, a special commission. Many artists, you must understand, chose to celebrate our glory in many forms, but Micanal was a man of exceptional wisdom. He claimed that capturing our magnificence in a painting or tapestry was insufficient, and he devised a new art form, especially for us.'

Eri was tucking into his sandwich, handing pieces of it over to Helcate, who had swallowed his down in one gulp.

'That's extraordinary.' Vintage glanced under her eyelashes at the dragon. She sensed that while Vostok was reluctant to share war-beast secrets with a mere human, she still could not resist talking of past glories. 'How did that work exactly?'

For a moment, Vostok was silent. They were in a part of the palace gardens that had yet to be infiltrated by the human settlers, and the sun was just edging towards the horizon, turning the sky orange and grey. The only sounds were the calls of the birds in the trees, and the determined sound of Eri chewing, although Vintage occasionally caught the scent of wood smoke on the wind. The cooking fires were not that far away.

'Back when Ygseril lived, in the bloom of his youth, sap was abundant.' Vostok stretched out her claws in the grass, flexing them like a cat. 'It fed and nourished the children of Ebora, and some even took it and, through a process that took many years, created nuggets of hard resin.'

'Amber!' cried Vintage. 'Your great tree-god produced amber?'

'It was, as you might imagine, beautiful. Light gold in colour, and shining with its own inner light. Artworks of the time often used it, or Eborans would create exquisite jewellery from it. Micanal the Clearsighted discovered a way to store dreams within the amber.'

Vintage blinked. 'I am sorry, my lady, I am not sure what you mean.'

'No, I thought you might not.' Vostok pulled her claws back through the grass, creating neat lines of dark earth against the green. 'Dream-walking. You know of it?'

'Well, of course. The famous Eboran art of dream-walking, where they can enter and even shape another's dreams. Tor claims to be quite good at it, although as usual I would take that with a pinch of salt.'

'As well as being an artistic genius, Micanal was a talented dream-walker. And the amber of Ygseril was not like any ordinary lump of tree resin, Lady de Grazon. It had a . . . presence. Micanal was able to store images and sensations inside the amber, to be experienced by us, when we wished.'

'But that's incredible!' Vintage looked at the boy, but he was leaning against Helcate, chattering away to the small war-beast about flying, and how they would explore Ebora together one day. 'I had never even heard of such a thing, not in all my years of studying Ebora.'

'There is no reason that you should,' sniffed Vostok. 'The amber record was for us alone.'

'But I have never even seen pieces of this amber, not in any museums or collections.' She paused. 'I might have read something, once . . . The old library in Reidn had a catalogue of Eboran artworks, but I must have assumed it was listing ordinary amber. Even so . . .' A terrible thought formed. 'Of course, when Ygseril died, or appeared to have died, I imagine those pieces of ancient sap became incredibly sought after. Not, I assume, that they helped at all.'

Vostok shifted her huge muscled shoulders: a dragon shrug. 'And Micanal's great work is gone. Perhaps you are right, and some Eborans desperate for sap found the amber record and ground it down, or smashed it to pieces. All those dreamscapes, lost.'

'We have one.'

Eri was sitting with his legs crossed, leaning against Helcate's back; the war-beast appeared to have gone to sleep. The boy looked up at them with half-hooded eyes, as though he was also sleepy.

'What?' snapped Vostok. 'Micanal worked only for us. He swore that this art form would be dedicated to us alone. You could not have possessed anything like it.'

Eri's eyes widened slightly, and he glanced at his bucket as if for reassurance – for the first time that afternoon.

'I suppose. My parents have one, though. They keep it hidden and safe. It is one of their most precious things.'

'This isn't some bauble, child,' huffed Vostok, drawing herself up to her full height.

'Eri, my darling, is it still there, at your home? At Lonefell?'

The boy was looking down at the grass now, rubbing his fingers free of crumbs. 'I don't see why not. Everything there is . . . everything there should be the same as I left it.'

'Then we must go there immediately!' At Vostok's low growl, Vintage turned to the dragon. 'Do you not see, my lady? It might not be exactly what we need, but it could be a clue!' She grinned, and in a fit of confidence, pressed her hand to the dragon's shoulder. 'I have spent much of my life looking for clues – empty spaces and broken things – and I know a good one when I smell it. Eri, my dear, do you think you could lead us back there?'

The boy was silent for a moment. Helcate, who was awake now, leaned his long foxy nose under Eri's chin and pushed him, as though trying to wake him up too.

'Probably. I can probably take you there.' The boy took a deep breath. 'But not now. It's getting late, and I don't want to go there in the dark. Please.'

* * *

126

Tor reached down and, taking hold of either side of his boot, wrenched it from the mud. It came away with an obscenely wet sound, and he took a moment to sigh noisily.

'We could have flown. We could have flown all the way there. Tell me, Kirune, do you have some terrible affection for mud? Or were your wings simply too tired to make the relatively short distance?'

The great cat lifted his head to glare at Tor, the pupils in his enormous yellow eyes expanding briefly, as though he were contemplating making the Eboran his prey. And then he rumbled deep in his throat and kept walking. This part of the forest was alive with the sound of moisture; freshly melted snow dripping from trees, the soft sound of rivulets of ice water trickling around their feet. It was fresh, and cold, and the scent of the forest was a deep-green companion all around them.

'These are my best boots, you know. Eboran leather, which means, of course, that no one is even making boots like this anymore.'

'Do you always mewl like an infant?' rumbled Kirune.

'Everyone else will be there by now,' Tor wiped his hands on his coat, resolving to look more carefully at where he was putting his feet.

'Ebora is my home,' Kirune said firmly. 'I want to walk all parts of it. Smell it. Taste it. Then I will come to know it.'

'Well, I hope you are enjoying the mud. And I hope the directions the boy gave us are accurate. Do you suppose Vostok stopped to have a ramble around the woods?'

'The snake.'

'You might not like her, Kirune, but she knows more about what is going on here than anyone. We need to listen to her.'

'Perhaps you should fly with the snake, then. Perhaps she would enjoy your mewling. She treats us all like cubs. I think she must like it very much.'

127

Tor opened his mouth to reply to that, and then closed it. What was the point? Ahead of them, the thick pines were becoming thinner, and it was possible to see what must be an overgrown garden, and beyond that, looking tired and ghost-like in the early morning light, was a grey stone house. It was not built in the Eboran style at all; it was tall and narrow, and there were three floors, all with unusual circular windows. The roof was peaked and angular, unlike the usual low and unob-trusive roofs of Ebora. It was an oddity, standing out here all by itself, and looking at it, Tor was reminded of other places he had travelled – perhaps the owners had once been travellers themselves, and had sought to reflect their experiences in their home.

They trampled through the gardens, Kirune pushing down overgrown bushes with ease. Once they were through the outskirts, Tor noticed that at least part of the garden had been regularly tended: there were neat rows of exposed earth, a shovel sticking out of the ground next to a pair of wooden buckets. Seeing those, he thought of the boy Eri.

'There they are,' muttered Kirune. 'The snake is here.'

Indeed, it was hard to miss Vostok. She stalked around the furthest corner of the house, her long neck low and her snout near the floor, as though she were scenting the place. With her came the boy and Vintage – Vintage was carrying the boy's bucket. She spotted them and waved, and they waited by the door as Tor and Kirune made their way over.

'Did you get lost, my darling?' asked Vintage brightly when they arrived. Tor watched her take in the mud on his boots and the corresponding mud that was spattered up Kirune's legs and dotted on the fur of his belly. She pressed her lips together briefly, and then smiled at them. 'Noon has decided to go scouting for food with Fulcor, but she might join us later. We've already ascertained, somewhat awkwardly, that the door is too small for Vostok to enter without causing damage to the house, but I think Kirune should be able to slip through.' She paused, then bowed slightly to the big cat. 'Your lithe frame should have no troubles, my lord.'

'Whatever you find, you will bring out here,' said Vostok. 'So that I may see it.'

Eri opened the door for them, with Helcate at his ankles. He hesitated for a moment on the doorstep, looking around at them as though he wasn't sure why they were there, but then Helcate head-butted him gently in his side, and they went through. Kirune followed, also pausing on the stoop to meet Vostok's eyes. He let his gaze linger long enough to be an obvious insult, and then he padded into the interior, brushing against a wooden cabinet and causing the ornaments there to tremble precariously.

'We will be back shortly, my lady,' said Vintage. 'I'm sure it won't take us long to find what the boy is talking about.'

The door led directly into a sprawling living room, well arranged to Tor's eye, but absolutely crammed with things. Paintings and tapestries on every wall, every cabinet stuffed with artworks and pieces of framed parchment. Even the furniture seemed needlessly ornate; chairs and tables carved and painted with myriad animals, plant life and complex interlocking shapes. There were bookcases everywhere Tor looked, all heaving with leather-bound volumes or stacks of rolled documents.

'Vintage, it's like you exploded all over this place.'

She swatted him lightly on the arm. 'I didn't miss you *at all*.' Stepping into the centre of the room she looked around with as much curiosity as Tor had seen when they were exploring the Wild. 'Early period imperial ceramics and later period paintings, all of them exquisite. Such a collection, and just gathering dust out here in the middle of nowhere! I cannot wait to see what books are on the shelves . . .'

Tor cleared his throat. The boy Eri was standing with his

arms by his sides, looking as though a strong breeze might blow him down at any moment. Helcate, as ever, crouched by him, looking with every appearance of concern at his friend.

'Vintage, we are not at a piece of Behemoth wreckage here. This is someone's *home*.'

She stopped on her way to the nearest bookshelf and whipped off her hat. 'Of course it is, my dear, of course. *Ahem*. Eri, my darling, would you like to . . . find your parents for us?'

The boy swayed on his feet, blinking rapidly. Vintage met Tor's eyes, her eyebrows raised in alarm.

'They're not here at the moment,' said Eri eventually. 'The thing you're looking for, it will be in Father's study. He won't mind us looking.' He rested his hand on Helcate's furry head, and seemed to find some strength there, because his face became more animated. 'All the important things that remind them of . . . before, are kept in there. Letters and maps and things. I'll show you.'

Eri led them from the living room up a flight of stairs to a broad landing leading to several more rooms. There was, Tor realised, an odd smell about the place. Nothing he could quite pinpoint, but it made him think of Esiah Godwort's house, abandoned and touched with madness. Kirune kept going up the stairs and disappeared around a corner, his striped tail vanishing from sight. Tor looked up the stairs after him, considering demanding that he come back – it seemed Kirune did not care if wandering around a stranger's home was impolite – but the inevitable snub would be too embarrassing. Instead, Tor followed the others into the study. It was similarly packed with books and scrolls, and dominated by an enormous desk, bristling with drawers. The surface of it was covered with a light layer of dust.

'My father keeps all his favourite things in here,' said Eri. He went over to the desk and pulled out a long thin drawer that ran the length of it. Inside was a sheet of cream velvet, dotted with small objects at evenly spaced intervals. Vintage was at his shoulder so quickly Tor didn't even see her move. 'It's here, see? The one in the middle. I knew it was still here.'

Even in a drawer full of extraordinary objects – just glancing at them Tor spotted several things he knew would make a fortune in certain Sarn markets – the amber tablet stood out like a new leaf on a dead tree. It was about the length of his palm, and a pale yellow colour, much paler than amber from other trees – even Wild ones. It seemed to shine, nestled in the velvet, and tiny flecks inside it caught the light and shimmered, like gold. On the surface was an extremely delicate carving of three faces, each so detailed it could only have been of a real person.

'Micanal the Clearsighted,' breathed Vintage. 'I've seen enough portraits to recognise him. And are the other two your parents, Eri?'

But the boy had gone utterly rigid. His eyes were locked on the faces, his own caught in an expression of dismay so clear that Tor felt his stomach turn over. Gently, he put his hands on the boy's shoulders and turned him away from the drawer.

'Eri? Are you with us, kid?'

Turning him away seemed to break the spell, and Tor felt him go loose under his hands. Eri looked down at Helcate, and then back to Vintage.

'Those are their faces. Micanal was a very good friend, someone they talked about often. I think they missed him . . . miss him a lot.'

'A very good friend.' Tor straightened up and met Vintage's eyes. 'Micanal was known for having lots of *very* good friends, but this looks like a special gift. May I look more closely at it, Eri?'

The boy shrugged, and then nodded, not quite looking at

the drawer. The amber tablet was pleasingly heavy, and cool to the touch. Tor turned it over and over, running his fingers over the deftly carved faces.

'Vostok said he had worked out a way to store information in the amber,' said Vintage. 'That would make it even more valuable, of course. Can you make out anything unusual about it, my dear?'

Tor grimaced. 'If you mean is it singing a song only my delicate Eboran ears can hear, then no. It's a very beautiful thing, and certainly more evidence that Micanal was the greatest artist we ever had, but I can't see how it can help us.'

'Let's take it outside to Vostok, and see what she says. Is that all right with you, Eri?'

The boy had leaned his face into Helcate's furry neck, but they could still make out his muffled assent.

Outside, the day had brightened, filling the garden with chilly sunlight. Vostok had wandered over to a pond and was sitting watching a small number of bright red fish flitting under its green surface.

'Ornamental fish,' she said as they approached. 'I had forgotten . . . These were called fire dabs. Once, the Nest had a lake, and there was a fish of every colour in it. I imagine they are all dead now.'

'We found one of Micanal's amber tablets,' said Tor, holding it out for the dragon to see. 'Even I, oaf that I am, can recognise the great artist's work when I see it.'

Vostok sat up, her horned eyebrows raised. 'And that is certainly Ygseril's own amber. Well.' She sniffed. 'Your parents, boy. What is the nature of their relationship to Micanal? Can we speak with them?'

Vintage hurriedly stepped in front of Eri. 'What can you tell us about it, my lady? Is there information stored in it as with the tablets Micanal created for you?'

'I imagine so, yes. Tormalin can access it for you.'

132

There was a moment's silence, into which Tor cleared his throat. 'I can?'

Vostok hissed through her teeth. 'So much has been forgotten. You must dream-walk to find it. It is as simple as that.'

'Dream-walk into what?' Tor looked down at the tablet in his hands. 'What are you talking about?'

'Ygseril's amber is, as you might imagine, unique. It holds his essence, the essence of a god, and consequently can act like a dreaming mind. Micanal, in his genius, crafted dreamscapes within the amber.'

'I take it that means that war-beasts can dream-walk too?' asked Vintage.

'Of course! And we are much better at it than Eborans. However,' Vostok sniffed, 'I am not some go-between for you. If Micanal meant this amber tablet for his Eboran associates, then I am not interested in unravelling it. Tor can do it.'

Vintage nodded curtly. 'Of course, my lady.' She turned to Tor. 'Get on with it, then, my dear.'

Tor looked around at them all. The boy was still quiet, but he was watching the dragon with interest at least, while Helcate was curled at his feet. Somewhere in the gardens, two birds were calling to each other.

'You want me to do it now? With you all watching me?'

Vintage rolled her eyes. 'Stage fright? You? Please.' She began to herd them all towards a nearby stone bench. 'We could have a significant clue here, Tor. Perhaps it won't solve our problems, but it could solve the mystery of the Golden Fox expedition – wouldn't that be wonderful?'

'I can barely contain my excitement.' Tor sat down on the stone bench, the amber tablet held in his hands. It was warming up to his touch. 'So, I should just treat this thing as a dreaming mind?'

'You will see it there, in the netherdark,' said Vostok. 'If, of course, you are at all competent at dream-walking.'

Tor grimaced and closed his eyes. It was not easy to slip into the netherdark with three pairs of eyes watching him – Kirune, he sensed, was still in the house somewhere – but eventually he broke through. It was eerily empty, with no sleeping minds nearby, but Vostok had certainly been right about the amber tablet; it blazed in front of him, a cold and flickering light, very like a dreaming mind, yet somehow less dense. His own curiosity piqued, he pushed through the soft membrane into its shifting light, and stepped out onto a wide stone plaza. He recognised it immediately; it was the circular courtyard in the southern gardens of the palace, often used in the summer for celebrations and festivals. He remembered such occasions dimly; clutching his sister's hand, they would watch fireworks or eat cakes. His own memories were so distant he could no longer trust them, but whoever had crafted this dream remembered it with startling clarity.

'It's magnificent.'

Men and women stood all around the plaza. They were tall and lithe, their skin shining and healthy, their eyes like rubies. To Tor they seemed too tall and imposing, and he wondered for a moment if his own childhood memories were superimposing themselves on the dreamscape, but, looking closer, he realised they simply *were* larger than life. Micanal, he reminded himself, was an artist, one not necessarily interested in the depiction of reality, but in reflecting an inner truth. This was the Ebora of hundreds of years ago, when she was at her peak – her god still lived, there was no crimson flux, and it was a place unlike anywhere else on the face of Sarn.

Tor walked among the figures. They turned and smiled at him, expressions of mild curiosity or simple benevolence. He found himself smiling back. Some of them were wearing armour, pieces of silver and white enamel that glittered in the sunlight. A soft wind blew through the blossom trees and tiny fragile petals whirled around them, a delicate and fragrant snowstorm,

134

and as Tor looked up, he saw Ygseril's branches spreading over them, heavy with leaves. Ygseril, Root-Father and Branch-Mother, cared for them still.

Movement above the branches. A great flock of war-beasts were flying over slowly, the sun winking off every scale and pearly feather, every claw and shining eye. Hundreds of them, certainly more than Tor had ever seen in his life, so many that for a moment the plaza was cast into darkness, and Tor heard the crowd who stood with him sigh, all at once. It was such a sound of longing that he found he had to swallow rather hard, and he hoped that those watching him as he dream-walked could not read the emotion on his face.

Then the flock of war-beasts had passed, and with them the sun had gone, turning the sky a pitiless grey. Tor looked to the other Eborans, a cold hand closing around his heart, and saw that it was already too late; the glory that Micanal had crafted was already fading, and the beautiful faces had grown old and cracked. As he watched, his people visibly diminished, becoming a shadow of something else. Beautiful skins split open, weeping bloody tears. Ygseril's branches were bare and dead, as were the small trees that had given up their blossoms so recently. Then, in the way of dreams, the people were all gone and Tor stood alone in a street outside the palace. This was the Ebora he recognised: empty, ramshackle houses, nature creeping her green fingers into every space and absence they had left behind. Now that he looked, the street was littered with enormous bones, the skulls and ribcages of legends that had passed into another time, and they, too, were choked with weeds. The smell of wolf was thick in his nostrils.

Tor took a slow breath. He was afraid, despite everything, and a terrible anguish threatened to close over his heart. Again, he wondered if those watching him would be able to read such emotions on his face – he sincerely hoped not.

'My dear friends, all this we know already.'

Tor looked around, but the voice came from everywhere at once. The street remained empty.

'You and I, we have lived through it. What use is there, I ask you, in staying in this graveyard?'

'I couldn't agree with you more, Micanal,' muttered Tor.

'You have your own reasons for staying, I know,' continued the voice. 'And perhaps you are right: seclusion from the horror of what Ebora has become could save you. Anything is possible.'

As the voice spoke, the giant bones began to sink into the road, and the buildings crumbled into dust. The landscape rippled and flexed, turning into something else.

'But I want to show you a different hope, my friends, in the only way I really know how to.'

They were no longer in Ebora, or at least in any part of it Tor recognised. He stood on wide stretch of beach. Under his feet, amongst the stones and sand, were tiny objects that didn't belong there: delicate teacups, glass pots of ink, sealing rings and golden daggers studded with precious gems.

'What were these, Micanal? Did they have a particular meaning for you? Or for Eri's parents?'

The sea was a dark band of grey, and on it sat a bristling collection of golden ships. The day was an overcast one, and in the distance the clouds were tall and ominous, but the ships still shone, as though they existed in their very own bubble of light.

'Well, that's not especially subtle, but perhaps you were pressed for time.'

The prow of each ship was carved into the shape of a war-beast head; griffins, wolves, great cats like Kirune, and several dragons. They were all beautiful, and as Tor watched, they came to life, bearing teeth and rolling eyes. Micanal's voice rolled over him again.

'They come with us in spirit, my friends, I do believe that. Because I think we are returning to their true home.'

With a lurch Tor found himself above the sea, the ships now speeding along below him. Their sails were wide and white, and they clipped along through the waves in precise formation. Tor thought of the remarkable giant fish he'd seen off the coast of Jarlsbad, which swam, he had been told, in 'pods'. The sky was ablaze with oranges and purples as the sun set to the west.

'It is far, and it is dangerous. The Barren Sea has earned her name, my friends, not because there's nothing in it, but because it is so empty of traffic – no one with any sense would try to cross it. Passage is dangerous, but not impossible.'

Night crowded into the sky, then, a purple bruising that turned black and star-lit, and Tor watched, entranced, as the stars grew brighter and brighter, each of them blazing like comets. A scattering of them glowed with coronas of startling yellows and blues, and Tor was wondering if this was more of Micanal's artistic licence when the significance of the stars became clear. Several distant islands – each surely no bigger than the central city of Ebora itself – began to glow with the same light.

'It's a map! Vintage is going to be crowing about this for months.'

The journey continued, nights burning into days, days sinking into nights so swiftly and so often that Tor quickly lost count. Always the incandescent stars, turning in the sky, and distant landmasses that appeared and vanished like beacons. Once or twice the sea boiled and unidentifiable shapes wrestled just under the surface, but the ships sailed deftly around these unseen dangers each time. Looking at them made Tor think of all the stories he'd heard growing up about the Barren Sea: a timely reminder that the Wild, and the unsettling beasts that populated it, did not exist solely on the land.

'My friends, I know that you believe as I do – that the true roots of Ygseril lay to the north of Sarn, that the key to Ebora's

137

salvation could be there too. The terrible losses we have suffered do not need to be the end of us.'

Far to the north, a great light was growing in the sky – a shining white essence that made the sunlight look dowdy. Within it, it was just possible to make out something. Another landmass, perhaps?

'You have your own reasons for staying, and I understand them. But if you should ever change your minds, I have every confidence you can find us. Please accept this gift of hope from me – it is all we, as a people, have left.'

The light in the north grew and grew till everything else was lost – the sea, the sky and the brave ships were all swallowed up in it. Tor winced against the light but looked for as long as he could, hoping to see some final clue. There was nothing, save for a delicate tracery of connecting lines, or branches . . . He blinked. *Or the cracks on the inside of a tablet of amber.*

He was awake, still sitting on the stone bench outside Lonefell. His rear end was cold and numb.

'Well?' demanded Vintage. The shadows had grown longer, suggesting he had been in this position for some time, but Vintage looked as though she hadn't moved an inch since he'd started dream-walking. 'What did you see? Clearly it was something.'

'It was certainly something.' Tor rubbed his hands over his face, wincing slightly at the stiff texture of his scars. 'It's the Golden Fox expedition, Vintage, which I know very well you are familiar with as you have lectured me about it often enough – the legendary journey Micanal the Clearsighted took to find the origins of Ygseril. It's a map to where they went, if you can believe it.'

'Extraordinary!' Vintage's grin threatened to split her head in two. 'What a time of wonders – and horrors – this has turned out to be. It seems that Eri's parents were close with him, so much so that he shared his plans with them. Should we assume he took the other amber tablets with him?'

Vostok rumbled deep in her throat. 'It's possible. Micanal was an honourable man. I believe that the loss of all the war-beasts would have encouraged him to complete his work, not abandon it.'

'Imagine what that could be worth to us, now . . .' Vintage pushed her springy curls back from her forehead. 'Even if he didn't finish it.'

From behind them came the heavy footfalls of Kirune. The big cat looked up at their faces, and shook his coat out.

'There is a dead body in the house,' he said.

15

Some time later, Vintage and Noon stood together in the living room of Lonefell, staring with some trepidation at Eri's bucket, which stood in the middle of the floor, still covered with its length of sacking. Noon had come looking for them as the night began to draw in, flying out across the city on the back of Fulcor, the bat she had stolen from the Winnowry when she had escaped.

'One of us is going to have to look in it,' she said. 'We may as well get it over with.'

Vintage sighed, her hands on her hips. 'What could have possessed the boy? Why, by the bones of Sarn, would he go to such . . . lengths?'

'A long time by yourself can do strange things to you.' Noon met the older woman's eyes, and she smiled hesitantly. 'I wasn't really alone at the Winnowry, with all the other fell-witches there, but it's not as though I spent much time with other people. Normal time, I mean.' She thought of the purgings, and of pressing her fingers to the iron grill in the floor, always unable to reach Fell-Marian. 'It's easier to keep things inside than to . . . than to look at them very closely.'

'We don't even know when they died, but I imagine it was

140

a very long time ago. He has been looking after the house and the property by himself, pretending that everything is all fine and shipshape, when actually his mother is a mummified creature in a nightie, and his father . . .'

'Where is the kid now?'

'In one of the bedrooms. Helcate is with him. My dear, I thought he would never stop screaming.'

Noon frowned at that. Where was the boy's human comfort? Had they given him up to the war-beasts? Were they so afraid of his grief?

'Look, it can't be so bad.' She stepped forward and in one movement whipped off the piece of sacking. Inside the bucket was a collection of yellowed, polished bones – all quite clean, and apparently well cared for. A pair of eyeless sockets stared back up at her. 'Just bones, that's all,' she said, feeling some of the tension ease out of her own chest. 'This was a human being once. Well, an Eboran. Should we . . . bury them or something?'

Vintage joined her at the bucket. Her expression of dismay had been replaced by a more familiar one: curiosity.

'Well, it looks as though Eri's father died some time before his mother. You can see that he has scrubbed the bones, but I can't imagine him doing that until the body was quite thoroughly decomposed. Otherwise he'd have had to remove a lot of flesh . . .' Her voice trailed off. 'Anyway, my darling, I'm afraid I know very little about Eboran burial customs.'

'I'm assuming the usual approach isn't just to carry them around in buckets, though. What about Nanthema? Did she know Eri's parents?'

Vintage looked up at her, a touch of amusement curling the corner of her mouth.

'Noon, Eborans don't all automatically know each other.'

'No, all right. I suppose not.' Noon cocked her head to one side. 'Where is she, anyway? I haven't seen much of her since you both arrived. Are you . . . sharing quarters together?'

To Noon's surprise, Vintage dropped her gaze. 'I'm afraid that Nanthema has had to suffer something very similar to poor Eri, and . . . I think she's having trouble coming to terms with everything that has happened. She needs some time alone. No, my dear, I think we will have to deal with this without the intervention of our Eboran friends. We should ask the poor lad what he wants to do.' She paused. 'What do you imagine could be learned about Eboran physiology from examining a complete adult skeleton?' She caught Noon's look, and nodded reluctantly. 'Come on. Let's go and talk to the boy about his bucket.'

It was a sad room, Noon thought, and all the sadder as the shadows of the evening began to pool in the corners and paint the walls grey. It was crammed with things, just like the rest of Lonefell, with bookcases full of books and several bright tapestries on the walls, but everything was covered with a thin layer of dust, and in an uneasy way it made her think of her cell at the Winnowry – loneliness and a kind of secret despair was written all over it. *Or maybe I think that because I know what the kid has been living with all these years.* She had the bucket in her hands, and she put it down on the floor very carefully, so as not to rustle the contents.

'Eri, darling? How are you doing? Do you feel up for a couple of visitors?'

The boy was curled on the elaborate four-poster bed, with Helcate curled around him like some sort of over-sized dog. As Vintage approached the bed, Eri looked up. His face was creased and damp but no longer obviously hysterical.

'I don't know what you must think of me.'

'Oh, what a thing to be worried about!' Vintage perched herself on the edge of the bed. 'I think you are a young man who has been through a very tough time.'

'I am hundreds of years older than you.'

'That's not the point, my dear.' Helcate sat up and peered at them. In the gloom his eyes were like silver mirrors.

'I . . . My parents took me to Lonefell when I was very young, too young to remember anything clearly. I have images of people who might have been my grandparents, but I could have imagined it. They, my mother and father, I mean, said that Ebora was going through a terrible change, and that it was safer if we kept ourselves apart from it. We lived out here by ourselves for so long that Ebora became like a story, and . . . so did other Eborans. There was just us, and I was happy. Mother and her garden, Father and his stories.'

Noon came to the foot of the bed and curled one hand around the bed post. 'They thought they were keeping you safe out here by keeping you isolated? Locking you up?'

'No. I mean, it wasn't like that.' Eri leaned against Helcate, visibly taking support from the war-beast. The bed creaked with their weight. 'I was safe. I was happy. They didn't like me to go far, but Mother taught me how to hunt, and Father made me a bow. I used to . . . I used to hunt rabbits . . .' Some fresh tears spilled from the boy's eyes, glistening in the poor light. 'But the things they feared came for them anyway. One winter, Father started to cough, and he said, "Oh, the seasons, they change and they take my breath away for a time," but that wasn't what it was. The cough got so that he had to lie down all the time, and then his skin started to split. He bled a lot. Towards the end, he shouted about the humans, about how they had ruined us.' Eri's gaze flickered up to Noon and away again. 'But I don't think he meant any of it. He was just scared.'

'The crimson flux.' Noon looked at her feet, thinking of Tor. 'There isn't any outrunning it, then.'

'He died, and Mother was sad, and it all seemed so wrong.' Eri's words were coming faster now, as though he'd broken through some interior dam. 'She couldn't look at him, couldn't look at his . . . body, so I said that I would take care of it.'

143

There was a long silence then. Noon stood and listened to the boy's thick breathing. Tor had drunk so much of her blood when he was healing, and no doubt a fair amount of other people's before hers – any single sip of which could summon the crimson flux. Whatever risks he was taking, he had clearly decided it was worth it.

'You have to understand,' said Eri eventually. 'It had just been us three for so long, and it seemed wrong for us to be apart. I put Father in one of the old rooms we didn't use, I dressed him and cleaned him and I talked to him like I always did, but by then Mother was starting to suffer too.' He coughed thickly into his hand. 'Not the disease, but a kind of wasting away. She became weaker, tired all the time. Her hair turned white and her skin crumpled. The knuckles of her fingers became swollen, and eventually she couldn't remember Father, or sometimes she did but she didn't remember that he had died.'

'She grew old,' said Vintage simply. 'No more Ygseril, no more sap. Something else that couldn't be run from.' She patted the bed lightly. 'I am truly sorry, my dear.'

'She died too. A long time after Father. When I went to see her and I saw that she had gone, the idea of moving her out of that bed . . . why should I? It was only ever just us three, and I didn't think that would ever change. We could all just stay here. No one else mattered anyway. So I kept hunting rabbits and deer, pickled the things from the garden, just like Mother had shown me, salted meat and stored it up for winter. And there were all the books and the stories. I could always read about Ebora, and it was like . . . like I went back there, in my mind, even though I don't really remember it.' He looked at the bedclothes, embarrassed. 'I talked to Mother and Father still, and I had the stories to keep me company. And I never thought I would see a real war-beast.'

'Oh Eri, my dear. It's an attractive thought, the idea that

144

nothing ever needs to change, but unfortunately that's not a choice we get to make.'

'Speaking of choices, you need to think about what you're going to do, Eri.' Noon kept her voice soft, but the boy still flinched. 'This is still your home, but . . . I don't think there is anything here for you anymore.'

'Helcate,' murmured Helcate.

'We should lay your parents to rest,' said Vintage. 'Let them stay here, in the place where they were happiest.'

The boy looked up then, staring across the room, and Noon knew he was looking at the bucket of his father's bones. Of course he'd known they'd brought them into the room.

'And after I've done that, you'll let me stay with Helcate? Wherever you go, whatever happens, I will have Helcate?' There was an edge of that hysteria to Eri's voice again, and Noon saw Vintage frown at it, but the older woman simply patted the bed again.

'Of course, my darling. You and Helcate will be firmest friends for all your days, I am sure of it.'

In the end, Kirune dug a hole in the garden, working swiftly and quietly and without any complaints, to Tor's surprise. He and Noon wrapped the skeletal remains of Eri's mother in a pair of thickly embroidered blankets, and together carried her down to the garden. By that time, it was fully dark, and a clear night had given them an audience of stars. The corpse they laid carefully in the dirt, and then the bucket they settled by her feet.

'Today we say goodbye to friends we weren't quite lucky enough to meet,' said Vintage. Eri was standing next to Helcate, and she squeezed the boy's shoulder. There were two spots of pink colour high on his cheeks, and his eyes were shining too brightly. 'Is there anything you want to say, Eri?'

The boy seemed to shiver all over at the question.

145

'No. I mean, I suppose. Mother and Father, I . . . am sorry. I can't stay here anymore. I love you.'

'Helcate,' murmured Helcate.

Afterwards, Vintage took Eri back indoors while Tor and Noon shovelled the dirt back into the hole. Kirune had offered to help, but Vintage had pointed out, in a low voice, that the big cat covering up the hole might look a little too much like he was hiding his own excreta. Tor paused to remove a rock from the pile of dirt, and caught Noon looking at him closely.

'What is it? Do I have something on my face?'

'No,' she said. For a moment it looked as though she might say something more, but then she bent back to her shovel. 'No, it's nothing.'

16

If she kept looking to the east, all Hestillion could see was green hills and lakes, largely untouched by the Wild and given hard edges here and there by dirt roads. If she turned and looked behind her, she would see the Behemoth, crouching like a growth amongst the wreckage it had caused while the queen's various creatures scuttled around it. She kept looking to the east.

'What do you think, Celaphon? It's beautiful, isn't it?'

With some effort, the war-beast raised its head to take in the view, his eyes narrowing as though he were looking at a painfully bright light.

'Outside. You brought me outside.'

'Yes, sweet one, remember? We've been out here for an hour or so. Fresh air and real sunlight on your scales. Doesn't it make you feel better?'

Celaphon didn't answer. He lay partially in her lap, his body limp and much lighter than she liked. His brief growth spurt had not lasted, and if anything, the energy it had cost him seemed to have made him even more sickly; he ate only listlessly and with no enjoyment at all. A few feet away from them two homunculus creatures waited with a platter of fresh meat and fruit, largely untouched, and behind them stood one of the queen's experiments – the looming man-creature with his stunted wings. Since Hestillion had last seen the creature the queen appeared to have given the thing more defined features – she could see the angle of its nose now, and a thin slit of a mouth.

That morning, Hestillion had taken Celaphon his breakfast and had been unable to wake the war-beast up. He hadn't responded to her shaking, or to her panicked shouts, and in the end she had screamed at the homunculus to fetch the queen. As it happened, Celaphon had awoken before the queen arrived, but Hestillion had siphoned the rapid beating of her heart and her terror into a severe scolding, demanding that she and Celaphon be allowed outside the corpse moon to breathe free air. To her surprise, the queen had agreed. She'd not even argued the point.

'You see those lakes, Celaphon? There will be fish in those lakes, big fat ones. We could go and catch them and then you could eat all the fresh fish you like. Would you like that?'

Celaphon shifted in her lap as though he were about to answer, but instead he only coughed weakly. Hestillion nodded and drew him close, trying to ignore the plummeting feeling in her stomach. The war-beast was dying, dying as surely as the people and plants being consumed by the Jure'lia. Dying as surely as Ebora. When Celaphon died, she would have nothing left at all, no connection to her home or her history – she would just be a traitor and a prisoner, and no doubt her life would also end when finally the queen got bored of her.

Hestillion bit her lip and focussed on the distant lakes. She had brought Celaphon out here for the sunshine, but it had quickly clouded over, and the edges of the lakes were growing blurry as a cold rain began to fall.

'The creature is dying.'

148

Hestillion looked up, blinking into the drizzle to see the Jure'lia queen standing over them. When she didn't reply, the queen crouched down, bending her long insectile legs to bring herself closer to the war-beast.

'It weakens so quickly. Unfinished, as we said. He will die before the night comes fully.'

'What does it matter to you?' Hestillion held Celaphon a little closer, hoping that he couldn't hear them. 'You must have seen many die in your time.'

'Oh yes.' The queen's face creased into a smile of genuine pleasure. Behind them, an industrious slopping and crunching indicated that the maggots were doing their job. 'Many of the old enemy died. Pulled to pieces, suffocated, pierced with pieces of us. Always satisfying, but this . . .' The queen stood up straight again. 'We will give him the Growth. Then he will not die. Not from being too small and weak, at least.'

Hestillion rubbed some rainwater away from her eyes, wincing at her sore fingers. 'The Growth? What are you talking about?'

'You know of it, Hestillion Eskt, born in the year of the green bird.' The queen turned to look at the homunculus, and at some signal Hestillion could not see, the creature put down its tray of food and began to toddle back towards the Behemoth. 'You used it to free us.'

'The golden fluid stuff Tor brought to Ebora? That's what you're talking about? And for what it's worth, I wasn't trying to free you. We were trying to bring Ygseril back to life.'

The queen tipped her head to one side, as if to indicate that Hestillion's intentions hardly mattered now.

'We secrete the Growth naturally and store it in pods. We take it with us to every new world, Hestillion Eskt, because not every world teems with life as this one does, and we need your life to feed on. Without the life we consume, we do not have the material to change.'

149

'Your maggots eat organic material to secrete the varnish.' Hestillion frowned. 'And your growth fluid . . . what? Encourages more organic material if there is not enough?'

'Yes, precisely. It takes what is dormant and weak and awakens it, fills veins with green life and hastens the pulsing rhythms. Feed it to your beast and see what happens.'

'You seek to poison him!'

'Not at all. Lady Hestillion, if we wished harm on the thing you have been harbouring within us do you not think it would be dead already? We control everything that happens within the corpse moon. Here, look.' The homunculus was returning from the Behemoth, and it carried within its stumpy arms a familiar golden pod, just like the ones Tor had brought to the Eboran palace. The creature came and placed it at her feet. 'Give the beast this to drink, and it may become strong enough to live. Or, it will die in a few hours' time, and become another piece of organic material for our maggots, as you call them, to feed on. It hardly matters to us, but we think you will be a more interesting guest with your companion alive.'

Hestillion picked up the pod, weighing it in her hands and listening to the thick slosh of the liquid inside. Now that she saw it again, she realised that it strongly resembled the gruel pods the Jure'lia had been supplying her – it was simply a different, more attractive colour – which rather suggested that the gruel was 'naturally secreted' too. She pushed that thought away quickly.

'How much?' she murmured.

'What? You speak so quietly.'

'I said, how much!' Hestillion glared furiously up at the queen. 'How much is safe? Will it hurt him? Can you even tell me that?'

'Pain, or death,' said the queen. 'You people make so much of these choices, when really they are no choices at all.'

Hestillion uncapped the pod. The fluid inside smelled like

deep running water, making her wince, and with her other arm she lifted Celaphon's head. For an awful moment he didn't respond, and Hestillion thought she had simply taken too long to decide, but then he shifted weakly, bringing his snout up to the lip of the pod.

'Is it like the porridge?' he asked, his nostrils flaring. 'It does not smell like it.'

'It's just like the porridge, sweet one. Drink it up, and then we can go fishing.'

Hestillion tipped the pod and Celaphon dutifully drank it down. She felt him stiffen as he realised it wasn't like the porridge after all, but she held him a little tighter and in the end he consumed all of the golden fluid. When it was done, she dropped the pod and turned his head to face her.

'Well? How do you feel, Celaphon? Any stronger at all?'

For a moment, nothing happened. Celaphon's sides rose and fell with his shallow breaths, and she could hear his throat wheezing with some new exertion. Then suddenly he stiffened in her lap, rolling off into the grass with a strangled cry.

'Celaphon?'

The small war-beast began to scream. It was a high-pitched, inconstant noise, reminding Hestillion of the great brass kettle her mother had used to make tea – for a dizzying second she was back there in Ebora, watching as steam escaped from the long spout – and she saw the homunculus take a hurried step backwards.

'Celaphon, I'm sorry, we're just trying to help you! Please, try to be brave.' She moved to his side and laid a hand on his heaving shoulder: it was as hot as her mother's kettle would have been.

'Come away from it,' said the queen. 'It may not be safe.'

Hestillion ignored her. 'Celaphon, please, I promise, this is good for you –'

The small dragon began to jerk all over, as if suffering a fit, and then as Hestillion watched, jagged plates of scales began to burst out of his flesh. They were a dark purple, darker than his original scales, and they forced their way out along his spine and behind his shoulders. Plates with pointed serrated edges like leaves erupted across his forehead and behind his stumpy ears, and his tail grew a line of thorn-like spikes. There was, Hestillion realised, another noise beneath his shrill screaming; a sort of creaking, like the sound a frozen lake makes before the ice shatters.

'What is that? What is happening to him?'

'The bones are growing,' said the queen. She sounded interested, as though the day had taken an unexpected yet pleasing turn. 'His flesh may struggle to keep up, but . . . your creatures have always been formidable. Perhaps even this runt will survive it.'

The eruption of growths appeared to have stopped, but Celaphon was shaking all over, and there was the faintest impression of movement under his scaly hide. Hestillion fought a wave of nausea and forced herself to stroke his fevered brow.

'Celaphon? How are you feeling?'

The war-beast opened his eyes. 'Hungry. I am so hungry. Can we eat now?'

'Of course you can, of course.' Hestillion leaned down to scoop him into her arms and was surprised to find that he was much heavier than he had been moments ago. Next to her, the queen gestured to her experiment, who was still gravely standing and staring at nothing.

'You, help the Lady Hestillion to take her war-beast back inside. And bring the food.'

17

'I have had a new commission, the first in years, and it is from a human.

'He is a wealthy merchant from Mushenska, and he wants a portrait, of all things. Specifically, he wishes to come to Ebora and sit for it, bedecked in all his finery, no doubt. It is such an extraordinary request that I sat and looked at the missive for some time, trying to tell if it were a jest of some sort. Eventually, Arnia caught me peering at it, and when she read it, she laughed. I asked her what was so amusing, and she told me that it is a human demonstrating his bravery – and his wealth – to other humans. To commission the legendary Eboran artist Micanal the Clearsighted was in itself outrageous – what human could have the money? To imagine that he would turn his exquisite eye to such a dismal subject . . . Arnia smiled while she said this, enjoying my discomfort, I think. But the real point, she claimed, is the sitting. For a human to come here, so soon after the Carrion Wars, was an act of bravado. Like placing your head within a war-beast's jaws.

'The Carrion Wars are over, I said, needlessly. We did

not mention the flux – there is never any need to mention it; daily, we hear of new deaths. Arnia, however, shrugged at me. It doesn't matter, she said. We will forever be monsters to them.

'There were lines at the corners of her eyes today, and her hand, when it touched mine, was dry.'

I cannot call to mind any artworks by Micanal that depicted humans. It is unsurprising that we are so beneath their notice, yet it is also important to remember that Micanal and his twin sister Arnia were among the most celebrated Eborans of their time. I have been lucky enough to know Eborans who were less picky with their company.
Extract from the private journals
of Lady Vincenza 'Vintage' de Grazon

'So the question is, how soon can we go?'

Vintage wetted her lips with her wine – it was annoyingly fine – and looked around at their faces. They had gathered once more in the largest courtyard, with all the war-beasts present save for Helcate, who was in Eri's room with the boy; he was still sleeping off the grief of Lonefell's revelations. Now they were being treated to the warmest spring day Ebora had seen so far; the warmth of the sun was a reassuring weight on the top of her head and shoulders.

Vostok snorted. 'Go? Go where?'

'My lady, to find Micanal, of course. Or to find the place that he described within the amber tablet.'

Tor cleared his throat. He had been sitting with his face turned up to the sun, his hands curled around a glass goblet, but now he leaned forward. 'Let's be clear, Vintage. He didn't describe this place at all, aside from some mysterious misty light. What he crafted in the tablet was a description of the journey.'

'Yes, exactly.' Vintage beamed at him, enjoying the look of exasperation that passed over his face. 'A map. He meant Eri's parents to join him, so he showed them the way. No reason at all why we can't follow it, once you've made yourself useful by writing it all down.'

'Hold on.' Noon was standing with Vostok. She was still wearing her dusty travelling clothes, worn at the knees and patched in places. She had also started to wear small pieces of Eboran clothing, Vintage noticed; a soft leather pauldron embroidered with silver leaves, a belt studded with tiny turquoise stones. Vintage amused herself briefly by imagining they were love-gifts from Tor; there was something almost bashful about how the girl wore them. 'Why would we want to go to this place anyway, Vin? All I remember about this fox expedition thing is that they never came back.'

'Ah, well.' Vintage settled herself more comfortably in her seat. 'In the Ebora of old, there were two schools of thought concerning the origins of Ygseril. One, that he grew straight out of the ground here, and that the lands of Ebora themselves were blessed. The second movement believed that the seed, or nut, or fruit, that would become Ygseril travelled here from somewhere else – supposedly somewhere far to the north of Ebora, across the Barren Sea. This was what Micanal believed.'

'Vintage, you realise you are giving a lecture on Eboran history in Ebora, to an audience of mostly Eborans?'

Tor's look was innocent enough, but Vintage inclined her head. 'You are, of course, quite right, my darling. Nanthema? Would you do the honours?'

Nanthema jumped at the sound of her name. She had been looking away from the group at the wide doors leading back into the palace. She looked paler than usual, and had replaced her normal eyeglasses with the ones with smoked glass, so that her eyes were hidden.

'Oh. The Travelling Seed theory, yes. Somewhere, it was postulated, there had to be a tree from which Ygseril had been dispersed, and for various reasons, a great many Eborans thought it was beyond the Barren Sea somewhere. However, no one had ever been able to find it, not even flying over the sea on war-beasts. Micanal the Clearsighted gradually became obsessed with the idea, especially after Ygseril died and the crimson flux began to decimate us. It was, he thought, the only thing that could save us – find a new seed, start the cycle again.'

'I remember his work so clearly,' said Aldasair. He was sitting with Jessen, his hands folded loosely in his lap. 'So much about that time is lost to me, but not Micanal's art. He really was the best we had.'

'Having experienced his dream-crafting, I am inclined to agree with you,' said Tor. 'This history lesson is very fine, Vintage, but I still don't understand why we should attempt this.' He gestured around the courtyard, as if taking in all of Ebora, and the dangers waiting for them beyond it. 'It's not like we aren't already busy.'

Vintage tutted at him. 'Out there somewhere is, potentially, the source of your tree-god. You don't think that could be useful?'

'But this Micanal person never came back, did he?' Noon looked around at all of them. 'For all we know, his ships sank and he drowned. Or maybe he got to an island, and there was nothing there, and he couldn't come back.'

'Or he found what he was looking for and decided to stay, believing that the old Ebora was lost forever. Anyway,' Vintage took another gulp of wine, 'there's the other reason to go and look – the amber record. It seems very likely to me that when Micanal left for the Barren Sea, he took his masterpiece with him. By all accounts it wouldn't have been finished, and perhaps he had good reason to believe that the place he was looking for would help him do that – if it did hold the secret of Ygseril's origins, or some other clue to the history of his people. I find it hard to believe he would just leave his unfinished masterpiece behind. Even if he reached a distant, shit-hole of an island and died there, that could mean the amber tablets are just lying around, waiting for us to pick them up.'

'And you believe these stones will help Sharrik and the others to remember who they are?' asked Bern. The big griffin was asleep, his huge form stretched out on the warm flagstones, but Bern was attentive enough for the both of them.

'They're not stones, darling, but yes. Even if they do not cause old memories to resurface –'

'They will not,' rumbled Vostok.

'– then they will at least contain vital information on war-beast history and lore – hints on how they fought, how they worked together. It would be incredibly valuable for the war we are about to face. There's something else that could help the war-beasts.' Vintage reached down into her satchel and tugged out a heavy leather volume. She didn't look at any of them directly as she held it up. 'Micanal's journal. I found it in Eri's father's study.'

'You stole it?' Noon's eyebrows vanished up into her fringe.

'I borrowed it.' Vintage stroked the leather cover. 'This is such a gift, do you not see? It contains writings from before the Eighth Rain, right up through the Carrion Wars and the beginnings of the crimson flux. Unfortunately, I can find little of the Golden Fox expedition in here, and I suspect his plans were drawn up fully in some other, later journal, one that he likely took with him. However, with a deeper and more considered reading, there will be more. I have only just started to discover what it can tell us . . .'

'What it can tell you, you mean,' said Tor. 'Did you even ask the boy?'

'I didn't want to distress him further, of course. We are, as

Vostok has wisely said, at war. Anything we can learn from Micanal could help us.'

Silence pooled within the courtyard. Somewhere, birds were singing. Vintage concentrated on that, rather than the uncertain expressions worn by those around her.

'Do you think this Micanal person could still be alive?' asked Noon eventually.

Vintage looked at the other Eborans, and when they did not speak, she shrugged. 'If he found another source of sap? Certainly. He was old when he left, but not ancient. Even if he hasn't found a new tree-god, he could easily still be clinging to life.'

'All right, perhaps we should take a look,' said Tor. 'I think Kirune and I can follow the map easily enough, such as it is.'

'If there is to be an expedition, then I should be a part of it,' said Vostok. 'I knew Micanal, after all.'

'But you think it is pointless,' hissed Kirune. The great cat had been stalking around the far side of the courtyard ignoring them, but apparently he had been listening after all. 'Perhaps you should stay here and prune your feathers.'

Vostok hissed through her nostrils, plumes of soft grey smoke jetting into the warming air. Noon placed a calming hand on the dragon's neck.

'Me, Tor, Kirune and Vostok. It's safer if two pairs go.'

'And myself, of course,' said Vintage. 'If you think I am missing this, you must be out of your mind.'

Tor grimaced. 'Vin, someone has to stay here.' He looked around the courtyard uneasily. 'Someone with some sense, at least.'

'Not a chance, lad. Now, let's see how much of that tablet you can transcribe before dinner, shall we?'

'Darling, I don't want to suggest that I'm the sort of person who has become reliant on having a dragon cart her around, but why exactly did you send Vostok away? Shouldn't we be preparing for the journey across the Barren Sea?'

Noon smiled to herself. Vostok had brought them to the foothills of the Bloodless Mountains, a broken mess of a region bristling with trees newly budding for spring and unexpected outcrops of steely grey rock. Here, they were faced with a sharp incline, the earth under their feet loose and black. Ahead, the trees grew thicker.

'There's something I need to show you, first. And it's best if Vostok doesn't come any further. Come on, it's not that far and I *know* you've walked further than this.'

'Surely there is nothing up here a dragon should be afraid of, and if there is, I should like to severely question your motivations for bringing us up here alone—'

'Vintage, you get what a surprise is, yeah? It's a surprise. Which I told you at least nine times on the way over.'

She glanced over her shoulder at the older woman and shared a grin with her.

'It's good to have you here, you know,' she said, turning away quickly so Vintage wouldn't see her face. 'Another voice of reason to drown out Tor's ego.'

'Oh! Yes.' Vintage put on a sudden burst of speed, catching up. The trees crowded in on either side the higher they climbed, and both their faces were shrouded in dappled shadow. 'I wanted to ask you about that, my dear, because clearly I missed a lot at some point. Was it at poor Esiah's house? In Ebora, after the Ninth Rain fell? But that doesn't seem right, I can't imagine Vostok being anything other than outraged. On the road here, then, that seems most likely.'

'What –' Noon cleared her throat. 'What are you talking about?'

Vintage chuckled and elbowed her in the ribs, none too gently. 'Oh please. Tor watches you, you watch him, it's all quite adorable. I met one of his old, uh, companions, did I

159

ever tell you that? Sareena, lovely girl, spends a lot of time on her hair but no nonsense about her, and you know, he never looked at her the way he looks at you.'

'Vintage!'

'Come on. I never had much opportunity for girl talk at home. I have a sister, of course, but she was younger and, well . . .' For a brief moment the brightness in Vintage's eyes seemed to fade a touch. 'Well, it was difficult. For a number of reasons. We were close, but not close when it came to those sorts of things.'

'Hmm. Well.' Noon narrowed her eyes at Vintage. 'Me and Tor . . . it's weird. I grew up thinking his people were inhuman monsters. *Knowing* that they were. Eborans are so strange – even knowing him like I do now, Tor seems almost unreal, like a figure from an old story. So do Nanthema and Eri, if I'm honest. But Tor is – I don't know what he is.'

'He's just as bloody complicated as the rest of us, of course. Are we nearly there?'

'Can you see that big outcrop of rock ahead?' Noon pointed above the tree line, where a rounded crest of moss-covered rock broke through the canopy. 'That's where we're going. So what about you and Nanthema, then? What's going on there?'

Noon took no small measure of glee in the way Vintage's step faltered, but then the older woman briefly squeezed her arm, and looking at the expression on her face her pleasure turned to guilt.

'Well, my darling, I suppose I'm not the only one with a beady eye, am I?' She sighed, pushing a twist of tightly curled black hair back under her hat. 'Nanthema. I don't think she wanted to come back here at all, you know. What is it with Eborans and running away from Ebora?'

'You must have loved her very much,' Noon said quietly. 'I mean, to look for her for so long. To be thinking about it, all that time.'

160

She risked a look at Vintage, and was surprised to see the older woman looking sternly at her boots – it wasn't an expression she associated with Vintage at all.

'For Nanthema, you see, no time has passed at all. She was trapped inside the heart of that Behemoth for more than twenty years, but she did not feel the years crawling by. To her, she should have stepped out into the world exactly as it had been, and it was not. And I am not who I was twenty years ago.' The shadows of the rock face were close now, creating ominous green and black shapes ahead. 'If you don't mind, my darling, I'd rather not talk about it at the moment. So much for girl talk, aye?'

'Sorry.'

'Do not worry yourself. I started it, after all, and if I can't – oh! Well, that's quite a thing.'

The trees had parted to reveal the dark chasm in the rock face ahead. It was tall and narrow and filled with shadows, while creeping vines of unusual size and thickness twisted around the entrance. When Noon had last been here, they had been covered in hard buds, but now they sported bright-yellow flowers with thick, fleshy petals like the fingers of babies. She paused, and looked behind them, but the forest they had walked through looked normal enough, so she put it from her mind.

'Come on. Do you have your old travelling lamp? I can make one, if not. It gets quite dark in there.'

'What do you take me for, darling?'

Vintage retrieved her lamp, and when it was lit they made their way into the cave. Yellow light skittered up the walls, revealing more of the vines within, and the craggy ceiling. The floor was dry and stony, and they had to look carefully at their feet to avoid tripping, which was what ultimately spoiled Noon's surprise.

'Noon, is this guano on the floor here? It is, isn't it? Is this where your bat has been hiding?'

Noon sighed theatrically. 'You have to be so bloody clever, don't you? Although you're not completely right, still. Up here, look. Hold up your lamp.'

Vintage did as she was bid and the warm yellow circle of her light revealed a cosy nook, high in the back of the cave. It was filled with a great furry pile, which gradually resolved itself into two giant bats – a black one and a white one. Fulcor, her sleep disturbed, turned her big solid head to face them and uttered a shrill but oddly welcoming chirp.

'Goodness, it's the two of them!' Vintage grinned and then advanced rapidly, no longer mindful of the rocks. 'That's the Winnowry agent's bat, isn't it? The one that tried to recapture you.'

'It is. His name is Gull.' When Vintage glanced at her, Noon shrugged. 'It was sewn onto his harness. Vintage, be careful, will you? You're going to break a bloody leg.'

Vintage paid no attention at all. Instead, she peered up at the bats, one hand hovering near her pack as though she wanted to remove a notebook. 'Well, isn't that interesting? You know, my dear, we know almost nothing about the Targus giant bats as a species, or at least we know nothing of their natural habits. The Winnowry have had them kept in their towers and used as steeds so long the poor creatures are institutionalised.'

'How very unlike the Winnowry,' said Noon drily. 'That's not all of it, though, look.' She stood up on her tip-toes and reached out a hand to Fulcor. She had put a handful of dried fruit in her pockets before they'd left, and the great bat shuffled around, nose twitching with interest. Gull, the big black bat next to her, opened his eyes a crack, obviously wondering where his source of warmth had gone, and it was possible then to see a smaller shape nestled between them. It was covered in grey fur so thin that its pink skin was visible underneath, and it clung to its father with oddly delicate wings.

162

Vintage made a noise, threatening to drop the lamp. Noon laughed.

'You see, this is why I keep Vostok away. The Winnowry's giant bats are pretty tough, but I reckon babies are still scared of dragons.'

'But this is simply wonderful! When was the pup born? It's still quite early in the spring for such things, but I have read theories that bats can mate, then the female holds the male spermatozoa in a special sac until the conditions are right, which can sometimes be several months and then, when there's enough food around, the spermatozoa is permitted to—'

'It was a few weeks ago,' said Noon hurriedly. 'I think they must be making it up as they go along. Neither of them can know what they're really supposed to do, but they're free now, so they're having to learn everything from scratch.' She smiled. 'I've brought little bits and pieces of food that we can spare. I think they take turns hunting, with one staying here to look after the little one.'

The quality of light in the cave changed, turning abruptly darker. Noon turned back to the entrance and saw a low shape crouched against the faint daylight. For a confused second, Noon thought that Vostok had come to get them for some reason, and then as the shape moved – a low, sinuous and silent creep – she corrected herself. It was Kirune, it had to be; perhaps the war-beast had been exploring the area alone and had heard their voices. But as it moved further into the cave, Noon realised that although the thing was big, it was not nearly as big as Kirune, and its eyes were long and narrow and faintly pink in the lamplight.

'Vin . . .'

Warned by the tone of her voice, Vintage turned around, her smile vanishing as she caught sight of what was approaching them. The thing moved utterly silently, and to Noon that was somehow the worst of it: a Wild-touched monster should come

163

roaring and frothing, like the thing that had attacked the winnowline. Vintage put the travel lamp down on a handy rock and retrieved the crossbow from her belt. Above them, the bats had smelled the predator and were beginning to shift about. Fulcor gave a series of high-pitched squeaks.

'Not to worry, darling.' Vintage's voice was soft, painfully casual. 'I'll just sting its nose and we'll soon see its backside.'

She raised her crossbow even as the Wild-touched cat crept closer, and although Noon didn't see the bolt fly, she saw the creature jump backwards as several inches of wood suddenly appeared in its bulky flank. The cat hissed, an oddly discordant noise that made the hair stand up on the back of Noon's neck, and then it continued creeping forward.

'Shit.'

Noon looked around. There was no vegetation she could see on the ground, and the bats themselves were out of reach. As the Wild-cat moved further into the lamplight, it was possible to see exactly how worm-touched it was; its pinkish eyes looked runny and diseased, its long fangs too big for its mouth so that drool ran continually in thick strands over its lower jaw. In every way it looked subtly wrong, as oddly shaped and unnerving as every worm-touched creature Noon had ever seen. It had bunches of long black hair sticking out of its back periodically, like quivering whiskers. Above them, both the bats were shrieking now.

'Vintage! I need your help.'

The older woman understood instantly, and stretched out her hand. Noon grasped it, and siphoned off the life-energy she needed. Her heart was thumping painfully in her chest but she forced herself to watch Vintage's face carefully; it would not do to drain the woman to the point of unconsciousness. Meanwhile, the Wild-cat was creeping ever closer. It was no longer looking at the two humans facing it; the thing's strange runny eyes were focussed on the family of bats. Noon motioned

164

Vintage to get behind her, and glanced back up at Fulcor and Gull.

'Can't they just fly away?'

'The pup won't be able to fly yet, my dear, and they won't want to leave it.'

'Oh. Right. Well, fuck this, then.'

Sweeping both hands low by her sides, Noon funnelled the energy into two bright flowers of green fire. More light than heat, she threw them gently ahead of her, intending them to float towards the cat and frighten it away. Dimly, she remembered cold winter nights on the plains when all the fires were built up as high as they would go. Predators were afraid of fire, everyone knew that.

Instead, the winnowfire – so bright that it filled the cave with a shifting eldritch light – flew along the ground at the height of the thing's legs and rather than turning tail and running, the creature sprung up into the air. Clearly it intended to leap over the fire, but instead the cat landed in the midst of it, and in the time it took Noon to take a startled breath the worm-touched monster was a torch. The eerie green of the winnowfire vanished to be replaced with a more familiar orange and suddenly the cat was barrelling towards them, jaws yawning wide with agony.

'Fuck, the thing's mad! Vintage, look out!'

They scattered to either side of the cave, Noon crashing her toe painfully into an unseen rock, but they needn't have worried. Although the thing was lit up like a beacon and the stench of its burning hair filled the cave, it still seemed to be focussed on the young bat family. It flew past Noon and Vintage, howling and hissing, and leapt madly up the wall. Fulcor, already very distressed, leapt away from her roosting place, and a second later, startled and no doubt terrified, Gull followed, and the young baby bat was falling.

'Vintage!'

But the older woman was already moving. Noon watched in horror, too far away to do anything useful, as the two big bats flew around the ceiling of the cave in obvious distress and Vintage threw herself over a pile of rocks to arrive just under the pup as it made its descent. There was a bellowed swear word from the scholar, loud enough to be heard over the howling of the Wild-cat, and then Noon was moving, summoning every last piece of life-energy from within her. The cat itself was writhing on the cave floor, a quickly blackening mess of claws and teeth, and standing over it, Noon sent a hot stream of bright-green fire from her cupped hands – as intense and narrow as she could make it. The worm-touched creature stiffened, its back seeming almost to curl in on itself, and then it was still. The winnowfire had simply cooked everything inside it in an instant. Clouds of foul-smelling black smoke billowed off it. Noon coughed into her hand.

'Vintage? Are you all right? What about the pup?'

'The pup is fine, darling. The dear thing has quite dribbled all over my shirt.' She paused, and when she spoke again her voice was tight. 'You know you were joking earlier about my breaking my leg?'

18

They were bringing the growth fluid as quickly as Celaphon could drink it, which was turning out to be very quickly indeed. Already he had outgrown their old quarters, and the queen had crafted them a new set of rooms without even needing to be asked. Ten times the size that he was, Celaphon lay stretched out on the porous floor, his snout buried deep into a pod while a small team of the homunculus creatures, armed with rags and bowls of water, cleaned his shining scales for him. This was something else Hestillion had not asked for, and she stood watching them work, her lips pressed into a long, thin line. There was no doubting he was better, she told herself. There was no doubt he was no longer dying.

'There is normal food too, Celaphon,' she said, observing a small servant of the queen busily polishing the claws on his back foot. 'Fresh meat, fresh fruit.'

Celaphon grunted into the pod. 'That's good. This is also good. There is more of this?'

'There is always more,' murmured Hestillion, more to herself than the reclining dragon. 'It is oozed out of the walls, or something like it, so there will always be more.'

Celaphon was unlike any war-beast Hestillion had seen, unlike

167

any in the paintings and books she had grown up with. He was still a dragon, and a mighty one, his shoulders broad and thick with muscle, his jaws bristling with teeth. Horns twisted from his head like a riot of branches. But his beautiful deep-purple scales were tinged in places with a deep, oily green, and along his belly were patches of white, like fading sunbursts. They put Hestillion in mind of mould – chalky growths on books that had been left to rot. His wings, once covered in fine silky black feathers, were now the leathery wings of a bat – the feathers had all fallen out, covering the floor in a shifting tide of darkness. And all along the back of his spine were the serrated plates, dark green and black at the edges. Again and again Hestillion thought back to the war-beasts she had seen as a child, and to the books and paintings she had poured over when they were gone, but she could think of no beast that looked quite like him. Try as she might to ignore it, there was no missing the link between what he was becoming, and the worm people.

'He is unique,' she said aloud. One of the homunculus creatures turned towards her, rag in hand, then returned to its work. 'No other war-beast was born this way, or raised this way. Of course he's different.'

The wall to her right flexed open, and the queen stepped quickly through. She came over to Celaphon, looking him over with apparent satisfaction, and turned her porcelain gaze onto Hestillion.

'We have found another ship, as you would call it. We wondered if you would like to come and see it.'

'A Behemoth? What do you mean, you've found it?'

The queen waved a hand dismissively. There was something different about her movements; they were jerkier, less controlled. As if she were excited about something.

'We are all connected. But so long apart, the connections have eroded, broken down. We must reconnect if we are to function again. Will you come?'

Hestillion smoothed her dress down. It was one of the finest the Jure'lia had scavenged for her; the skirts were a dowdy brown, but the bodice was constructed from panels of a soft velvet the colour of autumn leaves. Hestillion almost thought it worthy of wearing in Ebora itself.

'Very well. Celaphon . . .?'

'I will stay here,' said Celaphon. One of the queen's scuttling creatures pulled an empty orb away from his nose, and reattached a new one. Hestillion nodded and followed the queen from the room.

'How much of that can he safely eat, would you say?'

The queen led them down a series of shifting corridors. Walls oozed and melted out of their way as she followed her own path through the Behemoth.

'What can he eat safely? That is an interesting question, Hestillion Eskt.'

'You know well what I mean. He has been gorging himself on it for days now. I thought the pain of the growth spurts would have held him back, but instead he seems almost . . . addicted to those changes. He will not stop eating the stuff unless we – unless I – step in.'

The queen's pace was quickening, and she did not look at Hestillion as she answered.

'Why step in? Do you not wish to see what he can become?' She paused at a section of wall, and slowly it began to bleed back from her touch. A circle of diffuse daylight appeared there, hazy and orange from the oncoming evening. 'We have lived without change for a long time, Lady Hestillion Eskt, but we begin to see how it could be fascinating. We are interested to see what will become of your runt war-beast.'

Hestillion did not know what to make of that. The hole was now door-sized, and a blustery wind filled the stuffy corridor, bringing with it the scents of sea salt and wood smoke and even grass – all scents Hestillion didn't realise she missed.

Tears sprang to her eyes, and angrily she wiped them away with the back of her hand. Outside, she could see a sky bruised orange and purple and daubed with darkening clouds. Hanging in the midst of it was a mirror version of the corpse moon: a fat, oily green grub. She couldn't see the ground without hanging out the door.

'Look,' the queen gestured to the other Behemoth. 'It is hard to feel them, so rotten are our connections, but we tasted them on the wind as we passed over this land, and we moved without thinking, searching for that taste. Do you have a word for such things?'

'Instinct, I suppose?' Hestillion frowned. After the musty warmth of her rooms, the wind pushing back her hair and gusting around her skirts was cold. 'What must you do to . . . reconnect with them?'

The queen grinned as though she had been waiting for Hestillion to ask.

'We will show you. Here.'

Stretching out one overly long arm, the queen reached out for the Behemoth, and just as though it were a beloved pet being called for dinner, the huge thing began to grow closer to them, gradually blotting out the fiery colours of the sunset sky. Hestillion's stomach turned over at the sight of it – guest here she might be, but it was impossible to shake the sense of a monster looming over her. She looked up into the queen's face. All the animation that had been there previously had seeped away, smoothing the lines from the corners of her eyes and her mouth and making her look far from human. Instead, her eyes were wide and glassy, like lumps of polished black rock, and her thin lips were moving slightly, murmuring things Hestillion couldn't hear. And then the surface of the approaching Behemoth split open like a wound.

'Show us your heart,' muttered the queen. 'So that we may beat as one again.'

170

The wound became a tunnel, a deep hole lit with bunches of the strange fronds Hestillion had seen all over the corpse moon. The floor below them shifted, causing Hestillion to stumble, and then they were moving towards the approaching Behemoth, propelled on a platform of shifting black ooze outside of the corpse moon. Without really thinking about what she was doing, Hestillion glanced over the side of the small platform to see the ground far below; they were at the coast somewhere, a wide strip of golden sand below them kissing the darkening sea. There were no settlements she could see, but she had smelled the wood smoke, and so there must be people somewhere. With some difficulty she dragged her eyes away from the distant ground just in time for them to be swallowed up by the new Behemoth.

'When you are not inside the corpse moon, what happens to it? Does it all . . . die?' She imagined all the squat little creatures that tended Celaphon dropping to the floor, their questing limbs and oozing bodies still.

For the first time in a while the queen turned to look at her, a genuine expression of puzzlement flitting over the simple features of her face. 'Of course not. We are still there. It merely grows quiet. The heart of its memories is still with us. And, soon, we will be here fully too.'

Ahead of them, the tunnel was coming to an end, funnelling into a wide and vaguely familiar chamber. At the heart of it was an immense crystal, a deep yellow in colour. The queen stepped down off the platform and Hestillion followed. The floor was soft underfoot.

'Here it is, another piece of our history. It holds us together, you see.' The queen approached the crystal, her arms held out before her as though she were greeting an old friend, and indeed her face was creased in what appeared to be genuine pleasure. 'For so long we have been apart, shattered into separate pieces . . .' Her voice wavered. 'You cannot know what that is like, Hestillion Eskt, born in the year of the green bird. To be suddenly alone when all you have ever known is connection. To be alone in the dark while you felt the distant pieces of yourself decay.'

'I wouldn't be so sure about that. I think you would be surprised what I could know about such things. I have watched my people die, because of the Jure'lia, and what you did to us.'

'We did not kill your god.' The queen narrowed her black eyes. 'He killed himself, to trap us. But we did not come here to talk about our old prison. We intend to show you what these crystals mean, if we can. No one has ever been given this honour. Do you feel honoured?'

Hestillion held herself still. All at once it seemed as though the queen was very brittle, as though she was a thing made of hollow grass pods that could be blown away on the breeze at any moment. Whatever this was, it was important to the Jure'lia, and it made her vulnerable somehow.

'Yes,' she said simply. 'I will be very glad to learn more about you.'

'Here then, look. A memory in a great chain of memories, linking us each to the other.'

The queen snatched up Hestillion's hand, her elongated fingers closing and melting, shifting into one immovable fist. And then she laid the other hand gently against the crystal.

The effect was immediate. Instead of being in the crystal chamber, Hestillion stood in another landscape, one that was so alien to her it seemed an insult somehow, something crafted to upset and disorientate her. The sky was red – not the red of a sunset or even the early morning, but a deep, dusty blood-red, created by a continually roiling bank of murderous clouds. They passed overhead, too fast, and it was possible to see pockets of storms boiling in their midst – forks of lightning licked and flickered in too many places to count, and there

172

was a low booming, growling noise that seemed to roll back and forth across the landscape.

And what a landscape it was. Hestillion and the Queen stood on a thin wedge of orange rock, one of the few solid places rising out of a confusion of simmering yellow lakes. Steam rose in neat pillars from places where the water was clear. Mostly, though, the surface of the liquid was teeming with a knitted mass of fibrous yellow material. It looked like algae to Hestillion, except that it was moving, shimmering and vibrating slightly all over. Next to her, the queen let out a long sigh, just as though she had sunk into a hot bath.

'Yes, the connection. It comes back. We are a little larger, and our eyes are many. We remember this place, Lady Hestillion, and now we all do. A world that was acrid and almost familiar. The taste of the colours reminded us of some distant spawning place.'

'Where is it?'

The queen tipped her head to one side, considering the question. 'Somewhere very far from the place that birthed you, Lady Hestillion.'

'You hardly need to tell me that. You were here once, then? This is a memory?'

'Yes. We were here. We came and it was so deliciously hot here, so little needed to be done. We ate a little, took back the energy our long journey had taken from us, and then we burrowed, deep and warm and dark. We became our travelling forms again.' She looked around the red and yellow landscape, as if trying to take it all in. 'It was a good place. Easy.' She turned to look at Hestillion, her expression once again unreadable. 'No resistance.'

Hestillion smoothed the panel on her dress. A world of endless storms. 'And how does this connect you to your . . . ship?'

The queen did not answer immediately. Her head moved

173

slowly, turning from one side to the other as she looked out across the strange landscape. To Hestillion she looked a little like a bird of prey, an owl perhaps. Something with infinite patience. Eventually she said, 'We do not know how to explain it to you. You have blood connections back in the tree-place? Where we were trapped?'

Hestillion blinked at this unexpected line of questioning. 'A brother. My brother Tormalin was there.'

'Yes, good. Are there things that the two of you experienced together, that no one else did? Memories that belong only to the two of you?'

So many. She thought of the pair of them sneaking into Father's study together to look at the sword. The old idiot had kept it in a drawer, wrapped in an ancient oilcloth – he barely even bothered to hide it from them. She remembered how cold the hilt had been, and how unexpectedly heavy in her arms. She remembered Tor grinning at her in the dark, full of mischief. They had heard stories about this sword. And she remembered killing the wine merchant's boy in sacrifice to Ygseril, the blood seeping into her dress while Tor looked at her solemnly and said, 'They have already tried that.' She thought of standing in their mother's room with him, holding hands even though they were too old for such things by then, and watching their mother cough herself to death. *So many.*

'Of course I do.'

'They connect you, do they not? A unique bond. Together you are something that you are not, alone. Each memory crystal reminds us who we were and who we are, going back through every new world and every new body. Memories go deeper than your bones.'

Hestillion shivered. 'It is . . . quite extraordinary.'

'So we must find each of our wandering ships, and connect with them again. Gather our memories together, and we will be whole again. Once we are whole, this place will fall to us, and grow warm, as it should.' The queen's face filled with a beatific smile, strangely beautiful and frightening, like a forest fire. Hestillion looked away.

'And how do I fit in with all this . . . connection? I do not share your memories. Neither does Celaphon. We are not a part of your great chain.' Although, as she said it, Hestillion realised that wasn't true – Celaphon *was* connected to them. His very flesh was changing to be a part of them. 'I am not a part of this.'

The queen turned to look at her, her mask-like face creased in thought as though troubled by the question.

'We will return to the corpse moon,' she said instead. 'Our connection here is strong again, and I know you do not like to be away from your runt for long.'

19

'I am most inordinately put out by this, you know.'

Tor had to smile. Vintage *did* look put out; her normal easy confidence and cheery determination had been replaced with what his mother would have called *being an utter ratbag*. She had insisted on coming with them to the edges of the central city, and riding solemnly on the back of Sharrik for much of a day had put her in an even fouler mood. The big griffin moved gently enough, but with her ankle carefully splinted and wrapped and set sticking out side-saddle, Tor suspected that Vintage's dignity had taken something of a knock.

'Just look after yourself,' said Noon. 'Don't go jumping down any holes and falling out of buildings. Broken ankles can heal badly.' She paused. 'You're lucky it *wasn't* your leg.'

Vintage tutted. 'My dear Bern here has wrapped it up quite admirably, don't you worry about that.' She patted the beefy arm of Bern, who was standing next to her. Under her other arm she had slotted the crutch the big human had constructed for her – Bern was so useful, Tor reflected, that he could almost come to dislike him. Or at least he would, if he wasn't so bloody likeable. 'I am just so distressed that I can't come with you. I'm sure, you know, given a little more time, Bern could construct some sort of harness that could carry me and my ridiculous foot quite comfortably during flight . . .'

'Vin, we'll likely not be gone too long.' Tor patted the satchel at his waist, which contained the amber tablet. Vostok and Kirune had both been carefully laden with bags of supplies, but he had elected to keep the tablet with him at all times, given that it was the source of their map. The dragon and the great cat waited behind them, both pacing and eager to be on their way. For once, Kirune had allowed himself to be saddled and ridden by Tor, who was anxious to get going too, just in case the war-beast changed his mind. 'A few days maybe, a week – less than that, if we can't find shelter quickly.'

Vintage made a low grumbling noise in her throat.

'It will be my honour to help the Lady Vincenza while you are gone,' said Bern, apparently oblivious to Vintage's grumbling taking on a more pronounced note. 'I have seen injuries like this many times in Finneral. Rest, and then gentle exercise are what is required.'

'Rest! Ha. Rest, when the entirety of the Jure'lia could be on us at any moment.' Vintage shook her head. 'Sharrik and Jessen can keep up the perimeter patrols while you are gone, and I will keep my ear to the ground for any rumours that come our way. Just because we haven't seen them for a while doesn't mean they've all decided to take up embroidery instead.'

'Which is exactly why we must be swift,' said Vostok, stepping forward. She had grown in recent days, Tor realised, and Kirune looked almost small next to her. 'Enough of these delays – I prefer to fly in daylight, and it is almost all gone.'

They mounted, carefully strapped themselves in, double-checking that all the baggage was secure. Bern had rustled them up enough water and food for a reasonably long journey – Tor had peeked in the bag and been alarmed to find a lot of it was *dried* – and Vintage had insisted they take writing materials to make notes on anything they found. *What we will find*, he thought to himself, *is a lot of miserable bloody ocean and not much else*. He had, at least, managed to smuggle in a couple of bottles of wine.

Vintage waved them off somewhat jerkily, which Tor chose to put down to the pain of her broken ankle rather than any sentimentality on her part, and they rose together into the air, sending leaves and dust and debris whirling in all directions. Sharrik's feathers were ruffled and pushed back, but the big griffin just watched them leave placidly, and in moments they were high over the outskirts of the city. Tor allowed himself a grin. Noon might be used to flying with Vostok, but Kirune allowed such impositions rarely, and even if they were flying off on a fool's mission, he intended to enjoy the occasion.

They rose higher and higher, until the scanty warmth of the afternoon was bitten away by the cold teeth of a chilly wind. The larger buildings of the great city were long gone, and below them passed the parts of Ebora Tor was least familiar with. When he had left all those years ago, he had headed to the south, knowing very well there was nothing of interest to the north of Ebora save for a lot of dangerous forest and the Barren Sea. And it seemed he had been right; in the ensuing years, the northern forests had only grown wilder and denser, with patches of actual Wild dotted here and there like ugly growths on the skin of the world. These, he reminded himself, were more signs of the Jure'lia pestilence – the strange growth fluid they carried within their ships had poisoned Sarn, turning patches of the countryside strange and dangerous. Here and there were glimpses of old road, some paved with flat stones, others just scratches in the dirt. For some reason, the sight of them made Tor uneasy. Where were the people who should be using those roads? Dead, of course, or hiding.

It was fully dark before they reached the coast. The sea was the roar of a monster in the blackness, and the sight of that flat band of nothing, lit only with intermittent starlight, made

178

Tor sit up a little taller in the harness. The thought of flying over it, towards roots only knew what, suddenly seemed like an incredibly bad idea, and he was glad when Noon gestured that they should land.

'I think Vintage is going to be mad about this forever,' said Noon when they had landed and made their makeshift camp. A merry little fire was burning, casting long shadows across gritty sand that looked grey in the moonlight. Kirune had stalked off into the darkness the moment Tor had got his bags off him, but Vostok was sitting with them, her long form curling a great circle around the fire so that the worst of the wind was kept off them. 'Imagine coming through everything she did, including fighting your way off a bastard Behemoth, only to break your bloody ankle in a cave.'

'Humans are so fragile,' murmured Vostok.

'She has never been particularly cautious.' Tor opened one of the sacks and eyed a piece of dried beef doubtfully. 'What happened to the bats, anyway? Are they still in the cave?'

'Yeah.' Noon was sitting with her arms around her knees, a thick Eboran cloak over her shoulders. It dwarfed her a little, like a child wearing her father's shirt. 'It turns out there's a patch of Wild not that far behind the cave, which is where that ugly cat thing came from.' She paused, looking around at the lonely beach. In the night, the boom and hiss of the surf sounded like it came from all around them. 'We could try to move them somewhere else, I suppose, but Vin was worried that might cause them to abandon the baby.' She made a snorting noise. 'There's no way Fulcor would do that, but they're living their own lives now, and I think we have to let them get on with it. Bern said that he'd keep half an eye on them while we're gone.'

'Huh. Bern.' Tor caught Noon giving him a look for that, but he couldn't think of anything to follow it up with. 'So do you really think we're going to find anything out here?' He gestured to the huge canvas of black that hung to one side of them.

179

Noon shrugged. 'How would I know?' Then she smiled. 'Vintage seems pretty convinced. What do you think, Vostok?'

The dragon turned her head slowly, her violet eyes like jewels in the firelight. 'The Micanal I knew was a very determined man. If there was something to find in the Barren Sea, I think if anyone was going to find it, it would be him. Once, many centuries ago . . .' She stopped, staring into the fire, and Tor felt a shiver work its way down his spine. He was used to being the oldest person around, often by a very long way, but he was a child in comparison to Vostok. 'I was a different shape, of course,' she continued. 'I was war, and claws, and power. We all were. A few of us were intrigued by this idea that Ygseril, and, by extension, all of us, came from some place far to the north. I confess, mostly I wished to spread my wings and get some exercise – we were far from the last battle by then, the Jure'lia having scuttled back to their hiding places – but some of my friends were very convinced. We flew out over the sea more than once, looking for anything that seemed likely, but we never found anything.'

Tor sat back from the fire, dumbfounded. 'So you've done this before? Why are we bothering, exactly?'

'It was different, then. We did not have a map, or any indication of where it might be. Whatever Micanal knew when he created that amber tablet, we did not know it then. And besides,' she stretched out her claws, 'mostly I must admit we were enjoying ourselves.'

'Let's get some sleep,' said Noon, dragging a set of blankets from her pack. 'It's a long day tomorrow, and I've already got a sore arse.'

Tor agreed, but in the end, while Noon slept, he sat up with a smuggled bottle of wine in one hand, looking out into the dark. He wondered where Kirune had gone.

Deep within the palace, Eri also lay awake. He knew that some of his new friends had gone on a journey together, and that caused a seething nest of feelings in his stomach, so intertwined and strange that he couldn't isolate any of it. Instead, he lay on the enormous bed they had given him – with sheets that were clean and unfamiliar – and turned back and forth, sometimes staring out the long windows that reached to the floor, and sometimes just looking at Helcate, who lay on the far side of the bed, his patchy tail dangling off the end. The war-beast was also awake, and it was possible to see his eyes glittering like wet stones.

'Everything is changing,' he whispered. Helcate blinked solemnly. 'Everything was the same for so long, Helcate. Now things change *daily*.'

'Helcate,' said Helcate.

'I know. I think it's scary, too. But it's . . . better? Better than living with that silence all the time, or the empty larder. Do you remember, in the winter, when the snows had fallen so deeply I couldn't get out of Lonefell at all, and the silence would get so loud it became a noise? Like bells ringing, bells ringing everywhere.'

Helcate blinked again, and Eri shifted on the bed. 'No, that's right, you weren't there. Of course you weren't. It's just . . . I don't miss the bells. And when you talk to people here, they talk back to you.' He thought of the steel bucket, and of the soft clattering noise it made when you moved it around. There was no more bucket now; Father was buried, along with Mother, in their garden, underneath the sprouting peas and dormant carrots. He pictured the grave as clearly as he could, trying to force it over the image of the bucket. They were at rest. 'Do you want to go for a walk, Helcate?'

They slipped off the bed together, padding silently to the door. Beyond it the corridor was shrouded in shadows, save for a soft yellow glow that seemed to be coming from around the corner. With nothing firmer in his mind than a need to be up and about, Eri wandered towards the light, with Helcate close at his shoulder.

The palace was, to his mind, extraordinary. Lonefell was so different, with its peaked roof and its winding staircases that led to floors and floors, and that was all he'd ever known, whereas the Eboran palace was like a sprawling maze that never ended. He could turn down corridor after corridor, passing closed doors and windows onto gardens, huge paintings that stretched for a hundred feet or more, or statues of tall people with sharp faces he almost thought he recognised, and never would he find a single staircase.

Turning the corner, he found an open door, light streaming from it in a wide and inviting arc. He and Helcate approached it and peeked within the room, to see the Eboran called Aldasair sitting at a desk covered in slips of parchment. His head was bent over his work, long auburn hair falling in messy curls around his face, but at some soft movement he looked up, meeting Eri's startled gaze.

'Hello, Eri, Helcate. Can I do something for you?'

Eri hung in the doorway for a moment, uncertain, until Helcate's cold nose in the small of his back propelled him into the room.

'What are you doing?'

Aldasair looked back at the papers on the table, as if for a moment he couldn't remember why he was there. Neatly stacked to one side was a thick deck of Tarla cards – Eri recognised them as something his mother had once owned. They had played games with them, sometimes.

'Oh. Yes. I'm reading through the letters that have made it over the mountains to us. There are many of them, from all over Sarn.' He picked up one especially battered and stained envelope. 'This has come all the way from Jarlsbad.'

'People are writing to you? You must know a lot of people.'

Aldasair smiled faintly. 'Oh no, not me. Humans all across Sarn have heard that the war-beasts live, you see. When they were born from the tree, those humans who were here to witness it carried word out across the Tarah-hut Mountains, and now the echoes are coming back to us. They all want to know when we will be coming to save them, how long they must endure the sight of the Jure'lia in their skies.' Aldasair's smile faded. 'I'm not sure what to write back, but Bern says that we should. So that people know we are trying, and so that we can ask for help, too.'

'What sort of help?' It seemed incredible to Eri that a place like Ebora – like this echoing, twisting palace – could need assistance at all.

'Logistics, Bern calls it.' Aldasair ruffled his hands through the papers. 'We are such a small force, but the war-beasts we have eat a lot of food. The people we have here require care too, and with only four war-beasts to fight, we will need human armies too.'

'Five,' said Eri. 'You have five war-beasts.' He patted Helcate on the neck.

'Helcate,' said Helcate.

'Of course, you are quite right. And so, I have many letters to write. I spent so long not talking to anyone, and suddenly I am talking for all of Ebora.'

Eri took a few tentative steps into the room, and for the first time Aldasair seemed to fully take in his presence. He sat up straighter in his chair.

'Eri, do you need anything? It is very late, and I understand that children sleep at this time . . . Would you like food? Some wine? Should I get Vintage?'

Helcate came into the room fully, snuffling at the ashes in a brazier. Eri shook his head. 'No, I am fine. You said you didn't speak to anyone for a long time?'

'Yes. For many years, there was just the silence, the dust. Tormalin had left, and Hestillion came and spoke to me sometimes, but often I would imagine she was a ghost or a shadow, and she would get impatient and leave me again. She would always come back eventually, because even I was better company than the spiders and the wolves.' He blinked rapidly, as if remembering something. 'But it is better now, Eri. Ygseril lives, even if he sleeps so deeply we cannot tell, and there are real voices in these corridors again. Now, I have people to talk to every day.'

'And you are better for it?'

'Of course.' Aldasair smiled, and it was more believable this time. 'We should not be alone. Other people give things meaning. I forgot for a long time, and . . . maybe you forgot too.' His voice had softened. 'It is acceptable to remember, Eri. It is to be encouraged.'

Eri nodded, looking at Helcate, who was now busily scratching his ear with one back leg. He was much bigger than he had been, and even in the relatively spacious room it was clear it wouldn't be long before he would be too big to roam the palace freely.

'I will be fine,' he said firmly, trying not to think of the bucket, or the shiny yellow expanse of his mother's skull. 'I have Helcate, and we will never be apart.'

'Good. That is good.' Aldasair's attention had wandered back to the letters, and as he held one up to the candlelight his handsome features creased into a frown. Eri watched as he read through it again a second time, and then retrieved its envelope from the debris on the table.

'What is it?' he asked.

'Another plea for help,' he said. To Eri, the young Eboran man looked uncertain again, 'but I think Bern will want to see this one.'

20

In the morning they discovered Kirune someway up the beach. He had found an inlet, partially walled by rocks, where a great many fish appeared to have some sort of spawning ground. He had been in and out of it since sun up, his fur wet and stiffening with salt, and there was a big pile of fish on the sand. As they approached, Kirune had several fish hanging by their tails from his mouth.

'Breakfast!' said Noon, brightly. Tor looked less impressed, staring glumly at the heap of fish.

'I suppose one of us will have to gut those.'

'Not necessary,' said Vostok, who lowered her head and took a great mouthful, crunching through fine bones and scaled skin with every sign of enjoyment.

'Ugh,' said Tor.

'Are you all right?' Noon peered closely at the tall Eboran's face. He looked even paler than usual, much of the lustre missing from his shining skin, and there were brownish circles under his eyes. 'You look hungover. Did you drink the wine you smuggled in already?'

He looked away from the fish to raise his eyebrows at her. 'You knew about that?'

'Well, I have known you longer than five minutes, so yes.'

'I'm fine, actually. I suppose I'm just not a fan of sleeping on cold, desolate beaches while listening to a dragon snoring like a horde of wheezing dogs falling down a mountain.'

Vostok sniffed. 'I snore *majestically*.'

'This is great, Kirune,' said Noon, trying to make eye contact with the big cat. He was pulling himself out of the water with another huge mouthful of fish, several of which were spiritedly trying to escape. 'You've given us the best-possible start.'

One of the fish slipped from his jaws and went slipping and skipping along the sand. Kirune instinctively leapt after it, his enormous paws thumping the wet sand into sudden dents, but in doing so he dropped more of the fish, who peeled off in all directions.

Tor laughed delightedly. 'The great hunter returns!'

Kirune turned and hissed menacingly, dropping the rest of the fish.

'At least I have done something useful. I do not stink of the drink you consume when you think you are alone.'

Tor looked taken aback. Noon stepped between the two of them, feeling Vostok's irritation like an itch on the back of her neck. A thought came from the dragon, for once as clear as a comet in the night sky: *We should go by ourselves.*

Not knowing whether the dragon would pick it up or not, she sent back, *I don't have the map in my head, do I? And besides which, I'm terrible at reading them.*

Aloud, she said, 'Come on, let's get a few of these filleted. Tor, if you don't know how, I can teach you.'

'Of course I know how. What do you take me for, a human child?'

Anyway, if I have to do much more of this bloody peace-keeping lark, I'll have murdered them both by sundown.

*   *   *

Kirune and Vostok ate their way through the pile raw, while Tor and Noon roasted as many as they could over the fire. They ate several, and they were unexpectedly delicious, the flesh pink and smooth. By the time they were packed up and ready to start their real journey, the sun was lighting the grasslands to their right with a soft, golden glow – still the sunshine of early morning, but getting later on in the day than Noon would have liked. After seeing the stark stretch of black sea the night before, she was very conscious of how reluctant she was to fly over the sea after sundown.

'You know where we're heading?' she asked Tor as he strapped himself into Kirune's harness.

He shrugged, then catching her look, relented. 'As well as I can, yes.'

'We may have to come back to this beach,' said Noon. 'More than once, maybe. If we don't find dry land in time. Vostok, you must let us know if you start to get tired.' A strange thought suddenly occurred to her. 'Can you swim?'

Vostok snorted. In the morning sun her scales were liquid gold. 'Of course I can swim. However . . .' She turned her elegant head towards Kirune, who was pushing up long runnels of sand with his claws.

'Oh shit. Kirune, can you swim? In the water?'

The war-beast growled, deep in his throat. 'I fly. I don't need to swim.'

'If he had his root-memories, he would be able to,' said Vostok in a matter-of-fact tone. 'Through our many Rains, we would often have cause to swim. Many of us did it for pleasure.'

'Well that's just great,' said Tor. 'Perhaps this is something we should have discussed before coming all this way.'

'Kirune will not drown,' said Vostok firmly. 'I can pull him through the water if needed.'

'I would rather drown!' Kirune hunched his shoulders, causing Tor to rock forward in the harness.

'Fire and blood . . .' Noon rubbed a hand over her face. 'Let's just go.'

Despite everything, it was a joy to fly. Vostok took off in a flurry of sand and white feathers, with Kirune close on her heels, and in moments they were up above the water, leaving behind the white lines of surf and the bleak grasslands. Below them, the sea was grey as slate, fringed here and there with foam.

'Tor!' she called across to him. He had tied his long hair back in a thick tail, and she could see from the colour in his cheeks and the quick smile he turned on her that he was glad to be on their way too. Despite everything. 'You take the lead! You know where we're going.'

For once not contradicting her, he leaned over Kirune, murmuring words that were lost in the wind of their flight, and the war-beast moved in front. Noon felt a faint murmur of annoyance from Vostok, but it was slight, and immediately pushed to one side.

They flew on until the early afternoon, Tor curving them slowly northwest as they travelled. For a long time the Barren Sea remained exactly that, until Noon found herself looking away from it and scanning the sky instead, but there was little to see there either, save for the occasional seabird. Eventually, when the sun had reached its apex and was heading towards the west, Tor and Kirune began to fly much lower and closer to the water, moving down until they were only around ten feet above it. Intrigued, she touched Vostok on the shoulder, and they swept down to join them.

'What is it?' she called across. 'Was there something on the map?'

Tor shook his head and pointed downwards, so Noon looked again. The thing was so large that at first she missed it entirely, and she frowned, wondering if this was one of the Eboran's obscure jokes, but then their shadow passed over, blotting out some of the light on the water and she saw it: a huge, pale shape just under the waves, a blunt head at the front, and an elongated tail-end. Once she saw the one, she saw others, some even larger, and the one below them was easily as long as Vostok from nose to tail.

'What is it?' she cried out, startled.

'Whales, I think,' said Tor, sounding pleased with himself. 'Vintage has talked about them before. Enormous fish that aren't really fish.'

'What does that mean?'

'How should I know? Big bastards, though. If Kirune could get one of those in his jaws we'd be eating for months.'

Noon snorted, amused by the image. And then, as if they'd summoned it, the huge creature began to get bigger, more defined. It was rising to the surface, she realised.

'They breathe air,' added Vostok. 'Big stupid animals, really.'

Leaning out over the harness to get a better look, Noon kept her eyes on the creature's back, fascinated. The biggest animals they had ever seen on the plains were the hairy bison that migrated across their grasslands twice a year. But as the creature broke the surface she regretted her curiosity; the broad back was covered in ridged, pale-green skin, and all across it were wet, blinking eyes. There had to be around a hundred of them, deep blue and rolling at them with apparent interest. Here and there were a handful of holes, gasping in air like gaping mouths.

With a wordless cry, she jumped back in the harness and Vostok rose up swiftly, putting a good distance between them and the strange whale. When Noon looked up, she saw that Tor and Kirune had done the same thing, and Tor's mouth was turned down at the corners.

'I don't think I needed to see that *at all*.'

'What was it? Something Wild-touched, out here?'

'Behemoths did not always crash on the land when we

189

brought them down,' said Vostok. 'The seas are every bit as dangerous, and as poisoned. We would do well to remember that.'

Together they rose higher into the sky, and it was possible to see at least twenty of the enormous beasts, uncertain shadows under the dark water. Without having to discuss it, they put on a burst of speed, moving ahead of the group of mutant whales. The sea around them was featureless, and as they moved further from the shore, a deeper blue. Noon turned around and looked over her shoulder awkwardly. The dark, crumpled line of the Eboran coast had been behind them for part of the morning, but now it was completely out of sight.

'How much longer will we be flying before we have somewhere we can land?' she called to Tor. He twisted in his harness to glance at her, and his brow was furrowed in concentration.

'Further than I'd like. But there should be a big collection of rocks, not far from here. We can sit there for a while, get our bearings.'

Noon rested her hand against Vostok's neck, wondering if the dragon remembered the place from her previous lives, but the war-beast didn't venture an opinion.

'Let me know if you're getting tired,' she said, leaning forward so that only Vostok could hear. 'We don't want to fly you ragged.'

Vostok snorted. 'I could fly all day.'

As it was, they flew for another two hours before Noon's tired and watering eyes latched on to a dark blemish on the Barren Sea. She opened her mouth to point it out to Tor, but he was already turning Kirune in its direction, and Vostok followed suit without having to be prompted. It looked ridiculously tiny to Noon at first, certainly not big enough to house two war-beasts comfortably, but as they gradually drew closer, she saw that it was actually quite sizeable, if not remotely inviting. Tor was not far off in his description of it as a

190

'collection of rocks'; black and grey and blasted with salt and barnacles, the stones were jagged and sharp, appearing to have been thrust out of the sea with some force. As they circled, looking for a place to land, Noon saw a number of small mounds in the very centre, and at almost the exact same moment that she spotted them, they erupted with hundreds of black birds, all sporting brightly striped beaks. They rose up in a noisy, outraged crowd and then fled in all directions. The mounds, she realised, were sad-looking nests made from sticks, bleached feathers, old shells and an impressive amount of bird shit. The nests were in a big heap in the very middle of the bleak island, protected from the wind by the wall of jagged rock.

Vostok and Kirune landed on the outer edge, where the waves crashed and hissed constantly, like the ranting of some sea god. Noon felt the hairs go up on the back of her neck as she wriggled from the harness.

'This bloody place sounds haunted.'

Kirune seemed to have an even lower opinion of the place, picking up his paws and growling back at the hissing of the waves. Noon didn't blame him; the island was barely comfortable for her to walk on, with her tough boots and small feet. Vostok, with her more flexible body, had arranged herself around a series of pointed rocks, her long tail curling around one tall shard multiple times.

'How lovely,' said Tor as they picked their way towards each other over a mixture of sand and stones. The air was thick with water and salt. 'The birds are welcome to this place, I can tell you that.'

'Was this one of the landmarks on the tablet?'

Tor nodded. The endless wind had blown much of his black hair out of its tail, and now it swept across his face, hundreds of incredibly fine strands in constant movement.

'We're on the right track, at least.'

'And our next stop?'

'Far enough away for me to need a break. Do you think you can find anything to burn on this horrible little rock?'

Noon looked around. There was very little natural vegetation that she could see, other than some patches of orange and yellow lichen. She thought of clambering into the centre of the island and raiding a few nests for sticks, but they would likely be wet anyway.

'Bern packed some firewood for us. We can use that, if we're sparing.'

'Of course he did. Come on then, before I expire from sheer misery.'

When it was done – ignited with winnowfire fuelled by Vostok – Noon thought it had likely not been worth it, and she looked with anxiety at the dry sticks as they blackened and spat. They couldn't afford to waste their supplies, and with the constant spray and moisture in the air, it was unlikely that she or Tor would warm up or dry off, although Tor was practically sitting on top of the fire in an attempt to do so. She looked up again. Clouds were moving in from the east, chasing the sun across the sky.

'So, it's getting late. We can either eat something quickly here, and get back up there, or we can stay here overnight.' She grimaced as she said it. 'Will we get to the next stop by nightfall?'

Tor sighed heavily, and pulled his hood up over his head in one terse movement. 'Yes? Maybe? I transcribed everything I could from the amber tablet, and Vintage matched it up with the best maps we could find, but this still feels like a very precarious way to navigate the Barren Sea.' He sniffed. 'The seas are not for us, is what my grandmother used to say. Nothing in them but salt, nothing beyond them but woe. She was full of cheery observations like that, my grand-mother.'

'It will be even harder in the dark, and the clouds are moving in thick.'

'You sound just like her.' Tor held his hands out to the fire. 'Perhaps we would do better to be cautious for now.' He turned around to Vostok, and raised his voice. 'What do you think, my lady?'

The dragon bowed her head. 'This place is bracing. It is no discomfort for me to stay here for the night.'

Noon looked at Kirune, who had done his best to get comfortable a short distance from the fire. His thick grey fur was dark with moisture, and his tail flicked and jerked irritably. She suspected that he would have preferred to leave, but would sooner chew his own tail off than show himself to be less hardy than the dragon.

In the end, Noon did her best to cook some of their fresh fish with winnowfire – burning a few to blackened pieces in the process – and as the sun set and the clouds moved in, the sea seemed to grow a little calmer. Vostok and Kirune ate several fish each, bones and all, and then, to Noon's surprise, curled up next to each other and promptly went to sleep. She almost wanted to ask the dragon if she were feeling all right, but she could sense the weariness in Vostok's muscles and recognised that the war-beast was getting rest where she could.

'Fish for breakfast, fish for lunch,' said Tor, manoeuvring slippery pieces of hot pink flesh from between silvery skins with his fingers. 'Or is this dinner? Supper? I suppose it's better than dried meat at least.'

'So why did your grandmother hate the sea?'

Tor glanced up from his fish supper, his eyebrows raised. 'You didn't have stories about the sea where you're from?'

Noon shrugged. 'Maybe. I don't remember any. We lived on the plains, remember? You have to go a long way to see the sea.'

'Ah. Well. It was death, the sea. Life and earth were inextricably linked, the soil being the only place where roots could grow. The only good water was fresh water – seawater was poison.' He waved a piece of fish tail in the air. There were tiny scales stuck to the back of his hand – Noon could see them catching the light of the fire, like minute flecks of heated steel. 'Superstitious nonsense, of course.'

'I find it hard to believe that the mighty Eborans were afraid of anything.' She glanced at Vostok and Kirune, each breathing evenly and deep. 'You had the best weapons. What could possibly worry you?'

Tor grunted. 'The Jure'lia for a start, but that wasn't to do with them, at least not directly. At least the dangers we face on land are visible. On the sea, there could be anything waiting underneath. It's poisoned, just like the rest of Sarn, and there have been monsters under the waves for as long as we can remember. At least on the land, you know the ground itself will not betray you.'

'That's one way of looking at it.' Noon was thinking of the huge, deformed whales they had seen, and how in Esiah Godwort's compound a parasite spirit had risen up through the mud. There were no parasite spirits now; with the revival of Ygseril, all the old souls of the war-beasts had dissipated, too weak and confused to return to the tree-god's roots. All save for Vostok, who she had carried safe inside her until the dragon had been born again in the Ninth Rain. Noon looked out over Tor's shoulder; the sea was an inky blue now, thick and unknowable. Perhaps this wasn't the best subject for dinner talk.

'Were all the places you saw like this? Miserable rocks?'

'Mostly. Some were bigger, and even had trees, grass. But the dream Micanal crafted moves very fast – he wasn't giving us guided tours of these places, and besides which, these images he created are hundreds of years old. These tiny islands could have changed by now, or disappeared entirely.'

194

Dusk proved to be the dangerous time. Their conversation had lulled, and they were both sitting in a contemplative silence. Noon had just started to think about retrieving her bedroll, because, despite the cold and the hiss of the sea, her eyelids were getting heavier and heavier, while the thick clouds were casting everything into an early darkness. Later, she realised that if they had gone to sleep, there was a good chance that they could have been killed.

She had just fought down another huge yawn, and was about to tell Tor she was going to get her head down for a bit, when she spotted a faint glow at the edge of the rocks. It was so soft that at first she thought she was imagining it – that it was just her eyes getting used to the dark beyond the fire, creating images where there were none – but when she looked to her left she could see more of it there, too.

'What's that now?'

Tor's head jerked up – he had evidently also been on the verge of nodding off – and he looked where she was pointing.

'Ah. I wonder if this is one of these strange lichens Vintage has talked about before. At length, of course. Some sort of natural light, produced by something or other.'

'I don't know.' Very slowly, Noon stood up. 'Do those rocks look like they're the right shape to you? I mean, don't you think they've changed shape?'

It was difficult to tell. The firelight was continually dancing and flickering in the wind, sometimes even dying down to near embers before flaring back up again, and to Noon it looked as though the rocks were constantly moving. She looked over to Vostok and Kirune. The big dragon had her head tucked under her wing, and looked very determinedly asleep.

'What are you talking about?' Tor sounded annoyed, sceptical even, but he had stood up too, and he reached over his shoulder to rest his fingertips on the hilt of the Ninth Rain. 'Rocks don't change shape.'

The edges of the rocks seem to flex somehow, growing limbs in the dark, and then all at once the whole island teemed with movement. Noon yelped and jumped back towards the fire. Starfish, enormous things as big as dogs, were crawling out of the water and over the rocks at speed, their long tapered limbs waving in the air. Noon had seen pictures of starfish in her mother's books, years ago, and they had seemed pretty and charming, but she had never imagined them to be so big, or to move as they did. On the underside of each limb were hundreds of tiny fronds, and these were reaching out and clutching at the rocks, propelling them along. The starfish were glowing slightly, filled with a faint inner phosphorescence that only made them more eerie.

'By the roots!' Tor had drawn his sword, an expression torn between surprise and disgust on his face. 'How many of them are there?'

Noon just shook her head. They were already surrounded, and the starfish weren't slowing down. One of them was within reach of her boot, and it reached one long arm out to slide over the leather – it stretched more than she thought possible. Noon skittered back, casting around for something to steal life energy from – she desperately didn't want to touch the knobbly, slimy skin of the starfish – but there was nothing to hand.

'Vostok!'

The dragon was awake instantly, her head up and whipping around to survey the situation. Tor was poking at the starfish with the Ninth Rain, but it was doing little to keep the tide of them back. In one smooth movement the dragon uncurled her tail from the jagged rocks and reached out with it to poke Noon in the back of the leg. Next to the dragon, Kirune had jumped to his feet, his big yellow eyes like lamps in the growing gloom.

Noon reached down and slapped a hand against Vostok's slick scales. Immediately her chest was filled with a boiling heat, sending spikes of warmth through her whole body, and in the dark she smiled.

'Any time you're ready, Noon.' Tor was busily trying to shake a starfish off his own boot, and Noon saw with rising alarm that although several of the strange sea creatures around him were dead, missing arms and leaking dark fluid, there were more and more crawling over the rocks. It wouldn't take much for them to be overwhelmed.

Holding her hands a palm's width apart, she funnelled a bright stream of green winnowfire out and across the teeming animals. Almost immediately the air was filled with a high-pitched keening noise, like a thousand kettles boiling at once. Noon winced, and intensified the fire stream. A smell, like boiling seaweed, assaulted her nostrils, and with a wet pop first one starfish exploded, and then another. Next to her, Tor staggered as several starfish shoved into him at once, and then a moment later a number of them rushed her; it was like being hit in the shins by a horse. Noon crashed into the stony ground, narrowly avoiding the fire. Several sharp rocks punched her in the rear end and lower back, and she let out a bellow of rage. At almost the exact same moment, a stream of violet fire appeared from overhead, and the shrieking of the starfish grew deafening.

'Are you all right?' Tor's voice was terse with impatience.

'I'm fine.' Noon struggled to her knees, still reeling from the strength of the starfish. 'The bastards must be made of muscle!'

A shadow passed over her, and Kirune landed amidst the creatures. He was a whirling thing of claws and teeth, and Noon had to turn her head away as pieces of starfish flew in all directions. A strong arm curled around hers and lifted her to her feet; it was almost entirely dark now, but in the intermittent light from the fire and Vostok's flames she could see the rueful expression on Tor's face.

'Micanal didn't see fit to include *this* in his bloody dream-walk.'

197

Noon opened her mouth to reply, but Kirune suddenly roared and leapt back from the melee, shaking his head violently from side to side. His wings unfolded and shook out, and he half leapt into the air in his distress.

'Kirune!' Tor dropped Noon's arm and went to the war-beast, but the big cat hissed and swiped at him with one giant paw. 'What is it?'

Noon looked around. Between the four of them, they had killed an impressive number of starfish – it was no longer possible to see the rocks for their dismembered corpses – but there had been no let-up in their numbers. More and more were marching over their fallen brethren, and she had a sudden vision – the sea floor teeming with millions of moving starfish, this small island a tiny obstruction in the midst of some mysterious migration. The things might not stop coming all night. They might not stop coming at all.

'We have to get out of here, Tor!'

Tor wasn't listening. He had managed to reach Kirune, and was holding the cat's great blocky head between his hands. He turned towards Noon, and he looked very pale.

'I think they stung him, poisoned him or something.'

There was a thick yellow fluid oozing from between Kirune's jaws, and the cat was holding his mouth open at an awkward angle, as though it hurt to close it. Meanwhile, Vostok had stepped down across their fire, her bulk taking up almost all space as she sent an unceasing stream of violet flames into the heart of the massing starfish.

'Grab your stuff, Tor, and get on Kirune. We need to find another island before he gets any worse. Vostok, help me!'

'We can't leave.' Yet even as he spoke, Tor was grabbing his pack and tying it to Kirune's harness. He kicked a starfish back towards the rocks. 'It's too dark, you said so yourself.'

'Then I'll light the way. Come on!'

They scrambled back onto their war-beasts. Kirune was

198

whining pitifully now, and in the brief glance Noon gave him she could already see that his jaws and throat were swollen. Would he be able to fly? She felt a stab of panic, deep in her stomach, but pushed it firmly to one side; they needed to get out of here, then they could think. When finally they got up into the air, it was to leave one pack of fish behind, but when Noon made motions to go back for it, Tor shouted, 'If there's one thing we can get more of, it's fish. Let the five-legged bastards have it.'

Rising up above the island, Noon leaned out over Vostok's side and looked down. The faint glow of the starfish extended far beyond the limits of the island; a stretch of more than half a mile across glimmered faintly below the black water.

'Tor! Which direction should we be heading in?'

For a terrible moment, she thought he wouldn't know – in all the confusion she had no idea herself, and the clouds had completely hidden the moon and stars. But then he pointed, and placing her fingers against Vostok's neck, Noon produced a bright ball of flame in her other hand. It lit up the night like their very own sinister moon, and they flew out across the sea once more.

21

'Here, have some of that. It will help, I promise.'

Nanthema was curled on the low-padded seat nearest the fire, her legs tucked underneath her and a blanket pulled up to her neck. For the last two hours or so she had been staring into the flames, looking but not seeing, her face slack. She had not roused when Vintage had left the room, and had taken little notice when she had returned, even though carrying the small cauldron of hot soup while hobbling on her crutch had caused her to crash around somewhat, nearly knocking over an elegant side table.

When Nanthema eventually lifted her head to look at her, Vintage smiled. 'Don't worry, I didn't make it. I'm not a natural cook, as I'm sure you remember, but it's amazing what the plains folk can do with some dried meat and some old tubers. I think there's some sort of animal milk in it – I must find out which, as I tasted a little and it is very rich. Some warm food, that's what you need.'

The pot was on the small table, steam rising from it steadily. Vintage had smuggled a spoon and a small bowl in one of her large pockets, and these she placed next to it. Her ankle ached fiercely, but Nanthema's lack of response plagued her more.

'I'm not hungry,' she said eventually.

'Nan, please.' Vintage shuffled over to the seat opposite and lowered herself carefully, leg sticking out in front of her. 'You have to eat. I can't imagine the horror of what . . . I know this must be incredibly hard, but you are still alive, and I would prefer you to stay that way.'

Nanthema looked back to the fire. 'Can you imagine what it was like for them at the end? I find that I can. I imagine it a lot. Mother, shrinking in that bed, becoming a wasted, hollow version of herself, watching the house fall to pieces around her. By then perhaps all of their friends were dead, and no one came to visit them. Father, half crippled with age himself, trying to look after her, trying to feed and clean her.' She looked back at the pot of soup, her eyes too bright. 'He made her soup, I expect. She would cough it up, I expect.'

'You can't do this to yourself forever.' Vintage shifted on the seat, wincing as an arrow of pain travelled up her leg. 'Ebora needs you.'

'Ebora.' Nanthema repeated the word as though she'd never heard it before. 'Ebora. I knew when I went that I probably wouldn't see them again, Vin, but I thought that I would have the option to, for a while at least. To me, I only left Ebora a handful of years ago, barely no time at all to an Eboran. It's as though they have aged and died overnight. They must have wondered why I never answered their letters.'

They weren't the only ones, thought Vintage. Out loud, she said, 'It's only natural to grieve. You've had a shock.'

'It's like I left the room for a moment, and when I returned everything has been ruined, or changed,' said Nanthema. She was looking away from the fire now, but she still did not meet Vintage's eyes, and her mouth creased at the edges as though she could taste something sour. 'Like a broken mirror of my old life, like something poisoned. My parents are long dead, my home a stinking ruin. The Ebora I knew has been infected with humans, humans who camp on our beautiful lawns and let their children play in our sacred streams. The war-beasts who should be here for us in this time of war are a sham, a bad joke.'

'Nan,' Vintage leaned forward, 'you can't mean that? Yes, they have some problems, but they are still extraordinary beings.'

'You can't know,' Nanthema shook her head. 'You didn't see them when they were *real*. No, everything is ruined.'

Vintage looked down at her hands, trying to ignore the slow blossom of dismay seeping through her chest. She had always thought Nanthema optimistic, the sort of person who looked for the brighter things and cherished them, but in truth, had she ever been with Nanthema when she was truly challenged? Had she ever witnessed the Eboran woman deal with a real setback? Or was the truth that Nanthema had always been able to buy her way around problems, or simply leave and abandon anything that could prove tricky? It was easy to appear optimistic when the path was always smooth.

'There is hope,' she said firmly. 'It may not look like it, but while we are here, while we all have each other, there's always a chance.'

'Human platitudes,' said Nanthema, looking back at the fire. If she saw how the words wounded Vintage, she didn't show it. 'The stories you people tell yourselves.'

Vintage opened her mouth to reply, only for the brief silence to be broken by a series of rapid knocks at the door. Turning sharply away from Nanthema, Vintage called, 'Come in!'

Bern stepped into the room, the lines of his face unusually stern, with Aldasair at his heels. There was a piece of parchment in Bern's fist, and from the crumpled state of it he'd apparently read it a number of times.

'Lady de Grazon, I'm sorry.' His eyes flickered to Nanthema and back to her, taking in a lot in that brief glance. In contrast,

202

Aldasair had his hands clasped in front of him and he was looking at the floor. 'Could we have a word?'

Nanthema stood up, casting down the blanket and moving towards the door.

'You don't need me here for this.'

She slipped out of the room quietly and was gone. Vintage smoothed her face into an expression of cheerful query. 'Bern, of course. What is it you need? There's some soup here going spare, if you fancy it.'

'I was opening our letters,' said Aldasair, 'and there was one from Finneral. For Bern. Would it be possible for me to have a drink?'

Vintage raised her eyebrows, then gestured to a side table where a bottle of red wine was already decanted. 'Help yourself. It's almost as fine as that from my own estate.'

Bern held out the letter to her. 'We might have a problem. But it could turn out to be a blessing. I'm not sure, but I would like to have your take, Lady de Grazon.'

'Please darling, call me Vintage.' She took the parchment. Bern's big fingers had smudged the ink here and there, but it was still perfectly legible. There was a complex sigil in the upper right-hand corner, an interlocking series of lines that made her think of the tattoos that snaked their way up Bern's arms, and the handwriting was small and neat.

'Well, my Finneral is a little rusty, but I shall give it a read.' To one side, Aldasair was pouring glasses of wine, his fingers trembling slightly.

'To Bern the Younger, fourth of his name:

'I hope this finds you well, by the stones. I have heard all you have done to assist our Eboran neighbours, even staying behind to help rebuild what is left when most of your own people had returned to Finneral. Now news reaches us that you have bonded with an Eboran war-beast.

203

We are sceptical, of course – gossip that comes across the
mountains contains as much grit as it does diamond dust
– and find it difficult to believe that the—'

Vintage paused, pointing at a word.

'What does this mean?'

Bern pulled on his beard with one hand. 'Skrodahl. It means,
uh,' he glanced briefly at Aldasair, 'cursed blood-drinkers.'

'I see.' Vintage cleared her throat.

'. . . find it difficult to believe that the Skrodahl would
part with so precious a possession, but perhaps they truly
are that desperate. As it happens, if this is true, there is
a chance you could do your people a great service, Bern
the Younger. The Broken Field is awake, it is moving, and
we are all in terrible danger. We fight daily to contain it.'

Vintage stopped. 'The Broken Field? I will admit, I only have
the most rudimentary knowledge of Finneral culture, but this
sounds significant. Like something I should know about?'

Bern had been standing with his arms crossed, and now he
shook his head from side to side. Not in negation, she sensed,
but in a great reluctance to speak. Eventually, he sighed heavily.

'It's not a secret,' he said. 'Not really. We just don't talk about
it. When I was a lad, we would tell stories about it, but only to
each other, and only after dark, and if we got caught we got a
hiding. Aldasair, could you pass me a goblet of that wine, will you?'

He downed the alcohol in a series of loud gulps, and then
nodded emphatically, as though that was what he had been
missing all along. 'It's a worm-people ship,' he said. 'A very
old one, broken into pieces over our land during the Third or
Fourth Rain, we think.'

Vintage blinked. 'A Behemoth? In Finneral? Why have I
never heard of such a thing?'

'Because it's not really a Behemoth, it's just the bits of one, ancient and corroded and broken. Hundreds of years ago my people buried what was left of it under a pile of sacred stones—'

'Stones!' Vintage flapped the letter at him. 'Stones will hardly do any good!'

'They're very large stones. As far as we were concerned, it was a buried corpse. An evil one, mind. Just read the rest of the letter.'

'*The sacred stones still stand in most places, but in several areas, portions of the creature have broken through. It is difficult to describe. The thing is not complete, as you know – the initial crash and the slow disintegration of hundreds of years has seen to that – but since the corpse moon awoke, the pieces have grown lively. I can think of no better word. At night, the Broken Field glows and flickers, like lamps being lit and extinguished, again and again, while a kind of black liquid has appeared at the edges of the stones, seeping up, and then draining away again. It doesn't move as it should. And recently, this has all grown worse. The ground shakes, and sometimes the stones lift, almost into the air. And other things. The black liquid has begun to form shapes, skittering, clutching things that venture beyond the Broken Field. We have chased them back, and they are quick to be reabsorbed, but I fear they are slipping out past our guards at night. People have gone missing. A few young people at high summer, who grow restless and want to explore Sarn – this is normal, the handful who slip off, their eyes bright with the prospect of adventure. But it is not yet the trav-elling time, and those who have gone are not the young people, itching to be elsewhere. They are our treasured elders or the children. Those who might be slow or*'

unworldly, or too trusting, or less able to defend them-
selves.

'*I believe that the Behemoth is rebuilding itself under*
the stones. Slowly and with difficulty, perhaps, but we
have had reports of other wrecks coming back to life, and
I fear we are close to a catastrophe.'

Vintage stopped again, smoothing the paper between her
fingers.

'What are they taking people for?' she murmured. 'Not eaten
and emptied, like the drones, but taken.'

Meeting impatient stares from Bern and Aldasair, she
coughed lightly into her hand, and continued:

'*I say it is difficult to describe, Bern the Younger, so come*
and see it. If you truly have bonded to one of the Skrodahl's
war-beasts – and your father assures us that you have –
then you could be our only hope of defeating the thing.
I ask, not just for selfish purposes, but because this
Behemoth is injured – as weak and as vulnerable as a
newly born seal pup. This could be an easy victory for
Sarn, and I sense that we will desperately need those in
the near future. Bern the Younger, come home to Finneral,
and bring your new friends with you.

'*I would say I look forward to your reply, but in truth*
I hope that the next time I hear from you, it will be
to hear the sound of legendary wings, and to see a
shadow over Finneral that has not been seen for centu-
ries.'

The letter was signed with another of the Finnerals' complex
interlocking symbols. Vintage peered at it closely, before carefully rolling up the parchment and resting it contemplatively
against her lips.

'Well, this is interesting, isn't it, my darlings? On the one hand, a massive shit in our collective breakfasts – help needed, and desperately, when half our fighting force is somewhere over the Barren Sea. On the other hand, as the letter says, a chance for an easy victory. And a chance, potentially, to learn more about our enemy.'

'There's something else, too.' Bern nodded towards the letter, which Vintage passed back. 'You see this sigil here?' He indicated the sigil in the top right corner. 'Do you see how it's slightly different to the one underneath the letter?'

Vintage narrowed her eyes. It wasn't immediately obvious, but there was an extra flourish to the bottom of the second shape, and on that part of the design alone, the ink was a slightly different colour – greener, somehow. Not noticeable from a glance, and even if you did see it, you would likely assume it was a mistake. She nodded.

'Well, that in itself is a message, you see.' Bern took a deep breath. 'It means this letter comes directly from Valous, the Stone Talker.'

Vintage blinked. 'The Stone Talker? You mean . . .?'

'We don't speak of her outside Finneral,' said Bern hurriedly. 'Only a handful of us even know that she didn't die in the conflict with the Winnowry.' Bern glanced around, as if Winnowry agents might be hiding in the curtains. 'But if this letter is from her directly, then it's very serious. They knew I would recognise this sigil. I would be very grateful if the knowledge doesn't go beyond this room.'

'You can absolutely rely on my discretion, of course.' Vintage shook her head; despite everything, she felt a smile curling the corner of her mouth. 'I had hoped that the rumours were true. It's such a victory against the Winnowry, even if you must keep her continued existence a secret. How old is she? She must be . . . well, I heard about those rumours when I was in my teens –'

'What are we going to do?' said Aldasair. He seemed to have calmed down a little, as though he had passed the problem and, therefore, the decision on to Vintage and he could relax. His eyes, though, were still glassy. 'Do we . . . do we have to send Bern away?'

Vintage bit her lip to keep from smiling, and then sighed noisily. 'It's not the best situation, is it? But what good are we doing here, anyway? Feeding and training, it can only do so much, and you need experience. Perhaps one way to do that is to take on an already wounded enemy.' She paused. 'And perhaps it is best that Vostok is not here, after all. I suspect that such a mission would insult her dignity. How long will it take you to fly to Finneral?'

Bern raised his eyebrows. 'There's a question I never expected to hear. I'll be honest, Lady de Grazon, I don't rightly know. A few days?'

'You should go. Go now.' Sitting up and hobbling forward, she grasped Aldasair's arm briefly. 'Go together.'

They both looked shocked. 'And leave you here alone, Lady de Grazon?'

Vintage shook her head at them, her throat suddenly tight with words that couldn't be said. What should she say to them? That she saw their youth, the potential of them, and wanted them to take the chance? Those were the sorts of things that elderly women in stories said, wise, and ancient and toothless. *Well, balls to that.* Her own mistakes were not yet unfixable, after all.

'I will have Eri and Helcate here, and besides which, you won't be gone that long. A week, perhaps, maybe a little more, and we could have Tor and Noon back at any moment, making the place look untidy again. Go home, Bern the Younger, and show them what a fully operational war-beast is capable of.'

* * *

'Good luck. Let's hope we don't need you too soon,' murmured Vintage.

She was standing in the central plaza, watching as Sharrik and Jessen became distant points in a sky almost too bright to look at. Around her, the busy ecosystem of traders and messengers that had grown up around the Eboran city was in full flow, and she took a brief moment of pleasure in the sound of so many voices, so many languages, ebbing around her like the tide of a great sea. It was true that their situation was dire – so few war-beasts, and those they had were lost and confused – but she strongly felt that where there were people, there was hope.

There was a tug at her sleeve, and shifting the crutch awkwardly she turned to see Eri, his pale face looking especially delicate in the sunlight. Helcate was at his elbow, as ever.

'There are people asking to meet you, Vintage.' Eri smiled uncertainly, and Vintage returned the smile, unable to worry too much on such a sunny day. 'A man and a woman. They said they've travelled a long way.'

'Then let's not keep them waiting, Eri. Lead the way. Not too fast, though. I am so dreadfully slow with this ankle.'

Eri led her to the chamber to the side of the palace entrance that had, over the months, evolved into a sort of receiving room. It was clean and lined with tall windows, and it contained several heavily padded chairs – very inviting for those who had travelled across Sarn – and there was a well-stocked drinks cabinet. Vintage dismissed Eri and Helcate, and stepped inside. A slim man stood at the window, the bright sunshine outlining a sharp profile. He had brown skin, not quite as dark as her own, but warm against the soft green tones of the walls, and his tousled hair was black. A neat black beard, heavily hooded eyes and a pair of sharp cheekbones added to the impression of a quietly handsome man, although he wore an odd, mismatched collection of clothes: soft, dark leather trousers, worn at the knees and scuffed all over; tall black boots, and a long jacket that had been patched repeatedly – much too warm for the weather, even though spring was still melting away its icy bones. He did not seem surprised to see her enter the room, as though he had listened to her progress from a great distance.

The woman sat in one of the comfortable chairs, sprawled as though she were determined to enjoy the rest as much as possible. She was young, not much older than Noon, in Vintage's estimation, and she had blond hair, shaved close to her scalp at the sides but left long and messy on top. Her eyes were blue and narrow, making Vintage think of broken glass, but then she was standing, and whatever expression had been in those sharp eyes vanished. The young woman smiled, and Vintage noticed for the first time a sizeable scar at her throat; it was a jagged red line, and she thought that the young woman had been very lucky to survive that particular injury.

'Lady de Grazon?'

'Hello, and welcome to Ebora.' She shook her head, grinning. 'I never thought I would be the one saying that, somehow. And please, call me Vintage, it's so much easier.'

'Thank you. This is my partner, Okaar,' the woman gestured to the man at the window, who did not move. 'And I'm Tyranny Munk.'

'I beg your pardon?'

The woman grinned lopsidedly. 'It's a long story, Lady Vintage. Maybe I'll tell you sometime, but I reckon you want to know why we're here, first off.'

'You're from Mushenska?'

The woman nodded. She wore a simple vest of bright-orange cloth, loose brown trousers and boots that looked like they had fallen down a mountain several times. There was a thick silver chain around her neck, and hanging from it was a fat gold ring. The skin on her bare arms and across the sweep of

210

her breastbone looked blindingly white to Vintage, caught as she was in a shard of light from the window.

'I was born there. I'm guessing you can tell from the voice?'

'I've been there often enough to recognise that twang. Can I offer you and your companion a drink?'

The woman accepted on behalf of both of them, and Vintage poured three cups of steaming-hot tea; Aldasair, ever thoughtful, made certain that there was a pot brewing in the receiving room as often as possible.

'If you've come from Mushenska, you've travelled a long way. What can I do for you, my dear?'

The woman calling herself Tyranny glanced towards the man at the window – if he reacted in any way to her questioning look, Vintage did not spot it.

'Actually, we've travelled from Jarlsbad, and we're here to offer our help. I think . . . I think something we have could be significant. To your cause. To everyone's cause, really.'

Vintage took a sip of her tea. It was bitter and spicy all at once.

'We're happy for any help, as you can imagine.'

'Yeah, I bet. Well,' Tyranny tipped the cup of steaming-hot tea down her throat without a blink. 'Well. You know, I can't believe I'm in Ebora finally. War-beasts, the Wall, Ygseril, all of it. We saw the branches as we came down from the mountains. I'm not sure anything can prepare you for that – all this history, in one place.' She looked up, and caught Vintage's eyes, smiling lopsidedly again. 'Sorry, it's just all been a lot to take in, you know?'

Vintage nodded. 'By the vines, yes, I know that well enough.' Behind them, the man called Okaar was quietly blowing on the surface of his tea; he had yet to take a sip. 'We are still figuring everything out here, and I will admit to a certain amount of chaos. But I like to think we still have time for a cup of tea and a chat.'

211

'I feel like I haven't had a decent cup of tea in years.' Tyranny nodded to the offer of another cup and drank it straight down, even though it must have been scorching hot. 'I will not waste too much of your time, Lady Vincenza. I am a business woman, and I have a proposition for you.'

'And your friend?' Vintage nodded to Okaar, who was cradling his tea in his hands. 'He is your business partner? And does he ever speak?'

'Forgive me, madam.' Okaar's voice was low and musical, and Vintage immediately decided it was a crime that he did not speak more often. He had an accent that was decidedly not Mushenska – some minor region of Jarlsbad, perhaps. 'My plains speak is not as smooth as Tyranny's, and so I am often quiet.'

To Vintage's ear, his plains speak was word perfect, but she nodded graciously.

'Anyway, all you really need to know is that I've been successful, and lucky. One of the things I have done as part of my, uh, business, is provide muscle for those people travelling through the Wild.' Seeing the look of surprise that passed across Vintage's face, Tyranny tapped her little finger against the rim of the cup. 'I grew up in some of the, uh, rougher bits of Mushenska, and I came to know some fairly . . . muscly people. The Wild is a dangerous shit-hole, you know that, but if you're rich enough, you can create a safe path through it. However, some of the richest clients wanted more than just a quick run through the Shroom Flats or the Howling Forest. Some of them really wanted to *experience* it. Do you see what I mean?'

'I'm not sure that I do.'

'Hunting,' said Tyranny. Her lips turned down at the corners, just for an instant. 'They wanted to see the Wild-touched creatures, and kill them, if they could. Take home some bloody awful carcass and mount it on their walls – by Sarn's bloody bones, why you'd ever want to look at something like that I don't know, but what they required were guides, and people to keep them safe. These rich types, they want to experience the Wild, but they don't want to experience it so hard that they end up with their insides on the outside, you see. So the people that I provide for these expeditions . . . maybe they're pretty tough. Maybe they are willing to take big risks for a large chunk of cash no one is going to look at too closely, you see?'

'How extraordinary.' Vintage thought of what it would be like to track a Wild-touched beast through the forest for days, a team of men with axes and crossbows at your back. Perhaps you took it down all at once, or perhaps you just wounded it several times, until it was weak enough to kill. She found herself siding with the beast.

'I know. A few years ago, I went on one of these expeditions myself. To see that everyone was behaving, and partly, I guess, just because I was curious. We travelled through a dense stretch of Wild, and came across a smattering of Behemoth remains, parasite spirits, the whole works.'

'Where was that?' Vintage took a sip of tea to cover the sharpness of her words. 'I mean to say, I am quite familiar with a large number of Behemoth remains.'

'If you don't mind, Lady de Grazon, I'll keep that information to myself for now, for reasons that will be obvious eventually.' Tyranny Munk was still smiling, although Vintage thought she detected a little more ice in those blue eyes. 'I found something at the site, you see, that changed my life. Set me on a different course, I suppose you'd say. Could I have a little more of that tea?'

'Of course, let me get you a fresh cup. My dear Okaar, do you need another?'

The man inclined his head. 'No, thank you.' His original cup was still full.

'So, it was late evening. The rich arseholes had insisted we make camp near the ruins, close enough for us to see the lights of the parasite spirits coming and going, and my guides had to sit up, winnow-forged blades on their laps while the rich arseholes got drunk and told ridiculous stories about previous things they'd killed. I can't tolerate that sort of thing, Lady de Grazon, so I wandered off a little way. I reckon I hoped they'd drink themselves to sleep. And I found something, just sticking out of the mud, the moonlight shining on it, just so.'

The woman paused, and Vintage realised she was hanging on her every word. 'What was it?'

'I knew it wasn't part of the Behemoth. I have seen those ugly lumps before, and the stuff we call moon-metal is all green and black and unsightly, like a bruise, but this thing was a bright, shining silver, even spattered as it was with mud. I took it, and put it in my pack, and brought it home. Eventually, I got someone I knew to look at the thing – she had identified all sorts of things I'd, uh, acquired, in the past – and she told me what it was.'

Tyranny put down her cup of tea – she had already drunk it, in one gulp as she had with every cup – and reached for her pack, which was slung against the comfortable chair. She pulled a silver object from it, a piece just slightly bigger than the palm of her hand, and passed it to Vintage.

'Oh my goodness.'

It was a silver horn, twisting into a partial spiral at the very end. It was covered with the most delicate etching, a repeating pattern of leaves and branches that Vintage recognised instantly – she had seen it often enough, all over the Eboran palace. It was embedded with jewels too, bright green and blue gems, and around the bottom edge there was a jagged tear, as though it had once been attached to something larger.

'Is this . . .?'

Tyranny smiled and nodded, the expression of someone

sharing a thing she knew would receive the proper degree of awe.

'A piece of Eboran war-beast armour. Just a tip of something larger, a helmet probably. Once I knew what it was I went back. Took my guides along again, but with no paying guests this time, and what I found was . . . a hoard. Three almost complete sets of armour, most of it intact. There were huge curving chest pieces, as big as boats, another helmet – it looked like a big silver skull in the dirt. The finest chain mail I'd ever seen, too, and several things I couldn't guess at. I had it all collected, cleaned up, and brought back home, all in secrecy, and I started out on a new business venture – Eboran artefacts. Specifically, war-beast armour. I became, if you don't mind me saying so, the person you went to if you wanted to buy a piece, and I made a fairly tidy fortune.'

Reluctantly, Vintage passed the silver horn back. She pursed her lips behind her teacup, then took a sip. 'Then surely, my darling, I should have heard of you. I may have been away from it for a few months,' she gestured to the room, to the tall windows looking out across the Eboran gardens, 'but there was a time when I knew everyone in that trade. Eboran history and the Jure'lia are my passion. I got quite a reputation, actually, for chasing people down for what they knew, or what they were keeping to themselves.'

'Forgive me, Lady de Grazon, but you are a respectable lady.' Tyranny looked serious, but there was a hard glitter in her eyes that suggested she was amused. 'And I . . . am not. These trades and deals were often less than, uh, above board. There is, believe it or not, a lively black-market trade in Eboran items, or items related to Ebora. Sometimes one of the real scholars would find out and dabble – your friend Esiah Godwort had his fingers in some dirty pies, once upon a time – but mostly we wouldn't have been even a whisper to you.'

'Well.' Vintage sniffed. The idea that there could have been

215

a brisk trade in things she dearly wanted to get her hands on, yet she had been oblivious to, was outrageous. The suggestion that Esiah knew about it when she did not was extremely vexing. 'That seems quite extraordinary.'

'But I'm not here to boast to you about what a great businesswoman I am,' Tyranny put the small piece of armour back in her pack. 'With permission, I'd like to show you something a little bigger. It's in our caravan, on your lawns.'

Vintage gathered up her crutch, and slowly led the way back outside. It was late morning, and the gardens were finally beginning to warm up.

'The thing is, Lady de Grazon, everything has changed. We've lived in danger, and with a poisoned world, for such a long time, I think we'd got used to it. Looking up at that thing, hanging in the sky every day,' Tyranny nodded to the space where the corpse moon used to be, 'we were so used to it that it was all a bit of a fucking surprise when they came back, wasn't it?'

Vintage chuckled dryly. 'It was, rather.'

'I saw one. A bloated, bug thing, all these tendrils moving over it.' Tyranny's mouth was a thin, tight line. 'It was in the distance, but that was close enough, and I realised it wasn't all ancient history. Here we are.' She gestured to a covered caravan on the other side of the plaza. The roof was tightly bound leather, and it looked well cared for. There was a child sitting at the front, dark and lithe just like Okaar. Vintage couldn't tell if it was a boy or a girl – they wore their black hair long and straight and half over their face. 'It can't be about money now, Lady de Grazon, that's what I realised. It was to be about survival. Hoy, Jhef, give us a hand.'

The child hopped down easily enough and vanished around the back of the caravan. Tyranny led them round, and the kid was rapidly unlacing the leather cover at the back, long brown fingers moving as though they'd done it a thousand times.

'So I would like to offer you this. My contribution to the war effort.'

The leather flaps fell back. For a moment, Vintage could see nothing but shadows. It was a bright day, and her eyes were full of dazzle. But then they adjusted, and she could see a treasure trove crammed into the back of the wagon.

'Well, fuck me sideways,' she breathed.

Every piece of war-beast armour imaginable, and several that could never have been imagined in a thousand years. There were great rolls of chain mail, huge golden greaves studded with gems, enormous gauntlets with sharpened claws and elaborate helmets designed to accommodate horns, or feathers, or long, pointed ears. There were other, even more elaborate confections in the back of the wagon, huge wire nets glittering with gold and gem dust, meant to be worn over wings, and headdresses of beaten metals – looking with her scholar's eye, Vintage judged that these were largely ceremonial.

'What . . . where did you . . .?' She turned sharply to see Tyranny regarding her with a sunny smile.

'Everything I could scrape together, since that ugly bastard crawled its way back down out of the sky. I had to spend a lot of money and call in an alarming number of favours, Lady de Grazon, but I think it's a pretty reasonable collection, and I have brought it all here, for you. To be a part of the war effort.'

'For me?'

'Well, I guess they're really for, you know, your friends.' Tyranny looked around a little cautiously, even glancing up at the sky. 'The war-beasts. It should be theirs, really. It all belonged to them once. Or the fancier, more ridiculous bits you could sell, if you wanted – wars need coin, I don't think that ever changes, and I'd be happy to help you with that. Some of the items in there, I don't mind telling you, are richer and more extravagant than anything you'd find in an

217

emperor's favourite armoury. They obviously had – have, I mean – refined tastes.'

Vintage looked back at the trove; it was difficult to look away for long. 'If you are under the impression that I have access to the riches of Ebora, or that I am able to make financial decisions for them, well—'

'Oh no! You misunderstand me, Lady de Grazon.' Okaar stood at Tyranny's back, with the child standing next to him. Instantly, Vintage saw the family resemblance; surely a sibling or a son or daughter. 'This is all a gift.'

Vintage, still full of thoughts of how looks were passed through blood, cleared her throat. 'I beg your pardon?'

'For you, to use as you like. Like I said, these are rightfully theirs anyway. They might well be pleased to see it. All I ask, Lady de Grazon, is that . . .' The young woman seemed to run out of words, and a faint blush of pink bloomed across the top of her cheeks. 'That we might be allowed to meet the war-beasts, and to help you, however we can.'

The child looked up at that, long black hair falling away from a finely boned face, and on some deep, deep level Vintage felt a bell tolling: a long, low note, warning of danger. But she pushed it away.

'My darling, of course.' She reached out and impulsively squeezed the woman's bare arm. Her skin was very warm, almost feverish. 'I'll find some rooms for you all, in the palace. You must all stay here, with us.'

218

22

'I returned today from my journey to the Nest. I had hoped it would inspire this final, great project, as if by being in that place I would be able to imagine them more clearly, but in truth it simply filled me with an aching melancholy. I feel like I am full of cold river water, silty and bitter.

'When I came back to our suite, Arnia had company – Lord Tethras. I must admit to not being best pleased. Tethras was, for want of a better word, one of our key generals during the Carrion Wars. He led our armies down across the plains, and supervised that butchery. My most striking memory of him is of a figure streaked with gore, hair flat and almost black with it, a severed head clutched in one claw-like hand – it was so striking that I thought to make a painting of it, once, but could not quite stomach it. Who would want to look on such a thing? Then, he was vital, almost unnaturally strong, but now as he sits at our table, taking tea, he looks thinner, washed out. His hands are thin and clasp the cups too firmly, as though he is afraid of dropping them, and his eyes are watery and restless, moving around the room in a jittery fashion. When he saw me, though, he smiled.

'Arnia explained that Tethras had found something he thought I would be interested in, so I was polite, even though I was tired from my journey and eager to get to my bed. When he spoke, though, it was with the tight and considered voice of someone who is trying not to cough, and so I looked at him again – was his skin chalkier than it was? Did he look old, or ill?

'Micanal, Arnia chastised me. Pay attention to our guest, please.

'He claimed to have found a piece of the Forbidden Texts, so I smiled and nodded, quite sure then that he had the flux, and his mind had already turned, but Arnia caught my insincerity and turned her sour eye upon me.

'Look at this, she said, and she passed me a slim wooden box with a glass lid. Inside it was a scrap of parchment, yellow and brown and daubed with erratic letters in greenish ink. The earliest priests of Ygseril were said to have written the Forbidden Texts at the very dawn of Ebora, and then at some point in the intervening years the writings were taken from their hiding place and burned. It is one of the great tragedies of our history, and I have often wondered what truths we lost in that conflagration. As with all stories, fanciful rumours emerged that parts of the text had survived. Even I, dreamer that I am, could never quite believe it.

'A forgery, I said, slightly too quickly. A fine one, though.

'Tethras smiled at me, and somehow this was worse than him being offended. Look at it, he told me. Read it. I know you think as I do, that Tree-father did not spring from the ground without a seed. Read it and tell me what you think this says, about our past, and our future.

'It was not easy. This form of Eboran language died out thousands of years ago, but I knew enough that I could piece it together. The scrap told of an island in the

220

Barren Sea – I looked up at that, and caught Arnia's eye. She was sipping from her cup, watching me. There is an island, and it is called Origin.

'It is our past, and perhaps our future too.'

I have heard of this mythical island before – the place that supposedly birthed the seed that became Ygseril – but have never seen it named. This appears to be the beginning of the trail that led to the Golden Fox expedition. There is very little else in the journal about it that I can find, and I suspect that once he became serious about his intentions to find this 'Origin', Micanal made his plans elsewhere, perhaps in a journal he eventually took with him.

Extract from the private journals
of Lady Vincenza 'Vintage' de Grazon

It had been a bad day.

They had made it to another island, flying through the night and much of the next day, in the cold, tense silence that spoke of a mutual panic. Eventually, Tor had spotted another dark shape nestling within the steel-coloured sea that looked familiar from Micanal's dream, and they had landed with some relief. This island was larger, and significantly less bleak – rather than bare rocks and lichen, there was a thick covering of dark trees, and even a grotty little beach, the sand grey and somehow tired-looking. Vostok had led them into the small forest, and Kirune had followed, his head hanging low and his wings drooping. Noon, to Tor's surprise, had let the dragon lead and dropped back to walk next to Kirune, placing a hand on his great beefy shoulder, and to Tor's even greater surprise, the big cat hadn't shaken her away. They had found a small clearing and stopped there, busying themselves with the tasks of making a camp – Noon had made two fires, a large one for the war-beasts and a more sensible one for the two of them, while Tor had assembled a quick dinner from their packs. Kirune had thrown himself down, stretching out with a growl that was really more of a groan. The light was strained in the dark forest, the shadows long and deep.

When they had eaten, Noon put down her bowl and wiped her sleeve across her mouth. Vostok lay between the two fires, her long tail curling around them like a creeping vine, while Kirune was crouched with his back to them. The hiss and roar of the sea was distant here, clouded by the trees on all sides.

'We almost didn't make that,' said Noon eventually. 'I think Kirune was very close to dropping straight into the sea.'

'Believe me,' said Tor, 'no one was more aware of that than me.'

'We have to look at his head,' said Noon. 'See what's what.'

Tor let that sit for a moment. The taste of fish in his mouth was like an oily coating.

'I'm sure he'll love that.'

Noon raised an eyebrow. 'That doesn't really matter, does it? We've still got to look.'

Tor waved his arm in Kirune's direction. 'Go ahead, see what you can do. I read once of a festival entertainment in Jarlsbad where men would put their heads inside the mouths of wild cats for the delight of the crowds. I'm sure you'll be great at it.'

Noon stood up. 'Fine. I'll just get Vostok to hold him down, then.' She looked at him. 'Tor, he could die.'

Sighing, Tor stood up and followed her over to the bigger fire. In truth, Tor was reluctant not because he was lazy, but because it was hard to see the big cat in such a state. The sting from the giant starfish had caused one side of his head to swell up, making his fur stick out wildly and closing his right eye. His neck looked wrong too, oddly lopsided, and on the floor in front of him was the fish they'd given him to eat. Kirune had taken a few dainty bites from it and left the rest.

222

'How are you feeling, Kirune?' At the sound of Noon's voice the war-beast lifted his head warily, lips peeling back from his teeth briefly in a half-growl.

'I am fine.'

'You don't look fine, old chap.' Tor grimaced. He had hoped, as they flew over the Barren Sea, that the salty air would calm the swelling, or the sting would simply dissipate by itself. Instead, it appeared to have got worse. 'Will you let us take a look at it?'

Kirune growled, low and dangerous in the back of his throat, but when Noon stepped forward and placed her hands gently on his thick neck, he did not snap at her, or even protest. The fell-witch gently prodded him all over, pressing her palm against the whiskers on his snout and peering closely at the fluid running from his partly open jaws.

'Well.' Noon stood back. 'Fucked if I know what I'm looking at, but I reckon it's bad. What do you think?'

'Centuries of time on my hands, and I never bothered to learn anything about medicine. Your guess is as good as mine.'

'Vostok? Do you have any ideas?'

The dragon roused herself, bringing her long head over to them. In the shadows, her violet eyes looked as purple as orchids. She looked at Kirune for a long moment, then shook her head.

'A long time ago, we would have had Eboran men and women who cared for our health. Once, I remember a similar injury was suffered by one of us, and they lanced the wound with long silver needles, applied a hot poultice . . . but I believe that was a snake bite, not Wild-touched. I cannot say what they would do about this.'

'We'll have to go back,' said Noon immediately. 'Forget about this island thing and go back to Ebora.'

'For what?' said Tor. 'I don't want to be pessimistic, but it's not like we have anyone at the palace who knows war-beast medicine either.'

'There are other Eborans,' pointed out Noon. 'They could know something.'

Tor grimaced, thinking of them. The few Eboran survivors were old and decrepit – one or two he had spoken to appeared to be losing their minds. They kept asking after people who were long dead, or demanding their share of non-existent sap.

'Noon, if we have any war-beast experts amongst us we would have found them by now.'

'I don't want to go back,' said Kirune. His voice was muffled. 'I am *fine*.'

'It could go away by itself,' said Vostok, but for the first time that Tor could recall she sounded uncertain. 'War-beasts are strong. We can withstand injuries that would fell humans easily.'

'Or,' said Noon, 'it could fester badly enough for Kirune's blood to turn bad, or become sore enough so that he can't eat anymore. And then what?' She shook her head. 'We had a healer on the plains, and the Winnowry had a place they took you when you were sick, but I don't know anything about it. We shouldn't be the people caring for him when we just don't know.' She shot a look at Tor. 'Vintage would have a better idea. Or Nanthema would.'

'I will not go back!' Kirune raised himself to his full height, holding his head up with obvious effort. 'You cannot make me, human.'

'Kirune, this isn't about saving your bloody pride here.' Tor took a slow breath, and lowered his voice. 'Being ill isn't a weakness. Being hurt isn't a weakness.' With some difficulty he resisted touching the scars on his face. 'You have to think about what is best for Ebora here – we all do. What is best for Sarn. We can't afford to lose a war-beast.' He cleared his throat. 'I cannot afford to lose you.'

For a second, no one spoke, and suddenly Tor wished that he was somewhere else; anywhere else, but preferably some smoky tavern in Mushenska, halfway into his second bottle of wine with someone warm and friendly on the bench next to him. He could feel Noon looking at him, her dark eyes too shrewd for comfort, and then Kirune was speaking.

'You think I am nothing. That I am born wrong and weak. I am as strong as any of you, and I want to see this place more than any of you. I will not turn back. You cannot make me. I might not breathe fire, but I can fight.' Yellow eyes like lamps flickered to the dragon and then back to Tor. 'I can fight, with tooth and claw. Go home if you want, but I am carrying on.'

Tor blinked. It was easily the most he'd ever heard Kirune say at once. Vostok had turned her head away, shaking it slightly, and Tor was reminded of his sister shaking her head over some foolish notion of his.

'Tor, how far are we from this place, anyway?'

He met Noon's eyes gladly. 'Not so far, actually. Or at least, not so far according to Micanal's instructions, but there's also a pretty good chance that there's nothing there at all aside from a big stretch of empty sea and a lot of embarrassment.'

'I don't think you're born wrong, Kirune.' Noon spoke softly now. 'I think you've been born into a bad time, but so have the rest of us, haven't we? We can't help when we are, or who we are.' She straightened up and exchanged a look with Vostok. 'Let's stay here for the night, then, rest up. This at least doesn't look like the sort of place that might get invaded by a horde of marauding star fish, and we can get going again in the morning light. Kirune, you'd better eat the rest of that, though,' she pointed at the partially devoured fish on the ground, 'because you're our best fisherman, and it might be a while before we get any more like that.'

Kirune actually seemed to puff up a little at that praise, and he dutifully picked up the fish in his jaws and choked it down in one go, trying his best, Tor thought, to make a point of how his throat did not hurt and he was completely capable of eating.

'At least we're not so exposed here,' said Tor. Tall black trees rose to either side, while above them the sky was a strained orange, late afternoon filtered through a coming sunset. 'It would take Wild-touched starfish some time to negotiate through this forest.'

'Since we're staying here, I'm going to have a look around.' Noon stretched her arms over her head as she spoke, and Tor distinctly heard the pop of bones in her shoulders – very like the crackle and snap of the fire.

'If you're looking for some exciting nightlife, I suspect you will be disappointed. I think even the birds turn in early here.'

'Fresh food would be nice, wouldn't it? Nuts, berries, mushrooms, birds' eggs.' Noon lifted her arms and dropped them. 'Foraging is something I dimly remember from home.'

'Why not? A spot of food poisoning would round this trip off nicely,' Tor said. Noon turned to go, not judging this worthy of an answer. 'It's getting dark. You won't be able to see these nuts of yours soon.'

Leaning extravagantly against a tree, Noon held up one fist. A glove of green fire popped into existence around it, chasing strange shadows through the trees.

'I have my own lamp, don't I, Bloodsucker?'

He smiled wanly as she disappeared into the trees, swiftly becoming a bobbing circle of emerald light, growing weaker all the time. Vostok watched her go too, before curling up into a scaly heap, head tucked carefully under her wings. Kirune was already lying back down, his tail twitching miserably. The silence here, Tor realised, was eerie – just the hiss of the distant sea, coming from everywhere and nowhere, and the steady breathing of the war-beasts. When Noon's light had completely vanished, no doubt hidden behind a series of thick tree trunks, the darkness seemed to come in all at once, seeping in at the corners and pooling in the deep places. He had, he realised, a distinct sensation of being watched. All the hairs on his neck stood up, and after a moment he drew the Ninth Rain and laid it across his lap.

'I'll just stay here then, shall I?'

Despite her confident words, Noon quickly found herself discouraged. It was all very well claiming to know about foraging because of expeditions you went on as an enthusiastic nine-year-old, but that was a very long time ago, and they were in a strange place – she had no way of knowing if the things growing here were poisonous or edible. Vintage would have had a better idea, no doubt, but then she suspected that if Vintage had been along for the ride they'd never have found themselves on the Island of Bastard Stinging Starfish in the first place. Instead, she found herself frowning vaguely at splotches of luminous fungi, and kicking at the roots of a bush with her foot. It was while she was doing this – wondering what Tor would say if she came back empty-handed – when a round face appeared on the far side of the bush, looming out of the shadows.

Noon yelped and leapt backwards, managing with some difficulty not to summon the winnowfire to her hands. The face resolved itself into a tall, lean man, his own eyes wide with something like wonder. He had long black hair, tied into plaits that hung either side of his face, and warm tan skin, just like Noon's. He wore, as far as Noon could tell, clothes woven from bark and some dark, flexible material, and at his belt were a series of small knives – they were strangely coloured, although it was difficult to make out in the rapidly dimming light. The man stepped around the bush, holding out one hand in an unmistakably placating gesture.

'Hello? I will not harm. Hello?'

Noon blinked. The man with the long plaits spoke a strange

227

version of plains speech – familiar enough for her to follow, but with an accent she didn't recognise. It took her a moment to puzzle out the words.

'Fucking hell. I didn't think there was anyone else on this island! What are you doing here? What's your name?'

The man smiled hesitantly. 'We are island people, we live here. My name is Tidewater. You are not from the island. You are . . . new?'

'New, yes. Do you have a whole village here or something? Houses? A settlement? Where did you even come from?'

'Small places, yes.' Tidewater came closer, and Noon could see that the dark woven material that connected the softened bark plates of his clothing was made up of hair. Human hair. And the knives at his waist looked very much like the multi-coloured beaks of the strange birds they had seen at the starfish island; they had been cut and sharpened into tools. 'Many small places, throughout.' Tidewater gestured around him, taking in the whole forest. 'I will take you to one, if you would like?'

Noon smiled. The man looked so much like the people she had grown up with, and he was strong – the muscles on his arms were clear even in the fading light, and he held himself with the easy confidence of someone able to run and climb at a moment's notice. 'Sure. Show me where you live, Tidewater.'

The man nodded, and turned away. Noon followed him through the trees. Tor would no doubt be outraged by this decision – he would not be happy about being left out of such a discovery – but communication with the man was so fragile. Noon was not convinced she could explain to him that she needed to collect her friend first, and there was always the chance that these people had some food they could trade, or even medicine.

'A friend of mine is sick.'

Tidewater turned to face her as they walked, his forehead creased with concern.

228

'He has been stung, here.' She touched the side of her jaw. 'It's very sore. Do you have a healer? Any medicine?'

The man's mouth turned down at the corners, evidently confused by the words.

'I mean, someone who looks after people. Makes things better?'

Tidewater brightened at that, and nodded. 'We do. I will take you.'

They walked for some time, the shadows growing deeper all around while Noon's doubts about her decision to go with the man grew. Eventually, the light changed, and Noon realised she was looking at a series of small campfires filtered through the trees.

'This is your place? Where you live?'

'One of the places,' said Tidewater.

It was a very small settlement indeed, squeezed into a tiny clearing. Noon saw one large hut and four smaller ones, made from wood and bark and what looked like a fair quantity of mud. One central fire, just outside the biggest hut, appeared to be a cooking fire, and propped over it were several sticks, each with a pair of skewered squirrels slowly turning brown. A man stood next to the carcases, tending them carefully to make sure they didn't burn, and there were a handful of other people. Tidewater called to them as they entered the settlement, and Noon saw several pairs of eyes turn to her. Mouths dropped open.

Everyone began to talk at once, and almost immediately Noon lost track of what they were saying. Words and phrases she had known all her life were eaten up by a storm of terms she had never heard before, although most of them felt familiar, as if she were glimpsing the shadows of some shared history. Several people appeared to be angry or alarmed, judging by the tone of their voices, while others – including an ancient man with thick bolts of white hair running through his braids – were staring at her in something like awe.

'I'm sorry,' she said. 'I don't . . . I can't follow what you're saying. Could you slow down?'

Tidewater clicked his tongue with irritation.

'They want to know where you have come from. How you got here. No one travels on the sea, it is death.'

'From the monsters and the poisonless. Do you come from them? We must know.' This was from a short man wearing a cuff of brown and black feathers around his throat. He had a kind face, but even so, he looked worried, and Noon sensed that her sudden appearance had ruined his day in ways she couldn't understand.

'She could be a monster!' A young woman with fierce eyebrows stepped forward. She was carrying one of the beak-knives in her hand, holding it so that Noon could see it.

'Do not call me that.' Noon felt the first stirrings of anger, but Tidewater shook his head brusquely.

'Of course she is not. Look at her! I think she is a message, a sign.'

'I'm just visiting,' Noon's jolt of anger had quickly dissipated to unease. The idea of explaining who she was and what she was doing on this island abruptly seemed not only complicated, but also deeply unwise. She didn't know what she had walked into here, but her instinct was to get away again, before they decided she was some sort of messenger with a secret message, or a monster – and she had had more than enough of being called a monster. 'I'm not a monster, and I don't know anything about poison. Do you have a healer? My friend, he's . . . further back in the forest, and he is sick.'

This caused a flurry of more chatter, and again Noon lost the sense of what they were saying. The young woman with the eyebrows brandished her knife, but Tidewater shouted her down, and then the older man with the cuff of feathers came directly over to Noon, a torch in one fist. He still looked wary, but he nodded to her.

'If you are a message from the gods, then we should see your friend, and help him. Messengers from the gods usually come with a test, or a price.' He smiled thinly. 'And if you're a monster, well, I am one old man, and not worth the wear and tear on your teeth.'

'I'm not a bloody monster.'

'You do not look like one.' He took a breath. 'Come, take me to your friend. I will heal them, if I can. Tidewater, walk with us.'

The rest of the camp stayed behind, although Noon could feel their eyes on her back all the way into the trees. Tidewater moved on ahead, walking confidently along a path only he could see, while the short man walked beside Noon.

'My name is Borrow,' he said. 'This island is Firstlight. What is your name?'

'Noon. I . . . my name is Noon.'

The shadows were thick now, and with a crackle of shame Noon realised that if she had not been with them, she might not have been able to find her way back to the camp. There was also the question of what would happen when they did get back there – Tor's surprise at visitors was, on reflection, the least of their problems. If these people were shocked to see her, what would they think about a dragon and a giant winged-cat?

Borrow was oblivious to her discomfort. He smiled, nodded. 'You have a name like ours, I think. A name taken from something significant on the day of your birth, yes? Your mother, she saw the noonday sun, perhaps. We must be the same.'

'I think so. I come from the plains, beyond the Bloodless Mountains. I mean, I was born there.' Borrow looked at her blankly. 'Perhaps you travelled from there? Once, a long time ago, and came to Firstlight?'

The man looked disturbed by the question. 'We fled,' was all he would say.

231

Orange light danced between the trees ahead, and Noon swallowed hard. 'All right,' she said, trying to sound casual, 'what you will see might seem alarming, or scary, but it's all fine. I promise.'

It was too late. Up ahead, Tidewater gave a shrill cry, and Noon saw the huge bulk that was Vostok rise from her resting place, firelight glinting over her scales like a cascade of embers. There was a growling cough as Kirune sprang to his feet, and Tidewater actually leapt backwards, colliding with a tree.

'Who's there?' It was Tor's voice, unnaturally gruff in his surprise. 'Noon, if that's you, you're about to get set on fire or filleted.'

She ran forward, ignoring the growing expression of terror on Borrow's face.

'It's me, and some friends! Everyone bloody calm down, all right? Vostok, it's fine, stop it. Tidewater? Borrow? It's safe, honestly.'

'Who are these people?' demanded Vostok. In that moment, Noon saw her as a stranger would – a huge scaled monster with long jaws full of teeth, a head bristling with horns. Tor was standing to one side of her, partially hidden in her shadow, although Noon could easily see the glinting blade of the Ninth Rain. 'Why are there humans here at all?'

'Blood and fire, Vostok, they *live* here.' Noon turned back to the two islanders. All the colour had drained from Tidewater's face, but even as she watched he seemed to be recovering from his shock. The knife he had whipped automatically from his belt was slowly being lowered, and his eyes were flickering between the dragon and the great cat with a growing expression of amazement. Borrow was leaning against a tree for support, an expression of bemused dismay on his creased face.

'These are your friends, then?'

'Um, yes. This is Kirune, here, the one with the . . . claws.'

She cleared her throat and carried on quickly, hoping she wouldn't have to explain further. 'As you can see, he's got a swollen mouth and throat, it's making it very difficult for him to eat. He was stung by a huge starfish, and—'

'But you are . . . stories! Old stories, lies.' Now he had overcome his initial shock, Borrow was shaking his head back and forth – he had looked away from Vostok and Kirune, as though the sight of them was painful.

'This changes everything!' said Tidewater, hotly. 'What does this mean, Borrow? If the old stories weren't lies . . .'

'We are not lies!' thundered Vostok. 'And you will show more respect!' Tidewater stumbled back, colliding with the tree again, and Tor stepped forward laughing, sliding away the Ninth Rain as he did so.

'The first lesson, my friend, is don't aggravate the dragon.'

This time, Tidewater gave a genuine shout of fear. He drew his knife again, but instead of brandishing it he threw it to the ground, and with that he turned and ran. Borrow gasped.

'No!' He turned an anguished expression on Noon. 'You told us you did not come from the monsters.' To her horror and shock, she saw that tears were leaking from the old man's eyes. 'Instead you feed us to them.'

'Well, that's rude,' muttered Tor. 'Listen,' he raised his voice, 'that was all a long time ago!'

'Tormalin is not a monster,' said Noon, all too aware that Borrow had likely grown up with all the same stories she had and that the word of a stranger would not change that. 'Please, we won't be here long. If you can help Kirune at all – the big cat – I would be really grateful.'

Borrow pressed his lips together in the expression of someone enduring terrible pain. 'If I help you, will you go?'

'Yes, we'll be gone in the morning, I promise.' The campfire was the only light in the gloomy clearing, but Noon still caught the shudder of relief that passed over Borrow's face. It hurt her, for reasons she didn't care to dwell on. 'We're not staying here. Actually, we're looking for another island, a place not far from here. Perhaps you've seen it, or know it from your travels? Have you seen . . . have you seen more people like Tormalin? In another place?'

Borrow scowled at her, and she sensed she had pushed her luck too far.

'There is nothing beyond Firstlight. Nothing. And the sea is dangerous. When we take ships out to fish, we do not go far.' His expression softened a little. 'New one . . . Noon. You should go back to your home. There is nothing for you but cold rocks and sea and pain beyond Firstlight. Do not waste your life on it.'

Turning away from her, he removed his pack and rooted around in it. After a lot of rummaging he retrieved a fat draw-string bag, made of tiny leather patches.

'This,' he said, throwing her the pack. 'It eases pain. We make it from the bark of a tree. A little is normally enough but,' he glanced at Kirune, who was sitting remarkably still, big paws held in front of him like a well-behaved tent-cat, 'for your creature, the whole pack. Boil up water, soften it like a stew.' Borrow drew himself up to his full height, and Noon sensed that his responsibilities as a healer were briefly outweighing his terror. 'It was a starfish that stung him? I would also put heated material, here.' He mimed holding something to his throat. 'Rags, doused in hot water, then squeezed. It will chase the poison out.'

'Thank you. I mean it.' Noon took a step towards him. 'You can't know it, but this could be really, really important. Kirune is one of our war-beasts, and they are our best hope of surviving—'

'Enough, please.' Borrow turned away, shouldering his pack. He looked ill, as though speaking to them made him sick, and he would not meet her eyes. 'Do not follow me back, because my people will kill you. If he comes,' he gave Tor the briefest of glances, 'I will *tell* them to kill you.'

'Wait! When you talk about monsters, what do you mean? Where did you even come from?'

But Borrow was walking back into the trees, and in moments he was nothing but a vague, moving shadow, lost to the growing night.

23

'He is simply too big.'

It was a thought that had been battering around the inside of Hestillion's head for some time now. Celaphon had outgrown her apartments, causing the queen to craft another, huge chamber within the corpse moon for him, and even inside that he loomed uncomfortably. And it was more than simply taking up too much space – he had grown bigger than any war-beast she had known, or heard tell of, and something about it was . . . wrong. He looked, more or less to proportion – perhaps his wings could be bigger – but she found herself frowning when she stared at him, as though something were slightly off balance and her mind was trying to figure it out, even when she wasn't conscious of it. The war-beasts she had known were large, but lithe, and compact. They were like jewels; whether they had black fur, yellow scales or soft blue velvet the colour of the sky, they looked deliberate. Like things created. Celaphon looked like an experiment. Or an accident.

'It is interesting, Lady Hestillion Eskt.' The queen wasn't disagreeing, Hestillion noticed. They were on a great plateau far to the west. The corpse moon lurked behind them, perched on the edge of the clear land like some great wart, while a carpet of dark-green trees spread out below them. Despite his new bigger quarters, Celaphon had grown restless, demanding that he be let out to fly, to stretch his legs. The queen had calmly ignored these requests, sending along more of the growth fluid instead, but when the war-beast had started crashing his great bulk into the soft walls over and over again, she had steered the corpse moon to a remote place and opened a hole in the side of the Behemoth. Now, she and Hestillion stood on hard, scrubby grass and watched as the huge dragon repeatedly tried to take off. The wind from his wings battered them so constantly that Hestillion found she was endlessly wiping at her watering eyes.

'Interesting? War-beasts are born knowing how to fly. I don't understand it. He has no memory of his former lives, and it seems there's no natural instinct there either.'

'Or, what we have done to him has made it impossible,' said the queen lightly. Some distance away, Celaphon lowered his head, bristling as it was with blackened horns, and thumped his bat-like leathery wings up and down, up and down. He lifted his front legs awkwardly, and for a brief second he was almost propelled backwards by the force of his own wing beats. Instead, his tail dragged along the ground and he dropped back down, heavily enough for Hestillion to feel the tremor of his impact through her slippers.

'It's an abomination, what we have done.' Hestillion curled her hands into fists. Her fingers were icy cold despite the long fur vest she wore over her robes. 'You will kill him, and me, I suppose, when you've finally had enough of this farce.'

The queen turned to face her. There were more details to her clay-like visage lately – tiny lines, like cracks under the glaze on the finest tea set, clustered at her forehead and the corners of her mouth. Even her eyes, once black like pools of wet ink, were lightening at the edges – splotches of yellow were growing there, like blossoms of mould. The queen raised her approximations of eyebrows, opened her mouth, and then, curiously, closed it again.

'We think,' she said eventually, 'that perhaps you should try instructing him.'

'Me?' Hestillion shook her head lightly, then laughed. The sound felt dry and old in her throat. 'Instruct him? I was never a paladin of the war-beasts. I was a child during the Eighth Rain! The closest I got to one was standing in a crowd of well-wishers on a feast day.'

'Even so, you are the only connection he has to that past. Memories, the bridges they build, the paths . . . they are important. You understand this, yes, from what we showed you?'

Celaphon was running now, four huge muscled legs in slightly ungainly motion. He picked up as much speed as he was able to, and then his wings opened like a tent being erected. There was a resounding crack, and briefly he had all four feet off the ground. His wings beat down again, and again, and he lifted, uncertainly, into the air.

'By the roots!' cried Hestillion. Without thinking she touched the queen's sinewy arm. 'Look! He almost flies.'

And as she spoke he crashed to the ground again, hard enough to tear up huge lumps of black earth. He bellowed a wordless shout of rage and frustration. Hestillion cupped her hands around her mouth.

'Keep going, sweet one! You are getting there!'

Celaphon turned his head in their direction, and his pearly white eyes looked blank, as though he didn't know what they were, or why they were making noises.

'Celaphon?'

The dragon seemed to brighten then, and he turned around to start running again.

'He takes comfort from your voice,' said the queen. 'Imagine if you were there with him, murmuring your encouragement into his ear. He would fly sooner, do you not think?'

Hestillion's stomach tightened. Once, in her youth, she might have dreamt of flying a war-beast – they all had dreamed of that, after all. But in her dreams the war-beast had been a silvery griffin or a sleek red fox.

'He would gain nothing from that,' she said quietly.

'Were not your beast creatures paired with warriors, during our wars?' There was a teasing note to the queen's voice. 'A partnership, always. Or at least, that is what we witnessed with our many eyes, as we tore you all to pieces. Often, we would see the Eboran warriors standing over their wounded creatures, ready to die for them.' She tipped her head to one side. 'But you do not share this bond?'

Hestillion bit her lip. The flame of anger that had ignited in her chest was hot and unexpected. 'That is not what I said. Celaphon is precious to me, above *all* things.' An image of her brother pushed its way into her head, but she firmly ignored it. *Lost*, she reminded herself. *Lost to me, and taken up instead by a filthy human fell-witch.* 'A piece of Ebora, as it once was. There can be nothing more valuable to me than Celaphon.'

'Then go to him. Help him with this.' The queen shifted, and crossed her arms over her chest. 'If you are afraid of falling off, we can craft such a thing that will hold you in place.'

'Afraid?' Hestillion thought of the day she had cut the wine merchant's boy's throat, of spinning herself further and further into the netherdark to find her god. 'I have never been afraid. Very well. Bring me a saddle, or a harness, or whatever is needed, and I will gladly fly with Celaphon.'

The queen laughed at that. 'Jump, I think you mean. The creature is not quite up to flying. But very well–' she paused. – 'You should warn him, of what is about to happen.'

Hestillion held herself very still. 'What . . .?' But the queen had half turned towards the corpse moon, and a narrow port opened in the side of its shining greenish flesh. A thin line of the black ooze spooled out of it, flying up into the air in a curving arc. It spread its tendrils against the pale blue of the morning sky and flexed, heading towards Celaphon. Realising what the queen meant, Hestillion called out to the dragon, and he shifted his bulky head around to face her, but he just looked blank, as he did before. The spooling black fluid reached him and split into a number of forks, spinning around his broad chest, belly and neck. Celaphon bellowed with outrage, stumbling backwards in an attempt to get away from the substance that was the heart of the Jure'lia, but there was no escaping it. As Hestillion watched, the stuff wove itself into something that could, if squinted at from the right direction, be seen as a series of straps and a harness. Celaphon was shaking himself like a wet dog, trying to dislodge it. Inwardly cursing the queen, Hestillion ran across the scrubby grass towards him, calling his name.

'It's all right, Celaphon. Sweet one, please, don't panic.' He lowered his head and snorted indignantly at her; his breath was hot and smelled sickly sweet. 'It's just something to help me to help you. Look, see?'

She reached up and tugged at one of the straps, realising as she did so that it wasn't truly a strap at all – the harness was formed to his body and needed no adjusting, but the fluid had given her these hanging pieces to help her climb up his side.

'I will just sit there, at the base of your neck, do you see?' She hitched up her robes as best as she could, and began to climb. The fluid-harness felt warm and dry under her hands, like the fevered skin of someone ancient and wrinkled. 'And then I can help you.'

'Help me?' rumbled Celaphon. He was standing calmly now, his thick neck twisted so that he could watch her progress. 'How?'

Roots be damned if I know.

'Back when there were many war-beasts, Celaphon, they always had Eboran companions.' She was making her way

240

steadily up his side, arm over arm up the series of handholds. Dimly she was aware that she must look quite the sight; fine silk robes hitched up around her knees, her pale calves flashing in the sunlight. Her blond hair was in disarray, floating around her head like gossamer seaweed caught in a playful current. 'They made sure that their war-beasts lived in great splendour, and had the finest foods.' She thought of the echoing chamber inside the corpse moon, and the thick white gruel from the pods, and moved on quickly. 'But they also rode into war with them, and helped them fight. They were a source of strength to each other, for all of their lives.' She was over his side and looking at the broad expanse of his back. There was something like a seat in the centre, a mound of the rubbery black material that was raised above everything else – there was, she realised, probably one of Celaphon's fibrous plates underneath it – so she made her way over to it. 'It is right that I should fly with you, Celaphon.'

'Are we at war, then?'

What a question. Somewhere behind them, she could sense the queen's amusement. She refused to look.

'Here we are. This will be better, won't it? You don't have to do this alone.' Hestillion settled herself on the seat, and it shifted under her, moulding itself to the shape of her body. A thick belt slid its way across her stomach. Luckily, Celaphon had turned his head away from her again and therefore did not see the expression of disgust that cramped across her face. The bare skin of her legs was in contact with the leathery harness, and it felt like an invasion, a personal insult.

'Let's try this again, then, Celaphon. When you were running and flapping your wings earlier? Do that again for me, faster this time.'

Hestillion made her voice as firm as possible but her heart was in her mouth as Celaphon began to move. Standing and watching, it turned out, was very different to being on top of

the war-beast as he ran. Enormous muscles bunched and shuddered beneath her, throwing her back and forth, and she could
hear the bellowing rattle of his breath. He picked up speed,
and the landscape around them jumped and dropped wildly.
Hestillion had to hold on tightly to avoid being flung off,
despite the thick belt holding her in place. She clenched her
teeth together to stop from chomping through her own tongue,
and then his wings started beating; a thunder like nothing else,
and her ears were full of a whistling wind.

'Go!' she yelped out between her teeth. 'Fly, Celaphon!'

The war-beast leapt, and Hestillion felt her stomach drop
away alarmingly. For a handful of seconds, the scrubby grassland and the line of dark trees vanished, and everything was
the eternal blue sky. In that moment, Hestillion grasped something of the joy of flying.

But it was temporary. Celaphon crashed back down to the
ground, and in the violence of it Hestillion bit her lower lip
– the white-hot flash of pain and the taste of her own blood
was a revelation, and her heart stuttered in her chest. When
her head stopped ringing, she could hear Celaphon bellowing
his rage.

'I hate this!' His anguish and his pain were in every syllable,
fresh and honest in the way that, in Hestillion's experience,
only the very young could be. She rubbed a hand across her
chin and blinked at the crimson smear there. Leaning forward
so that she could touch Celaphon's scales, she pressed her hand
to him, trying to make a connection.

'Listen to me, sweet one. We will get there, I promise you.'
Her voice was low and rough, and her lip throbbed steadily.
'Together, if we work together, we will have you flying like a
bird soon enough. You have to trust me. Listen to my words.'

Celaphon grew still. All around them, the scrubby grass moved
in the wind like a living thing, and somewhere in the distance,
a bird was calling – something swift and lethal, seeking prey.

'And breathe fire?' asked Celaphon. 'Will I do that eventually too?'

Hestillion swallowed hard around the taste of bitter pennies. 'Maybe, my sweet. Maybe.'

24

Finneral was mostly coast, it turned out. A thick green strip along the edge of the sea, studded with fat grey boulders and larger outcroppings of rock, like misshapen buttons on an emerald jacket. The sea to their left was a deep, appealing blue, and Aldasair found himself warming to the place more and more the further they flew over it. Eventually, the rocky ground erupted into a single mountain peak, green and grey and topped with snow, and as they approached it, Bern leaned back in Sharrik's harness and shouted over his shoulder.

'Stone-Father!'

Aldasair nodded, although he had no idea what that was. Following Bern's lead, they began to fly lower, swooping over fields dotted with houses built from grey stone, many with herds of goats and sheep that scattered in all directions at their approach. Jessen was silent as they flew, her black fur rippling constantly in the wind, but Aldasair could feel her mind, close at hand and comforting in its calmness – she was not concerned about this trip. She wasn't nervous, or worried, so there was no reason that Aldasair should be. Of course not.

Gradually, the number of houses and dwellings they saw increased, and eventually Sharrik swept closer, slowing down abruptly. Bern was leaning over in his harness again, pointing below them this time.

'What is it?'

'We've been spotted. See?'

Aldasair scanned the ground below, and saw a beacon being lit at the edge of a meandering stone wall. The man who had lit it was staring up at them, and it was possible to see that his mouth was hanging wide open. Aldasair looked away in time to see another beacon lighting up to the north, a bright point of light competing with the sunshine.

'What does that mean?' he called back.

Bern shrugged. 'That someone should come to meet us soon, I think. They won't want us landing right in the middle of Kotra. We'd cause a bloody riot.'

Kotra, Bern had already told him, was Finneral's central city. They flew on, passing the second beacon and continuing to scatter herds of sheep and other animals, until Aldasair caught more movement below. A figure riding on the back of some animal he could not make out, at full pelt across a lush green field. He heard Bern give a joyous shout and Sharrik began to circle, stretching out his long furred legs to land.

'We stop here?' asked Jessen, her voice soft even over the whistling wind.

'It looks like it.'

Jessen followed her war-beast brother down, making a much more graceful spiral than Sharrik had done. When Aldasair climbed down the harness, Bern was already there, standing with his hands on his hips, talking excitedly to the woman on the mount. It was the mount that caught Aldasair's eye first, for he had seen nothing like it outside of their own war-beasts. It was a great bear, almost certainly Wild-touched from the size of it, with shaggy, dark-brown fur. Incredibly, it wore a thick mantle of stone across its back, held in place with leather straps, and this was where the woman was sitting. It also wore

245

a band of polished stone across its forehead, and it regarded them with small, intelligent black eyes. The woman was short and stocky, with a long braid of blond hair hanging down over her shoulder, brighter than beaten gold, and she wore a leather eyepatch over one eye and a coat of black-and-brown striped fur. The one remaining eye was a very familiar green.

'Well, it's good to see you, you great lump,' she was saying to Bern. 'We had thought you might never come back. Here, look, then, here's the other.' She looked down at Aldasair steadily, a glint of mischief in her one good eye. She looked, to his eyes, slightly older than Bern, but then he found predicting how old humans were a strange and confusing science. 'How're you, young man? Some fine beasts you have there. By the stones, Bern, your father will be beside himself.'

Bern cleared his throat. 'Aldasair, this is my mother, Rainya. She should introduce herself, but she'll be too busy showing off to you now.'

Rainya made a snorting noise at that, while Aldasair blinked rapidly. Despite their shared blond hair and green eyes, it was difficult to imagine someone of Bern's sheer bulk being created by this diminutive woman. Uncertain what else to do, he bowed stiffly.

'It is my honour to meet you, Lady Rainya.'

She raised her eyebrows. 'Well. Polite. I like that. And these two? Will you not introduce me, son of mine?'

Bern shook his head in a fashion that suggested that he was quite used to this behaviour from his mother, but to Aldasair's surprise Jessen stepped forward and lowered her long black snout.

'Thank you for welcoming us to Finneral, Lady Rainya.'

The older woman pressed her lips into a long thin line, and touched her braid. Aldasair felt another flutter of panic, sure that they had offended somehow, but then Rainya took a long breath through her nose, her good eye shining with unshed

246

tears. 'It's my honour, or a dream, I can't tell which,' she said, before laughing. 'To see you both, what a blessing it is.'

'Bern is my human,' said Sharrik proudly. 'Thank you for birthing him, Mother Rainya.'

She laughed raucously at that, grinning and winking with her one eye at her son. 'Did you hear that, so? First time anyone has ever thanked me for that, I should say. Come on, you'll come on foot now, will you? Your father is in his hunting lodge and it's not that far from here, if you even remember.'

'I haven't been away that long,' said Bern as he climbed back into the harness. Aldasair followed suit, and soon they were following Rainya on her giant bear. The grass here was thick and lush, reaching up to the bear's belly, and they passed three tall stone statues; they were each as tall as Sharrik, and appeared to be statues of women, their faces serene and beatific. They all faced the thin strip of sea in the distance, and when Aldasair looked around, he realised he could see lots of them, dotted all over the landscape. In the distance was a dark-green smudge that gradually resolved itself into a small forest, and sitting in front of it was a long, low building of grey stone, with a curved roof of pale-yellow wood. There was a cheery little streak of smoke coming from it. Bern's mother was keeping up a steady stream of chatter, punctuated with little pauses as she turned in her saddle to get another look at Jessen and Sharrik – every time she did so her eyebrows leapt up, as if she were surprised by them all over again.

'The seas have been good and calm for the spring, thank the stones, because we'll need all the bloody food and trade we can get now, no doubt. Did you hear of the attack at Coldreef? Destroyed the whole bloody place, those wormy bastards, and what am I even talking about? You were there! Stones shatter, what a time to be alive. I have to tell you, son, I never thought I would see it, never thought you would either,

247

let alone see you flying a bloody great griffin! I just hope your poor father's head can take it, that's all I'm saying.'

'Da will outlive us all,' said Bern. 'As well you know.'

As they drew close to the low stone building, Aldasair could see people streaming in and out of three main doors – children carrying baskets, men and women with armfuls of firewood. There was a paddock to one side of the building that seemed to be the focus of all the frenetic activity.

'Is this your doing, Ma?'

Rainya flapped a hand at her son irritably. 'You expect us not to make a fuss? Did you spring from a pebble yesterday?'

'We're here for a serious reason, Ma.' He leaned forward and buried one big fist in Sharrik's neck feathers, scratching the griffin behind his ears. 'You know about the letter, I reckon?'

Rainya fiddled with the reins, not looking at them. 'Ah so.'

'It made me think things were pretty bad.'

'They are.' She turned around in the saddle and flashed him a warning look. 'Dark things are happening here, don't be getting me wrong. Young people lost, their poor families going out of their minds, and that evil thing lurking . . . It should have been dealt with a long time ago, but how could we have known?' She sighed heavily. 'But it's not every day your son comes home with an Eboran war-beast and an Eboran prince!'

Bern looked briefly panicked. 'Ma . . .'

'I am sorry, Lady Rainya, but I am afraid there must have been a misunderstanding,' said Aldasair. He had been lulled by the sound of their voices, happy simply to listen to their bickering back and forth, but he hardly felt like he could let that pass. 'Although it is true that I have been living in the palace for some decades—'

'Decades! Would you hark at him? He looks no more than twenty!'

'I am not royalty. Our family are minor nobles, and that only because everyone else was dead.'

248

'Sounds good enough to me,' said Rainya cheerfully. Aldasair glanced at Bern and was surprised to see that his cheeks were faintly pink. 'Here we are, look. They'll be talking about this for years. If we live that long, of course.'

By the time they reached the lodge there was a fair crowd gathered to meet them – men and women dressed in furs and leathers, their hair and beards dressed with tiny polished stones, their bare arms and necks patterned with ink; children with their eyes so wide they looked like they might fall straight out of their heads. A tall, skinny man with a big nose and long ginger braids jumped forward.

'Greetings! Welcome, uh, welcome to, uh, this place.' He seemed to choke then, and Aldasair looked at Bern, wondering if they should offer to help the man, but he recovered his wits. 'We have prepared a great feast for you, mighty ones!'

Rainya was dismounting. She passed the reins of her bear to a young girl, who was dwarfed by the creature. 'He means the war-beasts. We've food for them in the paddocks. Bern, Aldasair, you're with me. Come along so.'

They climbed down from the war-beasts. Aldasair exchanged a look with Jessen – he felt, in one quick jolt, her discomfort at being separated from him – and then the crowd shepherded them into the nearby paddock. He heard Sharrik exclaim with pleasure over something – it had to do with roast meat, from the scent – and then Rainya led them into the shadowy interior of the lodge. The difference from outside was startling. Inside was a stifling heat, and deep shadows. Small, round windows poked fingers of dusty light across the room without managing to illuminate much, and after his eyes adjusted to the darkness, Aldasair saw that they were in a long room lined with several wooden tables. There were three fireplaces that he could see, burning fiercely despite the mild day outside, and at the nearest, a huge wooden chair covered in furs. Sitting in it was a man even bigger than Bern. Aldasair knew, without being told, that this had to be Bern's father – it could hardly have been anyone else. He was tall and broad across the shoulders, looming even though he was sitting down, and he had a chest like a re-inforced barrel. He did, in contrast to Bern, have a sizeable belly, and as he shifted in the chair, Aldasair saw that his left leg was missing from the knee down, and in its place was a thick wooden peg, carved all over with alarming snarling faces. The man's hair and beard were a shade darker than Bern's – his beard was, in fact, a deep, nutty brown – and his eyes were blue, but there was no missing the resemblance from the cheek-bones and long, straight nose.

'There you are, lad. Perhaps they'll all stop running around like headless chickens now you're here – I'm not sure Finneral has ever seen a carry-on like it.' His voice was low and musical.

'Father.' Bern was shifting from one foot to the other. Aldasair watched him with interest, wondering what subtle piece of human interaction he was missing. As far as he could see, Bern's parents had been nothing but utterly welcoming, yet Bern looked as uncomfortable as Aldasair had ever seen him. 'You look well.'

Bern the Elder chuckled. 'I still get about. Here, love, give me a hand, will you?' Rainya came forward, and Bern the Elder took her hand in his massive paws. With barely a hint of effort the tiny woman yanked him to his feet. Standing, the big man almost seemed to fill the long hall. He bent and planted a noisy kiss on the very top of the woman's head, and she swatted at his arm.

'Get off me, ya great oaf.'

Bern the Elder grinned and came forward, looking directly at Aldasair. Out of the chair, he moved with no difficulties at all, his wooden peg striking the floor with strong, confident knocks.

'It's getting up and sitting down that gets me,' he said, as though he had been reading Aldasair's mind. 'Lost the thing –

what was it, my love, two years ago now? Bitten clean off by a Wild-touched monster.'

'He fell off his bear and had a nasty break, he means,' supplied Rainya.

Bern the Elder grinned all the wider. 'When you're as big as me, your leg doesn't take kindly to being landed on by the rest of you. So, you're our Eboran prince, are you?' He looked Aldasair up and down once, then nodded. 'Seems about right. Has he been treating you well, our Bern?'

Once again Aldasair had the impression there were currents under the surface of the conversation that he had no comprehension of.

'I'm sorry . . .?'

'I may have written home,' said Bern stiffly, staring at the wall. 'About you. I mean, about Ebora, the war-beasts, and so on. Important things.'

Aldasair rallied as best he could. 'Bern has been an enormous help. He has helped us bring Ebora back, from death and dust and devastation, in so many ways. I can say in all honesty that we could not have done it without him. We will be glad to lend any aid we can to his people.'

Rainya and Bern the Elder exchanged a quick glance, the meaning of which Aldasair couldn't fathom, and then Bern's father slapped his son firmly on the shoulder – a lesser man would have been pelted across the room.

'Come on then, you. We've someone who wishes to talk to you.'

'Already?' Bern's blond eyebrows climbed his forehead. 'I thought we would rest at least, eat, perhaps bathe?' He touched a hand to his beard; during their long journey it had escaped its bonds, bristling and curling at the edges.

Rainya snorted laughter. 'She has seen worse than you, no doubt. And besides,' the merriment faded from her face, 'these are bad times, Bern. It's not like anyone expects you to solve

251

this problem overnight, but I think the sooner we put our heads to it, the sooner Finneral can rest easy, so. Besides which, she has travelled a long way to see you.'

'She's here?' Bern looked thunderstruck. 'So close to . . .?'

'Aye, well, come on.' Bern the Elder began to herd them easily back towards the door. He had been right; his wooden leg was no concern to him once he was up and moving, and Aldasair felt he could resist no more than he could turn the ocean tides. Even the mighty Rainya was neatly herded out the door with the rest of them. 'A short walk in my forest, that's what we're after now, isn't it? Nothing like a bit of a walk when you've had your arse in the saddle for days, that's what I say.'

And that is exactly what they did. As they walked around the back of the long hall, Aldasair glanced over at the paddock and was rewarded with the sight of Sharrik and Jessen in the midst of a great crowd. Both wore garlands of white and blue flowers around their necks, and a stream of people were carrying trays full of steaming meats to them. Sharrik was speaking, and although Aldasair couldn't make out the words he recognised the expression of pleasure that crinkled his eyes, and even Jessen was content, her eyes narrowed and relaxed.

The forest was cool and green. Rainya went ahead, her blond head alternately shining like gold in the sun, then darkened to steel with shadows by the canopy. The place smelled of good things – dark soil, newly budding leaves, the lives of small animals – and Aldasair found himself strangely moved by it. Here, he felt, was a place untouched by misery or by illness, or even the worm people. Here, perhaps, was Sarn as it was meant to be. He felt calmer by the moment.

'I hunt here sometimes, Lord Aldasair,' said Bern the Elder. 'Aye, I can still hunt! I had my arms-man make this cunning bow, like you wouldn't believe.' He tapped Aldasair with his elbow. 'The bastard thing could take down a charging ox! I will show it to you later.'

'Bern . . .' murmured Rainya.

'Not that we have ox in these woods, of course. Wild boar, that's what I take down most here, and some deer. The deer are the most useful, their hides are beautiful and Rainya makes coats out of their skins for the young'uns, but the boar put up more of a fight, which I prefer. Sometimes I have to finish them off with my knife!' He grinned.

'Da . . .' Bern still looked strangely uncomfortable. Aldasair made a note to ask him if he was quite well when they were alone together again.

'Quit your nonsense,' said Rainya, companionably enough. They were in the thick of the woods, and all the hubbub of the lodge and its merry paddock had been left far behind them. Instead, they walked in a noisy green silence, the rustle of leaves and the calls of birds all around. Ahead on the right was a tall stone monolith, at least eight feet tall, the foot of it stained dark with moisture and speckled with moss and lichen. There was the figure of a woman carved into it, long braids hanging either side of a gently smiling face, and she carried a pail in one hand, an axe in the other. Rainya saw Aldasair's curious glance, and smiled. 'The stone maidens. You'll see them all over Finneral – this one is in pretty good shape, but many are worn by the weather, and you can barely see their faces, save for the hint of a smile. They all look out to sea.'

'It is beautiful,' said Aldasair, and meant it. As they passed the stone maiden he brushed his hand over the stone: a cold, gritty kiss against his fingers. 'Why do they face the sea?'

'We don't know,' said Bern. 'They've been here longer than us, but Ma is right, they really are all over Finneral – you'll find them up on the peak of Stone-Father, and on the coast. There are even a few under the water. You can see their heads poking up sometimes, when the tides are low.'

'And what a job that must have been,' added Bern the Elder. He caught his wife's hand and squeezed it quickly. 'It's a particular type of stone, not from round here, as far as we can tell, but once a lot of very determined people brought it here, carved all these bloody women, then set them down all over Finneral.'

'Sarn is full of mysteries,' said Aldasair, thinking it was something the scholar Vintage would say. 'Is there a pattern to them? The locations?'

Bern the Elder raised his eyebrows. 'I did know a man who intended to map them all once. I thought he was a little worm-touched in the head myself, but perhaps he was on to something. If such a thing exists, Lord Aldasair, I will get you a copy.'

'Oh, I didn't mean to be—'

'Nonsense,' said Rainya. 'It's the least we can do. We welcome curiosity about Finneral, so we do, especially from such a distinguished guest.'

Something small and round dinged off Bern the Elder's shoulder and bounced off into the undergrowth. He grunted and looked around, only for another small projectile – they were pine cones, Aldasair saw – to bump off the back of his head. There was a shout of laughter from the trees behind them.

'Stones and arses,' muttered Bern's father. 'The woman is a menace.'

Rainya turned back, squinting at the trees. Her lips were twisted into a fond smile. 'Stone Talker? Our son is here.'

A woman emerged from the trees, flanked by a pair of huge boar. To Aldasair's eyes they looked Wild-touched – they were much too big to be natural, and their eyes were a fiery red – but they accompanied the small figure of the woman peacefully enough, and she even rested a hand on the flank of one of the monstrous creatures, as though it were a dear friend. The woman herself was short, and obviously extremely ancient for a human. Her tanned skin was speckled with darker freckles, and her face was a piece of parchment that had seen much use – the words of her many years were written there plainly enough. She grinned at them quite happily, though, and she hadn't lost any teeth. Her head was entirely clean-shaven save for a single white braid, which was threaded with polished stones of many colours, and it hung heavy and fat over her shoulder. The rest of her wiry frame was mostly hidden under a deep fur shawl.

'King Bern! I brought Peren and Nevin to see you. Haven't they grown into fine beasts?'

Bern the Elder made some harrumphing noises while Aldasair tried to make sense of what he had just heard.

'King . . . Bern?'

Bern shot a pained look at his father, then turned to Aldasair. 'It's not like you think. There are lots of kings in Finneral.'

'Well thank *you* very much,' muttered Bern the Elder.

'They're really more like warlords,' continued Bern. 'War parties left over from our wars with the Sown. I'll . . . I'll explain it later.'

While they had this oddly fraught exchange, Rainya had come forward to pat the boar on their snouts, and they were grunting happily.

'Never mind all that,' she said. 'Lord Aldasair, this is Valous the Stone Talker.'

Remembering all he had learned about diplomacy since the awakening of Ygseril, Aldasair swept a deep bow in the old woman's direction.

'It is a great honour to meet you, my lady.'

The Stone Talker smiled. 'It's one not many people get, I suppose.' Her voice was rough, but warm. 'I'm still their great secret. It is . . . interesting to meet an Eboran. You were too young for the Carrion Wars, I suppose?'

'I only remember them dimly.' Aldasair felt a familiar cold

255

fog edging in at the corners of his thoughts, and pushed it away firmly. 'It was a bad time.'

'It certainly was,' said the Stone Talker, her mouth twisting. 'Murder on a scale we had never seen outside of the Jure'lia. Our great mythical heroes sweeping down from the Bloodless Mountains to turn on the people they had always protected. The Finneral people were too far away to take those losses themselves, but when a dog runs rabid, you know it will come for you eventually, and we learned of the suffering of the plains people with heavy hearts.'

'But surely,' Aldasair felt his grip on the situation loosening, 'surely you were not alive then?'

The Stone Talker rumbled laughter. 'Oh no. I am not quite that old. But one of my roles as Stone Talker is to know our histories, to keep them and preserve them for whoever comes after me. And the many sorrows of Sarn are written into its very bones.' She looked up at the treetops, as though looking for a sign, and a stray shaft of sunlight settled on her face. It turned her hazel eyes golden. 'If you know where to look, you can read those sorrows like lines on a scroll.' She shook herself, and plucked at her shawl. 'Peren and Nevin were born in the woods to the north of here. We call those woods the Sorrowing Wood, because they are Wild woods, and because they are full of dangers. King Bern here liked to hunt in them once.'

'I still would,' said Bern's father. 'But apparently I risk too much.' He shot a look at Rainya as he said it.

'He went hunting wild boar, and found the biggest beast the Finneral people had ever seen,' continued the Stone Talker in her broken voice. 'It was, by all accounts, an epic hunt.'

Bern the Elder visibly brightened. 'That it was! You were there, Bern lad, you remember that? We tracked her for days, careful as you like, in woods much less friendly than these.'

'I remember, Da.'

'King Bern took the beast down singlehandedly, with spear

256

and sword,' continued the Stone Talker. 'There were songs sung, ale passed around. A great celebration. And then as the songs quietened we heard the sounds of snuffling, of whining. The great worm-touched beast had left behind two young, both equally worm-touched and now, very vulnerable. Do you remember, King Bern?'

Instead of answering, Bern's father made a low grumbling noise in his throat. The Stone Talker smiled. 'I would not let them kill the young. They might have come from a long line of beasts, but they were in trouble, and alone in the world. Killing such is not the action of a warrior, I told them, but the action of someone who looks only for pointless revenge.'

'You were at the hunt, Lady Stone Talker?' asked Aldasair.

'I was. Do you see, my friend?' She placed her hand on his arm briefly. 'Your people are vulnerable, alone in the world now. It would be easy, too easy, to take revenge. And then we would lose a powerful ally.' She nodded to Peren and Nevin. 'I raised them both myself – it's possible to do that, if you listen closely to the patterns nature shows us. Even worm-touched nature is understandable, if you're willing to listen. Gentle as lambs, the pair of them. They know who helped them, and they are grateful. Something to remember.'

'Stone Talker, do you wish to accompany us to the Broken Field?' Bern's face was very still, and again Aldasair felt like he was missing some vital interaction.

The Stone Talker took a long, slow breath, her shoulders rising and falling under the thick fur shawl. All at once she looked unspeakably old, as though a strong breeze would tatter her to pieces. 'Listen to me go on. We should go there before it gets dark. I am too old to look at that place in the moonlight.'

257

25

They went immediately. Nearby there were four horses waiting for them, looked after by a tall woman with bristly brown hair, and to Aldasair's surprise the Stone Talker rode on one of her boar – he still hadn't figured out which was Peren and which was Nevin. The beasts kept up with the horses easily, and the Stone Talker led them to the northwest, winding down paths that appeared and then vanished again, following signs that Aldasair could not fathom. Eventually, the forest began to thin – the towering pine trees were replaced with stumps, each carefully topped with some sort of hard brown substance. Seeing Aldasair's curious glance, Bern nodded towards them.

'There's a fair amount of Wild around here, and we do what we can to keep it back. Cut down the trees and seal them over. The Broken Field is enough trouble all by itself without a thriving Wild forest. Not that it does much good, mind.'

Aldasair could see what he meant. Despite the stumps and the dead wood lying around, this clearly wasn't a dead place. Smaller trees were already growing, racing to take the place of their older brethren, and they were strange themselves, with bark of black and red and green, with twisted branches and strange, tumorous lumps. There were patches of fungi too, things like bloated hands and lacy fringes, like the hems of elaborate skirts. Aldasair saw several things that looked like fat sleeping infants, their pale bodies curled in on themselves, but they were just more strange mushrooms. They made him deeply uneasy. He knew about the Wild, had even seen it on the edges of Eboran territory, but after centuries spent in the echoing corridors of the palace, he had neatly parcelled these memories away as old nightmares. The reality of the Wild was a hollow feeling in his chest.

The first they saw of the Broken Field was the stones, although Aldasair hardly thought that was an impressive enough name for them. The land fell away below them, revealing a shattered landscape littered with enormous monoliths. Each was huge, taller than the palace of Ebora, with several appearing to be almost as tall as Ygseril himself, and they were all shapes – roughly square, narrow and sharp, or round, like boulders. Every one of them had been carved all over, with the interlocking geometrical shapes that Aldasair recognised from the Stone Talker's letter, and all of the grooves had been filled with paint – red and black symbols shining against the rough grey stone.

'Ah, this place,' said Rainya. Her cheerful face was creased with distaste. 'I'm glad to say we don't have many scars in Finneral, but this is the biggest of what we've got.' She frowned fiercely. 'I wish we could lay about it with your axes, Bern my lad, and chop the whole bastard thing out of the ground.'

'All of Sarn must bear its scars,' said the Stone Talker. 'Do you see, Eboran, the efforts we have gone to, to keep this monster contained?'

Aldasair nodded slowly. Underneath the stone monoliths there was the broken ground, uneven and strange. There was black soil there, and enormous flat plates of rock, some overlapping each other, some shattered into shards as big as carts.

The Stone Talker led them on, and as they edged closer to the site, Aldasair felt the hairs on the back of his neck stand up. He could not see the Jure'lia here, but he could feel them. He sincerely hoped it was his imagination.

'You covered it up,' he said. He spoke softly, but all four of his companions turned to look at him as if startled. 'The pieces of the old evil. You found them and then you buried it all deep, hoping it would never awaken, and, just to be sure, you weighted everything down with rocks. Giant stones.' He blinked. 'Vintage said that stones would never work.'

'What is Vintage?' asked Rainya.

'A friend of ours, Ma,' said Bern. 'She's an expert on the Jure'lia. I think you'd like her.'

'It was the best we could do,' said the Stone Talker, shifting atop her boar. 'Your people, Aldasair, and our own warriors, brought this Behemoth down and, for once, it did not survive the collision with the earth. Our ancestors buried the remains of it, and the stones you see here are the most sacred guardians of Finneral, here to keep us safe.'

'But they didn't,' said Aldasair. 'They have failed you.'

The Stone Talker snorted, not entirely in good humour. 'You could say that. With the release of the queen from your dead god's roots, everything suddenly became much more . . . lively. The stones, which we thought so immovable, began to shift. At night, the place glows, and it moans, like something haunted. It is a horror waiting to happen.'

Aldasair wondered how much the Stone Talker knew about his own role in the awakening of Ygseril – he had, after all, walked across the roots and poured the worm people's strange golden fluid over the god's roots. And he had watched as the old nightmare had boiled up into life again. Bern had been there, and it was entirely possible that he had told them all of this in his letters. For reasons he didn't understand, he felt a soft pain in his chest, as though a hook had embedded itself

260

there. Did Bern blame him for what had happened? Did he see him as another selfish Eboran monster, like his cousin Hestillion, acting without caring for the fate of Sarn?

'Can we look at it more closely?' asked Bern. He was standing in his saddle, craning to get a better view. 'I'd like to know everything we can before we bring Jessen and Sharrik here.'

Together they moved off down the slope. The good sounds of the forest, as faint as they were – the rustling of leaves, the calls of birds and insects – faded away, and were replaced with a tinny silence. Even the air seemed to lie heavy here, and for the first time since arriving in Finneral, Aldasair felt a prickle of sweat break out across his back. There was a smell too, sweet and strange, like something rotting. When they reached the Broken Field, the horses grew skittish, refusing to travel across the black earth and shattered stones, and they all climbed down from their mounts.

'There is a Behemoth buried under there.' Aldasair meant to phrase it as a question, but the words fell from his lips like stones. Of course the Jure'lia lurked here. It could hardly be anything else.

The Stone Talker nodded.

'It's fixing itself, we think. There have been reports of this happening across Sarn – old Behemoth wrecks rumbling into life and joining all their broken pieces back together. Or at least it's trying too. The sacred stones are not just physically heavy – they carry the weight of the will of the Finneral people.'

'We have had those reports too,' said Bern. He glanced at Aldasair. 'In Ebora, I mean. This cycle, this *Rain*, is different. They weren't chased off to wherever it is they go, to come back good as new centuries later. They fell and rotted into the ground, and now they've risen from their graves.' When the Stone Talker turned to him, he shrugged. 'Vintage knows a lot about this, and so do the Eborans. The worm people are like wounded animals, weak and injured.'

261

'Unfortunately,' added Aldasair, 'so are we.' He turned to the Stone Talker and addressed her directly, looking straight into her hazel eyes. 'Ygseril was weakened when he brought forth the war-beasts, my lady, and we only have five to fight for us, and one of those an infant. And there are other . . . difficulties. We are not what we once were.'

The old woman tipped her head to one side, squinting at him and considering his words.

'But they are strong? They wish to fight?'

'Of course,' said Bern, a gruff note to his voice. 'They are legends brought to life.'

As if in answer to this statement, the ground under their feet began to tremble. Startled, Aldasair turned back to the Broken Field. The enormous carved stones were shifting, just slightly, and the flat plates of rock they stood on were moving too – the quiet, heavy air was split with an unhappy squealing. Aldasair's heart leapt into his throat until he realised that it was simply the sound of the rocks being squeezed together and shifting across one another. Nevin and Peren pawed at the ground and shook their ungainly heads.

'You see?' The Stone Talker gestured to the Field. 'It grows lively, even during the day.'

Unsheathing one of his axes, Bern walked down to the very edge of the field, and after a moment Aldasair followed him. Bern the Elder, Rainya and the Stone Talker stayed where they were.

'What do you think?'

Bern did not answer immediately. He looked out across the Field, his face unusually sombre.

'Look. Where the dirt is at its darkest.' He pointed with the axe. 'Can you see it?'

Aldasair looked where he pointed, and frowned. The dirt there was black, and it looked wet too, although nothing else here looked like it had recently been touched with rain.

'The black fluid that came up through Ygseril's roots.'

Bern nodded. 'It's the worm people, definitely. All I can think of doing is to move everything back – clear away the sacred stones in the centre there.' He gestured again with the axe. 'Dig down, and kill anything underneath. We don't know what's under there, or how put-back-together it is, but we do have the advantage of being directly above them.' He tugged on his beard with his free hand, and sucked in air through his teeth. 'Curse my stones, it's a big job, though, even with our war-beasts. We'll have to have everyone down here, ropes and platforms, and we'll need to be on our guard constantly, in case anything gets too wakeful.'

'What's that?' Something had caught Aldasair's eye, some piece of colour that sat out of place with everything else. Ignoring Bern's look of concern, he stepped onto the nearest flat plate of rock and moved to where it met the next plate. There was a sticky, bubbling crust of black fluid there, oozing between the two plates, and, wedged in it, something red and brown. He reached down and pulled it free, grimacing at the sucking noise as the black ooze reluctantly gave it up, and then turned the object over in his hands. It looked a little like a long soft leather sock, embroidered with red and yellow stitching – Aldasair saw flowers and fish there, entwined with each other. 'What is it? A boot?' he asked.

Bern appeared at his shoulder and his face fell at the sight of it. 'It's a betrothal boot,' he said, taking it from Aldasair and holding it gently as though it were something newly born. 'One of the traditions we have in Finneral. When a couple are falling in love and thinking of marrying, there are these little . . . steps, we have. Like steps in a dance. An unasked for task is undertaken and completed. One brings the other's parents the first catch of the day for a week or two. The couple take a walk together around the base of Stone Father, usually on the night of a full moon, and in the weeks leading up to their

263

moving in, they will work together on a piece of clothing.' He held the boot up. 'Traditionally, it is embroidered with their family's sigil. In this case, a flower of some sort, and a fish. This would have been treasured by someone, and I don't know why it would have been left out here.' He sighed heavily. 'But perhaps I do. The Stone Talker said in her letter that people were being taken by this thing.'

They returned to the others, and when Bern passed the boot to his mother, she turned it around in her hands, shaking her head.

'Terralah. She vanished early last week. She and Rold were due to be married at the end of the summer, and he has been going out of his mind.' She looked up from the boot, her eye blazing. 'What does this mean? What are they doing to our people?'

'We'll stop them, Ma.' Bern squeezed Rainya's shoulder. 'No one else will be lost to this evil place.'

A high-pitched shriek filled the air as the stones began to move again, and Aldasair wondered if Bern was right.

26

'Fuck this fucking storm!'

Next to Tor in the makeshift oilskin tent, Noon poked a foot out from under her heap of blankets and kicked him in the leg.

'Can you keep it down? I'm trying to sleep.'

Tor gestured wildly to the slick walls of their tent, well aware that she wouldn't be able to see his actions and doing it anyway. Outside, the howling wind rose a few notches, as if actively competing with him, and the sound of the rain, like handfuls of pebbles being thrown at their tent, grew in volume.

'Could you ask the storm to keep it down, then? I don't know if you've noticed but we could very well be lost.' He ran a hand over his face. 'I can't reach the netherdark with all this roots-damned racket, and if I can't do that, I can't dream-walk into Micanal's stupid roots-damned amber map.'

A sound rather like muttered swear words came from under the heap, and then part of a face poked out of the blankets. In the light of their tiny fire, now down to glowing embers, he could see the stark shape of the bat-wing tattoo on her forehead and a pair of dark, narrowed eyes.

'Maybe you should join the war-beasts.'

Vostok and Kirune had chosen to fly out and away from this particular miserable excuse for an island, looking for clear skies above the storm. Noon, who had been nodding off in the harness despite the wind and the rain, had insisted they rest, and despite his increasing concerns about the whole mission, Tor had to agree. They had been flying in circles for two days and two nights, trying to find the next stage of the blasted map and failing, and he had put Vintage's written notes away, reasoning that a fresh look at the amber map might help. But privately, he wasn't convinced; it looked more and more like they were wasting their time out here, that Micanal had been mad and desperate after all. The only bright spot of the process had been Kirune, whose swollen face had shrunk back down to normal proportions with the medicine given to them by the strange little man on Firstlight.

'Yes, thank you, useful advice as ever.' Tor turned back to the dim glow of the fire, turning the amber tablet over in his hands. It was too gloomy in the tent to see the delicate carvings, but he could feel the shape of them, cool under his fingers. 'To be honest, I'm not sure I have the strength. You'd think it would be the easiest thing in the world, but the reality is quite different. Finding the netherdark takes focus, and keeping yourself from being overwhelmed in the dream requires a presence of mind. When did we last have a decent night's sleep? I fear that if I close my eyes I will just drop off.'

Noon sat up, her mouth open to speak, but at that moment the storm bounced and rattled against the tent walls with extra violence, and they both sat still, waiting for it to pass. When it had quietened a little, she cleared her throat.

'Do you want to . . . would it help?'

The dragon was far away. Or at least, Kirune was – Tor could sense it, and he was sure that Vostok would be keen to explore at least as far as the giant cat would.

'It might.' He looked down at his boots. 'It has been a while.'

In that matter-of-fact way she had, Noon pulled the blankets back, rolling up her sleeve as she did so. It was all very practical, even sensible. He needed to be at his peak, if they were going to succeed at this ridiculous mission. Without human blood, he was weaker, and would only grow more so – it was a reasonable solution to an inevitable problem. So why was his heart beating faster at the thought of it?

'I have my own . . . blade. Would you like me to . . .?'

Noon nodded as she shifted around to sit next to him. She held out her arm, then seemed to hesitate.

'What is it?'

'We never really talked about it. The crimson flux, I mean.' She paused, eyeing the knife as he slipped it from his belt. 'Vintage and I talked to Eri about his father dying, and it was . . . Am I putting you at risk? By doing this?'

Tor smiled. 'No more risk than usual.' He took her hand and turned it face up, baring the paler skin of her underarm. 'What I mean is, *I* am the one who takes the risk. I have been taking this risk for a long time now, and it's my decision, in the end.' The veins at her wrist were dim blue threads, warm and alive under his touch. 'If I've doomed myself to die that way, then I've probably already done it. And it's that or die of unnatural old age. Those are our choices these days.'

'Unnatural old age,' snorted Noon. Some of the tension had eased from her shoulders. 'Anyway, you don't know that. What if we do find this island place of Micanal's? What if there is another tree? More sap?'

'Then I will be free to outlive you by five hundred years or so.' He had meant it jokingly, but all at once the dismal little tent seemed all the darker, and the storm outside more threatening. Noon's face was in shadow, and he couldn't see her expression.

'Do it, then,' she said, and he heard the effort it was costing her to speak lightly. 'Before *I* die of old age.'

267

He cut her, and the blood rose up black against her tan-coloured skin. Bending his head to drink, he kept her hand cupped in his, and the old familiar sharpness slipped down into his gut, sending out its threads of life and warmth to every part of him. His heart was still beating too quickly, but now it was strong too – impossible to believe that such life could ever end. Her skin tasted of sea salt.

When he lifted his head again she was staring at him, her eyes wide. The dragon, he remembered, was far away.

'Noon . . .'

'I've missed you, you know. Bloodsucker.'

A look passed over her face, almost angry, and then she reached up and kissed him. Somewhere, the sound of a storm faded, growing faint under pounding in his own head. When they broke apart, he grinned.

'We really should find more comfortable places to do this. We were just at a palace full of empty rooms.'

She pressed a hand to his shirt, warm fingers slipping between the silks to find his skin. 'Maybe we don't get to . . . Oh shit. Wait.'

'Wait?'

But she was turning away from him, and a second later he heard it too: the beating of enormous wings. Something heavy landed outside.

'Look, if we're quiet, maybe she'll go away.' Again he tried for levity, but before he could register the reaction on Noon's face one side of the oilskin tent was abruptly lifted up and away, letting in a huge gust of freezing wind and rain, and a long dragon nose. Tor scrambled to his feet while Noon shouted with alarm. The tiny fire winked out in a smear of black smoke.

'What's going on in here?'

'Roots be damned!' Tor snatched up the amber tablet from where it had fallen into the dirt. He was suddenly furious, and he found himself shouting over the wind. 'What's going on?

None of your business, that's what! Look what you've done to the tent. And I could have lost this!' He waved the amber tablet at Vostok, and felt a strange surge of triumph in his belly. This was so at odds with how he felt – humiliated, angry – that for a moment he was too confused to continue; until he saw the grey shape of Kirune skulking in the background. He was sensing the big cat's feelings, not his own.

'None of my business?' Vostok rose up on her hind legs, huge white wings held out to either side to keep her balance. Her feathers shivered constantly in the wind. 'Noon is my companion. Anything that concerns her concerns me.'

'Hold on,' Noon was on her feet too, her hands held out towards them both. A gust blew her black hair across her forehead, obscuring her eyes until she pushed it irritably out the way. 'Shut up the pair of you.'

'Believe me, Vostok, *this* definitely doesn't require your concern, your approval, or even your knowledge!' Tor squeezed the tablet between his fingers. He could still taste Noon's blood in his mouth. 'So give us a bit of space!'

'Son of Ebora, I assure you it certainly does concern me! Noon and I are a unit, which is more than can be said for the rest of you.' Vostok's eyes flashed purple and white in the storm light. 'We are a weapon, a sword. We do not have time—'

'I said shut up!' Green winnowflame popped into existence, twin-gloves around Noon's clenched fists. Tor hadn't even seen where she had taken the energy for that. The green flames were guttering and hissing in the rain and wind, casting wild shadows around the slick dirt and grass. 'Listen, you both need to . . . I can't . . . This is the last thing we need right now!'

Kirune slunk between them, his wings folded tightly at his back. He looked around as though noticing them there for the first time, and finding them all beneath his notice.

'If you've finished your squabble,' he said, in what Tor

269

thought was a fair impression of Vostok's imperiousness, 'you should come with me. I have found this island for you.'

'You have not found it.'

The storm had passed, and they were flying high above a calm sea again, sunlight jumping from waves like shoals of iridescent fish. Vostok was far to their right, with Noon bent low over her neck – her eyes endlessly sweeping the water. Tor leaned over so that his mouth was closer to Kirune's ear. Days of flying over the sea had turned the war-beast's fur stiff and unruly.

'You should just admit it now, or Vostok will only take even more pleasure in showing you up. It's nothing to be embarrassed about. You were flying in a storm, the visibility must have been terrible, and it would certainly be easy enough to see islands where there were none.'

Kirune's growl reverberated through his chest and up through his harness.

'I saw it. It was strange, though, like lots of lights, or pieces of water.'

'You're not even making sense now.'

'It was here. We keep looking, we will find it.' Kirune paused. 'You do not like the snake either. I can feel it.'

'You really shouldn't call her that. And I like Vostok well enough.'

Kirune hissed. 'You do not. You do not like her because she keeps you from humping the witch.'

'She keeps me from *what*?'

'I know what humping is,' said Kirune, suddenly haughty. 'I have heard the humans speaking about it. The snake is protective of her little warrior. She wishes their bond to be the only one the witch has.'

'Roots save us. You know, Vostok is right. Any chance we ever had of working together, of being a team, all went out

270

the window long ago. Drained away into the dust.' Tor sighed heavily, shifting in the harness. 'I am sick of looking at the bloody sea. Sick of looking at the lot of you, if I'm honest. We should go back now, so I can have a hot bath, drink several bottles of wine and sleep for at least a decade.'

'Hoy!' Noon was waving at him from the back of Vostok. 'What's that? Do you see it?'

He looked where she was pointing, and made a disgusted noise. 'Has the sea air driven you all mad?'

'No! It is there.' Kirune leapt forward, diving towards the stretch of sea Noon had been pointing at. To Tor it appeared to be exactly the same as every other piece of water nearby – grey, featureless, cold.

'This is ridiculous. Can't you see there is nothing there?'

And then something ahead of them changed. At first Tor thought it was a trick of the light, that he had spent too many hours squinting hopelessly at the sea and his eyes were too tired to be reliable. It looked like there were shards of light hanging in mid-air, as though they approached some huge edifice made of glass, only visible by the muted sunlight bouncing off it, and then he saw that there was a pattern to it – like the diamond-shaped panels in an elaborate Jarlsbad window. Slowly, like a giant whale moving under the waves, his stomach turned over. Now that he could see the pattern, he could see that there were pieces missing, and beyond that, landfall.

'Can you see it?' Noon's voice was high and excited.

'I can.' He thought of what Vintage would say when she heard that they had found this, and she hadn't been there to see it first. He grinned. 'Can we get through this barrier, do you think?'

Noon lifted her hand and a small green fireball, no bigger than her fist, flew from her outstretched fingers towards the light barrier. It passed clean through, with no apparent disruption to the shapes in the light.

'I think it's passable,' she called back. 'But there's really only one way to find out.'

Before Tor could open his mouth to advise more caution, or perhaps suggest that as a son of Ebora he should take this risk, Vostok surged forward. She and Noon passed through the barrier as smooth as silk, and were quickly reduced to snatches of scales and feathers glimpsed through the diamond-shaped holes.

Kirune didn't need to be told to follow them. Passing through the light barrier was strange – a cramp of cold moved through Tor, and then was just as quickly gone. He felt Kirune shiver underneath him. Beyond the light barrier was a sizeable island, much bigger than any they had passed so far, and it was unbelievably green and lush. A thick forest coated it from coast to coast, bristling with trees that Tor did not recognise from the northern regions of Sarn; they had huge, glossy green leaves, or were heavy with blossoms – tiny points of startling colour from where they were. The beach that they could see was capped with white sand, and even the seawater looked bluer. He blinked rapidly, wondering if he were imagining things again.

'This must be the place,' he called to Noon, who nodded vigorously. 'Shall we land?'

As they swept down, Kirune rumbled low in the back of his throat. 'There is another one of these walls of light,' he said. 'In the middle of the island.'

Tor looked up sharply, and caught a glint of something far to the north before they dipped below the treeline and approached the beach. Normally, he would be inclined to dismiss it, but Kirune had been right about the island, after all.

'Another mystery. Let's tackle them one at a time, shall we?'

27

The beach was wide and empty, and sweltering.

Once they had landed and unstrapped themselves, Noon turned back to look at the sky they had left. It was blue and hot, like the midst of high summer on the plains, but every now and then she caught a glimpse of a diamond-shaped patch of gloomier, cooler sky.

'Does this place have its own weather? What sort of magic is that?'

Tor shrugged. He was already pulling off his jacket. 'I can tell you it's not Eboran magic, at least. But I think if Micanal was looking for an unusual island, this Origin, as he called it, then this must be it.'

Vostok had stretched out on the beach, rolling back and forth so that the hot sand rubbed and cleansed her scales – Noon could feel her pleasure at that, after days of damp and cold – while Kirune had gone loping off up towards the thick line of trees. After a moment, he called them.

'There is something here. Come and see.'

It turned out to be a great number of rounded stones, sitting neatly in several rows. They were a light greenish-grey, and each one had been inscribed with what Noon recognised as

Eboran writing in an elegant hand, and each had a single leaf carved on it too.

'Well,' said Tor. He looked faintly bemused, his mouth pursed into a frown. 'We know for certain that Micanal was here, at least.'

'This is his work, then? What are they?'

For a moment, Tor did not speak. He looked up and down the row, as if he were counting the stones.

'Gravestones, Noon. They're gravestones. Each one is inscribed with a name, and a short line.' He pointed at the nearest. 'Keanla the Solemn, "forever looking homeward, my friend". And next to it, Gwidinal Brightest Song, "May the stars be bright for you".'

There were around forty of the stones, all along the shallow slope that looked out to sea. 'I mean, they're not necessarily gravestones, are they?' Noon pushed her hair back from her forehead. 'Are there any dates?'

'There aren't, but those leaves . . . A long time ago, when Ygseril was alive and we were very far from the Eighth Rain, when an Eboran died, he or she was given one of Root-Father's leaves to take into the grave with them. Death leaves. Micanal did not have any leaves to give them, but he did what he could anyway.'

'All of them, dead?' It was Kirune, his big head hanging low.

Tor sighed. 'It looks like it. We don't know the exact number of people who went with Micanal on his fool's voyage, but this certainly looks like most of them.'

'You should look and see if Micanal's name is on here anywhere, or his sister's. If he died, someone else might have taken on engraving duties.'

Tor grimaced at that, but he went and did it anyway. It was eerie, watching him walk past the stones, his head bowed to read the names, and despite the heat Noon felt a cold shiver move down her back. This place looked beautiful – the white sands, the trees thick with the scent of flowers – but it was like listening to a piece of music where one of the instruments wasn't tuned properly. Something was off.

'He's not here, and neither is Arnia.' Tor returned to her. His hair was loose and untidy from the time spent in the air, and his shirt gaped open. 'So. We know they got here, and we know a lot of them died.' He smiled lopsidedly. 'One of those good news–bad news situations, I suppose.'

'Hmm.' Noon looked at the trees. They were beautiful and lush, not Wild-touched at all, but healthy and green and welcoming. Yet something about that made her wary. *Maybe I've lived in a poisoned world too long*, she thought.

'It's been a rough few days,' she said eventually. 'What do you say to spending today resting up and eating? We can explore the island properly tomorrow.'

Tor shrugged, and they made their way back to where Vostok lay in the sand, the sky beyond flat and blue.

They slept that night on the edge of the tree line, still within sight of the sea. Noon built the fire, as usual, but kept it small – thanks to the strange warmth of the island they did not need it to heat their bodies – and together they set up the pair of oilskin tents, and then ate a good chunk of their stores. There were fruits and seeds everywhere, and small animals in the trees and in the undergrowth, and it was obvious to all of them that it wouldn't be difficult to find food here. Vostok curled her great bulk around the camp, twining her tail around the trees, and Kirune sat some distance off, watching as the shadows grew long.

'You are certain you are happy to take this first watch?'

The great cat turned his lamp-like eyes on Tor, and then just as smoothly dismissed him. 'I can watch. It is not hard. I see in the dark.'

With a shrug at that, Tor climbed into his own tent and did

what he could to make himself comfortable. Noon had already retired; he could hear her tiny, flute-like snores coming from the other tent. The separate tent. The tent that he didn't share with her. Sighing heavily, he rescued one of the smuggled bottles of wine from his pack and took a few long swallows from it. He did not expect to sleep, not after everything they'd been through, but apparently his body had different ideas. The wine eased his aches and clouded his head, and Tormalin the Oathless slipped into a deep sleep. He began to dream.

In the dream he was at home. It was the time of the crimson flux, and the sounds and smells of illness permeated everything. He was walking down a corridor in the palace, and it was dark. The lamps hadn't all been lit, and those that had been were guttering, caught in some breeze he could not feel. Everywhere was the sound of laboured breathing; wheezing and gasping and creaking, as though the very palace itself was caught in its death-rattle.

'I suppose it is,' he said softly, and then jumped at the sound of his own voice. It had yet to break. He came to a slightly open door, and saw that it led to his family suite. He stood for a moment looking at it, before pushing it open further, knowing what he would find when he stepped inside.

An overturned table. Chairs on their sides. There were dark stains on the pale rugs, and dirty glasses on every surface. On one of the sideboards there was a tall decanter, filled with something dark that wasn't blood, and on the floor there was an Eboran woman. She sat with her skirts up around her knees, and there were deep gashes at her wrists. The red pus of the crimson flux oozed from cracks that covered every inch of her skin, while the black Eboran blood of a mortal wound ran from her self-inflicted cuts.

'Mother,' he said. 'Mother.'

She lifted her head to him, and tried to smile. It was a terrible thing.

'Tormalin, my dear, could you help me with this? Help your mother now, please. Be a good boy for once.'

'I can't do that,' he said faintly. 'You know I can't. And you shouldn't ask me.'

'It's just so hard,' she said, looking back down at her bubbling wrists. She spoke as though she were complaining about getting a stain out of her gown, or mud off the windows. 'Everything is ending, so why won't I?'

'Mother . . .'

He came into the room, and this was the centre of it all for him: the yawning pit of despair had first opened up here, truly. This was where he had first thought of running, when he felt those tendrils begin to envelop him. In this room of sickness and horror.

'Just be a darling and help me, would you? Your father . . .' She stopped and her shoulders shook, but no tears came.

'Did you ask Hest this too? Was she here? No, I don't think so, because Hest would have helped you. She's never had any trouble spilling blood.'

His heart beating rapidly in his chest, Tor looked away from his mother, trying to distract himself with the details of the room. The beautiful painted wallpaper, the screen his father had made from pinkish rose-wood, the elegant ceramic shapes Hestillion had made when she was just a child. She had been so good at that, yet she hadn't kept it up. And all the time the tendrils of despair were looping around his heart, threatening to tie him here forever, to keep him in this terrible room with its terrible occupant. It was a trap. It was always a trap.

'It's been an absolute pleasure to see you again, Mother, but I really must be going.' He stepped backwards, making to leave this room, this time, this horror, when a figure at the far window caught his eye. She was standing in the gardens, looking in through the glass doors, and she was so utterly different from everything else that it very nearly kicked him out of the

277

dream altogether. Instead, the tendrils of despair fell back and the room seemed to brighten somehow. Tor stepped over his mother without looking at her, his eyes on the woman.

She was Eboran, tall and long-limbed. Her skin was a warm brown and her hair was a cloud of black curls; her red eyes were full of wonder. When he got to the door it had vanished, and then he was standing in the garden with her.

'Who are you?'

They both said it in the same moment. Tor shook his head. The dream was shifting around him, becoming insubstantial, but the woman remained unchanged. He could see every detail of her, from the faint pinkish shine on her full lips, to the delicate silver hands embroidered on her belt.

'You are in my dream!'

'Finally, someone has come.' She smiled broadly, and Tor found himself returning it. There was no resisting a smile like that. 'You have no idea . . . I thought you must all be dead, that it all ended centuries ago, but . . .' She grinned even more widely. 'You are so young!'

'No, I . . .' He looked down at himself, expecting to see the child he had been when he had first walked into that terrible room, but he was back as he should be. The woman's skin was smooth and luminous in the manner of an Eboran in full health. 'I'm no younger than you. Who *are* you?'

'If you have made it here, then surely you can guess?' Her eyes glittered, letting him know that she was teasing him. 'You can't know what this means to us, you can't. To even be able to dream-walk somewhere new.' She looked around, and for the first time a troubled expression moved over her face. 'Although this is not what I would choose, if I am honest. I am sure you will find other, less dark places for me to explore.'

Tor followed her glance. It was the gardens in early winter, crisped with frost. Even under the coating of white lace, it was

278

possible to see that things were overgrown, uncared for. There were shapes in the bushes he would rather not think about.

'I'd be glad to, my lady, if I might know—'

'We will see you soon, young prince,' she said, and then she was gone, and with her the dream was shredded into tatters. Tor woke in stuffy darkness, the wine bottle within reach of his outstretched fingers. The morning was still a long way off.

'They will find us today, I think.'

Noon looked up from her tea, her face still creased with sleep.

'Who? What? What are you talking about?'

'Sleep poorly, did you?' Tor took a sip of his own tea, enjoying the way Noon scowled at him. 'I didn't sleep too well myself, very disrupted dreams – disrupted, as it turns out, by Arnia herself.'

Vostok raised her head and peered at him, violet eyes narrowing, while Noon rubbed a hand over her face.

'Blood and fire, Tor, if you don't start making some bloody sense I swear I will—'

'She dream-walked into my dreams last night. A tall Eboran woman with black hair and brown skin. I have seen enough paintings of Arnia to know who it was, and really, who else could it be but her? It means we have found them.' He tore a bit of dried beef with his teeth. '*Mmf*. And she said "we" a lot, so I think we can assume that her brother the great Micanal the Clearsighted is still here too. And now they know that they have visitors.'

'This is extraordinary,' said Vostok. 'To think, Eborans who knew us in our previous lives, are still living here.'

'I can't believe it,' said Noon. Seeing Tor's face, she smiled slightly. 'I mean, I believe you, but I can't believe we succeeded! The map, the fucking starfish, the people on that island who wanted to kill us . . . This place was supposed to be a myth.'

Tor swallowed down his salty beef with a gulp of tea. 'Well. We don't know yet if they can help us.'

279

'Did she mention where they were? This is a pretty big place.'

'No. But they'll know we're on the coast, since we've only just arrived. She must have been casting out into the netherdark, looking for another mind, night after night.'

'What? Every night?' Noon raised her eyebrows. She had slept awkwardly on her hair and it was sticking up at the back. 'Every night for how many years? This Arnia woman would have had no idea we were coming, no reason to expect anyone would arrive after all this time, so why do that?'

Tor frowned. 'I don't know, do I? It's something to do, I suppose. In any case, I think we should stay around this area and wait for them to find us. Vostok, Kirune, perhaps you could fly up and over the forest – I expect you will give them something of a shock, but you'll definitely be visible from the ground at least.'

The dragon snorted, as though she wished to contradict him, but instead she stalked away through the trees to find enough space to unfurl her wings. Kirune stood up and stretched, muscles rippling under his grey fur, and he followed her.

'Are you sure about this?' asked Noon. She had finished her tea and was looking a little brighter now. 'How do you know you didn't just dream a version of this Arnia woman? Like, wishful dreaming.'

'How do you know you are not dreaming now?' snapped Tor. 'It is different, that's all. I know dream-walking in a way you never can, and she was as bright as a beacon on a dark night. Solid, in the way that dreams are not. I wouldn't expect you to understand.'

'I'm sure I don't,' Noon said dryly. She stood up and stretched her arms over her head until the bones in her shoulders popped. 'I will leave you to your deep and important Eboran thoughts while I go and find a bush to piss in.'

28

It was midday by the time Vostok and Kirune returned. Both seemed agitated, and when Noon ran her hand down Vostok's cool snout, she felt a static shock from the dragon.

'What is it? What did you find?'

'There is something here, certainly,' said Vostok. 'Or some-one.'

'A road,' said Kirune. 'Leads through this forest. And at the end of it, smoke, the smell of food.'

'We didn't venture any further than that,' continued Vostok. 'We saw another wall of lights in the centre of the forest, much like that which we passed through to get here, but in a dome shape. It . . . made us uneasy.'

'It made *you* uneasy?'

Vostok shook her long head and raked her claws through the dirt. 'I cannot explain it. But if Micanal and Arnia are here, they are at the end of that road.'

'We should walk it, then,' said Tor. 'If they are coming to find us, they will come that way, and we don't want to miss them.'

'If they are coming for us at all,' murmured Noon. She ignored the look Tor gave her. 'Take us to the road, Vostok.'

It was not much of a road at that, more like a wide stretch of dirt leading off into the thick forest. Trees towered to either side of them, and the place was alive with the sounds of bird-song and small furred animals calling to each other. Noon took a long, slow breath, taking in the scents of green things and living earth. Tor had washed his face and tied his hair back, and had even wrestled into a clean shirt from his pack. He looked keenly down the road, clearly expecting to come across these ancient Eborans at any moment.

'You know, this place is weird.' Noon nodded at the tree they were just passing; its leaves were fat and heavy, a green vine had grown around its trunk, and it was festooned with silky yellow flowers.

'You've just realised it's weird? Congratulations.'

'I mean, it isn't Wild. These plants and trees are exotic, but they're not mutants. Nothing here looks too big, or the wrong shape. It's just very green, and very beautiful.'

'It does not smell of the Wild,' added Kirune.

Tor grunted. 'Yes, well. Thankfully, there are still some places in Sarn as yet untouched by the Wild.'

'But, I haven't seen anything like this. Have you?' Noon bit her lip. She couldn't quite put into words what she was feeling, and Tor seemed determined to dismiss her thoughts. 'It feels different. To anything else. That's all. All this greenery. Wild without being . . . Wild.'

Tor kept his eyes on the road in front of them for that whole afternoon, clearly convinced that they would see their hosts appear there at any moment, but in the end they walked the entire stretch of dirt until they came to a grove of fruit trees. These, unlike the rest of the unruly forest, had clearly been planted by someone; they lined up in neat rows. White and pink blossoms were thick on every branch, and the tepid breeze blew small, fluttery snowstorms towards them. Beyond the grove was a large, low house made of blond wood, and to

Noon it looked like a house from one of Mother Fast's stories: something enchanted, magical, and not entirely to be trusted. Every inch of it was carved: images of trees, leaves, sea creatures, birds and animals jostled alongside figures in armour and robes. In some places the carvings were indescribably tiny and detailed, and along the windowsill tiny creatures – birds and mice and small cats – had been carved as though they were peeking in through the glass. It made her think of Eri's house, Lonefell, where every piece of furniture seemed to tell a story. The place had three chimneys, with long lines of grey smoke curling from each.

'The roof.' Tor pointed. 'Do you see? It is a ship, turned upside down. It is Micanal's ship, and these carvings are his work. They couldn't possibly be anyone else's.'

'Blood and fire.' Beyond the big house were more, similar houses, all with ships for roofs. 'They brought the ships all the way up from the beach, and turned them into their homes. They knew they would never go back, then, I'm guessing.'

'So quick to abandon Ebora,' murmured Vostok, who missed the angry look Tor cast her.

'Hello!' Noon cupped her hands around her mouth. 'Hello? Anyone there?' The wind picked up, sending a flurry of white and pink petals towards them. Kirune swiped one big paw at the blossoms, looking briefly kittenish. 'Hello!'

'You know, I don't think I will ever get tired of us going into spooky places so that you can yell hello.'

'Shut up. Hello!'

Footsteps from behind the house, coming at a run. For no reason that Noon could think of, she touched her fingertips to Vostok's neck and took a quick snatch of life-energy, but then the figure was coming around the corner of the house. The woman stumbled, and shrieked, dropping a basket she had been holding to press her hands to her mouth.

Arnia was just how Tor had described her. Tall and beautiful, with brown skin and sharp, almost sculpted cheekbones. Her red eyes were very wide, and when she pulled her hands away from her face, she was smiling widely, revealing two rows of perfect teeth.

'You are real!' she gasped, then laughed a little breathlessly. 'By the roots. War-beasts! Living war-beasts . . .' She stumbled towards them and stopped, leaning on the house wall for support. 'Forgive me, lords, ladies. I will need a moment.'

Tor went to her immediately, all charm and smiles. 'It's our honour. Arnia, isn't it? I am Tormalin, this is my friend Noon of the plains folk, and these are the war-beasts Vostok and Kirune. Why did you not come to meet us? I felt sure, after our conversation in my dream, that you would not hide away from us.'

Arnia nodded vaguely, her eyes on the two war-beasts. She seemed to be having difficulty dealing with their existence.

'Ygseril lives, then? I . . .' A rigid expression passed over her face, and then it cleared. Noon noticed that she hadn't looked directly at her at all yet, but then she could hardly keep her gaze from Vostok and Kirune. 'There is sap? You have sap in Ebora?' Her voice now was hard, almost bitter.

Tor shook his head. 'I am afraid not, my lady. It's . . . a long story.'

Arnia seemed to recover herself somewhat. 'And you've had a long journey. Oh! You must come and see my brother. He won't have heard you come. Hurry, look, come on.'

She turned and walked rapidly away from the elaborately carved house and into the trees. Noon looked at Tor, and he shrugged.

'It's what we came all this way for.'

Some distance from the house was the entrance to a tunnel, shored up with timbers that looked like they had been there some time – vines curled in and out of gaps, while a thick layer of moss had taken root on the lowest parts of the struts.

Arnia was standing outside, lighting an oil lamp. When she saw them, her eyes skittered back and forth again, as though she didn't know where to look.

'I am not certain . . .' She grimaced. 'I do not think you will fit down here, graceful ones.'

Vostok inclined her head. 'In any case, I have no affection for being underground.' Kirune didn't say anything; instead he curled his tail around himself and sat neatly on the grass.

Inside, the tunnel smelled powerfully of damp and dark earth, and the rough steps led downwards very steeply at first before levelling out into a long, low corridor. There was the sound of water dripping, and bristly tree roots hung from above, gently touching their heads with dry fingers.

'What is your brother doing down here? Is he digging for something?' asked Noon, but she received no reply. Eventually, the tall Eboran woman led them out into a wide chamber, and Noon had to fight the urge to flee. Nothing of the above forest spoke of the Wild, but this place was certainly strange, and she half expected some worm-touched monstrosity to lurch at them from the gloom. The room was a twisting maze of giant green roots, all of them glowing with a faint phosphorescent light – here and there some of the bigger roots had been carved with unsettling images; faces frozen in expressions of pain, mouths open wide to scream, or strange scuttling things with many legs. One root was covered entirely with hands, their palms open and empty. Standing in the middle of this great twisting confusion was a man with his back to them. He had his hands pressed to the roots, and on the ground by his feet was a box full of tools.

'Brother? You remember I told you visitors were coming and you didn't believe me? Well, I have brought them to you.'

The man turned and looked at them, and the first Noon saw of Micanal the Clearsighted was the terror on his face, and the shame. Like his sister, he had brown skin, but his hair was a white fuzz across a shining pate, and his red eyes were rubies lost in a web of wrinkles. He wore an old silk robe that had once been finely embroidered with dancing figures. As he looked at them, his wide mouth was pinched into an expression of dismay, then, as he took them in, it slowly fell open. His hands – long-fingered and covered in rings – were shaking. Arnia grinned, an expression of triumph on her face.

'You see? And this isn't the half of it, Micanal. Wait until you see who is waiting outside.'

'What is this place?' Tor's voice was unsteady, and looking at him in surprise Noon saw that he was deeply shaken, although she had no idea why. 'What . . .' He gestured at the lightly glowing green roots. 'What is all this? You must tell me. Is there . . . did you find the place that Ygseril came from? Is there a new tree-god here?'

The atmosphere in the cavern changed then. Arnia's triumph faded, her face becoming stony, while Micanal seemed to gather his wits. He rubbed his hands together, flaking away dirt and dust.

'Forgive me,' he said. 'I was miles away. Or at least, I wish I was.' He smiled, and his face lost all the naked confusion and terror that had been there a moment ago; instead, he looked faintly pained. 'To put you out of your misery, no, there is no tree-god here. I called this place Origin, and I still do, but . . . Never mind. Ebora lives, then? What joyous news.'

He came forward and gripped Tor's hand. 'Look at you, so young. There are others like you, I trust?'

'It's a long story,' said Tor. He was still looking past the old man to the roots. 'I am Tormalin the Oathless. You are Micanal the Clearsighted? It is an honour, lord.'

Micanal chuckled at that. He turned to Noon, smiling. 'A fell-witch? Is the Winnowry here also?'

'I'm Noon. And no, I left the Winnowry behind. I have nothing to do with them anymore.'

286

His eyes flicked up to the bat-wing tattoo on her forehead, as if the existence of that alone proved she was wrong, but he smiled and squeezed her hand anyway. His grip was surprisingly strong, and he had been strikingly handsome once – somehow the creases at his eyes and the white hair only threw that into sharper relief. He shared the same cheekbones as his sister, and he was similarly tall and long-limbed, but whereas she looked no older than a human woman of thirty, Micanal looked ancient, worn down by hundreds of long years. Hadn't Vintage said they were twins?

'There are war-beasts, Micanal.' Arnia sounded terse, and there was a hardness in the lines of her face that hadn't been there before. 'Outside, waiting to meet you.'

Micanal lowered his head, but not before Noon had seen the sparkle of tears in his faded ruby eyes.

'The dream of Ebora lives. I can barely fathom it.'

'Come, you must all have dinner with us.' Arnia was already turning away, leaving her ancient brother where he stood. 'We'll have a feast, or at least, as much of a feast as I can provide you.' She laughed, a sound like sunlight on water. 'We've all got so many questions, I doubt we'll even have time to eat more than a few mouthfuls, but I'll give you a spread to rival old Ebora.'

The sky was all colours.

Hestillion had never thought of it as such. The sky, to her, had always been the space that Ygseril's branches filled, or else it had represented a great absence – there were no more war-beasts to fly across it. When she thought of the sky at all, she thought it blue, or black, starry or sunny, and left it at that. The colour of the sky was a subject for poets, and they had all died with their words clogged in diseased chests.

But with Celaphon, the sky was a revelation. During their hesitant – and frequently disastrous – flying lessons, Hestillion had discovered the pearly silver of early dawn, the hot-anvil blue of late afternoon, the pink of mid-morning, the silent orange inferno of dusk. Clouds too, sometimes stretched across the sky like yellow lace, sometimes stacked like purple bricks, solid and ominous. It was like an entire world had opened up. They saw no birds – birds did not stay in the sky when Celaphon was flying.

The sky this afternoon was grey, blanketed with low cloud from edge to edge, and the breeze was freshening with every moment. There would be rain soon. She tipped her head back, thinking that she would welcome a good downpour; her chambers on the corpse moon had a space for her to wash in, but she was beginning to think it was impossible ever to feel properly clean in that place.

'Higher, my sweet one, if you can manage it. Let's leave the ground behind today.'

Beneath her, Celaphon's huge muscles bunched and strained, and they moved up, and up. The movement was still uncertain, and the big dragon seemed to find the idea of *rhythm* difficult, but he was managing to stay in the air for longer and longer stretches of time. She leaned forward and placed her bare hand on the scales of his thick neck.

'That is wonderful, Celaphon. You get better every day.'

'I fly,' he rumbled in response. As he had grown bigger, his small uncertain voice had been replaced with something hoarse and deep. Hestillion sometimes missed his old voice. 'It is good. It hurts, but it is good.'

'It hurts you, sweet one? What do you mean?'

But Celaphon did not answer. Instead, he beat his wings furiously, taking them up so swiftly that Hestillion found herself clinging to his harness. To fly with him she wore thick leather trousers and boots, and a dense fur vest. Her hair she tied back in a long braid, and she had even found a soft fur hat she could pull down over her ears. The queen had given this new outfit a long look, but Hestillion had lifted her head and turned away – robes and gowns were simply impractical.

'You are doing so well!' Hestillion shouted into the wind, wondering if she would lose the useful little fur hat. 'You are glorious, my sweet.'

Celaphon turned in the air – a little awkwardly, losing height – and once again the land below them came into sight. They were over the swamps of the far southeast now, a strange simmering land that Hestillion did not understand, and the corpse moon hung in the air just above the uncertain ground, not quite trusting its weight. The queen was not watching them today, or at least she was nowhere to be seen. Hestillion leaned forward in the harness, so that she could murmur directly to the war-beast.

'Take us higher, Celaphon,' she said. 'Let's see how far we can go.'

He obliged, and in moments the corpse moon was an ugly egg in the distance. The grey sky embraced them.

'Do you feel that, Celaphon? There is so much space, Sarn is so big. We could . . . we could go anywhere.'

As soon as the words were out she felt a tightening in her stomach, a sliver of panic in her belly, but the queen was not here to witness her rebellion. It was true, after all – they could go anywhere. There must be some distant corner of Sarn, some high, lonely place where no one would come for them and they could live out the last of their days together, quietly and without fuss. She began to list places, summon maps from her memory she had not thought of in years. There were mountains she had read about, further south than this; or a desert; so far away it was the other side of the world.

'And we could always keep moving,' she murmured, no longer really talking to Celaphon at all. The wind and the height were turning her hands and face to ice, but she barely noticed. 'There is no reason we should stay in one place. Just take what we want, when we want, and move on. We wouldn't have to think of Ebora, or our brother, or of Sarn at all, if we didn't wish it.'

'Hestillion?' Celaphon's voice was tight with something. She patted his neck to reassure him.

'Just think of it though! You could eat whatever you liked, we could go hunting.' She grinned at the thought of her hunting, like a human on the plains. 'The two of us alone, in peace.'

'Hestillion, we are not alone.'

'Yes, I know that, sweet one, but we could be, now that you have your wings. All we must do is make our minds up, save our strength, and then fly—'

'We are not alone *now*.'

Hestillion looked up, her heart skittering in her chest. The smooth blank greyness of the sky had been broken by several strange, pale shapes, oddly misshapen men with huge wings – more of the queen's experiments, let loose. Something in her recoiled at the sight of them, and close on the heels of that came a hot surge of despair in her chest. All her dreams of solitude and freedom seemed to boil away at the sight of the flying creatures.

'What do they want?' demanded Celaphon. The things were hanging in the sky around them, untroubled by the wind from the dragon's wings, their inky eyes expressionless.

'She is just testing them,' said Hestillion. 'The queen makes these things, and she wants to see how they work, that is all.'

'I don't like them,' declared Celaphon. 'I would eat them, if I could.'

'Well, I should imagine they would not taste pleasant, and—'

One of the creatures folded its wings and dived at them. Hestillion gave a shriek, and Celaphon dropped in the air. It wasn't quite enough to avoid the creature, which collided with Celaphon's flank before flying off again.

'What is happening?'

Hestillion turned around in the harness, looking back towards the corpse moon, but she couldn't see the queen there.

'My sweet one, I don't know. Let us just—'

All of the flying creatures began to dive at them. Celaphon bellowed, striking out with his thick legs but missing them, and they dropped again. Hestillion gave a breathy cry as her stomach collided with her throat.

'Remember the flying, Celaphon! Don't lose your focus!'

'But they vex me!'

And indeed they did. To Hestillion they looked like a swarm of biting red-fly, come to drink the blood of a much larger animal. Again and again they swept towards the dragon, colliding with him and knocking into him. Twice one of the flying men-creatures nearly knocked Hestillion from her harness – the third time, she grabbed hold of the edge of a wing and yanked it viciously, but it was greasy to the touch and it slipped away.

'Celaphon, you have to dodge them.' What was the queen thinking, to send these? Or had they escaped? 'Move out of their way, or smack them aside. You are so much bigger and stronger!'

'But I hurt.' Celaphon twisted in the air, huge wings flapping faster even as they lost more height.

'Just move! Quickly! You can outfly them.'

The queen's experiments were coming faster and faster, battering at them like fat bluebottles at a window. Hestillion shouted at Celaphon to move, to fly up out of their range, or sweep down below, but he was no longer listening. Instead, the big dragon was making ominous keening noises in the back of his throat, and there was a deep thrumming sensation working up through his muscles – Hestillion could feel it through her legs. He was, she realised, trembling.

'Celaphon, please, you have to listen to me!'

Another of the flying man-creatures landed next to her, and

Hestillion lunged for it. This time she dug her nails into its arm and dragged it towards her.

'What do you want from us?'

The creature just looked at her blankly; it was like looking for meaning in a bowl of porridge. She made an odd, guttural noise, something she was sure had never come out of her mouth before, and tore the thing's arm right off, tossing it into the void below. The winged creature looked in surprise at the tattered place where its arm had been. It had no blood or bones, just stringy white flesh.

'We are strong!' Hestillion bellowed in its face. 'Ebora is strong!'

The creature tipped backwards off Celaphon's back and was gone, but the others were keeping up their attack, and the war-beast was beyond tired. His wings shook violently with every stroke, and then they were falling out of the sky. Hestillion wrapped her hands around the harness straps and pressed her legs to his sides, wondering if this was where it all ended, after all. Instead, their descent ended in an enormous splash.

Thick green swamp water rose up on either side of them like a curtain, and then they were doused in it. Hestillion gasped – the freezing swamp mud was like a physical blow – and for a few moments she couldn't get her breath. When eventually she felt like she could speak again, she glanced up to see some tiny shapes flitting away above them. The queen's experiments were returning home. She wiped away the swamp mud from Celaphon's neck, grimacing as she did so. The stuff stank.

'My sweet one, are you all right?'

The dragon's sides heaved. His wings lay flat in the muck, looking like nothing more than a thick skin upon the swamp water.

'Pain,' moaned Celaphon. 'I hurt, so much. So much.'

'Your wings? Is that what hurts?'

292

He shuddered all over in way of a reply.

'We should leave right now,' muttered Hestillion. 'Leave these monsters behind us.' But even as she spoke she knew it was impossible. Celaphon could hardly walk, let alone fly. They were still as much prisoners as they'd ever been. Hestillion pressed her hands to Celaphon's scales, trying as ever to find a connection with him. 'My sweet one, you must listen to me. Listen to me and do what I say. That is the only way. When we were flying and those things were attacking us, you should have obeyed me. Do you understand me, Celaphon? Do you understand that you must obey?'

'But the pain.' Celaphon's voice was very close to how it had been when he was an infant. 'Everything hurts, all the time.'

Hestillion bit her lip, and then leaned down so that she was speaking next to his ear. 'I do not care about the pain,' she told him. 'You will obey me.'

'He did not perform so well, your war-beast.'

Hestillion very carefully did not turn at the sound of the voice. She was towelling off her hair, having just managed to wash all the swamp mud from it.

'You did that to us.' It wasn't really a question. 'This wasn't a random incident.'

'We thought it would be amusing,' said the queen. 'And it must learn how to fight. It won't do that jumping around in mud by itself.'

The towel was crusted with filth. Hestillion dropped it on the floor. 'Why must Celaphon learn to fight, exactly?'

'Have you forgotten what your creatures are called, Lady Hestillion Eskt? They are war-beasts. War is in their nature.'

Hestillion had taken off the leather trousers and boots, and cleaned them as best she could. The fur vest was too caked with muck to do anything with immediately, so she had left it to soak in the basin she used for her own baths, and she had changed into a simple yellow robe and black slippers. Once, these clothes, made of fine silk from Mushenska, would have been a comfort, but now she felt vulnerable in them, exposed somehow. She longed to put the leather trousers back on. Instead, she pulled her hair back from her face, still damp, and quickly tied it into a braid. That, at least, was an improvement.

'Perhaps war isn't in Celaphon's nature. We know already that he is not like the war-beasts of the past. He is gentle.'

'We do not believe you,' said the queen. She stalked fully into the room, making herself shorter in order to do so. 'But regardless. It is the time of the last extermination, we promise you that. And your people will insist on calling it war. So, your creature lives in a time of war, whether he is gentle or not. You are not gentle, Lady Hestillion Eskt, born in the year of the green bird. We saw you tear the limb from one of our creatures.'

Hestillion straightened up, meeting the eyes of the queen. 'If you did not wish them harmed, you should not have sent them to me.'

The queen grinned then, an uncanny splitting of her face. 'Good. We shall have more of these tests. My little war-queen.'

29

I have, with no small difficulty, recovered one of my coin caches, and for the first time in days we were able to sleep in proper beds, and have access to hot water. I felt better once we were behind the doors of our room, I must admit. The people in this small town are anxious and tense, and the sight of Nanthema seemed to push them in all directions. Twice during dinner, tavern customers approached us asking for news. One young man demanded to know what Ebora was going to do about the worm people, and I watched Nanthema's face grow still as she withdrew into herself. I told him we don't know. That our news is no different from anyone else's.

Later, when we were alone . . . I do not know how to write about this, but I feel I must, for my own sake, if nothing else. I have not been a hermit these last twenty-odd years. With the loss of Nanthema, I might have returned to the vine forest, but I did not sign up for any vow of celibacy – I am not some forlorn heroine in an old story, locking herself in the attic for want of her true love. I have too much to do, for a start. Yet I was reluctant, *when Nanthema came to me that night. I am older than I was, and she is as beautiful as ever – imagine your lover aging twenty years overnight . . . Imagine being the one who has aged.*

Still, war and the end of the world looming tends to put anyone in the mood, and we did share a bed that night. Was it like the old days? No, of course not, and yet there were times when I listened to her breathing and tasted her skin when I could remember them better than I have for a long time, and I will admit that for a while I was lost in that fantasy. And I believe she was too. In the morning, with a cold light streaming in through the window, she turned to me in bed and, for the barest moment, I saw an expression of surprise flicker across her face. She recovered well: stroking my cheek, she told me, 'Vintage, you age beautifully.'

Extract from the private journals
of Lady Vincenza 'Vintage' de Grazon

Once empty and filled with echoes, the ballroom of the Eboran palace now shone with treasures. Vintage stood leaning on her crutch, trying to take it all in. She had made several pages of notes already, but had had to stop when her hand started to cramp up. There was so much to see here it almost made her angry – she couldn't possibly catalogue all of it, and sooner or later Sharrik would return and then she wouldn't be able to keep the war-beast away. Everything that was newly shining with polish and fresh leather would, no doubt, be dented in minutes. She grinned.

'Did you ever think to see such a thing, Nan?'

Nanthema looked back from the window. It was another bright spring day, and the light made her look ethereal, unreal.

'You forget that I *have* seen it before. Their armour, the things they liked to wear, back when they were alive.'

'They are alive *now*,' said Vintage mildly. 'I can't wait for them to see what we have.'

'Do you think it will make much of a difference?'

Not for the first time in the last week or so, Vintage bit down a caustic reply. Just lately Nanthema had been reminding her of her eldest niece – a sulky child who had been capable of giving everyone the silent treatment from roughly the age of three, something more or less unheard of for a toddler. It was important to remember that Nanthema had witnessed the decrepit remains of her parents, and had been brought back to Ebora much sooner than she would have wished. Not looking at the Eboran woman, Vintage hobbled carefully over to the nearest piece Tyranny had brought them. It was a huge gauntlet, with long razor-sharp claws, all carefully sharpened.

'Look at this thing, it looks bloody lethal. I must say, this opens up a whole area of study I never imagined – weapons of war-beasts. I'm quite sure I've never seen anything written about them, and certainly no diagrams.' She sucked in air through her teeth. 'Of course, Nan, it *must* make a difference. Every small advantage we can get is worth chasing after, if it means we could save more lives.'

Nanthema did not reply, but Vintage could feel her scepticism like a wall of cold bricks at her back.

'Why were all of these things out in the world? Such artefacts should have been here for us to find in the first place.'

'Much of it was sold,' said Nanthema. 'What use was there in keeping it?' She took a breath and for a time some of the old light came back into her eyes. 'Long before I left, an emergency council was drawn from the survivors. It was their job to plan Ebora's survival, and it was decided that non-essential items would be sold, as quickly as possible. We were sick and dying, barely able to produce the food we needed, so we had to rely on trade. What could be more useless than the armour and trinkets belonging to the war-beasts? They were all dead.

They were not coming back. Our art and our possessions were valuable, but war-beast artefacts had never been on the market before. It was shameful, of course, so much of it was traded directly with governments and criminals, and never spoken of publically.' She smiled a chilly little smile. 'I believe that if they had lived long enough, the emergency council would have started chopping up Ygseril himself, selling him off as firewood.'

'That is incredible,' said Vintage quietly. 'And it must have been hard. Like giving away the possessions of a loved one.'

Nanthema shuddered, and Vintage turned away.

'I wouldn't need all that long to catalogue it all, make some sketches. And it's not like they can wear all of it at once, although I suspect Sharrik will certainly give it a try.'

'And when will he be coming back?' It was Tyranny, appearing at the ballroom door. The woman could walk utterly silently when she wanted to. Vintage envied her that; clacking around marble floors with a stick was so undignified.

'My dear! As I said, I am not certain when we'll see our war-beasts return, but I'll be sure to introduce them to you. The pieces are looking fine! We cannot thank you enough for your assistance with the cleaning and repairs.'

Tyranny beamed at her. 'My pleasure. Is this where the war-beasts were born? I must admit, I'd love to see the place where they came back to this world. It would feel very . . . historic.'

'Oh no, this is just a very large and handy room. Not that the Eborans are short on large rooms, as you can probably imagine. There is a special chamber for the war-beast pods, one that has always been used for the purpose.'

'And they all hatched in there?'

'Not all of them, no. And I'm sure we'll show you the room, my darling, but that will have to wait until the war-beasts have returned. It's their history, after all.' She gestured to the pieces of armour. 'Just like these are.'

Tyranny nodded, her face serious again. 'Of course, I wouldn't dream of being a pain. Actually, I popped along to ask you to dinner, Lady de Grazon.' She half turned and nodded to Nanthema too. 'And the Lady Nanthema, of course.'

'I'm busy,' said Nanthema, before the other woman had finished speaking, and again Vintage thought of her niece's stubborn face, her little brows drawn down over her wrinkled nose. Tantrum incoming.

'But *I* would be delighted, of course.'

'That's wonderful.' Tyranny smiled back. 'We brought some special foods and wines with us just in case we could convince the Eborans to eat with us. Nothing as tasty as your own vine-forest wine, I'm sure, but I've dabbled in the trade myself over the years and I'm happy to claim we've got a few bottles that you won't sniff at. Please, join us this evening.'

When the younger woman had left again, Vintage turned to Nanthema, no longer quite able to keep the frustration from her face.

'What is so offensive about dinner, exactly?'

'I don't trust them.'

'You don't trust them to make dinner?'

'Vin,' Nanthema pinched the bridge of her nose, half smiling, and the sight of it filled Vintage with hope. 'You know what I mean. What do they want here? Humans are . . . I don't really believe they are here out of the goodness of their hearts. They are too interested.'

'You underestimate the lure this place has,' said Vintage, but she also put her hand on Nanthema's arm and squeezed it. 'We are careful. They do not have the run of the palace, and all of Sarn's valuables are locked away. I have pressed several of the strapping young people Bern left behind into guard duty, and the Hatchery is watched constantly. Don't worry, Nan, your inheritance is safe from sticky-fingered humans.'

'That's not what this is about.'

'Then tell me. Please, I want to help. I care about you.'

Nanthema looked startled again, and abruptly she seemed very young – certainly she looked closer in age to a stroppy toddler than Vintage's forty-six years. Silently, she reminded herself that despite appearances, this woman was over four hundred years old.

'Vin, I have tried to explain, but you're so tied up in all this,' she gestured at the glittering pieces of armour, 'that you're not seeing it. From my point of view, I've only been away a handful of years, yet everything has changed. Ygseril is alive – at least partially – but my people are more or less dead. The palace is full of humans, and there are war-beasts in the skies again. There are *humans* riding war-beasts! Except that they are not the war-beasts of my childhood, but something lesser, something almost insulting. And you . . .'

Vintage waited, one eyebrow raised.

'And I am what, exactly?'

'Older. You are older.' Nanthema smiled faintly. 'The Vintage I left behind was desperately eager to see Sarn, desperate to leave her old life behind. That's what I liked about her. I wanted to leave the old life behind too. But you've brought me back here. And it's not just old now. It's broken.'

A swarm of sorrow and anger threatened to close Vintage's throat, so she closed her fist around the top of her stick, squeezing until the pain pushed everything else aside. She thought back to the months when she had been at home or at college, writing endlessly to Nanthema about when she could finally leave and join her. Nanthema had never, she belatedly realised, offered to come to meet her, to help her smuggle her things out of her dorm, or even to wait in the nearest village with a carriage, ready to whisk her away. Oh no. Nan had just carried on with her travels, from Reidn to Jarlsbad and back again, sometimes posting Vintage presents, things she thought she might find interesting, but never really committing to a plan. While Vintage sat at her dorm window, smelling the soaps she had sent or leafing through the pages of a new book, Nanthema had been doing exactly what she wanted to do – and that only included Vintage if she happened to be there at the time. The realisation was like a splash of cold water to her throat. Tor was self-interested too, but at least he didn't pretend to be anything else. In the end, when Nanthema had vanished, Vintage had given up on her hopes of adventure and returned to the vine forest to take up the running of the estate. If she had vanished on Nanthema, it would not have made even the barest scratch on her plans.

'The key phrase there, my darling, is "left behind". As charming as you apparently found me, you couldn't quite be bothered to wait, could you? And I am sorry if I am not as innocent or as free from responsibilities as when you left. Some of us do have to grow up.'

Nanthema shook her head. 'Humans! You think you know so much, when you are only here for a blink of an eye.' She took her glasses off again, viciously rubbed them on her sleeve, and put them back on her nose. 'I hope you enjoy your dinner.'

With that, she stalked from the ballroom, her footfalls somehow flat and empty.

The corridors were not dark and silent. Eri liked this very much. As he and Helcate made their slow way from one room to another – Helcate was large enough now for Eri to ride him with his own special harness – they passed many tall windows filled with the night sky, but always they could see the lights of the humans too, many-coloured lamps or the cheerful glow of campfires, and they heard the distant chatter of human voices. Once, Eri was sure, the very idea of even hearing a human voice would have terrified him. To his parents, humans were some sort of very special secret, a dark piece of history that it was best to leave behind – histories and conversations carefully gave only the slightest of details or left them out altogether, so in the end Eri had built a picture of them from the hole they left behind. Vintage had been the first human he had ever met. He thought that probably she had been a good one to meet first.

'I like Vintage,' he said to Helcate. 'And I like the lights and noise.'

'Helcate,' said Helcate. Somewhere nearby someone was telling a story, their voice tight with the joy of it, and then a number of people laughed, a tide crashing together.

'They spend a lot of time with each other,' Eri continued. 'I've noticed that. They like to be in big groups. Maybe it's because of how long they live. What if they try to know as many people as possible, because they might all be gone tomorrow?' Eri frowned and patted Helcate on the head. He didn't want to confuse the war-beast, and the ways of humans were confusing. 'I'll ask Vintage about it.'

'Helcate.'

They rounded another corner to see that the lamps at the end of this corridor had been extinguished, leaving the far side in a shroud of shadows. Eri and Helcate paused, looking at it. The dark did not worry Eri; in Lonefell he had gone many long winter nights with no lamps at all, because he had needed to save the oil. In those situations you either learned to love the dark or go mad – it was one of the things his father had told him, from his place in the bucket.

This was different, though. There was movement in the dark – a quick flitting of someone moving stealthily from one side to the other, and then standing, very, very still. It was so unlike all the open noise and movement outside that for the first time Eri became afraid.

'Hello? Is anyone there?'

Silence. Eri listened very hard, but all he could hear was the sound of his own breathing and the soft presence of Helcate inside his own head. That settled it, then. Everyone knew that humans always had to reply when you spoke to them – they loved speaking so much, they could not help themselves. Humans did not understand what silence was at all.

Eri turned Helcate aside, and they sought out the brighter lights of another corridor.

With the war-beast armour removed from it, the caravan was warm and cosy. Every surface was filled with cushions, the walls draped with tapestries – gaudy, certainly, but finely made. Vintage ran her thumb over one, noting the tiny silk stitches.

'The silk of Reidn can't be bettered, in my opinion, although don't let Tor hear me say that. I must admit, my dear, when you asked me to come to yours, I did think you would mean your rooms in the palace.'

Tyranny looked up from the glass goblets she was polishing. Through the open back doors, Okaar stood over a neat little cooking fire, stirring something thick in a pot, and beyond them it was possible to see all the small human encampments making their dinners for the night in the Eboran palace gardens.

'Not that I'm complaining,' added Vintage quickly. 'This is an utterly charming location for dinner. And goodness knows, I have seen enough of the inside of that place lately.' She tapped on the wooden crutch for emphasis.

'Are you comfortable enough?' Tyranny passed a glass of pale golden wine. 'I can always get more cushions. It's a bumpy journey from Jarlsbad and we like to be well padded.'

'I'm absolutely fine, my dear.'

'We thought it would be easier for you to get to know us if you saw us in our home,' continued Tyranny. She had poured herself a glass, and was peering at the liquid closely, as though it owed her money. 'I mean, I move around a lot, so this caravan has become a sort of home, and Okaar has become my family.'

303

Vintage nodded, sipping her wine. It was a good, if not especially subtle, way of getting her out of the palace. She thought of all the burly and skilled men and women standing guard on various doors, and her smile deepened.

'Where is your young friend whom I saw here before?'

To her surprise, Okaar answered. His voice was still soft, but it carried easily enough from the cooking fire. 'Jhef has grown close to some of the other young people here. She is of an age where she would rather chase moonbugs than eat. They run wild together.'

'I was the same when I was a kid,' said Tyranny, half a wistful note in her voice. 'Head to toe in mud and filth, ragged and big-eyed and no real morals to speak of.' She grinned. 'I like kids.'

'Jhef is your sister, Okaar?'

The lithe young man began to serve the stew into bowls. His every movement, Vintage noticed, was measured and precise. He would, she knew, serve everyone exactly the same amount of stew.

'You are very observant, Lady de Grazon. She is my youngest sister.'

'Many siblings?'

'Many.' He brought the bowls into the caravan, navigating the steep steps with no difficulty. Vintage kept her eyes on him, watching closely. She could not quite make out what his relationship with Tyranny was, but it did not appear to be romantic.

'This stew is wonderful.' And it was. Vintage had tasted spices like this before, on some of her furthest travels, but never combined in such a way. 'You are a talented cook, Okaar.'

'What do you think of the wine?' asked Tyranny. She nodded at Okaar. 'We have a bet on, you see. Okaar thinks it won't be sophisticated enough for your palate, but I spent a bloody fortune on that bottle, and if I know anything, it's that you pay for quality when it comes to booze.'

'It is very fine. From the northern region of Crest? My father used to insist that they get a different quality of light up in the northern hills, and that's why the grapes produce such a delicate flavour. Tell me, Tyranny – for such a young woman you seem to have fingers in a lot of pies. Who are you? Really?'

To the young woman's credit she only looked surprised for the briefest second, and then she covered it up with a rueful smile. Vintage, knowing she would be tempted to fill the silence, drained off her glass of wine without a blink. If they wanted to get her drunk, they would need to open a few more cases yet.

'You're a clever woman, Lady de Grazon. You have something of a reputation for it, after all. But there is nothing much more to know about me, I promise. I am what I said I am, a woman who found something interesting, and decided to make a business out of it.'

'Why Tyranny, then? Tell me why they call you that.'

This time there was a flicker of discomfort, visible in the way her pale-blue gaze shot to Okaar, in the way she shifted her shoulders.

'Well, Lady de Grazon, I'll be honest with you, that's not a very nice story, and it doesn't – how would you put it? – show me in the best light.'

'Please, darling, call me Vintage. A story with blood, is it? I assure you, I have a strong stomach. And this is a time of war. Perhaps we need people with some bloody stories in their past.' She reached over and refilled her goblet herself. It *was* very good wine.

'If it puts you off Okaar's excellent stew, then don't blame me.' Tyranny was still smiling, her posture still relaxed, but nevertheless there was a new tension here. Vintage sensed that the young woman was giving up something valuable by telling this story, but that she had decided the stakes were worth it. Interesting.

305

'I grew up in Mushenska, I've already told you that. I was a street scrap, a pocket shark, but I kept my head down then. When I was fourteen or fifteen, I joined a gang called the Salts, run by a woman called Reanne O'Keefe. It was a good place to be, because the Salts were feared and respected, and all the alleys of Mushenska seemed a little drier and a little safer while I was there. We did all sorts of jobs, but mostly stealing to order. "Go to this big house, take this fancy thing, bring it back here to be sold on." The only problem with being a Salt was O'Keefe herself. She was a bloody nightmare.'

Tyranny grinned, and Vintage got a glimpse of the child she had been: old before her time, sharp and street-tough.

'A temper like you wouldn't believe. She distanced herself from the main population, like, but sometimes she would make a flying visit, and we would all try to stand in the darkest corner because if she caught your eye, it was likely you'd get a beating for it. You'd be looking at her the wrong way, you see. She had a couple of associates who did the day-to-day running of the gang, but I don't think she was close to them, either. And everyone wanted to be a member of the Salts, so if she needed to have someone taken outside and beaten to a pulp, or just have their eyes cut out, or whatever, there was always someone eager to take their place.'

Vintage dropped a meaty lump back into her stew with a plop.

'Anyway, O'Keefe had this warehouse out on the docks. She'd bought both the places next to it too, and kept them empty, and anyone who particularly offended her, she'd take them to this warehouse. The Hole, we called it, because no one who went in there ever came out again. Sure, if she had someone's legs broken, you'd see them hobbling around afterwards, begging for small coins, or the ones she'd blinded would gather behind the fish stalls. You always know where you are, with that smell, and sometimes the mongers would pass you scraps. But if you got taken to the Hole, you were never seen again.'

'I knew Mushenska had its criminal element,' said Vintage. 'But this seems somewhat . . . extreme.'

Tyranny shrugged. 'It's a big city, the biggest on Sarn, I've heard some say. You can hide a bloody lot in a place like that. And who cares about some blinded pickpockets? Anyway, my particular friend, Aaron, he came a cropper with O'Keefe. When out stealing one day, he'd found these drawings, you see. Drawings of nude people. Happy nude people. I'm sure you get what I mean?'

'I do.'

'Well, we were still young enough to find this funny – more than funny, really, we were in fits over it, and Aaron had even found a bit of charcoal somewhere and had started *adding* to the pictures. We happened to be laughing over these drawings when O'Keefe made a surprise visit to the gang-house. She found us, in a corner, wheezing and clutching at each other in mirth. You know how, sometimes, when a situation is very serious indeed, it can be even harder not to laugh? Well, I very nearly pissed myself that day, with the effort of keeping the giggles in. O'Keefe was not amused. She declared Aaron for the Hole, and he was dragged away. Done and dusted.'

'She didn't punish you?'

'I don't think she even saw me. Aaron was holding the papers, and he had the charcoal. I've never seen a rage like it. The poor little bugger.'

Tyranny stopped. She seemed to have lost her taste for the story, and instead poured herself another glass of wine. Okaar had finished his stew and was sitting very still, his face expressionless.

'So.' Tyranny cleared her throat. 'I got it into my head that I had to save Aaron from the Hole, and I'd always been good at sneaking. I got some soot and grease and covered up my face and head,' she briefly touched her free hand to her blond hair, 'because this caught the light too much. I went quickly, using all the short cuts I knew, running so fast I don't think I even breathed once, and I came up to that row of warehouses with the Hole in the middle, and I slipped past the Salts guarding it, easy as that. In through a window, into the dark. That place – I can still smell it.'

When Tyranny didn't continue, Vintage cleared her throat. 'What did it smell of?' But the young woman just shook her head.

'There was nothing there, just three floors of darkness and dust, and that smell, until eventually I heard voices coming from the cellar, and light coming from cracks in the door. I heard Aaron shriek, just once, and I think it was the bravest thing I ever did in my life, opening that door. I was just a slip of a thing then, it was easy enough to get around a door and close it again, but none of them were looking at me anyway.' She had another sip of wine. 'The basement had a stone floor, and in the middle of it was a deep pit. The Hole really was a hole, you see. From the top of the old stairs, I could already see that they had thrown Aaron into it. I wasn't armed, save for my little sticking knife, and there were three of them. I wonder what I thought I was going to do. I do wonder that sometimes.' Tyranny smiled faintly, as if she wished she really could ask. 'Anyway, Reanne O'Keefe touched one of her guards on the hand, and he staggered. And then she stepped up to the pit, and she sent green flames shooting from her hands – endless waves of them, over and over, curling over Aaron and turning him crispy and black. He screamed for a bit, but not that long really. I reckon his throat was all burnt up pretty quick, and when he was dead, she kept burning him, on and on until there was nothing, nothing but ash and a few sticks of bone that didn't even look like bones anymore. And that was why anyone who went into the Hole vanished.'

Vintage nodded slowly, watching the young woman closely. 'She was a fell-witch.'

'She was. And that was her secret. That's why she wasn't close to anyone, and that's why she hated anyone that was. She had to hide it all the time, in case the Winnowry came for her.'

'What did you do?'

'I ran from that gods-cursed place and went straight to the Winnowry offices. I told them who Reanne O'Keefe was, and where they could find her, and extracted promises that I would be protected. Several Winnowry agents came for O'Keefe in the end, and that whole row of warehouses was burned down in the process. The pit in the stone floor was still there – is still there, if you go and look. I used to throw any rude pictures I found into it, to keep Aaron's poor old ghost entertained.'

'And what became of O'Keefe?'

Tyranny shrugged. 'Who cares? Probably rotting in a cell in that big, ugly, fucking building, or doing the Winnowry's dirty work. Eventually I told the Salts what I had done, and what O'Keefe had been doing, and how I intended to run them from now on. That's when they started calling me Tyranny. It was a little bit of a joke, you see. No matter what sort of a cold bitch I was, I was nothing to the tyranny of O'Keefe and her Hole.'

Vintage poured herself another glass of wine. A companionable silence grew in the small caravan, while outside the sounds of other people cooking and talking drifted through the still night. Somewhere, Nanthema was sulking, no doubt, or perhaps she had snuck off to carry on her own adventures in a place very far from Ebora. At this thought, Vintage felt a thin dagger of sadness pierce her heart. The world was so full of sorrows and pains, why did they have to add to it? She resolved to be more understanding of Nan's concerns.

'And what of the Salts? Are they still your gang?'

'Oh, I left them behind a while ago, although I daresay there's a chair there for me at the dinner table, should I ever need it. It's a hard job, running the streets of Mushenska, and it makes you a hard woman. Selling things to the rich – goods or unusual experiences – is a much less unsavoury job.'

'And now you are gifting your wares. For the war effort, no less. Your story is one of slow redemption, Tyranny Munk.'

The young woman lifted her glass to that, but the smile on her face did not quite melt the ice in her eyes. 'You could say that. We'll have to wait and see, I suppose.' She lifted a finger and pushed some strands of blond hair across her forehead. 'Perhaps your war-beasts, when I meet them, can provide me with some sort of peace.'

For the first time, Vintage caught a change in Okaar's expression that did not look calculated – he covered it up swiftly enough, his dark-brown eyes becoming impassive once more, but it had been there, Vintage was sure. Something Tyranny had said here had not been agreed between them previously, and Vintage suspected that much of what they said was carefully rehearsed and planned. She filed that thought away for future consideration.

'I shall drink to that,' she said, and raised her glass.

30

When the giant stone fell, it cracked with a sound like an avalanche. Beneath Aldasair, Jessen flinched, and he twined his fingers through her fur as much to reassure himself as her. Next to him, riding easily on Sharrik's harness, Bern muttered under his breath.

'Stones be damned, that's hardly good.'

'What is it?'

Bern nodded to where the huge stone had landed. The thing had toppled off the row of logs they had been using to transport it away from the Broken Field, and although it hadn't fallen on any of the Finneral men and women there – who had been very sensibly keeping far back – it had shattered into three large pieces. 'It's bad luck for the sacred stones to shatter like that, and three is an unlucky number too. They'll all be shaking their heads over this around the campfires tonight, that's for sure. Another bad omen in a place riddled with them.'

'It's going well, though.' And that was true. Over the last few days they had, very gradually, been moving the giant rocks and the great flat pieces of stone away from the field, exposing the broken Behemoth beneath. It was an extremely tense process; with each piece moved, they waited for the Jure'lia creature beneath to surge into life, or for the black fluid that shifted underneath it to take some terrible form. Aldasair was sure that they were all waiting for a swarm of burrowers to begin leaking through the gaps to eat them from the inside out, but even so the Finneral men and women worked steadily, bringing their horses and their equipment to get the job done. Aldasair thought they were very brave. And every time a stone was lifted, he and Bern were there, with the war-beasts, ready to take down anything that looked too lively. So far, there had been nothing; every time they got close, the black fluid would rapidly drain away from them, leaving the dented and strangely soft-looking pieces of the Jure'lia ship, oily and unsettling to look at. They had found no bodies. Aldasair wasn't certain if this was good or bad news.

'Hoy, boys. How about some lunch?' Rainya was approaching them, riding her enormous bear. Her golden hair was tied into a tail at the back of her head, and she was carrying a sack, which she threw to Aldasair. To his own surprise, he caught it.

'What's next, Ma?'

'You see that long flat rock in the middle there? Reckon you and Sharrik could manage by yourselves? Our poor animals are knackered.'

'We are very strong!' declared Sharrik, puffing out the thick blue and grey fur on his chest. 'We can move it easily. We do not even need lunch.'

'Well I need lunch,' said Bern. Aldasair opened the bag, and threw the bigger man a bread roll from it. Inside Bern's big fist the thing looked tiny, so Aldasair threw him another one, before tearing into one himself.

'The Stone Talker sends her thanks,' said Lady Rainya quietly. 'She's been watching all this, from a distance, as ye ken, and she says that although the ghosts are restless, it seems that peace may be possible here after all.'

312

'*Hmph*,' said Bern, around a mouthful of roll. 'Let's not plan any parties yet.'

As though he had summoned it, a man in the centre of the field began to shout and wave. Aldasair jumped down from Jessen and passed the bag of rolls back to Bern's mother. Bern joined him, and together they moved rapidly to where the man was standing. He was a short man with a shock of carroty hair, and as they got closer Aldasair realised he had been crying; his face was wet and his eyes were red and swollen.

'I can hear her,' he said as they each climbed down from their war-beasts. 'I can hear Terralah under there. She says she can't shout, because the weight is on her chest. She's under the stone.'

'A woman is under there?' The stone was long and thin, the very same one Rainya had pointed out to them moments ago. To either side of the stone it was possible to see the oily silver-green pieces of moon-metal where the Behemoth was gradually being revealed, but they were ripped at the edges, ragged.

'She can't be,' said Bern, not unkindly. 'I'm sorry, Rold, I really am. How long have you been out here, man? Take yourself off, have a drink. It's too hot, and you know you burn easily.'

For a moment Aldasair thought that perhaps this small man, Rold, would strike Bern, but instead he dissolved into more tears.

'I can hear her, Bern, so, it's her very own voice. Come here and listen. Listen. Please. If you don't hear it, I will go and have a drink, and a sit-down, as you say.'

Stepping cautiously over the moon-metal, Aldasair approached the edge of the flat stone. Behind them the men and women were still working to move the shards of the sacred rock, but their calls and shouts fell oddly flat here; the Broken Fields did seem to absorb the voices of the humans. Bern sighed, squeezing Rold's shoulder gently.

313

A dry voice, like a thing made of old leaves, dry and wracked with pain, faintly called, 'Help me. Please. You have to . . . I need to get out, please. Please.'

'By the stones,' moaned Rold. 'You hear her now? Please, Bern, please.'

Bern had turned the colour of porridge, but he carefully moved Rold to one side and approached the stone himself.

'Terralah? Terralah sweetheart, is that you now?'

There was a low hissing noise, like air escaping from something. Gingerly, Aldasair got to his knees and peered under the edge of the rock. There was a dark space below there, thick with shadows. Anything could be under there, waiting. Anything at all.

'I can see something . . .' Aldasair pressed his face to the gap, trying not to breathe in the strange sickly scent of the Jure'lia. 'I can just about . . .'

As his eyes adjusted to the dark, he saw it. The white curve of a shoulder, a dimmer space amongst the shadows, and a portion of white forehead, eyes lost beneath it. He saw the woman move, just slightly; she must be pinned with terrible force. He scrambled to his feet.

'She's under there. We have to move the stone now, Bern.'

Sharrik was there immediately, thrusting his huge curving beak under the edge to get a purchase, while he and Bern took the sides. Aldasair saw the man Rold staring at him, and knew what he was thinking as clearly as though it were written on his face: Aldasair was skinny, weak-looking. How could he help lift such an obstacle?

'I am strong,' he said across the stone. 'I am stronger than you, than any human.' He nodded in what he hoped was a reassuring manner, but Rold only looked confused.

'Carefully!' he cried when the stone began to shift. 'You could crush her still.'

In the end, they flipped the long flat stone rather than lifted

314

it, and underneath it a young woman lay on her belly, her long yellow hair pressed to her back. Even to Aldasair, who knew little of such things, she did not look well; the lower portions of her legs had been crushed so that the flesh was black and purple, and torn. Shards of bone were poking through the skin, and her feet were mere shreds of flesh. Likewise, the skin on her arms was strangely livid. Rold reached down for her, his hands shaking.

'Terralah? Terralah, you're free. You're free my love.'

The young woman turned her head, and it was all wrong – a slippery, boneless movement – and when her hair fell away from her face, they saw that her eyes were empty holes, the edges shining with a tarry black substance. Even so, she grinned at them.

'Freerer than you know,' she said in her voice of dried leaves.

Rold fell back with a cry, but Bern was already there, one of his axes held high over his shoulder, and he brought it down without hesitation, severing the woman's head from her neck. It rolled a short distance away, thankfully falling so that the hair was covering its face, and in the violence of it the body itself moved, revealing something smooth and glass-like underneath.

'That's why they were taking people?' Bern sounded sick, and he was glaring at the edge of his axe as though he'd never be able to make it clean again. 'As what, a joke? A way to upset us?'

'What is this?' Using his foot, Aldasair cleared some of the rubble away. The object underneath the woman was still partially buried, but it looked like a huge green crystal, and strange lights moved in its depths. 'Did not Vintage say something about crystals within the Jure'lia ships?'

'I want a place on the harness to store weapons.'

Hestillion lifted her chin, expecting this request to meet some

315

mockery, but the queen said nothing, her mask-like face unmoving.

'When you mentioned that our war-beasts were always paired with an Eboran companion that was correct, but of course they were also warriors. They fought alongside their war-beasts and, yes, died alongside them. If you insist on testing Celaphon with your hideous creations, then I insist I be permitted to help him. I am no warrior, and I did not study the martial arts as Tormalin did,' she paused to swallow the knot of pain produced by the thought of her brother, 'but if I must learn as Celaphon learns, then so be it. And you know I am of no threat to you, even armed, since you control every inch of this place – are you even listening to me?'

The queen's stillness had become unnerving. It was as though she had become a statue between eye blinks.

'Do you hear what I say?'

The queen roused herself, her long neck bending towards Hestillion. 'A signal. Another part of us has awoken.' She turned, and the portion of wall directly behind them become transparent. Beyond it, Hestillion could see the forests of what-ever land they happened to be over now; she had lost track again.

'Somewhere far to the north, another part of us is waiting.'

'You sound much warmer when you speak of these other parts.' Hestillion watched the queen's face closely for a reaction. The lines around the corners of her eyes grew momentarily tighter.

'The temperature of our voice is not subject to change.'

Hestillion surprised herself by laughing. Her chest felt light, too light, but it had been such a long time since she'd experienced anything as simple as laughter.

'That is not what I mean, and I think you know that.'

The queen straightened her shoulders.

'We have spoken of it before. The connection we feel, that

316

you feel to your brother. No matter how distant he is, you feel it. You long to reaffirm that connection.'

'Don't apply your logic to me,' said Hestillion sharply. 'There is little I would like to reaffirm with my brother.'

'Even so, Lady Hestillion Eskt, born in the year of the green bird, I think that you understand what we feel.' The queen stalked over to the greasy transparent panel, and touched it with the pointed ends of her fingers. 'We'll go to this place immediately, and collect that which has been missing.'

31

'I have eaten so much I might actually die.'

'Shut up.' Noon threw a piece of fruit at Tor, which bounced off his shoulder. Arnia had been as good as her word, and had thrown them a feast that rivalled even the food at the Sea-Heart Inn. They had eaten it all on a long table outside the house with the ship for a roof, and now they sat and watched as Micanal walked with Vostok between the trees. Arnia herself had not eaten much of her food, and disappeared soon after dinner, murmuring something about some tasks she could not leave undone. It was difficult, Noon reflected, not to feel a sense of peace here, as the sun set through the leaves, and the warmth of good food spread through their bellies. All of which just put her more on edge.

'I am serious,' said Tor. 'It won't be the crimson flux that carries me off, or extremely advanced old age. It will be that pie. I don't even know what that fruit was, but I wish to eat it every day forever.'

'Where do they get all this stuff?' said Noon, looking at the remains of the spread, which had included meats and cheeses and even a sort of sour wine. 'And where is everyone else? Are you telling me that Arnia makes all this cheese herself?'

'Please do not ruin a perfectly good cheese by worrying about where it came from.'

Noon snorted at him, and looked back at Vostok. The dragon was talking quietly with the old man, even lowering her head in a deferential way, which only made Noon feel more ill at ease. Kirune was asleep in front of the fire; at least the big cat did not change his ways so easily.

'Arnia and Micanal didn't come here alone. What happened to the people in those graves we saw? And wine – I'm sure Vintage would be able to tell us how much effort goes into making a bottle of wine, but even I know you don't just milk it from a wine-cow. Are you even listening to me?' She smacked Tor on the knee, and he jerked back into an upright position. He had been on the verge of falling asleep.

'Look, it's been a long bloody journey, Noon. There will be answers, I'm sure of it. I have questions myself. Why does the lovely Arnia look as fresh as a newly ripe fruit, for example, but Micanal is so frail? Why did they come here? And why did they stay?'

'And what's with the weird bloody field of lights around the island?'

'That as well. I hope they have more of this wine, because I sense we will get through a lot of it.'

'If she comes to you in your sleep again, tell me.'

Tor raised an eyebrow. 'My dreams are private, thank you very much.'

'When it suits you, perhaps.' Noon turned to him, trying to make him meet her eye. 'Something weird is going on here, and I don't think it's entirely safe. Micanal looked less than pleased to be found in that underground cavern, and Arnia's face when she realised Ygseril is alive . . . We've only got tiny pieces of the story here. Vintage would tell us to be careful.'

Tor sighed heavily. The scarring on the right side of his face had faded a little, she realised, and his hair had almost entirely grown back. Her blood had helped, perhaps, or it could even be Kirune's influence; they understood so little about the link between war-beasts and their companions. Thinking of this, she reached out towards Vostok with her mind; the dragon was calm, if intensely curious. As though she had somehow summoned them, the old Eboran and the dragon turned and headed back towards the house. Micanal looked very grave, and a shade paler than he had during dinner.

'The lady Vostok has explained some of what has brought you here, and my heart is both joyful and wounded. To know that war-beasts live once more in the world, and that they suffer so . . . More and more I feel that the long lives of Eborans are a curse, that we should live long enough to see this.' Noon frowned slightly. Vostok had told him everything already, which was unusually trusting for the dragon. 'She also told me that you came here in the hope of being able to see my great final project – the history of the war-beasts, which I was preserving within the amber tablets. Well –' He stopped, and pressed his lips together as though he didn't trust himself to speak further. 'You are right; I did bring them with me when we left Ebora all those years ago. I thought that this sacred place would lend a kind of magnificence to the project, and that whatever answers we might find here about Ygseril would help to complete it.' He smiled bitterly. 'What a fool I was. Come, please, the two of you, walk with me. I know it grows late, but now the idea is in my head I know I will not sleep until I have shown this to you, and when you get to my age you need your sleep quite desperately.'

Noon glanced at Tor, who looked about as nonplussed as she felt, and together they followed the old man back towards the trees. When Vostok made to follow, Micanal turned to her apologetically.

'My lady, I am afraid that the trees will grow very dense here, and it will not be a comfortable journey for you. I am

320

sure that your companions will explain everything to you when they return.'

The shadows within the trees were thick, and, all around, the birds were singing the sun down. Noon felt as though they walked through the body of a great living thing, something made of lots of separate parts, each with its own inner life. The last time she had felt like this had been when they had walked through the belly of the Behemoth on Esiah Godwort's land, but there she had felt threatened, too. This island seemed to offer the opposite of that. She didn't trust it.

'Where are we going, Micanal?'

The old man looked at her. In the growing dark, she couldn't see his eyes.

'There is a place I must show you, and there I will explain what I can.'

'Well, as long as we don't need to be able to actually see the place.' Tor squinted up at the canopy, where the patches of sky were turning violet. The day took a long time to die here, but Noon suspected the nights would be very dark indeed. 'We'll be stumbling around in the pitch-black soon enough.'

'Perhaps, then, your good friend could light the way?'

When Noon turned to the old Eboran in surprise, he touched her arm lightly, just once. 'We had fell-witches in Sarn during my time in Ebora. Little about their ways have changed, it seems.' He tapped his forehead.

'Oh.' Noon reached up and attempted to pull her fringe over the tattoo, knowing what a pointless gesture that was. 'Fine. What were the Winnowry like in your day, Micanal?'

Micanal looked down at his feet as they trudged through the undergrowth. 'They were powerful. Unbending. We did not see them often in Ebora. As I'm sure you know, the gift of the winnowfire is one that Eborans do not possess. But I travelled widely in my youth and would see them. I even heard about their actions during the Sixth Rain, when, briefly, they fought

321

alongside us against the Jure'lia, and I can tell you that they were not thought kindly of by our people.'

Noon pressed her hand to a tree trunk as they passed and siphoned off a little of its green life. It tickled against her palms.

'I don't think they're thought kindly of by anyone,' she said. 'Least of all by the women they imprison.'

Micanal nodded, but did not venture a further opinion. For a time they walked in silence, and when it became impossible to see where they were putting their feet, Noon summoned a small ball of winnowfire to dance just above her fingertips. The forest was revealed to them anew, in shades of emerald.

'The light!' said Micanal. 'It is so beautiful, in its way. I have known these trees for centuries, yet they look quite different. I should like to paint it so.'

'Micanal,' Tor cleared his throat, 'when I read about the Golden Fox expedition, it always said that you took a good number of our people with you. I don't mean to be rude, but where is everyone? Did . . . did the disease take them all in the end?' Then he spoke quickly, as though to cover up any pain his words might have caused. Noon noticed he did not mention that they had found the gravesite. 'The palace was decimated, with no more than one or two from each family surviving, and sometimes not even that.'

The old Eboran bowed his head, as though dealing with some physical hurt, and for a long time he didn't say anything.

'Yes,' he said eventually. 'They all died of the flux. We were very unlucky.'

In the greenish gloom, Noon tried to catch Tor's eye. The old man was lying. Why would he lie about that?

'Their bodies,' she said quickly, 'did you bury them?' Micanal looked startled, so she continued. 'It's such a tragedy. We might like to pay our respects.'

'I . . . This is very difficult for me to talk about. Perhaps

322

we could continue this discussion another time. Please, walking this far is not so easy for me these days. Forgive me if I must walk in silence.'

It was another hour before Micanal spoke again. The night fell thick and suffocating, and Noon found herself looking up at the night sky, seeking out the stars as some sort of comfort. The air around them seemed to be alive with insects – their trilling calls, the buzzing brush of their bodies against bare skin – and her back itched and tingled to be within four walls again. *You were stuck in a cell for ten years*, she reminded herself. *Don't let a few bugs put you off your freedom.*

'Here, it is just here.'

Noon jumped slightly at the sound of the old man's voice. 'Please, be careful. It could be easy to miss in the dark, and that would be unfortunate.'

Lifting the winnowfire to light the way ahead, Noon saw that the ground fell away just in front of them, and they stood on the edge of a great crevasse. The island continued some fifty feet away; she could just make out the far side, with its sheer cliff facing them. There was the sound of running water coming from below. Abruptly, she felt it was very important not to be within arm's reach of Micanal. She took a few soft steps back.

Tor, however, had gone right up to the edge of the cliff and was peering over into the black.

'Unfortunate is right. This is an impressive drop.'

The old man nodded. He seemed to be finding it difficult to talk again. As casually as possible, Noon leaned against a nearby tree and siphoned off some of its life energy, while keeping her eyes on Micanal. If he made any sudden moves, she could simply blast him off the cliff. Somewhere, distantly, she felt Vostok responding to the tension thrumming through her, but she pushed the dragon away.

'Micanal, what does this place have to do with your project?'

He looked up at her as though he'd forgotten she was there, and she felt a pang of shame. He was ancient, and clearly struggling with something, and she was planning to set him on fire. *I guess that's my answer to everything.* The old man turned back to the cliff face, and sighed.

'This is where it is. Down there. I threw it down there, oh, years ago. If the river hasn't carried it out to sea, that's where it still is.'

Tor stood up straight, clearly startled. In the light from the winnowfire he looked both impossibly handsome and utterly indignant.

'You did *what*?'

'Forgive me, I must sit for a while. My knees are staging a rebellion these days.' Micanal, with some awkwardness, seated himself on the dirt floor. His knees popped like knots in the fire. When he was settled, he waved at them both with a touch of impatience. 'Are you two just going to loom over me like that?' With a smile in his voice he added, 'Have some respect for your elders.'

Reluctantly, Noon sat, although she still made sure that she was out of the old man's reach. Tor sat next to her, leaning on her shoulder briefly to lower himself to the ground. Much to her own annoyance, she felt a burst of warmth at this unexpected touch.

'I could not finish the project,' said Micanal. 'It was as simple as that. Young woman, you cannot guess at the despair we felt as we left Ebora, sure we were leaving it to its ruin, but there was hope, too. We – I – was sure this place would be the rebirth of our people, a place to find a new start. I wanted to take our past with us into that new start, and the most impor-tant part of that was the war-beasts. They had been our companions for as long as we could remember, a living, breathing part of Ygseril, and century after century they had fought with us and died for us. They are honour in its purest form, a weapon and a shield.' He paused to cough into his hand. 'Ygseril and the war-beasts are so closely bound. With the tree-father dead, I knew that if we found a new tree-god here, on Origin, the war-beasts born from them would likely not know their own histories, so I saw it as my duty to give them that record. To paint the lost war-beasts, in dreams, for all the Eborans that were to come.'

'That is exactly what we need,' said Tor, leaning forward. 'Our war-beasts don't remember their past lives. With this history of yours, they could learn it.'

'What *did* you find here?' asked Noon. 'Because I'm guessing it wasn't another tree-father.'

'If we had known that Ygseril was shamming death, well . . .' He seemed to lose the sense of what he was saying, then, but Noon noticed he had not answered her question, or even acknowledged that she had spoken. 'It was to be my greatest work, and indeed I completed a great deal of it on the journey here, locking myself away in a cabin. Sea voyages are so dreary.'

'I have never been in a boat, so I wouldn't know,' said Noon. 'What did you find on this island, Micanal?'

The old man sighed. 'We did not find another tree-father. That is not what we found. The hope that we could start anew died with our friends as the flux came for them, and eventually working on the war-beast record became tortuous for me. To look at their glorious forms, and to know that they were lost forever to history, was too much. One day, I came here to this crevasse, and I threw all the amber tablets down here. Even if I regretted it, I would not be able to fetch them back. By that time, old age had its painful fingers in my joints and I was no longer capable of even attempting to climb down such a cliff.'

'Arnia could have, though,' said Tor.

The old man blinked, and scowled, so briefly that Noon almost missed it. 'Arnia has never had the slightest interest in my work, and certainly would not risk herself to retrieve something I did not want anymore.'

Next to her, Noon could feel Tor wanting to ask another question, but something was holding him back. *No new tree-father*, she thought. *So no sap. Then why has Arnia not aged as her twin has?*

'You were our greatest artist,' said Tor softly. 'Micanal the Clearsighted, it pains me to hear that you discarded what must be a work of supreme genius.'

Micanal smiled slightly at that. 'You are kind.' He sighed, and all the wind seemed to go out of him. All at once, the old man seemed smaller, less mysterious. Just an old man at the end of his life who had seen everything he cared about destroyed or ruined. 'It is good to see your face, you know. A young Eboran face. That, at least, is a blessing I did not expect.'

'So, what we came here for, is down there?' Noon nodded towards the crevasse. In the dark, it was little more than a yawning absence next to them, a difference in the air.

'Yes. At least, I assume it is. Ygseril's amber is quite heavy and it could well be exactly where it landed, all those years ago. Or perhaps the current has moved it, or animals might have burrowed under the pieces. I am afraid I could not tell you. Since I threw them away, I have not been back here.'

Noon looked at Tor. 'Then we could get them back. Easy enough to fly down there with Vostok and Kirune and have a hunt around in the mud.'

'Hunting around in the mud, my favourite. It's just like being back with Vintage.' Tor cleared his throat. 'Micanal, you do not object to us retrieving your work?'

Noon sat up. She wanted to kick Tor. There was more at stake here than the ego of an old man. And if he objected, how could he stop them exactly? But Micanal shrugged.

'Do not ask me to look on them again, but other than that,

326

you can retrieve them with my blessing. I would recommend doing it in daylight, however.'

'Good idea.' Noon stood up, and picking a tree nearest the edge of the cliff, pulled life force from it until the bark under her hand grew blackened and flaky. She repeated the process with several of its neighbours. 'There. We should know this place when we return, so that you don't need to come back with us.' She walked to the edge of the cliff and released the winnowfire she had built within her chest in a big blast of flame. For a few seconds, the crevasse was lit with an eldritch daylight, and she thought that she saw movement on the far side, just for a moment. When the winnowfire had spent itself, she blinked rapidly at the after-images floating across her vision.

'Did you see something, then? Moving on the far cliff?'

Tor came up next to her, shaking his head. 'You just blinded me, witch, so no, I did not.'

'Come on,' Micanal was abruptly on his feet and heading back into the trees. 'Let's start making our way back. I have no wish to be out here all night.'

32

'Bread, and ale, and somewhere to sit. These are the good things in life, lad.'

Aldasair looked up to see Bern the Elder looming towards him, a foaming tankard in one hand and what appeared to be half a loaf in the other. It was late, and Aldasair had found a quiet spot on the porch of the hut where they were staying. The place looked over the Broken Field, and had a dusty, unused quality to it – Bern had explained that once there had been a guard that lived there, keeping an eye on the Field, but since the Jure'lia had appeared to have been defeated, that particular tradition had been gratefully abandoned. Currently, the Field was quiet, although it still glowed faintly, and Aldasair found that his eyes were drawn again and again to the exposed crystal. They had left it where it was for now, with plans to move it with special precautions later – Vintage's suspicions were one thing, but all they truly knew was that it could be dangerous.

'Of course,' Bern the Elder settled next to Aldasair with a grunt. 'Bread is best when it has a big chunk of something's flesh in it. Have you eaten, lad? Of course you have. Rainya will have taken one look at you and decided you need fattening up.'

'It was an excellent dinner. You have all been very kind.'

'Ah. Well. We need to be kind to neighbours now, I reckon. Even the Sown, the ugly bastards.' He paused. 'They sent us horses to help, you know. With the Broken Field. They may be ugly but they aren't stupid – if that thing gets out, it won't be just the Finneral who suffer.'

'Are you really a king?'

Bern the Elder laughed, a hoarse sort of bark that made Aldasair jump. 'I'm guessing kings don't look much like me where you're from?'

'We do not have any kings.'

'Ah. I don't suppose you do, now that you say it. You've had a hard time of it.'

'Yes. Much of what Ebora was is gone. The buildings are in ruins, our roads are overgrown. The library, even, was destroyed.' He brightened slightly. 'Your son rebuilt the Hill of Souls for us and it gave me hope.'

'Yes, he told us about that.' There was a different tone in Bern the Elder's voice, but Aldasair could not decipher it. 'But I don't mean your people, lad. I mean you. You've had a hard time, going through those cold years alone.'

Aldasair nodded hesitantly. 'I don't remember much of it. When I try to think of all those years I spent in the palace, just wandering, I cannot separate the days. Instead there is a grey sort of fog, in my mind. Perhaps that is for the best, though.'

'You're safe here, Aldasair. You can be whoever you need to be, in Finneral.'

'I am not sure what you mean?'

'I mean, our lad Bern is very fond of you.' Bern's father took a big bite out of the bread, and chewed on it for some time. 'That's what I mean. You can be part of a family here, if you want it.'

Aldasair nodded slowly. Family. He could just about remember

329

his mother and father, although the memories associated with them were difficult; like wild animals waiting in the dark, he had no wish to poke them into life. His two cousins were the only members of his family left alive, and Hestillion was apparently lost to them. Tormalin, who had come back to them just before the Jure'lia arrived, was now his only family, and he had always been flighty, hard to pin down.

And Jessen, he realised. Jessen was closer to him than anyone, save for perhaps Bern. Vintage, too, was not far from his thoughts when he conjured the word 'family'.

'Family doesn't have to mean blood,' he said quietly. 'It doesn't even have to mean Eboran.'

'That's the spirit, lad. To answer your question, I am a king of sorts, which makes Bern a prince. Don't say it to his face, though, he gets very touchy about it –'

Aldasair's first warning was a cold tremor moving through his chest, and then on the tail of that, a note of panic from Jessen, as clear and as sharp as a lightning bolt. He stood up.

'Something is wrong!'

Bern the Elder levered himself off the porch with a huff, scanning the Broken Field below as he did so. 'Is it the carcass? Moving again?'

Jessen was coming, with Sharrik close behind. In the hut behind them were raised voices as Bern picked up on whatever was alarming the war-beasts.

'No, I don't think so.' He looked up. It was a clear night, with stars dusting the sky from horizon to horizon, but there was a hole above them. A dark space where there should be stars. 'There's a monster up there.'

'This is more than just a settlement.'

Hestillion had pressed herself up against the transparent section of wall – she was no longer afraid of falling through them – and peered down at the lands below the corpse moon.

She could see farmland and woods, and in the distance, a stretch of coast, and everywhere there were roads and clutches of houses. She saw lights and smoke, and all the other small signs that suggested the place was home to a large number of people.

'One more place that humans fester in.'

The queen had been striding back and forth throughout the whole journey, her jagged shoulders rising and falling. Hestillion was quite sure she had never seen her so agitated.

'What is wrong with you? What vexes you so much about this one?'

'It is broken.' The queen gestured viciously at the window. 'Now we are close, we can feel it. This piece of us is scattered and . . . flattened, held down even. They have tried to bury us, like one of their own dead.'

'And this upsets you?'

The queen pulled her lips back from her teeth. 'It will be harder, but the core still lives, and still calls to us. The humans here will pay.'

She stood back from the window, and grew very still. Hestillion was beginning to recognise these moments; the queen would send herself out through the ship and beyond, travelling through connections that Hestillion could only guess at, and in these times she could be everywhere. The corpse moon itself was beginning to drop slowly, edging down through the sky. A movement from the ground below caught her eye; a big stretch of land that appeared to be glowing faintly – she had assumed it was Wild-touched – was beginning to shift and move, the stones and rocks scattered across it bucking and tumbling like it was in the midst of a very specific earthquake. And then, in the centre, she saw a green light flickering – another crystal, like the one at the heart of the corpse moon. She was looking at the remains of a Behemoth, being summoned into life by the Jure'lia queen. The black ooze, looking like

331

dark water from this distance, began to seep out of the cracks in the ground.

'They are fighting back,' said Hestillion. People with torches were appearing, and she saw the orange pinpoints of flaming arrows appear. 'They must know it is useless, I can't imagine . . . wait!' She pressed her forehead to the transparent wall, barely able to understand what she was seeing. 'There are war-beasts there! Two of them!'

This got the queen's attention. Her sharp-angled face twisted at an unnatural angle.

'Would Celaphon like to meet them, do you think?'

Hestillion did not move. *Perhaps*, she thought, *if I keep very still, she will not ask the question.*

'It is time, my little war-queen. War has come, and who do you think will win it? How can you best stay alive?'

'By the stones, the bloody thing is waking up!'

Bern and Sharrik were flying low over the Field, with Jessen and Aldasair close behind. Below them, the oily pieces of the Behemoth were shifting themselves out of the dirt and stones, urged together by the black fluid. As they watched, it almost seemed to form fingers, pushed the pieces into place like someone completing a puzzle.

'What can we do? The corpse moon is right on top of us.'

Bern lifted his head and looked. The Behemoth above them was lowering all the time, and Aldasair thought he could almost feel the connection between it and the remains on the ground – as if they were reaching out to each other. A hatch was opening in the side of it, a flexing of moon-metal flesh that would very soon release all the horrors they had seen at Coldreef. A great many people had died there, or lost their homes. And the Finneral people had been so kind to him.

'There are only two of us,' cried Bern. He looked stricken. 'I'm not sure what we *can* do.'

332

'We have to push the corpse moon back,' said Aldasair, as firmly as he was able. He caught the surprise in Bern's glance and pretended not to have seen it. 'The dead one is only this lively because it is close – if we can force it away, we'll buy ourselves some time. And we have to stop it birthing any horrors. Look! Quickly now, go!'

The hatch had opened to its fullest extent, and things were beginning to crawl out, moving too quickly on multiple limbs. The six-legged burrower-mothers dropped like seeds, and it was possible to see the head of something else still making its way towards the opening, blunt and glistening and pale. A maggot.

Aldasair leaned forward, feeling Jessen bunch her muscles, and they shot ahead, closely followed by Sharrik and Bern. The griffin was bellowing some war cry, and he crashed fully into the belly of the corpse moon, raking his claws across its flesh as he went. Jessen landed with more precision, and with surprising agility, propelled herself to the edge of the aperture. The maggot was still in the process of being squeezed out, and it was accompanied by several of the scuttling mothers; they appeared to be excreting some sort of clear fluid, which they were using to ease its passage. Aldasair coughed into his hand; he was fairly sure brave warriors didn't vomit on the battlefield, but he was close to it.

Jessen bent her head and snapped up one of the mothers between her jaws and worried at it, severing a few of its limbs before letting it drop and grabbing another. Sharrik scrambled further within the hole and actually tore at the end of the maggot with his huge beak. Aldasair saw the slippery white flesh of the thing tear open and the thing shifted backwards slightly, but he also saw the sticky clear fluid dripping down onto Sharrik's wings.

'Be careful, Sharrik! That stuff may ruin your wings.'

Bern looked up, and struck at the interior of the passage

333

itself with one of the Bitter Twins. Immediately the whole thing convulsed, and the pair of them were thrown back out. Sharrik's wings snapped open, spattering fluid everywhere, and the hole sealed over as if it had never been there.

'Look!'

Below them, the warriors of Finneral had gathered and were loosing fiery arrows up towards the corpse moon, but already they were meeting trouble on the ground. A few of the burrower-mothers had escaped and were bearing down on the humans, and the black fluid oozing up through the ruins was forming itself into the shapes of strange, scuttling humanoids. Even as he watched, Aldasair saw several men and women falling, either pulled down by the fluid-creatures or overwhelmed by the mothers.

'We will help them,' he said, pulling his own sword from its scabbard. It felt very unfamiliar in his hand. 'You and Sharrik, do what you can to drive this thing away.'

Bern nodded once, and they split up, Jessen diving back to the ground in what was almost a freefall. Once there, they barrelled straight into a pack of the mothers, scattering them, and there was a small cheer from the humans. Aldasair leaned out over Jessen's side and swept his sword at the mobile fluid – it danced back out of reach. He was just urging Jessen forward again, hoping to put them between the worm-fluid and the humans, when the area ahead of them exploded with green fire. His heart leapt, thinking it must be Noon, that Noon and Tor had joined them after all, and all would be well, but when he turned to look he saw the Stone Talker, riding high on one of her giant Wild-touched boars, her arms bare and held in front of her. She was building a huge ball of winnowfire there, her hands shaking with the effort. There were two warriors standing with her, Bern's mother and father, and they were each riding a bear.

There was a roar from above. Another of the holes had opened in the side of the corpse moon and more mothers were pouring forth. Sharrik was there, tearing them to pieces with his claws and beak, but he was being overwhelmed. One of the creatures was on his back, and Bern was wrestling with it, hand to hand. As Aldasair watched, one of its wiry legs wrapped around the big man's neck.

In seconds, he was in the air again, Jessen flying as fast as the arrows; faster. They came in so quickly that they nearly collided with Sharrik, but Aldasair was able to reach across and tear the mother from Bern, and with one convulsive movement he tore the thing in half. It was fibrous inside, and stank. Dimly, he thought of telling the red-headed man *I am strong, stronger than you.*

'Thanks!' Bern was grinning, his cheeks flushed and his eyes bright. 'Stones arses, I thought I was dead for a second there . . .'

The stars vanished again as something huge appeared in the sky next to them. Again, Aldasair experienced that strange cramp of joy – Vostok! She had come to help them after all!

But it was not Vostok. This dragon was twice as large, and it was purple and black and green, the colour of a particularly bad bruise, although its eyes were white and blind-looking. It bristled with horns and ridges all along its back, and sitting in its harness was a woman with a pale, serene face. Her eyes were red, and her blond hair was pulled back from her face in a severe braid.

For a long, heart-stopping moment, Aldasair did not know where he was, or what he was doing. That could not possibly be his cousin: she had been stolen by the worm people and was likely to be dead; she would never wear such filthy leathers, or carry such a lance. She could not be riding a dragon. Nothing that he was looking at made sense.

'Hestillion?' As if her name were the key, all the pieces rushed into place. Hope fluttered in his chest again. He twisted

335

in the harness to speak to Bern. 'It's my cousin! She will help us, she must have found—'

The enormous dragon knocked them both out of the sky.

There was a period of blankness, of a whistling noise in his ears, and then Aldasair was struck with what felt like a brick wall covered in fur and feathers. A strong arm looped around his chest and pulled him upright. Bern was shouting something, but Aldasair's head was spinning too badly to make it out. In front of them, more green fireballs were lighting up the night, and they were crashing against the enormous purple dragon, which was shaking its head and roaring.

'Where . . . where is Jessen?'

'She's on the ground. We have to get to her.'

This was easier said than done. More movement was happening around the corpse moon. A figure was easing down from its belly in a column of dark green fluid, a human-shaped thing with a white mask for a face. It was heading directly to the crystal, its arms outstretched, and something about that sent a curl of terror straight down Aldasair's back. Another hole had opened and more mothers were scuttering out, floating down towards the humans on the ground, and that was when he spotted Jessen – the great black wolf was lying, half stunned, on the Broken Field. The oozing humanoid creatures were converging on her.

'Quickly!'

But Sharrik was already moving. The huge griffin crashed next to the wolf, stumbling slightly on the uneven ground, before moving to stand over her. Aldasair slipped down from the harness and went to her, kicking away one of the burrower-mothers as he did so.

'Jessen? Jessen?'

She lifted her head, her orange eyes open a crack. 'Aldasair. Who was that? Who hurt us?'

'I don't know.' He smoothed his hands along her snout, and was glad to feel her reaching back to him. 'I don't know who that was, not truly. We will stop them, though. Can you get up? We need you to get up.'

'I've met that woman,' said Bern, in an undertone. 'She was at the palace, before the worm people came.'

Jessen got to her feet and Aldasair climbed back into her harness. He could feel how unsteady she was, but also that she was gathering her strength. *Family*, he thought. Above them, the dragon was turning about, moving out of range of the Stone Talker's fireballs, while the skeletal figure, descending on its ropes of green and black fluid, was moving ever closer to the Broken Field. She would be there in moments.

'The dragon. It can't breathe fire, or it would have done so by now. You and Sharrik should go and drive it back,' he said to Bern. Somewhere, he had lost his sword. 'Give me one of your axes, and I will join you in a moment.'

Bern did not hesitate. He unhooked one of the Bitter Twins from his belt and passed it to Aldasair. 'Be quick. That bastard thing is huge.'

Sharrik leapt, and they were gone in a shower of feathers. For a second, Aldasair wasn't quite able to tear his eyes from them: the brilliant blue griffin, the man with the shining yellow hair, and waiting to meet them, a dragon from some sort of nightmare. Shaking his head to clear it, he urged Jessen to turn.

'Run!' he hissed into her ear. 'To the crystal!'

They had to leap over several burrower-mothers, and one fluid-creature nearly tangled Jessen's legs beneath her, but Aldasair swiped at it with the axe – it felt much more natural in his hand than the sword ever had – and they got to the crystal just before the Jure'lia queen did. Aldasair leapt from the harness, half falling, and then he was there. He gripped the axe in both hands, and held it high over his head. The

337

surface of the crystal was slick under his knees. There was a hairline crack running through the centre of it already, some injury from its initial crash, and he focussed on that.

'No!'

The shout seemed to come from all around, an exclamation of despair that moved the very stones under him, and then he brought the axe crashing down with every bit of strength he had left. He had half expected it to bounce off, perhaps catching him in the face with its rebound, but instead the crystal shattered. A high, moaning wail filled the air, reverberating strangely around his head, and then all the glowing light and the shifting fluid grew utterly still. Above him, the queen of the Jure'lia hung on her ropes – despite the smooth surface of her mask-face, her fury was like the sun; he felt the heat of it on his face.

A bellowing roar brought his attention upwards again. Sharrik and the dark dragon were locked in an embrace, Bern lost somewhere in the middle. He had a sighting of Hestillion, her eyes wild and her mouth open as she shouted something, and then he saw the dragon's claws raking across Sharrik's furry flank. Blood leapt into the sky, and he heard Bern shout out.

Ignoring the queen, Aldasair climbed back onto Jessen and they were in the air again almost faster than he could pull himself into the harness.

'Family,' she murmured to him as they flew.

'Family,' he agreed.

They were too late. A great mouth in the side of the corpse moon opened up, lined with tendrils of black fluid, and the dragon dragged Sharrik and Bern inside. They were gone almost instantly, and the mouth began to close.

'No!'

Jessen flew faster than she ever had, flattening her ears and pulling up her legs to close the distance more quickly, but the wall of the corpse moon was a smooth and bruise-covered blankness. Aldasair, hardly aware that there were tears in his eyes, leaned out of his harness and crashed the edge of the axe against it, again and again, although it made barely a mark. The corpse moon was moving up and away again, away from Finneral, but he did not care. Jessen's pain and his pain were one, and he could think of nothing else.

And then a voice, which again seemed to come from all around.

'Very well.'

The side of the corpse moon split open again, and the two of them were eaten up by the darkness.

33

'Whether it's searching out parasite spirits, worm-people junk or fabulous artefacts, it always seems to end with me knee-deep in mud.'

'It's funny how it also seems to end with you moaning about something.' Noon, who was bent at the waist and peering intently through the murky water, straightened up briefly to cup some water in her hands and throw it at Tor, splashing the back of his shirt.

'I am going to prove I am the adult here and not respond to that.'

Luckily, the water in the crevasse came up to the top of Tor's thighs and the current was sluggish, meaning they could, more or less safely, search for the missing amber tablets. Less luckily, the floor of the crevasse was covered in a layer of silt and mud, and every movement caused swirls of the stuff to darken the water, making spotting anything at the bottom extremely difficult. The crevasse was also wide enough for the sun to make it down there, meaning that the centre of the little river was a headache-inducing collection of lights bouncing off the water. They had been searching since the sun had risen, and Tor was already too hot and too wet, and certainly too covered in mud.

Vostok waited above, her long tail hanging over the cliff's edge, while Kirune was upstream some way, bathing himself. He was causing even greater tides of mud, but Tor didn't feel much like telling him to stop it.

'I can't help feeling like this is a hopeless task.' He straightened up and pushed his hair out of his face. 'Even if we find the tablets, we've no way of knowing if they'll actually help Kirune and the others. Meanwhile, anything could be happening at home.'

'So, do you want to give up in ten minutes, or wait until lunch?'

Tor turned to Noon in surprise, and then caught the expression on her face. 'Yes, all right, I am moaning again. I'm just being a realist.'

Noon bent her head back to the water. She was soaked from head to foot, her black hair now a collection of inky wet curls, and her cheeks were flushed from the heat. 'The amber tablet we have is pretty heavy, right? Maybe the things sank into the mud, and they're still there, sitting on some lower bedrock. We could get Kirune to try digging around.'

'Or the river was different when Micanal helpfully chucked them away. Deeper, stronger. They could easily be anywhere.'

'We've come a long bloody way, and eaten that bloody awful salted beef for days. I'm not giving up after only . . . ow. *Ow*.'

'What is it?'

'My neck. It's seized up, or I've pulled something.' She stood up straight, wincing and rubbing her neck.

'Come here,' said Tor, before striding over to her. 'Let me have a look.'

'You can't *see* a strain, Bloodsucker.'

'Now who's moaning? Let me just . . . here.' He walked behind her and placed his hands on the back of her neck, the smooth stretch of her shoulders. 'You've got big knots here, which doesn't surprise me, given all the flying and riding and

341

sleeping on rocks, and how much staggering around in mud we've been doing.' Carefully, too aware that he was strong enough to snap her neck if he wanted to, Tor began to knead the muscles in Noon's shoulders. She jerked a couple of times as he reached an especially sore spot.

'Ow! Is this supposed to be helping?'

'Just let me do my work.' Her skin was warm, and he could smell her too now; good clean sweat, the scent of her hair, all tangled up in the minerals of the river. 'We spent a year on this at the House of the Long Night. Usually, of course, it involves oils scented with violet-wort and king's-blossom, but hopefully the results will be the same.'

Noon snorted. 'Hmm. That does feel better actually.' With his hand on the side of her neck, he could feel her pulse, light and quick. Growing faster. 'Much better.'

He bent his head to her ear, not at all sure what he was about to say, when a voice carried down from above.

'How goes the search?'

It was Arnia, her oval face framed with her cloud of black hair as she peered down from the cliff edge. She was smiling broadly, as sunny as the sky. Noon stepped away from Tor, smoothing her hand over the back of her neck.

'Slowly,' she called up. 'Have you come to help?'

Arnia laughed. 'I will bring you some lunch soon, though.'

When they eventually got Kirune to shepherd them back up to the clifftop, Arnia had laid out a lunch for them on a blanket, complete with more of the sour wine. She was wearing a robe of white silk embroidered with tiny golden suns, which looked quite incongruous in the middle of a vibrant forest, but with Vostok stretched neatly behind the blanket, it could almost have been a scene from an Eboran painting; the war-beast and the lady dining together. Arnia looked exquisite, and as she reached to pour the wine, her sleeve pulled up to reveal rows and rows of delicately carved wooden bracelets – they were covered in interlaced hands. Seeing Tor glance at them, she smiled.

'Made for me by my brother.'

'We shouldn't have too much of that,' said Noon, nodding at the wine. 'Not if we're going back down there.'

'Oh, you haven't finished looking, then?'

Noon picked up a slice of cured meat and pressed it whole into her mouth. 'There's a lot of mud to sift through.'

Arnia shrugged as if it didn't matter at all. 'Well, it is good to have your company.' She looked at Tor as she said this, and he returned her smile. 'It's been so long since I've had anyone to talk to other than my dear brother. You are like the past of Ebora, and its future, come to visit us.'

Tor took the offered glass of wine. It *was* too sour, but after hours in the sun and mud, he thought he could get used to it.

'Why haven't you tried to leave?' Noon was picking up more of the ham, apparently to see how much of it she could stick in her mouth at once. 'Your brother seems very nice, but I can understand wanting to find other company after . . . how many years have you been here?'

A shadow passed over Arnia's face, and the sunny smile vanished. 'We thought Ebora was dead. The grief of it . . . I can't expect you to understand what it feels like to watch everyone you've ever known die, but it's not something you recover from, even after centuries.'

'Oh, I don't know.' Noon swallowed her mouthful of ham, and Tor thought he recognised the overly tight smile on her lips. He began wondering if something was going to be set on fire shortly. 'I think you'd be surprised by how much I could understand about that. And you left while there were still people alive in Ebora, didn't you?'

'Once we were here, this seemed like a paradise of sorts. It wasn't what we had hoped for, no, but there was a peace here, away from the cities and the politics, and the memories. We

343

turned our ships into houses, and we decided that this was where we would spend the rest of our years.'

'And then everyone got the crimson flux and died anyway?'

'Noon,' said Tor. He glanced at Vostok, wondering what the dragon was thinking of this aggressive tone, but her violet eyes revealed nothing.

'No, it's fine, Tormalin. I know it is difficult for the shorter-lived species to understand our struggles.' Tor saw Noon roll her eyes at that from the corner of his vision, but Arnia was looking at her glass of wine and missed it. 'Did I hear correctly? That you studied at the House of the Long Night?'

This was quite a change in direction. Tor nodded graciously. 'For over a decade, my lady. Our numbers were greatly reduced by then, I'm afraid, but there were still those who remembered.'

'It is good to know that the old traditions are being kept alive.'

'Well, this has been charming, but we've still got a lot of searching to do.' Noon stood up, brushing crumbs off her damp trousers. 'Vostok, would you give me a lift back down the river please?'

'Do be careful,' said Arnia, 'not to come up on the wrong side of the crevasse when you are finished. You could get quite lost, and there are larger, more dangerous wild animals on that side of the island.'

They left Arnia still sitting on the blanket, her golden dress sparkling and her face raised to the sun.

They searched for the rest of that day and well into the evening, until the shadows grew so deep that Tor managed to walk into the cliff face twice, and they did not locate a single amber tablet. Wet and sunburned and aching, they returned to the grove of houses. Micanal and Arnia had opened up one of the empty homes for them to stay in, and they were both too exhausted to take much notice of it, although Tor did note that the walls were all hung with pieces of Micanal's art, alongside works by lesser artists – he wondered how many of the Eborans who had set out on the Golden Fox expedition were his surviving students.

Noon had been in an especially grumpy mood on the way back, so Tor retired straight to bed. He lay there for a while, listening to the soft pads of Kirune circling the house, and eventually drifted into a thick, smoky sleep. When he began to dream, he almost recoiled from it – rest was what he really wanted, of both body and mind – but he soon recognised that this was not a dream of his own making, and that made him curious. In the dream, he was on a ship. It was beautiful, with huge white sails like clouds, and the masthead was carved with foxes chasing each other. Everywhere he looked he saw Eborans, men and women who looked happy, excited and healthy. Seeing them all together it occurred to him that he could not remember a time when he had been around so many healthy Eborans; nothing that wasn't hazy with distance and memory, at least. He saw these faces clearly, and his heart lifted at the sight of them. They wore not the usual finery of the Eboran palace, but simple, tough, well-made clothes – the sort of clothes necessary for a long voyage – and they moved around the deck of the ship with ease and knowledge.

'Arnia?' he called. 'This must be your doing.'

She appeared from behind a group of Eboran ladies, grinning sheepishly.

'I thought you would like to see the Golden Fox expedition as it was,' she said, 'rather than how it ended. We had so much hope, you see.'

'Did you bring those who could sail? Or did people learn?'

'We learned, mostly. We built our own ships too.'

'A purely Eboran enterprise.' For some reason, this made Tor think of his sister. She had chosen to turn away from the world too, while he had walked out into Sarn. 'Have you ever thought what would have happened if you hadn't come out here?'

A crease appeared between Arnia's eyebrows. 'We all would have died. There is no mystery in that.'

'Or you could have gone beyond the Wall and out into Sarn.' Tor watched as a pair of young Eborans, perhaps only three hundred years old, turned over a crate to play cards on it. 'There's a lot to see out there. You'd be surprised.'

Arnia turned her head and walked to the rail. The sea was vast and silvery, stretching out in all directions. Tor knew it wasn't easy to hold such a large dream together; Arnia was quite a talented dream-walker.

'I hope you will stay,' she said suddenly, still not looking at him. 'I know that's not very fair of me, Tormalin the Oathless, but I hope it anyway. What is there for you back in Ebora? The last dregs of our people, dying, and the Jure'lia returning to finish the job they started with the Eighth Rain.'

Tor joined her at the rail, trying to look at her face, but she just continued to stare out to sea. 'But we have to fight. You must see that.' He half laughed, thinking she must be teasing him, but her expression only grew stonier. 'Without us, and the handful of war-beasts we have left, Sarn is doomed. I know you remember what the Jure'lia are. If we don't stand against them, who will?'

She lifted a shoulder. 'The Jure'lia may never come here. We are hidden, and distant. This could be the only safe place left on Sarn. You could live here with us. Perhaps that should be your duty.' Arnia turned to him and pressed her hand to his arm where it rested on the rail. Her touch was shockingly warm, and her gaze very direct. 'I have so much to show you here. And I think you would understand it too, like no one else has.'

Tor cleared his throat. There was something going on here, something strange under her words. She was concentrating on them so fiercely that the light of the dream had dimmed around them, the sounds of sea and sailing growing faint, but all he could think of was her warm hand on his arm. Slowly, she slid it under his sleeve.

'What . . . what do you mean? What is here that you need to show me?' He struggled to concentrate as the dream grew darker and darker until she was the only bright thing.

'I am so lonely, Tormalin the Oathless. Can you imagine what it has been like for me here, with only my *brother* for company?'

'My sister isn't too fond of me either.' She was leaning towards him now, and he found that he was searching her face for the least sign of aging or of the flux, but there was nothing. Arnia was flawless, untouched by the curses of Ebora. 'What did you mean, we are hidden here? The lights that surround the island – do you know what they are? Did you see them when you came here?'

She blinked. He could smell blood, sudden and sharp, and then he was awake, lying in the bed. He had, he realised with some exasperation, an erection, so he stood up and walked around the room a little, letting the night air cool his skin. By the time he was feeling vaguely back to normal he was fully awake, so he left the bedroom and walked into the parlour. One of the siblings had left a bottle of the sour wine on the table there for them, and he hoped a glass might ease him back to sleep. However, Noon was already there, her feet curled under her in the dark and a goblet of wine cradled in her hands. She looked up at him with no surprise at all, and Tor was thankful that she would not be able to make out that he was blushing in the shadows. He found another chair and sat in it with a huff.

'So,' said Noon softly. 'What do you make of all this, then?'

He contemplated a flippant comment, then decided he didn't have the energy for it. 'I think Vintage would say it all stinks like a week-old fish.'

'Mmm.' Noon sipped her wine, and made a face. 'Ugh. I saw someone as we were leaving tonight. On the other side of the crevasse.'

'You saw what?'

'I didn't say anything because I think they had been watching us for some time, and I didn't want them to know I'd seen them. They looked human to me, though, from what I saw. Too short to be an Eboran. It's interesting that Arnia specifically warned us away from that side of the island, isn't it? Has she visited your dreams at all?'

'No,' said Tor, before taking a big gulp of the wine. He wondered if he had said anything in his sleep. 'So there might be people living here already, is that what you think?'

'I don't know what I think.'

Silence weaved itself between them, growing thicker and heavier. Tor thought about the people who had built this house, and then supposedly died in it, probably coughing their lungs into shreds.

'Do you think,' Noon said eventually, 'that Arnia could have found the tablets and moved them?'

'What? No. Come on, Noon. Not all of my people are devious monsters, you know. And think about what you're saying. You're suggesting that Arnia climbed down there in the dark, after Micanal had shown us the place, retrieved the tablets, climbed back up – still in the dark – and hid them somewhere. All to, what? Vex us slightly?'

'To stop us from leaving straight away. And yeah, that's exactly what I'm saying. Even Micanal said she was capable of doing it, because she is still young and strong, and he's not. And what is that about, anyway?'

Tor shifted in his chair. 'I agree that this place is strange, and there are undoubtedly a lot of questions I'd like the answers to, but I think you are seeing plots where there are none. Arnia is just a lonely woman, not some scheming creature.'

348

'Mmm. Lonely, and desperate, maybe. They've been here *centuries*, Tor, alone. You don't think that might have made them a bit unstable?'

'You are thinking in human terms, witch.' It was growing lighter outside, the deep blues of night becoming the greys of dawn. 'A human would go mad, certainly, stuck here for so long with no other company, but Eborans are made of sterner stuff. We can endure.'

'And I suppose you left Ebora just because you were bored?'

Tor put his glass down on the table, with a little more force than he'd intended. 'I imagine you will want us back down in the mud pits as soon as the sun is high enough, so I am going to see if I can grab a few more hours' sleep.'

34

At first, Aldasair thought he had gone blind.

He felt his eyes open, but he simply went from one utter darkness to another. Carefully, he lifted shaking fingers and touched his eyelids. He could feel the creases there, and the working muscles. Dim colours burst and spread in his vision, his eyes trying to make shapes from too little information. Alarmed by this, he squeezed his eyes shut and reached out around him. He was lying on a soft floor, slightly warm to the touch, like skin – a spike of terror surged up his throat, and he swallowed it down. He ached all over, his left side and his left arm in particular, as if he'd landed on it with some force. Awkwardly, he clambered to his knees and began to crawl.

A pale light blossomed into life, revealing a strange grey room with softness where there should be corners. The light itself came from a fistful of fronds growing straight out of the wall, and twenty feet away Bern also lay on the floor, unmoving.

'Bern?'

The big human didn't reply. Aldasair wobbled towards him only to find a soft, transparent barrier in his way – it stretched across the whole room, cutting him off from Bern. Touching it made him think of the way unseen cobwebs could ambush you in corridors, and with a shudder of revulsion he pulled himself free of it.

'Bern? Are you well? Can you hear me?'

Bern did not move. His head was angled away, so that Aldasair could only see the bright pinkness of one ear, and the curve of his jaw. The light was dim enough for him not to be able to tell if Bern's chest was rising and falling, and again, terror and panic threatened to swallow him whole. The idea that this was all a nightmare rose up in his mind, sudden and extremely persuasive: he had never left the empty, silent corridors of Ebora, and he was asleep in a room somewhere, covered in dust – his mind finally completely untethered from the rest of him. Looking at Bern's unmoving body, he almost wished it were true.

He tucked a stray lock of hair behind his ear, and looked around the room. There were no windows. And no doors.

'Jessen?'

'You have never taken prisoners before!'

The queen had been dangerously calm since their abortive attempt to reconnect with the crashed Behemoth. Hestillion's cousin – her *cousin*, of all people – had smashed the crystal to pieces before the queen could reach it, and this meant that the memory it had housed was irretrievable. It was, as far as she could tell, a profound loss. Without it, the chain that bound the Jure'lia together was weaker.

'We are doing many things we have not done before,' said the queen. 'As are you.' They were standing outside a pair of hastily constructed cells. The two war-beasts were being kept separate, although they could see each other through the transparent wall. They couldn't be behaving any more differently. The magnificent griffin, with his blue and black feathers and thick fur, was roaring intermittently and shouting insults. He had given up trying to break through the wall when its fibrous

351

material grew soft and sticky, gumming up his claws, but he still paced the cell, swearing by all the roots that he would shred them to pieces. The beautiful black wolf was sitting at the back of her cell, her long brush of a tail swept neatly over her feet. She watched, with amber eyes, and did not speak at all. Hestillion found that she could barely look away from them both.

'Besides,' continued the queen, 'what would you have preferred? Did you intend to kill them all, on the battlefield? Would you have let your war-beast tear them apart? One of them is blood to you, is he not?'

Hestillion bit her lip. She had no answer to that question, just as she had no answer to any of the questions that had been plaguing her since she had climbed into Celaphon's harness and urged him to fly into battle. All she knew was the fierce joy she had felt at the power of him, and then the shock of seeing Aldasair, his auburn hair flying behind him as he flew straight at her. He had believed in that moment that she was rescuing them; she had seen that in every line of his body.

'Are you going to kill them?'

The queen seemed to consider it. 'We have killed so many of your beasts, over the years. Two more would hardly make a difference. But this is a new sort of war, and it might be helpful to know things – how many beasts we must face, where they are, what they plan. Information is a weapon for us to use, in this war. We can ask them questions. If they don't want to answer the questions, we can take pieces of them away until they do.' She seemed to brighten, lips peeling back from her teeth in an approximation of a smile. 'Hestillion Eskt, would you like to sleep in a wolfskin blanket?'

Hestillion swallowed hard. Such a suggestion was perhaps the most offensive thing an Eboran could utter. He or she would be exiled for even thinking it. *But I am already exiled*, she thought. *I exiled myself.*

'I could ask them,' she said. 'They may speak to me.'

'Yes. We would like to see, when you speak to your blood kin. To your cousin.' She tipped her head to one side. 'We saw him, when we crawled back up through the roots. He was one of your people then, so yes, we should very much like to see what he makes of you now. But first you must go to Celaphon.'

Hestillion dragged her gaze from the war-beasts to the queen. 'What? Why?'

'Your creature is throwing himself against our walls again. It seems he is upset about something.'

Upset was something of an understatement; Celaphon had worked himself up into an incoherent rage. When she arrived in his vast quarters, she found him throwing himself from one side of the room to the other, flapping his enormous wings and apparently trying to take off, despite the fact that there was nowhere to go. He very nearly crashed into her, and it took several minutes of Hestillion screaming his name before he even seemed to notice she was there. He turned his strange, blind-gaze onto her, his chest and shoulders heaving with the effort.

'Celaphon, sweet one! Whatever is wrong?'

The dragon opened his jaws, bearing all his terrible teeth. Hestillion suspected that if he'd been able to breathe fire, she would be a pile of ash and cinders on the floor.

'You. Where were you? I have been alone.'

'I was with the queen, observing the prisoners. She wanted my advice.' Hestillion straightened up. 'Celaphon, you have been alone before, many times. What is the reason for all this noise?'

He began to pace, tail lashing behind him. 'The prisoners. The other war-beasts, you mean. Who we caught. Who we defeated.'

'Yes. They are being kept in cells not far from here.'

353

'They are very different to me.'

There was a hint of a question there.

'They are, sweet one. All war-beasts are different from each other, that's just in their nature.' She cleared her throat, abruptly nervous. 'Some will be dragons, like you, others are griffins, flying wolves, giant cats . . .'

'That's not what I mean. I mean I am different. I feel it when I look at them, like—' He shook his head, like a dog with a wasp in its mouth. 'Remember when you would sing to me, when I was small.'

'I do.'

'It is like, when I look at them, I hear a song, but it is wrong. The notes hurt each other, the words are bad. But I should know it! I should know the song.'

Hestillion didn't know what to say to this. 'They are our enemies. That is how it must be.' Inside, her stomach rolled, and she felt as though she were standing at the very edge of a great drop. How had things come to this?

Celaphon ceased pacing and threw his weight down on the floor. His big, lumpy head continued to move back and forth, as though he were watching something she could not see. She went over and sat on the floor with him, placing one hand on a giant claw.

'There is something else,' he said eventually. 'They flew together. They moved together. Did you see this?'

Reluctantly, Hestillion nodded. 'I would never have thought it of Aldasair, of all people. He has always been something of a halfwit, spoilt by our aunt and indulged by my brother. But he and the black wolf were of one mind. And when we knocked him from the war-beast's back, the other flew down and caught him without hesitation. And, and' – she sat up straighter in her outrage – 'the other rider was a human! They have hatched new war-beasts, and have let humans defile them.'

'They all hear the song, between them,' said Celaphon glumly.

'And it is not wrong to them, or broken. All I have is this poison song, and I am alone with it.'

'Sweet one, it will come. I promise you, we will be connected in the same way they are, eventually. It takes work. You must listen to me, obey me, do as I say and our . . . song will be mended.'

'I want to meet with them. I want to speak to them.'

'If the queen allows it.'

'A connection.' Celaphon sighed, an enormous rattle from deep within his chest. His breath smelled of dead things. 'I want to feel a part of something larger, like they are.'

'Yes.' Hestillion thought of the shattered crystal, and the way the queen travelled through the Jure'lia, thinking and feeling every part of it at once. 'I know, sweet one.'

There were eyes in the ceiling.

It had taken Aldasair some time to notice them. He had spent hours watching Bern, trying to decide if the big man was breathing or not – he thought he had caught a wisp of his beard moving, so he still had hope – and then, eventually, he had lain on his back and seen it. The ceiling was made from the black fluid that seemed so much a part of the Jure'lia, and there were things, floating in it. White orbs, some with veiny protuberances, were oozing out of the fluid, moving as he moved. They were watching him.

After a while, Aldasair stood up and moved to the transparent wall and sat with his head down. He heard the wet noises the eyes made as he moved, and ignored them. Instead he spoke to Bern.

'I can feel Jessen nearby, and I'm sure that means that Sharrik is here somewhere too. She is unhappy, and frightened, but not in pain. I wish that you were awake, Bern. I think maybe you are hurt and needing to sleep it off. I'm not sure how humans heal exactly, but I imagine it involves sleep.' He paused.

'Your parents must be very worried. They must have seen us get taken by the Behemoth, and they probably think you are dead. At least, I think the Broken Field is safe now, or safer than it was. When I broke the crystal something went out of it, and I don't think it will be stealing your people anymore. I doubt that makes up for getting you hurt, though.'

Aldasair swallowed and looked at his boots until he felt like he could speak again. 'Please do not be dead, Bern. I don't think I could stand it.'

The wall in the neighbouring chamber peeled back, and a slim figure stepped through it. She wore tough, beaten leathers and a stained shirt.

'Cousin. I wish I could say it was good to see you.'

Slowly, Aldasair climbed to his feet. His cousin looked whip-thin, her cheekbones jutting from her face like knives, but she also looked more vital than when he'd known her in Ebora, and she carried herself differently. Her red eyes flashed danger-ously at his appraising glance.

'I thought you were dead,' he said.

She smiled coldly. 'Perhaps you wish that I were.'

'We were not sure if you were taken by the Jure'lia, or if you went willingly.' He limped a step closer. 'My friend. Can you tell me if he's alive?'

'Which do you think, cousin? Do you think I was snatched, or that I held out my arms to be taken?'

'I think it hardly matters, now.' He watched with some small degree of satisfaction as she thinned her lips at that. 'The war-beast pod you took with you has hatched, then.'

'Yes.' She grinned. There was no humour in it. 'I have my own dragon now, loyal to me.'

'What have you done to the poor thing?'

She took a step back, as if he had struck her.

'He is magnificent,' she said, her voice low and terse. 'A true warrior. What is this?' She pointed to Bern's inert form. 'And why has it been permitted to fly with a war-beast? I have had to put up with Tormalin's bizarre affection for humans, but I didn't believe I had to worry about you.'

'This is Bern Finnkeeper the Younger, a prince of Finneral and my friend. He and Sharrik have bonded.' Aldasair stopped, aware that his voice was beginning to shake. '*He* is a *true* warrior.'

'Humans are not friends with us, Aldasair. They are afraid of us, and rightly so.' Her tone had switched to reasonable, so like her usual faintly annoyed tone that Aldasair felt dizzy. It was almost as though he were back in the echoing palace, and Hestillion was the only voice of reason; reminding him to change his clothes, to eat, to lie down in a bed every once in a while. Her words seemed too plausible, suddenly. Why should a human be a friend to him? His people had murdered humans in their thousands. He squeezed his hands into fists.

'He has pretended to be your friend to get close to the war-beasts,' Hestillion continued, in that same infuriatingly reasonable tone. 'And it worked, didn't it?' She laughed. 'And why wouldn't it? You were so very lonely, Aldasair. You must have been such an easy target.'

'Why did you betray Ebora, Hest?'

He said it to make her stop talking about Bern, but he saw immediately that he had struck home somehow. Her whole body shook, making her look like a willow caught in the wind.

'I . . . I gave everything to Ebora, to tree-father,' she spat. 'Centuries spent nursing the dying, and then reaching for his soul through the netherdark. And he was there, all along, wasn't he? Yet he didn't answer. He still chose to ignore me. It was I who was betrayed!' She stopped, breathing too hard. She stepped over to Bern and kicked him viciously in the stomach. To Aldasair's mingled horror and delight, the big human rolled over with a groan, his face screwed up with pain.

'Bern! Bern, it's me, I'm here.'

357

'Do you care so much about this human, Aldasair? I'm not sure what the queen wants done with the pair of you, but I'm sure I can make some suggestions.'

The eyes in the ceiling were moving wetly, straining to take in every detail. Aldasair took a few slow breaths, trying to calm his wildly beating heart. Bern was still alive, and this meant that he could not take risks. They were all in a lot of danger. When he spoke again, he kept his voice as calm as possible, looking Hestillion directly in the eye.

'Cousin, whatever has been done to you, I am sorry. I still love you.'

She stood over Bern, unmoving. Her face looked bone-white save for two points of hectic colour high on her sharp cheekbones.

'Your war-beasts. What are they called? The griffin keeps shouting and will not answer questions, whereas the wolf does not speak at all.'

'Her name is Jessen. She doesn't speak much generally, but I imagine she will have little to say to our captors. Tell her that I am alive and well and thinking of her, and she might respond to that. The griffin is called Sharrik. I strongly advise that you do not enter the cell with Sharrik. He is very powerful.'

'Celaphon is powerful too,' spat back Hestillion. 'The griffin would not dare to act if I bring my own war-beast.'

Aldasair blinked. 'You named that creature after a flower?'

She hissed at him, then pulled her lips back from her teeth in a sneer. In that moment she looked more like the queen of the Jure'lia than any Eboran Aldasair knew.

'Where is my brother? And his pet witch?'

'I don't know,' he replied, which was true enough. 'They were not with us in Finneral. They could be anywhere.'

'The other dragon. She lives?'

'Vostok is alive, and very strong. They all are, Hestillion. And they are all ready to fight the worm people.'

All of the anger seeped from her and she just looked tired and sad. He saw in her the cousin who had helped him back up when he had fallen and grazed his knee, or told him the names of all the birds in the garden. He remembered that she had had a special fondness for the emerald-lark, because she had been born in the year of the green bird, and once he had learned how to imitate its call, just to please her. He hadn't thought of that in centuries.

'Oh Aldasair,' she said. 'You will all die. Everything will die. Do you not see the inevitability of it? The Jure'lia will not stop until we are destroyed, and we've already done half the job for them. The fight is for nothing, except to prolong your own suffering.'

She went back to the wall, which split open for her again.

'Celaphon will want to speak to you all, in time. I suggest you show him the respect he is due.'

Hestillion stepped through the hole, and it sealed up behind her.

35

'This should be the place.'

Vintage paused, ignoring the steady throb in her ankle to survey the overgrown garden. It was a section to the northeast of the palace grounds, far from the human encampments and, consequently, still in something of a state. Bern had not yet ventured this far when he had been tidying away debris, and despite the sunshine of the bright morning it was a dark place, the grass choked with weeds and the dank smell of rot hanging over everything. It was a strange garden to her eyes – in Catelenia, gardens were lush things, full of gaudy flowers and straining with fruit trees – but this place was a garden of boulders. To either side of her black stones, smooth and shaped by expert hands, sat in regulated patterns on what must once have been a very fine lawn. There were seats carved into the boulders, and between one or two, even miniature bridges. It was all hopelessly overgrown, but she found that she could almost imagine Eboran families lounging here, drinking sweet wines and enjoying the air.

'Perhaps they watched some sort of game from here,' she murmured aloud. In Catelenia, there was a sport played with polished balls and bats on lawns, something Ezion had been quite accomplished at in his youth. She could imagine that too: a genteel game on the grass, music playing while the Eborans watched from their rocks.

'It should be around here somewhere.'

The pattern of boulders came to a stop at a dip in the ground like a shallow basin. It was full of a type of thorny bush, but just ahead she could see that it was obscuring something – a structure that poked out of the dip like a standing stone.

'There you are!' Leaning heavily on her crutch, Vintage shuffled closer to the edge of the dip, only to find her good foot slipping out from under her on the slimy undergrowth. With a shriek she fell awkwardly, handing with a thump at the edge of the thorns. Her ankle stabbed with pain, and for a moment she just sat, fists at her sides and jaw clenched.

'Sarn's bloody arse,' she hissed. The grass she had landed on was damp, a fact rapidly becoming clear to her own behind. 'Sarn's bloody, bloody arse.'

The crutch had landed next to her, and she had begun to pull herself awkwardly to her feet, turning so that she was on her knees, when she heard footsteps. After a moment, a slim figure appeared between the boulders. It was Okaar.

'Are you quite well, Lady Vintage?'

She had to laugh at that. 'I'm completely fine my dear, except that, apparently, I think it's reasonable to go stamping about in the damp with a broken ankle.' She held up an arm, and immediately he came over and helped, quite gently, to put her back on her feet. 'What are you doing out here, anyway?'

'I am looking for Jhef,' he said, in his low, musical voice. 'She promised to help the Sown with their puppet festival, but now, of course, she is out exploring. My sister is very clever, but has no concept of the passing of time. It seems I have found you instead.' He paused, looking around the strange boulder garden. 'What are *you* doing out here?'

361

'I'm looking for a work of art.' She patted his arm and he let her go. 'I have been reading Micanal the Clearsighted's journal, and it's all quite extraordinary. In one of the entries he speaks of a sculpture he made for these particular gardens, and I thought I would seek it out.' She turned and gestured to the thicket. 'I think it is in there somewhere.'

'Then I think it is lost.' He looked down at her foot. 'How painful is your ankle? It appears to be swelling up. Would you care to accompany me back to the main gardens, Lady Vintage?'

Vintage grimaced. 'Now that you mention it, I doubt I have done it any good by rolling about on the ground.' She nodded at the hidden garden. 'It's a shame, though. Tor would point out that I have no patience, but I know it will nibble away at me, knowing such a masterpiece is hidden out here.'

'Tor?'

'Tormalin the Oathless. My friend. He is away with the war-beasts.' Vintage shook her head. 'If you wouldn't mind giving me a hand, Okaar, I should make my way back.'

'One moment, please.' He nodded at her formally, before pulling a long knife from his belt. Vintage had time to see that it was well-used and well-maintained, with scratches on the blade and an often-repaired handle, before Okaar was moving methodically through the bushes, cutting them back and throwing the branches to one side. Very swiftly he had forged a path through the overgrown foliage and it was possible to see something at the centre of it – a figure of slick, white marble.

'There it is! A lost piece of Micanal's work. It's possible, Okaar, that we are the first humans ever to look upon it.'

Okaar nodded, although Vintage could not tell if he was genuinely impressed – his face was as impassive as ever. The sculpture was of a beautiful Eboran warrior, her sword arm raised in triumph. The weather had ruined her somewhat – the marble was cracked and stained, with moss creeping across her breastplate and at the corner of her stern mouth – but there was no doubting that she was the work of a master. Something about it, standing alone yet crowded with weeds and thorns, made Vintage feel melancholic. Forcing herself to smile, she waved Okaar back.

'Thank you, Okaar, for sharing that with me. It was kind of you to recover it.'

The slim young man returned her smile. 'Tyranny can also be impatient. I have grown used to solving problems for her as swiftly as possible. It is the easiest path, much of the time.'

'Well, she is lucky to have you, in that case. Shall we walk back together?'

By the time they reached the main area of the palace gardens, Vintage's ankle was throbbing steadily, and she was not quite able to keep from grimacing. Okaar gestured to their caravan, which still sat just outside the main human settlement.

'I have something that could help with the discomfort, Lady Vintage. I would be glad to share it with you.'

Once inside the caravan, Okaar began briskly moving around the small space; fetching a pillow to elevate her leg, setting the small stove to warm, and wrestling a bottle of dark liquid from out of a tiny compact cupboard, along with two tiny glasses.

'Even I would say it's a little too early to drink, my dear, but if it will help my ankle . . .'

'It is not alcoholic,' said Okaar, smiling faintly. He pulled the cork from the bottle with a soft pop and poured too measures. 'This is *kyern*, a restorative. We drink it in Goddestra when we have had a shock. Tyranny refuses to drink it, and I'm afraid even Jhef turns it down, but perhaps you would like to try?'

'I would love to.' Vintage sipped at her tiny glass, and was surprised at the powerful flavour that flooded her mouth, both cloyingly sweet and refreshing. 'Well, it certainly wakes you up.'

Okaar tipped his own glass back in one mouthful. He nodded once to himself, then addressed her. 'Yes, it is good. A real kick in the face, is how Tyranny describes it.'

'Ha, yes, that seems about right.'

He put the glass down and retrieved a round glass pot from where it had been warming by the stove. This he brought over to Vintage, along with a long length of yellow linen. 'This is what I meant to use on your ankle, Lady Vintage. It will take down the swelling. If I may?'

Feeling vaguely foolish, Vintage nodded, and Okaar carefully lifted her foot into his lap, examining the splint and the padded sock Bern had constructed for her. To hide her own embarrassment, Vintage cleared her throat.

'So, you are from the Goddestra Delta? A little further west of Jarlsbad than I guessed.'

'Yes, although I certainly have family in the great city.' He peered closely at her foot, then opened the jar. A strong minty smell immediately filled the caravan. 'We travel a great deal – Jhef and I have not seen them in some time.'

'Hmm.' Vintage watched with some concern as Okaar scooped a handful of faintly pink gunk from the jar and began to lather it right over the ankle area of the padded sock. 'If I were to ask you, Okaar, do you think there is any chance you would tell me what it is you do for Tyranny Munk, exactly?'

He looked up, a sliver of white showing around the dark irises of his eyes, and then just as swiftly he recovered from his surprise.

'A lady as experienced as yourself, I am sure, does not need to be told.'

Vintage tipped her head to one side. Okaar was carefully wrapping her ankle with the linen, hands moving deftly and without hesitation. She did not know what he had meant by that laden comment, but she was content to let him think she did.

'Your work. I imagine it is not as straightforward as Tyranny likes to make out.'

Okaar shrugged, tucking pieces of linen away neatly. Already, Vintage could feel a deep heat encircling her ankle.

'She was a criminal. My circumstances were . . . similar. And yes, we have not left that life as far behind as we might say. Sarn is a hard place, Lady Vintage, and people do what they must to survive in a poisoned world.'

Vintage sighed. 'I understand that well enough. Is my ankle supposed to be this hot?'

'Just give it a moment.' He sat back, and from a bucket of water took a damp cloth, with which he began to clean his hands. 'Tyranny is a complex woman, Lady Vintage. I have known her many years, and she can still be unpredictable, even to me, but I do believe she seeks a redemption of some kind.' He smiled ruefully. 'She would not like me to say it, of course, because she is practical down to her bones, but I believe she feels she was meant to find that piece of war-beast armour, and that it, in turn, was meant to lead her here, to help you, now.'

'That is an interesting way of looking at it,' said Vintage carefully.

Okaar chuckled, a bare, dry sound that Vintage immediately liked. 'You also, are a practical woman, Lady Vintage, and you believe I am speaking, uh, I believe you would say, horse shit.'

'Ha! Yes, well, my darling, I have certainly heard my share of it over the years. Oh, my ankle is cold now, is that supposed to happen?'

Okaar looked pleased. 'Yes, great heat and then great cold. It will help the swelling. Would you like another glass of kyern?'

Vintage was just leaning forward to take the glass when a

flurry of raised voices from outside made them both sit up. It was usual for the palace gardens to be noisy, especially as the morning eased into afternoon and people gathered for lunch, but there was a sharp cadence to these voices that made Vintage uneasy. Looking up, she caught a similar expression of concern on Okaar's face, and without a word he helped her up and they headed back outside. At first Vintage could not make out the problem, although she could see plenty of people standing and staring, distracted from their daily tasks of skinning and tanning, or fetching water. They were all looking towards the central gate, where a large group was approaching.

'What is this now?'

'Let us go and see,' murmured Okaar, but when he made to take her elbow, she shook him off.

'I'm quite all right, darling.' She shifted the crutch back under her armpit. The ankle did feel better, almost pleasantly numb. 'Keep an eye on me, if you don't mind, just in case it looks like I'm about to go arse over tit.'

Moving swiftly down through the crowds, Vintage kept her eye on the new group, attempting to take in as much about them as possible before the inevitable confrontation. There were around ten of them, and they were an impressive bunch. They were all riding fine black and bay horses, which were shaking their heads and stamping impatiently, and each man and woman wore a combination of furs and armour that took the form of overlapping enamelled plates, scratched and dented but clearly well made. Their attire was too warm for the brightening spring day, and Vintage suspected that they must have set out on their journey in the depths of winter. There were two figures at the front who appeared to be the leaders. A tall, stocky man rode at the front, with a beard so black it was almost blue and a ring of black hair that circled back from his ears. The top of his head was carefully shaved, and there was a tattoo of an octopus there, its tentacles held in

366

graceful loops. *Yuron-Kai, then,* thought Vintage, and on the heels of that, *a long and hard journey, yet he still takes time to shave his head each day. Interesting.*

Next to him was a woman, her hair just as shining black, and cut quite severely across her forehead into a fringe. She was tall and wiry, and sat watching the crowd with a considering look on her face. The thick metal plates that covered her chest had once been painted with a red octopus, but years of hard wear had chipped much of it away.

'Hello! Hello, welcome to Ebora!'

With Okaar's help, Vintage pushed through the people standing around gawking, to the gate itself, which was still standing open. The man on his fine black horse scowled down at her, while his people milled about behind him, not quite approaching the gate.

'You are human,' he said. His plains speech was heavily accented.

'You noticed? That's encouraging.' Vintage smiled up at him in what she hoped was a cheerful manner. 'Won't you come through the gate? You must have had a long journey—'

'You are human.' He cut her off, looking over her head to the palace beyond. 'Where are the Eboran lords? We wish to be properly greeted.'

Inwardly cursing, Vintage took a breath and raised her voice. Next to her, she felt rather than saw Okaar look at her in surprise.

'Who are you? What do you want here? State your business.'

The bearded man looked back at her, black eyebrows raising fractionally.

'We are Yuron-Kai.' He paused, as though for dramatic effect. 'I am Sen-Lord Takor. This,' he indicated the woman with the severe fringe, 'is Sena-Lord Kivee. As for our business in Ebora . . .'

Sena-Lord Kivee urged her horse forward, pulling at a heavy

sack strapped to her saddle. She tipped it up and let its contents fall at Vintage's feet. It was a corpse, the body small and pressed in on itself, its skin turned purple and yellow. It was flat, too flat for any human corpse, and without any surprise Vintage noted the holes where its eyes should be, and the gaping slash at its throat that revealed a black, rubbery substance, long since dried. A drone.

'This was our son.' Sena-Lord Kivee's voice was clipped and smooth, her eyes difficult to read, although Vintage thought the glitter in them was due to more than just the sunny day. 'Our son, this abomination. Where are the Eboran sen-lords? Where are their beasts? For they are not in the skies over Yuron-Kai. That is our business in Ebora.'

Vintage sighed, her eyes on the sad, shrivelled thing at her feet. How long had his mother been travelling with that thing strapped to her horse? She could smell the preservatives they had packed it with, sharp and sour in her nose. It was possible to see a leather cuff on the shrivelled arm, the red octopus painted there a twin to the one on Sena-Lord Kivee's chest.

'Please,' she said eventually. 'Do come inside.'

Tyranny Munk had been in the receiving room, drinking rapidly from a fresh pot of tea – she seemed to have taken a shine to it – when the congregation from Yuron-Kai were led in. Eight of them came, with two insisting on staying with their horses, and they stood with straight backs behind the chairs and loungers, looking uncomfortable and overdressed while their two leaders glared around at the artful furnishings. Tyranny had picked up her cup and sauntered to the corner of the room, but she did not leave. Instead, Vintage saw her exchange a significant look with Okaar, who had also been careful not to leave her side. This was less than ideal, but, Vintage reasoned, she had no time to deal with it now. She murmured to one of the Finneral guards on the door, asking for someone to fetch

Eri and Nanthema, if they could find them, then hopped awkwardly to the centre of the room.

'My lords, you have come a long way. Will you not sit? Are there any refreshments you would prefer? There is tea, but I can find you something stronger, if you prefer.'

Sen-Lord Takor glanced at the padded chair as though it were a dog making a mess on the carpet, and did not sit.

'I will say again, where are the Eboran sen-lords? Where are their beasts? We are owed an explanation.'

'They are coming.' Vintage moved towards the chair, then thought better of it. Walking with the crutch was straining all sorts of muscles and she longed to sit down, but having this conversation with the Yuron-Kai lords looming over her seemed like an unfortunate start. 'I am Lady Vincenza de Grazon.' When they did not react to this, she cleared her throat and continued. 'Perhaps you can tell me what happened.' Seeing a flicker of indignation on Sena-Lord Kivee's face, she held up one hand. 'The worm people, of course, but details here would be most appreciated. Ebora is isolated, as I'm sure you know, and any information we can gather is useful in our fight.'

'We were visiting our outer camps,' said Sena-Lord Kivee. 'There had been a hard snow, and since the corpse moon left the skies, a bad feeling was in the air, like panic among horses. Our people, Vincenza de Grazon, are familiar with the horrors of the worm people. Our lands bear their scars. When the nights are long and dark, it can become tempting for the weak and cowardly to abandon their families for places they believe to be safer, like the soft bright cities of Reidn, even Mushenska.' As his partner spoke, Sen-Lord Takor's mouth twisted, revealing what he thought of such places. 'So we patrol. Our people were afraid, and rumours were flying around all campfires. We watched the skies, and told them – Ebora will wake, and come. We had heard those whispers too, you see, that the

369

tree-god had birthed new beast warriors.' Sena-Lord Kivee paused. It was painfully quiet in the room, the sounds from the palace garden seeming to come from miles away. 'But the worm people came, their ugly ship birthing forth monstrosities, and our people were slaughtered, and although we fought, we were slaughtered too. Those who died got up again and fixed cold hands around our throats. Our son, who had been riding with us to learn the ways of a sen-lord, was overwhelmed by the monstrosities and I could not reach him, I could not –' She stopped again, then stood up a little straighter. 'Where was Ebora? Where were their knights? In the past, we have fought together. The history of Yuron-Kai is riddled with such tales. But in this Ninth Rain, they have let us die. We fought alone, and watched our families eaten. Eaten. Where was Ebora? *Where?*'

'A blood debt is owed us.' Sen-Lord Takor rested his hand on his belt, where Vintage couldn't help noticing he kept a short sword and three daggers of various sizes. 'It will be paid.'

'My lords, I am sorry for your loss. You must know of the losses Ebora has also faced in recent centuries?' Vintage kept her face very still. Out of the corner of her eye she could see Tyranny, an empty cup held in her hands. The young woman was watching intently. 'The death of the tree-god, the crimson flux. Ebora is not what it once was.'

'The tree-god lives again,' said Sena-Lord Kivee. 'Our son does not.'

'What happened?' To Vintage's enormous surprise, Tyranny stepped forward from her corner, putting the teacup down on a nearby table. 'You weren't all killed, were you? Because you're standing here now, with faces like smacked arses. So what happened?'

Vintage watched the confusion pass over the Yuron-Kai lords' faces – she imagined they were trying to decipher the plains speech for 'arses' – and, for a moment, she wondered if Lord Sen-Takor would simply take out his sword and murder them all. Instead, he frowned at the blond-haired woman.

'The worm people's ship was damaged,' he said shortly. 'It seemed to have difficulty remaining in the air. They killed many hundreds, and we cut down the walking corpses, but when it birthed its great worm, the thing did not live long enough to produce the green fluid. Shortly after that, the worm people's ship left.'

'There were holes in it,' added Sena-Lord Kivee. 'In the side of the ship. And the behaviour of the creatures was erratic.'

'Interesting,' said Vintage. 'This would add up to what we have observed too – that the Jure'lia are weakened and confused. It certainly does not reflect their usual methodical patterns, as observed in previous Rains. My lords—'

At that moment, there was a scuffle at the door and Eri arrived, his eyes wide at the sight of so many people in the receiving room. Vintage looked beyond him, hoping to see Nanthema, but instead she saw Helcate, his scruffy snout resting on Eri's shoulder. Vintage felt her heart sink.

'What is this?' asked Sen-Lord Takor coldly.

'Lords, please allow me to introduce Eri of Lonefell, and Helcate, our youngest war-beast.'

'Youngest? It is a runt!' Sena-Lord Kivee looked to her partner in disbelief. 'A runt and a child? Is this what Ebora is? Where are your true beasts?' She changed her stance, gripping the back of the chair in front of her. With some dismay, Vintage saw that her knuckles were turning white with the force of it. 'You dare to lie to us? We have heard reports from several scouts, and from travellers through Yuron-Kai, that there is both a dragon and a griffin – enormous, powerful war-beasts. Yet you insult us by bring us this half-formed thing?'

'Hel*cate*,' said Helcate.

'The war-beasts you speak of, along with others, are away

371

on missions right now.' Vintage raised her hand. 'Due to the hardships Ebora has suffered, their forces are greatly reduced, and they cannot possibly be everywhere at once.'

'It's true,' added Tyranny. 'We came here to see them too, but they're busy. As you might expect at a time of war.'

'Are you letting that child raise it?' demanded Sen-Lord Takor. 'Clearly you do not know what you are doing. A human woman, greeting us at the gates of the Eboran palace! Do you think to stay here and be safe by keeping the war-beasts to yourselves?' He shook his head. 'The remaining pods should be given to us for raising. Raised in Yuron-Kai, they would be warriors such as the previous Rains have seen. Greater, even.'

'Hold on! How do you even know about those?' Vintage glared around at the gathered warriors. 'And such a suggestion is ridiculous! You think you can just walk into Ebora and start taking their property?' She shook her head, annoyed with herself. 'Not even their property, but their sacred children. It is an outrage! I will not hear it said in my presence again.'

To her surprise, Sena-Lord Kivee looked at her partner, and she seemed to sense a reprimand in that glance. The bearded man made a grumbling noise, and clasped his hands behind his back.

'Yuron-Kai demands the assistance of the Eboran lords.' Sena-Lord Kivee let go of the chair back, her voice soft but still dangerous. 'We will not stand by and suffer more losses. You will mark these words.'

36

In the silvery dawn light, the grey war-beast pods looked eerie and misshapen, like gravestones in a forgotten graveyard. Eri went to each one in turn, telling it good morning and hello. It was the first thing he did each day, and each day he hoped that he would find a new war-beast waiting to greet him back. They remained inert.

Once he had greeted them all, he went back to Helcate, who was waiting in the centre of the Hatchery, and they sat companionably for a while. Eventually, they would both be hungry and they would wander down to the palace's sprawling kitchens to see what the humans were cooking that morning, but for now Eri liked to watch the pods, just in case. Sometimes he felt like everyone else had forgotten about them.

'But they are your brothers and sisters,' he said to Helcate, who was resting his furry head on his front paws. 'They just need more sleep than the rest of us. I know you're feeling lonely, since the others went away, but you just have to remember that the rest of your family is in here. What's it like having so many brothers and sisters?'

Helcate yawned cavernously. 'Helcate.'

'Oh. Well, you are nearly as big as Kirune now, and your

wings work beautifully. So I am sure you will fly and fight with them when they all come back.' Eri pulled his fingers through the beast's fur. 'I suppose Kirune could have grown while he was away, but you're pretty big.'

There was a noise at one of the tall windows. It was still quite dark out, the shadows lingering as long as they could before the sun chased them off, but Eri thought that he could see a shape there. He looked back to the huge double doors; human guards stood outside them at all times, but there was no sound of activity from the corridor. He heard another noise, and this time it was identifiable enough: a hesitant *tap tap*.

Cautiously, Eri stood up and moved to the window where the shadow waited. The person outside was no taller than him, and they stood close to the frame, almost as though they were making themselves look as small as possible.

'Helcate,' said Helcate.

'I know,' Eri whispered back. 'I'm just having a look.' In a slightly louder voice, he said, 'Who's there?'

'It's Jhef. Can you let me in?'

Eri stood very still, his hand resting on the sill. It had been a while since anyone had dusted it. He knew who Jhef was – she was the sister of the man Okaar, who had come with the war-beast armour. He and Helcate had looked over every inch of it, of course, and been annoyed to find that almost all of it did not fit the war-beast yet.

'I can't let you in here.'

'Why not?'

Eri had to admit he did not really know why not. When he didn't answer, the girl spoke again.

'I just want to have a look at them. I've seen you come in here every morning. What's so interesting? Can't you show me?'

'I'm not supposed to, that's all.'

374

Jhef made a snorting, disgusted noise. 'That's no reason for anything at all.'

Eri turned and looked back at Helcate. The war-beast was sitting up, his long raggedly tail curled around his feet, but he didn't venture an opinion. There had been lots of things Eri wasn't supposed to do at Lonefell – leave the grounds, explore Ebora, ask questions – but the world was different since the corpse moon had fallen from the sky.

The window had been locked with a pair of steel arms that were screwed in place. They were rusted, and even appeared to have been painted over at some point, but when the pods were placed in the Hatchery someone (probably Bern) had come and opened each window to air the place. They had all been carefully locked again, but it was no great feat to remove the screws. When he pushed the pane up, there was a terrible screeching noise, and he stopped, heart thumping in his throat, but no guards came. Perhaps they had fallen asleep.

He had only pushed the window up a few feet, but the girl slipped through it like an eel, barely making a sound. She grinned at him in the gloom of the Hatchery; her clothes were all dark, and her black hair hung partially over her face, but her eyes were very bright.

'Hello. You're Eri, aren't you?'

She did not sound like anyone he had ever met, with a music to her voice he had not heard from the other humans.

'That's me. This is Helcate.'

Her eyes grew wide, and she slipped further into the chamber. She made no sound at all as she walked.

'A war-beast! We've seen him from a distance, but not close like this.' She flashed Eri another smile. 'He is very beautiful.'

'Helcate,' Helcate agreed.

'Thank you for letting me in, Eri. It was colder out there than I thought. Your country is very nice to look at, but not very warm. Okaar is always dragging us to cold places.'

'It's still spring here, and the snows have only recently gone,' pointed out Eri, reasonably enough. 'Okaar is your . . . brother?'

She made a face. 'My big, overbearing brother. Do you have brothers and sisters Eri? Where is your family?'

Eri thought of the bucket. 'Oh, far away from here. I don't have any siblings, but I have Helcate.'

She padded silently over to Helcate and stood looking up at him. Helcate's big blue eyes were like lost pieces of summer sky. Outside, the sun was finally breaking free of the horizon and the chilly light revealed the dust on top of the war-beast pods. Eri found himself feeling oddly ashamed.

'When did Helcate hatch? How old is he?'

'He was the last to hatch.' Eri found he was glad to talk, as if that might distract from the empty, sad atmosphere of the room. 'It was on the eighth day of the Turning month, in the year of the Crawling Spider.' Realising how formal he sounded, he cleared his throat. 'I mean, he's much younger than the others, and look at how big he is!'

'The process can take that long? It sounds unpredictable.' Jhef looked around the room, and the assessing expression on her face confused Eri, but then she caught his eye and it vanished. 'I did not realise there were so many beasts waiting to be born here! Thank you for showing them to me.'

Eri scuffed his boots over the floor, trying to ignore the worm of worry that was growing in his gut. He did not feel that he had been showing the girl the war-beast pods, but it seemed that is what she thought he had done. He suspected Vintage would not be too pleased about that. When he didn't answer, she wandered over to the nearest pod.

'How heavy are they? Probably not heavy for an Eboran to lift – Okaar says you are all very strong – but a human would have trouble, wouldn't they?'

'I don't know.' Eri shrugged, and then in a quieter voice said, 'I haven't really met any humans before.'

376

'You haven't? Well, I haven't met any Eborans either, although there're quite a few more of us than you.'

She smiled in a certain way, and Eri realised she had been making a sort of joke.

'Ha ha,' he said, hoping that was the right response and distantly wishing the ground would open up and carry him away. 'Ha, yes, although my people did try to lessen your numbers at one point.'

There was a horrible period of silence, and then Jhef seemed to brush off his attempt at humour. She reached out to touch the inert pod, then thought better of it.

'I hope one hatches before we leave, Eri. That would be incredible. Something hardly any other human has seen. Are there still guards outside the door?'

Eri blinked. 'Yes, they stay there all day and all night.'

'Sorry, I will speak more quietly.' She pushed her hair back behind her ear, revealing her long face fully for the first time. 'I don't want to get you in trouble. Do you think one will hatch?'

Again, Eri felt oddly ashamed, although he could not tell if this was because he had somehow revealed the vulnerability of the war-beasts, or because he felt responsible somehow for their failure to hatch.

'I don't know,' he said simply. 'We just have to wait.'

'But don't you have any idea? I mean, is one of these pods more likely to give you a war-beast than another? You say hello to all of them each morning, don't you? Are any warmer than the others, or do they move?'

So many questions. 'Sometimes I think some are warmer than others, but then I think it is where they are warmed by the sun.' Jhef was looking at him attentively, and as the room grew brighter he could see that there was a scar on her chin – a tiny curve of white against her brown skin, like the half-moon shape on his fingernail. 'This one, though.' Hesitantly, he walked over to the pod that was third closest to the back of the room. It was just slightly smaller than Helcate's pod had been. 'Helcate sometimes feels something from this one.'

Jhef looked impressed. 'He does? What does he feel?'

'It's hard to describe.' Eri frowned, trying to think of the right words. 'It's like when you can hear someone talking in the next room, but can't make out what they're saying. And sometimes I have touched it, and it is warm. It's not much, really.' He shrugged. 'But if I had to choose one to hatch next, it would be this pod.'

Jhef smiled. 'I hope it does, and soon. What does Helcate eat? What are his very favourite foods?'

'Oh, he will eat most things. He's always hungry!' Eri smiled. 'I think it's because he's still growing. But there is a cheese the humans make . . . I mean, the Finneral people have a cheese made from goat's milk, and he loves that. He got into their tent and ate a whole wheel of it to himself, and I thought they would be very angry, but instead they laughed. They said they would send for more of it.'

From the corridor outside came the sound of male voices, low and fogged with recent sleep. It was the guard changing over, and Eri found his throat growing tight.

'If they find us in here . . .'

'Shall we go to the kitchens?' Jhef didn't look at all concerned at the noises from the guards, but she was making her way back to the open window. 'You can slip out this way with me, and I can show you all the secret ways I've found.'

Eri stopped by the window. The gardens beyond were bright with icy sunshine, glittering on the dew. He knew what it would feel like to run his hands through the grass, that sudden burst of chilly wetness, but then he looked back at Helcate.

'I can't,' he said. 'Helcate won't fit through the window.'

The girl looked blank, and in that moment she looked much older than she had, and much more like her brother. In the next eye blink, the blankness was gone and she seemed happy, if slightly disappointed.

'Of course, that's silly of me. I'll leave you, then.' She went back to the window and slipped back out into the bright morning. 'Thank you for showing me the pods!' This last was a whisper, and then she was gone. Eri couldn't see how she could disappear in such clear sunlight, but when he went to the window and peered out, there was nothing to say she had been there at all.

'Oh,' he said, feeling as though he had failed some sort of test. He thought of the dew and the secret ways, and felt a sour bloom of disappointment in his chest.

'Helcate,' said Helcate.

37

It appears that Tethras – Tethras, of all people – truly has stumbled upon something extraordinary. He has produced more fragments of the Forbidden Texts, and although they are vague and, in some cases, extremely cryptic, they all seem to point to something significant in the midst of the Barren Sea. My mind begins to turn in all directions, and I cannot sleep at night. Can I let this go? Can I stay here and watch the last of my people die when there is a chance of redemption?

Tethras is staying in our apartments, and there is no question now that he has the flux. Arnia spends a great deal of time with him, nursing him or easing his passage, I do not know, but sometimes, when he is well enough, he will sit by the fire with me and I hear the story of how he came to find such wonders, although his telling is frac-tured and strange. The flux seeps into our minds sometimes, and I think that might be the cruellest part of it.

He was hunting. Despite the disaster that was the Carrion Wars Tethras was never quite able to let go of his hunger for human blood, and that is not as rare as an outsider might think. Just because it is poison, this does not mean it no longer soothes our aches and wakes our minds – but most Eborans who still partake find willing human donors, and sample only enough to keep old age at bay. For Tethras, the chase, the killing, the feast . . . these were all a part of it. He heard that there was a human settlement on the very edge of Eboran territory, so he travelled there, meaning to pick them off one by one, at night perhaps. He would make a game of it. All this he told me with a gleam in his eye, and I think he wanted to become something like an evil spirit to them. Something to warn their children of at bedtime, a creature of darkness. Just as they expect us to be, he told me, smiling. But he underestimated his own bloodlust. He found them living in an old abandoned temple, and in a fit of rage he killed them all. 'How dare they?' he asked me, as though his slaughter were in response to some insult rather than an attempt to relive his war days. When he had drunk his fill, he explored the temple, and found it to contain more than just the corpses of his unfortunate victims. A buried room, an iron chest. The keys to our future, perhaps.

Arnia joined me as I walked the palace grounds, and she spoke of ships, and maps. Slowly, our ideas are forming, and hope is such a fragile thing I feel I cannot look at it directly. In the soft light of dusk Arnia's face was gaunt, and I know she looks upon my skin, still smooth and unlined, and sees time running out for her. She has always been the practical one.

Extract from the private journal
of Micanal the Clearsighted

Noon stretched her legs out under the table, wriggling her toes. Her boots, which were thick with river mud, had been cast down by the table, and they ate again outside, another balmy early-evening sky overhead.

'You have yet to find the tablets, then? I do not envy you the task, not in this sun, pawing through all that mud. Here, have some more cake.'

Arnia was in fine form, standing and smiling as she served up big slices of a moist fruit cake. As at every meal, she ate very little herself, but still seemed full of a restless energy.

'If you helped us, we might find them more quickly.' Noon watched the woman's face for a reaction, but she just smiled all the wider.

'And have you leave me all the sooner? I could hardly do that.'

Noon tried to catch Tor's eye, sure that he must see that this could practically be an admission of guilt, but the stupid Eboran was already halfway through the bottle of wine and seemed quite happy to be fed endless food and lies. Vostok crouched at the far end of the table with the old man, and they were talking together quietly, taking little notice of the rest of the company. For the first time since arriving on the strange island, Noon felt a real lurch of fear. Tor, with his beautiful face in profile, Arnia poised as the ethereal hostess, moving gracefully around the table, Micanal with his long fingers interlaced, his head bowed. And the dragon, pearl scales shining in the evening light. They were all figures out of a story – living, breathing myths and monsters – and she was the only human: weak, short-lived, a footnote to their history. What was she even doing here?

'Where is Kirune?' She wasn't sure why, but the big cat's cool demeanour was something she suddenly missed.

'He is off exploring,' Tor said, toying with a piece of bread. 'He likes to prowl the woods.'

'Lord Kirune must be careful,' said Arnia. 'As I said before, much of this island is not safe. I would not like Kirune to find himself in danger.'

'Danger? What would a war-beast have to fear here?'

382

But Arnia did not answer the question. Instead, she put down the bottle of wine she had been pouring for Tor and brushed her hands together.

'Do forgive me, but I am feeling so tired today. I think it must be all the excitement of having guests.' She smiled wanly and looked around at them all, her gaze lingering longest on Tor. Micanal looked up from his conversation with the dragon, and Noon thought he looked at his sister with something approaching contempt, but the expression, if it had ever existed at all, was gone in a moment. 'I will go to my bed, I think, but please, finish the food and drink here. You will need to keep your strength up if you will be searching more mud tomorrow.'

Noon watched her go. They had set the table at the back of the house, but curiously, she walked around the side, apparently heading to go in the front door.

'You know, I think I'll follow Arnia's example. My back is killing me, and I could do with resting it.' Tor looked up at her in surprise but without much interest.

'Do what you will. I'll be here a little while yet.' And he poured another glass of wine.

Noon headed towards the house they had been given to sleep in, but once inside, she kept going and left via the back door. Moving as quickly and as quietly as she could she slipped into the trees and used them as cover to reach Micanal's and Arnia's dwelling. She got to it just in time to see Arnia not, as she had claimed, retiring for the night, but walking off to where the trees were densest. She had apparently grabbed a shawl to wrap around her shoulders, and her face was still and intent. Keeping a fair distance back, Noon followed her into the forest, her heat thumping thickly in her chest.

It was not easy. Noon had never followed anyone before, and her every footstep seemed impossibly loud, breaking every twig in the forest and finding every patch of dry leaves to

383

crunch, and Arnia moved very quickly, clearly at home among these trees. It was growing darker too, and for several long moments Noon was sure she had lost the woman, one more shadow in a forest full of them. Once, Arnia stopped and looked behind her, searching the forest for something, and Noon pressed against a tree, barely daring to breath. She was uncertain why she was so frightened of the idea of Arnia catching her. It wasn't that it would be rude – she was fairly sure that the Eboran woman didn't like her anyway, or at least thought she was barely worth noticing – but more a sense that she would genuinely be in danger. For all her smiles and welcoming demeanour, something about Arnia had a sharp edge, and Noon had no wish to be caught on it.

Arnia moved on, and Noon followed, picking her way with even more care. Eventually, they came to the chasm, although much further up than the route Micanal had taken. Here the foliage was thicker, so that it was difficult even to reach the edge, and Noon thought that perhaps this was where she had hidden the tablets, but instead Arnia headed deep into a tall cloud of bushes, disappearing utterly from sight. Noon froze. To follow her into the thicket was too much like walking into a trap, and there was hardly anywhere she could go from there, since the crevasse loomed beyond it. Confused, Noon back-tracked, edging away from the bushes to get a better view, and that was when she saw Arnia moving across the bridge.

It should have been obvious. It was a rickety thing of ropes and planks, but it was hung heavily with the vines and plants that had grown around it, and against the cliff faces with their own vibrant foliage it seemed to vanish into the background. Noon doubted that she would have spotted it at all, especially in the dark, if it hadn't been for Arnia's tall figure walking across it, her shawl across her shoulders.

'If the other side of the island is so bloody dangerous,' murmured Noon, 'then where is she going?'

She waited for Arnia to cross to the other side, and then cautiously she made her way to the bushes that had concealed the entrance. Here, it was possible to see that they had been deliberately planted; they were too regularly spaced to be anything else.

'Right. Fine. So why hide a bloody bridge?'

The bridge stretched in front of her, ending on the other side in the midst of a very similar patch of foliage. Arnia could be over there right now, waiting for her to walk across the bridge – she would be an easy target, and there could be no denying that she had been following the Eboran woman.

'I am a weapon,' she reminded herself. The bridge was covered in leaves and vines, so it would hardly be difficult to summon winnowfire there. And Eborans burned just like anyone else.

Just then, she felt a stirring from Vostok, clearly summoned by Noon's feelings of aggression and fear. With a pang of guilt, she held the war-beast back, pushing her away as lightly as possible. A dragon suddenly appearing at the crevasse could hardly be easily hidden.

The bridge swung alarmingly as she stepped out onto it, and the water below seemed very far away. It occurred to her that it would be the easiest thing in the world for Arnia to wait until she was halfway across and cut the ropes, and then winnowfire would be no help at all. But she walked on, biting her lower lip until she reached the other side. There was no sign of Arnia, and Noon felt a stab of annoyance – to have followed her this far and lost her – but then she heard, quite clearly, the crack of a branch as someone who did not care how noisy they were stood on it. She moved in that direction, her head up to catch every possible noise, and saw that there was a path of sorts below her feet – a dirt path, worn into the ground by someone who came this way often, even daily. This, she had no doubt, was where Arnia kept disappearing to at all hours of the day.

385

Crouching slightly, she moved on. The light was leaching from the day as every second passed, but she caught sight of Arnia in the distance again, and quickened her pace. It would not do to get lost out here, and the Eboran woman clearly knew where she was going. They walked in this secret tandem for another hour, until the sky overhead was a deep purple punctured with stars, and Noon had started to wonder if the woman was just mad and really very keen on long walks, when, ahead of them, Noon spotted a series of orange lights. Torches, burning in the night, and below them, a fence made of wood. It didn't look especially sturdy, at least not in comparison to settlements out in the Wild where every care was taken to shelter from the monsters that habitually haunted Sarn. There was something out here, then, something they hadn't been told about.

Arnia walked towards a gate, or a hole in the fence, and vanished from sight. Noon stopped, her heart thudding thickly in her chest, and then, after a moment, she approached the fence, coming close enough to be able to see through the gaps. The movement she saw beyond the wooden panels, so unexpected after so long in the forest, made her jump. The fence circled an enclosure of huts made of wood and mud, and no more than twenty feet from her she could see a group of humans, varying in age. As she watched, more appeared at the doors of the hovels, all watching Arnia as she walked through the settlement. To Noon they looked like they had been plains people once – their skin was tan like hers, and their hair was black, although here and there she saw paler faces. It was difficult to tell in the uncertain torchlight. All of them looked undernourished, with not enough flesh on their bones and hollows around their eyes, and their clothes were mended and patched so much that they appeared to be holding together with twine only. All of them were staring at Arnia with awe. Noon felt her throat tighten. Earlier she had been afraid that she was the only human here. Now it turned out that was not true, and she was filled with dread.

In contrast, Arnia looked totally unconcerned. She walked past most of the humans as though they weren't there, pausing once to exchange words with a young woman who had a child of about four or five years old clutching at her skirts. Noon could not hear the words, but when Arnia bent down to smile at the child, a shiver seemed to pass around the crowd – some unspoken fright. The Eboran woman straightened up and walked out of sight. When she did not immediately come back, Noon settled on her haunches, checking that she was not visible to the people in the settlement. Most were returning to their huts, their heads down, and to Noon they looked like people waking from a long sleep, their eyes unfocussed.

'What would Vintage say?' murmured Noon. She rested one hand on the wooden plank, and tried to look at the strange village as the scholar would have looked. There were around fifty people that she could see, and enough houses for perhaps twice that. Some of the buildings were bigger, and they had holes in their roofs through which smoke escaped. She also saw tanning racks, rows and rows of them, and, to her surprise, livestock; a pen off to one side containing fleeten, of all things – the swift little creatures of the plains – and even a cow, one of the big shaggy creatures from Finneral. There was a man carrying buckets of milk, and through one open doorway she saw a spinning wheel. As unassuming and rustic as it was, Noon thought this was a place of great industry. One woman, who stood closest to her, had tough pads on her hands that Noon recognised; the weavers of her tribe had carried the same marks from long hours of work. She smiled slightly to herself, thinking that Vintage would be impressed with that observation, when she saw that the woman was crying. Her arms were at her sides and her shoulders shook, and no one came to comfort her, as though despair were a constant companion not worth commenting on.

The night seemed colder, then. Noon looked behind her, into the darkening trees, and saw other signs; paths leading away into the dark, even ruts where barrows were used frequently, and pegs hammered into tree trunks to allow easier climbing. There would be a lot of fruit here, she guessed – they had seen plenty of it on their way from the beach on this strange, warm island. She thought of the wine Arnia had poured for them, and wondered which fruit these ragged people collected for it.

Inside the enclosure, she caught the sound of raised voices, and heard enough of it to recognise the same odd version of plains talk that Borrow and Tidewater had used on the island of Firstlight. Perhaps they were related, or had come from the same place, once, a long time ago. The man who was speaking was short and sturdy, his muscles like ropes on his arms and legs, and he had a thick, dark beard. He was gesturing in the direction that Arnia had disappeared, and another, younger, man was taking his arm, trying to turn him away from it. The younger man looked both annoyed and scared – whatever this conversation was, he did not want Arnia to hear it. Noon pressed herself to the fence as close as she dared, trying to make out more words, but the wind had changed direction, keeping the voices of these mysterious settlers distant. She caught brief snatches that seemed to make little sense.

'. . . You are all caught in a madness . . .'

'. . . That's enough. I am sorry for you, that you are so blind to what we are, that you cannot see the Poisonless . . .'

'. . . If you would listen to yourselves. The night ruins . . .'

'. . . We don't have time for this. The roots are our concern, our duty . . .'

Noon frowned, half certain that her understanding of their language was not as correct as she thought, when Arnia re-appeared. All talk in the settlement stopped, and the older man pulled his arm roughly away from the younger one. He stalked off into the huts while Arnia left the enclosure, once again not looking at any of the people who stood staring at her. She walked rapidly, her arms bared to the night and her head high – the smooth skin of her forehead shone in the torchlight. She seemed to have left her shawl behind.

Before she left to follow Arnia back to the far side of the island, Noon took one last look at the villagers. They were going back to their own business: carrying waterskins, fetching food. She lifted out of her crouch, wincing slightly at a sharp ache in her lower back – the river had yet to yield any amber tablets – and saw that a little girl of four or five was standing and watching her, one pudgy fist pressed to her mouth. Her dark eyes were very, very wide.

Noon slipped back into the trees.

It was a long and fraught journey back. Arnia seemed more alert than she had done earlier, and many times she stopped and turned around, looking back where Noon was following. By this time it was so dark that Noon could only really see the dimmest outline of the tall woman, but Arnia had no apparent difficulty in finding her way, and when she turned and looked back, Noon couldn't help thinking of those red eyes, seeking her out. The Eboran moved faster than she had before, as though she was eager to get back by sun-up. When eventually they crossed over the chasm and came to a part of the forest Noon recognised, she dropped back, letting Arnia complete her journey alone; out from under the trees, she would have no cover. After a reasonable amount of time had passed, she continued, feeling some of the tension drain out of her chest.

The clearing with the houses was quiet when she got there. Dim lamps shone in the windows of the siblings' home, and in the building she shared with Tor. Belatedly, she wondered if he had come to find her and then stayed up, waiting for her to return. That would be awkward. Uncertain what to do next, she stood on the edge of the trees. The sky was a deep grey, the colour of old dust, and the horizon was tainted a dirty orange. It would be dawn soon, and the new day would bring more questions without answers. Noon had no idea whom she could truly trust, and, to top it all off, she'd had no bloody sleep.

A prickle on the back of her neck alerted her to the presence of Vostok, and then a bare breath later, she saw her; the dragon was, improbably, crouched in the branches of one of the tallest trees. In the dark she would have been well hidden in the shadows of the canopy, but as the day lightened her bright scales stood out like polished silver pennies. Despite herself, Noon smiled.

'What are you doing up there?'

The dragon lowered her long head. Her feathered wings were tucked tightly along her back.

'Can you climb up here to me?'

Noon blinked at this strange request. 'I don't know. It's been a long time since I've climbed a tree. A lot of grass on the plains, so I didn't get to practise that often.' When Vostok didn't answer, she shrugged. 'I can try.'

After hours trekking through the woods in the dark it was the last thing she needed, but Vostok let her long tail drape down the length of the trunk, and using that as a handhold when there wasn't a natural one, Noon eventually hauled herself up onto the thicket of branches where Vostok had arranged herself. It was cool among the leaves, full of a rushing whisper as they brushed against each other, and it smelled of sap and salt. As huge as the tree was, Noon was still amazed it was holding the dragon's weight.

'What is it?' She realised belatedly that she could not feel Vostok as clearly as she normally did, as though the dragon were holding back somehow. 'Has something happened? Did you find the amber tablets?'

390

Vostok turned her head so that her great violet eye was close to Noon's face.

'I did not think this would be so hard. I thought that I had come to terms, somewhat, with what we have lost, but speaking to Micanal the Clearsighted makes it sharp again.' Vostok turned her head away. 'I am finding it difficult to sleep. Being in the trees reminds me, a little, of home.'

'Of Ygseril?' When the dragon dipped her head, Noon pressed her hand briefly to her snout. 'I don't trust this place, Vostok. I don't trust Arnia. This is a place of lies.' She took a breath. 'Arnia goes somewhere on the other side of the island, and there are humans there! Humans scraping an existence off the land. Why wouldn't she tell us about that? And Micanal must know.'

Vostok didn't say anything for a time. When she did speak, it was softly, using a tone Noon was sure she had never heard the dragon use before.

'They are my link to a very distant past. They alone understand what I have lost.'

'Did you know them? Before?'

'A little. I was fond of Micanal's art, of course. Many of us were. And he created many special pieces for the Nest, which we supervised and instructed him on. His sister, I only knew as a figure in the background, a shadow. She would bring him messages sometimes, or food, if he was working late. I never heard her speak, that I remember.'

'That doesn't sound much like the Arnia we know.'

Vostok tipped her head to one side in her equivalent of a shrug.

'When Micanal began speaking of a great record, a way of preserving our history, we were all of a mind that it was a magnificent idea. When I knew him, in my previous form, it was little more than that – an idea. As our most celebrated artist, we trusted him to do it, and to do it well. He was an honourable man.' She paused. 'I remember that there were war-beasts who regretted that they were not bonded to him, even though he was not a warrior and would be of little use should a Rain fall.' The dragon sniffed. 'It was vanity to think such things. War-beasts must always remember that they are weapons, that their goal is always victory. No matter how beautiful art is, or how entrancing songs are, our place is always, ultimately in battle. But Micanal was a charming man, dignified and trustworthy. He was highly honoured among us.'

'I'm not sure that he's so trustworthy now, Vostok. They are lying to us, I'm sure of it. And if he valued you all so highly, why would he throw the amber tablets into the crevasse? You would think those dreams he had crafted of the lost war-beasts would be precious to him. And the humans! He must know about them. What are they doing here?'

'The amber tablets are likely a lost cause anyway. Such things cannot replace the lost root-memories of the lesser war-beasts.' Vostok pulled her serpentine neck up and away, so that her head rose into the branches. 'And humans are hardly my concern. You say that Micanal is acting strangely, that he is not trustworthy. Perhaps you are not understanding him. You know very few Eborans, after all. You do not know our people, or who we are. Not truly.'

Noon straightened on the branch, feeling her face grow hot. The life energy of the tree was a greenish tingle against her fingers, seeming to thrum with her own anger.

'Well, humans concern me, because I bloody well am one. I'm sorry if that is a disappointment to you, but this is what you're stuck with.' Underneath the anger, she felt like she had been struck in the chest. Of them all, she had hoped for Vostok's understanding, but the dragon was holding herself at a distance. 'And your great and wondrous artist is not what he appears. Neither is his sister.' She shuffled to the edge of the branch, preparing to scramble back down the trunk, but Vostok lowered her head. The dawn light played across her milky scales, briefly dazzling, and Noon remembered that she was sitting in a tree with a dragon.

'You go to Tormalin now, I expect.'

Noon stopped. 'What do you mean by that?'

'He will hurt you, little weapon. Eborans always end up hurting humans – either through malice, through inattention, or boredom. His eye has already started to stray, and if you cannot see that, your dull human senses are of even less use than I thought.'

Noon left the tree a little faster than she meant to, scraping the palms of her hands against the bark in her haste to get away, and she stalked back to the rows of houses without looking back. She didn't want Vostok to see what was on her face, even though she knew the dragon could feel it plainly enough – just as she felt the thin thread of the war-beast's disgust.

38

When Hestillion had been young, there had been a brief fashion among the Eborans to own hunting hounds. Pets generally were an unpopular concept with them, because the lifespans of normal animals were so very brief, but for some reason there was a short span of years when the big, shaggy wolfhounds from the east were popular, and Hestillion's father had given in to the craze. She remembered that she had been vaguely scared of the thing, as it had long legs, and was taller than she was at the time. It had had short, wiry grey and blond fur, and Mother had let Tor name it. He was not frightened of the hound, and he named it Mouse, as everything had to be a joke with her brother. Once, she and Tor had been out in the forest with their father and Mouse, and a pair of wolves had approached them, slinking silently out from between the trees. They weren't worm-touched but they were big, healthy animals, and her father's hand had dropped to the sword at his belt. Hestillion remembered very clearly that she had been exasperated by that – there was no chance, by all the roots, that their useless father would be able to protect them. Mouse, though, had jumped out in front of their small group, and he had put his head low to the ground and growled, prowling back and forth as though he were standing over his own pups. His wiry fur had stood up on end, and his mud-brown eyes flashed, and the wolves had slunk off again. What she was seeing in the massive chamber now made her think of that day; Celaphon growling and prancing, making himself look as large as possible, while the two smaller war-beasts looked on.

'I defeated you,' he hissed, 'because I am stronger!'

They were still separated from each other by the thin transparent walls, which Hestillion thought was all for the best, as the great griffin looked murderous with rage. Her cousin and the human man had been moved into the chamber with them, and there was no mistaking the aghast expressions on their faces as they watched the enormous dragon strut back and forth. The queen was a dark presence by the wall. She had been silent so far, simply watching.

'Let me out, and I will fight you, one warrior to another!' shouted the griffin, whose name apparently was Sharrik. The tall blond man, the one her cousin had been so concerned about, was back on his feet, although he looked pale and shaken. He stood next to Aldasair, but she could see him muttering words to the griffin, attempting to calm him. 'Let us see how you fare when we are not fighting your entire worm-army at the same moment.'

'War-beasts should not fight at all. Not against each other.' This was the great wolf, Jessen. Hestillion lifted her eyebrows. Aldasair's war-beast had hardly spoken at all so far, but her soft voice was ringing with tension. 'You are our brother.'

Celaphon stopped pacing, his tail swishing back and forth. This seemed to have thrown him. The wolf stepped forward.

'We were born from the same branches, we were nourished by the same roots. Why do you fight us?'

Hestillion glanced at the queen, expecting her to step in, or halt the discussion, but she stood unmoving, her cracked-glaze face perfectly still.

'I am different to you,' said Celaphon simply.

'That is no reason to fight.'

'He is not like us,' added Sharrik, hotly. 'He is tainted. I can smell it, and I know you can too, sister.'

The collar of jagged plates around Celaphon's jaw expanded, and he rose up to his full height. If he truly went berserk in here, Hestillion did not know what they could do to stop it. She stepped lightly in front of the dragon.

'Celaphon is stronger, hardier and fiercer. He is a war-beast unlike anything that has come before, and you are afraid.'

'Yes, I am,' said Jessen, her orange eyes on Hestillion. 'We should all be afraid, as should you, Lady Hestillion.'

Before she could reply to that, Celaphon lowered his head again, snorting hot blasts of foul-smelling breath.

'They are connected. How are you connected? Why am I not? What is the bond between you?'

The war-beasts looked at each other.

'We do not know what you mean,' said Jessen eventually.

'You fly together, think together, aid one another,' spat Celaphon. 'When one is threatened, the other comes for them. There is a bond. What is it? What is this connection?'

When no one replied Celaphon hissed at their silence. 'It is some magic you keep to yourselves. You call me brother, but you hide it from me.'

'There is nothing.' Aldasair had approached the transparent wall, and, annoyingly, he looked genuinely concerned. 'Nothing that could not also be yours, if you flew free with us.'

The queen had appeared at Celaphon's side. For the first time that Hestillion could recall, she was looking directly up into the dragon's face, regarding him as though he were a fellow being and not just some curious artefact.

'Celaphon,' she said. Hestillion was almost certain that she had never used his name before either. 'If it is a connection you seek, then we can give it to you.'

The dragon didn't answer, but continued looking down at the Jure'lia queen. His strange, pearly eyes looked blank.

'Have we not fed you? Brought you life when you were dying? Made you stronger and more powerful than any other?'

His reply was a murmur. 'Yes.'

'Then trust us. Come with us now.'

'What are you talking about?' asked Hestillion. She pitched her voice low, reluctant to let her cousin see her question the queen so directly, but she saw him out of the corner of her eye, clearly listening.

'Come, both of you, then. We will explain it as we go.'

'I have never seen anything like it.'

Aldasair spoke quietly. They still shared their cell, but the two war-beasts were sleeping, curled up together for comfort. He and Bern sat on the other side. They had both tried leaning against the wall, but the warmth and softness of it was unnerving. Aldasair was sure his shirt had stuck to it a little when he pulled away, as though it were slightly sticky.

'It is obvious they have . . . done something to him, poor creature.' Bern looked as serious as Aldasair had ever seen him. In the gloomy light, the broad planes of his face looked as though they were carved from marble, and his eyes were dark. 'Some worm-people taint. Sharrik is upset by him. It's like . . . looking at a wound that is festering, or a lamb born with one too many legs.'

'He was birthed here, grew here. In this sunless place. None of his brothers or sisters were with him, just Hestillion.' He shook his head, still disbelieving. 'I do not know her anymore. My own cousin.'

'Do you know why she did this?'

'No! I . . . I'm sorry. When the humans started coming to Ebora I could not understand them at all, all the ways they spoke and the looks they gave each other. I remembered their

397

languages, but the rest of it was a mystery. At least, I thought, I understood Hestillion. But I do not. There was some poison growing in her.' He stopped, remembering how she had become obsessed with the Hall of Roots, how she would not let him see her. 'I should have seen it, still, I think. If I were not so . . .'

'You cannot live other people's lives for them,' said Bern, shifting on the soft floor. 'And you can't always know their hearts.' He sighed. 'My head aches like a bastard.'

'I thought you were lost to me.' When Bern looked up, Aldasair turned away, not quite able to meet his eyes. 'You and Sharrik. Eaten by this monster. And then when we were in here, and I couldn't reach you, and you did not move . . . I thought I had lived through all my worst days, Bern, but I was wrong. I would live another thousand years in that empty palace of the dead, rather than lose you.'

The words were out before he'd even known they were coming. He felt stricken with horror, betrayed by his own mouth. Sitting up very straight, he tried to ignore how Bern was looking at him, because he had no idea what it meant. Years and years of never speaking and in a handful of moments he had exposed something he hadn't even known existed. He thought of a frail underground root, suddenly meeting sunlight, and shrinking, shrinking . . .

'Aldasair.' Bern's voice was so strange – rough, somehow, broken – that Aldasair turned to him in concern. The big man looked as though he were struggling with something, and then he reached over and took Aldasair's hand and squeezed it.

'Aldasair,' he said again, and now his green eyes looked brighter than the shadows. 'You look like you've just swallowed a goose, and you shouldn't, you shouldn't feel any shame over your words, because I . . . By the stones, Aldasair, I want you.'

'You want what?'

In the corner, the war-beasts shifted in their sleep, and both Bern and Aldasair jumped guiltily.

'I don't know how it is in Ebora, but in Finneral, we love who we love.' Bern looked anguished now, as though he too were struggling to swallow a goose. 'I don't know; you might find it horrifying, or disgusting even, but what I know is that to fly with you is happiness, and to see you hurt is sorrow.'

'Oh.'

'So . . . how do Eborans feel? About . . . this sort of thing?'

Aldasair blinked rapidly. Bern was still holding his hand, the warmth was like a balm against his skin. He felt dizzy, his mind caught in a vortex around the words *we love who we love*.

'I don't believe it actually matters. I don't believe it matters at all.'

Bern leaned forward and rested his forehead against Aldasair's, his eyes closed. The warmth and closeness of the man felt like the only thing that mattered just then.

'Then let's keep our eyes open, because we need to get out of this place. The sooner the better.'

'What do you mean to do?'

The queen had taken them out of the chamber, throwing back the walls to make room for Celaphon's huge bulk as easily as a woman turning aside a curtain. When they had arrived at the central crystal chamber, the walls had fallen away entirely, opening up the room to the corridors beyond. The blue light of the crystal seemed to splash eagerly against the walls like some unlikely summer sea, and in it Celaphon looked grey, as though he had been turned to stone.

'I still do not like it,' he said.

'This, Celaphon, could give you the connection you crave.'

'How?' demanded Hestillion. 'What are you talking about?'

'The crystals contain pieces of our memory,' said the queen, calmly ignoring Hestillion's tone. 'And through those memories, we are together. We could give you a piece of this, Celaphon,

399

to carry within you, and through it you would be joined with us.'

'Joined with you,' said Celaphon, his voice flat.

'Every part of us, you would feel. It is a connection unlike anything else.' The queen reached out and held her hand in front of the crystal, not quite touching it. 'To you also, Lady Hestillion Eskt, born in the year of the green bird, I offer this boon.'

Hestillion swallowed hard. Her bond with Celaphon was a tenuous thing, coming and going depending on his moods; half the time she thought she imagined it. Was this a way of strengthening it?

'How can you know that will work?'

'On your war-beast? Certainly it will. He is already half our creature, anyway. On you, we are less certain, but you are strong.'

'How . . . How could you even do such a thing? Give us a piece of that?'

'It is not easy,' said the queen. The shadowed places on her white, mask-like face collected the blue light like rock pools. 'We must grow the crystal a little, which costs us a great deal of effort. And then we must break it off, and it must be accepted by your body. It will be a slow and painful process.'

Celaphon had been staring at the crystal in silence, but now he lowered his head to speak to them more directly. 'And what of my brothers and sisters?'

A flicker of annoyance passed over the queen's face. She drew herself up, looming over Hestillion. 'What of them?'

'Will this connect me to them?' If it were possible for a dragon to look stubborn, Celaphon was making a good show of it. The queen made to reply to that, and then paused. She looked back to the crystal, her brow creased, and it was such a human expression that Hestillion felt a set of cold fingers walk down her spine.

'If we gave them pieces too, it is possible. There will be resistance from them, which might make it difficult . . . but there could be unexpected benefits, too.'

'What do you mean?' asked Hestillion.

'I am uncertain. But perhaps they will be more tractable. Our memories will spread through them, changing them. They may not wish to fight us any longer. Or they may fight for us.' The queen shrugged, another chillingly human gesture. *Did she learn it from me?* 'We can kill them, if it does not prove useful.' The queen looked pleased with this logic. 'Yes, kill them now, or use them, kill them later.'

'They are my brothers and sisters.' There was danger in Celaphon's voice, and Hestillion tried to send a note of caution to him. 'I will fly with them.'

'You wanted to destroy them earlier,' pointed out the queen. 'It does not matter. Will you accept this boon, Celaphon Eskt, born of the corpse moon?'

Hestillion felt like she'd been struck, but she held herself very still. Celaphon did not seem at all concerned by the queen's phrasing, and he reached out towards the crystal. 'Yes,' he said. 'I will. How do we do it? Make it work, now.'

The queen turned to Hestillion. If there was triumph on her mask-like face, she couldn't see it. 'And you?'

Celaphon would not be turned away from this path now, and where he went, so would she.

'Do it.'

The queen smiled, a thin stretching of her lips, and she turned back to the crystal. She reached out again, but instead of touching it, strings of black fluid began to fly out from her body, encircling the crystal. In her time aboard the corpse moon, Hestillion had observed the queen becoming more solid somehow, as though the black fluid her body was composed of had set, turning spongy and dark green, and evidently this fresh liquefaction cost her some considerable effort. Her eyes closed tight, sending thin cracks across the white material of her face. After a moment, drops of grey liquid formed on her forehead, building there, and then oozing greasily down her face. The rings of black fluid now fully encircled the crystal, and the light inside it was growing dimmer and dimmer. Abruptly, it flickered out, and with a sound like dry leaves being crushed underfoot, the top section of the crystal sprouted several new shards. They stood out from the rest of the smooth crystal like a set of broken fingers – clearly attached, but wrong somehow.

The black fluid flowed back into the queen with a snap, and she shook herself all over before placing a hand on the blue surface. There was a sharp cracking sound, and the extra section of crystal broke away and fell to the floor. Despite herself, Hestillion jumped.

'There.' The queen reached up and swiped away the lines of dirty grey from her face, which was glistening slightly. 'Not something we should like to do very often.'

The ship was very quiet. Too quiet. Hestillion realised that several noises, soft hums and clicks that she had grown so used to that she no longer heard them, had ceased while the queen had been growing the crystal. There was something unsettling about that, as if they stood within the bowels of something utterly dead, and she found that she was relieved when the light within the crystal blinked back into life, and the soft murmur that was the life of the corpse moon eased back into existence around them.

The queen had retrieved the newly formed piece of crystal, and held it up to them. It looked like a huge blue sapphire, a slightly brighter colour than the rest of the object. It winked with internal fires.

'The next stage will not be so comfortable for you, Celaphon.' The queen smiled. 'But you will trust us, I believe.'

39

'They aren't here, Noon.'

Tor stood and waited while Noon made a point of sifting through a final patch of mud before turning around to face him. The witch looked pale and drawn this morning, with dark circles under her eyes, as though she had missed a few nights' sleep, and she had been distracted and quiet, not even responding to his usual taunts. It had been another hot day – as all the days appeared to be – and her cheeks bore isolated patches of bright pink.

'Not in this bit, no,' she said, squeezing her eyes shut and rubbing them with her fingers. 'We've looked through a lot of mud today, though. We're probably getting close.'

'Noon.' Tor took a breath and held it, watching her closely. 'You must see that this is a pointless task? The amber tablets aren't here. We're a good two hundred feet away from where Micanal said he dropped them, and we've been that far up the other end too. The things are lost.'

Noon dropped her hands and glared at him. 'You're giving up?'

Tor grimaced. 'I'm saying it's pointless. We're not going to find them, we're wasting our time.'

She pressed her lips together, then bent and swished her hands back and forth through the water, washing off the mud.

'Not up for a bit of heavy labour? Is that it?'

Tor rolled his eyes at that. 'Noon, I'm twice as strong as you. But that's not my point.' He composed his features, trying to look as reasonable as possible. 'Anything could be happening in Ebora, and we have two of the strongest war-beasts here – in the middle of nowhere, on an impossible quest. It's irresponsible.'

Noon raised her eyebrows. 'That's pretty rich, coming from you.' She sighed loudly. 'Fire and blood, I don't want to be here, Tor, but . . .' She ran her still-wet hand through her hair, making it stick up in odd spikes and whorls. 'I don't want to go back empty-handed.'

'What? You want to make Vintage proud?' Tor smiled.

'What if I do?' Noon shook her head brusquely, dismissing his comment with annoyance, and Tor felt a pang of regret; he had hit closer to home than he'd intended with that barb. 'There are mysteries here, Tor, and I think we could discover some important things, if we could just figure them out.'

'Or, we could just get Micanal and Arnia to come back with us.' Seeing nothing but flat hostility in the set of her mouth, he carried on before she could comment. 'Micanal's memories could be enough. His knowledge could bring the war-beasts back together. If nothing else, I think it's got to be a better plan than endlessly trudging through all this shit for artefacts that probably don't exist.'

Noon narrowed her eyes. 'Have you talked to them about this?'

'Well, no. Although Arnia has, well, she has indicated that she would like us to stay. Here on the island.'

'Us?' Noon laughed, a narrow and bitter sound. 'You mean you.' She paused, as though she were going to say something more, but shook her head instead. 'You don't know anything about that woman.'

'I know that she is Eboran, just as we were back before everything came falling down around our ears.'

'And what does that mean?'

It was infuriating. She had been nothing but difficult since they had found this island. 'I don't expect you to understand, when your history with your people is such a brief thing. How could you know what it's like to watch your people die?'

Noon straightened up, looking away up the river. He could not tell what she was looking at, and the sun was too bright on her face for him to make out what her expression was.

'Fine. Sure. What would I know about that? Maybe you're right, maybe this island isn't doing us any good at all.' She turned around, and all the blush had dropped from her cheeks. 'But do me a favour, Tor. Talk to Micanal again, and see what you can find out. Perhaps he'll be more open with you alone. Appeal to his vanity, or whatever. He and Arnia are lying to us. I think it would be useful to go back to Ebora with some bits of truth, at least.'

'Will you be happy to leave, then?'

Noon shrugged. 'It's probably up to Vostok and Kirune, isn't it?'

He left her there, still stubbornly rooting around in the mud, and went to look for Micanal, but the old Eboran was not in his home, or in any of the houses that Tor could see, and he wasn't wandering the trees flanking their empty little settlement. Tor found himself kicking at clods of mud and frowning at the birds. Where could Micanal be? Why was he suddenly so absent when Tor had made up his mind to attempt to extract some answers? There was no reason to go far, and indeed, with his creased face and white hair, he did not look like he should be out exploring the island.

'You are thinking like a human,' he muttered angrily to a bush. 'He might look ancient, but he is still Eboran.'

As he wandered further from the houses, he gradually became

405

aware of the stillness of the forest. Everything seemed to hang in a hot, green haze, and the bird calls sounded like the slow, descending notes of exotic instruments. Strange blossoms, purple and white and yellow, hung heavy from the branches of trees, their petals fleshy and somehow unsettling. Eventually, he realised he had walked to where they had first met Micanal the Clearsighted. The tunnel entrance loomed out of the greenery like a fat square of black velvet, impossibly dark within. He could see no lit torches this time, and could hear nothing at all from the hole – if anything, it seemed too quiet, as though it ate up any noise that got too close – but, he reasoned, this was as good a place to search for Micanal as any. There was a small oil lamp wedged into the dirt by the entrance, obviously left there for the old man's use, so he bent and lit it, waiting for the dirty orange glow to seep into life before he moved into the tunnel. As an Eboran he could see reasonably well in the dark, but there was no need to trip and break his neck for the sake of showing off to no one.

The tunnel was much as he remembered it. Dark dirt floor, smelling pungently of the earth, and half-seen wooden structures holding up the walls and ceiling. After a short time, he found the strange central chamber, and here he paused. The warmth of the oil lamp was a hot circle against his hand.

'So.' There was no sign of the old man. Instead, he found himself facing the wall of green roots, their tapering ends reaching for him, or diving down into the black earth. 'What is this bloody place, exactly?'

Standing here alone, without the distraction of Arnia or her brother – or Noon, for that matter – he could see that the roots were an unusually bright green, the colour of the pond algae that had grown on the southern palace lakes, perhaps, and they held a strange inner glow of their own. He closed his eyes, and was surprised to see a very faint after-image hanging there.

'What would Vintage do?' he murmured, thinking of Noon's

406

words, and, smiling, he stepped forward to take a closer look. 'I don't know, probably fall down a hole, get blown up, something useful like that.'

Up close, the roots were very smooth, smoother than from any tree he had seen – Ygseril's roots, of course, were wrinkled and horned and ancient. He slid his free hand over the nearest, and grimaced slightly at the touch. There was nothing definably terrible about it; the surface was simply smooth, polished almost. But even so, he felt a twinge of dismay, as though he'd just realised some heart-rending truth. Micanal, he remembered, had looked similarly horrified when they had found him down here, and at the time Tor had assumed he had simply been taken unawares. But perhaps it had been due to the strangeness of these green roots.

Stepping back, intending to leave and find some sunny sky to stand under, his boot collided with a wooden crate. It had been covered with a dark cloth, which was why he had not spotted it sooner. His skin still crawling from touching the roots, he reached down and whipped away the material. Underneath was a small pile of furry things, which at first he did not understand, until he kicked the box again and one of the objects rolled stiffly over. It was a large rodent of some sort, obviously dead, and underneath it was a thinly furred black hare, as well as other dead animals. There was other equipment in the crate, delicate-looking instruments of glass, and thick rubber straps. Someone, presumably Micanal or his sister, had carefully packed the items amongst the dead animals, to stop them clinking against each other.

'Well, that is charming.'

Tor glanced back to the wall of green roots. Did he imagine it, or were there more little furry bodies back there, staring sightlessly at him with beady eyes gone dull with dust? He had destroyed parasite spirits, carved up Wild-touched monstrosities and faced down the Jure'lia queen, but something

407

about this worried him on a deeper level. There was a mystery here they weren't even close to understanding, but he sensed that the answers would be bad news.

He left the chamber and the tunnel, extinguishing the oil lamp and putting it down again without really thinking about his actions. His mind was full of the slick touch of the roots, a touch that upset him for reasons he couldn't understand, so that when he turned around and saw Arnia standing waiting for him, it took all of his self-control not to yelp with surprise.

'Tormalin,' she said warmly. 'I went and peeked at the river, but it was just your human woman there, so I came looking for you.'

'She is not my woman,' he said, in a terser tone than he had intended. He walked rapidly towards her, trying to wipe his hand on the side of his trousers. He felt like the roots had left a film of something behind, making his hand feel too hot. 'Actually, it seems we are all missing each other today. I was looking for your brother, but I can find no sign of him.'

Arnia shrugged. She was carrying a bottle of the sour wine in her arms. 'He has days when he will wander in the forest, tired of my company. I must admit I am surprised he leaves us just now, with such fine visitors.' She smiled. 'Will you join me? I know a beautiful spot just nearby. It's beyond the sight of the houses.'

Tor still felt disgruntled from the touch of the roots, but it had been a long morning trawling the river, and his throat was dry. He summoned what he could of his courtly manners.

'I'd be delighted. Lead the way.'

The spot Arnia led them to was a little pocket in the forest, clear of trees yet tightly surrounded by them. The grass was long and lush, and above them the sky was a hot blue circle. Arnia had apparently been here before, and recently; the grass in one patch was trodden down, and there was a thick blanket cast over it, held down with a pair of thick glass goblets.

Looking at the little scene, Tor felt a rush of unreality. He recognised the pattern woven into the blanket, a blanket Arnia must have brought with her when they came to the island; it had been fashionable back when he was very young, and his mother had owned thick curtains with it on. On some level, he recognised that Arnia was attempting to manipulate him with this set-up, but she could not have known that it would remind him how old she truly was, and how the Ebora she had left behind had been a very different place. Mysteries on top of mysteries, just as Noon had suggested.

'What are the green roots in the underground tunnel? Where do they come from?'

The questions were out before he knew he was going to ask them. Arnia looked briefly bemused, then brushed past him to reach the blanket.

'That's not quite the response I had hoped for, but very well. Come and sit.'

Tor did as he was bid. The blanket was warm from the hot sun, and when Arnia pressed the goblet full of wine into his hand he was glad of it. She sat next to him, her legs curled under her.

'We know very little about Origin, you must realise. The island did not hold the answers Micanal hoped for, or the future we all wanted. But it was warm, and secluded, and there was no death here. Only the death we brought with us. Do you understand?'

Tor sipped at his wine. 'I think I do. You mean that it wasn't Ebora.'

Arnia swirled the liquid in her glass, staring off into the trees. 'Ebora was a graveyard. Everywhere you looked, you knew that there was death, just out of sight. People dying in their rooms, or being buried anywhere there was dirt enough to cover them. Many lost their minds too – not just because of the flux, but because of the horror of it, and the creeping misery of growing old too soon.' Her lips turned down at the corners, a deep line growing between her brows. 'I'm sure you don't need me to tell you that.'

'You do not.' He thought of Aldasair, his clothes growing dusty as he gave up changing them, as he gave up moving at all. He hoped that his cousin, so recently brought back from the brink of that misery, was doing well.

'My brother saw much of the Carrion Wars. I doubt that is generally known these days – people have always preferred his paintings of happier times, his sculptures of our war-beasts – but he travelled among the armies, and saw the aftermath of it. He told me of the piles of human bones that were stacked, high as hills, at the ends of battles. He told me that all of Sarn was a graveyard, and we were all just ghosts. And he was right.' As she spoke, she shifted on the blanket, bringing herself closer to him. 'This place is not a graveyard, Tormalin the Oathless, which is why you should stay here, with us.'

He looked at her. Under the sun her skin was a brown so warm it seemed almost to glow, and her eyes were bright drops of human arterial blood. A curl of her black hair lay against her cheek, glossy as ink.

'I ran away once,' he said softly. 'I ran halfway across Sarn to get away from that graveyard.'

She smiled slowly. 'You see? You have always been wise.'

'That's not what my sister would say. Or Vintage. Or Noon.' It felt strange speaking their names here, as though he were invoking some last spell of protection, but it had no effect on Arnia, who only smiled more widely.

'Then maybe they don't know you like I do.'

He knew it was coming, but somehow he still felt a soft bloom of shock when she leaned forward and kissed him. She did it firmly and with no hesitation; it was not stealing a kiss, but claiming something she thought of as hers. A hundred

410

thoughts collided in his head at once – how long since he'd kissed an Eboran? Where would this go? And underneath all that, *Noon*. Arnia tasted of the sour wine, and sunshine, and something else. A taste like pennies that was familiar but somehow wrong. Her tongue slid into his mouth and now he did jump back – that taste had grown abruptly stronger, turning the taste of her to ashes.

'Please relax, Tormalin. Can you understand how lonely I am, I wonder? How long I have been here, alone, with only my fingers for company?'

Absurdly, he felt his cheeks grow hot. Despite everything, his body was responding to her, and the grass under them was very soft.

'The House of the Long Night was an old, favourite discipline of mine. I would be glad to refresh myself of the techniques.' She kissed him again, and this time he let her do what she would, putting the taste of her from his mind and concentrating instead on the hot press of her hands on his chest, pushing him down onto the blanket.

'I feel that perhaps you are avoiding my questions.'

'Do you mind, truly?' Her hair, a tumble of black curls, brushed against his face. 'I don't think you do.'

Tor had the sense that they weren't alone a handful of seconds before he heard the whisper of soft footfalls against the grass. He leaned away from Arnia, trying to see over her shoulder – he fully expected to see Noon, her face flushed with outrage, her fists coated in green fire perhaps – and he hoped to get out a few words of explanation before she turned them both to ash. Instead, he was startled to see Kirune padding towards them; for his size, the great cat moved almost silently.

'You must come with me,' he said.

A flicker of annoyance passed over Arnia's face, sharp and ugly and then gone in an instant. She pulled herself up from

411

Tor but did not remove her hands from his chest. Tor cleared his throat.

'I'm a little busy, Kirune. I don't have time for your nonsense right now.'

Kirune looked at them both in that particularly dismissive way of cats, his yellow eyes still, and then Tor felt a rush of powerful emotion in his chest. It was his link to Kirune, but he had never felt it so strongly. It was a command, edged with cold anger, and he felt his legs flexing before he'd made any sort of decision to get up. Arnia made a startled noise, straightening her skirts as she was ejected from Tor's lap.

'I am sorry, my lady.' Tor found that he couldn't take his eyes from Kirune. No war-beast magic, just the simple wonder that their connection finally seemed forged, and that there was some strength behind it. 'It seems I have business elsewhere.'

He left her there in the glade, not quite daring to look back – her outrage and disappointment was like a cold knife at his back – and followed Kirune into the forest. They were heading away from the houses, towards the crevasse. Once they were a decent distance from Arnia's secret hiding place, he hesitantly laid a hand on Kirune's meaty shoulder, slowing him.

'Do you want to tell me what this is about, then?'

To his surprise, Kirune did not shake him off. Instead, the big cat looked up, eyes narrowing as he focussed on the canopy.

'Need more space,' he said. 'Then we can fly.'

'Fly? Should we not go back for your harness, in that case?' The war-beasts had shed their harnesses soon after arriving.

'No. You can hold on. I will not drop you.'

Tor fell silent. The idea of flying above the trees with nothing securing him was not something he relished, but this new openness from Kirune felt like a development he should encourage, and given how volatile the cat was, he knew that contradicting him could destroy this fragile alliance.

And the cat did not drop him. When eventually they found

412

a space large enough for Kirune to comfortably leave the ground, Tor clung to the beast's back tightly, hands gripping thick wads of dense grey fur. But the war-beast was careful, considerate almost. The island fell away below them, green and simmering under the bright sunshine. They headed inland, passing quickly over the crevasse, which flashed briefly below them as a fat silver ribbon. Tor thought of Noon, still toiling down there in the mud, then pushed the image from his mind.

'Do you feel like telling me now? I am certain no one else can hear up here.'

Kirune did not answer immediately. Several seabirds that had been flying in a sort of formation scattered before them, a few of them evacuating their bowels as they did so. *No bird wants to see a flying cat*, thought Tor.

'I went looking,' rumbled Kirune eventually. 'Around. I wanted memories, but there is nothing. So I went looking. This island smells strange. I do not like it.'

'Well, it's warmer than home at least.'

'I claimed the trees and the rivers, even though they smelled wrong. I went into caves, and found nothing bigger than myself. I ate many things. I hunted.'

'You have been busy.' Tor felt a pang of guilt. He and Noon had been so focussed on the amber tablets, he realised, that he had thought very little about what Kirune must be getting up to.

'I found things that are troubling,' said Kirune, and then in the same tone, as if the two things were related, 'you were going to mate with that woman.'

'Well . . .'

'She also smells wrong, but in a different way.'

Tor grimaced. 'I shall have to remember to come to you for advice about my love life in the future, Kirune. I had no idea you had such opinions.'

'I do not care who you rut with.' Kirune sounded dismissive

413

again. 'But the Noon witch, I respect her. It is not respectful, what you do.'

They were flying lower, the trees coming up to meet them again, bringing with them their thick jungle scent. Tor sank his hands deeper into Kirune's fur, trying to make sense of what the big cat was saying.

'You respect Noon? I can't get you to talk to me civilly, and you respect Noon? Besides which . . .' He shook his head lightly. 'Never mind all that. What did you find?'

'Fell Noon might be bonded with the snake, but she is a warrior. Her green fire is strange, but she has the heart of someone who fights.' And then, 'I cannot tell you what it is. I must show you. I will not waste words on you, when you will see with your own eyes.'

Ahead of them now, Tor could see the fall of uncertain lights hanging over the forest, which they had first glimpsed flying towards the island. Uneasily, he realised he had put that particular mystery from his head too. Now that they were closer it was possible to see that they covered the centre of the island like a dome. Before they reached the strange wall of lights, Kirune dropped down, his wings beating slower and slower until they were descending through the trees. There was a crack of small branches being broken and the scuffling noise of smaller animals fleeing the scene, and then they were down on the ground again. This far into the island the forest was dense, and the air so close that Tor could taste that jungle scent on the back of his tongue. Sweat broke out across his back and over his forehead. It wasn't the Wild, he reminded himself, although the virulent growth of the plants and foliage all around made him uneasy.

'You say you saw nothing out here bigger than you? Does that mean there were things not much smaller than you too?'

Kirune ignored him. 'Get off me.'

Tor got down. Despite his pleasure in Kirune's new closeness, he was glad to get his feet onto solid ground. All around them the air echoed with bird calls.

'Here. It is here.'

At first Tor couldn't see what Kirune was indicating with his big, blocky head, and he opened his mouth to question whether the cat was seeing things, but then he remembered that Kirune had, for the first time, come to him for help. He forced himself to look closer at the confusion of plants and trees.

'Do you see it?'

Tor frowned, about to own up, and then he did see it: something that looked like a broken glass panel in the shape of a diamond, hanging in mid-air. Now that he could see it, he could also see the faint outlines of surrounding panels – it was like looking at an elaborate pattern on a length of fabric that suddenly resolved itself into a series of interlocking figures. Faint traceries of light, like veins in a leaf, were visible all around the area where the panel was broken. There was a hole there, he realised, large enough for either of them to pass through.

'Yes, I see it. This is like the wall we passed through to get here, the one that concealed the island.'

Kirune had grown agitated while Tor examined the panels, pacing back and forth through the undergrowth.

'This also hides something. It is solid, unlike the sky-wall. It is a dome, but broken here.'

Tor looked at him. 'You have been through?' He could sense something like reluctance from the cat.

'For a little while. I went quickly, came back.' Kirune shook out his fur, sending droplets of moisture flying. 'You should look.'

Tor reached for his scabbard only to realise that he had left his sword belt, and the Ninth Rain, back at the house. Of course he had. He hadn't wanted to get water and mud on his fine sword. Cursing himself silently, he approached the hole in the strange wall and ducked through.

'If there's anything hungry through here, Kirune, I will expect you to protect me.'

The space beyond the transparent wall had shown only more forest – thick and vibrant and cloying – yet when Tor stepped over to the other side, he stood in a space where the trees were thinning significantly. There was no birdsong either. After a moment, Kirune followed him through.

'All right, this is certainly strange, I will give you that.' He sighed. 'As if we don't have enough mysteries to deal with.'

'It gets stranger,' said Kirune drily. Tor followed the direction of the war-beast's baleful yellow eyes. Behind them, rising out of the black dirt, was a strange smooth structure, breaking through the earth like the back of a sea monster. It was green, and came up to his waist. There were no markings on it, no blemishes of any sort, and its shape was irregular. His first thought was of a huge fungus – he'd certainly seen such things in the Wild, and particularly in the Shroom Flats – but then there was the way it rose out of the ground like much of it was still underneath. He moved forward, thinking to touch it, and then saw that there were similar, larger structures behind – looming green shapes, stretching back into the forest. The further back they went, the more they seemed to take on an understandable shape. That one was almost a wall, with a corner. Behind it, something like a tower.

'What is this?'

'It was hidden,' said Kirune. Tor nodded. For once, the cat had bitten straight down to the bones; perhaps what it was didn't matter as much as the fact that someone had put up a wall to hide it.

'How far in have you been?'

'Not far,' said Kirune, something unspoken in the rumble of his voice. And then, very reluctantly. 'I touched it.'

'So? Did something happen? Did it harm . . .' He stopped. The roots in the tunnel. These strange mounds were the same colour, and he was sure that if they were glowing slightly, he would not be able to see it in this sunshine. Steeling himself, he stepped forward and pressed his hand to the nearest mound. Immediately, revulsion closed his throat; again, it was too smooth, and unpleasant in a way that he could not name. He swallowed hard as his heart thudded in his chest. 'It's all connected. The roots in that tunnel are a part of this, whatever this is.'

'Could it be a new tree-father?'

Kirune spoke so softly, and with such a painful note of hope in his voice.

'I don't know,' said Tor, truthfully enough. 'I don't think so, though. It doesn't . . . Ygseril never felt like this, but it does not feel like the Jure'lia either. It's not quite ugly enough, for a start.' Tor stared off at the rising green monuments. 'We'll walk a little further in, and then go back. For my sword.'

The deeper they went into this new part of the forest, the more the trees fell away and the more green shapes they saw rising from the black dirt. Soon, several of the green shapes seemed to be joining together, forming something like a series of walls, before sloping back into the ground again. Some of the pieces rose up higher and higher, until Tor saw a few that were higher than the trees. There was still no birdsong, and Tor found that he was grinding his teeth together, his hands pressed into fists so tight that his fingernails threatened to pierce his palms.

'Do you feel that too?'

Kirune was stalking next to him, his tail low. 'I do. I do not like it.' He snorted. 'I am fearless. But this place . . .'

'It's all wrong, but I couldn't tell you what it is. When Vintage and I explored the Behemoth sites, there was a sense of misery about those places, but that just made sense. Those were the bodies of alien creatures, decaying, seeping their poisons into the earth. And there were the parasite spirits, of course.' He glanced at Kirune. 'Now that we know what they

417

were, it seems reasonable that they seemed to carry with them a sense of melancholy.'

'My fallen brothers and sisters.'

'But this . . .' It made him think of his family's suite on the day he'd found his mother, her skin oozing the puss of the crimson flux and her slashed wrists dark with blood – here, he felt not decay or disgust, but a sense that everything he had believed in or held dear had been a lie, and not an especially kind one. The strong were not strong. He shook his head and ran a hand through his hair, grimacing at the sweat there. 'This place feels wrong in a deeper way. Come on, not much further and we'll head back.'

He half expected the big cat to protest but Kirune simply lowered his head. They moved on. The trees became sparser, until the green shapes were all they could see ahead of them.

'We shall have to climb over it,' said Tor, as they came to a long flat stretch, almost like a smooth pavement. The thought of walking on it made his toes curl up in his boots.

'Or we could stop,' said Kirune.

'Just a little further. Past that wall there.' The shapes had grown increasingly taller, until they sprouted like towers and walls all around. It was strange to see such things without windows or doors, without any kind of markings at all – like walking through a half-formed, blind city.

'I don't like it.'

'Wait. Look!' Tor dropped his voice to a whisper and rested his hand on Kirune's shoulder to pause him. They had rounded one of the corner pieces, and beyond it, just visible in a gap between a pair of the green blocks, something was moving. Several things.

Tor felt his throat close up with a strange mixture of fear and disgust, and next to him Kirune made a peculiar noise in the back of his throat, almost like a kettle coming to boil. The things moving beyond the green architecture were unlike anything he had seen before, and his mind seemed to veer away from them, as though they offended his sense of reality. They were very large, four-legged things, with long limbs that bent oddly at the knee, like a chicken's leg. Their necks also were long, tapering to neat arrow-shaped heads that looked largely featureless, although it was difficult to see from that distance. Their skins were all as white as chalk, and looked as smooth as the green shapes around them.

'We should go,' said Kirune.

Tor nodded. He could see nothing threatening about them, no teeth or claws or obvious weapons, but, nonetheless, he was frightened. It was partly to do with the way they moved, slow and fluid, almost as though they were underwater.

They began to back away, keeping their eyes on the strange beasts in the distance. Too late, Tor became aware of movement to the right of them; the tall green tower, which had been empty and featureless before, now sported one of the strange white creatures, and it was scampering down the tower, spider-like, towards them. Its head was lifted up and staring straight at them, and Tor caught a glimpse of bulbous crimson eyes, and a mouth lined with sharp teeth.

'Run!'

Kirune leapt away, then belatedly seemed to remember his wings. He shook them out hurriedly, turning to meet Tor, but the scuttling white creature was unnaturally fast and it caught Tor before he had even closed half the distance. The head whipped out like a snake's and teeth like daggers sank into Tor's shoulder and then yanked him back. The pain was terrible, and for a moment everything seemed to dim at the edges as Tor struggled not to pass out. Another tug, and the pain travelled through him like a lightning bolt, snapping his consciousness back to him in a blink. Kirune was bellowing his rage and pounding towards him, but Tor could see what the cat could not; the white beasts running down the green

419

walls from all around, as if they had simply melted up through the green surface – all of them seemed to defy gravity with their scampering. Kirune, for all his fierceness, would be overwhelmed in moments.

'Go!' The thing's bite was like a vice, impossible to escape from. If Tor struggled at all, he sensed it could tear his arm off. 'Fly, Kirune! To Noon, go!'

The war-beast blinked, clearly confused and even a little hurt by the command, but then he saw the creatures flanking him. With three enormous beats of his wings he was in the air and out of their reach, although Tor saw several of the things stretching their narrow heads towards him as if they meant to tear at his flesh.

'Fly!'

Another of the things had reached Tor, and it stood looking him over, red eyes wet and glistening in its head. They looked like big bubbles of human blood, and he could see nothing comprehensible in them. Beyond the thing's shoulder, he could see that Kirune had got away; he was a fleck above the trees, flying faster than Tor had ever seen. He hoped the big cat would remember where to find the way out.

'What are you?' he spat at the white creatures. Many had circled him, their heads bobbing and weaving like snakes. 'What do you want?'

The one that stood over him lowered its head slowly, seeming to examine Tor. It opened its mouth, and Tor wondered if it was going to talk. Instead, it darted forward and sank its teeth into the soft flesh of his thigh – slowly, almost as though it were testing the solidity of it.

Tor screamed, a high-pitched wail that he was immediately ashamed of, but the pain was too great to bear stoically. As he shrieked, the being that had his shoulder began to move its head back and forth; a dog worrying at a piece of meat.

This is where I die, then. The thought shot across his mind like a comet, burning everything in its wake. There was no chance that Kirune could reach Noon or Vostok in time. These things would have pulled the flesh from his bones in minutes. All those years of avoiding the flux, of running from his home, and then rebirthing the war-beasts, and he would die on this roots-forsaken island in the middle of nowhere, eaten by abominations. Abruptly, he was filled with rage, and he kicked out wildly with his one free leg. His boot connected with the head of one of the creatures, and it drew its long neck back.

'That's it, you bastards! I'll have your fucking eyes out, I'll—'

The creature that had a hold of his shoulder – he was aware that his shirt was soaked with blood, both the clear and the black of a deadly wound – was dragging him back, further and further. The tall tower of green stone was still behind them, as far as he could tell, so he could not understand where they were going, until he glanced over his free shoulder and saw that the creature was sinking back into the green surface of the thing. He knew a moment of pure terror: he would not bleed to death after all, but suffocate slowly within that terrible, smooth substance. He kicked out again and used every bit of strength left to him to pull away, no longer caring if he did lose his arm, but the creature was implacable. He felt the stuff at his back, somehow cold and hot at the same time, and felt himself sinking into it. It pushed across his shoulders and up his neck, slipped around his waist and over his legs. Everything it touched turned numb, and very swiftly there was little he could do save for gasp air into his lungs, thinking that perhaps if Noon got here soon, within the next handful of moments, perhaps then . . .

The green substance slipped up around his neck, turning his ears deaf, pressing against his cheeks. Where it touched the scars on his face it seemed to sting. He thought of Noon, wondered if she would look for him, if she would care. And then everything was green.

40

'Something is wrong.'

Vintage jumped, guilty for several reasons all at once. For a start, she was reading through Micanal the Clearsighted's journal, the one she had liberated from Eri's parents' home, and the boy stood in front of her, looking as solemn and as innocent as ever, Helcate waiting patiently at his back. And more to the point, she was sitting quite comfortably on one of the gently rolling hills in the palace gardens, one that just happened to overlook the suite she had given to Tyranny Munk and Okaar – it was entirely possible, with her seeing-lens, to watch the strange pair through the enormous windows that looked onto their central living space. She had been doing so, every now and then, for the last few days, just on the off-chance she might catch them doing something interesting. So far she had seen very little that could be construed as suspicious. She had also been keeping half an eye on the contingent from Yuron-Kai – since their initial meeting, they had been a brooding presence in one of the larger suites. The situation had been explained to them, at length, and they had reluctantly agreed to wait for the return of the war-beasts and their warriors. Vintage suspected that their patience would not last much longer, however.

She slipped the glass back into the big pocket on her jacket and moved a sheet of parchment to cover the writings in the book.

'What is it, my dear?'

The boy stood up a little straighter. For all his solemnness, he looked much better than when she and Nanthema had found him on the road. The hollow pits had vanished from his cheeks, and he had put on a little weight, covering up his stick-like ribs. He also, to Vintage's eye, appeared to have grown a little taller, although he still carried the creases at the corners of his eyes that would look so odd on a human child. Helcate, likewise, looked healthier; he wasn't as big as his war-beast brothers and sisters, and he was scrawny around the flanks, but she could see muscle under his short, curly fur, and his blue eyes were bright and alert.

'The other war-beasts. There is something terribly wrong.'

'What do you mean?' Vintage grabbed her stick and levered herself to her feet rapidly. 'Have they come back?'

'No.' Abruptly Eri's face was a picture of misery. She watched as he screwed his eyes closed and opened them again in an effort not to cry. 'I don't know if they can! Helcate can feel them, and he is very upset.'

'Helcate,' said Helcate.

Vintage transferred her attention to the war-beast. 'Can you tell me what you mean, Helcate?'

The war-beast dipped his head, his nose pointed to the floor, and shook the fur out on his neck. It shouldn't have been a recognisable gesture, but Vintage found she could read it well enough: sorrow and shame that he was not capable of what she asked.

'There, darling, don't take on so. Eri, tell me everything that you suspect. Quickly now, as we walk back to the palace.'

The boy put his hand on Helcate's flank as they moved down across the grass.

423

'He can't tell what's happening to them exactly. It's not like they can talk in their heads among each other or anything. But he feels them, very distantly.' Eri sighed suddenly. 'And they are afraid.'

Vintage thought of Noon and Tor, of waving them off on some stupid quest to find something that probably didn't exist anymore, or never had done. *Foolish woman.*

'Can you tell me anything else? Any more detail than that?'

They were away from the open grass and passing down through the neat rows of flowering bushes, all the branches heavy with unopened buds. The leaves were waxy and green, and gave off their own sharp scent. Vintage made a note to find out what these plants were, and if an oil could be extracted from their leaves.

'Jessen is afraid. She feels trapped. Blind even. Helcate thinks that she cannot see the sky. Sharrik is afraid, but he is also angry. He longs to fight something.'

Vintage's stomach turned a slow somersault. She had assumed that it would be Noon and Tor in trouble, because they had ventured out over the Barren Sea, but instead it was the friends she had sent to Finneral – together, for their own safety. Abruptly she wanted to kick something, but her leg was too stiff.

'Aldasair? Bern?'

'I'm sorry,' Eri shook his head slowly. 'Helcate cannot feel them. But then, he can't feel them usually, so maybe that's all right?'

'Yes, let's hope so.' She squeezed the book under her arm. 'This situation in Finneral must have been worse than I thought. How long would it take a messenger to get to us, if there were bad news? Weeks perhaps, or if they sent a bird . . .'

Eri looked up at her with wide eyes. 'I don't know. I'm sorry.'

She did her best to smile at him. 'Oh don't listen to me, I'm rambling. We shall have to send our own message. It will take a while, but that can't be helped.'

'Kirune is scared too,' said Eri.

This time Vintage's stomach dropped like a stone. She pursed her lips, and forced herself to speak calmly.

'Kirune?'

Eri nodded. 'Helcate says that Kirune doesn't like anyone to know how he feels, but it bleeds through anyway. He panics, he doesn't understand what's going on.'

They were nearly back to the palace courtyard. The plains folk and the people from all across Sarn were as busy as ever, men and women back from hunting, or greeting new traders. She saw some of them look over towards them, their eyes automatically seeking out the war-beast, and she saw that sunny look of awe on many faces. They would be wondering where the others had gone, and what was she supposed to tell them?

'Right. The contingent from Jarlsbad have beautiful messenger birds, sleek, lethal predators, every one of them. I'm sure we can ask a favour of them.' Vintage looked around the packed square, seeking them out. 'The trick will be not letting on that there's a problem.'

'We shouldn't tell them?'

'No, my dear.' Vintage looked at the boy and was seized with an impulse to ruffle his hair. She reminded herself that not only was he centuries older than she was, he was also a teenage boy who might find such things embarrassing. 'We'll have to keep it to ourselves for now. Things are under control here. People are bringing us food and supplies, happy in the belief that they're aiding the fight against the worm people. Without that structure, we would be in a lot of trouble indeed, and if they should find out that the war-beasts are in real danger, it could be disastrous.' She took a slow breath. Nanthema was there, across the square, walking away from

425

the caravan that Tyranny and Okaar had travelled in. 'I will have to tell Nan, at least,' she murmured.

'We could take the message!' Eri reached out and patted Helcate's ruff of fur. 'We can fly to Finneral, if you give me a map. And explain it to me, maybe.'

The small war-beast sat up straighter. 'Helcate!'

'Oh no, my dear, I can hardly send you into a danger we don't yet understand.' She saw the flash of disappointment that crossed Eri's face, so she smiled to lessen it. 'And I need you both here. You are Ebora's last defence. It would be a great help if you could speak to the Jarlsbad leaders for me, though, ask if we might kindly borrow one of their messenger birds.' Eri might only be a boy, but he was still an Eboran, and Vintage guessed that being asked by him would be more impressive. Plus, they would assume it couldn't be a dreadfully serious message if a supposedly teenage boy was asking them. 'Could you do that for me, Eri?'

The boy nodded briskly. 'Easily.'

He sped off, with Helcate close on his heels. Vintage adjusted the crutch so that it sat more comfortably under her armpit – her ankle, she told herself, was feeling better every day – and set off in pursuit of Nanthema, who was heading back inside the palace. The woman was walking slowly, apparently in deep thought, but they were still some way down one of the vast corridors by the time Vintage caught up with her.

'Nan? A word.'

She quickly ran through what Eri had told her, watching the Eboran's face as she did so. This section of the palace was largely empty, the sounds from the campsites outside drifting in through the tall windows, but Vintage kept her voice low anyway.

'The boy says this?'

'He does. We'll send a message by bird, and hope we hear something soon. What else can we do?'

426

Nanthema frowned. 'So the boy has a true bonding with his war-beast, and the beasts themselves have bonded with each other. I doubt it is a true connection, as the fully formed war-beasts of old would have had, but nevertheless that is interesting. I have always wondered how such things worked.'

'Nan, I think you're missing the main meat of what I told you there.' Despite the empty corridor, Vintage lowered her voice further. 'Jessen and Sharrik are in trouble, and Kirune as well, by the sounds of it. Which means Noon, Tor, Aldasair and Bern could all be in serious danger.'

Nanthema turned slightly, and the cold daylight filled the glass of her spectacles, turning them into opaque white squares. Her eyes hidden and her mouth solemn, it was hard to know what she was thinking. The silence stretched out between them.

'Well? Aren't you going to say anything?'

Nanthema grimaced slightly, as though Vintage had interrupted her from admiring the view out the windows. 'You don't like what I have to say about these things. That we shouldn't be here at all. That these war-beasts are a mistake.'

'A mistake? How can they be a mistake? They are here, your tree-god birthed them, they are real!'

'I wish you could understand.' Nanthema moved away from the window and her crimson eyes were visible again. They glittered oddly. 'I really wish you could see things as I do, but I suspect that you are just . . . too human.'

Vintage drew herself up to her full height, ignoring the twinge in her foot. 'If I were feeling especially spiteful, I might say something about you being too Eboran, but I have known some Eborans in my time, Nan. Dear, confused Eri, and quiet, compassionate Aldasair. And Tor, a vain layabout with a high opinion of himself and a tendency to avoid responsibility, who still came back here when he thought there was a chance he could save his people. And if I am too human? Then I shall take that as a compliment.'

With that she turned and walked back down the corridor. The crutch made a loud, rhythmic rapping against the marble floor, but she was glad of it, as it broke up the icy silence from behind her.

41

It was, Hestillion thought, like some sinister ceremony.

The queen had taken them to the same enormous chamber where she had been creating her odd, flying humanoids, but she had expanded it to accommodate Celaphon and his bulk. The flying men and the wizened little homunculi that brought Hestillion her food and took away her waste all waited in silent rows, lined up by the flesh walls, while in the centre of the chamber a huge shallow pool of steaming white liquid waited. Hestillion pulled her furred vest closer around her chest, feeling cold, although she was quite sure the temperature hadn't changed.

'Celaphon, you will get in.' The queen still carried the shard of crystal in her hands.

'And then what?' asked Hestillion. The blank faces of the flying men were unsettling. Celaphon, meanwhile, was stepping into the pool. It was deeper than Hestillion had guessed; he sank in up to his belly, vapour rolling off him in waves.

'Then we . . . graft the crystal onto him. The fluid allows us to make changes – as we made changes to the others.' She gestured with her long fingers to the figures standing at the wall.

'Changes,' echoed Hestillion flatly. 'Will it hurt?'

'Yes, we would imagine it is very painful.' The queen paused, turning the crystal over and over in her long hands. 'We feel a connection to all of our extensions, but it is possible for us to make that connection dim. And these others,' she nodded to the flying men and the homunculi, 'they do not always have mouths to scream.'

With that cold thought nestling in her throat like a small lump of ice, Hestillion turned to watch Celaphon in the water. He was looking around with every sign of curiosity, but she guessed from the way he was holding his head away from the liquid that he did not like the smell of it. With the black horns bristling from his head and neck and the thick, fibrous plates lining his back, he looked very little like the small, feeble dragon that she had torn free of the pod – yet in his fastidiousness she could see a shadow of that past self.

'Watch closely, Lady Hestillion Eskt, as you will be next.'

The queen strode over to Celaphon and a small platform grew out of the floor, long and tapering with a flat surface at the top. She put the crystal on it carefully, and then held out her arms to the war-beast. Slowly, the dragon lowered his head, and she placed her hands to either side of his enormous jaws. She should have looked small in front of him, or at least diminished somehow, but she did not. She looked powerful.

'Trust me, Celaphon,' she said, and she pushed his head under the steaming liquid.

Hestillion bit her lip, certain that Celaphon would rise back up, roaring and outraged, but he meekly stayed where he was, his thick neck leading straight into the pool. The queen's hands began to work quickly, kneading the scales on the dragon's broad forehead. To Hestillion's surprise – and no small amount of horror – they began to move, as though they rested on top of a malleable paste instead of flesh and bones. There was a rumble from Celaphon, but it sounded more like an exclamation

430

of surprise than a pained outburst. When the queen had arranged his flesh to her liking, she plucked the crystal from the platform and placed it in the hollow she had made. The reaction was immediate – Celaphon's entire body shuddered, and a noise came from under the liquid, a terrible, strangled roar that forced a storm of air bubbles up to the surface. But he did not pull his head away from the queen's grip, and she continued her work without a change on her mask-like face. Hestillion edged forward, wanting to get a better view, and watched as the queen methodically pulled red flesh and black scales back around the edges of the jagged crystal.

Celaphon had stopped his guttural roaring, but he still shuddered in place, sending sharp waves through the white liquid, which lapped at the edges of the pool with increasing violence. Where it spilled, however, it was absorbed into the floor and was gone in moments.

'Nearly there, my sweet,' murmured Hestillion. The crystal was almost in place – it was not a smooth fit, jutting from the dragon's forehead, but the scales were closing up around the edges as if it had always been there. *No blood*, thought Hestillion.

'There.' The queen stepped back, and Celaphon raised his head – slowly, as though it weighed more than the rest of him. The crystal rose from the centre of his forehead in a series of jagged peaks. 'Now let me just . . .'

The Jure'lia queen reached up and tapped the crystal with a single finger, once. It flickered, light racing across the surface, and Celaphon staggered, as though he'd been struck by some-thing much bigger than himself. Mindful of the hissing waters, Hestillion leaned over the edge of the pool to place her hands on his shoulder. His scales were hot under her fingers, and he was trembling.

'Celaphon? Are you well? Talk to me?'

'There is so much,' he said. 'Endless, a line, a thread. Passing back through . . . great emptiness. But I am caught on the end of the thread.'

'Calm yourself,' said the queen. 'You are part of us now, and what you can feel is the line of our lives, stretching back to the very beginning. This is a connection, is it not? What you were looking for?'

'Crawling, noises, skittering.' Celaphon began to shake his head, whipping it back and forth. 'Darkness, heat, no air, no air, I can't breathe.'

Hestillion rounded on the queen, panic thick in her throat. 'What have you done to him?'

'We have given him what he wanted.' The queen was watching Hestillion closely, her eyes narrowed. 'It is an honour beyond anything experienced by anyone on this world before. He sees what we are, truly. A connection to something greater. Isn't that what you once sought?'

'I don't know what you mean.'

The queen tipped her head to one side, as though Hestillion were a curious insect doing something unexpected.

'Do you not?'

Hestillion turned back to Celaphon. 'My sweet one, please, are you all right?'

The dragon had grown very still now, and there was a new light in his pale eyes. He looked away from her, at the fleshy walls and the rows of silent Jure'lia servants. Not one of them had moved during the grafting process.

'I can feel it all. Is this what they feel?'

'Who, my sweet?'

'My brothers and sisters.'

'What they feel is less,' the queen cut in sharply. 'The bond that we have, now, Celaphon, is eternal. And now, we will rest and then gather another shard. Lady Hestillion Eskt, born in the year of the green bird, it is your turn.'

*　*　*

432

The pain was not so terrible, if she did not focus on it.

The Jure'lia queen had reduced the size of the pool before Hestillion climbed down into it, and she lay with her face turned up to the ceiling, waiting as the pale water soaked through her clothes. It did not burn as she had thought it would, but the scent of it was stronger and that was unpleasant, at least partly because she could place it: the smell of silt at the edge of a cold running river, or the smell at the back of an old wardrobe full of clothes long since forgotten – it was both yet neither of these. It was the moving that was distressing. When she moved, her body moved too much. As though her bones stayed in one place, but her flesh moved an extra inch or so. She thought of herself as a reflection caught in moving water, parts of her being sliced away in ripples of light. It was best, all in all, not to move.

'Are you ready?'

The queen crouched over her. Somewhere, out of sight, Celaphon was at the back of the chamber. He was quiet, coming to terms with the new sensations he claimed to be feeling.

'Why do you ask me, truly?' Hestillion could see the queen's face, hovering white above her. 'You could force this on me.'

'But I do not.' The queen paused, appearing to correct herself. 'We do not. You can walk away from this connection, Lady Hestillion, but we will not offer it again. We think you have some idea what it means.'

'Yes, it might kill me. And it is at the very least the final severing of any ties I have to Ebora, and to my brother. They will not have me back after this.'

But it was also a connection to the power that Celaphon wielded, a chance to help him become what he was meant to be. It was a way to understand the Jure'lia fully, and to be a part of the future they were building for Sarn: an alien future, yes, but one perhaps where she could continue to live. And regardless, there was no way back now, no path that led back

433

to the sunny palace gardens, laughing with her brother and her cousin. All of that was closed off to her, forever. She realised the queen was waiting.

'Oh, just do it,' she said tersely. 'If you can.'

The queen's long arms arched over her, clutching in one hand a new shard of blue crystal; she had retrieved another, while Celaphon and Hestillion waited in the eerily silent chamber. Her free hand settled around Hestillion's neck, curling around it as snugly as a scarf. The queen's skin was dry and hot.

'Do not move.'

With one finger from the hand still holding the crystal, the queen pressed against Hestillion's breastbone. She felt a moment of pressure, uncomfortable yet not quite painful, while the pale waters shifted and lapped around her body. Then, the finger sank in, as easily as if Hestillion were made of uncooked dough – yet still there was no pain.

'I don't understand, how are you doing that?'

'Not moving includes not talking,' said the queen. She moved the finger in slow circles, drawing out the hole she was creating, making it larger. From her awkward vantage point, Hestillion could not see the interior of the hole, but her heart was beating harder and harder, and she half feared to see it rise up through it, a desperate purple muscle, finally abandoning her.

Happy with the aperture she had created, the queen took the blue crystal and began to sink it into Hestillion's chest. Watching it, she felt a sudden terrible urge to laugh; giggles jammed in her throat, threatening to spill out, and she grimaced with the effort of keeping them in. *Roots save me, what have I done?*

With the crystal in place – it protruded almost two inches from Hestillion's breastbone – the queen began to push the flesh and skin around it back into place. Now, there was pain, and Hestillion gleefully seized on it, cherished it; anything to stop this dreadful need to laugh.

434

'Where is my blood?' she said suddenly. She felt like she'd had several glasses of wine on an empty stomach.

'Be quiet,' replied the queen, although without any heat. Her head was down, intent on her task – long fingers the colour of swamp moss patted and cajoled flesh and skin, patting them into place like pieces of clay. 'There, it is done.'

And then, without a word of warning, she pressed on the crystal and it winked with sapphire fire. In the first instance, Hestillion felt a shaft of agony impale her through the chest, instantly stopping her breath and expelling every other sensation. In that moment, she knew she must be dead. Her vision turned black at the edges, turning the chamber into a place of shadows. Then that pain moved out through her body, shooting to the tips of her fingers, crackling across her eyes, the lobes of her ears, the soles of her feet. Everything tasted blue, and then . . .

The first thing she felt, thankfully, was Celaphon. His bulk was reassuring, almost seeming to block everything else out. She felt his own wonder, and his confusion, and then a moment later, his joy at being connected with her. She knew, for a handful of seconds, what it was to be a dragon, scales moving over muscles, wings folded carefully away lest they catch on anything. She was him, standing on all fours, the weight and the power, the potential. And there was pain too, a sense of his body warring against itself. Parts of him did not sit well with others, grinding and catching, being in conflict. He was always in pain, she realised. It was a part of him.

Celaphon, I'm sorry.

Go, he said. *See all of it.*

He pushed her away, gently, and she span out of herself, belatedly recognising the enormous void that was waiting for her. Dimly she was aware that she was still lying in the pool of pale water, her eyes turned up to the ceiling – she could see herself, in fact, could see her hands lying palms up like pale dead fish – she was in the ceiling, she was in the walls, in every strange malformed creature that lined the walls.

'Be careful.' The queen's voice echoed from somewhere distant. 'Do not lose yourself, Hestillion Eskt.'

How?

Celaphon's presence, a huge weight of pain and power; the flying men, barely aware of where they were; the homunculi, still and waiting; the breathing flesh of the walls, the teeming multitude that was the corpse moon. She felt every part of it, within herself and outside herself. The queen too, a dark nexus at the heart of it, a part and yet apart. Hestillion felt her essence speeding towards her, as helpless as a leaf heading towards a waterfall, and there was the strangest sense of doubling, of being caught between mirrors . . .

It was too much. When she awoke, she was no longer in the pool but in her own room, lying on her bed with her arms by her sides. Nausea rolled and pitched in her stomach, but she didn't have the strength to move. With one hand she reached up and tentatively touched the blue crystal protruding from her chest. The corpse moon was heavy with silence.

'What have I done?' She swallowed hard, feeling her tongue sticking to the top of her mouth. When had she last had anything to drink? 'Celaphon?'

He was not with her, but she could feel him nearby. She sensed his warm concern for her, as though she were a baby with a fever.

There is so much to see, he said. *But our queen says you are still weak. Rest. My brother and sister will soon receive the gift.*

She felt a stab of alarm at that, but already she was sinking back into unconsciousness.

Our queen, she thought. *Ourselves.* And then she was gone.

42

Noon was, secretly, more than ready to give up. Her head was too hot, her back ached, and her boots were more mud than leather now. The sun glinting off the water seemed to mock her, and when she reached up to push her hair out of her eyes her hair was too hot to touch. Time to get out of the heat. She had just pulled her boots free of the thick river mud, ready to head to the makeshift rope ladder Tor had slung over the side of the cliff face, when a shadow passed over her, moving very fast. She squinted up at the sky, sheltering her eyes with one cupped hand, and she saw Kirune, his wings outspread and banking erratically. He was turning in the air and coming straight for her.

'Kirune?'

He crashed into the water just ahead of her, sending up a wave big enough to drench her and nearly knock her onto her backside. Spluttering, she waved her arms, attempting to stay upright. The big cat was upset, that was clear enough, and as he bore down on her she had a handful of seconds to wonder if he had just decided he'd had enough, and he was going to eat them all.

'Kirune? What is it?'

He wasn't wearing his harness. He shook himself all over, sending drops of water like diamonds scattering all over the crevasse.

'Tor. He has been attacked. Taken. You have to come with me now. Now!'

'Taken by who?'

As she stumbled over to him, wading through the warm water, she threw out her awareness to Vostok, hoping that the dragon was nearby.

'I don't know,' snapped Kirune. Then, 'Monsters. Monsters in a secret part of this place.'

Noon felt her insides turn to ice. *Vostok? Where are you?*

'All right.' She climbed onto Kirune's back, all too aware that she didn't have a harness to tie herself into. 'Take me there. Can you do that?'

Kirune did not reply, but instead his wings cracked open again like the sails of a ship caught in a storm, and they were in the air. Noon dug her fists into his fur and gripped his torso as well as she could with her thighs. Very swiftly they were above the island, the green canopy falling away below them.

'Can you tell me what this secret place is? Why you were there?'

The war-beast grumbled low in his throat, as though vexed by so many questions. 'I was exploring. I found a thing that felt bad. I got Tor to come and see. But . . .' He trailed off. 'There were lots of monsters. Tor told me to go, and get you.'

'Fire and blood.' Noon leaned forward, trying to get a sense of where they were going by peering over Kirune's head, when a patch of forest below them shuddered, and Vostok arose from it, feathered wings beating frantically.

'What is it?' she called. 'Do we fly to battle?'

'It sounds like it!' Noon called back. 'Tor has been attacked.'

The dragon came up next to them, her violet eyes winking in the sun.

438

'Very well. Lead the way, Brother Kirune.'

As if spurred on by the dragon's words, Kirune put on a sudden burst of speed, apparently caring little if Noon could keep her precarious seat on his back. With no other choice, she lay fully against his back, pressing her cheek into his dense grey fur. She could smell him, wild and familiar, and the scent of the river mud on her boots. Somewhere beneath his fur, she could feel the thunder of his heart. They flew on for some time, until abruptly he slowed.

'Here,' he said, 'it is the barrier we passed through. This is where we found it.'

Cautiously, Noon sat up. Kirune was descending, with Vostok beside him, but she had time to see the odd flickering wall of lights, and recognised it as the same barrier they had glimpsed when they had first found the island.

'There is a hole at the bottom,' continued Kirune. 'It is where we passed through.'

Once they had landed, Noon gladly hopped from the big cat's back, trying to ignore how badly her legs were shaking. Vostok was hissing with displeasure; the forest here was thick, and she found herself hemmed in by too many trees.

'It hides the truth,' said Kirune, as if this explained everything. The hole was obvious, surrounded as it was with multiple hairline cracks of white light. 'The monsters are beyond there.'

'Great. Vostok, can you get through it?'

'We have to help him,' said Kirune. He was, Noon realised with growing alarm, becoming panicky again.

'We will. Vostok?'

The dragon had been grumbling and poking at the edge of the hole with her snout.

'It will not keep me out.' She pushed her head and shoulders through, straining against the strange barrier, and then abruptly more pieces of it winked out of existence, as though the violence of Vostok's passage had shattered them. She was through, and

Noon quickly followed with Kirune. Beyond the barrier the forest was much sparser, but Noon barely had time to consider that, as immediately Kirune was racing off ahead, his great paws kicking up clods of black dirt.

'Climb up,' said Vostok, 'we'll follow.'

Noon scrambled up her side, boots sliding unhelpfully against her slick scales, until she was seated just beyond the dragon's shoulders. She took a little of the dragon's life energy, just a touch, more a comfort than anything.

'If there are monsters, we should approach slowly,' said Vostok, but she was already thundering after Kirune, and although Noon murmured agreement, in her mind she saw Tor, how he'd been after the explosion in Esiah Godwort's enclosure; wounded, helpless, close to death. She had no wish to see that again.

Quickly it became apparent that this part of the island was unlike anything they had seen before. Strange pale green hillocks, as smooth as glass, burst out of the black earth, increasing in frequency until they appeared to be moving through the ruin of a slowly emerging city. But there was nothing there that Noon would have expected to see in a city – no windows or doors, no discarded carts, no wells or roads.

'What the fuck is all this, then?'

'I do not know,' said Vostok. The dragon shuddered under her.

'What is it? What's wrong?'

'This place. Can you not feel it? It is like . . . walking through despair.'

Noon blinked. The whole place was eerie, and Kirune's distress was gnawing at her guts, but she couldn't have claimed to be sensing anything else from the strange green shapes. She leaned close to the dragon, trying to feel what she felt, and caught a sense of deep wrongness, a horror that was difficult to put into words. Instinctively, she separated herself from it.

'I'm not feeling what you are, that's for certain. What is it, Vostok? Have you felt anything like it before?'

'No,' the dragon replied immediately.

Ahead of them, Kirune had stopped. The green structures had completely replaced the trees, and some of the towers and walls were so tall they couldn't see beyond them. The big cat was looking around slowly, his shoulders hunched.

'This is where they were,' he said. 'Monsters, white things. And they took Tor inside there.'

Noon looked at the smooth green tower he indicated, expecting to finally see a door or a window of some sort, but there was just more of the smooth green material.

'Are you sure?'

Kirune bared his teeth in a hiss. 'Yes. I am no idiot.'

She climbed down from Vostok's back and clambered up a slope towards the smooth lump of green rock that Kirune had indicated. She pressed her fingertips to it cautiously, half fearing that she might sink through it, or it might burn her, but there was nothing. It was unpleasantly slick, but she still did not feel any of the unsettling horror that Vostok was experiencing. There were no birds singing. There were no noises here at all, save for their own breathing. Again she thought of how alone she was on this island.

'Well. Let's look around and see what we can find.'

It was the scent that Tor noticed first.

The smell was overwhelming. Sharp and yellow-green, coating his tongue and stinging his nose. It was like being inside a large, unripe fruit.

He opened his eyes. He was standing pressed against a slightly inclined smooth green wall, while below him the floor sloped away vertically out of sight. His thigh and his shoulder were throbbing steadily, but at least there didn't appear to be any of the awful white monsters in here with him. The walls around him were smooth and rounded as well, and he had just enough time to realise that there was nothing below his feet and that he was somehow stuck to the wall, when, slowly, he began to peel away from it. There was tacky stuff there, like glue, adhering to his coat and the back of his head, sticking them to the smooth surface.

He panicked, scrambling at the wall, but despite the unpleasant stickiness there was nothing for him to get a purchase on and within seconds he was sliding down the sloping wall, pitching forward into a long tube lit from within by green light. Tor rammed the heels of his boots ahead of him, attempting to arrest his progress, but only succeeded in turning himself around and sending him rolling down the tube horizontally. There was a breathless sense of falling, of crashing, and then he hit a pool of lukewarm water with a tremendous splash. He rose up gasping, half convinced he would drown – the water was somehow thick, and it sought to clog his mouth and nostrils – and then he sat back. He was in around three feet of water, sitting in the bottom of some sort of huge, featureless cavern. It was not dark in the chamber, but lit with a warm, yellow-green light, like that of sunshine passing through spring's first leaves. Further up the faintly glowing walls were large round holes, clearly similar to the one he had just fallen out of.

'Ygseril's balls,' he murmured to himself, before swiping his wet hair back from his face. 'I'm inside the island. Or under it. Or some bastard thing.'

Tentatively, he poked at his leg. The white monster had easily punctured the leather of his trousers, and now his flesh oozed black blood from several deep wounds. From the feel of his shoulder, it was in more or less the same state, which was not good news. Awkwardly, he stood, swearing repeatedly as his black blood swirled amid the silvery water, like ink on moonlight . . .

He stopped, barely daring to breathe. A memory, something from his earliest childhood, suddenly rose as clear and as painful as a knife under the ribs. He remembered his mother holding him in her arms, a fine cup in her other hand. It had been painted with shining red dragons, and they caught the light and glimmered and flashed, like living things. He had wanted to hold the cup for himself and had reached out for it, but his mother had just shaken her head before pushing the lip of the cup towards his mouth.

Did he remember what it tasted like? He thought not. Centuries of absence, and centuries of human blood had gradually eroded it, but he thought that he would know if he tasted it again.

In the memory, they were in the Hall of Roots. There were lots of other Eborans there, pressed in all around, talking animatedly, laughing and greeting each other, but it had not been a special day. It was just one Sap Day of many – once every moon's cycle, but when you lived for hundreds and hundreds of years, they seemed to come around so often. Tor, even as a child, small enough to be carried by his mother, had already seen nearly a thousand of them. His sister, Hestillion, had already sipped from her own cup – hers was painted with green birds, of course – and she stood impatiently clutching at their mother's skirts, anxious to be away again, to find somewhere they could play. The sap had been silvery and thick, coating his throat and burning in his belly, and at the time he had been impatient with it – the same thing, every month, boring old sap.

'Boring old sap,' he whispered, looking at the pool of shining liquid around him. Hands shaking, he cupped them together and watched as it pooled between his clasped fingers. Would he remember what it tasted like? Would it heal him, take away his scars and seal up the oozing wounds on his shoulder and thigh? He raised his hands to his mouth; it smelled of nothing in particular, save for a strange mineral coating on the back of his throat. It could equally be poison, but then given there was no obvious way out of the cavern and he was bleeding mortal-blood, it seemed that the risk hardly mattered. He lifted his cupped hands to his lips.

'It is not what you are seeking, child.'

Tor jumped, the silvery water falling away through his fingers. Standing on the far side of the chamber was a tall figure that hadn't been there before. It was white, like the monsters that had bitten him, but it was more Eboran in shape – slim and upright, with legs and arms. Too many arms, in fact. With some difficulty, Tor scrambled to his feet, ignoring the roaring pain in his leg.

'Who . . . what are you?'

The figure came forward, and more details resolved themselves. It was around eight feet tall, much taller even than he was, and it had two long sets of arms, the second positioned just behind and below the first. It had a long, smooth face, with a nose that was a long, flat afterthought, a slash of a mouth, lips pressed tightly closed when it was not speaking, and eyes like a deer's – large and black and set almost diagonally below its smooth brow. There were marks on its cheeks and forehead, like dabs of crimson paint, and it wore long, thick robes that were decorated in a similar fashion – slashes of colour against white. Tor did not recognise the material; it looked a little like wool, but it was much denser and lined with a faint fuzz. Long pale hair, as white as its robes, was tucked carefully behind a pair of ears that ended in a tapered point.

'You are not who came before.'

The voice was soft and faintly male. Tor wiped his hands on his trousers, once again wishing he had not left his sword behind.

'Who came before? Who are you?' He stopped, trying to think what the most important questions were. 'How could you know what I'm looking for?'

444

The strange many-limbed man was peering at him closely, frowning at the wounds on his thigh, and the way his shirt was stuck to his shoulder with blood.

'It is not the sap you were raised on.' Before Tor could respond to this, he continued, 'You bleed black. How strange. I imagine that this is not good?'

Tor raised his eyebrows. 'You could say that. Enough black blood and you'll have a corpse rattling around in your big . . . whatever this is. And what are those monsters outside?'

The man clasped all four of his hands together, long fingers interlocking with an eerie grace. Tor realised that the shape of the man, how he moved, should all appear deeply wrong to him, yet it did not – if anything, it felt familiar on some level he did not understand, and that in itself was frightening.

'They prevent infection. There are tiny animals in your blood that fight infection. Did you know this?'

'Tiny animals?' Tor snorted. His leg felt heavy now, even as his head felt lighter and lighter. It was difficult to make sense of what the man was saying, and for an alarming moment he wondered if he were simply caught in a dream created by Arnia, some sort of test or punishment. But as real as dreams could seem, there was never really any mistaking reality for one. 'You might have tiny . . . cats or dogs in your blood, but I certainly don't.'

'Hmm.' The man bowed his head slightly, the skin around his huge liquid eyes crinkling. 'Then, meat – you salt meat to keep away rot? And flies?'

'I can't say that I've ever done it personally, but yes, I suppose we do.'

'Then the things you encountered outside are like salt. They hold us as we are supposed to be, fight off infections, eat away that which is not needed. They are caretakers.' He paused, and then huffed. Despite his strange appearance, it was an oddly familiar gesture. 'It is not a very good analogy, actually.'

'Salt monsters. Fine. And what is this place? What are your salt monsters protecting?'

'That is more complicated, child.'

'Well, I've been savaged and pulled into a giant green tube, so I would appreciate some answers, no matter how complicated they are.' He took a deep breath, ignoring how badly his head was spinning. 'And I'm four hundred years old. I am hardly anyone's *child*.'

'Come. First, we must stop the black blood.'

The figure turned and walked away, heading straight for the smooth, green wall of the chamber. Tor hesitated, watching the swishing of the man's robes through the pool. Keeping his eyes on the man's back, he briefly dipped his fingers into the silvery water and tasted it; it was not Ygseril's sap. The disappointment of that held him in place for a few agonized seconds, and then he began limping after the man; it seemed that the only way he was likely to get out of here was with someone else's help. It looked as though his new friend was about to walk straight into the smooth green expanse, when the wall ahead of them split open as though someone had just struck it with an axe blade. There were fibrous threads hanging from the place where the wall had split, and the sharp scent of foliage grew stronger.

They stepped through into another chamber, only this was long, and the walls leaned towards each other until they came together in shadows that loomed far above their heads. In the centre of the room there was a spindly structure, a thing of spirals and curves and more fibrous threads, which curved off to meet the wall on the left. As they drew closer, Tor realised it was a staircase of sorts.

When the man led them to the bottom of it, Tor was dismayed to see that the thing did not look sturdy at all – in fact, he doubted it would take his weight, let alone the combined weight of him and the man with four arms.

446

'I do not believe I can climb that, friend,' he said, gesturing to his leg.

The man peered at his leg again, as though he had forgotten what one was. 'I am sorry,' he said, 'but I cannot help you. It is stronger than it looks, this structure, and I promise that there is help beyond it.'

Tor opened his mouth to reply, when the man seemed to shatter and break apart in front of his eyes. It was as though he were a reflection on the surface of a pond, and someone had tossed a rock, sending all the pieces of him into fractured bits. And then just as quickly, the pieces rearranged themselves until once again the man was a solid figure in front of him, his long fingers still interlaced.

'As I said, I cannot help you,' he repeated, as though this explained everything. 'I cannot touch you. What is your name, child?'

Tor swallowed. It had to be the blood loss. Had those salt creatures some sort of poison on their saliva, like some Wild-touched monstrosity?

'Tormalin the Oathless,' he said, before pressing his lips together. They were starting to go numb. 'I am Tormalin. What is your name? Who are you? What are you doing on this island? You can't ignore all my questions forever.'

'Tormalin, follow me.'

Despite his better judgement, he did. The strange man flowed up the erratic staircase as though it were barely there, while Tor pulled himself up by grabbing a hold of the twisted pieces of greenish material. It was solid enough under his weight, although every awkward step caused a fresh wave of blood from the punctures on his leg, and he could feel the blood from his shoulder wound trickling down the centre of his back.

When eventually he reached the top, he followed the man through a dark opening into a wider room, much smaller and closer than the cavern they had been in. In here, roots, just like those in Micanal's underground excavation, sprouted from the walls, alongside several large oval-shaped objects that Tor took to be mirrors, although their surfaces were a deep, dark red.

'Come here and rest yourself, Tormalin the Oathless.' The man gestured to the walls. 'And you will be healed.'

Tor did not move. 'How? What is going to happen?'

'I do not believe you would understand if I told you. Stand here, against the tendrils.'

When Tor still did not move, a flicker of impatience moved across the man's face – as alien as his appearance was, Tor found he recognised that emotion well enough. 'Tormalin, you are dying as I look at you. The children here are strong, but not invulnerable – surely you have learned that by now?'

A wave of light-headedness moved through his body. Thinking of Kirune, and wondering if the cat had escaped and if he had, if he'd fetched Noon, he walked over to the wall and the things the man had called tendrils.

'With your back to them, please.'

Tor did as he was told, the tendrils making uncomfortable knots against his back, and then waited. Nothing happened. He glared at the strange man, but he simply stood and fiddled with the thick cuff of his robe, removing some invisible grain of dust.

'Well?' snapped Tor eventually. 'You were the one who told me I was about to drop dead. How is this supposed to be helping me?'

'It is doing its work,' the many-limbed man said mildly.

Perplexed, Tor looked down, to see several green tendrils sticking up through the material of his trousers, all bunched around the area where he had been bitten. They were moving slightly, as though they were underwater weeds caught in a current. He could feel nothing there but the pain of the bite, yet they had clearly wormed through his flesh. There was, he could just make out by turning his head slightly, a similar gathering of tendrils just under his collarbone.

'Oh.' He looked away hurriedly, swallowing down the wave of bile that threatened to close his throat. 'I . . . what is this?'

'It will close your wounds.'

The man stepped back, and all around him, the red mirrors shimmered with a light source Tor could not see, and then faces began to appear in them – similar to the man who stood before him, with their smooth noses and bulbous, inky eyes, although each had a different collection of coloured marks across its skin. One that Tor could see had braided its white hair, while another wore a chain of some dark material flecked with red.

'Eeskar.' One of them spoke, and its voice sounded to Tor as though it came from a very great distance. 'Another one comes? So soon?'

'Yurn, the incident you think of was many turns ago,' replied the man who had brought him to the chamber, who Tor assumed must be Eeskar. 'You are poor at watching the times.'

'I do not remember it,' said another of the mirrors. This was the one with the braids, and its voice was higher and softer than the others. As Tor watched, the image seemed to shatter and re-arrange itself, just as Eeskar had done. 'They are small, are they not? And unfinished, somehow.'

'Degradation,' said Eeskar, sorrowfully. He bowed his head slightly. 'Of us, now, and of the seed, then. We cannot expect endless successes.' He straightened up again, turning to look around at all the mirrors – the faces followed him as one. 'That is why there are many seeds. You know this.'

'It seems a waste,' said the one called Yurn. 'Such material, turned into this. A shadow, an echo of what it should be. Of what we are.'

'Were. What we were,' said Eeskar, sternly. He looked back to Tor, and to his surprise the man smiled, his huge doe eyes creasing at the edges. 'Yes, they are small and weak, a ripple cast by a mighty rock, but they are still a delightful simulacra. Not a success, no, but neither is it a thing to look on with disgust.'

'Speak for yourself,' muttered the one with the braids.

'Who are you?' The strange conversation had almost made him forget his wounds, but now that Tor spoke he could feel a tightness in his leg and shoulder that was replacing the pain. Whatever the tendrils were, they were succeeding. 'What is this place? You have to give me some answers!'

'Always questions,' said Yurn, dismissively. 'The last one asked questions, and it didn't like the answers, but still they ask.'

'Tormalin the Oathless,' Eeskar lifted all four of his arms, the thick sleeves falling back to reveal limbs that seemed to have too many elbows. 'We are the beginning of you.'

43

Another empty room, another sad collection of shadows and dust.

Vintage paused in the doorway, taking the opportunity to lean there and rest for a moment. Micanal's journal was wedged firmly under one arm, with the crutch under the other, and various bits of her were aching to retire to her rooms for the night, but it was so difficult to sleep when so much of the palace lay empty for her to explore. And, of course, Nanthema could well be in her rooms. Just lately the atmosphere between them had grown thick and charged, like the air before a storm; when they were together, she half expected the light to take on the strained, yellow quality of sunshine before a cloudburst.

Cautiously, she shuffled forward into the semi-dark. The emptiness of the palace had surprised her at first. Only a handful of the humans had chosen to take up suites in the palace, with most choosing to camp in the gardens instead. She had asked Bern about it – had Tor objected to humans cluttering up his ancestral home? Did Aldasair not want strangers poking around the Eboran furnishings? Bern had smiled a little, looking oddly apologetic, and then he had explained that many of the humans who had made the long journey to Ebora were convinced that the palace must be haunted, or cursed. You have to remember, he said, that to most of these people the Eborans were near mythical creatures, unknowable beings who had turned into monsters and thirsted for human flesh. At best, they think it's unlucky to sleep in their vacant beds.

Vintage had shaken her head at that, and Bern had grinned. 'As a woman of science, I reckon you find those sorts of attitudes frustrating,' he'd said.

Standing in one such abandoned chamber, it wasn't so difficult to imagine the place was cursed. Vintage put Micanal's journal down on a nearby table, and looked around. This place had been an artist's studio once, and there were wooden easels crowded at the walls, hunched together like uneasy skeletons. On another table towards the window there was a murky collection of glass jars, one with an extremely ancient paintbrush sticking out of it. Seeing those, her heart quickened in her chest, and with trembling fingers she opened the journal to a page she had marked with a strip of leather. This was Micanal's studio – one of many, actually – with what were likely his very own tools, just lying scattered about. Forcing herself to take it all in properly, she scanned down the page to the entry that had brought her here.

I went to the summer studio today. I have been avoiding it, for it is so close to the Hatchery and I have found it difficult even to walk in that part of the palace. But I am the only one who uses it now, and I feel some strange pull towards the old places, as though they are ailing relatives I should be caring for in these final days (of course, all my true blood relatives save for Arnia are dead). I don't know if I meant to do any work there, or if I simply meant to clean it up, but when I got there I found a woman I did not know, crouched in the corner of the room, as if hiding from the daylight. I have made a brief sketch of her in these pages, from memory.

Her feet were bare. She sat with her arms over her head, and from them I could see that she had the flux, oozing red cracks in chalk-white skin. From between her arms she looked up at me, deep shadows around her eyes. I surmised from her clothes that she was not from the palace, or even central Ebora, but one of the outer settlements near our borders. Her feet, as I looked more closely, were dark with dirt and blistered. I must admit, I felt a tremor of shock that such as her had come so far, and then somehow crept so deep within the palace. And to here, this place that was mine.

I asked her what she was doing here. She told me, haltingly, that she had come to the palace because she was dying, and she wanted to be near Tree-father when she died. Wanted to be on his roots, if she could.

A wave of revulsion closed my throat. Have we not done enough? Has Ygseril not suffered enough? We dare to bring our diseased selves into his presence, to rot on his sacred roots?

She continued speaking in her dry, broken voice, ragged from coughing. She had made it this far, she explained to me, but was too exhausted to go any further. She had never been to the palace before, and she kept getting lost. Outside, it was possible to see Tree-father, but once she was within the twisting corridors she had become confused. Perhaps I could help her. Carry her there. Her time was short.

I said no more to her, and left. I have not been back.

Vintage closed the book, and looked to the corner nearest the window. She could imagine the woman easily enough – the sketch included by Micanal was a brief thumbnail, but extremely evocative – crouched in the dust, her feet sore and bleeding. She would have gone to the window to see if she could see Ygseril, but the room was facing in the wrong direction – there was only a garden, one of hundreds dotted around. She could imagine Micanal too, straight-backed and imperious, looking down on this woman who had invaded his sanctuary. It made her frown.

Was this why they had left? The presence of illness in the palace had become too difficult to avoid, in the end, so they had sought to outrun it. *Just like Tor.*

Gathering up the journal, Vintage left, walking back out into the corridors without much sense of where she was going. What sort of people were Micanal and Arnia, truly? What sort of situation had she sent Tor and Noon into? More disappointment and sorrow seemed likely. She was so caught up in her thoughts that she very nearly walked straight into Tyranny Munk, who was standing in a corridor gazing up at painting that stretched lengthwise for a good ten feet or so.

'Lady Vintage! You made me jump. Have you seen this? I don't think I've ever seen anything like it.'

'I'm sorry, my dear, I was miles away.' Vintage turned to study the painting. It was a stormy landscape, depicting a great stretch of broken grassland, with dark mountains brooding in the distance. A war was raging there, thousands of figures frozen in violence, but the far end of the canvas was rough, and scratched here and there with charcoal marks. The painting was unfinished. 'I had thought all the big paintings and artworks had been squirrelled away, but this has been left out. How interesting.' She peered closer at the tiny figures, and realised with a slight lurch of her stomach that it depicted the Carrion Wars – humans were being torn apart by tall figures in shining armour. Splotches and smears of crimson, tiny faces contorted in pain. 'It is by Micanal the Clearsighted. I imagine this must be one of the pieces he was

454

working on when he left, and some poor soul has framed it and put it here, unfinished as it is. He really was truly revered here.'

'This must be worth a fortune.' Tyranny met her eyes and grinned. 'Don't worry, it's much too big to hide under my shirt. It's a fairly grim subject too, what do you—'

They both turned to look up the corridor as a flurry of shouts broke the silence. Voices raised in demand, and outrage, then a shout of warning. A moment later, Vintage heard the distinctive sound of sword against sword.

'What is that?' Tyranny was frowning.

'Sarn's arse, it's coming from the Hatchery. Come on.'

Vintage moved off down the corridor as fast as she could, the crutch clattering a din on the marble floor. Tyranny Munk came close on her heels. When they turned the corner to the wider passageway that housed the Hatchery doors, Vintage was alarmed to see a small but violent battle taking place outside them. Immediately, she spotted the guards Bern had assigned to watch the Hatchery, a pair of Finneral warriors with stones in their hair and their distinctive short swords in their hands; facing off against them was Sen-Lord Takor and three of his soldiers. All were still standing, but the clamour of sword against sword was deafening, and the Yuron-Kai were known to take hand-to-hand combat very seriously. As she watched, one of their soldiers slammed a Finneral woman against the wall, hard enough for Vintage to hear the flat crack as her head hit the stone.

'What is going on here? What, in the name of Sarn's broken bones, do you think you're bloody well doing?'

'They tried to force their way inside the Hatchery!' shouted the other Finneral guard, his voice tight with outrage. Sen-Lord Takor stepped back and met Vintage's eyes, letting his soldiers continue the fight without him.

'There is nothing but chaos here,' he snapped in his accented plains speech. 'If you will not let us in, we must force our way in and take what we need.'

'You will do no such bloody thing!' Vintage patted her belt, only to remember that of course she hadn't brought her crossbow with her – she hadn't thought she would need it. 'Tell your men to step down, Sen-Lord Takor, or you can consider yourself at war with Ebora, *and* at war with me, and I promise you, at least one of those is a bloody dangerous thing to be.'

'What Ebora?' Sen-Lord Takor snorted – it was, Vintage guessed, as close as he came to laughing. Behind them the fight continued. The Finneral guard who had shouted had taken a punch to the face, and his nose was bleeding freely. Vintage felt a surge of anger. 'Ebora is long gone. What's in that room should be given to those able to do something with it.'

'How dare you! How dare you accept our hospitality, and then start a bloody brawl in the corridor!' In her anger, Vintage took a moment to curse Nanthema. If she had made herself more visible, taken more of an interest, they could well have avoided this situation. 'I will not have it, sir. I will not!'

She turned to ask Tyranny to go and get more help, but the young woman was already moving towards Sen-Lord Takor, her hands held up in a placating gesture.

'Lord Takor, I understand your frustration.' She walked up to him casually enough, not looking at the curved sword he held in one hand. 'It's a bad situation all over. But you have to think about it another way.' She placed a hand lightly on his upper arm, just as though they were friends chatting in a bar. 'You see, just down that corridor, there's a painting . . .' She pointed with her other hand, and obviously confused, Sen-Lord Takor looked where she was gesturing.

Vintage saw it coming, but only just. Abruptly, Tyranny's posture changed, and her pointing hand was suddenly flying back in the form of a fist. It connected neatly with Sen-Lord

456

Takor's jaw, and he went down like a sack of stones – she had knocked him out cold. The man's soldiers looked around, stunned to see their commander unconscious on the floor, and the two Finneral guards took immediate advantage, knocking the weapon from the hands of one and driving the other two back. Vintage stepped up, carefully keeping her own surprise from her face.

'Take him back to the rooms we assigned you,' she barked. She made sure to make eye contact with each of them, and was pleased to see the confusion and indecision on their faces. It was useful. 'And you can tell Sena-Lord Kivee that we shall be having words about this later. Go!'

Sheepishly, they went, carrying Sen-Lord Takor between them. The two Finneral guards were looking at Tyranny with something like awe, while she was shaking out her hand and wincing.

'Fuck. Ow. Not done that for a while.'

'Not that you can tell, my darling.' Vintage patted her arm. 'Thank you. Now, we're going to need extra guards here, I think. Perhaps we should close off this whole corridor. Norri,' she said, addressing the female guard, 'could you run—'

'It's all right,' cut in Tyranny. 'I'll go.' The young woman had broken out in a sweat, and was holding her hand awkwardly.

'My dear, are you quite well?'

She grinned. 'I just need to get something cold on this. Okaar will have the stuff, and I'll call in on your people as I go, get a few more warm bodies along here for you.' She nodded to Norri and the other guard before hurrying away up the corridor.

'What a punch!' said the male guard, putting away his sword.

'What a woman,' added Norri.

'Yes, well.' Vintage adjusted the crutch, and passed a hand over her forehead. 'Thank you for holding them off. I suspect our future relations with the Yuron-Kai are going to be somewhat strained.'

44

Aldasair could hear Bern screaming from wherever the queen had taken him – somewhere towards the heart of the Behemoth. The human's agonised yells echoed and shivered around him, seemed almost to bleed from the walls – the hopeless sound of someone suffering terribly.

It had been going on for hours, and at first Aldasair had thrown himself at the barriers, shouted at the eyeball-filled ceiling, bellowed for Hestillion to come and justify herself. Nothing had happened, although he had made his throat raw and painful. Then, as the screaming went on and on and did not stop, he thought of how perhaps he could end his own life, so that he would not hear it anymore. He knew that Hestillion and the Jure'lia queen would come back for him too – it had been decided, they told him, that he and Bern would be bonded first to the worm people, in order to make Jessen and Sharrik more tractable – but this now seemed like the most attractive possibility; after all, if they came for him, they would be finished with Bern.

In the next chamber, separated from him by the clear membrane wall, Sharrik lay on the floor with his head resting on his paws. The big griffin looked strangely small, as though he had somehow shrunk over the last few hours, and his feathers trembled slightly with each breath. Jessen sat with him, gently resting her muzzle on his broad back, and Aldasair could feel her quiet attempts to comfort him.

'They cannot hope to do the same to you.' Aldasair got to his feet and approached the membrane. 'As powerful as they are, you two will be too strong for them.'

Jessen didn't lift her head, but her eyebrows rose slightly.

'You saw what they did to Bern. This place isn't a room or a prison – it is them. We are at their mercy here.'

Aldasair stood very still. He did not want to remember – he wanted the memory to vanish into fog, like so many of his memories of Ebora – but instead he saw Bern again, his stricken face as they had taken him. First, they had thrown up a wall to separate them, clear mucous shimmering across the room like a thrown net, and then a small force of the wizened creatures made of greenish ooze had rushed him. Bern had fought them, tearing the small things to gooey pieces, but the floor had grown soft, trapping his feet and sinking him up to his shins. Then the creatures had swarmed into one thing, swamping him like a suit of supple armour until they had complete control. After that, it had been a simple enough job to take him away.

'It is worth fighting,' Aldasair said, too aware that he sounded uncertain. 'Enough confusion, enough trouble . . . it might give us a chance.'

'It hurts,' rumbled Sharrik. 'It hurts.'

'I know, brother. You must be strong for him. Send him your strength.' For a second, Jessen's long pink tongue whipped out and she fussed at Sharrik's feathers, grooming him like a mother with her cub, and then abruptly the screaming stopped. Aldasair felt his skin grow cold, a terrible chill circling around his neck like an icy hand. Perhaps no one could suffer that long and live.

'He lives,' said Sharrik after a moment. He lifted his shaggy head, his eyes focussed on the section of the wall where an opening most often appeared. 'My human lives.'

They waited. Aldasair found that he could not sit and wait, so he paced, back and forth, feeling his own anxiety mirrored in the war-beasts. When, finally, the opening peeled back to reveal the queen and a horde of her creatures carrying Bern, he found that he was more angry than frightened. He stood still and waited, watching the queen carefully.

'Interesting,' she said. Her mask-face looked oddly brittle; hairline cracks, grey against the white, seemed to bunch around her mouth and eyes, and there was a delicacy to her movements that Aldasair hadn't noticed before. Was it possible for the worm-queen to grow tired? 'Such a . . . process. The human did not enjoy it, we fear.' She gestured with one long finger to where Bern lay, prone on the floor, his golden hair stuck to his forehead with sweat. Aldasair could not see immediately where the crystal had been grafted, but he was sure it must have been – he had seen the rock that now stuck out of the dragon's forehead, and the matching shard nestling in his cousin's chest. 'It will become easier, we believe.'

'When will you take your next victim?' The words felt like poison on Aldasair's lips, hot and bitter. 'Can you bear to wait to create your next monstrosity?'

The queen tilted her head towards him, as though surprised that he could speak at all.

'No. The connection is a fine web. Too much weight too quickly, would break it.' She gestured, and the homunculi seeped into the floor. As she walked away, a new transparent membrane leapt up in her wake, while the one immediately in front of Aldasair dissolved, leaving him in a new cell with the unconscious Bern. 'You may have him back.'

Aldasair knelt by the unconscious man. He looked gaunt, with purple shadows like bruises under his eyes, and his cheekbones looked too prominent, as though he'd been lost in a wilderness for weeks, not tortured for a few hours. Even his blond hair was darker, soaked in sour-smelling sweat.

'Bern? Bern, it's me.'

The big man's eyelids flickered and he grimaced. He shifted on the floor, and brought one hand up to rub his forehead, and that was when Aldasair saw that the blue crystal had been sunk into the palm of his hand. It looked heavy and awkward, the flesh around it rigid and white like a network of old scars.

'I keep falling.' Bern's voice was ragged from the screaming. 'Over and over. I think I've found something solid, and then it falls away again. Like I'm out . . . on the ice . . . and . . .'

'Bern!' Sharrik was up on his feet and standing as close to the membrane wall as he could get, with Jessen at his shoulder. 'Brother! I am here!'

'Brother. I know you, I know you . . .'

'You know us all, Bern.' Aldasair took his other hand and squeezed it, not liking how cold and clammy it was. 'We're all here with you.'

'By the stones, there is such a darkness, such a huge space . . .' Bern jerked and shuddered, and for a second his face screwed up like a child waking from a nightmare. 'I keep falling through it, or I'm being dragged through it, from point to point. I can feel it all at once, but it's too much.'

'Can you sit up?'

Aldasair pulled him into a sitting position, and was gladdened to see him smile as he saw Sharrik and Jessen.

'Aldasair, I feel this place too. It's a living thing, and now it's like it's a part of me.' He grimaced again. 'I think I'm going to be sick. How long was I gone? Have they done it to the rest of you?'

'A few hours. The lights here dimmed, and even went out for a while.' Aldasair swallowed, deciding not to mention that he'd been afraid that they would be trapped there until they

461

died of hunger and thirst, blind in the dark. 'The queen has not touched the rest of us yet.'

'I would not wish this on anyone. I can feel her, crawling around, like rats in my head.' He held up his hand and peered at the blue crystal erupting from his palm. 'I will not be able to swing an axe with this.'

'They will regret injuring you, brother.' Sharrik's voice was a low growl. 'I will shred their guts to pieces. I can feel the poison that is in you, and I will taste their blood for it.'

'Yes,' said Jessen, her amber eyes flashing. Aldasair felt a current of outrage from her, and under that, fear, mixing with his own. 'We will kill them. But first, we must survive this poison.'

The walls were breathing.

Hestillion couldn't believe she hadn't noticed it before, because it was deafening. Not that she could hear it. There was no noise, but a sense of pressure in her head; pressure building, pressure releasing. Pressure building, pressure releasing. She glared at the wall of her chamber and willed it to stop, or choke, but the breathing went on, regardless of her. On some level she knew that she could never stop that – it was like willing her own heart to stop, or willing herself blind.

She stood up and crossed to the table that held her basin of water, the jug and her combs – all of which had been looted from a town they had destroyed – and stripped off all her clothes. Methodically, she washed herself with a clean cloth and a small nub of yellow soap, scrubbing her hair with particular violence to remove the smell of the changing pool. Very quickly, the water turned dark grey and silty, and she wished one of the squat homunculus creatures would bring her fresh water, but she was too exhausted to shout, and still squeamish about the things seeing her in the nude – they were undoubtedly spies for the queen, after all.

Squeezing the water from her hair, she was startled when a

small greenish creature stepped awkwardly through the opening in the wall, carrying a fat jug full of fresh water. She watched as it set the jug by her feet and then retreated. She listened to the soft patter of its stubby feet disappearing back down the corridor, a crease of puzzlement between her eyebrows.

'It heard me.'

Hestillion dropped the cloth, her nakedness forgotten, and formed a new thought in her mind.

Run back to me.

Silence. The breathing of the corpse moon again, and behind that, the presence of the human man – his pain and his horror, his disgust at what had been done to him – but she pushed those away hurriedly. She did not want to think about the human, because when she did, she felt uncomfortably close to him, could almost feel what it was to be in his large, short-lived body. Instead, she touched the crystal at her throat and cast her thoughts out towards the corridor.

I said run back to me!

This time the response was instant. A rapid patter of small feet outside, like her father drumming his fingers on a leather chair, and the wizened creature appeared again at the entrance, peering in with its eyeless face. Abruptly, she was disgusted by it, and instead she reached out with her mind and imagined the opening squeezing shut. A second later, it did, hiding the homunculus from view.

'Ha!'

She grinned, dizzy with triumph, which made her think of Celaphon. Swiftly, she pulled some clothes from the chest that had been provided for her and dressed. Clad in black velvet leggings and a dark-green jerkin tied with a crimson belt, she left her chamber – gesturing the door open with a flick of her hand – and made her way to the vast room that had been allocated to Celaphon. She found him crouched up next to the transparent strip that ran the length of the east wall, his huge

463

head moving steadily back and forth as he tracked their progress over the landscape. Much of the room was filled with the expanse of his wings, which he had spread out behind him like the canopy of some vast tent.

'Celaphon?'

'I knew you were coming here,' he said without looking at her. 'You are a part of it, this web. I see you like a bird, small and green, so tiny that you fly perched on my horns. Is that strange?'

Hestillion blinked. 'No, it is apt, my sweet.'

'And the other, this human,' he turned to her, his white eyes shining like pearls, 'I can feel him too, and he is a bright, shining weapon. Powerful, strong. He is strong for a human, I think, and brave. He fought us well, and now he is my brother.'

'You feel him so clearly?'

'Yes. You do not?' He paused, and then, 'An axe! He is an axe in my mind, silver and . . . stones, too. A great core of stone, not cold, but solid.'

'I have been avoiding him, I think.' Hestillion smiled slightly, still full of satisfaction over her new mastery of the corpse moon. 'I do not have the best history with humans. Not many Eborans do.'

Celaphon snorted, blasting her with rotten breath.

'He is worthy of our glory, I think, even if he is human. He is a weapon, like me.'

Hestillion noticed he did not think of her as a weapon. Hesitantly, with her eyes on the view beyond the window – a vast tract of Wild, twisted trees reaching up for them like the hands of the dying – she reached out for the man her cousin had called Bern. Almost immediately, she found him. His pain and misery made him easy to find, like a broken tooth turned black in the mouth, and she could tell that he was with Aldasair, because there was a narrow line of comfort there, light against

464

sprawling darkness. Curious, she moved towards this, noting as she did so how it was almost like moving through the netherdark.

The surrounding darkness, the vastness of the Jure'lia that held them all within its web, was a busy thing, filled with scuttling movement and ancient thought. It was undoubtedly alien, and yet she was also a part of it. Somewhere within that vastness, she felt the presence of the blue crystal that lay at the heart of the corpse moon, and then linked to that, the other crystals in the hearts of other ships. Together, they created the net that held all of the Jure'lia together. And the queen was all of it, of course, a thrumming essence that changed and shed its shape but never really died.

Hestillion moved away from that and reached out for the line of light that was the connection between Bern and Aldasair. Her cousin was only a faint presence, more an absence than anything else, a darker space in a sky made of night, but that line burned like a comet. She touched it.

And instantly fell back, confused by what she felt there. Love and kinship, deeper than anything she would have believed possible between an Eboran and a human. Of course her brother had his pet witch, with her messy hair and belligerent look, but sex with humans had ever been a popular pastime with her people – they were so disposable, after all. But this was something else. Curious, she turned her attention to Bern himself.

Stone, like the foundation of a building, as Celaphon had said, and honour too. It oozed out of him like the scuttling creatures oozed from the walls of the corpse moon. He was a *good* man, kind and thoughtful, sometimes rash and impatient, but always thoughtful. She had a flash then, and saw him within in the Hill of Souls, of all places, carefully sweeping away dead leaves and the tiny skeletons of mice and birds, mending the skylight and the door, washing down the stone shelves and . . . In her physical body, Hestillion reached out for Celaphon's muscled leg and leaned on it, trying to understand what she

465

had perceived. Bern, this barbarian from Finneral, had carefully taken each of their old war-beast statues and stored them in a box, handling them delicately, as though they were babies. It was an act of hope, of kindness, of . . . courting. He had done it out of affection for her cousin, as a demonstration of his admiration.

Hestillion broke away. Her stomach was churning.

'Do you see what he is?' asked Celaphon cheerily enough. 'A warrior. He is strong. He will be a great ally for me. All of them will be – my brothers and sisters.'

The landscape below them was terrible and dark, the setting sun leaching the last of the light from the trees.

'An ally,' said Hestillion, faintly. Except that wasn't true. Bern and her cousin, and her brother and even his pet witch – they were all enemies, and forcing this connection on them would not change that. And if they were the enemy – including this good, kind man – what did that make her?

A woman who made a choice.

The queen's voice was faint in her head, as though she were still exhausted from her efforts with the crystals. Hestillion did not answer, and instead drew as far into herself as possible, holding her thoughts close, like jewels. Because she knew perfectly well that it didn't matter if they forced the crystal on each of them, if they made them a part of the Jure'lia; they would always be enemies. And she would always be the woman who made a *choice* – a choice that had doomed her, and possibly doomed all of them. If they were all joined, that would only become more obvious. She also could not ignore the bright interest Celaphon had developed in Bern; she was a bird, and he was a weapon. It was not difficult to see who would be the most important to a beast of war.

'Sweet one.' She forced a smile on her face, feeling it pull at the edges of her mouth as though she too wore a mask. 'I am glad for you.'

466

45

Tor walked slowly, rubbing his shoulder. The roots had done their job, closing up the wounds so closely that there were no marks at all, but he still felt deeply uneasy, as though he could still feel the wriggling tendrils within his flesh. Eeskar had taken him from that room to another, filled with even more of the red mirrors, each with a strange alien face caught in it. Tor noticed that many of them stared at him blankly, as though he were of no more interest than a passing cloud, while others openly scowled or looked away.

'You are not Jure'lia,' he said. 'But you are not from Sarn, either.'

Eeskar nodded. 'You are perceptive. That is good. It's a trait we encourage.'

'But you speak Eboran. All of you do. How can you speak Eboran when my people do not know you?'

The man sniffed. 'You think you hear Eboran, yes. But in truth, our voices speak directly to you, without need for language.'

At the end of the room, the floor fell away into a low, sweeping chamber. In the centre of it there was what appeared to be an enormous glass box, completely empty. The edges of

467

it were etched with shapes and patterns that Tor felt like he could almost understand, and on the walls were hundreds and hundreds of the red mirrors. Eeskar walked over to the glass box, which was twice his height, and pressed his fingers to it – he had, Tor noticed, only three on each hand, and an elongated thumb. This last detail almost seemed too much, and he found himself looking around for a window or a door, some route to make his escape.

'Look, could you tell me whatever it is you feel the need to tell me, and then we can both get back to our lives? My war-beast will be worried, and he's no fun at all when he's anxious.'

'War-beast!' The cry came from one of the mirrors, but when Tor turned to look, he couldn't make out which one had spoken. 'What a name. Such a thing to call them! Truly this seedling was a mistake.'

Eeskar continued as though he couldn't hear the voice. He turned to Tor, slowly blinking his bulbous eyes. 'Are you certain you want to know, child? The truth of this is often something that the lesser peoples struggle to accept.'

'Lesser people?' Tor stood up straight, taking his hand away from his aching shoulder. 'Whatever it is, just show me.'

'Very well. This is what you stand within, Tormalin the Oathless.' The glass box filled with darkness, as though it were spooling out from Eeskar's hand. And then, gradually, the darkness became pierced with points of light, and Tor realised he was looking at the night sky. Within it, cradled by the night, was a shape a little like one of the sea creatures they cooked and ate in Mushenska: there was a fat, rounded head, garlanded by multiple tentacles, which were all braided and twisted together to form a point at one end. The thing was a pale greenish-white, like the delicate necks of snow flowers in the spring, and here and there green fires were burning in deep alcoves. As he watched, it moved through the night sky, many of the tapered ends of the tentacles moving slightly. He saw one curl up and brush at another, as though it were grooming itself. Tor squeezed his eyes shut and opened them again, but the vision was still there.

'What is this? What are you showing me?'

'Do you understand that although this image I am showing you is small, the object itself is very large?' Eeskar sounded concerned. 'It is a problem with explaining this, sometimes, with the lesser peoples.' When Tor glared at him, he carried on. 'Very well. We call this the . . . the closest words would be Seed Carrier. Our own home . . . well, the less said about that, the better. We left, and we came to many places. This place, which you call Sarn, was one of them.'

The images within the big glass box changed, and for a few moments Tor stared at it rapt, unable to look away. He had a glance of a beautiful jewel, perfectly round, blue and green and white, and then the Seed Carrier eclipsed it. A series of things followed that he did not understand; the green fires of the Carrier burned brighter, too bright – he thought of Noon then, accidentally causing an explosion on Esiah Godwort's estate – and then a sense of great movement, of shaking. The blue and green jewel loomed closer, and the fires turned orange and yellow and red, for a time obliterating everything else, and then he saw the carrier flying rapidly over oceans of steely green.

'This is Sarn? You are showing me Sarn?'

'You see how worthless this is,' said one of the faces from the mirrors. 'It barely understands.'

'It is Sarn,' said Eeskar, quietly. 'Watch.'

An island loomed on the ocean, a bleak place of rocks and black sand, and the Seed Carrier struck it at terrifying speed. Again, Tor only had a sense of great movement, and of fires burning out of control, green flames tracing up into the sky like lightning. When some of the smoke had cleared, Tor saw

469

that the Carrier was partially buried in the island's earth, black sand and soil blasted into a rough crater around it, and the tentacles were delving down through it, seeking to partially bury itself. The fires, meanwhile, had detached fully from the body of the Carrier, and sped off across the livid sky. Something about the bright lines of green fire made the hairs on the back of Tor's neck stand up.

'What happened there?' he asked. 'To that fire? What was it? Did it power your carrier?'

'It doesn't matter,' said Eeskar, too quickly, before making an odd swallowing motion; the muscles on his neck stood out in thick rings, and then he continued. 'Listen, child. Our work is, in many ways, a great experiment,' said Eeskar. His face and body were so strange it was difficult for Tor to tell, but he thought that from the way he grasped at his sleeves and his eyes grew wet, that this was a source of great passion. 'We do not know what we will find on these worlds—'

'Worlds?'

'We do not know what will already exist here. We do not know if the gifts we bring will make any difference at all. Our work must always, ultimately, be a melding.' He paused, the muscles around his mouth twitching. 'It is a risk, but, I think, an exciting one.'

There were some murmurs of dissent from the faces on the walls. Tor looked closely at the images within the box, watching as the Seed Carrier sank deeper and deeper into the black earth – pieces of it remained above, smooth chunks of greenish-white root poking through like bones in the dirt. His mouth was very dry, and his heart was beating too fast.

'I don't know what you're trying to tell me.'

Except that he thought he did, and that was even worse.

'A seed. Several are released, but . . .' Eeskar tipped his long head to one side. 'Often they do not take. Water swallows them, or there is no water at all. With nothing to nurture them,

470

our vital seeds can die. But here, we had one success.' He smiled then, and there was nothing alien about it – he was a man pleased with his job. 'Look.'

An object, not like a seed at all to Tor's eyes, but something like a network of lights, flew out from the heart of the Seed Carrier. As it left, a shining set of lights appeared behind it, sheltering the Carrier from prying eyes. The image changed. There was a landscape, lush and green and criss-crossed with silver rivers, all about the size of ribbons from his vantage point. Something about the shape of the land . . . And then the rivers all began to dry up, turning from silver to brown, and something was growing in the midst of the green land. A great tree, quickly overtaking the trees around it, pushing them out of the way and sucking their vitality from them so that they shrivelled and gave up the land to it. The great tree shot up and up, branches spreading like a blooming flower, and Tor saw new leaves uncurling, as bright as coins.

'No,' he said. There was a tightness in his throat, and he wasn't sure if he wanted to laugh or cry. 'Are you . . . are you telling me you gave us Ygseril?'

'That is what you call it, yes, I remember the other saying it. Well, actually, Ygseril gave us *you*. At the time we came here and tasted this world, you as a people did not exist. Other humanoids, yes, thinking animals that walked and talked and were growing cleverer and more adept all the time.' Eeskar gestured to the image of the tree. 'It is, as I say, always an experiment. We never know truly what will happen. Our seeds growing in different soils, absorbing the flesh and the spirit of that world, until each tree is unique.'

'I don't understand what you're saying.'

'Your ancestors came and they drank what you call the sap, and it changed them. It made them into you.' Eeskar smiled, his cheeks with their bright splotches of crimson creasing. 'I like to think that perhaps they simply worshipped it, recognising it for

471

the glory of something otherworldly, until someone was brave enough to taste the sap. And then gradually, over time . . .' Eeskar turned and beamed at Tor. 'Eventually, your people. You look a little like us, I think.'

'It is a failure,' barked one of the voices from the mirrors. 'Weak, an echo of us, a shadow.'

'We did worship it!' Tor curled his hands into fists. It was not the dismissive tone of the mirror-voice that riled him, but the kindly expression on Eeskar's face – like someone watching a dog try and fail to do a trick. 'We called him Root-Father and Branch-Mother, he was the centre of our lives, of our world. We thought ourselves superior, special, when actually – are you telling me you are our gods?'

'Oh no,' Eeskar's four hands fluttered up to his face and away, clearly dismayed by the very idea. 'You are just one of many, an experiment.' His big eyes blinked slowly, and he peered closely at Tor. 'An echo is right, or a shadow. There is too much of this world in you – ultimately its taint could not be overwritten. It is regretful that you should know this, child. But you did come here. You did ask the questions, and demand the answers.'

'Don't call me child!'

Tor made a grab for Eeskar's robes, intending to pull his head down to his level and attempt to twist it off, but instead his hands passed straight through the figure, and the image of Eeskar shattered and reformed, a few steps away.

'Oh dear,' he said.

'It is a savage animal,' snapped one of the voices in the mirrors. Tor could not tell if it was the same one as before. 'We should not let such things in here.'

'What are you? Why can't I touch you? And why are all your friends in the bloody walls?'

'More questions, Tormalin the Oathless, and I doubt you will like the answers.' The muscles in Eeskar's throat shuddered again. 'Perhaps I should leave you alone for a time, to contemplate what you have learned.'

'What? No, it's not enough, you have to finish what you—'

It was too late. The mirrors sank seamlessly into the walls, while Eeskar himself flickered and vanished. The huge glass box folded in on itself so smoothly and silently Tor began to wonder if it had ever really been there in the first place. Very quickly he was alone in the room, the walls softly radiating their filtered-sunshine light. His leg no longer pained him, but even so, he sat down on the floor. After a moment, he put his head in his hands.

46

The strange green architecture was only growing more elaborate the further in they explored. The ruins burst through the black dirt like the bones of some enormous creature, and just ahead of them now was something much larger. It looked like a great oval-shaped mass, lying slightly at an angle against the earth. All the other pieces seemed to converge here, and it was easily as large as the Behemoth wreck had been within Esiah Godwort's enclosure.

'It's not the worm people,' said Noon.

'You have already said that, more than once,' said Vostok. 'And I agree. This does not carry the stench of the ancient enemy on it, although it still makes me uneasy.'

'If I keep saying it, it's because the last thing I want to see are any of the Jure'lia's ugly bastard beasts appearing from nowhere.'

'There are marks,' said Kirune. The cat had been mostly quiet during their search, the hackles across his shoulders raised. 'It is not smooth, like the rest of it.'

'Your eyes are better than mine, Kirune,' said Noon. 'Let's go and have a look.' Not for the first time, she wished that Vintage were with them.

The huge ovoid shape was, to Noon's eye, a paler green than the rest of the structure, almost a pale yellowish white in places. As they climbed up onto the surface, she felt her leather boots slipping and was forced to climb in an awkward half crouch to keep from going flat on her face. Kirune and Vostok both grumbled with displeasure as they stepped onto it, but Noon did not ask them why; she had given up trying to understand the disgust they felt at this place. Just ahead, she could see one of the marks Kirune had spoken of, so she made her way towards it with the sun beating down on the back of her head.

'Here. What do you reckon this is?'

It was a hole in the smooth surface, as though someone had taken a spoon and scooped out a deep alcove there. Within it were other, smaller holes, with holes within those, leading back into darkness; none of these last holes were big enough to fit her fist in. The surface here was shiny and thick, as though it was covered in slightly warped glass, and as she ran her fingers over it, she felt a shiver work its way down her spine. She could not see it, but there were faces in the glass, and she felt like she knew them.

'Given that we do not know what this entire structure is, I hardly know what I can be expected to think of a hole in it.' Vostok lashed her tail to one side irritably. 'It is one more question we do not have the answer to.'

'But I almost . . .' Noon pressed her hand flat to the surface, reaching for any sense of a life force. There was nothing, but still the idea that she knew this thing, on some level, would not leave her. 'It must be reminding me of something else, that's all.'

Noon stood up, and shuffled a little further over the rounded structure. There were more of the alcoves, she saw, dotted all over. Some were much bigger, and some contained odd graceful shapes made from the smooth green material – struts with ladder-like interiors, things that looked like plants, and several that seemed to depict the phases of the moon.

'Kirune, are you quite certain Tormalin was taken within this thing?' Vostok sounded exasperated, but Noon could feel the clear current of fear beneath her haughty tone. 'We are no closer to finding a door.'

'Yes,' hissed Kirune. 'You should listen, snake. I—' The big cat stopped and lowered his head, then, shaking out his fur all over, said, 'I can feel him! Tormalin is close, inside, but he is afraid, and . . . disturbed. Pain, he feels pain.'

'All right.' Noon stood up straight, as best she could. 'Maybe we've done this Vintage's way for long enough. Time to burn the fucker down. Vostok? Do you want to see if we can blast our way inside?'

'And if Tormalin is just on the other side?'

'He is not so close,' said Kirune, immediately. 'Deeper, within. But be careful, snake.'

Vostok rumbled in the back of her throat, and then, turning away from them, roared a stream of violet fire out across the green expanse. After a moment, she refined her aim, focussing the stream on a certain point. Noon took a few steps back; the flames licked and curled across the surface, radiating back at them, but did not seem to be doing any real damage to the structure. The dragon kept it up for a number of minutes, until eventually she snapped her jaws shut and shook her head.

'It does nothing,' she said bitterly.

Noon blinked, trying to rid her eyes of the wavering after-images of fire. The green surface looked a little darker, as though it had bruised slightly, but there were no cracks, no blisters and no holes.

'Blood and fire. All right, let me try. Kirune, may I?' The war-beast glowered at her briefly, before turning his head to bare his neck to her. Impressed with this gesture of trust, Noon sank her hands into his fur gently, and steadily took a sample

476

of his life energy – slowly, so as not to alarm him. Then, obeying some instinct she didn't want to think too closely about, she walked over to one of the biggest alcoves. This one contained the series of circles that could be moons. Holding her hands cupped towards the hole, she summoned a stream of emerald fire and directed it into the hole.

Immediately, Noon sensed a change. The smooth surface under her feet began to vibrate slightly, and within the alcove, her fire was running along invisible channels, tracing shapes like leaf veins. Soon, the small traceries of brightly glowing green were escaping the hole and racing across the surface, but they did not move like fire anymore – they seemed almost to pulse, like a heartbeat. The faces that Noon had sensed when she had touched the surface were now visible; they were not human, but even so, she *knew* them. Like people caught in the blast of some bright light, she saw the shadows and the shapes that made them, and she saw that they were laughing.

'Noon!' Vostok's voice was urgent. 'You have opened a door!'

The fire leaping from her hands died, and Noon looked up to see a new shape in the surface of the structure. A piece of it had swung open, and there was a dark space beneath it. She could see immediately that it would be too small for Vostok to go through. She turned to the dragon, only to see her ruffle her feathered wings impatiently.

'Go! Quickly, before it closes, and retrieve the son of Ebora.'

'Watch for us. And watch for monsters.'

With that, she and Kirune ran for the hole.

47

The wall beyond the barrier spasmed open, and Aldasair scrambled to his feet. They had been waiting an indeterminable amount of time – he could not tell if it were night or day in this cell – for the queen to return and continue her work. So far she had not, but each movement and each scuttling creature turned his stomach over anew. The figure that stepped through the opening was that of his cousin, and he took a breath, trying to calm his heartbeat.

'Aldasair,' she said, in way of a greeting. She looked thin and drawn, as though she had lost weight since he had last seen her, and there was something strangely compelling about it, as though she were becoming a thing made entirely of sharp angles; a blade perhaps, or a broken mirror. The muscles on her arms stood out like rigid cords, and she wore a simple fur-trimmed tunic and leather leggings. The blue crystal glistened darkly in the centre of her chest.

'What do you want, Hest?'

She turned away from him to look at Bern. 'How are you, human? How are you dealing with this gift?'

Bern was standing next to Sharrik, the arm with the crystal embedded in it hanging awkwardly at his side. Like Hestillion, he was gaunt, and his eyes were deeply shadowed.

'Can't you tell?' he asked gruffly. 'I can feel you on the other end of this thing, another piece of grit in . . . whatever this is.' He paused. 'I have a constant headache, and I feel like I'm falling all the time. I've been sick a few times.' Next to him, Sharrik shook himself all over. 'We don't belong in that, you and me. You know that, don't you?'

'There is strength in it,' she said, although to Aldasair she sounded sick too. 'If you had any sense, human, you'd grasp that and make of it what you can. That's what I've had to do.' She drew herself up to her full height. 'Think about it, if you can. It will be important.'

'By the stones, I've no time for riddles.'

She looked up at the ceiling, and Aldasair thought she was being dramatically exasperated, until he noticed her scanning the black ooze that flowed above them.

'Never mind. Aldasair, when we fought, you moved to destroy the crystal that was half buried in the ground. What do you know about them?'

'Why should I tell you that?'

Hestillion sighed, a familiar expression of impatience.

'Would you prefer the queen asked you? Or she instructed her creatures to ask you, over and over? Or perhaps I could rip the information from your human's mind.'

'Bern doesn't know anything.'

'I could enjoy myself finding out, though, I am sure. Just tell me, little cousin.'

Jessen was sitting up, her stance tense. Aldasair could feel her anger, simmering under the surface.

'The scholar Lady Vincenza de Grazon discovered one of these giant crystals within the heart of some Behemoth wreckage, and she is very certain that they are important to the worm people. The Jure'lia.' He glanced at the black ceiling, but there were no eyes watching. 'I saw the queen heading towards it and if it's important to them, then it must be destroyed.'

To his surprise, Hestillion smiled. The smile looked strange on her newly angular face, but something about it hurt his heart a little; it was like glancing up and briefly seeing her as she had been, a little girl with yellow silk slippers.

'Listen to you, Aldasair. You speak like a warrior now. I would never have imagined such a future for you.' She laughed. 'But I could say that about any of us, I suppose.'

'Hestillion – Hest – it's not too late. You can come back, your brother loves you—'

She held up a hand, cutting him off. 'Listen to me. The crystals link them all together, each Behemoth to the next. When Tree-father killed them at the end of the Eighth Rain, that link was broken. Now, the queen must renew that connection, with each ship. Do you understand me?'

'That is why she sought out the crystal at the Broken Field.' Aldasair nodded. 'Vintage is a very clever woman.'

'Why are you telling us this?' asked Bern. He looked as serious as Aldasair had ever seen him. 'You've already picked your side.'

Hestillion ignored him. 'It is the queen's highest priority. Until she has done this, she is weak. They are weak, or at least, weaker. The Behemoths can be heavily damaged, they can be in rusted pieces, but if she can make contact with her crystals, then it can be salvaged. This is what I have learned while I am here.' She paused, fiddling with the fur trim on her tunic. 'There is a Behemoth nearby, and without its queen it is bumbling and confused. She is heading towards it now, to bring it back to the fold. This little project,' she touched the shard of blue crystal at her heart, and then gestured to Bern, 'will be on hold for a while.'

'Well,' Bern raised his eyebrows and shrugged, 'that's . . . nice?'

'Listen to me, human,' she rounded on him as if suddenly angry, 'you need to think about this connection, and what it

480

means for you. How it could make you strong. Do you hear me? And be ready.'

Her last words she delivered in a barely audible hiss, and then she stepped out through the opening, which closed up smoothly behind her.

'What do you imagine that was all about?'

Bern took a big breath and let it out slowly. He shrugged. 'Buggered if I know.'

Tormalin woke and sat up, wincing at the stiffness in his face and arm. He wouldn't have believed it possible to sleep after everything he'd been told, but he had, curled on the floor of the strange room Eeskar had left him in. He had even dreamed of Noon, wandering the Shroom Flats alone as he and Vintage had found her, except that in this dream she had been wearing elaborate Eboran armour: silver and shining like the moon, with a violet cape. Her eyes had burned green, and he had been afraid of her. Even so, he'd needed desperately to talk to her, and had been dragging himself through thick black mud to reach the stretch of Wild where she stood. In the way of dreams, he'd had the sense that time was very short for the both of them, but when he'd called her name the flames had escaped her eyes and enveloped her head, giving her a crown of emerald fire. He briefly considered the idea that Arnia had been inside his head, manipulating things, but he had had no sense of her there at all, and why would she give him a dream about Noon? Hestillion was skilled enough to craft such a thing, certainly but . . . He shook his head. He did not want to think about Hestillion.

'You are awake.'

Eeskar shivered into existence before him. Tor stayed where he was, watching the strange man carefully.

'What do you call yourselves?' he asked. 'I don't even know that, and you are not Eboran.'

481

'Ah, yes, that is true. Ebora is your very own name and place.' Eeskar seemed pleased by the question. 'Our true name would not make much sense to you, so you can call us Aborans. It is what we said to the previous visitor.'

'And who was that?' Tor paused. 'It was Micanal, wasn't it? He found you. He came looking for the origins of Ygseril after all, and that's what you are.'

'I do not recall what he called himself, but yes. He was not pleased by what he found here. For some reason he found it belittling. Distressing in a way I could not quite fathom.'

'The idea that we, that our entire storied history, is a mistaken experiment by people with no connection or love for us? Yes, I'm sure that was as welcome as a turd in his porridge.' Tor shook his head. 'Do you even understand what it means, what you've told me? We were random. The random result of humans drinking sap, and being changed by it.'

'It was a very long time ago,' said Eeskar, in a tone which Tor suspected he thought was reassuring. 'Thousands and thousands of your years. Your history is still ancient, and valuable.'

Tor laughed, although he felt a terrible tightness in his throat. 'You don't understand. We have . . . the things that we have done to humans, in the belief that we were better than them, when in truth we are the same. We are just like the Wild, a thing changed and corrupted by outside influences. No wonder Micanal was upset by the things he found out. No wonder he and Arnia never came back to Ebora. What would be the point? It was all a lie anyway. And the humans . . .' He thought of Noon, her untidy hair and her dark eyes. 'If they knew that their mythical heroes were nothing but a failed experiment . . . What would we be to them, then? At least Vintage will be pleased, I suppose. She loves this sort of thing – all these new questions for her to ponder.' He paused, thinking of Kirune and his frantic escape from the salt monsters. 'What of our war-beasts? Are they part of your experiment too?'

482

'Ah, the other spoke of these also. They do not occur with every seed, nor do they take the precise form you have witnessed – like you, Tormalin, they are a unique result of seed and world together.'

'Unique,' said Tor, not able to keep the bitterness from his voice.

'I understand that it is a difficult concept. Perhaps if I showed you some of the other beings that have received our influence, it would make more sense to you?'

Tor looked up at the man, taking in his multiple arms, his strange deer-eyes and narrow frame. 'Why are you still here? You've sent out your, seed, or whatever you want to call it, and you have wrought your changes upon Sarn. What's the plan now? Why are you all still sitting here, alone on this island? Don't you have other places you want to manipulate?'

Eeskar's bright manner evaporated. 'That is a less pleasing story.'

'Even so, I would like to hear it.'

'Very well.' Eeskar sighed, and abruptly seemed much less alien. 'Follow me.'

Just as before, the wall split open to emit them, and Tor followed the man down a narrow corridor towards a set of spirals steps leading up. It was darker here, and smelled musty, as though no one had been through there in a very long time. Eventually, though, a soft kind of light began to bleed through the walls until they emerged into a space with a domed roof. The covering was thin and white, and the sun was a bright, almost suffocating presence. On the floor, there were many long indentations, filled with what looked like soft white powder. Eeskar nodded to the nearest one, and Tor bent to examine it. There were larger chunks in there, which crumbled apart when he prodded them with a finger.

'This is where we are now,' said Eeskar. He cocked his head to one side, as if contemplating some impossible problem. 'We died a very long time ago, Tormalin the Oathless, and we put our bodies here so that we might still feel the sun on our bones.'

Tor looked up sharply and wiped his hands on his trousers. 'What are you talking about? I'm talking to you now, aren't I?'

'Child, I understand that this will be difficult for you to comprehend.' Eeskar smiled fondly, and Tor considered punching him in the middle of his strange bulbous eyes, until he remembered that he couldn't. 'I am a memory, an echo. When I spoke to your brethren, he told me of an ability your people possess called dream-walking. This was very interesting to me, as I believe it to be a perversion of our own abilities. We were able to leave the essence of ourselves behind, without physical bodies. We are confined by the physical limits of our home, but we are still able to think, to ponder. Many preferred that to oblivion.'

'The faces in the mirrors?'

'All dead, but still here, in a sense.'

'Then why did you die? Why didn't you just leave?' He looked around at the graves; there was no scent of decomposition, not even the whiff of old bones. They had clearly been dead a very long time. 'Was it a disease?'

'What? No. It was simply old age. Like you, we are very long-lived, but . . . we were not meant to stay here.' The image that was Eeskar shivered and flickered. 'The truth is, we did not come here alone – we could not have come here at all, or anywhere, in fact, without the partnership of another being from our home. She was a spirit of great energy and vitality. Through her, the Seed Carrier made its impossibly long journeys, over periods of time I doubt you could even comprehend. But then, here, in this place, she left us. And without her, we could not leave. We could not even move the Seed Carrier elsewhere.'

484

Tor dipped his toe into one of the graves, coating the end of his boot in a fine white dust. He wondered what Hestillion would make of all this: that Ygseril was an experiment, and they were the results. Not revered, not special or god-touched – just a mildly interesting side effect.

'A spirit?' He tried to picture it, but could only think of the parasite spirits, with their amorphous transparent bodies. 'Where did it go?'

'It doesn't matter. She did not come back – that is what matters.'

'So you were left here. And you all died?'

Eeskar dipped his long head. 'This world is not friendly to us, although in the early days we tried.' His face creased, an Aboran version of a grimace. 'Those were some terrible deaths. So, in the end, we came to accept that we had come to the end of our journey, thanks to the betrayal of our old friend. But,' he brightened, and touching the wall, produced a new cube made of glass. Images began to flicker across it. 'We did so much, in our time. Made so many changes. Do you see?'

Tor looked at the glass, and felt his stomach turn over. Moving across the surface he saw people who were not his people; tall beings with multiple limbs, or many eyes, or tails and wings. Many were a similar dusty white to the Aborans, but a great number were of all different colours and hues, with patterned skins or fur or scales. They ran through forests he barely recognised as such, or lounged on thrones of crystal in rooms taller than Ygseril. He saw buildings of steel and glass, skies of all colours, including one that seemed to contain a permanent orange storm. He saw beings moving through the night sky as easily as swimming in a lake, their bodies encased in strange bulky clothing, and people like giants, reaching down to grassy valleys to scoop up animals, eating them whole. He saw men and women who almost appeared Eboran, their eyes crimson and their bodies tall and strong, yet they each had bony protrusions from their foreheads, like the horns of a ram.

It was beautiful, and strange, and frightening. It was too much. He turned away.

'You do see,' said Eeskar, quietly. 'You understand, I think, why we have done this. Perhaps you will cope better than our first visitor.'

'I don't understand it at all,' said Tor, not caring how Eeskar recoiled from his harsh tone. 'But maybe I don't care as much as Micanal did. I—'

The room seemed to thrum. Tor put it down to the heat, or the strangeness of everything he'd heard, but when he glanced down at the graves, the powdery remains were crumbling and shifting, and the bulkier pieces fell about into smaller chunks. A pulse of green light travelled up through the walls.

'No,' Eeskar's eyes were bulging so much that Tor thought they might fall out of his head. 'No! What is this?'

From somewhere nearby came the crumping roar of an explosion. Although they felt nothing but the soft vibrating hum, Eeskar staggered as though he had suffered a physical blow.

'It can't be!'

'What are you talking about? What's happening?'

Eeskar did not answer but instead blinked out of existence. Tor stared at the space where he'd been for a moment, and then ran down the spiral stairs. When he was back in the corridor he caught sight of Eeskar again, and at the far end of the passage he could see more green light, and a pair of figures emerging from it.

'Noon!'

The young fell-witch looked annoyed, her cheeks flushed with colour and each fist wreathed in billowing winnowfire. Kirune came on beside her, his head bent away from the flames.

'Tor! Are you all right? What is this bloody place? Who is this bastard?'

486

Tor grinned despite himself, his heart inexplicably lighter at the sight of her scowling face.

'I have no chance of explaining it to you without, I don't know, diagrams or something, but Eeskar here . . .'

'YOU!'

Eeskar, he belatedly realised, was quivering with rage. As he came alongside the Aboran, he saw that stiff fans of flesh were rising from the back of his head – they appeared to be lined with bone and attached with thin strips of skin, like the wings of a bat. It gave him a strangely reptilian appearance. 'It cannot be you! After all this time, when all of us are already dead . . .' Eeskar howled with anguish, a noise of such complete despair that Tor felt his skin go cold. 'You come back NOW?'

Noon looked nonplussed. 'I don't know what you're talking about. We've come for our friend. According to Kirune, your monsters attacked him and took him away. You can give him back now, or I can burn you all to soot. It's up to you.'

'Noon, it's fine. I was attacked, but it's a long story, and . . . let's just go. Eeskar isn't even really here, he can't do anything.'

Eeskar reached out and touched the wall. 'We can't have much, but perhaps we can have vengeance.'

'What are you talking about?'

The walls pulled up like curtains, and beyond them were scores of the long-necked white beasts, their sharp mouths bared to show endless jagged teeth. They swarmed forward, making an odd chittering noise, so loud that Tor almost missed Eeskar's final words to him.

'I don't expect you to understand, child, but when you are faced with the extinction of all you know, a little petty revenge becomes an attractive option.'

And then he flickered out of existence again. Tor ran towards Noon and Kirune, who were looking around at the approaching monsters with twin expressions of confusion.

'So, he wasn't real, but these ugly bastards are.' Seized with impulsiveness, he leaned down and kissed Noon forcefully on the cheek. 'I am very glad to see you both. Did you bring my sword?'

'There wasn't time.' Noon shot him a look, although whether she was annoyed about the kiss he couldn't tell. 'Get behind me, both of you. I'm not in the mood to be subtle.'

Hoards of the white monsters were approaching, their heads weaving on the ends of their necks like particularly ugly snakes. Tor did as Noon said, although as he passed she reached out and touched his neck, taking his life energy as she had on the day they had first met. He felt his strength dim, like a candle tattered by the wind, but rather than the outrage and fear he had felt then, a sense of rightness filled his chest instead.

She is the weapon. It was Kirune, briefly forming a connection that was dazzling in its completeness. *The snake is right about that, at least.*

Noon raised her arms, and an ocean of fire flowed from her chest. The monsters with the misfortune to be in the front line of their attack went up like things made of paper and sawdust, their pitiful screams almost instantly silenced. The others, still alive but burning, burning, turned to run. Quickly, Noon's pure green flame turned an oily yellow as the creatures fell before it. Many more were melting back into the walls, sinking into the smooth green surface as Tor had when they had captured him.

But Noon wasn't satisfied with that. She took a few more steps forward, and released a new wave of flame, scouring the chamber from floor to ceiling. Tor put his arms over his face, feeling his scars tingle with the memory of their own burning. In moments, everything else in the room was dead or vanished, with only soot and smoke left behind.

Noon lowered her arms. Her eyes were very wide. Tor put a hand on her shoulder, and squeezed it.

'Come on, witch. Let's get out of here, before they send anything else for you to burn.'

48

The nights were never truly dark in Ebora. Vintage stood by the tall windows in her room, looking out at the lights that blazed across the palace gardens. Campfires and lamps of all colours, alongside the softer illumination of silk tents that were lit from within. She had been initially fascinated by these, convinced that the flimsy walls would not be warm enough for an Eboran spring – there was still snow on the Bloodless Mountains – but she had introduced herself to the travellers inside, who had turned out to be from Kuruknai, a very distant eastern state that she had never laid eyes on, and they had shown her how the silk was treated with a type of grease, just on the inner layer. It kept the heat in amazingly well, and even smelled quite pleasant, laced as it was with the oil of a flower they called bluesky-wort. She smiled faintly.

'All of this I would never have learned, if I'd stayed where I was.' She thought of the vine forest every now and then, but with no particular sadness or longing – walking away had been the best decision she could have made. 'I should have done it sooner, if anything, and then Nanthema . . .'

Turning away from the window, she began rifling through

the papers on the desk. She hadn't seen Nanthema for hours, although this was nothing particularly new; lately the Eboran woman seemed keen to spend time on her own, walking in the palace forests.

'Where the bloody hell is it?'

Micanal the Clearsighted's journal should have been on the desk, she was sure of it, but she had turned all the papers upside down several times and, after all, it shouldn't be so easy to miss a fat leather-bound book. She frowned, ignoring the distant ache in her leg.

'Am I getting old? Losing track of my things like some aged dear. Talking to myself like a lonely old baggage . . .'

The door crashed open and Eri half fell into the room. The boy's face was so white his eyes looked like dark holes, and his lips were grey with shock.

'My darling, what is it?'

'Helcate! He's sick! I think he's dying, Vintage, I think . . .' He stumbled against the door frame, his eyelids flickering ominously. Vintage limped over and took him firmly by the shoulders. Even through the fabric of his shirt he felt too cold.

'Calm yourself, Eri, it will all be fine. Look at me! Good, that's good. Now, calm down. Take a few breaths, that's it, that's it. Where is he?'

Eri nodded, and took a few more gasps of air, trying to follow her words. She felt a pang of affection for the boy that was as painful as it was sweet.

'In the courtyard. He likes to sleep there now as he's too big to be comfortable in my room, but it's just down the corridor from me. I couldn't sleep, so I went to see him and –' He gasped again, his crimson eyes too bright in the lamplight. 'I can't wake him up.'

'Come on,' Vintage snatched up her crutch from where it rested against the wall, 'give me your arm, lad, and we'll get there all the quicker.'

The corridors were silent, all the life of Ebora going on either within its rooms or outside in the palace gardens. The courtyard itself, when they got there, was lit with a pair of small oil lamps which Eri diligently lit each evening. Helcate was a furry lump, lying across the stones with his wings untidily spread behind him. Not far away from his snout was a partially demolished wheel of pale cheese. As they approached, Vintage could see that he was breathing, but his eyes were only partially shut; slivers of sky blue peeked out from between his eyelids. When Vintage waved her hand in front of his snout he did not respond, and they got no reaction when she briskly shook his shoulder.

'Why won't he wake up?' The boy's voice was thick, and she could tell he was on the verge of crying again.

'There, don't take on so, dear.' She squeezed his arm briefly. 'Perhaps he has a fever.'

She pressed her hand to the creature's forehead, noting as she did so that she didn't have the faintest idea what temperature war-beasts were supposed to be. His fur there, a curly mixture of blond and copper, felt warm but not worryingly so.

'Your bond with Helcate, Eri. Can you feel anything from him? Have you felt anything strange from him earlier tonight?'

The boy shuddered all over, and then swallowed. 'He is far away. Like, he's lost in a fog. Something in his mouth tastes bad. That's all I can feel.'

'Hmm.' Vintage smoothed her hands along the war-beast's jaw and then down his neck, searching for swellings or obstructions, but found nothing. 'Is there water for him here, my darling? What does he drink from?'

'Oh yes!' The boy jumped up and fetched, with little apparent difficulty, a huge bucket brimming with water. He set it down next to her, sloshing it only a little, and she reminded herself

492

that however young he looked, Eri was an Eboran, and significantly stronger than he looked. 'I filled it up fresh before I went to bed.'

Vintage dipped her hand in the water and sniffed it. No scents, no strange colour, no burning. 'My dear, rub some water on his face. Use my handkerchief, if you like.'

'That's all right.' Eri stripped off his shirt, revealing his narrow bony chest, and dipped the garment in the water. As he worked at gently wiping the war-beast's face down – it couldn't hurt, Vintage reasoned, and it kept the boy busy – she worked her way down the creature's body, looking for anything out of place. Carefully, she lifted the edge of his wing, and pressed her hand lightly to the mixture of feathers and fur underneath. When she lifted her fingers, they came away daubed with a slippery black fluid – not much, but enough for her to know that Helcate was bleeding in a spot just under his wing.

'Eri, my dear, perhaps you could try trickling some water into Helcate's mouth? A little water will do him good, I'm certain.'

The boy nodded, and began gamely wrestling with the war-beast's snout, while Vintage peered more closely at the thick matt of Helcate's fur. It was certainly small, a wound no larger than the end of her smallest finger, and the fur around it was damp, as though someone had wiped the area down. Leaning forward, she sniffed carefully; no poisons that she could detect.

She leaned back awkwardly, the crutch under one arm.

'Eri – '

The sky over the courtyard was abruptly filled with orange light, and with it came a chorus of noises; the roar of fire, and the panicked screams of a large number of people.

'Come on!'

Vintage snatched up her crutch, and together they ran back through the palace. When they got outside, Vintage stumbled

493

to the ornate gates and grasped them fiercely as her legs threatened to pitch her to the ground. The garden forest, that cupped the gardens in its green hands, was ablaze. The people in the caravans and tents were fleeing, some dragging their possessions with them but most leaving everything they had and running for the gates. As she watched, the fire grew higher and higher, curling dangerously towards the walls of the palace itself, and beyond that, Ygseril. She felt her heart stutter in her chest. Which way was the wind blowing? Could something like the tree-god even burn?

'I absolutely do not want to find out.'

'Vintage?'

'Eri, darling . . .' Her words were drowned out as the fire shuddered with even greater violence. Pieces of burning wood and foliage floated up into the night like fireflies, and several nearby tents turned into torches. 'Wait! Wait! You there!' She grabbed a passing man, his hair and beard elaborately braided with stones. 'The lake, we need to get water from there and put this thing out, do you hear me?'

'Lady, I am not staying here to burn—'

'Listen!' She shook his arm violently. 'If the tree-god goes up in flames, that's the end for Ebora, and the end for our war-beasts! What do you think will happen then? The fucking worm people, that's what!' Vintage shoved him in the chest. 'Get your people together, get buckets and axes, get water . . .'

A woman who had been fleeing with the man stepped up next to him. She had a baby clasped to her chest and a short sword at her belt. 'We need to create a space between the forest and the fire, it's the only way to stop it now.'

'Yes! Some bloody sense here, thank you – cut down the trees, don't give it anything to eat up. Go!'

Other people were having the same idea, and while children and animals were being moved away, men and women were coming back, their arms full of axes and buckets. The fire, meanwhile, was like a demon, roaring in the night. Where there had once been a thicket of beautiful trees, graceful and ancient, there was now a blaze almost too bright to look at; Vintage could feel the heat of it scorching her cheeks and crisping her hair. And it was still growing; as they watched, fat tongues of fire leapt up at the sky, turning the night into day.

'How has it become so fierce so quickly?' murmured Vintage. 'I have seen a few forest fires in my time, and they are frighteningly fast, but this is a cold place, a wet place, and no alarm was raised until it was burning far out of anyone's control . . .' The words died in her throat. She reached out for Eri and squeezed his arm again, taking some reassurance in his solidity.

'Lady Vintage?'

'My book!' She shook him lightly. 'Well, your book, technically. It's not missing at all, it's been stolen.'

'I don't understand. What book?'

'They must think it will tell them how to birth the war-beasts – never mind, come on. Let's go and see exactly how badly I have fucked up, my dear.'

The Hatchery was too dark, and the guards were missing from its doors – Vintage did not like to think what had happened to them. The faint fiery light from the windows only served to make the shadows deeper. Eri lit a lamp, and with a sinking heart Vintage followed him down the row of war-beast pods. There were three empty spaces, including the pod that Eri had been convinced would hatch next.

'I don't understand.'

And the poor lad really didn't, Vintage realised as she looked at his pale face. His eyes searched the room as though the pods might have rolled off by themselves somewhere.

'The book, a blood sample from Helcate, and three of the most valuable artefacts on Sarn.' She took a deep, watery breath. 'And Helcate, our only real chance of pursuing them,

495

drugged. I suppose we can be relieved they didn't try to take him too. I've no doubt they would have killed him if he'd resisted.'

'Lady Vintage? I don't understand what's happening.'

'The fire is just a diversion, a way to keep us busy, and of course if it just happens to burn down the palace, that will only increase the value of what they have.' Turning to Eri, she met his eyes. 'Eri, what is happening is that I am in a fucking rage, my darling, and someone is going to pay.'

'Why are we out here, Lady Vintage?'

Eri looked like a ghost in the moonlight, his hair silver and his face white. Vintage summoned up her bravest smile for him; Nanthema had been nowhere to be found, and the boy was her last ally. No sense in scaring him.

'We need to be away from all the light and the fuss, my dear.' They had walked some distance from the fires, but even so she could still smell the smoke, and the sound of the blaze was an ominous rumble on the edge of hearing. Her ankle was throbbing steadily, but it was a distant thing, unimportant compared to the anxiety curling in her stomach. 'We have to trust our friends to do what they can to save your palace, I'm afraid. And we have to hope that some old friends of mine will be willing to help us.'

She slipped the whistle out of her pocket and eyed it doubtfully. The instructions that Noon had given her were clear enough, but Fulcor had been living wild for months, and the great bat had her own young to take care of – it was doubtful she would pay any attention to the summons, let alone allow them to mount her again. Nevertheless, Eri carried the old Winnowry harness in his arms, ready.

'Now then. Think some good thoughts, Eri. We're going to need them.' Vintage put the whistle to her lips and blew three short blasts – the summoning notes. They sounded very small and very stupid in the darkness of the trees, and looking for some reassurance, she touched the crossbow at her waist.

'Is something supposed to happen?' asked Eri. Vintage ignored him, and tried blowing the notes again, putting a bit more welly into it this time. She frowned. Now it just sounded desperate. 'I would like to go and see if Helcate is awake yet.'

'Just a moment, please, darling, just a moment.' Vintage held her breath, and listened harder than she ever had in her life. The roar of the distant fire, the small sounds of the woods almost lost underneath it – and there! The leathery sound of wings, like an expensive book dropped from a great height.

'Fulcor!'

The great bat was a white smudge on the black sky, and then she was diving towards them. Behind Vintage, Eri gave a little shriek, but then Fulcor was on the ground with them, walking awkwardly on her wings, her black eyes bright and shining.

'Old friend! Do you remember me?' Vintage reached out and rubbed the short velvety fur on the bat's snout, before slipping some morsels of dried meat from her pocket. Fulcor munched these up merrily enough. 'Eri, my darling, let's see if we can get this harness on her, shall we?'

It wasn't easy. Living in the wilds of Ebora for months, Fulcor had lost some weight, and they had to fiddle about with the belts and straps for some time before Vintage was satisfied they wouldn't fall off, and all the while she was horribly aware that their thieves were getting further and further away. Her ankle was no help either, but eventually they were strapped in, with Eri sitting ahead of Vintage – 'You can see better in the dark, my dear, so I will need you to be lookout for us' – and with another round of commands from the whistle, they were in the air.

'*Wargh*,' said Eri, and then: 'This isn't much like flying with Helcate.'

'Hold on to your stomach as best you can,' said Vintage. Her own innards felt like they had been left behind on the ground, and the take-off had jerked her injured ankle so badly that she'd had to bite her lip to keep from crying out. 'We are going to have to work quickly, if we've any hope of stopping them.'

Up above Ebora, it was possible to see the true extent of the fire. It was still burning with alarming ferocity, but it had not reached the palace or Ygseril, and Vintage thought she could see a dark line on its nearest edge – people there had cut down the trees, and were flooding the area with water. There was a chance it wouldn't be a complete disaster.

'They have a lot to carry, but they have good, strong horses, used to carrying heavy loads – and they will be heading south-west, towards the Bloodless Mountains. They may have someone waiting there with fresh mounts, and if we don't reach them before that, I fear we will lose them as they make their way over the pass. Lots of places to hide there.' She took a breath, ignoring the tight knot of despair in her chest. Fulcor was heading towards the huge dark mass that was the mountains, a great absence of light against the night sky. 'But if you saw Helcate awake and chirpy at bedtime, they can't have gone too far. Keep your clever eyes open, my dear. If you see any movement, tell me.'

Vintage looked too, and soon found she was continually wiping her eyes as the cold wind pushed and stung. Once, Fulcor gave a piercing squeak that almost sounded like a query and, instinctively, Vintage looked up, but she could see nothing in the night sky ahead of them. The further they flew, the more she became convinced that she had guessed their actions incorrectly; perhaps they had fled on foot, hiding in some cave somewhere until the initial search had given up, or had they headed north? There was nothing there of note save the Barren Sea, but it was possible they had chartered a ship to meet them.

'Sarn's twisted bones,' muttered Vintage. 'I bet that's what they've done.'

'Lady Vintage? I saw something. Moving under the trees.'

'Could be wolves . . .' Vintage sat forward and looked at where Eri was pointing. The forest here was sparser as they got closer to the mountain, but despite the bright moon and clear night it was very dark. She waited, biting her lip, and then a paler shape caught her eye; a grey horse, moving steadily through the trees, with a rider. Next to it were the dark shapes of four more horses, two with riders and two heavily loaded with bags. Vintage guessed they had used much of their energy in the initial flight, and were now giving their horses a chance to breathe. One of the riders shifted on their mount, and for a moment a hood fell back to reveal blond hair that was almost white. The woman snatched it back up, but it was enough.

'Well, fuck me,' murmured Vintage. She had been expecting the Yuron-Kai – they had been missing from their rooms, and they had been intent on taking the pods for themselves, after all. But in truth, poison and misdirection was hardly their style. On some deeper level she wasn't surprised. She wasn't surprised at all.

'Vintage?'

'Don't worry, Eri, this will soon be sorted. Fulcor, quietly please, and not right on top of them.'

'What are you going to do?'

Vintage pressed her hand to the crossbow at her belt. The truth was, of course, that she did not know. Could she kill them? One of them was a child. But there was still the chance the war-beast pods could hatch, and that could be the turning point in defeating the Jure'lia – she couldn't let them just be lost.

Fulcor landed as softly as falling snow. Tyranny, Okaar and Jhef were points of movement in the distance, mostly hidden in the shadows.

'Stay behind me, Eri.' She spoke, barely moving her lips, her eyes trained on the movement through the trees ahead of them. There was just enough moonlight here to catch the shining flanks of their horses. 'We will go quietly, surprise them.'

The boy nodded, and cautiously they left the bat behind. Vintage had already cocked her crossbow in readiness, the weight of the extra bolts reassuring at her hip even as her ankle cramped with pain. If Nanthema had been around, if she'd been able to find the woman, she could have been limping into this fight with an ally instead of a frightened boy. She was just raising the crossbow, intending to keep it trained on the back of Tyranny's head while she shouted at them to stop, when she became aware of two things at once: one of the figures on the horses looked too tall to be either Tyranny or Okaar . . . and the wind in the trees was suddenly too solid somehow.

She whirled around in time to see Okaar dropping from the branches above like a cat. He had a long knife in one hand, and in an instant he had snatched up Eri and had the blade at the boy's throat. Jerking in surprise, Vintage felt her hand squeeze the trigger before she even knew where she was aiming, and Okaar abruptly flew backwards, three inches of steel bolt poking up from just below his collarbone. Eri scampered back, his hands to his neck, and Vintage was already preparing another bolt while the horses ahead wheeled around.

'Come any closer and he's dead!' With some difficulty she slammed the new bolt home and aimed at Okaar's chest. 'And if I miss, well, it's still a very long and horrible way to die, a bolt to the guts. I've heard that you can smell your own shit as you die, my dear, and I would not wish that on you.'

Okaar was as still under her attention as a trapped mouse,

his dark eyes betraying no emotion. Tyranny rode forward, her hood thrown back now to reveal her closely shorn head. Her cheeks were flushed.

'What makes you think I would care, old woman?'

'Oh please. An assassin this skilled? It would cost you a fortune to replace him. And I suspect his little sister would have something to say about it.' The girl Jhef was on her own horse, and her face was not quite as expressionless as her brother's; a flicker of unease twitched at the corner of her mouth, and she held herself too straight. The figure on the third horse was wearing a deep hood, and was keeping back from the others. 'Let's have a talk, shall we, my dear? I believe you have some things that belong to us.'

'Have I?' Tyranny smiled. 'I don't think you know quite as much as you think, Lady de Grazon.' She turned to address the hooded figure. 'Come forward, friend.'

No one moved. Vintage watched the flash of anger that passed over the young woman's face with some alarm. There were depths to her she had not glimpsed, and they appeared to be dangerous ones.

'You will come forward now, or we will bloody well leave you here, regardless of your help.' The hooded figure urged their horse forward, until it was level with Tyranny, and then, after a moment's clear hesitation, pulled down the hood. It was Nanthema.

'I did not agree to this,' she said, as though they spoke of borrowing books or which wine to drink with lunch. 'I wanted to leave quietly.'

'Nan? Nan, what have you done?'

'Lady de Grazon,' said Tyranny, cutting over her smoothly, 'wouldn't you agree that the war-beasts are a part of Ebora? That's what you told the Yuron-Kai, I believe.'

'I don't . . .'

'And surely such important Eboran relics belong to – well,

501

they belong to Eborans. Like this Eboran woman. Not, for example, this posh woman from the vine forests.'

For a second, Vintage was so angry that she considered shooting Okaar in the throat anyway.

'All we're doing really is helping Nanthema with her birth-right. And some other bits and bobs.'

'Other bits and bobs? You mean the journal of Micanal the Clearsighted, which rightfully belongs to Eri here? Or the blood you took from Helcate, what of that?' She shook her head, dismissing the cheek of the woman. 'Nan, what were you thinking? These people nearly burned down the palace! You would take the pods away from their siblings? Where, by Sarn's blessed bones, do you expect to go?'

Although it was a chilly night, a steady line of sweat was trickling down Vintage's back. It was hard to keep an eye on both Okaar, who remained on the ground next to her, and the figures on horseback. Her ankle ached steadily.

'It doesn't matter!' Nanthema shook her head lightly, half smiling. 'Anywhere but here. That's all I wanted, to go away, but you wouldn't listen. You're so caught up in this . . . what-ever this is.'

'It's the Ninth Rain, Nan.' Vintage adjusted her grip on the crossbow. 'You know very bloody well what it is.'

'Well, I missed twenty years of my life, Vin. And I'm just supposed to hang around Ebora, waiting to die? No.' She pressed her lips into a thin line. 'Tyranny can get me over the mountains, and across the plains. To Jarlsbad, if I want. Or Reidn.'

'And if the worm people come?'

'Then I will watch them from a distance.' For the first time she looked afraid. 'I thought they were long dead. That it was safe to poke around their old ruins. But they're not, and it's not. I'm not staying here to watch your half-made war-beasts die.'

502

'So, there you have it,' said Tyranny. 'I hope that's all you really need to say, because I'm getting bored.' Snake-quick, she reached across and grabbed Nanthema by the hair, yanking the taller woman's head down to meet hers, while her other hand became a fist of green fire. Winnowflames lit up the night, turning everything a sickly shade of blue-green.

Vintage took an involuntary step backwards. 'You're a *fell-witch*?!'

'I like you, Vintage, so I'm going to assume your new fondness for stating the obvious is the result of you taking a knock to the head or something. Back off, drop that clever little crossbow, or I will roast the face off this one here.'

Nanthema protested, pulling back, but Tyranny brought the fist of flame around to dance perilously close to her long black hair. The tall Eboran woman immediately stopped moving.

'I know you are strong, lady, but strong doesn't make much difference to fire. That's one of the things I learned in Mushenska.'

'So everything you told me about who you are – that was a lie?' Vintage kept herself very still. She had not lowered her crossbow, and Okaar still lay on the ground, his shirt dark with blood. She needed time to think, and she was remembering how talkative Tyranny had been while they had eaten dinner together in their caravan.

The young woman smiled, and it looked genuine enough. 'Not at all. That story was completely true, it's just that I . . . told it from a different angle.' She grinned. 'I tell it pretty well, don't I?'

'*You* were the leader of the Salts? You were O'Keefe, the woman who burned people in her pit?'

Tyranny inclined her head, even as she kept a firm grip on Nanthema's hair.

'Someone in your gang ratted you out, and you ended up in the Winnowry. Did you escape? Where is the tattoo?'

Tyranny snorted. 'They decided I was a special case. If you want to hide something, you don't put a bloody great sign on it telling everyone what it is. Do you really think all their agents fly around on giant bats with big wings printed on their heads? Speaking of which—'

A huge indistinct shape dropped from the sky, and suddenly Vintage was off her feet and face down in the dirt. She scrambled up, looking for Eri; instead she saw two enormous bats, both with Winnowry agent riders. One was a thin white woman with a sour face, and the other was a woman with brown skin and black hair held back by a scarf. She glanced at Vintage once and then dismissed her, turning to Tyranny with an aggrieved expression.

'What's all this? Do you have what you came for?'

There was no sign of Eri. With a bit of luck the boy had run off. Vintage was just lifting the crossbow again, when a pair of arms snaked around her throat, holding her still with an impressive show of strength.

'Do not move,' said Okaar. Vintage could smell his blood. He shifted slightly, then added, 'Sorry.'

'Shit.'

Tyranny and the Winnowry agent were engaged in a mild sort of argument. Vintage could see from the set of the agent's mouth that she was not pleased to see an Eboran with them, while the other agent had climbed down from her bat and was busily inspecting the large packs tied to the two spare horses. Seeing them, and knowing that the war-beast pods must be in there, Vintage felt her chest growing hot and tight.

'You weren't supposed to bring anyone out with you,' said the agent with the scarf. 'We want Eboran artefacts, not actual bloodsuckers.'

'She made it easier for us, so we drew up a deal.' Tyranny had doused her own flames and released Nanthema. She leaned back in her saddle, as if they were discussing the price of wine. 'There's no need to put your outraged face on, Maritza, I've got everything you wanted – blood samples, artwork, a fancy book. And *three* war-beast pods.' She grinned fiercely, although there was no humour in her eyes. 'You should be congratulating me. Us. For a job well done.'

Agent Maritza blew air between her teeth. 'And yet I turn up to find you arguing with a stranger, with an extra passenger for us and your pet assassin wounded. Perhaps our definitions of success aren't in alignment.'

Tyranny shook her head and looked away – a pointed dismissal. 'Whatever. I'll kill these two, and then you can take the goods away. We'll make the rest of the journey over land.'

'Two? What do you mean, these two? I thought you'd made a deal with this Eboran woman.'

Vintage stiffened in Okaar's grip. Tyranny had failed to notice Eri's absence.

'The kid. Where's he gone? There was a pasty little kid here . . .'

'Pasty?' said Vintage. 'You've got a cheek. Agent Maritza, my dear, can I ask what the Winnowry are thinking by committing an act of war against Ebora? Stealing their sacred property and murdering their citizens?'

'Ignore her,' snapped Tyranny. 'Jhef, go and fetch the kid, he'll be skulking around the trees here somewhere, I reckon. I don't think he has the balls to go running back to the palace in the dark.'

The girl slipped down from her horse silently, but by then Vintage had caught another noise on the breeze. She looked up, ignoring how Tyranny summoned her winnowfire into a fiery glove.

'I'll kill the old one first,' she said, and to Vintage's wonder there was a noticeable touch of regret in her voice. 'You should have just let us leave, Lady de Grazon. Contrary to what you

505

might think, I don't actually like killing people – not clever people, anyway. Okaar, step away.'

Vintage felt the man hesitate. She lifted her chin, still half listening for the noise she had heard before.

'Then why not get your man here to do it? If he's an assassin, I reckon he has a hundred different ways to kill me painlessly. But you want to burn me alive, don't you?' She put on her sunniest smile. 'Kill me, if you must, but don't pretend you aren't some kind of worm-spat monster, Tyranny O'Keefe.'

Nanthema's face was a mask of shock, white and almost unseeing inside its frame of black hair. Tyranny opened her mouth to reply to that, when abruptly a stream of something that looked like water blasted the side of her, splashing over her right arm, leg and part of her throat. She jumped back in surprise, and then started screaming as a thin white smoke began to rise from her clothes and skin. The horse, which had also been splashed by the substance, shook its head and began to buck convulsively.

'What is happening?' demanded Agent Maritza. 'What are you doing, Fell-Tyranny?'

'Helcate,' said Helcate.

The war-beast appeared above them, great wings keeping him hovering just under the treeline. In the darkness and the moonlight, he was an alarming sight, a shifting, strange thing – not griffin, not dragon. Something else. He opened his mouth, and a stream of fluid shot forth again, this time hitting the second Winnowry agent straight in the face. She went down bellowing with pain.

For a time, all was chaos. Okaar was immediately gone, and just as swiftly Vintage could not see the girl Jhef; they seemed to have vanished into the darkness. Agent Maritza scrambled down from her bat and swept a barrage of fireballs into the air, which caused Helcate to rise back up above the canopy.

Vintage limped rapidly over to where Nanthema sat, watching everything with a slack expression on her face.

'Vintage, I didn't think . . . I thought we would just be stealing and running . . .'

'Shut up. Which bags have the pods in?'

'There are two pods on the black horse, one on the other.'

Vintage reached for the bags on the nearest horse and pulled loose several straps, only to see Okaar running out of the dark towards her. He had a short blade in each hand, and Vintage scrambled to get her crossbow up and aimed at him in time. She fired, too high, and he easily ducked it before coming on, barely slowing up at all.

'Shit!'

There was a roar from Helcate and the war-beast dropped down from above them, partially landing on the assassin and knocking him heavily into the dirt. Amazingly, Okaar slashed at the war-beast with one of his blades, but Helcate spat forth more acid in a strange hiccupping movement, and Okaar was writhing on the ground, white smoke rising from his skin and clothes. Belatedly, Vintage realised that Eri was sitting on Helcate's back, his fists deep in the war-beast's fur.

'Stop it!' It was Tyranny. She had detached herself from her horse and was approaching them with a pair of fiery spheres hovering over her outstretched hands. Her neck looked like it had been badly scalded, and already there were fat, yellowish blisters puckering her skin. Agent Maritza came along behind her, her eyes wide with shock. 'Leave him alone!'

'My dear, are you out of your fucking mind?' Vintage turned the crossbow on them, newly loaded, but before she could get a shot off, a huge blossom of green fire billowed towards her. Vintage dived towards the horses in time to see Nanthema riding off on one of them. The bags she had managed to loosen had fallen onto the ground, and Vintage began to wriggle towards them before realising that the tail of her jacket was on fire. Gasping with horror – *the compound, the fire, it's all happening again* – she turned and rolled herself in the dirt. Helcate was advancing on the two fell-witches, hissing and snorting.

'I would have been happy with blood, but I can take a war-beast body back too!' shouted Tyranny, and she released another of the huge fireballs. Helcate leapt up into the air, beating once with his great wings, and although Vintage caught the sharp scent of burning hair, the fireball did not reach him. He hissed again, making the strange hiccupping motion, while, on his back, Eri looked stricken.

Whatever that is he is spitting, he has run out. Sarn's bones, our bastard luck!

Vintage raised her crossbow again, steadying it by resting her elbows on her knees, and fired. Tyranny staggered back from the shot, which had landed deep in the meat of her thigh. The fire she had been building winked out of existence, but Agent Maritza stepped up to take her place.

'Enough of this,' she said tersely. 'What a bloody mess.'

She raised her arms to put an end to them all, when Fulcor swept down out of the sky. She took hold of the agent with her flexible back feet and swept her up and into the trees, where Vintage could hear the woman shrieking with outrage. After a moment, a blossom of green fire belched out of the canopy, and parts of it started to burn.

'Fulcor!'

There was no time. Vintage limped over to where Tyranny lay on the floor, and struck her between the eyes with the butt of her crossbow. The woman did not go down cleanly; blood burst from the skin there and her eyes rolled back into her head, but she groaned and struggled in the dirt.

'Oh, bloody stay down, if you know what's good for you.'

Vintage looked around. Okaar was unconscious in the dirt, Nanthema had fled. The second Winnowry agent lay where

508

she had fallen, possibly dead – Vintage did not like to think what happened if you got that acid in your eyes, or if you swallowed any of it – and Helcate and Eri waited nearby, the war-beast breathing heavily, his blue eyes oddly silver in the poor light. He was bleeding from the shallow wound Okaar had given him, and as she watched, he staggered, going to his knees in the mud.

'He's so tired,' said Eri mournfully, who also sounded as though he might pass out at any moment. 'Everything is heavy.'

'I know dear, I know, I just—' The trees above were burning merrily, and there was no sign of the Winnowry agent. 'Fulcor? Fulcor!'

There was a high-pitched trill, and Fulcor swept back down towards them. She had black marks on her white fur and her ear looked a little ragged, but she came over and nosed at Vintage's pockets.

'Yes, my darling, just a moment . . .'

The small shape shot out of the dark much as her brother had done, and Jhef leapt up onto the horse still carrying the last war-beast pod. Seeing Vintage distracted, Tyranny scrambled up and threw herself at another of the horses, suddenly moving very swiftly for a stunned woman. Without a second look at her prone sibling, Jhef kicked at her mount and the two of them were away, Tyranny leaning over her saddle. In moments they were lost to sight.

Sighing heavily, Vintage rooted around in her pockets and removed a string of dried meat, which she passed to a grateful Fulcor.

'I will be honest with you, this hasn't been my best day.'

By the time they had gathered what they could – they had saved two of the three war-beast pods, and happily Micanal's journal had been in one of the fallen bags – the sky was a

509

dirty, rusty pink. Vintage could not bring herself to check whether Okaar was alive or not, and reasoned that if he was, he would be more likely to go after his sister than go back to Ebora. The Winnowry agent was certainly dead; from the purple hue of her face and the thickness of her neck, Vintage guessed that the acid had swollen her throat shut. Of the other Winnowry agent, there was no sign, and she was happy enough not to look for her. Their bats had flown off when the fighting had started, but if Agent Maritza was still alive, she would be able to summon them back.

'Should we not have gone after them? For the other war-beast pod, I mean.' Eri was standing next to Helcate, leaning heavily on the beast. 'It was precious.' He paused. 'And I think it was the one most likely to hatch next.'

Vintage sighed. She could not bring herself to ask the boy how he knew that.

'My dear, we are all injured and exhausted, Helcate most of all. And I'm afraid that if we had another fight, it would be down to him to protect us again.' She looked up at the beast, who looked back with his luminous blue eyes. 'How long has he been able to do that, anyway?'

Eri shrugged. 'Just now. He woke up and knew we were in trouble. He could feel that I was in the woods, in the dark by myself, so he came for me. When he knew that they were trying to steal our pods, he was angry. And then he just knew how to do it.'

'It is extraordinary.' Vintage paused. She felt bruised all over, her ankle was aching like a bastard, and her coat was singed. 'Extraordinary. I've never heard of a war-beast that could spit acid, certainly nothing in any book I've read, although it could simply be that the etchings we have taken to depict fire are . . . But perhaps we can talk about it when we get home.'

Although Helcate's leg had stopped bleeding, he was still

510

limping a little. Vintage went over to the big beast and patted him fondly on the nose.

'What about the thieves, though?'

'Helcate,' said Helcate.

'I doubt they will be back. And I shall have some interesting correspondence to send to the Winnowry. But for now, let's get back to the palace and see how much of it has burned down, shall we?'

49

The sky was white and heavy with snow. Hestillion narrowed her eyes against the cold and pulled her fur vest a little closer around her neck. In the distance, another Behemoth sat in the air like a fat grub, and the thin black line that joined it to the corpse moon seethed and convulsed. The queen was still close, moving slowly towards her wayward ship – it had, Hestillion suspected, been heavily damaged in the Eighth Rain. There were holes in its side, and a thick band of black fluid around its middle section like a wide stretch of scar tissue where it had tried to put itself back together. There wasn't much time.

Trying not to think too closely about what she was doing, Hestillion turned and headed back within the fleshy corridors of the corpse moon, her head down. She moved towards the cells, and as she did so, the lights dimmed, and the constant murmur of life quietened. Grimacing slightly, she broke into a run.

'Cousin!'

The prisoners still sat within their cells, looking morose. She felt a stab of impatience at this – they clearly had not thought at all on what she had told them in her last visit – and then roughly put it aside. Aldasair had risen to his feet. His hair, unwashed for days, hung in a thick, greasy tail over his shoulder.

'Hest?'

'The time is now. Are you ready?' She gestured to Bern, who was still sitting with his elbows resting on his knees. 'You, human, get up. I will need your strength.'

Her heart beating rapidly in her chest, Hestillion reached out for the corpse moon and *pushed* against it – the membrane separating them shrunk away. There, it was done; now it was simply a countdown to the moment the queen realised her betrayal.

A black shape, moving too fast to follow, shot across the room, and Hestillion hit the floor hard enough for all the air to be knocked from her lungs. The wolf brought her long snout down until she could feel Jessen's hot breath blasting over her face. The weight on her chest was agonising.

'What do you want, betrayer?'

'Aldasair . . .' Hestillion gasped air back into her lungs, and felt a stab of real panic at the enormous effort that cost her. 'There isn't time. Call off your dog.'

Dimly, she saw her cousin move into view, Bern just behind him.

'Why should we trust you, Hest?'

'Get her off . . . and I will tell you.'

Jessen jumped away, and Hestillion scrambled to her feet, blinking away black spots at the edge of her vision.

'Well?'

'I don't want you here,' she said. 'You exert too much influence over Celaphon and he is mine. And I cannot be joined to you with the crystal. I just cannot. Bad enough that I must know a human so well,' she nodded to Bern, 'but you as well? No.'

She couldn't miss the expression of disappointment that moved over Aldasair's face. Despite everything, he had still believed she would come back to them. She wanted to laugh, but there was no time.

'Do not give me that sad puppy look, cousin. We have a matter of moments while the queen is distracted. You, human. Help me move these walls.'

She moved over to the eastern wall, knowing that it was the swiftest path to the outer skin.

'I don't know what you're talking about.' The big man was on his feet, with his huge griffin behind him. 'I have tried my axes against these walls, and Sharrik's claws. They do nothing.'

'Idiot. You are a part of this ship now.' She touched the crystal at her heart. 'And it is a part of you. It is attached to you as your leg is attached to you, or your arm. And you can move your hand, can you not? Flex your toes? Think! This is your one chance to get out, so reach for that power and use it.'

To his credit, the big man came to join her at the wall, his brow furrowed. Aldasair followed with the two war-beasts. The lights in the room had grown so dim they were almost in darkness.

'You know of what I speak, don't you? I know it is unpleasant, but you must embrace the connection for a moment. Join me in pulling the walls aside and we might just get you outside in time.'

Bern looked at the blue crystal in his hand, an unmistakable expression of revulsion creasing his brow, and he placed it gently against the wall. Hestillion joined him and reached out. *A good man, a kind man, a risk-taker . . . The teeming dark, busy with webs, a dark intelligence at its heart, but looking away for now . . .*

The wall opened to their touch, revealing a dark corridor beyond.

'Quickly now, follow me, all of you.' They crossed the corridor and pulled the next wall open, and the next, and the next. Aldasair and the war-beasts followed. With each wall, it grew a little harder, until Hestillion noticed that the lights were gradually coming back on. There was a scuttling noise, somewhere down the corridor where they were, and Bern had broken out into a sweat.

'She's coming back,' he said.

'Yes.' Hestillion swallowed down her own panic. 'As fast as we can. We can't be very far from the outer skin now.'

They moved on, although now it was like pushing against a wall of treacle, rapidly turning to rock. The small intelligences of the homunculi were tickling whispers against her consciousness, growing stronger, and elsewhere, something bigger was barrelling towards them.

'This is it.' They stood in front of a curving grey wall, a row of holes behind them. 'One more push . . .'

The inner wall to their right exploded, throwing them all to the floor. Hestillion looked up, fearing to see the still visage of the queen, but instead Celaphon was looming over them, the thickly corded fans on his neck standing up in outrage. Something danced around him, some blue light, and then it was gone.

'What are you doing? Where are you taking my family?'

'Bern, keep working on that outer wall.' Hestillion stepped in front of them. 'Celaphon, sweet one. This cannot work. We have to get rid of them.'

'What do you mean? The connection works! I feel you and the human man, so clearly, and I am not alone. Together, we will be strong.'

Next to her, she could feel Bern commanding the wall to part, to split open and admit them to the sky, but the queen's influence was strengthening with every passing second.

'No. Remember when I told you to listen to me? That you must always listen to me? This gift changes nothing about that, Celaphon. I know what is best for you – for us. And to have

515

you connected to a human, to these lesser war-beasts . . . it would taint you. Poison what you are. And it would poison me, too.'

'Lesser war-beasts!' The idiot griffin raised his wings threateningly. 'Another battle and I will tear the scales from this abomination!'

In the growing brightness of the corridor, Celaphon's scales shone a deep, iridescent purple. He tipped his head to one side, his pale eyes narrow.

'Are you not my brother?'

'I do not know what you are,' said Sharrik.

An uneasy silence blossomed in the crowded corridor, and for a moment Hestillion found the words lodged in her throat like stones. She had felt, quite keenly, the sliver of misery that had moved through Celaphon like a blade, and knew that Bern had felt it too. Behind her, the big man laid a hand on the griffin's shoulder.

'Be ready, Sharrik,' he said. 'We are almost through here.'

'No!' Celaphon reared back, his huge blocky head hanging over them all, and the uncertain blue light Hestillion had seen before flickered into being around his jaws, at the ends of his teeth. There was no time; she did not know what Celaphon was about to do next, but she suspected it would be very bad for all of them. She turned quickly to Aldasair, catching his eye.

'Fly quickly, cousin, there will be enemies in the sky.' Then, looking back up at the dragon, she focussed everything she had on him, picturing him as he had been when he had first hatched from the pod: small, weak, certain to die. She conjured herself as his saviour, as his only friend, and threw it at him with every inch of her connection to him – both forged by the crystals, and the natural link of warrior-bond to war-beast.

You will do as I say!

The enormous dragon recoiled from her – again, that blade

516

of misery, of terrible confusion – and in the handful of seconds he was distracted, she joined her own strength to Bern's. The wall burst open, letting in daylight and a howling wind.

'Go! Quickly!'

Aldasair was already clinging to Jessen's back, and Bern scrambled onto Sharrik. The last Hestillion saw of her cousin was his pale face as he looked back, his auburn hair falling over his forehead and clinging to his cheeks. She saw the question he wanted to ask, and she shook her head firmly. With more strength than she thought she had left, she commanded the edges of the hole to seal back together, although it was a poor job; she could still smell the fresh air. It did not matter, though, as the queen was back. Already Hestillion could feel her curiosity, her sense that something was amiss. It would not take long for her to figure it out.

Celaphon looked down at her.

'You took my family. You forced them to go away.'

'I told you, Celaphon, I am your only family.' She smoothed her hand over the scales on his knees. They were hot, just as they had been when he was an infant. 'As you are mine.'

It was a subdued journey back. Vostok had been full of questions when they had emerged from what Tor referred to as the Seed Carrier, but the Eboran had just looked away from the dragon and shaken his head. The sun had set while they had been looking for him, and they had emerged into a thick jungle night, warm and still and eerily silent. There was no sign of the white monsters.

'I need to think,' he said. 'I just need to think for a while.'

Noon would normally have badgered him for more information than that, and she could feel Vostok's curiosity tingling in her fingers, but the Eboran looked so distracted and mournful she was willing to let it go. The place itself appeared to have suffered no ill effects despite her filling at least part of it with

517

flames, and as they walked away she noticed that the green lines of fire she had somehow awakened had faded and died. There were, indeed, a lot of questions to be asked.

When they arrived back at the clearing with the neat little homes and clambered down from their war-beasts, Tor took her arm gently.

'Can I talk to you? Alone.'

Vostok rounded on them, her jaws open slightly to expose her teeth.

'If you have something to tell us about Ebora, Tormalin the Oathless, I believe I should hear it too.' She twitched her head slightly in Kirune's direction. The big cat was crouched silently next to her. 'We should *both* hear it.'

'And you will.' Tor sounded unutterably tired, and to Noon he suddenly looked much older; it wasn't so difficult to imagine he was four hundred years old, with his lips pressed into a thin line and his brow furrowed. 'I promise, but I want to get it all straight in my head first, and to do that I want to talk to my . . . I want to talk to Noon about it.'

'You do not trust me.' It wasn't quite a question, and in Kirune's lamp-like eyes there was, Noon suspected, more hurt than anger. 'You cannot speak to me.'

'Kirune—'

'Go on, the two of you, go and get some rest now. Go hunting or something, I don't know.' Noon moved in front of Tor, almost chasing them away as she'd once chased the small herds of fleeten on the plains. 'There're a few questions I want to ask our hosts in the morning, and it's going to go down about as well as a shit in a pond, so go and get some rest. As soon as I know, you will both know. Go.'

Reluctantly, the war-beasts slunk off. Tor did not wait for them to leave, but instead headed to a small copse of trees, almost immediately vanishing into the dark.

'Here, where are you going? Wait!'

518

Noon brushed her fingers against a tree and formed a small ball of green light in her palm, almost entirely without heat.

'I want to show you something.'

It turned out to be Micanal's tunnel. They stood together in a pool of green light, looking at the strange smooth roots, but for a very long time Tor didn't say anything at all.

'What happened to you in there, Tor? Kirune said that you'd been bitten. Pretty badly, he said, but I can't see any wounds on you. The blood on your shirt and trousers looks dry to me, and you haven't moaned about it once, which is a pretty big giveaway that you're fine.'

Tor looked down at his shirt and prodded at the stain as though he'd never seen it before. He sighed.

'Best Eboran silk, this was. I have ruined so many good shirts with you, do you realise that? One of them I believe you had to cut off me with a knife.'

'Tor, I did not come down here to talk about your fashion choices.'

He sighed, and then, haltingly and with several pauses, began to tell her a very strange tale indeed: of being pulled through a solid surface, of waking in a tube-like tunnel; of being healed by roots just like the ones they stood in front of, and of the creature Eeskar, who had talked to him of his people's origins. Here, the story moved back in time to the impossibly distant past, when Eborans were apparently just humans, and the creatures had grown a tree to change them – to make them what they were now.

When he was done, Noon rubbed her hands over her eyes – it was as though he had transferred his terrible weariness over to her.

'I'm not sure I understood that,' she said eventually. 'You are the children of a people not from this world? Not from Sarn?'

'Nothing as grand as that, Noon. Eborans are simply humans

519

who stumbled over a magical tree.' He smiled at her, although it looked like it pained him to do so. 'We are an odd footnote in their history. Not even a particularly interesting or worthy one to them, it seems.'

'Fire and blood. But why tell me? It seems like if anyone should know, it's Vostok and Kirune. And the rest of the war-beasts.'

'And they will know. Of course, they must know. They also owe their existence to the Aborans, and the seed they planted thousands of years ago. But it is hard for me to take this in – hard to understand that our people are not really the god-touched heroes we have always been told.' He glanced down at her. 'Perhaps I simply needed to tell someone who wouldn't care either way. We are monsters to your people regardless of what our origins were.'

'You are not a monster to me, Tor.' She took his hand and squeezed it, and he squeezed hers back. 'I . . . care about you. And now, with Vostok, I am more linked to Ebora than any other human has ever been, I reckon.' His life energy lapped at her skin, more powerful and brighter than any other she had tasted; with some effort, she refrained from sampling it. 'What I want to know is, why didn't Micanal tell us this? He clearly knew, as did his sister.' She gestured to the green roots. 'Part of the truth is down here, in his bloody tunnel. The roots healed you, didn't they?'

'Eeskar spoke repeatedly of speaking to another of my kind – someone who didn't take his news well, either. This is why Arnia warned us to stay away from that side of the island.'

'Well. Partly. There's something else you should know.' Noon paused, painfully aware that this information was coming to him late, and explained how she had followed Arnia across the crevasse to a hidden human village. Tor stared at her incredulously.

'Why didn't you tell me this before?'

520

'You wanted to believe they were good, that they wouldn't lie to us, when that was obviously a steaming pile of horse shit!' Noon glared at the roots, ignoring the defensiveness in her own voice. 'I felt like I was on my own here, with you and your little family of Eborans. I mean, didn't you ever wonder how they were existing out here by themselves? Or was it easier to not look too closely at what they were telling us? You were so taken with them – especially with Arnia.'

'Noon, that is ridiculous.' But Tor looked away from her as he said it, and she suspected she wasn't too far wrong. 'At least you have deemed me worthy of all the facts now. We'll have to get answers from them. From both of them.'

They turned to leave the tunnel.

'Do you think those monsters will follow us back? The things from the Aboran ship, I mean. I might have pissed them off.'

Tor smiled faintly, then shook his head. 'I don't know for sure, but I suspect they can't. Eeskar described them as a sort of animal they use to defend the Seed Carrier, so unless the whole thing comes after us—'

'Tor!' It was Kirune, his bulky silhouette blocking out the dim light from the end of the tunnel.

'What is it?'

'The other two. They are not here.'

Tor and Noon emerged into the cool night air. The big cat looked agitated, prowling back and forth in front of the entrance.

'What do you mean?'

'They are not in their house. Vostok called for them, nothing. They are not in the clearing.' Kirune shook out his fur. 'They are gone, and you hide from us. Keep knowledge from us. Eborans are . . . disappointing.'

Tor sighed extravagantly. 'Come on, let's find Vostok, and I will explain it all to both of you, but I don't expect you will enjoy it.'

And they didn't. Noon sat on the porch of their dwelling, watching as Tor outlined the truth of Ebora to the war-beasts. She felt Vostok's growing anger and dismay as a tightening in her chest, and even thought she could sense Kirune's disappointment and confusion. When he was done, he spoke to them about the human village, about making their way there in the morning should Micanal and Arnia not show up, but they drifted away without agreeing to anything – Noon doubted they even heard him. Vostok and Kirune walked away under the trees together, and when Noon reached for the dragon – to give her sympathy, or comfort – she sensed that Vostok did not want to speak to anyone at that moment. Tor joined her on the porch, looking downcast.

'I fear we have only made our situation worse,' he said quietly. 'We came here to find something that would bind us all together, but instead . . .' He nodded to the patch of trees where the war-beasts had vanished. 'We are not just divided, but dispirited.'

'Are you glad that you know the truth, though?' Noon was thinking of the hole in her memories, the place where her mother and everyone she had known had died; she could approach the edge of the memory, but whenever she got close, a terrible sense of danger would push her back. 'It's weird, and disappointing, but it is the truth of who you are. Does that mean something?'

He looked at her, half smiling. His long black hair was loose, framing his face like a curtain. She realised that the scars across his eye and his cheek had become as much a part of him as anything else, and she knew only that she was glad to see his face, and to be sitting with him on this quiet night.

'I expect Vintage would have some fine words about the value of truth,' he said. 'But at the moment it simply feels like everything I knew about my people was a lie. We are not god-touched, and indeed Ygseril is no god. He is the spawn of some other race, an experiment.'

'He loved you, though,' she replied, smoothing out her trousers with her hands. Her fingers were red and rough from days of searching through the river. 'You told me that – that you felt his regard for you, when he returned.'

'Hmm. We were just like you once, you know. Humans who happened to wander across a certain tree. It doesn't sound like the beginning of much, to me.'

'Doesn't it make us closer, though?'

He looked at her then, and said, 'Do you want to go inside?'

It was slower than before, and they laughed more. The lamps were burning low, but still Noon felt vaguely self-conscious as she lost each item of clothing. Tor pulled off his shirt and threw it so extravagantly that he knocked a vase over that promptly shattered, and for a long moment they just held each other as they giggled helplessly. Then, though, he kissed her, kissed her throat and her neck, and she slid her hands down the smooth skin of his belly, grinning secretly into his shoulder at what she found there. Vostok had been present the first time, in a strange way, but now she was far away, and this was very much her own experience.

Eventually, Tor scooped her up and carried her to one of the beds – it was his, she realised belatedly, as it was untidy and strewn with clothes – and there he spoke softly of the rules of his House of the Long Night. This time, Noon had the patience to listen, although not for long, and eventually she pulled him to her with a hunger that seemed bigger than herself. He burned in her, a delicious brand, and as she tangled her fingers in his hair she murmured 'fire and blood, fire and blood', over and over.

Afterwards, they lay together in a tangle of limbs and sheets. Noon found herself staring at the window. It didn't seem possible, but the small patch of night she could see looked brighter than it had.

'I prefer this to the cave floor,' she said.

'Mmm.' Tor was twirling a section of her hair around his fingers. 'I think you are my favourite witch, witch.'

'I have a bad feeling about this place, Tor. Why did that . . . Aboran person react to me that way? He couldn't possibly have known me, but he seemed . . . I don't know. Horrified. Scared.'

'Well you are pretty scary.'

'Tor.'

He shrugged. 'I don't know, Noon. To be honest, I think so long alone has turned them strange. And they're not even really there, not physically.' She felt him shift in the bed, and knew that his mouth would be pressed thin with annoyance. 'Thousands of years stuck there, stranded, slowly dying, and then channelling what was left of them into mirrors, becoming reflections of themselves. It's not healthy, to be alone for so long.'

'Like Micanal and Arnia, you mean. I don't think they are as happy or as normal as you would like to believe.'

He shifted again, and she sensed him reluctantly agreeing with her.

'We'll find them, and get some answers. Soon.'

Hestillion waited.

There was little else she could do. She could feel Celaphon at the edges of her perception, a strange mixture of angry and cowed – he had not enjoyed her commanding him as she had, and he was outraged by the loss of his siblings, but had chosen to keep his distance from her for the time being. Her chamber was dark and still, the landscape beyond the translucent panel speeding away from them under grey skies. On the floor some distance from her scuffed boots, the Tarla card Aldasair had once given her lay crumpled and discarded. She stood looking out of the makeshift window, and did not turn when she heard the wall open behind her. Distantly, she was glad she was wearing what she now thought of as her battle clothes – a fur vest, leather leggings, her hair pulled back into a tight braid. This was more comfortable than her silk robes.

The queen's movements were almost silent, yet Hestillion felt no surprise at all when her long tapered fingers closed around her neck. Her touch was warm and papery.

'Hestillion Eskt, born in the year of the green bird, child of Ebora.' The queen tightened her grip, just slightly. 'You have disappointed us.'

'I did what I felt was necessary.'

'Our prisoners were interesting to us. We have developed an appreciation for . . . experimenting. We were anxious to see what would happen to these new shapes, how we could change them, and you have taken that away.' She paused, and when she spoke again her voice was much closer than it had been. Hestillion imagined the queen bending her strangely flexible neck, bringing her teeth closer to her throat. 'I could tear your head off. That would also be an interesting change.'

'Why don't you?'

Instead of answering, the translucent window grew cloudy and the lights grew dim. Hestillion felt a moment's sorrow at that; she didn't want to die in the dark.

'Yet you did not leave with them,' said the queen. 'It would have been easier, safer, to go. You could even have taken your war-beast – we think you know he would have followed you. Why?'

Hestillion closed her eyes, hoping she had judged this correctly. 'Why do you ask, when you can easily know the truth of me?'

Abruptly the grip on her neck vanished, and the queen moved to stand in front of her. She looked curiously diminished.

For the time being, she was not much taller than Hestillion, and her mask-like face was grey and solemn. Her eyes moved wetly as she peered closely at Hestillion. 'Know the truth of you. To learn what holds you together. Yes.'

She touched the crystal at Hestillion's heart, and Hestillion felt all her hiding places, all her shields and barriers stripped away pitilessly in one heart-stopping moment. She was alone and exposed within the heart of the Jure'lia, cradled within its sprawling, busy intelligence, and there was only the truth. She felt the queen looking her over like the skittering touch of thousands of spiders, and then just as swiftly it was done. The queen stepped back, becoming taller and more impressive again. A slick sheen moved across her mask-face.

'So. You have turned away from them. You have . . . "cut ties".' Her head tipped to one side. 'It is interesting to us that you could not bear to be joined so with your blood-cousin, with the war-beasts you prize so highly.'

'But you see that it's true,' snapped Hestillion. 'I have made my choice. There is no returning to Ebora – I will become something else instead, something new. There is no walking away from this path.'

'Yes, we see that it is true, Hestillion Eskt, the green bird of the corpse moon. But there must be a penance, we think, for such disobedience.' All her early gravity had vanished, and instead she sounded amused. 'You will find them and kill them, the prisoners. You will kill them for me, my little war-queen.'

50

They left as soon as the dawn light turned the trees a silvery, delicate grey. Vostok and Kirune stayed behind, in case the two Eborans should return. Both war-beasts were uncharacteristically quiet, keeping their heads low and together. Vostok in particular seemed almost mournful, and although Tor could not sense her feelings like Noon could, he watched the young witch's face and saw a line of worry growing between her brows.

'There's nothing to say they will be at this village you found.'

'No, but there will be answers there, I'm sure of it.' The crevasse was a dark slit in the ground ahead, and when Noon led them beyond a heavy thicket of trees Tor found himself willing the bridge not to be there. Perhaps if it was not there, he could go back to believing that the siblings were simply eccentric recluses. But it hung across the gap, oddly gossamer in the strengthening light, and it was solid enough as they crossed it; the bridge was old, but it was well cared for.

'Are you sure you know the way?'

Noon stopped, seeming to consider the question.

'Yeah, I'm pretty sure.' They started walking again. 'When I was a child on the plains, we were taught very early on to remember where you were at all times. To be able to find your way back from places. Kids who wandered off from the tribe and couldn't find their way back would usually die.'

'Killed by animals? Wild-touched things?'

'Sometimes. But mostly just being out under the sky too long. There are lots of places on the plains that are far away from any drinkable water, and it can get very cold at night. We would find their bones sometimes, when we came back that way, and we would take one bone, as evidence of what we had given to the land, and bury the rest.'

'It sounds like a hard place.' He glanced sideways at her. In the growing light, her face and the column of her neck looked luminous, and he felt an odd tightening in his chest. 'You don't talk about it very often.'

'A hard place. I suppose it was, but maybe no harder than being poor in Mushenska, and certainly better than being a prisoner at the Winnowry. It feels like it was another life – a dream I had, or someone else's life.'

'Memory is strange like that.'

They walked on until the sun was a hot presence overhead and the air was alive with the sound of birds and insects waking up for the day. Eventually, Noon laid a hand on his arm, and just visible through the trees ahead was a sprawling settlement, surrounded by wooden walls and a palisade. He could smell wood smoke, and meat cooking, and there was a murmur too – the sound of a reasonable number of people living their lives. After days at sea and in the relative seclusion of the twins' houses, it was a strange, almost alarming sound.

'What do we do? Just walk up to the gate and ask if Micanal and Arnia can come out to play?'

Noon grinned at him wickedly, and for a moment he considered suggesting that they find a secluded patch of grass instead. When had he started to need her so badly?

'Why not? Let's see what these people know of the great artist and his sister.'

They ghosted towards the main gate, but before they reached it Tor spotted something moving furtively in the shrubs to the far side of the settlement. He touched Noon's shoulder and they both stopped. It was a man, short and stocky, in his middle years for a human, and he had a thick black beard and skin that had likely once been tan like Noon's, but years of the island's hot sun had turned it as deep a brown as polished wood. He wore an outfit constructed from various small patches of fur and leather, and around his neck there was a necklace strung with a motley collection of coloured stones – red, brown, black and grey, and one bright piece of what looked like sea-glass, as green as Noon's fire. Although his appearance was somewhat odd, it was his behaviour that struck Tor – the man was moving slowing through the bushes, his posture that of an animal ready to flee at any moment, and all the time he kept his eyes rigidly on the settlement. His right hand compulsively reached for the stones at his neck, over and over, each time brushing the smooth surface of the sea-glass.

'Him,' Tor said, pitching his voice low. 'We'll circle around and grab him, and ask him some questions. It makes more sense than storming the place.'

'Grab him? You can't just wander around beating up whoever you like.'

'I'm not talking about a beating, Noon. Think about it – remember the people on Firstlight, how frightened they were to see me? How do you think this man will feel about new strangers on his island, and does he look like someone we can explain all this to quickly?'

The man was now tugging violently on his beard and glaring at the settlement with an expression of anguish. He stopped, then pressed his hands to the side of his head, looking at the ground.

'Fine,' said Noon, although she sounded unhappy about it. 'Quickly. I can stun him, just a touch.'

Moving quickly and quietly, they doubled back on themselves and took some effort to approach the man from the thickest part of the bush, but ultimately Tor sensed it was a wasted effort – the bearded man remained utterly oblivious right up until the moment Noon slipped a hand around his wrist and he sunk into a faint. Tor grabbed him under the armpits and hauled him out of sight of the village – he was remarkably light for a stocky man – and propped him up against a tree. Already, his eyes were rolling in their sockets as he fought to regain consciousness.

'You're getting pretty good at that,' Tor said to Noon. She raised her eyebrows at him.

'Are you saying I wasn't before?'

'The first time you did it to me I thought I'd been lightly tapped with a sledgehammer. You're using it with precision now . . . look, he's awake.'

The man was staring at them both with apparent horror, his mouth hanging open.

'Hello,' said Noon. 'What's your name?'

The man swallowed hard. 'Am I awake?' He spoke a version of plains speak that was very close to Noon's, just as the people on the other island had.

'You are, friend.'

His eyes skittered to Tor, and he blinked several times. 'Are you sure?' Then, 'I have seen you before, both of you.'

Noon glanced at Tor. 'You were the figure I saw on the other side of the crevasse that day, watching us. Why?'

When the man didn't reply, Tor took a hold of his shoulders. 'My name is Tormalin the Oathless. We're looking for a couple of Eborans – people like me. Have you seen them? Micanal and Arnia. They are brother and sister.'

The man's eyebrows had shot up to be hidden under the scruffy flap of black hair that hung over his forehead.

530

'Oh, I know them. We all know them, they—' He stopped, appearing to struggle with something. To Tor's alarm, he saw the man's eyes grow bright with tears. 'They are constant, they are gods, but I can't see it. Why can't I see it? My name is Fallow.' He took a deep breath and tugged viciously on his beard. 'I am an outcast, but I keep coming back here to look. To see my people, living on without me.'

Tor opened his mouth to ask if he'd seen Micanal or Arnia recently, but Noon spoke over him. 'Why have you been cast out, Fallow?'

'I dream differently,' he said, and each word was so coated in misery it made Tor's skin grow cold. 'In their dreams, they all sing together, but I am the lost note.'

'You mean the other people here all have the same dreams?'

'Yes, of course.' Fallow looked up at them as though they were mad, and his fingers closed around the piece of sea-glass again. 'Every night they sing and walk as one. I don't. My dreams are chaos, darkness.'

Tor glanced at Noon, but whether or not she had caught the significance of what the man had said he couldn't tell. If the villagers on this island were all dreaming the same thing every night, it was very likely that Micanal or Arnia were interfering with their dreams, crafting them all to be the same. Something about that caused the worm of worry in his gut to grow.

'How long have you been here, Fallow?' asked Noon.

'Here? Cast out, you mean?'

'No, on this island. When did you come to this place?'

'I was born here. My mother and father were born here, their mother and father . . . we were all born here.' He screwed his eyes up tight, trembling, then popped them open again. 'There were ships, hundreds of years ago, and we came here with our gods. But people – they forget there was ever another place, that there was a time when we didn't believe in these gods. Years ago there were others, people who couldn't dream the poisoned dream either, but they left. Made a secret boat and left, my grandmother said.'

'So you came here with Micanal and Arnia?' Noon rubbed a hand across her eyes. 'I mean, your ancestors did? Why?'

Fallow tucked his chin into his chest. 'I . . . I don't know.'

'You don't know?' Tor shifted, glancing back towards the settlement. 'Or you don't want to say?'

'I can show you. I can show you why we're here.' Fallow's voice was firmer, angrier than it had been. 'The others, they won't see it, because they listen to their dreams, but I have other dreams.'

Noon stood up, and turned away. For a moment, her left hand was surrounded by a corona of green fire. She grimaced, and it grew fiercer, and then it sputtered out. When she turned back, she looked rueful.

'I had to release the energy. Sorry.'

Tor smiled, half amused – he had thought of Lucky Ainsel, burping loudly after a meal – but the effect on Fallow was quite different. The man scrambled to his feet, his mouth hanging open.

'The fire!' Tor took hold of the man's arm, hoping to calm him, but Fallow shook him off. 'I knew it. It's the one dream I have over and over, but no one else has ever had it. That one day everything will end in green fire.'

The man was glaring at Noon with a wild expression. Noon shook her head, looking vaguely put out.

'What is wrong with everyone on this island? Has no one seen a fell-witch before?'

'They probably haven't, actually.' Tor sighed. 'Put that from your head, Fallow, and show us why you're all here. I think it might be the piece we're missing from all this.'

'I will show you.' Fallow glanced at Noon's hands, as if afraid they would burst into flame again. 'But we will have to go back inside, and they will not like it. I am not welcome.'

532

'Don't worry, we're with you.' Noon smiled grimly. 'And we're always welcome everywhere.'

They walked up and through the gate, with Fallow walking between them both. There were groups of people inside, all busy with one task or another. Tor saw rows and rows of tanning racks, men and women with buckets of water, crates of fruits and spits with animal carcasses speared on them. Everywhere he saw steam and smoke and he caught multiple scents on the wind – wood smoke, cooking meat, the strong scent of alcohol, of urine from the tanning, of overripe fruit and the sweet scent of bread baking. It was a hive of industry and work. The men and women wiped sweat from their brows absently, and even the children carried bags and pots, or sat with furs on their laps, cleaning or sowing. There was very little talking, even between the children; instead their faces were intent, or absent. Far to their right Tor saw a tall man with broad shoulders carrying a crate of green glass bottles; they clinked together and he shifted his grip – clearly these were precious items, and Tor recognised them as the bottles of sour wine Arnia was so free and easy with.

'This is where they get it from,' he said in a low voice. 'All that food, their wines, all produced here, by these people.'

'Their own private workforce.' Noon looked quietly furious, her eyes glittering darkly. 'Why do they do it, Fallow? What do they get out of it?'

'It's what we've always done, we've . . .'

His words died in his throat as a tall woman with a lined face began to march towards them. At first their entrance into the settlement had been masked by all the activity, but Tor could see many faces turning towards them now. One man dropped the bucket he was carrying, and several children vanished back inside the nearby houses.

'You are not to come here!' The woman had short grey hair, bristling close to her scalp, and her face seemed pinned to her cheekbones, the skin stretched thin and delicate, although judging from her voice and her stride, she was not that old. 'You've made your choices, Fallow. There is no place for you in the Poisonless, I won't . . .' She stopped, and her arms fell slack to her sides. 'What . . .? Who . . .?'

Her eyes danced between them. Tor sensed that at first she had taken Noon to be a resident of the settlement – with her black hair and warm skin, she would easily fit in here – but she had had a chance to see him clearly, and there was no mistaking Tor for anything other than an Eboran. Her mouth fell open, and she seemed incapable of speech.

'You see, Highsun? Change has come here, no matter what you think, or what the dreams say!' Fallow had drawn himself up to his full height, and he clutched at the stones at his throat. 'How do you explain this?' He gestured at Tor. 'Our lords have lied to us, Highsun.'

The woman looked utterly bewildered, and Tor felt a stab of sympathy for her. She was seeing the bones of her world exposed, and they were fragile things.

'There is no reason to be afraid,' he said, holding up his hands. 'We're not going to hurt anyone. We just want to know what's been going on here.'

'Where did you come from?' asked Highsun. 'What are you?'

A small crowd had gathered by this point. Tor swallowed down his unease, and forced himself to smile. 'We come from Ebora. You must have heard of it?'

'Ebora is no more.' This came from a young man to Tor's left. He was handsome, with a spare, wiry frame and a dark matt of hair across his chest, and he glared at them with open hostility. 'Everyone there died, save for our lords, who escaped because they were chosen. This is a test!' He turned to the others in the crowd. 'You are a fool if you cannot see it! Our lords are testing the Poisonless, to see who will fall for false dreams and lies.' He laughed, an ugly, short sound. 'This is just a dream, to test us.'

'I am no dream,' said Noon sharply. 'Why do you call your-selves the Poisonless? Don't you understand there is a whole world out there? Have you forgotten about it?'

'Highsun, I want to show them the temple.' Fallow was pointedly ignoring the young man. 'They must see it.'

'No! It is our most sacred place.' The young man pushed past the people he stood with to square up to them. Tor was a good head taller than he was, but his open aggression made the skin on the back of his neck tingle. He did not want to get into a fight with these people. 'Fallow has always been a blight, a rotten branch of the Poisonless. We should throw him out again, or kill him.'

'Whiterun is right,' said the woman called Highsun, although she sounded uncertain, and still she could not look away from Tor. 'The rites of the temple are the very core of who we are. It is not something to be gawked at.'

'Look at him!' Fallow gestured at Tor again. 'He is one of them. Can you deny him what he asks? We have spent our whole lives giving them everything. If there are other answers, we should know them.'

The small crowd were growing all the time, and an angry murmur was bubbling up from within them. Tor caught snatches of their conversations, none of it reassuring.

'This one.' Fallow grabbed Noon's arm this time. 'This one brings the green fire I told you of, in the dreams you dismissed.' Noon, seeming to sense that some sort of demonstration was needed, produced a tiny fireball with her free hand, letting it float there. The noise from the crowd increased. 'Are you so sure that you can just dismiss it?' said Fallow. 'I told you! I told you all.'

'Fine.' Highsun seemed to crumple somehow, growing thinner and weaker with a single word. 'Come with me.'

She led them deeper into the village. Everywhere they looked Tor could see abandoned tasks, men and woman standing next to their churning buckets and cooking fires, eyes wide and shocked. Eventually, Highsun brought them to a tunnel leading into the ground – immediately Tor was struck by the resemblance to the place where he had so recently spoken to Noon, and where he had first seen the strange green roots of the Seed Carrier, only this place was much better cared for. The wooden jambs had all been carved with images of foxes and hands, and there were lamps burning all around it, even in the midst of the day. The carvings were not as fine as Micanal's, he could see that at a glance, but they were numerous, and the black earth had been flattened with carefully placed pieces of grey slate, creating a proper floor. A woman stood by the entrance, a bucket filled with wet cloths in her arms, and she staggered back as they approached.

'Here,' said Highsun, as they crossed the threshold. 'These are the sacred mysteries of the Poisonless.'

Within the tunnel it was surprisingly well lit, with lamps and short candles wedged into the walls every few feet. There was also a powerful scent, pungent and somehow thick; the scent of unwashed bodies, of urine and shit and old food. As if sensing his disgust, Highsun glanced up at Tor defiantly.

'We care for them,' she said fiercely. 'We care for them every day of their lives.'

'What do you mean?' asked Noon. To anyone else the fell-witch would have sounded angry, Tor was sure of it, but he could hear the fear in her voice – the expectation that they were about to witness something terrible.

'Every one of them is chosen at birth to be the best and most valued of us,' said Highsun. Ahead of them the passage grew steeper, diving down into the shadows. There were, Tor noticed, a number of muddy footprints leading both up and down the passage. This was clearly a place that was visited often. 'They are the heart of the Poisonless.'

'That isn't an answer,' said Noon.

The tunnel ended and they entered a low-ceilinged cavern. It was lit with more candles and lamps, most at ground level, so at first it was difficult to discern what it contained. Tor saw a pair of women, their sleeves rolled up to their elbows, watching them come with wide eyes. They each wore dark furs and a rough sort of cloth that had been dyed black, and each had the shape of a hand painted on one cheek with a green, greasy-looking substance. One of them, he saw, was carrying a jug with a long, thin neck, while the other had a bowl of something that looked like yellow sludge.

'What is happening?' one of them asked.

'Don't worry,' said Highsun. 'Please, go outside.'

The women moved away, but neither of them left – instead they hung at the mouth of the tunnel, clutching the objects they carried possessively. Where they had been, Tor could see that to either side of the cavern the smooth green roots burst through the black walls of dirt, and impaled on them, there were people.

'Noon,' he said. 'Noon, you probably don't want to see this.'

'What? What can you see?' The witch barged passed him, blinking. She didn't see as well in the dark as he did, and it took her a few moments. She straightened up and took a step backwards. 'Fire and blood, what is this? *What is this?*'

'The Poisonless,' said Highsun stiffly. 'We care for them, from birth.'

The nearest person appeared to be a teenage boy. His head lolled awkwardly on his neck, and his eyes rolled in his head, but there was a ghost of a beard on his chin, and his sunken chest had a few scanty hairs across it. The ends of the green roots erupted from his flesh all over, sticking up like barbs through the thin meat of his thighs, his arms and his stomach. Tor even spotted them thrusting up through the boy's feet. He was pinned on the roots like a bird caught in a briar, though there was no blood. Tor thought of how the roots had burrowed

537

through the flesh of his shoulder and his thigh. There had been no pain, but that hadn't made it any less horrifying. The boy was pale, the skin on his face grey and stretched. As they stared at him, he turned his head towards them, although this seemed to cost him a great deal of effort.

'We feed them, and bathe them, and take away their waste.' Highsun's voice now was almost tender. 'There is always someone here with them, from the moment they take up the roots.'

'Why did you do this to them?' demanded Noon. Beyond the boy was an older woman, her hair long and grey and her flesh sagging. She did not look up at them; Tor did not think she was capable of it. And there were more. Wasted figures pinned to the walls, around twenty that Tor could see, and some of them, he saw, were very young indeed – children, their bodies riddled with the green barbs. The smell of the place was making it difficult to breathe.

'The Poisonless are chosen as babies,' said Highsun. The woman sounded less sure of herself than she had done. 'And given to the roots.'

'Take them down,' said Noon. 'Take them all down right now, or I swear I will burn this whole fucking village down.'

'She can't,' said Fallow. He had edged to the side of their group with his head down, not quite looking at the figures on the walls. 'They die if they are pulled away from the roots. Once they are infested they can't live without it.' He tugged on his beard. 'That's what happened to my sister.'

'You should not have tried to take her back,' said Highsun. Even in the dim light, Tor could see that her face was flushed. 'You killed her, Fallow, not the roots. But you wouldn't listen, and now you bring more lies here.'

'I don't understand.' Noon moved deeper into the cavern, approaching the roots and the people trapped there. Tor wished that she wouldn't. He did not want to look any closer at them,

538

but he was drawn there alongside her. 'Why do this at all? What's the bloody point of it?' She paused. 'Are you telling me these poor bastards have grown up like this?'

'They are chosen.'

'It's the dreams,' said Fallow. 'The dreams tell them that this is what they should do. Every one of them hears the same message. Except me.'

'Noon, look.' Despite his own crawling horror, Tor had moved closer to one of the prisoners on the wall. It was a woman in her middle age, although it was not easy to tell; her legs were stick-like, and the face she turned on them was sunken and loose, as though she'd lost her teeth. On her right arm, in a patch of skin clear of bristling root ends, there was a clear, almost surgical cut. It had been covered over with a balm of some sort – he could just about smell it, beneath the other smells in the cavern – but it was obvious enough to anyone who had spent much of his life making similar cuts in flesh. There was also a small clay bowl on the floor, and in it was a slim glass tube, narrower at the top and delicately etched with an interlocking pattern of leaves. At the sight of it all the warmth seemed to drain from the dark space.

'A cut here in the arm would be an easy place to draw blood from. And this,' he gestured to the bowl, 'this is a blood tube. They were very fashionable during the Carrion Wars, and we crafted many ornate ones – it was the graceful way to take blood from a human. Whether they were willing, or constrained somehow. I haven't seen one in hundreds of years. When the crimson flux came, most of them were smashed or sold.'

He turned to Highsun. 'Arnia and Micanal come here, don't they, and feed on these people? They drink their blood.'

Noon frowned. 'But the crimson flux . . .'

'The roots clean the blood somehow. Make it safe. That's why you call yourselves the Poisonless, isn't it? Because the blood of these hopeless creatures will not poison *them.*'

539

'The Lady Arnia comes most often,' said Fallow. 'Every day, if she can. It's why there are so many of them. She has a large appetite, and they need many Poisonless to let the others recover. The other, Lord Micanal, comes rarely. He takes only a little, and does not stay long.'

Highsun's mouth twisted. Beyond her, the two attendants were watching with slack, shocked faces.

'It's our purpose,' she said. 'Through us, the last of the Eborans live on.'

'They aren't the last!' Noon gestured viciously at Tor. 'Does it look like they're the last? You've been lied to, and you've eaten it up. Can these poor people even speak? What lives do they have?'

'They can't speak,' said Fallow. His face had been rigid with anger, but now it softened, his mouth becoming loose under his beard. 'Something in the roots keeps them from that. When I saw my sister, she looked at me, but she looked through me. It was a cold thing. Something else infests them.'

'I should kill you all for this. Burn this whole fucking place down.' There was a flat, dangerous light in Noon's eyes. Tor almost thought he could see the dragon looking out of them. 'It's a prison, full of innocent people, *children*, and you let those monsters use them.'

'Noon—'

'Their own families have done this to them. At least the Winnowry are cruel strangers. Do you take babies from their mothers? Do they even get to name them?'

'Noon, these fools aren't responsible. At least, not entirely.' He rubbed his hands against his jacket. The place felt grimy, and he too had a strong compulsion to use his sword on the lot of them. 'I think it's Arnia. She is a skilled dream-walker, and I believe she has been manipulating them over hundreds of years, over generations. She must have brought the ancestors of these people here in their ships, when the Golden Fox expedition

540

first crossed the sea. It was probably just a fall-back, something to have if this mythical place failed them. But then, they found something else.'

'I don't understand,' said Highsun. 'What do you mean, a dream-walker?'

'We can't let this go on, Tor.' Noon's hands were balled into fists at her side. He could almost smell the winnowfire waiting to jump from her fingers. 'This is worse than a prison!'

'Highsun, when did you last see Arnia and Micanal? Was it recently? Do you know where they might be now?'

The tall woman did not answer immediately. Instead, she was staring at the wall of prisoners behind them. To Tor she looked like a woman standing on black ice, about to plunge into something unknown.

'Yesterday,' she said eventually. 'Lord Micanal has not been here for some months, but Lady Arnia was here yesterday. She . . . she feasted greatly. I do not know where she is now.'

'It doesn't matter,' said Noon tersely. 'We should stop this, and then leave. Burn the whole island down, for all I care.'

'No.' At her furious look, Tor shook his head gently. 'I need answers, Noon. If they found this method for cleansing human blood of whatever causes the crimson flux, then where are the other Eborans? Arnia and Micanal did not come here alone. And I don't believe their travelling companions all died of that disease. Which means they lied to us.'

To his surprise, the witch laughed – it was a dry, strangled sound.

'Don't you get that yet? This whole island is a place of lies.'

He looked back once more at the prone people on the walls. Men, women and children caught like flies in a web, and feasted on by monstrous creatures. All at once, it was very easy to see why the people of Sarn hated his kind.

'Come on. They will not have left the island, and we have Vostok and Kirune to help us search.'

51

The journey back seemed faster to Noon, and she felt as if they walked in a nightmare. The vivid trees and plants, with their vibrant leaves and petals, were alien and hostile, one more part of this island that was false, a strange tropical paradise hidden in the midst of a cold ocean. Within her, the anger that had been slowly seething since they had arrived was a cauldron of rage, and periodically she took deep breaths to calm herself, to keep it inside. It was like the winnowfire, almost; a pressure within her chest and stomach that demanded to be released. She tried instead to focus on what would come next – soon, they would leave and travel back to Ebora, and leave this cursed place behind – but each time the images of the Poisonless would reassert themselves. A child's foot, utterly clean and painfully soft where it had never touched the floor; a twisted green root erupting a finger's breadth away from the dimple of skin that was someone's navel; a wasted arm hanging loose and boneless; clouded eyes rolling away from lamplight; the stained floor where years of waste and food had been dropped and inadequately cleaned. And the silence. So many stolen voices.

Inevitably, she thought of the Winnowry, women growing

old and wasted in the shadow of the Sisters' contempt and disgust. Faces covered in ash, the shame and the damp.

'Are you all right?'

Belatedly, she realised that she had been breathing hard. Tor looked ashen in the bright morning light, his face uncharacteristically grim and drawn.

'No. Are you?'

He shook his head. 'I wish we'd never come here.'

They didn't speak again until they emerged into the clearing. At first, Noon thought they were alone, until Vostok abruptly emerged from behind one of the houses, the limp form of Micanal dangling between her jaws.

'Fire and blood! Vostok, what . . .?'

The figure stirred weakly, and the dragon spat him onto the ground. The Eboran was covered in mud, his fine robes brown and sodden with it.

'I have found our host,' said Vostok. 'Micanal the Clearsighted claimed at first to know nothing of what we found on the far side of the island, and attempted to laugh off the idea that Eboran history is a fabrication, but eventually conceded that he had, in fact, spoken to Eeskar, as you have.'

'She tried to drown me.' Micanal was getting very slowly to his feet. 'A war-beast, laying its claws on an Eboran.'

'I did not *try* to do anything,' said Vostok. 'If I wanted your lungs filled with river water, they would be.'

'I was attempting to find the amber tablets.' Having gained his feet, Micanal was trying to brush some of the mud from his heavy robes. In any other situation, Noon reflected, it would have looked comical. 'It is right that you should have them, after all. And then you can return to Ebora.'

'He was hiding.' Vostok came forward, nearly knocking Micanal to the ground again. 'What is it? What else have you discovered? I can feel the horror nestling in you, bright weapon.'

'Prisoners,' said Noon. Gratefully, she passed her arms

around Vostok's neck and hugged the dragon briefly. Her strength was like a warm fire on a freezing night. 'Micanal and his sister have kept human prisoners here, feeding off them and torturing them, like parasites. Micanal, where is Arnia? I want to have a word with your bloody sister.'

'Oh no. Not that. Of everything . . .' Micanal passed a hand over his face, and age seemed to settle over him like a shroud. 'Of all the terrible secrets here, I had hoped you would not discover that one.'

'How could you do it?' Tor was fidgeting with his sword belt. Where Micanal looked older, he abruptly looked younger; a child realising that his parents were not gods after all. 'You saw the Carrion Wars, Micanal, you even wrote about them. Painted what happened there. How could you revisit that horror on more humans?'

'It was Arnia.' When Noon made a noise of disbelief, he held up his hands. 'She brought them with her, in one of the ships. She told me she was bringing servants from the plains, and I shrugged it off – Arnia has always been fond of her comforts, and I understood that this would be a difficult journey for her. With all the chaos of travel, of readying ourselves to leave, I did not realise that she had brought many more humans than I had guessed. The others who came with us did not know either – perhaps only the captain of our ship knew the true number.' Micanal sniffed. 'They were kept in the hold, with cargo.'

'Did they come willingly?'

'Yes, or she said they did. Being an Eboran servant was not such a terrible life, and we firmly believed that we would be sailing into a new golden age for our people. But it was not. It was something else entirely.' Micanal shuddered all over. 'From what Vostok has said, you have been there, and you've spoken to . . . *them*. To the *Aborans*. Tormalin, you must understand what such a revelation did to me. To our company.'

Vostok blew hot air down her snout. 'It made you a liar and a thief, it seems.'

'I lost my mind,' Micanal said simply. 'There was no new Ygseril for us to care for, and no sap to heal us. Worse than that, we were a by-blow, an accident of science, of no great interest to the people who had created us. Our storied history was a joke, made worse because I knew we had left behind the rest of our people to die in agony. We faced the end, even as we discovered that our beginning was a sham.' Micanal sighed, and passed muddy hands over his scalp. 'I wandered for a long time, not seeing or thinking. When I returned to my senses, Arnia had had her own conversations with Eeskar, looking for ways to make our existence tenable. She is, in her own way, deeply pragmatic, and she and Eeskar had found a way to make human blood palatable. By the time I had discovered why she had truly brought them, she had already twisted them into what they are now.' He took a shuddering breath. 'The followers who came with us had much the same opinion as you, I'm afraid. They had lived through the Carrion Wars, and had no wish to live at the expense of humans. There was . . . a confrontation.'

'You killed them?' Tor shook his head slightly. 'You mean you killed them? Those people trusted you!'

'She summoned the Aborans' monsters. Eeskar gave her a connection to them, and they . . . I had to stand with my sister. She has been my blood since the very moment I first opened my eyes.'

'What about the tunnel on this side of the island? Arnia said it was your project.' Noon watched the old man's face carefully, but he just shook his head.

'I thought there could be a way around it, a way for them to survive the roots, for it to be something they would only have to suffer temporarily. I tried, but the roots are so invasive. Human flesh ultimately cannot survive their removal.'

'And do you also walk in their dreams?' asked Tor.

'No, that was always my task. And I enjoyed it.' Arnia appeared from the trees, Kirune close behind her. She looked serene, her skin lustrous and shining, and Noon wondered if she had visited the Poisonless after they had – she did not seem surprised to see them, or concerned at their conversation with Micanal.

'You admit it, then? That you manipulated them?' Tor gripped the hilt of his sword. 'Not enough that you make them prisoners and drink their blood, you warp their minds too.'

'Oh please. You of all people have no place in pretending to be righteous. You drink the blood of humans too.' Arnia smiled and tipped her head to one side, so that her black curls tumbled over her shoulder. 'The skill of dream-walking has always been undervalued, I think. We never prized it in the same way we did art, or music.' She shot a narrow glance at her brother, and then shrugged. 'It's an incredible tool, but we use it as a way to pass the time. I'll admit, it has been some-what monotonous, pottering around inside the heads of humans for hundreds of years. They are so tiny in their outlooks, and so limited.' She looked at Noon and grinned. 'But you have seen the results for yourselves. The Poisonless regard us as gods, and live their entire lives serving us – and when they die, their children do the same.'

'You are monsters.' Noon's mouth felt awash with bile, but Arnia shrugged. Kirune had circled around the Eboran to move next to Tor's side.

'Do you think we care what you think of us, human? You people have always thought we were monsters. Why should we not take the title, and make it our own?'

Micanal bowed his head at that, but said nothing.

'You're no better than me. In fact, according to the weird six-legged thing Tor spoke to, you *are* me. Just humans who've been warped into something else.'

At this, Arnia lost her sneering smirk. 'Leave now,' she said. 'Take your false war-beasts with you and go. There's nothing you can do here. But Tormalin, you should stay. Stay with us. I know you wanted what I offered you – I felt it from your dreams, and from your body. Just think what I can give to you! Here, you can be young and strong forever, and never risk the crimson flux.'

Knowing she would regret it, Noon glanced up at Tor, and saw the guilty expression that flashed across his face. Something had gone on between them that she did not know about, and on the heels of that revelation she caught a murmur from Vostok – not of triumph, as her predictions were proved correct, but of sorrow. Somehow that was even worse.

'There's nothing for me here.' Tor pushed his hair back from his face. 'Ebora might be more or less dead, but we do have some standards.'

Arnia's composed expression crumbled into one of disgust. For a strange moment, Noon thought she might actually spit at Tor, but instead the woman flapped a hand at him dismissively. 'Get out. Leave my brother and me alone, then. Go back to your war and your disease and your deaths.'

Noon touched Vostok's neck and took a little of the dragon's life energy. It clouded her own hurt, softening it like a several glasses of wine all at once. She grinned.

'Or, I could kill you.' She stepped forward, and summoned twin gloves of green fire around her fists.

'Noon . . .' She felt Tor's hand brush at her arm, and she shook it off. Much closer and more immediate was Vostok's satisfaction. *Yes, shining weapon.*

Arnia and Micanal were backing away from the fire, and that was also satisfying.

'What? Do you think I will leave here and allow you to continue treating those people like slaves? Leave their children as food for you?' Noon laughed, and let the fires creep a little higher. It made so much sense. It was *right* that they should die for what they'd done.

'Noon!' This time Tor grabbed her arm and shook it, and she saw the white monsters from the Seed Carrier emerging from the trees on both sides of them. Their long necks weaved and danced like snakes, and their sharp teeth were bared in the sunshine. The sheer strangeness of their forms wiped all the building triumph from her body, and the winnowflames stuttered.

'The Aborans might not care much for us, but Eeskar is curious enough to speak to me,' said Arnia. 'We've worked together over the years. He was interested to see what the roots could do to human bodies. He's not interested in letting that experiment go just yet. So, he allows me to summon his creatures, just as he did when Micanal's idiotic friends tried to turn against me.' The Eboran woman gestured to the monsters, and they swarmed in at once – almost instantly they were surrounded. 'I gave you the chance to leave,' shouted Arnia. 'Remember that!'

Noon scrambled for Vostok's back, but the seed-monsters were alarmingly fast. Jaws closed around her boot and yanked her back down into the dirt, while Vostok whirled, her mouth boiling with violet flames. Tor had been luckier, and he and Kirune were in the air, circling above. Noon caught a glimpse of his face as he leaned over the war-beast's side, and then she was being dragged rapidly through the mud. A second later, and the air was full of fire the colour of an eventful sunset, and several of the creatures screamed. The monster dragging her sunk its teeth in and her foot lit up with bright, burning pain.

'Bastards!' With some difficulty she twisted around and sent a surge of green flame towards the long-necked beast. Her attack was narrow and focussed, and she watched with satisfaction as its smooth white skin turned yellow and then black, but it fell forward over her legs and her own fire licked dangerously against her trousers. Yelping, Noon rolled herself forcefully in the mud and felt the cold muck extinguish the flames, but then another of the monsters reached down for her, jaws gaping. She had a glimpse of Vostok behind it, and the sight chilled her blood; the dragon was covered in the white monsters, and despite her considerable size and strength, they were keeping her down on the ground – one of them, she saw, had ripped out chunks of the feathers from her wings, which were now falling down around them in a soft rain. Outraged, Noon sent a ball of flame directly into the maw of the monster gaping at her, only to be knocked to the ground again.

She had lost sight of Arnia and her brother, but Kirune swept down from above and she saw Tor's sword slicing through the monsters, a lethal silver blur, and then they were down in the clearing amongst them, Kirune lashing out with claws and teeth. Noon blasted the monsters nearest to her, the heat from her own fire pushing at her skin. With Vostok, Kirune and Tor all on the ground and in the midst of the monsters, she could not use the fire as she had done within the Seed Carrier itself – not without potentially killing her allies.

'Tor! Help me free Vostok!' Tor turned at the sound of her voice and without a second's hesitation jumped down from Kirune's back and ran towards the dragon, his sword dealing death as he went. Noon joined him, and with as much care as she could, threw her green flames against the monsters that were suffocating her dragon. One by one they fell away, burning, but more were swarming through the forest all the time, and it was clear they would soon be overwhelmed if they couldn't get back into the air.

'Get on Kirune and get away,' Tor snapped at her. He had his sword embedded in the neck of the nearest creature, and his face was set and furious. Ignoring him, Noon pressed her hand to the flank of the nearest creature, and ignoring her repulsion at the touch of its unpleasantly smooth skin, attempted to rip the life energy from it. The energy came in a rush, and it was unlike anything she had felt – slow and heavy and sharp, more like the energy of a plant than an animal. Something about it filled her with a kind of horror, and then beyond that she sensed something else. The creature was pressed next to another of its kind, skin to skin, and that was next to another. It would be so easy to just reach, and then take . . .

Noon jumped back, her hands held away from her. She had been filled with an icy black terror that had nothing to do with the chaos around her, and it was difficult to think, let alone fight. A long, muscular neck looped around her waist, pulling her towards a waiting pack of monsters, but her head was full of the smell of plains' grass, and the sound of the wind.

'Noon!'

She blinked once, coming back to herself. Tor was trying to reach her, his face wild with panic, while Vostok reared up, attempting to shake off the monsters that were clinging to her, and somewhere behind her she could hear Kirune roaring his displeasure. Noon let go of the energy that had been nestling in her chest – gladly, as it had been sitting there like a fat, oily snake – and the seed-monsters that were around her were abruptly blown into steaming, smoking chunks. She staggered, momentarily disorientated, only to see more of the things streaming out of the trees towards them.

And then . . . they all stopped. They paused as one, as if waiting for something, and Noon realised she had been hearing another voice under all the chaos. Slowly, she turned and peered through the smoke to see Micanal standing amidst the white bodies, with Arnia kneeling in front of him. He had hold of her hair in one fist, a sharp whittling knife held at her throat.

'Stop it,' he was saying. 'Command the monsters to leave.'

550

Arnia curled her lip, her beautiful face finally ugly in its outrage. 'Coward. You were always too weak, Micanal, too much of a dreamer. You would choose their lives over ours? You would die here, wasting away into nothing?'

'By the roots,' said Micanal. 'Yes, gladly. I choose that gladly.'

In a jerky, violent motion, he cut his sister's throat. Black Eboran blood spurted from the slash, and Noon saw the surprise and outrage in the woman's eyes before her brother pushed her down into the dirt. There were tears streaming down his lined face. He dropped the knife, and as if in response to that, the seed-monsters also fell, as if suddenly lifeless.

'What have you done?' shouted Tor. He stumbled his way across the fallen bodies of the seed-monsters, but it was clear the woman was already dead. She lay in an ever-increasing pool of her own blood; to Noon it looked like ink. With shaking hands, she rubbed at her eyes.

'It's the only way,' said Micanal. He bent to his sister's body and stroked her hair, pulling it gently through his fingers. 'Those humans are free now, and I can grow old and die. That's all I ever wanted to do, once we knew the truth. But I couldn't leave her alone, not here, in the shadow of our broken history. She was my sister. How could I ever leave her, alone?'

Noon looked at Tor in time to see an anguished expression pass over his face, and then it was gone.

'For what it's worth, Micanal, I am sorry. I'm –' He lifted his arms, then dropped them to his sides. 'I'm sorry that we even came here.'

Noon pulled her hands through her hair, feeling it stand up stiff and untidy with sweat. 'Come on,' she said. 'Let's get out of this shit hole.'

Despite their eagerness to leave, it was a few days before they were ready. Both Noon and Vostok had sustained some injuries in the fight, and Tor was keen to take supplies with them that weren't dried salted meat. Noon, without much guilt, spent some time gathering food and drink from the dwellings, and Tor filled one of their bags with fresh fruit from the surrounding trees. They didn't see much of Micanal. He took Arnia's body away and presumably buried it somewhere, and then he kept out of their way until the day they started to attach their travel bags to the harnesses.

The old man appeared out of the trees, a heavy-looking sack in his arms. Noon stepped back from where she was tightening the belts around Vostok and freed up her arms, half expecting a fight, but Tor waved her back.

'I thought you should have these,' said Micanal, passing the sack to Tor. 'It's why you came here, and perhaps some good should come of your disastrous visit.' He glanced uneasily at Vostok, who was watching him closely. 'If they help to bring your war-beasts some sort of connection, or peace, perhaps I will have achieved something after all.'

Tor pulled a long, golden object from the bag and held it up to the sunlight, where it glittered and glowed with an inner fire.

'The amber tablets. You had them all along?'

'No.' Micanal's lips twitched into a smile that lasted only an instant. 'I really did throw them in the river. I was in quite a melodramatic mood that day. I suspected that Arnia found them, and had hidden them away for her own purposes.' He sighed. 'Sometimes I fear that I did not understand my sister at all.'

'I know that feeling,' said Tor.

'But she only ever had a few hiding places, and I knew them all, so I went and had a look. I hope my last great work is useful to you, Tormalin the Oathless.'

Noon felt Vostok stir behind her, and she waited for the dragon to speak, but in the end she turned her head away. Micanal left, and she did not see him again.

* * *

552

There were some final visitors before they left. Vostok and Kirune had gone to fly one last circuit around the island, when Highsun and Fallow emerged from the trees, shading their eyes against the sun. To Tor, both of them looked gaunter than when they had last seen them, and the woman looked almost frail, as though something vital had been stripped from her in the last few days. Noon offered them some of the sour wine they had gathered, and Tor did not miss the sardonic look Fallow gave the bottle: his people had made it, after all.

'The dreams have stopped,' said Highsun, once they had all shared a glass. 'I don't know, really, how to explain what that's like to you. A presence, a reassuring voice that has been with us forever, is now gone.'

'Arnia is dead,' said Noon. 'She was the one who was manipulating you.'

Highsun nodded, gazing into the bottom of her glass. 'I assumed so. Did you kill her?'

There was a note of accusation there, but when Noon shook her head, Highsun seemed willing to let the matter go.

'And Lord Micanal?'

'He is still around,' said Tor. 'But I doubt he will be bothering you much from now on.'

'It is a hard time for the Poisonless,' said Fallow. 'For us, I mean. With the dreams gone, we've lost the backbone of what we were. Worse than that, is realising what lies we have eaten.'

'Lies that *you* never believed,' said Highsun sharply. 'And we exiled you for it, fools that we are.'

Fallow touched her arm. 'That doesn't matter anymore. We have spent centuries toiling in this place, working from sunrise to sundown to feed and clothe our *gods*. To know the truth of that is painful. But we will survive it. Now everything we make will be for us alone, and we will have good, rich lives, I think.'

'What will you do?' asked Noon. She had finished her glass

553

of wine already, and had poured herself another. Tor wanted to joke with her, to tell her that if she had too much she would fall off her dragon, but there had been an icy wall between them since the confrontation with Arnia: as thin as paper, but cold nonetheless. 'You can leave this place now, you know.'

Highsun and Fallow exchanged a look. 'There is more to tell you,' said Highsun, and here her voice became thick, and she looked at the ground when she spoke. 'Without the dreams, we can see clearly what we have done to ourselves. To our children.'

'As I said, it's been a hard time.' Fallow put his hand on Highsun's arm again, and this time he left it there.

'Whatever it was that kept them silent, it is gone,' said Highsun. 'Those who have been given to the roots began to speak to us – those who could, anyway. Mostly they had difficulty forming words. Because they've all been there since they were babies, you see, and . . .'

For a time, Highsun could only stand, swallowing hard as she struggled to get her sobs under control. Noon's face was a mask.

'Some of them spoke, and some of them cried. A few screamed. They all said the same thing, in truth. That they lived in terrible pain, had always lived in pain – a cage of it that existed inside and outside their bodies. They all wanted it to end.'

Tor took a slow breath and looked away into the trees. It was such a beautiful place. But it was like a beautiful veneer over something rotten and dark. When he looked back he saw the horror on Noon's face, stark and unavoidable.

'And you . . .?'

'It was swift,' said Fallow, and he sounded on the verge of tears himself. 'But it's an act that will have changed all of us who witnessed it. And we will bear those marks into the grave, every one of us.'

'They are not in pain anymore,' said Highsun, firmly, as though to convince herself of the fact. 'But I do not know that we can stay here. It is blood and lies, this island.'

'We have no ships of our own,' said Fallow, in a more business-like tone. 'The dreams always told us that we could never leave, so why would we? We can build our own, perhaps.'

'But it would be helpful to have outside help?' Tor smiled faintly. 'I think, Fallow, with everything my people have done to yours, we can probably find some way to help.' He cleared his throat. 'But it will take time, I have to warn you of that. Micanal and Arnia didn't lie about Ebora so much as embellish the truth. We aren't dead, but we're not exactly thriving either, and we'll probably need to have ships built.' He thought then of Bern, and the Finneral people with their coastal territories. 'Or it's possible we have friends who might help. The Barren Sea isn't kind to ships, but that's not to say we will abandon you out here.'

Fallow nodded. 'Thank you.'

'I'm sorry,' said Noon suddenly. 'I'm sorry for everything that was done to your people.'

Highsun pressed her hands to her cheeks, swiping away the tears that still ran there. 'Don't be,' she said. 'Don't you be sorry. If you hadn't come, we would never have known, and our children would have lived in torture for decades more. So please, do not say you are sorry.'

When they had packed everything, and the amber tablets were safely stored in a pack tied across Kirune's shoulders, the four of them left without speaking. To Tor it seemed that they flew under a new weight, as though tendrils of despair were pulling them back, but as they rose up and above the island, some of that lifted. He pressed his hands into the dense grey fur on Kirune's shoulder and felt a mixture of emotions from the big cat; sorrow, yes, but satisfaction too. They had got what they came for, after all.

As they flew out over the white strip of beach he caught sight of a tall figure on the shore, his brown skin striking against the sand. The man was looking out to sea, and if he saw them as they flew over, he did not raise his hand to them.

52

Jessen hit the ground too hard and half fell, half skidded into a heap. Aldasair loosened the straps on the harness and jumped down, before stumbling forward to press his forehead to the great wolf's neck.

'I'm sorry, my friend. You've done well, we're home now.'

Jessen was panting steadily, too exhausted to speak. Some ten feet away, Sharrik landed with a crash. They had been flying almost constantly, racing ahead of the corpse moon, through days that passed like eye blinks and nights that seemed a lifetime long, stopping only to drink from streams and grab the briefest of naps. They would lose sight of the Behemoth sometimes as weather moved in or they swooped low over valleys, but even then the Jure'lia queen would send out battalions of strange-winged men, who could not keep up but did keep them moving. Finally, they had sighted the familiar sweep of Ebora with her dark forests and dusty city, and at its heart, the silvery branches of Ygseril.

'I just hope we've made the right decision.' Bern climbed down from Sharrik, holding his injured hand out awkwardly as he did so. The big griffin was holding his head down, and there were white foamy gobs of sweat on his furry hide. 'We're bringing them right to where we don't want them.'

'Where else could we go?' It was a discussion they had had many times in the last few days, shouted between their war-beasts and wheezed over handfuls of water. 'We can't hold the corpse moon off by ourselves, and Ebora is the only place we might find help.'

Looking around the palace gardens, he stopped in his tracks. The northern forest was gone, and in its place was a blackened and ash-covered nightmare.

'What has happened?'

Inside the palace, they found Vintage and Eri. The older woman looked harassed, her tightly curled black hair escaping from its ties in little blossoms of chaos, but when she saw them both some of the tension dropped from her face.

'By Sarn's crooked bones, you gave me a bloody fright! Where have you been?' Without pausing for an answer, she grabbed hold of Aldasair and hugged him fiercely, nearly lifting him off the ground despite his height and her injured ankle. 'How are Sharrik and Jessen? Both fine?' She transferred her attentions to Bern, patting his face fondly. 'You both look bloody awful, if you don't mind me saying so. What's happened? Look, we've had something of a situation here, perhaps you should come and sit down.'

It took some time to sort through it all, with each party convinced that their story was the more urgent, but when Bern managed to explain how the corpse moon had been actively pursuing them, and was likely to appear any day over the Tarah-hut Mountains, Vintage grew very grave, and listened to the rest of their account in silence.

'You've been through a lot, all of you.' She sighed and touched a hand to her eye, although Aldasair could not tell if she was crying. 'Bern, I . . . May I see your hand?'

Bern held it out to her, the blue crystal appearing dark and dead in the dim light of Vintage's study. She took his large hand in both of hers, and carefully turned it back and forth.

Very lightly, she brushed her fingers over the place where skin met crystal, and then, curiously, fingered the bones in his wrist.

'This is very deeply embedded. And you say this is how the Jure'lia queen is following you?'

'I'm sure of it,' said Bern. 'There were times when we lost them, and the connection grew very quiet, and there we gained some time. I can feel them now, very far away, but getting closer. It's like someone is singing a song, and I can just hear it.' He raised his hand and looked at it, turning the palm back and forth so that the crystal glittered in the lamplight. 'I can't make out the words, and they are so strange, it makes me sick. Although it hardly takes their poison in my blood to tell them we would come back to Ebora.'

'We had to, Bern.' Aldasair turned to him, feeling a flush of an emotion he was unfamiliar with. 'Where else could we go for help?'

Bern the Younger shook his head slightly. 'As I said on the way back, more than once, I could have led them away. This connection is dangerous, Aldasair. We all know it.'

'My dears, what's done is done. We have to prepare as well as we can, with what we have to hand.' Vintage reached up and tugged distractedly at her hair, trying to push it back under one of the ties. 'I had thought our news was dire enough, but we do still have the war-beast armour Tyranny brought with her. Perhaps our run-in with the Winnowry won't have been a complete disaster.'

'But where is Tormalin? And Noon? Haven't they returned?'

'We're waiting for them,' piped up Eri, who had been mostly silent during the discussion, save for describing Helcate's new acid-spitting ability. 'We've had no word but Helcate can feel Vostok and Kirune, and they . . . well, they're still alive.'

'There is a chance they will return before the Jure'lia arrive,' said Vintage, although she didn't sound convinced, and when

559

Bern took a breath to argue, she spoke over him. 'Think about it. We estimated it would only take a few days of flying to find this secret island of Micanal's. They have been gone much longer than that, yet Helcate reports that they are alive. We can conclude from that, that they have found something out there, and are investigating it. They could be on their way back right now.'

'Lady Vintage,' said Bern, 'I enjoy your optimism, I really do, but I think we are all avoiding the obvious problem. If the Jure'lia come here, and we are not able to defend Ygseril, then all the war-beasts could die. The only sensible thing to do is for me to leave. Sharrik can take me some distance and then return to help you. He won't like it, but I can talk him into it.'

'No.' Aldasair saw the flash of anger in Bern's eyes, and ignored it. 'That is out of the question. And as the only Eboran here, the only adult Eboran bonded to a war-beast here currently, I forbid it.'

Bern and Vintage exchanged a look.

'I agree,' said Vintage quickly. 'And we don't have time to argue about it. Go and get some rest, the two of you, and Eri and I will see what armour will be suitable for Jessen and Sharrik. Go on, go.'

When they were back in the hallway, Bern and Aldasair walked for a distance together in an uncomfortable silence. For Aldasair, it was deeply unsettling; he had no words for what he was feeling, and did not understand his own anger towards Bern. After all, what he had said was correct – it would make the most sense for Bern to lead the Jure'lia away from Ebora, and he was only right to put it forward as their only viable plan. And yet Aldasair was outraged with him for suggesting it, and he knew well from the look on the big man's face that he was equally outraged with Aldasair for forbidding it. As they reached the door to Bern's own quarters, the bigger man turned to him stiffly.

'You know I'm right.'

Bern stood partially in shadow, a hulking form framed in the doorway. What light there was turned his hair the colour of beaten silver, and dusted the curve of his shoulder in moonlight. To Aldasair in that moment he looked like the statue of some forgotten hero, someone from centuries ago who had lain down his life and then been lost to the endless pages of history. It was too much to bear, somehow.

'I will not have you die for us.' Aldasair shrugged. 'There is little else I can say. Ebora might fall, all of Sarn might be taken by the worm people, but I cannot—' He stopped. Bern was a warm presence in the corridor, solid and real in a way he wasn't sure anyone else in his life had ever been. 'I spent so many years doing nothing, Bern. Being no one. I was empty, just a thing for gathering dust, and now I am full of *something*, and if that causes me to make poor decisions, then I will live with it. Or die with it. I don't care.'

Placing his hands on either side of the doorframe, he reached up and kissed Bern firmly on the mouth. The bigger man seemed startled at first, and then responded, pulling Aldasair through into the room beyond. His beard felt scratchy against Aldasair's chin and cheek, and something about that seemed to awaken his entire body – suddenly he could feel the weight of his own clothes, the breath in his lungs, and every inch of his own skin. He gasped, and Bern pulled away. In the dimness of the room he got the impression of almost military tidiness; Bern had made the bed before their trip to Finneral, and the surfaces were clear, uncluttered. A screen had been pushed back away from the window, allowing for the silvery moonlight to flood the room.

'Are you all right?'

Aldasair nodded, not quite trusting himself to speak. Instead, he listened to the new voice inside him that had recently begun to talk, very urgently, about everything he wished to see and do in this room.

Aldasair tugged at Bern's shirt, at his belt, and all sense of their earlier disagreement faded into nothing. Gradually, they lost their clothes, and Aldasair saw that a human's body was not all that different from an Eboran's. Bern was muscular, and he found himself particularly fascinated by the smooth planes of his stomach, the rigid mass of his thighs, and the thick patch of hair – darker than that on his head – that swept across his chest, and existed in sparser whirls across his lower belly and legs. Almost more interesting was the feeling of their bare skin together, and for some time Aldasair found himself lost in that alone, moving and touching in ways that he would have sworn, hours before, were completely unknown to him. When he looked back on that night in years to come he would always see the room in silver and black, a place and a time unlike anything he'd ever known – yet, ultimately, deeply familiar and enormously welcome.

'Aldasair,' by this time Bern's voice was low and rough, tight with need, 'are you sure?'

'I am, but . . . You might have to show me?'

Sex had always seemed to Aldasair to be something done by other people, probably in a place very far away – he imagined it to be something necessary, quick, simple. To his surprise, what he thought of as sex was like a shadow cast onto a wall, while he had completely missed the fire. He and Bern moved slowly at first, the bigger man taking the lead, until quite abruptly Aldasair realised that he could not wait, and they came together swiftly then, urgently – Bern's breath on his neck as sweet as wine, and joy beyond all things. Later, sleepy and yet utterly unable to sleep, Aldasair found himself exploring the bigger man's body again, trailing kissing across his chest and following the dark line of his hair down. When Bern pushed his hands into his hair, breathing in a way that only made his own desire sharper, Aldasair felt a shiver of power move through his body. How had he never known this? How many centuries had he wasted without it?

562

Yet the answering murmur of his heart told the truth; without Bern, he was alone. There was joy in the moment, and it was something they both needed.

The next morning they stood together in the war-beast's courtyard as Eri and Vintage took them through the armour they had acquired from the thief Tyranny O'Keefe. It was difficult to concentrate. To Aldasair the world looked very different in this new daylight. Normal things, like the water glinting in the ridges in an ornate paving stone, or the spider's web tucked secretly under the awning, looked edged in gold, and the air seemed especially clear and sweet. His breakfast that morning had been a simple bread roll with a quick smear of butter, but he had sat looking at it for some time. Did it taste better? He thought it did. And his mind felt clearer too, sharper, as though he had opened a pair of eyes he didn't know he had. He forced himself to look away from the spiderweb to the piece of armour that Vintage was holding up.

'Do you see the claws on the end? They are serrated.' The item appeared to be some sort of metal gauntlet, made from pieces of metal that slotted together to allow for great movement, and there were lethal-looking talons on the end. Vintage twisted the gauntlet a certain way, and the talons slid away into some hidden recess. 'It's outrageously clever, isn't it? I had no idea the Eborans were so fiendish with their armour. In any case, I believe this could be just the job for Jessen, if she is comfortable with wearing something so heavy.'

Aldasair looked to the great black wolf, who was sitting with her tail neatly curled around her forepaws.

'I think I should like it very much,' she said, her amber eyes shining. 'I have often looked at brother Sharrik's talons and admired them.'

Next to her, the griffin puffed out his chest. Helcate was with them too, and the little war-beast had grown significantly even during their short trip. He sat close to the other war-beasts, still dwarfed by them but clearly glad to see his siblings.

'What about me?' boomed Sharrik. 'I was promised a bejewelled harness. Fit for my glory!'

'Yes, well.' Vintage was still limping, the crutch wedged firmly under her armpit, yet she moved around swiftly enough. 'Come and look at this then, you beautiful brute.'

As she took Sharrik to the far side of the courtyard to look at some enormous confection of leather and silver, Eri approached them with an item Aldasair did not recognise.

'I thought this could be useful for you, Aldasair,' he said. His voice was still quiet and he had difficulty meeting his eye, but there was some new confidence in the way he stood, in the way he'd pushed his long, ash-blond hair from his face. 'It's too heavy for me yet, and Bern has his axes, Tormalin has his sword, and Noon has . . . well, Noon has herself. Perhaps you would find it useful?'

It looked to Aldasair like the quiver for a bow and arrow, yet much larger, and reinforced with steel rivets. Inside it were around fifteen narrow metal shafts, each sharpened to a lethal point. Carefully, he took one from the quiver and turned it over in his hands. It was indeed very heavy.

'Vintage says they've been weighted to be thrown, or dropped,' said Eri brightly. 'There were loads of them in the cache Tyranny left behind, but I found the best ones and cleaned them up for you. Agney, the Finneral blacksmith, showed me how to sharpen them too.' He cleared his throat. 'Do you think you can use them?'

'I think they will be perfect.' Aldasair slid the bolt back into the quiver. As functional as it was, someone had seen fit to cover it with an enamelled scene depicting dragons frolicking, each as green as an emerald, and there was a thick leather strap allowing the wearer to fit it comfortably across the shoulders or the chest. 'Thank you, Eri.'

The boy beamed with pleasure, and Aldasair felt a surge of affection for him. When they had first brought Eri here, he had reminded him uncomfortably of himself – of the time he'd spent lost in the corridors of the palace while everything died around him. To see him brighter, even in the face of oncoming disaster, was a reminder that things could get better.

As Eri wandered back to help Vintage wrestle a helmet lined with sharpened tusks over Jessen's snout, he felt Bern touch his shoulder gently.

'I have something for you too.'

He reached to his belt and slid one of his axes, the Bitter Twins, from its strap. When he held it out to Aldasair, he stood looking at it, wondering if perhaps Bern meant to use it to cut something – a lock of hair, perhaps?

'I can't use both of them anymore,' said Bern, a touch sadly. 'The bloody crystal that creature wedged in my hand means I can't grip it properly. So I'd like you to have it –' he paused and cleared his throat, his cheeks turning faintly pink – 'my love.'

'Your axe? I can't take that. The Bitter Twins are your weapon.'

Bern smiled, and any sadness there might have been vanished. 'You will make better use of it than me now, and I know you have the strength in those arms to use it.' He grinned then, suddenly and wolfishly. 'There's no one else I would want to take it.'

Hesitantly, Aldasair took hold of the haft and lifted the axe, thinking of how he had used it without thinking at the Broken Field. Like the lethal bolts, it was heavy, but it felt right in his hand, like he had been waiting to hold it for a long time – or as though it had been waiting for him, somehow.

'The queen will regret following us,' he said.

53

My dearest Marin,

This is my fifth letter to you, and I still have received no reply. I am choosing to believe that you are too busy, or the birds are getting lost, or perhaps the messengers have decided that they have better things to do. If you are busy, I hope it is a safe kind of busy, and not the sort of busy that involves you riding off into the Wild or following a Behemoth to see where it goes. Yes, I am aware this is hugely hypocritical of me. I imagine you rolling your eyes at this letter and it lifts my spirits.

And that is sorely needed. I write this in the few quiet moments I have while friends of mine prepare for a battle they are almost certain to lose. They are good, brave people, Marin, and I dearly hope there is a chance you will meet them when Sarn is a little less lively. As for myself, I intend to accompany them, to do whatever I can.

The world looks ever so dark today, Marin. Do your aunt a favour and keep your own light shining.

Extract from the private letters
of Master Marin de Grazon

The journey back was not eventful, so they did not break their necks to get home. It was a thought that would haunt Noon's dreams for some time afterwards – if they had rushed, if they had urged their war-beasts to fly through the night, would that have changed anything? If they had arrived earlier, could they have avoided what was to come? In the cold light of a bitter morning, she thought not, but when the sun sank and the lamps burned into the small hours, the question was like a stain she could not quite wash out.

It was late afternoon when they reached the stretch of land that she recognised as Ebora; there were the thick, dark forests, lying hot and green under a spring sun that was building in ferocity, and the intricate roads and ruins of the sprawling city. There was Ygseril, a cloudburst of branches above the palace, new leaves glinting and shifting – he was alive, yet inert, silent to them all. Noon raised her eyes to the horizon, taking in the familiar sweep of the Bloodless Mountains, wintery and harsh despite the warmth of the sun, and spotted something that should not be there. Her stomach dropped, and beneath her Vostok jerked with surprise – the dragon had spotted it too.

'Tor! The corpse moon, it's here!'

'What?' Tor sat up in his harness. He had been sullen and moody during the journey, spending the evenings staring at nothing, or glumly cleaning his sword. She saw shock settle over his face as he saw it – an enormous, bulbous green and black and silver mass, hanging in the sky just in front of the mountains. It looked obscene, the sunlight glistening off of its oily flanks.

'Fuck.'

'Vostok, is Ygseril . . .?' The dragon shivered, already beating her wings faster.

'He lives,' she replied tersely. 'But we are in trouble.'

The palace was coming up below them. Immediately, Noon could see all was not well. A huge part of the garden forest

567

was gone, burnt to miserable black stumps, and she could see no tents or caravans on the wide green lawn. There was only one person moving down there, a busy figure on the flat white stones, and as they grew nearer she turned her face up to the sky. Vintage waved frantically at them, her normally cheerful face pinched and grim.

'Tor, we have to land! Follow me.'

Vostok took them down with precision, and only as Noon stumbled out of the harness did she see Fulcor, the great white bat, crouched on the marble paving slabs, her black eyes glinting with curiosity. Vintage had been putting the harness on her, and she wore her crossbow at her belt.

'Could you cut it any finer, do you think?' said Vintage, as Noon hurried over to embrace her. 'Perhaps you'd like to come back in an hour or so, just to make sure it's a properly dramatic entrance.'

'What's happening?' demanded Tor. 'Where are my cousin and the other war-beasts?'

'Bern and Aldasair are already up there,' Vintage extracted herself from Noon and hobbled back to the bat, where she finished busily tugging straps into place. She continued to speak without looking at them. 'And Eri and Helcate, roots damn us all. I couldn't stop them. The boy insisted it was his place to fight, that it was what they were meant to do. I don't care if he's four times my age, he's a child!' She shot a look at them over her shoulder. 'If Vostok and Kirune are carrying anything heavy that isn't a weapon, ditch it now. You will need to be fast.'

Tor nodded once and returned to Kirune, swiftly unpacking their leftover supplies, packs of clothes, and the heavy bag containing the amber tablets.

'Vintage, what is Fulcor doing here? You can't mean to be going up there?' Noon glanced at the older woman's ankle – she was still limping. 'What are you doing?'

568

'Stop asking pointless questions. We have to lead the corpse moon away from Ebora, if we can. Most of Bern's people are in the palace – they have chosen to defend Ygseril, should it come to that – and I've sent most of the others out to hide in the forests, or to run as far as they can, but if the Jure'lia take Ebora now none of them will live anyway. We have to get up there, and we have to fight. Are you listening?'

'I . . . yes.' Noon glanced at Tor, who was already climbing back onto Kirune's back, his sword the only thing he was carrying with him. 'But what happened here? Why has the corpse moon come now?'

'There is no time for that,' said Vostok. The white dragon was looking at the mountains, her long neck outstretched as though she longed to be there already. 'I can see Sharrik and Jessen. They fight fiercely, but they are outnumbered. We must go to them, bright weapon.'

The surge of Vostok's courage was like a dash of cold water to the face. Noon hurried to her side, and began to strap herself back into the harness. Already, her chest felt tight with the powerful need to fight – enemies were on their territory, and they must be forced back at all costs. Vintage had, with some difficulty, wriggled her way onto Fulcor's back, and she was checking her crossbow.

'Oh, by the way,' she said, fiddling with the row of bolts sown into her belt. 'The Jure'lia have a dragon now, apparently.'

'Of course they bloody do,' said Tor.

'How?' asked Vostok sharply.

From the back of the bat, Vintage pressed her lips together, and glanced uneasily at Tor. 'It flies with the Lady Hestillion, so we must assume . . .'

'She has her own war-beast?' Tor twisted around in his harness to look directly at Vintage. 'The pod she took with her has hatched, then?'

'Vostok was right, we don't have time for this.' Noon leaned forward and pressed her hand to the dragon's warm scales. *No other dragon could be as fine or as lethal as you.* 'If they have a dragon, we can assume it won't like us much. Let's go – Aldasair and Bern will need our help.'

Once they were up in the air, both Kirune and Vostok put their heads down and produced a burst of speed that caused Noon and Tor to press themselves flat to the harness. Fulcor, as fast as she was, began to fall behind.

'Go ahead!' called Vintage. 'I will be right behind you.'

Already, the corpse moon loomed larger. It hung over the very outskirts of Ebora, where the foothills of the mountains met the crumbling wall that ran along the southernmost boundary of Eboran lands. Aldasair and Bern were there, and seeing them, Noon felt a surge of emotion wash through her that she couldn't quite identify – she didn't even know if it came from her or Vostok. Both the warriors and their mounts wore armour; glittering, spectacular armour unlike anything Noon had ever seen. Sharrik in particular looked like a flying fortress; he wore a helmet that glinted silver and gold in the sun, with a pair of jewelled horns bursting forth from the forehead. The helmet left his beak free, and she saw him roar, catching a glimpse of his sharp purple tongue. The harness he wore was covered with flat metal plates, interlocking like the scales of a fish, and Bern wore a matching chest plate – together they were a scene straight out of a storybook, one of the more fanciful books of tales Noon's mother had saved for bedtime reading.

Jessen's armour was less extensive, and immediately Noon saw how this was sensible – Sharrik was a hammer, heavy and strong, but Jessen was a thin-bladed knife, fast and precise. The great wolf's armour was something like a wiry silver vest covered with smaller interlocking silver plates – these ones were round, like coins, and the centre of each sported a dot of white enamel. The vest was clearly very flexible, reaching up and around the wolf's throat without impeding her movements, and on each leg she wore a gauntlet rimmed with claws like daggers. Aldasair too looked like a knight from an ancient tale, his white enamelled armour catching the sun and shining like it was ablaze. As she watched, he pulled a long, thin object like a miniature spear from a quiver at his hip and threw it, overarm. The spear soared through the air and sank into the chest of a grey humanoid figure with huge bony wings.

'Fire and blood, what is that?'

There were loads of the flying men, and they were strange half-formed things. With no faces to speak of and no hair they looked like they had been patted together from pieces of gangrenous dough, but they flew around the Behemoth like flies around a pile of dung, and lunged periodically at Bern and Aldasair, who were struggling to reach the corpse moon at all. Helcate appeared, previously hidden behind the bigger war-beasts, and Noon found herself grinning at the sight of him despite their dire situation. The little war-beast had grown, and was using his wings with confidence, his blue eyes bright and sharp. On his back Eri looked truly alive, his whole being bright with the joy of battle, his mouth open and shouting his triumph. They also wore armour, although it was less extensive and looked more decorative than the others: scarlet gems the size of fists glinting from the sides of Helcate's bronze harness, while Eri's mail shirt looked as bright as blood with its red enamel. As Noon watched, Helcate opened his mouth, the muscles in his long neck clenching, and he spat something, too swiftly for her to make out. Whatever it was, it landed on the nearest flying man and the thing *sizzled*, like fat in a hot pan, and dropped towards the distant ground.

Noon heard a shouted oath from Tor, and turned to see him staring at the little war-beast in shock.

'No time for bafflement, bright weapon,' said Vostok. 'We must join the fray.'

'Let's do it.'

Vostok dived into the thick of the action, parting the flying creatures with a stream of violet fire. Noon took a little of the dragon's life energy and threw a stream of winnowfire like a whip at those that had failed to get out of the way. From above and behind them, she heard shouts of greeting from the war-beasts and their riders. For a moment, her vision was filled with thick grey fur and then Kirune was up and past them, barrelling into a flying creature that had been falling on them from above. He bent his head to the thing's neck and tore its head away from its body, letting the rest of it drop.

'What's the plan?' shouted Tor. He was half standing in the harness, his sword in hand. 'Anything we should know?'

'We need to drive it back, away from Ygseril,' Aldasair shouted back. 'And it's very good to see you!'

Vostok swept up, her powerful wings lifting them easily away from the main milieu. Other creatures were scuttling over the surface of the corpse moon, things with too many black legs and other things that looked like larger versions of the burrowers, some as large as dogs. Noon grimaced, wondering if these were new, or if they simply hadn't seen them before.

'New abominations,' said Vostok. 'Something has changed within the old enemy.'

'It doesn't matter,' said Noon, leaning forward. 'I'm quite happy to burn anything it vomits up.'

The dragon folded her wings and they dropped towards the oily surface of the Behemoth. Noon reached out her arm and just before they came into contact with it, she released a rolling sheet of green flame at the burrowers and mothers closest to them. They popped and sizzled and curled up on themselves, and she laughed aloud.

'Dragon soul, witch-fire,' Vostok said. 'If we had known then . . .'

Noon opened her mouth to ask what she meant, but Sharrik and Jessen raced past them, flying in tandem. A particularly large burrower had leapt from the corpse moon onto Helcate, and Eri was gamely trying to fight the creature off with a short sword. Sharrik cinched the thing between his claws and flung it away from the smaller war-beast, and Jessen caught it between her jaws, savaging it.

A flicker at the edge of Noon's vision let her know that Vintage had arrived on the back of Fulcor. The big white bat was hanging at the edge of the aerial battle, and Noon felt a stab of anxiety – they couldn't possibly watch over Vintage at all times, and the older woman would be in enormous danger – but as she watched the scholar lifted her crossbow and neatly took down one of the flying men that were getting too close. Catching Noon's eye, she raised the weapon in a salute, then seemed to stiffen in the saddle, her gaze fixed on something behind Noon. She turned in the saddle, just as Bern began shouting, 'Watch out! Get back!'

A hole was appearing in the side of the corpse moon, puckering open to reveal some busy inner darkness. Blue light flickered deep inside it, like the spitting lightning from a summer storm on the plains, and something large moved towards the light. Something very large.

'Oh, *fuck*,' said Noon.

A monster was climbing out of the corpse moon.

Tor felt a tingle travel down his back as all the hairs on the back of his neck stood up. This, he thought, was what it was like to be a tiny prey animal – a mouse or a bird perhaps – when the owl flies over. Or, his mind supplied viciously, this was what it was like to be a defenceless human when the Eboran hunting parties rode forth during the Carrion Wars. The dragon pulling itself out of the newly opened aperture was twice the size of Vostok, and bulkier, with enormous muscled shoulders and a thick, wedge-shaped head. It was black and purple and in some places, particularly the stiff serrated plates that protruded from its back and neck, it was an oily, dark green – the same colour as the corpse moon. It rolled eyes that were milky and white, yet evidently it could see, as it turned its head to follow Vostok as she shot past, and its jaws fell open to reveal long, dagger-like teeth.

The monster lowered its head and unfurled thick, bat-like wings, and that was when Tor spotted the figure sitting on its back. Wiry and pale, Hestillion was wearing a strange collection of furs and leathers, utterly unlike the beautiful silks she had coveted in Ebora, and she sat poised in the harness, her sharp face intent, like a hawk's. Inevitably, she looked up and they stared at each other, sister to brother. Her eyes, as deep a maroon as his, widened a fraction, but the expression on her face did not change.

'Hest?'

She could not have heard him, but Kirune did. 'She is your blood,' he pointed out, less than helpfully, and then, 'and he is mine.'

Tor realised he was talking about the dragon. 'That might be true, but I don't think they are on our side.'

As if to prove it, the enormous dragon leapt from the side of the Behemoth. It did not move gracefully, but it was hardly slow, and immediately it set off after Vostok. The smaller dragon turned around to face it, and Tor caught a glimpse of Noon's face, partly lit by the glove of green fire dancing around her hand. She looked defiant, and furious, and he felt a strange clash of emotions pressing on his throat; fear for her, and something else that he wasn't about to look at too closely. Vostok opened her jaws and an elegant spear of violet fire shot down onto the larger dragon's upturned head. The monster bellowed, a discordant, deafening roar of outrage and pain. Tor saw it twist its neck to avoid the flames and had enough

574

time to note that it did not seem particularly injured before he and Kirune were hit violently from the side.

Swearing, Tor slashed blindly with the Ninth Rain and felt it sink into something solid. Wrenching his body around, he saw that one of the grey men had landed on Kirune's flank, with another clambering over it, so that Kirune's right wing was restricted. The big cat hissed in annoyance, but Tor already had his sword embedded in the upper arm of one of the grey men. Reaching behind him he grabbed the thing around the throat, grimacing slightly at the faintly sticky touch of its flesh, and yanked it towards him. It was bigger than a human, and its face – what there was of it – was slack and unresponsive. Tor could feel no bones inside the thing, only slightly spongy flesh, so he pulled his sword free and slashed at its throat. It gaped open, a bloodless wound that reminded him eerily of the white monsters that Eeskar had commanded, and he threw it from Kirune's side. The thing dropped out of sight, while the second one jumped away, retreating to a safer distance.

Turning back to the battle, he saw that the Behemoth had stepped up its attack. The large burrowers had unfurled glass-like wings from under carapaces and taken to the air, and a swarm of them surrounded Helcate and Eri, who were on their own. Several of these and a number of the grey men were keeping Sharrik and Jessen from getting any closer to the corpse moon, despite their best efforts – he saw Bern's axe held high above his head, its blade already dark with some unspeakable fluid, while Aldasair was stabbing a flying man over and over with something Tor could not make out. Taking up much of the air space was Vostok and the strange, purple dragon. They were locked in an embrace, two sets of wings beating frantically as each fought to subdue the other. Tor found he could hardly look away from the sight. Vostok seemed small and somehow wiry in the grip of the other dragon, and they snapped and lunged at each other viciously. Several times the enormous wedge-shaped head of the enemy war-beast came perilously close to where Noon was seated, yellowed teeth chomping at the space near her, and Vostok would drive him back, often simply crashing her head into his, or locking her own jaws around his throat.

'Noon!'

She could not hear him. Instead, she was intent on her fight, sending fireball after fireball of hot green flame crashing against the monster's wings, or blasting a funnel of fire directly at its head. Vostok too would roar forth her own flames, but the two dragons were in such close quarters it was clearly hard for her to be accurate. Hestillion, meanwhile, had a sword at her waist but had not drawn it – instead she seemed to be speaking to the dragon, her mouth moving all the time.

Sharrik had broken free of the enemies that had been holding them back, and he shot forward, Bern with his axe at the ready. Without hesitation they flew to the two dragons, Sharrik with his forepaws outstretched, claws ready. Tor saw the war-beast barrel into the monster's side, his powerful beak attempting to get some sort of purchase on its slippery scales, but the dragon's tail swung around and crashed across Sharrik's outer wing. The tail was not long and thin like Vostok's – it was shorter, thick with muscle and serrated plates, and Tor imagined it was like being hit with a log. Bern cried out, almost knocked clean out of the harness, and Sharrik dropped away, his wing held out awkward and stiff – Tor suspected that the big griffin had been stunned.

'We have to help.' Kirune had been leaping from flying enemy to flying enemy, dismembering neatly as he went so that they were followed by a rain of grey body parts, but he raised his head at Tor's suggestion.

'What can we do?' he said, reasonably enough. 'It is too big. If the loud bird cannot take it, how can we?'

Tor shook his head impatiently even as he yanked his sword

from the belly of a flying man. 'All of us together? We have to do something . . .'

The battle had drifted over the foothills until the mountains loomed over them, bringing colder air and the powerful scent of pine trees. Above, incredibly, the sky was still a bright, blameless blue, and Tor felt an irrational stab of annoyance at that; they could all die here, *all of Sarn* could die here, and the oblivious sun would continue to beat down on their broken bodies. All the while, more apertures were opening in the hide of the corpse moon, and through them were streaming a hideous parade of scuttling, whirring abominations.

There was a high, thin cry – more of anger than of fright – and Tor looked back to see the enormous dragon closing its jaws so close to Noon that she had to lean right back in her harness to avoid being bitten in half. Tor saw the problem immediately – she was strapped in so she couldn't fall, but it meant that she was trapped within range of the dragon's considerable bite. She could be torn to pieces in a moment, despite her flames.

'Right, that's it.' Tor sank his hands into Kirune's fur, attempting to convey his own sense of urgency. 'We're going in.'

'Up, up, up!'

Fulcor floated up on an air current, her pinkish wings spread wide. From above Vintage could watch the play of the battle while being mostly removed from it, which was handy because she was almost out of crossbow bolts and many of the things crawling from the inside of the Behemoth looked like they might chew the bolts up and spit them back at her. From above, it was clear they would be overwhelmed soon. They were a tiny force in the face of an enemy that could seemingly produce endless soldiers. Nervously, she slotted another bolt home.

'It's the Behemoth we have to defeat,' she murmured. Fulcor squeaked in response, and Vintage leaned forward to pat the fluffy patch of fur between the bat's ears. 'You are a brave one, aren't you? I hope your baby is all right, my darling.' She took a deep breath, trying to slow the racing of her heart. 'They will wear us down eventually, if we can't wrangle some sort of advantage. It can't just end here, it *can't.*'

Ignoring the various desperate struggles of her friends, Vintage focussed on the corpse moon. Like the Behemoth she and Nanthema had been inside when the Jure'lia woke up, it showed signs of having been inactive for a very long time. It was certainly in better shape than the rusted wreck on the coast, but there were darker patches on the skin that looked like recently repaired holes. She wondered if the surface were thinner there.

'And what of the queen?' she said aloud. 'We know from Bern and Aldasair that she is on board, but she hasn't shown her face, such as it is.'

A roar of outrage from Vostok echoed across the mountains, and Vintage transferred her attention back to the dragons. Kirune and Tor had joined them, the big cat doing what he could to get close enough for Tor to use his sword. It seemed that Vostok had attempted to fly out of the larger dragon's reach, but it had lunged after her and fastened its terrifying jaws around her tail, yanking her back down. For a moment the view was lost in a corona of violet flame, and then when that dissipated and the dragons loomed back into view, Vintage saw that the great brute appeared to be hiccupping. She blinked, trying to figure out what it could be doing: its throat, ringed with muscle and purple scales, was twitching and flexing, and it held its enormous jaws open, revealing a tongue the colour of bad cream.

'It looks like a bloody cat coughing up a hairball!'

It looked amusing for the briefest moment, and then a hot

spark of blue light burst into life deep within its throat. Vintage opened her mouth, to call a warning or shout for help, but before she could, a bolt of blue lightning shot from between the dragon's jaws, striking Vostok in the underbelly and from there branching out around her like a web of veins. Unlike real lightning, it lasted for a good three seconds, and then Vostok was limp in the arms of the giant beast. Vintage saw a flurry of white feathers, swirling madly in the cold air, but she could not see Noon. The larger dragon tipped back its head and roared its triumph – the noise echoed around them, like summer thunder.

'No! Oh no!'

It curved his great neck, clearly meaning to tear the smaller dragon's throat out. Vintage did not know if it could bite through Vostok's tough white scales but the power behind the creature's enormous jaws had to be considerable. Lost and horrified, she found herself raising her crossbow, although she knew that was next to useless.

'Someone help her!'

A bronze shape shot across the battlefield and collided with the purple dragon. It did very little, although the monster did turn his head to see what had hit him. It was Helcate, the small war-beast twisting in the air to bring himself around to face his enemy. On his back, Eri was half standing in the harness, his face set and fierce. He looked older suddenly, and Vintage had a glimpse of the man he would become, handsome and golden-haired. He shouted something, and Helcate opened his own jaws and spat – a steaming stream of acid shot through the air and hit the monstrous dragon across the face, sizzling on impact.

Vintage gasped. The bellow of rage and pain that rolled across them made the dragon's previous roar sound like a polite cough. Immediately, it dropped Vostok, who fell away towards the ground, and lunged after the smaller war-beast.

Fulcor was swooping down before Vintage was aware that she had even given the order. The dragon loomed closer, and she saw that Kirune – who had also taken something of a shock from the blast of electricity – was harrying its wings, attempting to slow it, but already it had a hold of Helcate. Helcate, with his soft fur and velvet muzzle, the more decorative and less useful armour, the only armour that would fit him . . .

'No!'

The dragon closed his jaws around the boney lump of Helcate's shoulder and shook him viciously. There was a howl of pain, as piercing and as terrible as the dragon's roar in its own way, and then the monster was bearing Helcate down to the ground. With no other ideas, Vintage urged Fulcor to follow, and so she arrived in time to see the purple dragon tearing Eri from his harness, while Helcate lay amidst a jumbled collection of rocks and grass and snow. Without really knowing what she was doing, Vintage yanked herself free of Fulcor and stumbled onto the ground.

'Leave him be! Drop him this instant, you big ugly bastard!'

The dragon took no notice of her at all. The scales around its eyes looked discoloured, a splash of mottled lighter purple where the acid had hit, and a clear fluid was running constantly from the creature's eyes. Vintage transferred her gaze to the Eboran riding him. The woman she knew to be Tor's sister was flushed and sweating, and as she met Vintage's eye, her face split into a wide grin – or at least, she bared her teeth. She did not look sane.

'Tell your monster to let him go.' Vintage raised the crossbow and aimed it at the Lady Hestillion. 'You might be strong, darling, but I suspect a bolt in the middle of your forehead would still ruin your afternoon.'

She tried not to look at the limp form hanging from the dragon's jaws. Abruptly she remembered that Aldasair had said the dragon's name was Celaphon; an oddly elegant name for such a beast.

'If you hurt me, he will kill you in an instant,' said Hestillion. She sounded calm, even serene, despite the glistening lines of sweat running from her temples.

In the moment of silence that followed, Helcate raised his head from the ground. The fur around his shoulder was torn and smeared with black blood.

'Helcate,' he said plaintively, and in Celaphon's jaws Eri twitched, his arms reaching for his war-beast. This seemed to trigger something in the great dragon. He dropped Eri onto the rubble and snow, then, turning his head to get a good purchase, he closed his jaws around the boy's torso and pulled up sharply, dragging his teeth through Eri's flesh.

The boy screamed. Mindlessly, Vintage ran, ignoring the pain in her ankle and loosing the bolt as she did so – it *thunked* harmlessly against the dragon's scales and fell to the ground – and threw herself down next to Eri, taking his hand. There was a great deal of blood already, seeping into the knees of her trousers, black and terribly final. The boy looked up at her, his face oddly blank with pain. A stray curl of ash blond hair had stuck to his forehead.

'Eri, look at me, look at me, it will be—'

Suddenly Vintage found she was on her back some ten feet away. Celaphon had knocked her to one side, and now he had his head bent to the ground in a terrifyingly busy fashion, turning back and forth to better savage the flesh underneath him. As she watched, the dragon pressed one enormous clawed foot to Eri's head, and then began to tug at his lower body . . .

Vintage looked at the ground. Stones and mud and tiny blades of grass. Dust and dirt and ice crystals, hard and old and grey, like grit. There were wet noises she didn't care to hear, but no more screaming. She blinked rapidly, willing herself not to pass out. She would die here if she did.

She looked up. There were shapes moving in the sky, a confusion of bodies blurred into shifting masses by the tears that were running freely down her face. The other war-beasts were still up there, she hoped, still fighting. The great dragon Celaphon dropped Eri's corpse and shook his head rapidly, thick eyelids like the scuffed leather on a boot squeezing over his eyes. It was as though he had just remembered the acid on his face, and with the heat of his anger spent, the pain was coming back. Hestillion was speaking again, leaning forward and murmuring soft words into his ear, and abruptly he leaned back and roared again, although whether it was in triumph or rage, Vintage could not tell. His wings unfurled with a dry crack, and he leapt back up into the air, heading back towards the corpse moon.

Gingerly, Vintage got to her feet, wincing at the newly awakened pain in her ankle.

'Oh, my dear.'

There was very little she could do for Eri save to close his eyes. She did so, her hand shaking badly, and then lurched unsteadily to where Helcate lay. Miraculously, Celaphon appeared to have forgotten the smaller war-beast, and although the bite across his shoulder looked painful, the black blood was already running clear. He would live. He lifted his head, looking past her to the mess on the ground, so she took hold of his snout, forcing him to look at her. His eyes were unfocussed, and with a feeling of sick pressure in the centre of her chest she saw that he was trembling all over, like a whipped dog.

'I am so sorry.' She gasped, trying to swallow the sob that threatened to close her throat. 'My darling, I can't . . .' Gently, she lowered her face to press her cheek against his. The fur that tickled her nose was coarser than it had been. 'I've seen some awful things, but this? What terrible times we have come to know.'

A shadow passed over them and Vintage jumped, thinking it must be Celaphon come to finish the job, but it was Vostok, being supported in the air by Sharrik and Kirune. The dragon was conscious, but her head was bowed, and as they landed she stumbled a little, trying to find her feet. Jessen landed lightly behind them, Aldasair sitting up very straight in his glittering white armour, which was now spattered with grey gore.

'What's happening?' called Vintage.

Aldasair urged Jessen forward. 'Celaphon has retreated to the corpse moon – I think Helcate's attack has hurt him more than we realised. Vostok has been badly stunned, she needs to rest.'

'I am fine,' snapped the dragon, some of her old imperiousness seeping back into her voice. 'You fuss over nothing.'

'It is *not* nothing,' said Tor. He had unstrapped himself from Kirune and was climbing up Vostok's harness. Noon, Vintage saw with a little flurry of dread, was slumped forward, her black hair covering her face.

'Noon! By Sarn's blessed roots, is she—?'

'She is unconscious,' said Tor. He put his arm around the witch's shoulder, pushing her hair back to touch her face. Something about that soft movement, the way he bit his lip as he did so, seemed to send a shard of pain into Vintage's heart. 'We need to get her out of here.'

'I felt something. What happened to Eri? Where . . .?' Aldasair stopped. He had seen the sad little corpse, the pieces of it littered on the snow and dirt. Jessen made a panicked, whining noise.

'That fucking bastard,' said Bern. He sounded ill. 'That fucking *bastard*. By the stones, I'll cut him into pieces, I swear it.'

'We failed Eri,' said Vintage, thickly. 'That monstrous thing killed him, killed him like someone swatting a fly.' She stopped,

583

aware that she was veering close to losing control, and there was no time. 'Helcate is injured. We need to get under the trees, find cover and hide if we can, until Noon and Vostok have recovered.'

'There was a cave,' said Kirune. 'I saw it as we came down. It is not far.'

'Vintage, we cannot just hide,' said Tor. 'We are in the middle of a battle! That thing might be resting for a moment, but it'll soon be back, and the corpse moon isn't going anywhere unless we make it.'

'No, Lady Vincenza is correct,' said Aldasair. Jessen had trotted over to Helcate, and was licking the fur around his wound. The Eboran looked up, frowning at the sight of the Behemoth, bloated and strange. 'We need to gather ourselves. And the Lady Noon is one of our strongest weapons, we need her back.' He turned back to them, his handsome face very still. 'Let's get under the trees, quickly now. Kirune, lead the way.'

54

Celaphon was still bellowing with pain. On some level, Hestillion registered it, even understood that it was something she needed to deal with, but she could not quite look away from her hands, and the spots of black blood on them. As innocent as ink.

She had felt it falling on her like rain as Celaphon had shredded the boy between his teeth, and the power and the glory of battle had faded, becoming a distant echo, a conversation happening in another room somewhere, and instead she had felt herself retreating into some inner darkness.

Not the first blood I have shed, she told herself, but that had been some simple wine merchant's boy, a human. This was one of her own, an Eboran child, something she had been quite sure did not exist anymore. When she had seen him flying with his diminutive war-beast she had registered some surprise – an unknown child – but he was an enemy and she was in the midst of battle glory, a feeling very like being drunk. He was something to be defeated. He had not looked like an enemy lying in the dirt, his eyes glassy and his guts looped around his knees.

Hestillion pressed her fingers to her lips, worried that she might suddenly vomit, and somehow this simple physical concern brought her back to herself. Celaphon had landed on the topmost side of the corpse moon, and he was shaking his head back and forth violently, hollering with pain. Taking a deep breath to steady her hands, Hestillion ripped the lower half of her tunic away. It wasn't much, but it was the best she could do. She couldn't see her brother and his comrades in the air, but they must still be close.

'Celaphon, my sweet. Turn your head to me, please.'

She had to repeat herself, finally shouting the words, before he turned around. Letting herself out of her harness, she shuffled closer, trying not to think about how far above the ground they were, or how, if he chose to fly, she would fall and die.

'That's it, good. How are your eyes? Can you see?'

Celaphon dropped his head mournfully. 'They burn! They hurt so much!'

The black and purple scales around his eyes and across his forehead were discoloured, turning a strange mottled yellow. Hestillion could clearly see the splash marks where the acid had hit him.

'Open your eyes for me.'

He did. Thankfully, they did not seem much changed. His eyes, Hestillion reflected, already looked blind. She spat onto the piece of tunic and very carefully rubbed at a section of scales. Celaphon made a noise of discomfort, but did not move.

'Does that help?'

'A little.' He still sounded very sorry for himself.

The discoloration had not changed in the spot where he had been splashed, but a lessening of his pain was a start.

'Well, I'm not sure I have enough spit for this.' She reached out to the corpse moon, feeling along the link to find one of the queen's scuttling creatures close by. The crystal in her chest itched.

The green skin of the Behemoth next to them peeled back,

and a tiny oozing homunculus emerged holding a dun-coloured pod.

'Bring it up here, then.'

The pod was heavy and sloshed satisfyingly in her hands, and when she poured it onto the tunic she saw that it was water – just what she had asked for. Briskly, and more and more aware that the enemy could be retreating, she bathed the dragon's face, taking particular care with his eyes. She could sense the queen quite clearly – watching, tasting their battle glory in small doses, like a wolf lapping at blood. The death of the boy had pleased her.

'An acid-spitting war-beast,' she said aloud. 'That is very rare indeed. Almost as rare as your lightning, my sweet.'

'I don't like it,' Celaphon said, sulkily. 'It is cowardly. It is not my brother. I don't *like* it.'

'Well, I'm not surprised.' An image of the boy's hand, upturned and slack in the dirt, floated across Hestillion's mind. She bit her lip, focussing on the pain. 'We will make them pay, my sweet.'

The cave was really more like a great horizontal crack in the mountain, very wide but not very high or deep. Packed in all together they weren't especially comfortable – Vostok was grumbling the loudest about having to keep her head lowered – but they were certainly invisible from above. Tor took a deep shaky breath and rubbed his hands over his face. Helcate was curled against the far wall, his nose pointing down at the floor.

'Are we all here?' Vintage looked drawn, dark circles under her eyes, and she was back to limping heavily. 'Is anyone other than Helcate injured?'

Tor looked at Noon, who had regained consciousness on their way to the cave. When they had told her about Eri, she had cried aloud, the sound of something wounded, and now she leaned heavily against Vostok with her hair in her face.

'I am fine,' she said, sensing their concerned looks. 'I don't much fancy doing that again, but it's nothing I can't get over.'

Silence pooled between them. Tor realised that he could feel Kirune's sorrow like a great heavy coat, and through that could feel the sorrow of all of them. Helcate most of all was a beacon of pain, his loss like an open wound, and it was making it strangely hard to breathe.

'The poor lad,' said Bern eventually. The big man's face was still wet from the tears he had shed. 'He was so brave.' He shook his head. 'They murdered him, and I felt it.' He looked around at them all, as though seeking an explanation. 'I felt him die. I hoped it wasn't that, but . . .'

'We all did,' said Aldasair. 'It's the nature of the bond between us and our war-beasts. They are bonded to each other, as family, so when they feel the passing, so do we.'

Bern made a choked noise. Sharrik bent his big head and nudged his shoulder. 'Bloody cursed stones, am I ever tired of feeling . . . all of this.'

'We should go, now,' said Tor. 'Sneak off while we still can, hide from them as long as we can. There's just not enough of us. We need to get an army to take down that thing.'

Vintage was already shaking her head. 'And leave Ygseril vulnerable? And what of all the humans and Eborans still living in your homeland? We can hardly leave the remaining war-beast pods, they could still be viable . . .' She seemed to lose some of her bluster at this, and looked down at the ground for a moment. Tor noticed that Helcate had raised his head and was looking at her keenly. 'Besides, there are some factors you aren't aware of yet, my dear.'

To Tor's surprise, Bern stepped forward and held up his hand. A thick shard of blue crystal protruded from the centre of it. Tor blinked.

'What happened? Was this in Finneral?'

'Your cousin and I were captured by the worm people.'

'What?' Noon's head snapped up. 'When? Vintage, why didn't you tell us?'

Vintage flapped her hands at her irritably. 'There was no time.'

'That weird sticky bitch wanted us to be connected to her people,' continued Bern. 'It's that dragon, Celaphon. He's a war-beast, but he's . . . warped.' Bern shook his head and rubbed a finger across his eyebrow. 'By the stones, I'm not sure how to explain all this.'

'You are doing well,' said Aldasair softly. 'And they need to know.'

'Well. Those crystals Vintage saw? There's one at the heart of every Behemoth, and they hold them all together, like the connections in a spider's web.' He laced his fingers together, demonstrating. 'By giving me a piece of this crystal, she caught me in that web. I can hear them, feel them, and they can feel me. When we escaped, the corpse moon followed us across Ebora, no matter where we hid. The Lady Hestillion also had a crystal joined to her body, as did the dragon.'

'My sister? She has joined so deeply with the Jure'lia?'

Bern met his eyes steadily. 'She has, aye.'

'A traitor to her own kind,' said Vostok.

'So you see, we cannot just run,' said Vintage. She had pressed her hands to the side of her face, a gesture familiar to Tor: it meant she was trying to think her way around a particularly thorny problem. 'And we can't hide for long.'

'How then? How can we defeat them?' Tor looked around the cave – he saw a bedraggled bunch, grief and sorrow etched into every face, clear from the curve of every shoulder. Jessen, the great black wolf, had curled herself into a circle on the cave floor, her nose tucked neatly away and her eyes shut. 'We are broken.'

'Eri,' said Helcate.

For a long moment, no one could speak. Tor thought of

the boy and his bucket of bones, and the slow sense over the weeks that he was returning to life somehow – it seemed impossible that he was gone. Eventually, into the silence, came Vintage's voice, sounding much older than her years.

'Oh my darling, I know. I know.' She went to the war-beast and heedless of the bloody wound on his shoulder put her arms around his neck and held him. 'I know, I know.'

'This connection.' Tor's eyes were stinging and there was a great weight in his chest. 'I'm not sure I can do this. I feel Helcate's pain, and it's wiping everything else from my mind. How can we do anything, like this? Losing one of us has destroyed us.'

'You are wrong.'

It was Kirune. The big cat had been silent so far, skulking at the back of the cave. His eyes, as they turned towards the light, flashed a ghostly winnowfire-green. 'We went looking for something that connected us. We did not find it. The amber tablets are not what we needed.'

'Thanks, Kirune. I really wanted to be reminded of that particular failure right now.'

'This pain is not weakness. It is strength.' Kirune padded forward slowly, coming to stand in the midst of them. 'Our grief binds us. Do you not feel it?'

'I do,' said Noon. She lifted her head. 'I can feel you all, sharper than before, but deeper too.'

Kirune shook out his coat. 'The witch understands. Eri was ours. We will not forget him. We will not forget this act.'

'Revenge, then,' said Vostok. The dragon had lifted her head also, almost mimicking Noon. 'Yes, revenge will unite us. We shall all be weapons, forged in the heat of revenge.'

'And love,' added Aldasair. 'Love binds us.'

Tor stared at them all. He wanted to rave at them, he wanted to shake his cousin. He wanted to take hold of Noon and convince her to run with him – they would go to Jarlsbad or

590

Reidn, or somewhere even more distant, and they would hide. Yet underneath all that, he could feel what they were talking about well enough: the raw pain of losing Eri had opened them up to each other, somehow.

Vintage stood up, pushing her hair back from her forehead. Her face was wet, but her eyes, when they met Tor's, glittered with some new emotion.

'The connection is the key,' she said. 'Bones of Sarn be damned, the idiots might just have bloody handed us the weapon on a plate.'

'Vintage, what are you talking about?' Tor's voice was terse, but there was a terrible feeling growing in his chest, and he had a horrible suspicion it was hope.

'We are connected,' she said. 'And so are they. And, thanks to the Jure'lia queen, Bern is connected to them. Do you remember how you escaped, Bern my darling?'

'We pushed our way out,' he said. 'There are parts of the corpse moon that will listen to me.' He grimaced. 'It was bloody awful.'

'If you can get out, then we can get in.' Vintage grinned. 'And I'm fairly sure we can do them a mischief while we're in there.'

'You mean to attack them directly?' Aldasair glanced at Bern, who shrugged.

'I do. The Jure'lia are still recovering – I saw that myself when I was in the air. And she hasn't brought any other ships with her, so angry was she at your escape. We have a very small chance, but I think it's worth taking.' Vintage removed a scrap of fabric from somewhere in her jacket and used it to sweep her hair back from her face and tie it in place. 'Get ready, my darlings. We are going to fuck them up.'

55

Flying with Helcate was a vastly different experience to flying with Fulcor. Vintage noted this as she gritted her teeth, hanging on, it seemed to her, for dear life. As the smallest war-beast catapulted her back into the heart of the battle, she could feel the immense power of his muscles, thrumming like the winnow-line engine, and with each movement her ankle echoed with pain. *I'm riding a near-mythical beast,* she told herself. *Possibly to my death, but even so.*

The others were spread out in a fan, and already the great dragon Celaphon was lifting from his perch on top of the corpse moon, ready to meet them. The other minions of the Jure'lia, the mothers and the burrowers and the strange grey winged-men, were a shifting cloud, like starlings at dusk – only significantly less beautiful. Looking to her side, she saw Sharrik and Bern. The big man's face was set and grim, and his steely determination was reflected in the posture of his griffin. Vintage knew that there were aspects of this plan they were unhappy with. Sarn's broken arse, she was pretty unhappy with it too, but what else did they have?

As the cloud of enemies swarmed down on them with Celaphon just behind, Sharrik ducked abruptly out of their fan formation, and Helcate followed suit. This was the first risk: if they did not drop away cleanly, then everything else would be several magnitudes harder, but Vostok shot forward, engaging Celaphon directly, and as they had hoped, the main force stayed with the other war-beasts. Meanwhile, the two of them flew fast and low, the rugged mountainside below a grey and green blur, and eventually they passed under the belly of the corpse moon. The shadow of it, colder than it should be, covered them like a shroud.

It took them some time to fly underneath, but eventually they came up on the far side, to the place that Vintage could not help thinking of as the Behemoth's arse. There were apertures here, some of which were pinched shut. Others were covered with a pearlescent grey membrane that made Vintage think of a fly's eye, made up of thousands of interlocking hexagons. One of these entrances was very large, several times the height of Sharrik, and she recognised it as the place where the Behemoth could birth its enormous maggots. It was inert currently, but when it was time, the thing would flex and excrete its monstrous offspring. Vintage grimaced. Excrete was the polite term.

'Are you sure you can do this?'

Both war-beasts were hovering outside the membrane. Bern raised his eyebrows at her.

'Stones alive, of course I'm not sure. This was your bloody idea!'

'Yes, well. Here's where we find out, I suppose.'

Sharrik flew as close as he could to the membrane, and Bern leaned as far out of his harness as he could go, the hand with the crystal embedded in it held out towards the Behemoth. He closed his eyes.

In the silence, Vintage listened. She could hear the sounds of battle. Once or twice she thought she heard Tor shouting, and every now and then, a roar. They would have very little time.

Sweat was running down Bern's face, and his hand was

trembling with the effort. Vintage bit her lip, telling herself that he needed to concentrate, but the sense of time passing was like a hand creeping up her back, reaching for her throat. The others could be in serious trouble, could be dead already. Bern and Sharrik might sense their deaths through the link they shared, but she wouldn't.

'How's it going?'

Bern's eyes popped open and he glared at her. 'I'm telling it to open up, that I belong here. But I have to do it quietly, in case *she* hears.'

'Hmm. Can you pretend to be one of her creatures?'

'Pretend?'

'Picture it, in your head. Imagine being that shape.' Vintage paused. 'You must know, better than any of us, what that might be like.'

For a moment, Bern looked utterly dismayed, and Vintage felt a stab of guilt. She had reminded him that he was on intimate terms with a murderous, monstrous enemy. But he closed his eyes again, and this time the membrane did peel back. Quickly, they flew inside. Bern unstrapped himself, then went to Vintage and helped her down. Her crutch was retrieved from Helcate's harness.

'I don't like this,' said Sharrik. 'I should go with you!'

'Sharrik, we've talked about this.' Bern patted the griffin fondly on the smooth black curve of his beak. 'You are too mighty to waste on this part of the mission. You are needed on the battlefield.'

'You have to help Vostok,' added Vintage. She shook her head, adopting an expression of deep uncertainty. 'I don't think she can defeat this Celaphon by herself.'

Sharrik puffed out his chest. 'I am mighty!' he said. 'I will fight, but I will listen for you, brother.'

'We'll call you when we're ready,' said Vintage. 'And take Helcate with you. I'm sure you could use his acid.'

The war-beasts left, and the two humans turned back to the chamber. The walls were an off-white, like parchment, and they appeared to be ringed with huge cords of what looked like muscle. The tunnel was taller than it was wide, the two walls meeting at the top, and there was a sticky residue on the floor.

'How are you feeling?' asked Vintage. The colour had rushed from the big man's cheeks, and the strands of blond hair falling across his forehead looked oddly colourless.

'I have to tell them, all the time, that we belong here,' he said. 'And I have to keep picturing the shape they expect. It's not easy.'

'Well, my darling, I have every faith in you.' She took his arm, and began to gently guide him forward. 'Just between you and me, I've never crawled up a monster's arse before. It's quite exciting.'

Noon gasped and tucked her head in as Vostok rolled through the sky. For a moment, everything was a spinning confusion – she saw clouds under her boot where it stuck out over the harness, saw the mountain passing lazily under her head – and then they were upright again and pulling an arc of violet fire behind them. The dragon called Celaphon came on behind, his jaws open so wide that Noon had the eerie sensation that they could fall straight down his throat and be swallowed whole. She turned around in the harness and sent a pulse of winnow-fire into his cavernous maw – the dragon swallowed it and shook his head as though he had a bee in his mouth.

They were caught within a furious net of action. All around them the minions of the worm people swarmed, but Aldasair and Tor were there, moving constantly to keep them away from her and Vostok. Tor's sword was a blur, cutting through the bellies of the grey men, or severing the legs of the flying burrowers, while Aldasair wielded one of Bern's axes. Noon would never have guessed it, but the weapon suited him, and when she caught sight of him – auburn hair blown back from his temples, crimson eyes wild, white armour glittering in the sun – she realised he looked like every picture she'd seen of the Eboran knights of the previous Rains. Jessen and Kirune were fast and lethal, taking their warriors from fight to fight, while their own teeth and claws plucked enemies from the sky like plums.

And she could feel them. The pain and the grief and the anger was never more than a thought away, and when she touched it, the others blazed into her mind, bright and familiar. *We are united.*

A surge of feeling from Vostok met that thought: pleasure, hope, ruefulness. And on the back of that, anxiety. *We've not won yet. We could still die here, bright weapon.*

As if he could tell what they were thinking – and perhaps he could, Noon thought with a surge of panic – Celaphon slammed into them, his enormous bulk almost striking Vostok from the sky. The smaller dragon twisted at the last moment, turning her body so that some of the force was dissipated, and Noon threw a sheet of winnowfire at Celaphon's wings. He dropped back, but only for a moment, and Noon could feel that the blow had winded Vostok.

'Bastard!' she yelled. 'What sort of creature fights its own family?'

There was a shriek from above, and Noon looked up in time to see Sharrik flying towards them with his wings tucked to either side of his body, as fleet as an arrow. Bern was not there, but that was a good sign – he and Vintage should be inside the corpse moon by now. The griffin struck Celaphon in the chest, and the two tumbled together in mid-air as Vostok turned to rejoin them.

'We take him down together,' cried Vostok. 'Yes, this is as it should be. Wait for me, brother!'

* * *

596

'Are you sure this is the way?'

Bern nodded, and they moved on. So far they had peeled back seven walls, making their way steadily into the heart of the Behemoth. Although Vintage had asked the question, she felt on some level that it was the right direction anyway. She had, after all, made her way to these crystal chambers before – once in the ruins in Esiah Godwort's compound, and once in the broken Behemoth where Nanthema had been trapped. It was simply that it was so quiet and eerie that she felt she had to speak, as though by speaking she were reminding herself that they were alive, and human.

She thought of Nanthema. The last sight she had had of her long-lost love had been her back as she rode away, her long black hair tied behind her and a bag of stolen goods next to her. Perhaps their relationship could never have worked. Vintage felt older and wearier than she ever had in her life, and from that perspective the idea of rescuing and taking up with a woman she hadn't seen for decades seemed faintly ludicrous. But even so, the fact that Nanthema had turned her back on her own people, had even conspired to steal from them with a Winnowry agent, was an insult and an outrage. *Nanthema should be here*, she thought hotly. *Sharing in the risk with the rest of us.* She thought of Eri, and a wave of sorrow moved through her. Eri, a boy who had grown up in complete isolation, had been willing to risk his life for a people he had never known, and he had died for it. With an almost physical feeling of disgust, Vintage felt the reservoir of affection she had carried with her for Nanthema for much of her life harden and twist into something else.

'Hold up.' Bern stopped. They had been moving through a series of small linked rooms, each filled with alcoves studded with faintly glowing fronds. Not for the first time, Vintage marvelled at the utter strangeness of the Jure'lia.

'What is it?'

'Something is coming. Be really still, if you can. I will try to shield us.'

A nightmarish shadow grew on the wall, coming from the next chamber, and then a tall, spindly creature scuttled through. It appeared to be constructed of the same greenish black fluid that formed so much of the Jure'lia's structure, and it had several pairs of insectile arms gathered at its centre, which were busily cleaning a pair of serrated mandibles.

It stopped just in front of them, although whether that was because it had seen them or not, Vintage could not tell; it didn't have any eyes that she could see.

She held her breath. The Behemoth was silent save for a residual hum that came from everywhere at once. Vintage tried not to think about the toothy mouth on the thing opposite, or how it could probably pull them apart if it decided too. Instead, she thought about her crossbow, and how quickly she could get it off her belt if she needed to.

After an indeterminable period, the spider-like thing moved on, disappearing quickly into the next chamber. Vintage and Bern stood still for a long moment afterwards, in case it should come back, until Bern shook his head.

'Let's go.'

'Take me closer.'

Kirune growled his opinion of that plan, and Tor could hardly blame him. The two dragons were locked in combat, hissing and roaring at each other, while blasts of green and violet flame periodically curled out dangerously towards the rest of them. Thankfully, Celaphon did not seem able to perform his little lightning trick very often, and so far they had only seen short bursts of it. Now they were aware of it, they could move to avoid the attack. But the purple dragon was still a formidable force in its own right, and getting right up next to

598

it was a job best reserved for the biggest war-beasts. Sharrik was harrying the monster, attacking its back end as Vostok shot fire into his face.

'I think it's time I had a word with my sister.' Tor swung his sword back and forth in short, brutal motions, disembowelling a flying burrower that had been attempting to tangle itself in his hair. Jessen flew past, a winged-man between her jaws, and Helcate was close by too – the little war-beast had rallied well, although his sorrow was still a beacon of pain amongst them all. Impulsively, Tor reached along that connection, seeking out the others. Noon was right, he could feel them. It was sharp and painful, like gripping a blade at the wrong end, but he had a purchase. *Whatever happens, we are together.*

Tor began loosening the straps on the harness.

'You are an idiot,' said Kirune, but even so the big cat broke away from the cloud of minions and slipped into the radius of the main fight, just in time for a green fireball to go floating over their heads.

'Shit!' Tor laughed, then patted Kirune on the back of his head in a way he knew he hated. 'If I fall, you'll catch me. Quickly!'

Kirune dipped sideways, and the huge dragon loomed into Tor's line of sight. His sister was there, her attention on Noon and Vostok – she was shouting commands at the dragon, he saw. Murmuring a vague prayer to Ygseril, Tor pulled the last strap away and jumped, the Ninth Rain held in one hand.

There was a sickening second when he was sure he had made the worst mistake of his life, and then he collided heavily with his sister, almost wrenching her from the harness. He very nearly carried on past her into the void below, but with his free hand he grabbed onto her leather vest. She squawked in outrage.

'What are you doing?'

'Shouldn't I be asking you that, sister?' He pulled himself up so that he was sitting behind her, pushing his boots through several handy loops. With his free hand he placed his sword at her throat. 'I always thought I was the rebellious one, you see. Do you always have to steal my thunder?'

'You idiot!' She struggled against him, so he pressed the blade a little closer. 'You'll fall and die, or your idiot allies will kill you by accident!'

'It almost sounds like you care, Hest!' He grinned. 'I just thought I'd give you a chance to explain yourself. Why did you betray Ebora? Why did you betray me?'

'Ebora! I loved it more than you ever did.' She turned her head to look at him, and despite all the chaos going on around them and the fact that he could die at any moment, Tor was struck speechless by the change in her. Hestillion had always been coldly beautiful, but all the softness of her beauty had been burned away, chiselled into something hard and alien. She was still striking, but striking in the way a frozen lake was, or a remote mountain. And at her throat there was a jagged shard of blue crystal, pinching the skin around it into hard, pinkish scars.

'Why, then?' All of his bravado had vanished. A stream of violet fire lit up the sky to their left, and the bellow of Celaphon's roar rumbled through them like an earth tremor. 'Why did you do it, Hest?'

Her eyes widened, and some of the severity seemed to drop from her face. She opened her mouth, and closed it again. When she did speak, he knew it was not to say what she had originally thought.

'Because Ebora is nothing compared to them. I will not die in obscurity. The glory will be mine for once!'

'I really wanted you to have a better reason than that.' Tor shifted his grip, turning the killing edge of the Ninth Rain so that it rested against her skin. With the violence all around them and the continual shifting of Celaphon, it took all his effort to keep the sword steady. He didn't want to cut her throat accidentally. 'Can you at least give me a good reason not to kill you, dear sister?'

Hestillion felt frozen. The glory of battle and the power of directing Celaphon was fading, and instead she was unable to look away from the face of her brother. His hair was streaming out around him, wild and black, and the ugly scar across his eye and cheek was only inches away from her. He looked furious, but also hurt. It conjured up so many childhood memories that it was like drowning; the time she had taken one of his wooden practise swords and then broken it falling out of a tree; when their father took her side in every quarrel; when she had cut the throat of the little wine merchant's boy. Always she had been hurting him, and always he came back, this expression on his face.

In a desperate need to escape the discomfort of this, she reached out to the Jure'lia and found, to her surprise, the queen there waiting for her. She was so close that Hestillion had to believe she had been watching her for some time.

Your blood is here. The queen's voice was like another mind in the netherdark, noiseless yet clear.

He is, and he's about to kill me.

He will not do that. And besides, you must fight. Kill those who slipped away from me. This one task I gave you.

Hestillion felt a faint smile twist her lips. Through her Eboran-eyes, she saw Tor frown as he tried to make sense of it.

I will die now, and Celaphon will be lost. The thought was comforting.

That is unacceptable.

Why is it? Why?

There was no answer. Hestillion blinked once, turning away from Tor to look back to the corpse moon.

'The queen is coming,' she said.

'It's not far now.'

Vintage nodded and lifted her crossbow. The closer they had got to the centre of the Behemoth the more scuttling creatures they had seen. Each time they had stayed very still, waiting for them to pass on by, and each time Bern had stood rigid, veins on his neck and forehead prominent with the effort. His skin looked grey and clammy.

Ahead of them was another of the segmented walls. Bern reached up for it as he had a hundred times before, and then stopped, his hand shaking.

'I can feel her,' he said in a strangled voice. 'She's very close. I . . . by the stones, this is too much.'

Vintage went to him and took his free hand in hers.

'Bern, you may be the strongest man I've ever known.' She glanced down the corridor; there were shapes moving at the end of it. 'I know you can do this.'

'She has eyes everywhere, always watching.' He shuddered violently. 'They are inside me, her eyes.' He gasped, and a tear spilled down his cheek to soak into the whiskers of his beard. 'The worm people are an infection and I . . . I'm dying.'

'Listen to me,' hissed Vintage. The shadowy shapes were growing closer. 'Remember Aldasair. Remember Sharrik – those who love you, Bern the Younger. A bit of blue rock in your hand doesn't change that.'

'I . . . but . . .' He swallowed. 'Her eyes, this place is made of them –' He paused, and then leaned his hand against the wall. 'She's moving away! Something has caught her attention outside.'

Vintage lifted Bern's big beefy hand and kissed it. 'I knew you could do it. Come on, my dear, let's get this business done and get out of this shit pot.'

602

The wall ahead of them split open to Bern's touch, and ahead of them was a smaller chamber, lined with greyish blocks and the peculiar light nodules. And in the centre of it was the crystal – tall and blue and shining like a nightmare.

'This is a bloody nightmare!'

Noon sat back in the harness, her hand covered in a glove of green fire she wasn't sure what to do with. In a display of poor decision making that was impressive even for Tor, he had jumped from Kirune's back onto the giant dragon, and now appeared to be having a terse argument with his sister – which meant that neither she nor Vostok could use their fire without potentially striking him.

'You will just have to be precise!' Vostok had backed off a little while Sharrik attacked Celaphon's head, his giant claws causing a terrible screeching racket as he dragged them across the dragon's scales. 'Remember what I have taught you!'

'I've already burnt Tor once—'

'Then he'll be used to it! There's no time to be hesitant, bright weapon!'

Noon raised her hands, forming the winnowfire into a series of flat discs, which she threw, one by one, towards Celaphon's wings. Several were batted away, but at least two landed, sinking into the thin skin stretched between the bones there, and Celaphon hollered his displeasure.

'Yes!' cried Vostok. She turned in the air and went after the injured wing, sinking her teeth into the leathery covering. Pulling away, she left a tattered edge to the giant's wing – not much, perhaps, but a start.

'Let's do the other!' Noon sat up, preparing more discs as Vostok circled the bigger dragon. She caught sight of Helcate, gamely spraying a horde of flying men with acid, and Aldasair below them, he and Jessen moving together like they had been fighting monsters for years. It was Aldasair she was looking at when she saw him glance above them, his eyes widening in alarm. The warning seemed to shoot through them all, travelling along the link between them like a flash flood.

'The queen!' he called. 'The queen is coming!'

Noon turned back to the corpse moon. A thin black thread was spooling out of it, moving faster and faster as it came towards them. The thing shifted and changed as it came, sometimes appearing to be almost humanoid, at others something more akin to the burrowers, a scuttling thing of legs and mandibles. It was coming straight for them.

Vostok swept up and breathed a stream of fire across it, but the path of fluid melted away from them, twisting out of range. Noon threw her own flames at it, pelting it with hot discs of flame that burned white in their ferocity, but while it curled away from them, another section of it suddenly grew, reaching directly for Celaphon. Reaching for Tor, Noon realised with horror.

'Tor, watch out!'

It was too late. The black fluid reached down, becoming at the last minute like a great claw, and it ripped Tor away from the dragon. His sword span through the air, a silver bird, and then it was lost to sight. The shifting form of the Jure'lia queen carried him up and away, her white mask-like face appearing at last. She was smiling.

'Tor!'

Noon watched, her skin crawling, as the black fluid rippled over Tor, covering his arms, his chest, curling around his neck like mud. It slid up into his hair, and fingers of it moved over his cheeks. She saw him shout something, but swiftly the queen closed up his mouth, swarming over his nose and his eyes.

'It's not going well.'

Vintage looked back from where she had been circling the crystal. Bern was leaning against the wall, his eyes shut.

'I've had to cut myself off from them, as much as I can anyway.' He opened his eyes and looked at the floor. 'But I can still feel them in the background – Aldasair, Sharrik, Tor. Something bad has happened out there.'

'Fuck my old boots.' Vintage rubbed her hands over her face. 'I had hoped inspiration would strike, my dear, once we were in here.' She gestured at the crystal. There was an alien landscape caught inside it, just like the one Nanthema had been trapped in. 'I know so much more than I did! But it's still not enough. You have your axe? I think we will need to do this the most obvious way, as much as that pains me.'

'Break it? If we do that . . .'

'We don't know what will happen. So, in the spirit of scientific enquiry, let's try it!'

Bern slipped the axe from its loop, and hefting it, came towards the crystal. Within it an alien landscape waited, but despite her curiosity Vintage was happy to ignore that. Theirs had never been an especially robust plan, and this was exactly where it could all go to shit. After all, hadn't Esiah tried to free his son from the crystal by smashing it, and failed? But it was the only idea they had, and Vintage was a firm believer in the potential genius of last-minute intervention.

Bern held the axe high and to his side, the considerable muscles in his shoulders and arms bunching, and then swung it. The blade hit the crystal with an unpleasant discordant ringing, but it did not break. As far as Vintage could see, there wasn't even a scratch.

'Go on,' she said. 'Keep going. It may need weakening.'

Bern did so, striking again and again and again. He did not seem to tire – Vintage suspected that, back in Finneral, Bern the Younger was no stranger to chopping wood – but the crystal did not shatter. Eventually, he stood back, the axe at his side.

'Try again.' Vintage swallowed down the surge of panic in

605

her throat. 'Perhaps try a different place? There could be a fault line . . .'

'These things were made to last for centuries. For longer than that.' Bern was staring at the crystal, although Vintage couldn't tell if he was looking at its surface, or the alien landscape beyond. 'Stretches of time we'll never be able to understand. I can almost feel how long it was, but if I go too close to that, I can feel my mind starting to get ragged at the edges. When Aldasair destroyed the crystal in the Broken Field, it was already cracked.' He smiled. 'There might be another way, though.'

Fastidiously, Bern slipped the axe back into his belt, and pressed his hand with its embedded crystal to the surface of the shard.

'Bern? Bern, what are you doing?'

'I'm going to give it something else to think about.'

For a long moment, nothing happened. Vintage glanced back to the door, wondering how they would get back if this went wrong, if the others would be able to pull them out before whatever had happened outside ended them all. And then, the shifting landscape of boiling green sky and yellow sea inside the crystal began to drop away in pieces, being replaced by something else.

'Bern?'

The big man was lost to her, his green eyes staring deeply into the crystal as though everything he'd ever wanted was inside. Gradually, she saw a new landscape forming. There was a sky white with snow clouds, and in the distance, a thick green band of trees that was almost black. She saw flagstones of marble, streaked with mud, and unlike the alien world it was replacing, there were people here – men and women and children, crowded around colourful tents and a tall, elegant fence. It was, she realised, a place she knew very well – the Eboran palace.

There were campfires and all the people, she saw, were wearing winter clothes. There was a figure standing in the midst of it all, looking lost, and he seemed to shine more brightly than anyone else there. It was Aldasair, somehow younger and less careworn than the Aldasair she knew, his long auburn hair a tangled mess, his clothes faintly dusty. Vintage could see every detail of him; the particular crimson of his eyes, the line of his jaw, the way his hair fell against the collar of the old-fashioned blue jacket he wore. It was a memory that blotted out everything else, and all around them, the Behemoth began to wail its protest.

'Oh Bern,' she said, taking his arm. 'You are a bloody genius.'

'We have to help him!'

Vostok was already diving towards the sticky, oozing presence of the queen, and Noon had her arms up ready to give everything she had. Tor had disappeared into a fat black cocoon, looking very much like he was waiting to be eaten by a giant spider, while the queen herself crawled around it in mid-air, like some vast hybrid between woman and insect. Fire, green and violet, tore through the sky, but the queen threw up a wall of shifting ooze, and it curled harmlessly against it.

Dimly, Noon was aware of the others. Kirune was coming towards them, teeth bared, while Sharrik, Jessen and Helcate had descended on Celaphon, crowding the big dragon so that he could not move or reach them. Noon felt a surge of gratitude at that, and again became aware of the connection between them all – how had they not felt it before? They were family.

'Let him go!'

The queen's face split open, revealing row upon row of small white teeth, marching all the way down her throat.

'This? He is already dead,' she said. 'We have seeped inside him and snuffed him out. Would you like his corpse? We understand that humans value that sort of thing.'

Noon screamed. In response, Vostok flew straight into the shivering web of fluid, jaws snapping wildly. The queen spun away from them carrying the cocoon, only to be faced with Kirune, his jaws wide. She recoiled, splitting into numerous threads as she did so.

'It will be good to kill you myself, for once,' the queen said. 'I feel I have missed so much.'

The spiralling threads curled around them, snapping around Vostok's chest and legs, tightening and shifting with every movement. Several fingers of the substance surged over Noon's stomach, crawling rapidly up to her throat. Repulsed, she tried to pull them away, only to find her fingers sticking to it. Kirune roared, and glancing up she saw he had been caught in the web too. The big cat was furiously thrashing back and forth, biting at the threads that held him.

'Vostok, can you move?'

The dragon roared her reply, her blast of violet fire cut off abruptly as the tendrils of the Jure'lia curled around her snout. Noon looked back to the cocoon that contained Tor. Perhaps, if she concentrated all of her winnowfire in once place, if she took all the energy she dared from Vostok, she could create an explosion big enough . . .

And then, all around them, the burrowers and the mothers and the winged-men began to drop from the sky. Hundreds of them, unmoving, their insectile legs held out at stiff angles, falling like a grotesque rain. There was a wordless, discordant cry from the queen and abruptly the bonds holding them grew slack, slithering back towards the corpse moon like thousands of panicked snakes.

'What . . .?'

The cocoon that was holding Tor dissolved and Noon found herself watching as he fell, turning helplessly through the open sky.

'Tor!'

Kirune was already there. The big cat dived, falling through the air and catching Tor like a kitten catching a ball of yarn. Meanwhile, the corpse moon, incredibly, was moving away towards the mountains and away from Ebora, although there was something lopsided about it. Celaphon and Hestillion had broken away from their own fight and had flown away as if startled. Sharrik and Helcate peeled off after the corpse moon to retrieve Vintage and Bern, and Noon found herself watching Kirune fly back up to them, Tor hanging from his teeth by his shirt.

'You knew he was not dead,' said Vostok, quietly. 'We all would have felt it.'

Noon sat back in the harness. Her head was thumping steadily, and her ears ached as though someone had punched her. At some point in the fight one of the burrowers had torn the flesh of her upper arm, and that side of her body was hot and sticky with blood.

'I know,' she said. 'But the idea of it was enough.'

For a long time Vostok did not say anything at all. Instead, they watched as Sharrik and Helcate returned from the Behemoth, carrying their precious cargo. In the distance they could still see the huge purple dragon, flying in circles over and over, until it turned away, following the corpse moon over the mountain. Weary and sore, Noon reached out to the others via their newly forged link and, as one, they flew back, heading towards the broken buildings of Ebora. The sun was sinking towards the horizon, Noon noticed with surprise. How long had they been fighting?

'It's over,' said Vostok. 'This battle has been won, at least.'

56

Tor sat up in bed, reaching to the side table for the bottle of wine. He poured himself a glass, but did not drink it. The taste of Noon's blood was still in his mouth and he wasn't quite ready to wash that away just yet. It had been three days since their battle with the corpse moon, and with Vintage's stern instructions and the blood, he was feeling quite recovered, but still – he was happy to rest a while longer. He was still having nightmares, ones that he could not dream-walk his way out of. In these dreams, the oozing mass of the Jure'lia queen swallowed him up again and again, flowing into his mouth and up his nose, cutting off his air supply and blinding him. The dreams would fade, he hoped. Wine would help, and blood.

'Were you tempted?' asked Noon. She was sitting in a chair by the bed, her legs drawn up to her chest. She still had a bandage around the top half of her right arm. 'When Arnia asked you to stay there?'

Tor pressed his lips together. 'I can honestly say that I was not. Staying in the same place forever. Does that sound like me?'

Noon made a small, noncommittal noise.

'It was another kind of trap,' continued Tor. He swirled the wine in the glass; it smelled of spring, grassy and sharp. 'A pretty one, maybe. One that looked a lot like how things used to be here. But it wasn't Ygseril's sap that was keeping Arnia young.'

'What they did,' said Noon slowly, 'was unforgivable. They didn't just steal the blood of those people, they took their lives too.' She looked up at him. Her hair had fallen to one side, exposing the crude batwing tattoo on her forehead. 'Generations and generations of lives. And it will be generations more before those people recover from it. Things like this, they leave wounds that fester. People who step on others, who crush them so they can live comfortable lives . . . they should be destroyed.'

Tor nodded, watching Noon carefully.

'Are you all right, witch?'

She smiled lopsidedly. 'It's given me a lot to think about, that's all.'

'We all have a lot to think about.' Tor took a sip of the wine. 'We might have won the battle, but the Jure'lia are out there still, and I don't think they'll let us get away with the same trick twice. We need to get stronger, and fast. The amber tablets might help, but we'll need assistance from other places too. Bern has sent messages to his family in Finneral, letting them know he's still alive, but perhaps we can forge a greater alliance with them.' He cleared his throat. 'I'm not quite sure what's going on between Aldasair and Bern, but I think we're going to be growing a lot closer to the Finneral royal family.'

'They are in love,' said Noon, simply. 'That's what is going on between them.'

There was a long silence then, and Tor regretted drinking the wine. All at once the taste of Noon's blood was all he wanted.

'Speaking of which,' he said, feeling suddenly faint for no reason that he could see, 'maybe we should have a talk. I have been thinking, that is to say, the last couple of weeks have made some things clearer to me that should have been, well—'

'Maybe later.' Noon untangled herself from the chair, not looking at him. 'I have some things to do.'

Tor watched her go. After a while, he filled his glass to the brim and drank it all down, ignoring how the sharp taste stung at his eyes.

It felt like all of Sarn lay below them, but in truth it was simply the low hills of the outer plains, and beyond that, the teeming stretch of life that was Mushenska. Noon leaned into the wind, enjoying how it ruffled her hair, and the tangy taste of the sea on her tongue.

'The others are not going to like what we do here.'

Noon smiled, although it felt strange and stiff on her face. Reaching forward she pressed her hand against the warmth of Vostok's scales.

'So what?'

The dragon laughed reluctantly. 'We don't need more enemies.'

'No. But they've been my enemy since I was eleven. They took my life and stole it, as they've been stealing the lives of women for hundreds of years.'

Beyond the lights and smoke of Mushenska, the grey sea stretched across the horizon, and, rising from it like a dark fracture against the sky, were the towers of the Winnowry.

'The actions of cowards,' said Vostok, disdain thick in her voice. Noon grinned, more naturally this time, and she narrowed her eyes at the sight of her old prison.

'Let's go and burn it all down.'

Acknowledgements

I look back at this book and I'm not really sure where it came from or how it came to be – except that I know, of course, that a whole bunch of people helped me to wrangle it into existence.

Big thanks to the brilliant Frankie Edwards, who has jumped on this runaway trilogy-train with all the enthusiasm and panache of a bad-ass Indiana Jones, and thanks as ever to the fabulous Claire Baldwin, who continues to keep it on the tracks – I couldn't ask for better editors. Love and gratitude to my extraordinary agent, Juliet Mushens, whose excellent advice was key to bringing *The Bitter Twins* to life. Juliet isn't just a fantastic agent of course; she just happens to be one of my very favourite people and dearest friends – saltmates 4 lyfe. Huge thanks as ever to those writer friends who offer endless support and periodically listen to my ranting (usually about people hating on Star Trek): Den Patrick, who knows where the bodies are buried; Adam Christopher, who advised on disposal; and Andrew Reid, who helped me put them there.

This book is dedicated to my dad, who wasn't in my life for long but certainly left an impression. I think he would have been dead chuffed that I became a writer, and I think he would have loved these books, with their weirdness and grossness and swearing. Credit must go to my mum, who not only put up with all my usual nonsense this year, but also looked after me while I recovered from an operation – this involved watching *The Crown* with me and baking me chocolate chip rock cakes, so I had a pretty good time for someone missing an organ. And of course as ever I must tip my hat to Jenni, my oldest friend and first source of wisdom.

Lastly, all my love and eternal gratitude to my partner Marty (known to some of you, for complicated reasons, as Doug) who continues to believe in these books, and my ability to write them, during those times when I'd rather crawl into Skyrim and never come out. Love you babe.